The Fantasy Hall of Fame

This authoritative companion and follow-up to the acclaimed
Science Fiction Hall of Fame acknowledges the importance of fantasy to modern literature, and enshrines the thirty favorite short
stories of all time.

Chosen by popular ballot among the one thousand professionals
who make their living creating America's bestselling dreams, these
are the undisputed classics: the unforgettable stories that influenced and shaped the imaginations at work in the field today.

Never before has such a feast of fantasy been assembled. Its
theme is not weirdness, or werewolves, or even wonder, but pure
excellence: the demonstrated ability to please those most demanding of readers—other writers—and to lodge in the mind of the literature itself.

Here are the stories that shaped the shapers. Here are the fantasy
stories that will live forever.

THE FANTASY HALL OF FAME

Chosen by the Members of the
Science Fiction and Fantasy Writers of America

Edited by
Robert Silverberg

HarperPrism
A Division of HarperCollinsPublishers

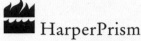 HarperPrism

A Division of HarperCollins*Publishers*
10 East 53rd Street, New York, N.Y. 10022-5299

Individual story copyrights appear on pages 559–562.

ISBN: 0-06-105215-9

HarperCollins®, ®, and HarperPrism®
are trademarks of HarperCollins*Publishers* Inc.

HarperPrism books may be purchased for educational, business,
or sales promotional use. For information, please write:
Special Markets Department, HarperCollins*Publishers,*
10 East 53rd Street, New York, N.Y. 10022-5299.

Cover design by Carl Galian

First printing: March 1998

Printed in the United States of America

Library of Congress Cataloging-in-Publication Data
is available from the publisher.

Visit HarperPrism on the World Wide Web at
http://www.harperprism.com

98 99 00 01 ❖ 10 9 8 7 6 5 4 3 2 1

Table of Contents

Introduction

IN 1992, THE SCIENCE FICTION WRITERS OF AMERICA—A TWENTY-seven-year-old organization of more than a thousand members, including just about every professional science fiction writer of importance—formally changed its name to the Science Fiction *and Fantasy* Writers of America. Thus it acknowledged not only the emergence of fantasy fiction as a powerful force in modern-day commercial publishing, but also the close relationship between science fiction and fantasy as literary forms.

To the casual reader and even to the not-so-casual writer, it may have already been clear that the two were related in a profound way, indeed were differing aspects of the same thing. Both fantasy and science fiction can readily be classed as types of "imaginative literature," the flamboyant cousin of "realistic literature." (And already we are lost in a maze of definitional confusion. Plenty of fantasy is grittily realistic in tone, except for its one conceptual departure from mundane norms. And a good many novels and stories that ostensibly are reality-based—Joyce's *Ulysses* and Kafka's *The Castle* are the first two that come to mind—take great leaps into the realm of the surreal.)

To those of us on the inside—the working professionals, that is—the distinction between the two genres has always been reasonably clear, if not entirely rigid. Science fiction is, mainly, that stuff that deals with androids and robots, spaceships, alien beings, time machines, viruses from outer space, galactic empires, and the like. These are all matters that are *conceptually possible* within the framework of scientific law as we currently understand it. (Although such things as time machines and faster-than-light vehicles certainly stretch that framework to its limits, and perhaps beyond them.) Fantasy, meanwhile, uses as its material that which is *generally believed to be impossible or nonexistent* in our culture: wizards and warlocks, elves and goblins, werewolves and vampires, unicorns and enchanted princesses, efficacious incantations and spells.

As soon as we set up these distinctions, we begin to find problems with them. Where does one classify a story about a virus from outer space that turns its victims into vampires? What about the tale of a computer program that generates angels, or one that provides a rational biological explanation for the werewolf phenomenon, down to the fangs and fur? The horrible mutant creature whose parents keep it chained in the attic—is he a denizen of a science fiction story, or a fantasy? And so on and on, far into the night.

Some will argue that the difference is one of tone: that a fantasy story has a certain vague and misty quality that would be inappropriate to a nuts-and-bolts science fiction story. Which is true, up to a point; but only to a point, for any of us could name a host of nuts-and-bolts fantasies and ethereal science fiction stories. There are those who would say that science fiction involves a rigorous examination of the consequences of postulating a single speculative idea, whereas fantasy is a free-form thing that has no rigorous rules at all—"tennis without a net," as one critic has called it. But a careful reading of the classics of fantasy fiction, including the stories in this collection, will make it obvious that the stories we classify as fantasy are every bit as rigorous in their exploration of their speculative concepts as science fiction stories are. (Consider, just as a single example, the chain of events that overwhelms the hapless protagonist of H. L. Gold's "Trouble with Water" after he rashly offends a water gnome. It happens that water gnomes, so far as we know, do not exist; but everything in the story that follows the giving of offense to the water gnome unfolds as logically and inevitably as the events of a story in which some rash scientist discovers how to generate a chain reaction by mixing toothpaste and distilled water. Q.E.D.)

Trying to set distinctions between science fiction and fantasy, then, is a difficult business. If they are not both, actually, offshoots of the same imaginative current, then it might be fair to say that science fiction is a highly specialized form of imaginative expression, a subgenre of fantasy.

At any rate, we know more or less what we mean when we speak of "fantasy" and when we speak of "science fiction," and we operate pretty well within those boundaries, putting the robot stories on the science fiction shelves and storing the unicorn fables over with fantasy. Certainly this was clear enough in the first half of the twentieth century, when fantasy fiction was something largely reserved for children (*Peter Pan, Alice in Wonderland,* fairy tales, stories about obsolete gods of antiquity) and science fiction, having been given its essential nature by Jules Verne and H. G. Wells, manifested itself in the United States in the form of magazines with names like *Amazing Stories* and *Astounding Science Fiction* and readerships composed largely of boys and earnest young men with an interest in gadgets and scientific disputation. The only American magazine dealing in the material we define as fantasy fiction was *Weird Tales,* founded in 1923, but that magazine published not only fantasy but a great many other kinds of genre fiction that might not be thought of as fantasy today—tales of pure terror, for example, with no speculative content.

Fantasy fiction *per se* did not have a real magazine of its own until 1939, when John W. Campbell, Jr., the foremost science fiction editor of his time, brought *Unknown* (later called *Unknown Worlds*) into being in order to allow his writers greater imaginative latitude than his definitions of science fiction would permit. Many of the same writers who had turned Campbell's *Astounding Science Fiction* into the most notable magazine of its type yet published—Robert A. Heinlein, L. Sprague de Camp, Theodore Sturgeon, Lester del Rey, Jack Williamson—also became mainstays of *Unknown,* and the general structural approach was similar: postulate a far-out idea and develop all its consequences to a logical conclusion. The stories about being nasty to water gnomes or selling your soul to the devil wound up in *Unknown;* those about traveling in time or voyaging to distant planets were published in *Astounding.*

But *Unknown,* though it was cherished with great fondness by its readers and writers, never attained much of a public following, and when wartime paper shortages forced Campbell to choose between his two magazines in 1943, *Unknown* was swiftly killed, never to reappear. Postwar attempts by nostalgic ex-contributors to *Unknown* to recapture its special flavor were largely unsuccessful; H. L. Gold's *Beyond* lasted ten issues, Lester del Rey's *Fantasy Fiction* managed only four. Only *The Magazine of Fantasy,* edited by Anthony Boucher and J. Francis McComas, managed to establish itself as a permanent entity, and even that magazine found it wisest to change its name to *Fantasy and Science Fiction* with its second issue. When science fiction became a fixture of paperback publishing in the 1950s, fantasy once again lagged behind: few fantasy novels were paperbacked, and most of them—Jack Vance's *The Dying Earth* and the early reprints of H. P. Lovecraft and Robert E. Howard are good examples—quickly vanished from view and became collector's items.

It all began to change in the late 1960s, when the sudden availability of paperback editions of J.R.R. Tolkien's *Lord of the Rings* trilogy (previously kept from paperback by an unwilling hardcover publisher) aroused a hunger for fantasy fiction in millions of readers that has, so far, been insatiable. Tolkien's books were such an emphatic commercial success that publishers rushed to find writers who could produce imitative trilogies, and the world was flooded with huge Hobbitesque novels, many of which sold in extraordinary quantities themselves. And a few years later Ballantine Books,

Tolkien's paperback publisher, brought out an extraordinary series of books in its Adult Fantasy series, edited by Lin Carter, which made all the elegant classic masterpieces of such fantasists as E. R. Eddison, James Branch Cabell, Lord Dunsany, and Mervyn Peake available to modern readers.

It was in this same period that the Science Fiction Writers of America was founded "to inform science fiction writers on matters of professional interest, to promote their professional welfare, and to help them deal effectively with publishers, agents, editors, and anthologists." No particular distinction between science fiction and fantasy was invoked in deciding membership eligibility; former contributors of elf-and-goblin stories for *Unknown Worlds* were every bit as welcome as were those writers whose work had dealt only in the abstrusities of nuclear physics. Nevertheless, the writing and publishing of science fiction, not fantasy, was plainly the primary concern of the organization's members in those early years.

In 1967 I edited an anthology called *The Science Fiction Hall of Fame*, the contents of which were chosen by vote of the membership to form a roster of the finest science fiction stories that had been published up until that time. There were two arbitrary cut-off points: no story could be longer than 15,000 words, and all must have been published prior to 1965, the first year covered by the newly formed Science Fiction Writers of America's own annual achievement award, the Nebula. Isaac Asimov's "Nightfall" proved to be the most popular story in the voting, followed by Stanley G. Weinbaum's "A Martian Odyssey" and Daniel Keyes's "Flowers for Algernon." Several subsequent Science Fiction Hall of Fame volumes followed, offering longer stories than the first one had been able to include.

But now the Science Fiction Writers of America has become the Science Fiction *and Fantasy* Writers of America; and, since fantasy fiction was excluded *a priori* from that first Hall of Fame volume, I was asked to compile a companion book that would do justice at last to our sister genre. In editing *The Fantasy Hall of Fame* I used the same approach as I had for the earlier book. Once again, there were arbitrarily imposed limits: no stories published earlier than 1939 (the beginning of the launching of the modern fantasy movement in the United States with the founding of John Campbell's magazine *Unknown*) or later than 1990 would be included, and the upper length limit for any story would be 17,500 words. (Once again, a second volume covering novellas may be published at a later time.) And I asked the nominating members to try to make some sort of distinction between fantasy and science fiction that would exclude science fiction stories from the roster.

The organization's members then nominated their favorite fantasy stories within the constraints of these rules, after which a ballot listing the qualifying nominees was presented to the membership at large for a six-month voting period. (Just to show how vague the line between science fiction and fantasy can be, three stories that *had already been published* in the older Hall of Fame books as science fiction were nominated for this one: Richard Matheson's "Born of Man and Woman," Jack Vance's "The Moon Moth," and Jerome Bixby's "It's a GOOD Life." They were ruled ineligible on grounds of previous enshrinement.)

A total of seventy-one stories, by forty-nine different writers, qualified for the ballot that went to the membership. It was understood that no more than one story by each writer would be included in the book, regardless of how many that writer had on the ballot, and the members were told that in cases where writers had more than one story on the ballot, they could vote for only one; but I stipulated also that the total votes accrued by each of the multi-story author's total votes would be credited to the story by that writer which ranked highest, thus sparing the more prolific and popular writers from having to compete with themselves for a slot in the book. (Ray Bradbury had four stories on the ballot; Theodore Sturgeon and Fritz Leiber had three; fifteen writers had two apiece.) Write-in votes were permitted, but those that came in were few and scattered and did not have a significant effect on the outcome.

Fritz Leiber's three nominees got him the highest number of total votes of any author, followed by Shirley Jackson (two stories nominated), Theodore Sturgeon (three stories nominated), Avram Davidson (two stories nominated), Peter S. Beagle (two stories nominated), and Ray Bradbury (four stories nominated.) The fifteen most popular authors, based on the aggregate vote totals for all their nominated stories, were:

1. Fritz Leiber
2. Shirley Jackson
3. Theodore Sturgeon
   Avram Davidson (tie)
5. Peter S. Beagle
   Ray Bradbury (tie)
   Ursula K. Le Guin (tie)
8. Roger Zelazny
9. James Tiptree, Jr.
10. J. G. Ballard
    Philip K. Dick (tie)
12. Harlan Ellison

13. Jorge Luis Borges
14. Robert Bloch
15. Terry Bisson

The fifteen most popular stories, ranked by individual vote totals, were:

1. "The Lottery," Shirley Jackson
2. "Jeffty Is Five," Harlan Ellison
3. "Unicorn Variations," Roger Zelazny
4. "Bears Discover Fire," Terry Bisson
   "That Hell-Bound Train," Robert Bloch (tie)
6. "Come Lady Death," Peter S. Beagle
   "Basileus," Robert Silverberg(tie)
8. "The Golem," Avram Davidson
   "Buffalo Gals, Won't You Come Out Tonight," Ursula K.
      Le Guin (tie)
10. "Her Smoke Rose Up Forever," James Tiptree, Jr.
    "The Loom of Darkness," Jack Vance (tie)
    "The Drowned Giant," J. G. Ballard(tie)
    "The Detective of Dreams," Gene Wolfe(tie)
14. "The Jaguar Hunter," Lucius Shepard
15. "The Compleat Werewolf," Anthony Boucher

("Or All the Sea with Oysters" by Avram Davidson would have tied for fourteenth place, but was it excluded from the book because of the other Davidson story higher on the list.)

And there you have it: those fifteen and fifteen runners-up, a definitive one-volume library of the modern fantasy short story, as chosen by the actual practitioners of the art in the United States in the year 1996. I am grateful to Martin Harry Greenberg for supplying introductions to the individual stories in the collection at a time when circumstances made it impossible for me to provide them myself.

—Robert Silverberg
October, 1996

THE FANTASY
HALL OF FAME

Trouble with Water

H. L. Gold

H. L. Gold reshaped the science fiction world with the creation of his maga-zine Galaxy Science Fiction *in 1950. His emphasis on relevant social satire attracted writers like Ray Bradbury, Robert Heinlein, Isaac Asimov, and others. His pioneering editorial work has unfortunately overshadowed his career as a writer. With only one novel, a collaboration with L. Sprague de Camp called* None but Lucifer, *and a handful of short stories collected in* The Old Die Rich, *until now his fiction had been all but forgotten. His impact on the genre, however, will never be.*

GREENBERG DID NOT DESERVE HIS SURROUNDINGS. HE WAS THE FIRST fisherman of the season, which guaranteed him a fine catch; he sat in a dry boat—one without a single leak—far out on a lake that was ruffled only enough to agitate his artificial fly. The sun was warm, the air was cool; he sat comfortably on a cushion; he had brought a hearty lunch; and two bottles of beer hung over the stern in the cold water.

Any other man would have been soaked with joy to be fishing on such a splendid day. Normally, Greenberg himself would have been ecstatic, but instead of relaxing and waiting for a nibble, he was plagued by worries.

This short, slightly gross, definitely bald, eminently respectable businessman lived a gypsy life. During the summer he lived in a hotel with kitchen privileges in Rockaway; winters he lived in a hotel with kitchen privileges in Florida; and in both places he oper-ated concessions. For years now, rain had fallen on schedule every week end, and there had been storms and floods on Decoration Day, July 4th, and Labor Day. He did not love his life, but it was a way of making a living.

He closed his eyes and groaned. If he had only had a son instead of his Rosie! Then things would have been mighty different—

For one thing, a son could run the hot dog and hamburger grid-dle, Esther could draw beer, and he would make soft drinks. There would be small difference in the profits, Greenberg admitted to himself; but at least those profits could be put aside for old age, instead of toward a dowry for his miserably ugly, dumpy, pitifully eager Rosie.

"All right—so what do I care if she don't get married?" he had cried to his wife a thousand times. "I'll support her. Other men can set up boys in candy stores with soda fountains that have only two spigots. Why should I have to give a boy a regular International Casino?"

"May your tongue rot in your head, you no-good piker!" she would scream. "It ain't right for a girl to be an old maid. If we have to die in the poor-house, I'll get my poor Rosie a husband. Every penny we don't need for living goes to her dowry!"

Greenberg did not hate his daughter, nor did he blame her for his misfortunes; yet, because of her, he was fishing with a broken rod that he had to tape together.

That morning his wife opened her eyes and saw him packing his equipment. She instantly came awake. "Go ahead!" she shrilled— speaking in a conversational tone was not one of her accomplishments—"Go fishing, you loafer! Leave me here alone. I can connect the beer pipes and the gas for soda water. I can buy ice cream, frank-furters, rolls, sirup, and watch the gas and electric men at the same time. Go ahead—go fishing!"

"I ordered everything," he mumbled soothingly. "The gas and electric won't be turned on today. I only wanted to go fishing—it's my last chance. Tomorrow we open the concession. Tell the truth, Esther, can I go fishing after we open?"

"I don't care about that. Am I your wife or ain't I, that you should go ordering everything without asking me—"

He defended his actions. It was a tactical mistake. While she was still in bed, he should have picked up his equipment and left. By the time the argument got around to Rosie's dowry, she stood fac-ing him.

"For myself I don't care," she yelled. "What kind of a monster are you that you can go fishing while your daughter eats her heart out? And on a day like this yet! You should only have to make supper and dress Rosie up. A lot you care that a nice boy is coming to sup-per tonight and maybe take Rosie out, you no-good father, you!"

From that point it was only one hot protest and a shrill curse to find himself clutching half a broken rod, with the other half being flung at his head.

Now he sat in his beautifully dry boat on an excellent game lake far out on Long Island, desperately aware that any average fish might collapse his taped rod.

What else could he expect? He had missed his train; he had had to wait for the boathouse proprietor; his favorite dry fly was missing; and, since morning, not a fish struck at the bait. Not a single fish!

And it was getting late. He had no more patience. He ripped the cap off a bottle of beer and drank it, in order to gain courage to change his fly for a less sporting bloodworm. It hurt him, but he wanted a fish.

The hook and the squirming worm sank. Before it came to rest, he felt a nibble. He sucked in his breath exultantly and snapped the hook deep into the fish's mouth. Sometimes, he thought philosophically, they just won't take artificial bait. He reeled in slowly.

"Oh, Lord," he prayed, "a dollar for charity—just don't let the rod bend in half where I taped it!"

It was sagging dangerously. He looked at it unhappily and raised his ante to five dollars; even at that price it looked impossible. He dipped his rod into the water, parallel with the line, to remove the strain. He was glad no one could see him do it. The line reeled in without a fight.

"Have I—God forbid!—got an eel or something not kosher?" he mumbled. "A plague on you—why don't you fight?"

He did not really care what it was—even an eel—anything at all.

He pulled in a long, pointed, brimless green hat.

For a moment he glared at it. His mouth hardened. Then, viciously, he yanked the hat off the hook, threw it on the floor, and trampled on it. He rubbed his hands together in anguish.

"All day I fish," he wailed, "two dollars for train fare, a dollar for a boat, a quarter for bait, a new rod I got to buy—and a five-dollar-mortgage charity has got on me. For what? For you, you hat, you!"

Out in the water an extremely civil voice asked politely: "May I have my hat, please?"

Greenberg glowered up. He saw a little man come swimming vigorously through the water toward him: small arms crossed with enormous dignity, vast ears on a pointed face propelling him quite rapidly and efficiently. With serious determination he drove through the water, and, at the starboard rail, his amazing ears kept him stationary while he looked gravely at Greenberg.

"You are stamping on my hat," he pointed out without anger.

To Greenberg this was highly unimportant. "With the ears you're swimming," he grinned in a superior way. "Do you look funny!"

"How else could I swim?" the little man asked politely.

"With the arms and legs, like a regular human being, of course."

"But I am not a human being. I am a water gnome, a relative of the more common mining gnome. I cannot swim with my arms, because they must be crossed to give an appearance of dignity suitable to a water gnome; and my feet are used for writing and holding things. On the other hand, my ears are perfectly adapted for propulsion in water. Consequently, I employ them for that purpose. But please, my hat—there are several matters requiring my immediate attention, and I must not waste time."

Greenberg's unpleasant attitude toward the remarkably civil gnome is easily understandable. He had found someone he could feel superior to, and, by insulting him, his depressed ego could expand. The water gnome certainly looked inoffensive enough, being only two feet tall.

"What you got that's so important to do, Big Ears?" he asked nastily.

Greenberg hoped the gnome would be offended. He was not, since his ears, to him, were perfectly normal, just as you would not be insulted if a member of a race of atrophied beings were to call you "Big Muscles." You might even feel flattered.

"I really must hurry," the gnome said, almost anxiously. "But if I have to answer your questions in order to get back my hat—we are engaged in restocking the Eastern waters with fish. Last year there was quite a drain. The bureau of fisheries is coöperating with us to some extent, but, of course, we cannot depend too much on them. Until the population rises to normal, every fish has instructions not to nibble."

Greenberg allowed himself a smile, an annoyingly skeptical smile.

"My main work," the gnome went on resignedly, "is control of the rainfall over the Eastern seaboard. Our fact-finding committee, which is scientifically situated in the meteorological center of the continent, coördinates the rainfall needs of the entire continent; and when they determine the amount of rain needed in particular spots of the East, I make it rain to that extent. Now may I have my hat, please?"

Greenberg laughed coarsely. "The first lie was big enough— about telling the fish not to bite. You make it rain like I'm President of the United States!" He bent toward the gnome slyly. "How's about proof?"

"Certainly, if you insist." The gnome raised his patient, triangular face toward a particularly clear blue spot in the sky, a trifle to one side of Greenberg. "Watch that bit of the sky."

Greenberg looked up humorously. Even when a small dark cloud rapidly formed in the previously clear spot, his grin remained broad. It could have been coincidental. But then large drops of undeniable rain fell over a twenty-foot circle; and Greenberg's mocking grin shrank and grew sour.

He glared hatred at the gnome, finally convinced. "So you're the dirty crook who makes it rain on week ends!"

"Usually on week ends during the summer," the gnome admitted.

"Ninety-two percent of water consumption is on weekdays. Obviously we must replace that water. The week ends, of course, are the logical time."

"But, you thief!" Greenberg cried hysterically, "you murderer! What do you care what you do to my concession with your rain? It ain't bad enough business would be rotten even without rain, you got to make floods!"

"I'm sorry," the gnome replied, untouched by Greenberg's rhetoric. "We do not create rainfall for the benefit of men. We are here to protect the fish.

"Now please give me my hat. I have wasted enough time, when I should be preparing the extremely heavy rain needed for this coming week end."

Greenberg jumped to his feet in the unsteady boat. "Rain this week end—when I can maybe make a profit for a change! A lot you care if you ruin business. May you and your fish die a horrible, lingering death."

And he furiously ripped the green hat to pieces and hurled them at the gnome.

"I'm really sorry you did that," the little fellow said calmly, his huge ears treading water without the slightest increase of pace to indicate his anger. "We Little Folk have no tempers to lose. Nevertheless, occasionally we find it necessary to discipline certain of your people, in order to retain our dignity. I am not malignant; but, since you hate water and those who live in it, water and those who live in it will keep away from you."

With his arms still folded in great dignity, the tiny water gnome flipped his vast ears and disappeared in a neat surface dive.

Greenberg glowered at the spreading circles of waves. He did not grasp the gnome's final restraining order; he did not even attempt to interpret it. Instead he glared angrily out of the corner of his eye at the phenomenal circle of rain that fell from a perfectly clear sky. The gnome must have remembered it at length, for a moment later the rain stopped. Like shutting off a faucet, Greenberg unwillingly thought.

"Good-by, week-end business," he growled. "If Esther finds out I got into an argument with the guy who makes it rain—"

He made an underhand cast, hoping for just one fish. The line flew out over the water; then the hook arched upward and came to rest several inches above the surface, hanging quite steadily and without support in the air.

"Well, go down in the water, damn you!" Greenberg said viciously, and he swished his rod back and forth to pull the hook down from its ridiculous levitation. It refused.

Muttering something incoherent about being hanged before he'd give in, Greenberg hurled his useless rod at the water. By this time he was not surprised when it hovered in the air above the lake. He merely glanced red-eyed at it, tossed out the remains of the gnome's hat, and snatched up the oars.

When he pulled back on them to row to land, they did not touch the water—naturally. Instead they flashed unimpeded through the air, and Greenberg tumbled into the bow.

"A-ha!" he grated. "Here's where the trouble begins." He bent over the side. As he had suspected, the keel floated a remarkable distance above the lake.

By rowing against the air, he moved with maddening slowness toward shore, like a medieval conception of a flying machine. His main concern was that no one should see him in his humiliating position.

At the hotel he tried to sneak past the kitchen to the bathroom. He knew that Esther waited to curse him for fishing the day before opening, but more especially on the very day that a nice boy was coming to see her Rosie. If he could dress in a hurry, she might have less to say—

"Oh, there you are, you good-for-nothing!"

He froze to a halt.

"Look at you!" she screamed shrilly. "Filthy—you stink from fish!"

"I didn't catch anything, darling," he protested timidly.

"You stink anyhow. Go take a bath, may you drown in it! Get dressed in two minutes or less, and entertain the boy when he gets here. Hurry!"

He locked himself in, happy to escape her voice, started water in the tub, and stripped from the waist up. A hot bath, he hoped, would rid him of his depressed feeling.

First, no fish; now, rain on week ends! What would Esther—if she knew, of course. And, of course, he would not tell her.

"Let myself in for a lifetime of curses!" he sneered. "Ha!"

He clamped a new blade into his razor, opened the tube of shaving cream, and stared objectively at the mirror. The dominant feature of the soft, chubby face that stared back was its ugly black stubble; but he set his stubborn chin and glowered. He really looked quite fierce and indomitable. Unfortunately, Esther never saw his face in that uncharacteristic pose, otherwise she would speak more softly.

"Herman Greenberg never gives in!" he whispered between savagely hardened lips. "Rain on week ends, no fish—anything he wants; a lot I care! Believe me, he'll come crawling to me before I go to him."

He gradually became aware that his shaving brush was not getting wet. When he looked down and saw the water dividing into streams that flowed around it, his determined face slipped and grew desperately anxious. He tried to trap the water—by catching it in his cupped hands, by creeping up on it from behind, as if it were some shy animal, and shoving his brush at it—but it broke and ran away from his touch. Then he jammed his palm against the faucet. Defeated, he heard it gurgle back down the pipe, probably as far as the main.

"What do I do now?" he groaned. "Will Esther give it to me if I don't take a shave! But how? . . . I can't shave without water."

Glumly, he shut off the bath, undressed, and stepped into the tub. He lay down to soak. It took a moment of horrified stupor to realize that he was completely dry and that he lay in a waterless bathtub. The water, in one surge of revulsion, had swept out onto the floor.

"Herman, stop splashing!" his wife yelled. "I just washed that floor. If I find one little puddle I'll murder you!"

Greenberg surveyed the instep-deep pool over the bathroom floor. "Yes, my love," he croaked unhappily.

With an inadequate washrag he chased the elusive water, hoping to mop it all up before it could seep through to the apartment below. His washrag remained dry, however, and he knew that the ceiling underneath was dripping. The water was still on the floor.

In despair, he sat on the edge of the bathtub. For some time he sat in silence. Then his wife banged on the door, urging him to come out. He started and dressed moodily.

When he sneaked out and shut the bathroom, door tightly on the flood inside, he was extremely dirty and his face was raw where he had experimentally attempted to shave with a dry razor.

"Rosie!" he called in a hoarse whisper. "Sh! Where's mamma?"

His daughter sat on the studio couch and applied nail-polish to her stubby fingers. "You look terrible," she said in a conversational tone. "Aren't you going to shave?"

He recoiled at the sound of her voice, which, to him, roared out like a siren. "Quiet, Rosie! Sh!" And for further emphasis, he shoved his lips out against a warning finger. He heard his wife striding heavily around the kitchen. "Rosie," he cooed, "I'll give you a dollar if you'll mop up the water I spilled in the bathroom."

"I can't, papa," she stated firmly. "I'm all dressed."

"Two dollars, Rosie—all right, two and a half, you blackmailer."

He flinched when he heard her gasp in the bathroom; but, when she came out with soaked shoes, he fled downstairs. He wandered aimlessly toward the village.

Now he was in for it, he thought; screams from Esther, tears from

Rosie—plus a new pair of shoes for Rosie and two and a half dollars. It would be worse, though, if he could not get rid of his whiskers—

Rubbing the tender spots where his dry razor had raked his face, he mused blankly at a drugstore window. He saw nothing to help him, but he went inside anyhow and stood hopefully at the drug counter. A face peered at him through a space scratched in the wall case mirror, and the druggist came out. A nice-looking, intelligent fellow, Greenberg saw at a glance.

'What you got for shaving that I can use without water?" he asked.

"Skin irritation, eh?" the pharmacist replied. "I got something very good for that."

"No. It's just— Well, I don't like to shave with water."

The druggist seemed disappointed. "Well, I got brushless shaving cream." Then he brightened. "But I got an electric razor—much better."

"How much?" Greenberg asked cautiously.

"Only fifteen dollars, and it lasts a lifetime."

"Give me the shaving cream," Greenberg said coldly.

With the tactical science of a military expert, he walked around until some time after dark. Only then did he go back to the hotel, to wait outside. It was after seven, he was getting hungry, and the people who entered the hotel he knew as permanent summer guests. At last a stranger passed him and ran up the stairs.

Greenberg hesitated for a moment. The stranger was scarcely a boy, as Esther had definitely termed him, but Greenberg reasoned that her term was merely wish-fulfillment, and he jauntily ran up behind him.

He allowed a few minutes to pass, for the man to introduce himself and let Esther and Rosie don their company manners. Then, secure in the knowledge that there would be no scene until the guest left, he entered.

He waded through a hostile atmosphere, urbanely shook hands with Sammie Katz, who was a doctor—probably, Greenberg thought shrewdly, in search of an office—and excused himself.

In the bathroom he carefully read the direction for using brushless shaving cream. He felt less confident when he realized that he had to wash his face thoroughly with soap and water, but without benefit of either, he spread the cream on, patted it, and waited for his beard to soften. It did not, as he discovered while shaving. He wiped his face dry. The towel was sticky and black, with whiskers suspended in paste, and, for that, he knew, there would be more hell to pay. He shrugged resignedly. He would have to spend fifteen dollars for an electric razor after all; this foolishness was costing him a fortune!

That they were waiting for him before beginning supper, was, he knew, only a gesture for the sake of company. Without changing her hard, brilliant smile, Esther whispered: "Wait! I'll get you later—"

He smiled back, his tortured, slashed face creasing painfully. All that could be changed by his being enormously pleasant to Rosie's young man. If he could slip Sammie a few dollars—more expense, he groaned—to take Rosie out, Esther would forgive everything.

He was too engaged in beaming and putting Sammie at ease to think of what would happen after he ate caviar canapes. Under other circumstances Greenberg would have been repulsed by Sammie's ultra-professional waxed mustache—an offensively small, pointed thing—and his commercial attitude toward poor Rosie; but Greenberg regarded him as a potential savior.

"You open an office yet, Doctor Katz?"

"Not yet. You know how things are. Anyhow, call me Sammie."

Greenberg recognized the gambit with satisfaction, since it seemed to please Esther so much. At one stroke Sammie had ingratiated himself and begun bargaining negotiations.

Without another word, Greenberg lifted his spoon to attack the soup. It would be easy to snare this eager doctor. A *doctor!* No wonder Esther and Rosie were so puffed with joy.

In the proper company way, he pushed his spoon away from him. The soup spilled onto the tablecloth.

"Not so hard, you dope," Esther hissed.

He drew the spoon toward him. The soup leaped off it like a live thing and splashed over him—turning, just before contact, to fall on the floor. He gulped and pushed the bowl away. This time the soup poured over the side of the plate and lay in a huge puddle on the table.

"I didn't want any soup anyhow," he said in a horrible attempt at levity. Lucky for him, he thought wildly, that Sammie was there to pacify Esther with his smooth college talk—not a bad fellow, Sammie, in spite of his mustache; he'd come in handy at times.

Greenberg lapsed into a paralysis of fear. He was thirsty after having eaten the caviar, which beats herring any time as a thirst raiser. But the knowledge that he could not touch water without having it recoil and perhaps spill, made his thirst a monumental craving. He attacked the problem cunningly.

The others were talking rapidly and rather hysterically. He waited until his courage was equal to his thirst; then he leaned over the table with a glass in his hand. "Sammie, do you mind—a little water, huh?"

Sammie poured from a pitcher while Esther watched for more of his tricks. It was to be expected, but still he was shocked when the water exploded out of the glass directly at Sammie's only suit.

"If you'll excuse me," Sammie said angrily, "I don't like to eat with lunatics."

And he left, though Esther cried and begged him to stay. Rosie was too stunned to move. But when the door closed, Greenberg raised his agonized eyes to watch his wife stalk murderously toward him.

Greenberg stood on the boardwalk outside his concession and glared blearily at the peaceful, blue, highly unpleasant ocean. He wondered what would happen if he started at the edge of the water and strode out. He could probably walk right to Europe on dry land.

It was early—much too early for business—and he was tired. Neither he nor Esther had slept; and it was practically certain that the neighbors hadn't either. But above all he was incredibly thirsty.

In a spirit of experimentation, he mixed a soda. Of course its high water content made it slop onto the floor. For breakfast he had surreptitiously tried fruit juice and coffee, without success.

With his tongue dry to the point of furriness, he sat weakly on a boardwalk bench in front of his concession. It was Friday morning, which meant that the day was clear with a promise of intense heat. Had it been Saturday, it naturally would have been raining.

"This year," he moaned, "I'll be wiped out. If I can't mix sodas, why should beer stay in a glass for me? I thought I could hire a boy for ten dollars a week to run the hot-dog griddle; I could make sodas, and Esther could draw beer; but twenty or maybe twenty-five a week I got to pay a soda man. I won't even come out square—a fortune I'll lose!"

The situation really was desperate. Concessions depend on too many factors to be anything but capriciously profitable.

His throat was fiery and his soft brown eyes held a fierce glaze when the gas and electric were turned on, the beer pipes connected, the tank of carbon dioxide hitched to the pump, and the refrigerator started.

Gradually, the beach was filling with bathers. Greenberg writhed on his bench and envied them. They could swim and drink without having liquids draw away from them as if in horror. They were not thirsty—

And then he saw his first customers approach. His business experience was that morning customers buy only soft drinks. In a mad haste he put up the shutters and fled to the hotel.

"Esther!" he cried. "I got to tell you! I can't stand it—"

Threateningly, his wife held her broom like a baseball bat. "Go back to the concession, you crazy fool. Ain't you done enough already?"

He could not be hurt more than he had been. For once he did not cringe. "You got to help me, Esther."

"Why didn't you shave, you no-good bum? Is that any way—"

"That's what I got to tell you. Yesterday I got into an argument with a water gnome—"

"A what?" Esther looked at him suspiciously.

"A water gnome," he babbled in a rush of words. "A little man so high, with big ears that he swims with, and he makes it rain—"

"Herman!" she screamed. "Stop that nonsense. You're crazy!"

Greenberg pounded his forehead with his fist. "I *ain't* crazy. Look, Esther. Come with me into the kitchen."

She followed him readily enough, but her attitude made him feel more helpless and alone than ever. With her fists on her plump hips and her feet set wide, she cautiously watched him try to fill a glass of water.

"Don't you see?" he wailed. "It won't go in the glass. It spills over. It runs away from me."

She was puzzled. "What happened to you?"

Brokenly, Greenberg told of his encounter with the water gnome, leaving out no single degrading detail. "And now I can't touch water," he ended. "I can't drink it. I can't make sodas. On top of it all, I got such a thirst, it's killing me."

Esther's reaction was instantaneous. She threw her arms around him, drew his head down to her shoulder, and patted comfortingly as if he were a child. "Herman, my poor Herman!" she breathed tenderly. "What did we ever do to deserve such a curse?"

"What shall I do, Esther?" he cried helplessly.

She held him at arm's length. "You got to go to a doctor," she said firmly. "How long can you go without drinking? Without water you'll die. Maybe sometimes I am a little hard on you, but you know I love you—"

"I know, mamma," he sighed. "But how can a doctor help me?"

"Am I a doctor that I should know? Go anyhow. What can you lose?"

He hesitated. "I need fifteen dollars for an electric razor," he said in a low, weak voice.

"So?" she replied. "If you got to, you got to. Go, darling. I'll take care of the concession."

Greenberg no longer felt deserted and alone. He walked almost confidently to a doctor's office. Manfully, he explained his symptoms.

The doctor listened with professional sympathy, until Greenberg reached his description of the water gnome.

Then his eyes glittered and narrowed. "I know just the thing for you, Mr. Greenberg," he interrupted. "Sit there until I come back."

Greenberg sat quietly. He even permitted himself a surge of hope. But it seemed only a moment later that he was vaguely conscious of a siren screaming toward him; and then he was overwhelmed by the doctor and two interns who pounced on him and tried to squeeze him into a bag.

He resisted, of course. He was terrified enough to punch wildly. "What are you doing to me?" he shrieked. "Don't put that thing on me!"

"Easy now," the doctor soothed. "Everything will be all right."

It was on that humiliating scene that the policeman, required by law to accompany public ambulances, appeared. "What's up?" he asked.

"Don't stand there, you fathead," an intern shouted. "This man's crazy. Help us get him into this strait jacket."

But the policeman approached indecisively. "Take it easy, Mr. Greenberg. They ain't gonna hurt you while I'm here, What's it all about?"

"Mike!" Greenberg cried, and clung to his protector's sleeve. "They think I'm crazy—"

"Of course he's crazy," the doctor stated. "He came in here with a fantastic yarn about a water gnome putting a curse on him."

"What kind of a curse, Mr. Greenberg?" Mike asked cautiously.

"I got into an argument with the water gnome who makes it rain and takes care of the fish," Greenberg blurted. "I tore up his hat. Now he won't let water touch me. I can't drink, or anything—"

The doctor nodded. "There you are. Absolutely insane."

"Shut up." For a long moment Mike stared curiously at Greenberg. Then: "Did any of you scientists think of testing him? Here, Mr. Greenberg." He poured water into a paper cup and held it out.

Greenberg moved to take it. The water backed up against the cup's far lip; when he took it in his hand, the water shot out into the air.

"Crazy, is he?" Mike asked with heavy irony. "I guess you don't know there's things like gnomes and elves. Come with me, Mr. Greenberg."

They went out together and walked toward the boardwalk. Greenberg told Mike the entire story and explained how, besides being so uncomfortable to him personally, it would ruin him financially.

"Well, doctors can't help you," Mike said at length. "What do they know about the Little Folk? And I can't say I blame you for sassing the gnome. You ain't Irish or you'd have spoke with more respect to him. Anyhow, you're thirsty. Can't you drink *anything?*"

"Not a thing," Greenberg said mournfully.

They entered the concession. A single glance told Greenberg that business was very quiet, but even that could not lower his feelings more than they already were. Esther clutched him as soon as she saw them.

"Well?" she asked anxiously.

Greenberg shrugged in despair. "Nothing. He thought I was crazy."

Mike stared at the bar. Memory seemed to struggle behind his reflective eyes. "Sure," he said after a long pause. "Did you try beer, Mr. Greenberg? When I was a boy my old mother told me all about elves and gnomes and the rest of the Little Folk. She knew them, all right. They don't touch alcohol, you know. Try drawing a glass of beer—"

Greenberg trudged obediently behind the bar and held a glass under the spigot. Suddenly his despondent face brightened. Beer creamed into the glass—and stayed there! Mike and Esther grinned at each other as Greenberg threw back his head and furiously drank.

"Mike!" he crowed. "I'm saved. You got to drink with me!"

"Well—" Mike protested feebly.

By late afternoon, Esther had to close the concession and take her husband and Mike to the hotel.

The following day, being Saturday, brought a flood of rain. Greenberg nursed an imposing hang-over that was constantly aggravated by his having to drink beer in order to satisfy his recurring thirst. He thought of forbidden ice bags and alkaline drinks in an agony of longing.

"I can't stand it!" he groaned. "Beer for breakfast—phooey!"

"It's better than nothing," Esther said fatalistically.

"So help me, I don't know if it is. But, darling, you ain't mad at me on account of Sammie, are you?"

She smiled gently, "Poo! Talk dowry and he'll come back quick."

"That's what I thought. But what am I going to do about my curse?"

Cheerfully, Mike furled an umbrella and strode in with a little old woman, whom he introduced as his mother. Greenberg enviously saw evidence of the effectiveness of ice bags and alkaline drinks, for Mike had been just as high as he the day before.

"Mike told me about you and the gnome," the old lady said. "Now I know the Little Folk well, and I don't hold you to blame for insulting him, seeing you never met a gnome before. But I suppose you want to get rid of your curse. Are you repentant?"

Greenberg shuddered. "Beer for breakfast! Can you ask?"

"Well, just you go to this lake and give the gnome proof."

"What kind of proof?" Greenberg asked eagerly.

"Bring him sugar. The Little Folk love the stuff—"

Greenberg beamed. "Did you hear that, Esther? I'll get a barrel—"

"They love sugar, but they can't eat it," the old lady broke in. "It melts in water. You got to figure out a way so it won't. Then the little gentleman'll know you're repentant for real."

There was a sympathetic silence while his agitated mind attacked the problem from all angles. Then the old lady said in awe: "The minute I saw your place I knew Mike had told the truth. I never seen a sight like it in my life—rain coming down, like the flood, everywhere else; but all around this place, in a big circle, it's dry as a bone!"

While Greenberg scarcely heard her, Mike nodded and Esther seemed peculiarly interested in the phenomenon. When he admitted defeat and came out of his reflected stupor, he was alone in the concession, with only a vague memory of Esther's saying she would not be back for several hours.

"What am I going to do?" he muttered. "Sugar that won't melt—" He drew a glass of beer and drank it thoughtfully. "Particular they got to be yet. Ain't it good enough if I bring simple sirup—that's sweet."

He pottered about the place, looking for something to do. He could not polish the fountain on the bar, and the few frankfurters boiling on the griddle probably would go to waste. The floor had already been swept. So he sat uneasily and worried his problem.

"Monday, no matter what," he resolved, "I'll go to the lake. It don't pay to go tomorrow. I'll only catch a cold because it'll rain."

At last Esther returned, smiling in a strange way. She was extremely gentle, tender, and thoughtful; and for that he was appreciative. But that night and all day Sunday he understood the reason for her happiness.

She had spread word that, while it rained in every other place all over town, their concession was miraculously dry. So, besides a headache that made his body throb in rhythm to its vast pulse, Greenberg had to work like six men satisfying the crowd who mobbed the place to see the miracle and enjoy the dry warmth.

How much they took in will never be known. Greenberg made it a practice not to discuss such personal matters. But it is quite definite that not even in 1929 had he done so well over a single week end.

———

Very early Monday morning he was dressing quietly, not to disturb his wife. Esther, however, raised herself on her elbow and looked at him doubtfully.

"Herman," she called softly, "do you really have to go?"

He turned, puzzled. "What do you mean—do I have to go?"

"Well—" She hesitated. Then: "Couldn't you wait until the end of the season, Herman, darling?"

He staggered back a step, his face working in horror. What kind of an idea is that for my own wife to have?" he croaked. "Beer I have to drink instead of water. How can I stand it? Do you think I *like* beer? I can't wash myself. Already people don't like to stand near me; and how will they act at the end of the season? I go around looking like a bum because my beard is too tough for an electric razor, and I'm all the time drunk—the first Greenberg to be a drunkard. I want to be respected—"

"I know, Herman, darling," she sighed. "But I thought for the sake of our Rosie— Such a business we've never done like we did this week end. If it rains every Saturday and Sunday, but not on our concession, we'll make a *fortune!*"

"Esther!" Herman cried, shocked. "Doesn't my health mean anything?"

"Of course, darling. Only I thought maybe you could stand it for—"

He snatched his hat, tie, and jacket, and slammed the door. Outside, though, he stood indeterminedly. He could hear his wife crying, and he realized that, if he succeeded in getting the gnome to remove the curse, he would forfeit an opportunity to make a great deal of money.

He finished dressing more slowly. Esther was right, to a certain extent. If he could tolerate his waterless condition—

"No!" he gritted decisively. "Already my friends avoid me. It isn't right that a respectable man like me should always be drunk and not take a bath. So we'll make less money. Money isn't everything—"

And with great determination he went to the lake.

But that evening, before going home, Mike walked out of his way to stop in at the concession. He found Greenberg sitting on a chair, his head in his hands, and his body rocking slowly in anguish.

"What is it, Mr. Greenberg?" he asked gently.

Greenberg looked up. His eyes were dazed. "Oh, you, Mike," he said blankly. Then his gaze cleared, grew more intelligent, and he stood up and led Mike to the bar. Silently, they drank beer. "I went to the lake today," he said hollowly. "I walked all around it hollering like mad. The gnome didn't stick his head out of the water once."

"I know," Mike nodded sadly. "They're busy all the time."

Greenberg spread his hands imploringly. "So what can I do? I can't write him a letter or send him a telegram; he ain't got a door to knock on or a bell for me to ring. How do I get him to come up and talk?"

His shoulders sagged. "Here, Mike. Have a cigar. You been a real good friend, but I guess we're licked."

They stood in an awkward silence. Finally Mike blurted: "Real hot, today. A regular scorcher."

"Yeah. Esther says business was pretty good, if it keeps up."

Mike fumbled at the Cellophane wrapper. Greenberg said: "Anyhow, suppose I did talk to the gnome. What about the sugar?"

The silence dragged itself out, became tense and uncomfortable. Mike was distinctly embarrassed. His brusque nature was not adapted for comforting discouraged friends. With immense concentration he rolled the cigar between his fingers and listened for a rustle.

"Day like this's hell on cigars," he mumbled, for the sake of conversation. "Dries them like nobody's business. This one ain't, though."

"Yeah," Greenberg said abstractedly. "Cellophane keeps them—"

They looked suddenly at each other, their faces clean of expression.

"Holy smoke!" Mike yelled.

"Cellophane on sugar!" Greenberg choked out.

"Yeah," Mike whispered in awe. "I'll switch my day off with Joe, and I'll go to the lake with you tomorrow. I'll call for you early."

Greenberg pressed his hand, too strangled by emotion for speech. When Esther came to relieve him, he left her at the concession with only the inexperienced griddle boy to assist her, while he searched the village for cubes of sugar wrapped in Cellophane.

The sun had scarcely risen when Mike reached the hotel, but Greenberg had long been dressed and stood on the porch waiting impatiently. Mike was genuinely anxious for his friend. Greenberg staggered along toward the station, his eyes almost crossed with the pain of a terrific hang-over.

They stopped at a cafeteria for breakfast. Mike ordered orange juice, bacon and eggs, and coffee half-and-half. When he heard the order, Greenberg had to gag down a lump in his throat.

"What'll you have?" the counterman asked.

Greenberg flushed. "Beer," he said hoarsely.

"You kidding me?" Greenberg shook his head, unable to speak. "Want anything with it? Cereal, pie, toast—"

"Just beer." And he forced himself to swallow it. "So help me," he hissed at Mike, "another beer for breakfast will kill me!"

"I know how it is," Mike said around a mouthful of food.

On the train they attempted to make plans. But they were faced by a phenomenon that neither had encountered before, and so they got nowhere. They walked glumly to the lake, fully aware that they would have to employ the empirical method of discarding tactics that did not work.

"How about a boat?" Mike suggested.

"It won't stay in the water with me in it. And you can't row it."

"Well, what'll we do then?"

Greenberg bit his lip and stared at the beautiful blue lake. There the gnome lived, so near to them. "Go through the woods along the shore, and holler like hell. I'll go the opposite way. We'll pass each other and meet at the boathouse. If the gnome comes up, yell for me."

"O.K.," Mike said, not very confidently.

The lake was quite large and they walked slowly around it, pausing often to get the proper stance for particularly emphatic shouts. But two hours later, when they stood opposite each other with the full diameter of the lake between them, Greenberg heard Mike's hoarse voice: "Hey, gnome!"

"Hey, gnome!" Greenberg yelled. "Come on up!"

An hour later they crossed paths. They were tired, discouraged, and their throats burned; and only fishermen disturbed the lake's surface.

"The hell with this," Mike said. "It ain't doing any good. Let's go back to the boathouse."

"What'll we do?" Greenberg rasped. "I can't give up!"

They trudged back around the lake, shouting half-heartedly. At the boathouse, Greenberg had to admit that he was beaten. The boathouse owner marched threateningly toward him.

"Why don't you maniacs get away from here?" he barked. "What's the idea of hollering and scaring away the fish? The guys are sore—"

"We're not going to holler any more," Greenberg said. "It's no use."

When they bought beer and Mike, on an impulse, hired a boat, the owner cooled off with amazing rapidity, and went off to unpack bait.

"What did you get a boat for?" Greenberg asked. "I can't ride in it."

"You're not going to. You're gonna walk."

"Around the lake again?" Greenberg cried.

"Nope. Look, Mr. Greenberg. Maybe the gnome can't hear us

through all that water. Gnomes ain't hardhearted. If he heard us and thought you were sorry, he'd take his curse off you in a jiffy."

"Maybe." Greenberg was not convinced. "So where do I come in?"

"The way I figure it, some way or other you push water away, but the water pushes you away just as hard. Anyhow, I hope so. If it does, you can walk on the lake." As he spoke, Mike had been lifting large stones and dumping them on the bottom of the boat. "Give me a hand with these."

Any activity, however useless, was better than none, Greenberg felt. He helped Mike fill the boat until just the gunwales were above water. Then Mike got in and shoved off.

"Come on," Mike said. "Try to walk on the water."

Greenberg hesitated. "Suppose I can't?"

"Nothing'll happen to you. You can't get wet; so you won't drown."

The logic of Mike's statement reassured Greenberg. He stepped out boldly. He experienced a peculiar sense of accomplishment when the water hastily retreated under his feet into pressure bowls, and an unseen, powerful force buoyed him upright across the lake's surface. Though his footing was not too secure, with care he was able to walk quite swiftly.

"Now what?" he asked, almost happily.

Mike had kept pace with him in the boat. He shipped his oars and passed Greenberg a rock. "We'll drop them all over the lake—make it damned noisy down there and upset the place. That'll get him up."

They were more hopeful now, and their comments, "Here's one that'll wake him," and "I'll hit him right on the noodle with this one," served to cheer them still further. And less than half the rocks had been dropped when Greenberg halted, a boulder in his hands. Something inside him wrapped itself tightly around his heart and his jaw dropped.

Mike followed his awed, joyful gaze. To himself, Mike had to admit that the gnome, propelling himself through the water with his ears, arms folded in tremendous dignity, was a funny sight.

"Must you drop rocks and disturb us at our work?" the gnome asked.

Greenberg gulped. "I'm sorry, Mr. Gnome," he said nervously. "I couldn't get you to come up by yelling."

The gnome looked at him. "Oh. You are the mortal who was disciplined. Why did you return?"

"To tell you that I'm sorry, and I won't insult you again."

"Have you proof of your sincerity?" the gnome asked quietly

Greenberg fished furiously in his pocket and brought out a handful of sugar wrapped in Cellophane, which he tremblingly handed to the gnome.

"Ah, very clever, indeed," the little man said, unwrapping a cube and popping it eagerly into his mouth. "Long time since I've had some."

A moment later Greenberg spluttered and floundered under the surface. Even if Mike had not caught his jacket and helped him up, he could almost have enjoyed the sensation of being able to drown.

Nothing in the Rules

L. Sprague de Camp

L. Sprague de Camp has been writing since the 1930s, and has more than three dozen novels, dozens of short stories, and many nonfiction works to show for his efforts. Known early on for his space opera novels, he was first critically recognized for the novel Lest Darkness Fall, *about one man's attempt to change history during the Roman Empire. In his wide-ranging career he has written everything from Conan pastiches to books on writing science fiction. He has been named Grand Master of Science Fiction by the Science Fiction Writers of America.*

NOT MANY SPECTATORS TURN OUT FOR A MEET BETWEEN TWO MINOR women's swimming clubs, and this one was no exception. Louis Connaught, looking up at the balcony, thought casually that the single row of seats around it was about half full, mostly with the usual bored-looking assortment of husbands and boy friends, and some of the Hotel Creston's guests who had wandered in for want of anything better to do. One of the bellboys was asking an evening-gowned female not to smoke, and she was showing irritation. Mr. Santalucia and the little Santalucias were there as usual to see mamma perform. They waved down at Connaught.

Connaught—a dark devilish-looking little man—glanced over to the other side of the pool. The girls were coming out of the shower rooms, and their shrill conversation was blurred by the acoustics of the pool room into a continuous buzz. The air was faintly steamy. The stout party in white duck pants was Laird, coach of the Knickerbockers and Connaught's arch rival. He saw Connaught and boomed: "Hi, Louie!" The words rattled from wall to wall with a sound like a stick being drawn swiftly along a picket fence. Wambach of the A.A.U. Committee, who was refereeing, came in with his overcoat still on and greeted Laird, but the booming reverberations drowned his words before they got over to Connaught.

Then somebody else came through the door; or rather, a knot of people crowded through it all at once, facing inward, some in bathing suits and some in street clothes. It was a few seconds before

Coach Connaught saw what they were looking at. He blinked and looked more closely, standing with his mouth half open.

But not for long. *"Hey!"* he yelled in a voice that made the pool room sound like the inside of a snare drum in use. "Protest! PROTEST! *You can't do that!"*

It had been the preceding evening when Herbert Laird opened his front door and shouted, "H'lo, Mark, come on in." The chill March wind was making a good deal of racket but not as much as all that. Laird was given to shouting on general principles. He was stocky and bald.

Mark Vining came in and deposited his briefcase. He was younger than Laird—just thirty, in fact—with octagonal glasses and rather thin severe features that made him look more serious than he was, which was fairly serious.

"Glad you could come, Mark," said Laird. "Listen, can you make our meet with the Crestons tomorrow night?"

Vining pursed his lips thoughtfully. "I guess so. Loomis decided not to appeal, so I don't have to work nights for a few days anyhow. Is something special up?"

Laird looked sly. "Maybe. Listen, you know that Mrs. Santalucia that Louie Connaught has been cleaning up with for the past couple of years? I think I've got that fixed. But I want you along to think up legal reasons why my scheme's O.K."

"Why," said Vining cautiously. "What's your scheme?"

"Can't tell you now. I promised not to. But if Louie can win by entering a freak—a woman with webbed fingers—"

"Oh, look here, Herb, you know those webs don't really help her—"

"Yes, yes, I know all the arguments. You've already got more water-resistance to your arms than you've got muscle to overcome it with, and so forth. But I know Mrs. Santalucia has webbed fingers, and I know she's the best woman swimmer in New York. And I don't like it. It's bad for my prestige as a coach." He turned and shouted into the gloom: "Iantha!"

"Yes?"

"Come here, will you please? I want you to meet my friend Mr. Vining. Here, we need some light."

The light showed the living room as usual buried under disorderly piles of boxes of bathing suits and other swimming equipment, the sale of which furnished Herbert Laird with most of his income. It also showed a young woman coming in in a wheel chair.

One look gave Vining a feeling that, he knew, boded no good for him. He was unfortunate in being a pushover for any reasonably attractive girl, and at the same time being cursed with an almost pathological shyness where women were concerned. The facts that both he and Laird were bachelors and took their swimming seriously were the main ties between them.

This girl was more than reasonably attractive. She was, thought the dazzled Vining, a wow, a ten-strike, a direct sixteen-inch hit. Her smooth, rather flat features and high cheekbones had a hint of Asian or American Indian, and went oddly with her light-gold hair, which, Vining could have sworn, had a faint greenish tinge. A blanket was wrapped around her legs.

He came out of his trance as Laird introduced the exquisite creature as "Miss Delfoiros."

Miss Delfoiros didn't seem exactly overcome. As she extended her hand, she said with a noticeable accent: "You are not from the newspapers, Mr. Vining?"

"No," said Vining. "Just a lawyer. I specialize in wills and probates and things. Not thinking of drawing up yours, are you?"

She relaxed visibly and laughed. "No. I 'ope I shall not need one for a long, long time."

"Still," said Vining seriously, "you never know—"

Laird bellowed: "Wonder what's keeping that sister of mine. Dinner ought to be ready. *Martha!*" He marched out, and Vining heard Miss Laird's voice, something about "—but Herb, I had to let those things cool down—"

Vining wondered with a great wonder what he should say to Miss Delfoiros. Finally he said, "Smoke?"

"Oh, no, thank you very much. I do not do it."

"Mind if I do?"

"No, not at all."

"Whereabouts do you hail from?" Vining thought the question sounded both brusque and silly. He never did get the hang of talking easily under this circumstances.

"Oh, I am from Kip—Cyprus, I mean. You know, the island."

"Really? That makes you a British subject, doesn't it?"

"Well . . . no, not exactly. Most Cypriots are, but I am not."

"Will you be at this swimming meet?"

"Yes, I think so."

"You don't"—he lowered his voice—"know what scheme Herb's got up his sleeve to beat La Santalucia?"

"Yes . . . no . . . I do not . . . what I mean is, I must not tell."

More mystery, thought Vining. What he really wanted to know was why she was confined to a wheel chair; whether the cause was temporary or permanent. But you couldn't ask a person right out, and he was still trying to concoct a leading question when Laird's bellow wafted in: "All right, folks, soup's on!" Vining would have pushed the wheel chair in, but before he had a chance, the girl had spun the chair around and was half-way to the dining room.

Vining said: "Hello, Martha, how's the school-teaching business?" But he wasn't really paying much attention to Laird's capable spinster sister. He was gaping at Miss Delfoiros, who was quite calmly emptying a teaspoonful of salt into her water glass and stirring.

"What . . . what?" he gulped.

"I 'ave to," she said. "Fresh water makes me—like what you call drunk."

"Listen, Mark!" roared his friend. "Are you sure you can be there on time tomorrow night? There are some questions of eligibility to be cleared up, and I'm likely to need you badly."

"Will Miss Delfoiros be there?" Vining grinned, feeling very foolish inside.

"Oh, sure. Iantha's out . . . say, listen, you know that little eighteen-year-old Clara Havranek? She did the hundred in one-o-five yesterday. She's championship material. We'll clean the Creston Club yet—" He went on, loud and fast, about what he was going to do to Louie Connaught's girls. The while, Mark Vining tried to concentrate on his own food, which was good, and on Iantha Delfoiros, who was charming but evasive.

There seemed to be something special about Miss Delfoiro's food, to judge by the way Martha Laird had served it. Vining looked closely and saw that it had the peculiarly dead and clammy look that a dinner once hot but now cold has. He asked about it.

"Yes," she said, "I like it cold."

"You mean you don't eat *anything* hot?"

She made a face. " 'ot food? No, I do not like it. To us it is—"

"Listen, Mark! I hear the W.S.A. is going to throw a post-season meet in April for novices only—"

Vining's dessert lay before him a full minute before he noticed it. He was too busy thinking how delightful Miss Delfoiros's accent was.

When dinner was over, Laird said, "Listen, Mark, you know something about these laws against owning gold? Well, look here—" He led the way to a candy box on a table in the living room. The box contained, not candy, but gold and silver coins. Laird handed the lawyer several of them. The first one he examined was a silver crown, bearing the inscription "Carolus II Dei Gra" encircling the head of England's Merry Monarch with a wreath in his hair—or, more probably, in his wig. The second was an eighteenth-century Spanish dollar. The third was a Louis d'Or.

"I didn't know you went in for coin collecting, Herb," said Vining. "I suppose these are all genuine?"

"They're genuine all right. But I'm not collecting 'em. You might say I'm taking 'em in trade. I have a chance to sell ten thousand bathing caps, if I can take payment in those things."

"I shouldn't think the U.S. Rubber Company would like the idea much."

"That's just the point. What'll I do with 'em after I get 'em? Will the government put me in jail for having 'em?"

"You needn't worry about that. I don't think the law covers old coins, though I'll look it up to make sure. Better call up the American Numismatic Society—they're in the phone book—and they can tell you how to dispose of them. But look here, what the devil is this? Ten thousand bathing caps to be paid for in pieces-of-eight? I never heard of such a thing."

"That's it exactly. Just ask the little lady here." Laird turned to Iantha, who was nervously trying to signal him to keep quiet. "The deal's her doing."

"I did . . . did—" She looked as if she were going to cry. " 'Erbert, you should not have said that. You see," she said to Vining, "we do not like to 'ave a lot to do with people. Always it causes us troubles."

"Who," asked Vining, "do you mean by 'we'?"

She shut her mouth obstinately. Vining almost melted. But his legal instincts came to the surface. If you don't get a grip on yourself, he thought, you'll be in love with her in another five minutes. And that might be a disaster. He said firmly: "Herb, the more I see of this business the crazier it looks. Whatever's going on, you seem to be trying to get me into it. But I won't let you before I know what it's all about."

"Might as well tell him, Iantha," said Laird. "He'll know when he sees you swim tomorrow, anyhow."

She said: "You will not tell the newspaper men, Mr. Vining?"

"No. I won't say anything to anybody."

"You promise?"

"Of course. You can depend on a lawyer to keep things under his hat."

"Under his—I suppose you mean not to tell. So, look." She reached down and pulled up the lower end of the blanket.

Vining looked. Where he expected to see feet, there was a pair of horizontal flukes, like those of a porpoise.

———

Louis Connaught's having kittens, when he saw what his rival coach had sprung on him, can thus be easily explained. First he doubted his own senses. Then he doubted whether there was any justice in the world.

Meanwhile Mark Vining proudly pushed Iantha's wheel chair in among the cluster of judges and timekeepers at the starting end of the pool. Iantha herself, in a bright green bathing cap, held her blanket around her shoulders, but the slate-gray tail with its flukes was smooth and the flukes were horizontal; artists who show mermaids with scales and a vertical tail fin, like a fish's, simply don't know their zoology.

"All right, all right," bellowed Laird. "Don't crowd around. Everybody get back to where they belong. Everybody, please."

One of the spectators, leaning over the rail of the balcony to see, dropped a fountain pen into the pool. One of the Connaught's girls, a Miss Black, dove in after it. Ogden Wambach, the referee, poked a finger at the skin of the tail. He was a well-groomed, gray-haired man.

"Laird," he said, "is this a joke?"

"Not at all. She's entered in the back stroke and all the free styles, just like any other club member. She's even registered with the A.A.U."

"But . . . but . . . I mean, is it alive? Is it real?"

Iantha spoke up. "Why do you not ask me those questions, Mr. . . . Mr. . . . I do not know you—"

"Good grief," said Wambach. "It talks! I'm the referee, Miss—"

"Delfoiros. Iantha Delfoiros."

"My word. Upon my word. That means—let's see—Violet Porpoise-tail, doesn't it? *Delphis* plus *oura*—"

"You know Greek? Oh, 'ow nice!" She broke into a string of Romaic.

Wambach gulped a little. "Too fast for me, I'm afraid. And that's *modern* Greek, isn't it?"

"Why, yes. I am modern, am I not?"

"Dear me. I suppose so. But is that tail really real? I mean, it's not just a piece of costumery?"

"Oh, but yes." Iantha threw off the blanket and waved her flukes.

"Dear me," said Ogden Wambach. "Where are my glasses? You understand, I just want to make sure there's nothing spurious about this."

Mrs. Santalucia, a muscular-looking lady with a visible mustache and fingers webbed down to the first joint, said, "You mean I gotta swim against *her*?"

Louis Connaught had been sizzling like a dynamite fuse. "You can't do it!" he shrilled. "This is a woman's meet! I protest!"

"So what?" said Laird.

"But you can't enter a fish in a woman's swimming meet! Can you, Mr. Wambach?"

Mark Vining spoke up. He had just taken a bunch of papers clipped together out of his pocket, and was running through them.

"Miss Delfoiros," he asserted, "is not a fish. She's a mammal."

"How do you figure that?" yelled Connaught.

"*Look* at her."

"Um-m-m," said Ogden Wambach. "I see what you mean."

"But," howled Connaught, "she still ain't human!"

"There is a question about that, Mr. Vining," said Wambach.

"No question at all. There's nothing in the rules against entering a mermaid, and there's nothing that says the competitors have to be human."

Connaught was hopping about like an overwrought cricket. He was now waving a copy of the current A.A.U. swimming, diving and water polo rules. "I still protest! Look here! All through here it only talks about two kinds of meets, men's and women's. She ain't a woman, and she certainly ain't a man. If the Union had wanted to have meets for mermaids they'd have said so."

"Not a woman?" asked Vining in a manner that juries learned meant a rapier thrust at an opponent. "I beg your pardon, Mr. Connaught. I looked the question up." He frowned at his sheaf of papers. "Webster's International Dictionary, Second Edition, defines a woman as 'any female person.' And it further defines 'person' as 'a being characterized by conscious apprehension, rationality and a moral sense.'" He turned to Wambach. "Sir, I think you'll agree that Miss Delfoiros has exhibited conscious apprehension and rationality during her conversation with you, won't you?"

"My word . . . I really don't know what to say, Mr. Vining . . . I suppose she has, but I couldn't say—"

Horowitz, the scorekeeper, spoke up. "You might ask her to give the multiplication table." Nobody paid him any attention.

Connaught exhibited symptoms alarmingly suggestive of apoplexy. "But you can't— What are you talking about . . . conscious ap-ap—"

"Please, Mr. Connaught!" said Wambach. "When you shout that way I can't understand you because of the echoes."

Connaught mastered himself with a visible effort. Then he looked crafty. "How do I know she's got a moral sense?"

Vining turned to Iantha. "Have you ever been in jail, Iantha?"

Iantha laughed. "What a funny question, Mark! But of course, I have not."

"That's what *she* says," sneered Connaught. "How you gonna prove it?"

"We don't have to," said Vining loftily. "The burden of proof is on the accuser, and the accused is legally innocent until proved guilty. That principle was well established by the time of King Edward the First."

"That wasn't the kind of moral sense I meant," cried Connaught. "How about what they call moral turp-turp— You know what I mean."

"Hey," growled Laird, "what's the idea? Are you trying to cast— What's the word, Mark?"

"Aspersions?"

"—cast aspersions on one of my swimmers? You watch out. Louie. If I hear you be— What's the word, Mark?"

"Besmirching her fair name?"

"—besmirching her fair name I'll drown you in your own tank."

"And after that," said Vining, "we'll slap a suit on you for slander."

"Gentlemen! Gentlemen!" said Wambach "Let's not have any more personalities, please. This is a swimming meet, not a lawsuit. Let's get to the point."

"We've made ours," said Vining with dignity. "We've shown that Iantha Delfoiros is a woman, and Mr. Connaught has stated, himself, that this is a woman's meet. Therefore, Miss Delfoiros is eligible. Q.E.D."

"Ahem," said Wambach. "I don't quite know— I never had a case like this to decide before."

Louis Connaught almost had tears in his eyes; at least he sounded as if he did. "Mr. Wambach, you can't let Herb do this to me. I'll be a laughingstock."

Laird snorted. "How about your beating me with your Mrs. Santalucia? I didn't get any sympathy from you when people laughed at me on account of that. And how much good did it do me to protest against her fingers?"

"But," wailed Connaught, "if he can enter this Miss Delfurrus, what's to stop somebody from entering a trained sea lion or something? Do you want to make competitive swimming into a circus?"

Laird grinned. "Go ahead, Louie. Nobody's stopping you from entering anything you like. How about it, Ogden? Is she a woman?"

"Well . . . really . . . oh, dear—"

"Please!" Iantha Delfoiros rolled her violet-blue eyes at the bewildered referee. "I should so like to swim in this nice pool with all these nice people!"

Wambach sighed. "All right, my dear, you shall!"

"Whoopee!" cried Laird, the cry being taken up by Vining, the members of the Knickerbocker Swimming Club, the other officials, and lastly the spectators. The noise in the enclosed space made sensitive eardrums wince.

"Wait a minute," yelped Connaught when the echoes had died. "Look here, page nineteen of the rules. 'Regulation Costume, Women: Suits must be of dark color, with skirt attached. Leg is to reach—' and so forth. Right here it says it. She can't swim the way she is, not in a sanctioned meet."

"That's true," said Wambach. "Let's see—"

Horowitz looked up from his little score-sheet-littered table. "Maybe one of the girls has a halter she could borrow," he suggested. "That would be *something*."

"Halter, phooey!" snapped Connaught. "This means a regular suit with legs and skirt, and everybody knows it."

"But she hasn't got any legs!" cried Laird. "How could she get into—"

"That's just the point! If she can't wear a suit with legs, and the rules say you gotta have legs, she can't wear the regulation suit, and she can't compete! I gotcha that time! Ha-ha, I'm sneering!"

"I'm afraid not, Louie," said Vining, thumbing his own copy of the rule book. He held it up to the light and read: "'Note.—These rules are approximate, the idea being to bar costumers which are immodest, or will attract undue attention and comment. The referee shall have the power'—et cetera, et cetera. If we cut the legs out of a regular suit, and she pulled the rest of it on over her head, that would be modest enough for all practical purposes. Wouldn't it, Mr. Wambach?"

"Dear me—I don't know—I suppose it would."

Laird hissed to one of his pupils, "Hey, listen, Miss Havranck! You know where my suitcase is? Well, you get one of the extra suits out of it, and there's a pair of scissors in with the first-aid things. You fix that suit up so Iantha can wear it."

Connaught subsided. "I see now," he said bitterly, "why you guys wanted to finish with a 300-yard free style instead of a relay. If I'd'a' known what you were planning—and, you, Mark Vining, if I ever get in a jam, I'll go to jail before I hire you for a lawyer, so help me."

Mrs. Santalucia had been glowering at Iantha Delfoiros. Suddenly she turned to Connaught. "Thissa no fair. I swim against people. I no gotta swim against moimaids."

"Please, Maria, don't *you* desert me," wailed Connaught.

"I no swim tonight."

Connaught looked up appealingly to the balcony. Mr. Santalucia and the little Santalucias, guessing what was happening, burst into a chorus of: "Go on, mamma! You show them, mamma!"

"Aw right. I swim one, maybe two races. If I see I no got a chance, I no swim no more."

"That's better, Maria. It wouldn't really count if she beat you anyway." Connaught headed for the door, saying something about "telephone" on the way.

Despite the delays in starting the meet, nobody left the pool room through boredom; in fact the empty seats in the balcony were full by this time and people were standing up behind them. Word had got around the Hotel Creston that something was up.

By the time Louis Connaught returned, Laird and Vining were pulling the altered bathing suit on over Iantha's head. It didn't reach quite as far as they expected, having been designed for a slightly slimmer swimmer. Not that Iantha was fat. But her human part, if not exactly plump, was at least comfortably upholstered, so that no bones showed. Iantha squirmed around in the suit a good deal, and threw a laughing remark in Greek to Wambach, whose expression showed that he hoped it didn't mean what he suspected it did.

Laird said, "Now listen, Iantha, remember not to move till the gun goes off. And remember that you swim directly over the line on the bottom, not between two lines."

"Are they going to shoot a gun? Oh, I am afraid of shooting!"

"It's nothing to be afraid of; just blank cartridges. They don't hurt anybody. And it won't be so loud inside that cap."

"Herb," said Vining, "won't she lose time getting off, not being able to make a flat dive like the others?"

"She will. But it won't matter. She can swim a mile in *four* minutes, without really trying."

Ritchey, the starter, announced the 50-yard free style. He called: "All right, everybody, line up." Iantha slithered off her chair and crawled over to the starting platform. The other girls were all standing with feet together, bodies bent forward at the hips, and arms pointing backward. Iantha got into a curious position of her own, with her tail under her and her weight resting on her hands and flukes.

"Hey! Protest!" shouted Connaught. "The rules say that all races, except back strokes, are started with dives. What kind of a dive do you call that?"

"Oh, dear," said Wambach. "What—"

"That," said Vining urbanely, "is a mermaid dive. You couldn't expect her to stand upright on her tail."

"But that's just it!" cried Connaught. "First you enter a nonregulation swimmer. Then you put a nonregulation suit on her. Then you start her off with a nonregulation dive. Ain't there anything you guys do like other people?"

"But," said Vining, looking through the rule book, "it doesn't say—here it is. 'The start in all races shall be made with a dive.' But there's nothing in the rules about what kind of dive shall be used. And the dictionary defines a dive simply as a 'plunge into water.' So if you jump in feet first holding your nose, that's a dive for the purpose of the discussion. And in my years of watching swimming meets I've seen some funnier starting-dives than Miss Delfoiros's."

"I suppose he's right," said Wambach.

"O.K., O.K.," snarled Connaught. "But the next time I have a meet with you and Herb, I bring a lawyer along too, see?"

Ritchey's gun went off. Vining noticed that Iantha flinched a little at the report, and perhaps was slowed down a trifle in getting off by it. The other girls' bodies shot out horizontally to smack the water loudly, but Iantha slipped in with the smooth, unhurried motion of a diving seal. Lacking the advantage of feet to push off with, she was several yards behind the other swimmers before she really got started. Mrs. Santalucia had taken her usual lead, foaming along with the slow strokes of her webbed hands.

Iantha didn't bother to come to the surface except at the turn, where she had been specifically ordered to come up so the judge of the turns wouldn't raise arguments as to whether she had touched the end, and at the finish. She hardly used her arms at all, except for an occasional flip of her trailing hands to steer her. The swift up-and-down flutter of the powerful tail-flukes sent her through the water like a torpedo, her wake appearing on the surface six or eight feet behind her. As she shot through the as yet unruffled waters at the far end of the pool on the first leg, Vining, who had gone around to the side to watch, noticed that she had the power of closing her nostrils tightly under water, like a seal or hippopotamus.

Mrs. Santalucia finished the race in the very creditable time of 29.8 seconds. But Iantha Delfoiros arrived, not merely first, but in the time of 8.0 seconds. At the finish she didn't reach up to touch the starting-platform, and then hoist herself out by her arms the way human swimmers do. She simply angled up sharply, left the water like a leaping trout, and came down with a moist smack on the concrete, almost bowling over a timekeeper. By the time the other contestants had completed the turn she was sitting on the

platform with her tail curled under her. As the girls foamed laboriously down the final leg, she smiled dazzlingly at Vining, who had
had to run to be in at the finish.

"That," she said, "was much fun, Mark. I am so glad you and
'Erbert put me in these races."

Mrs. Santalucia climbed out and walked over to Horowitz's table.
That young man was staring in disbelief at the figures he had just
written.

"Yes," he said, "that's what it says. Miss Iantha Delfoiros, 8.0; Mrs.
Maria Santalucia, 29.8. Please don't drip on my score sheets, lady.
Say, Wambach, isn't this a world's record or something?"

"My word!" said Wambach. "It's less than half the existing short-
course record. Less than a third, maybe; I'd have to check it. Dear
me. I'll have to take it up with the Committee. I don't know
whether they'd allow it; I don't think they will, even though there
isn't any specific rule against mermaids."

Vining spoke up. "I think we've complied with all the requirements to have records recognized, Mr. Wambach. Miss Delfoiros
was entered in advance like all the others."

"Yes, yes, Mr. Vining, but don't you see, a record's a serious matter. No ordinary human being could ever come near a time like
that."

"Unless he used an outboard motor," said Connaught. "If you
allow contestants to use tail fins like Miss Delfurrus, you ought to let
'em use propellers. I don't see why these guys should be the only
ones to be let bust rules all over the place, and then think up lawyer
arguments why it's O.K. I'm gonna get me a lawyer, too."

"That's all right, Ogden," said Laird. "You take it up with the
Committee, but we don't really care much about the records any-
way, so long as we can lick Louie here." He smiled indulgently at
Connaught, who sputtered with fury.

"I no swim," announced Mrs. Santalucia. "This is all crazy business. I no get a chance."

"Now, Maria," said Connaught, taking her aside, "just once more,
won't you please? My reputation—" The rest of his words were
drowned in the general reverberation of the pool room. But at the
end of them the redoubtable female appeared to have given in to
his entreaties.

The 100-yard free style started in much the same manner as the
50-yard. Iantha didn't flinch at the gun this time, and got off to a
good start. She skimmed along just below the surface, raising a
wake like a tuna-clipper. These waves confused the swimmer in the
adjacent lane, who happened to be Miss Breitenfeld of the Creston
Club. As a result, on her first return leg, Iantha met Miss

Breitenfeld swimming athwart her—Iantha's—lane, and rammed the unfortunate girl amidships. Miss Breitenfeld went down without even a gurgle, spewing bubbles.

Connaught shrieked: "Foul! Foul!" though in the general uproar it sounded like "Wow, wow!" Several swimmers who weren't racing dove in to the rescue, and the race came to a stop in general confusion and pandemonium. When Miss Breitenfeld was hauled out it was found that she had merely had the wind knocked out of her and had swallowed considerable water.

Mark Vining, looking around for Iantha, found her holding on to the edge of the pool and shaking her head. Presently she crawled out, crying: "Is she 'urt? Is she 'urt? Oh, I am so sorree! I did not think there would be anybody in my lane, so I did not look ahead."

"See?" yelled Connaught. "See, Wambach? See what happens? They ain't satisfied to walk away with the races with their fish-woman. No, they gotta try to cripple my swimmers by butting their slats in. Herb," he went on nastily, "why dontcha get a pet swordfish? Then when you rammed one of my poor girls she'd be out of competition for good."

"Oh," said Iantha. "I did not mean . . . it was an accident!"

"Accident my foot!"

"But it was. Mr. Referee, I do not want to bump people. My 'ead 'urts, and my neck also. You think I try to break my neck on purpose?" Iantha's altered suit had crawled up under her armpits, but nobody noticed particularly.

"Sure it was an accident," bellowed Laird. "Anybody could see that. And, listen, if anybody was fouled it was Miss Delfoiros."

"Certainly," chimed in Vining. "She was in her own lane, and the other girl wasn't."

"Oh, dear me," said Wambach. "I suppose they're right again. This'll have to be reswum anyway. Does Miss Breitenfeld want to compete?"

Miss Breitenfeld didn't but the others lined up again. This time the race went off without untoward incident. Iantha again made a spectacular leaping finish, just as the other three swimmers were halfway down the second of their four legs.

When Mrs. Santalucia emerged this time, she said to Connaught: "I swim no more. That is final."

"Oh, but Maria—" It got him nowhere. Finally he said, "Will you swim in the races that she don't enter?"

"Is there any?"

"I think so. Hey, Horowitz, Miss Delfurrus ain't entered in the breast stroke, is she?"

Horowitz looked. "No, she isn't," he said.

"That something. Say, Herb, how come you didn't put your fish-woman in the breast stroke?"

Vining answered for Laird. "Look at your rules, Louie. 'The feet shall be drawn up simultaneously, the knees bent and open,' et cetera. The rules for back stroke and free style don't say anything about how the legs shall be used, but those for breast stroke do. So no legs, no breast stroke. We aren't giving you a chance to make any legitimate protests."

"Legitimate protests!" Connaught turned away, sputtering.

While the dives were being run off, Vining, watching, became aware of an ethereal melody. First he thought it was in his head. Then he was sure it was coming from one of the spectators. He finally located the source; it was Iantha Delfoiros, sitting in her wheel chair and singing softly. By leaning nearer he could make out the words:

> "Die schonstte Jungfrau sitzet
> Dort ober wunderbar;
> Ihr goldenes Geschmeide blitzet;
> Sie kaemmt ihr goldenes Haar."

Vining went over quietly. "Iantha," he said. "Pull your bathing suit down, and don't sing."

She complied, looking up at him with a giggle. "But that is a nice song! I learn it from a wrecked German sailor. It is about one of my people."

"I know, but it'll distract the judges. They have to watch the dives closely, and the place is too noisy as it is."

"Such a nice man you are, Mark, but so serious!" She giggled again.

Vining wondered at the subtle change in the mermaid's manner. Then a horrible thought struck him.

"Herb!" he whispered. "Didn't she say something last night about getting drunk on fresh water?"

Laird looked up. "Yes. She— The water in the pool's fresh! I never thought of that. Is she showing signs?"

"I think she is."

"Listen, Mark, what'll we do?"

"I don't know. She's entered in two more events, isn't she? Back stroke and 300-yard free style?"

"Yes."

"Well, why not withdraw her from the back stroke, and give her a chance to sober up before the final event?"

"Can't. Even with all her firsts we aren't going to win by any big margin. Louie has the edge on us in the dives, and Mrs. Santalucia'll win the breast stroke. In the events Iantha's in, if she takes first and Louie's girl take second and third, that means five points for us but four for him, so we have an advantage of only one point. And her world's record times don't give us any more points."

"Guess we'll have to keep her in and take a chance," said Vining glumly.

Iantha's demeanor was sober enough in lining up for the back stroke. Again she lost a fraction of a second in getting started by not having feet to push off with. But once she got started, the contest was even more one-sided than the free style races had been. The human part of her body was practically out of water, skimming the surface like the front half of a speedboat. She made paddling motions with her arms, but that was merely for technical reasons; the power was all furnished by the flukes. She didn't jump out onto the starting-platform this time; for a flash Vining's heart almost stopped as the emerald-green bathing cap seemed about to crash into the tiles at the end of the pool. But Iantha had judged the distance to a fraction of an inch, and braked to a stop with her flukes just before striking.

The breast stroke was won easily by Mrs. Santalucia, though her slow plodding stroke was less spectacular than the butterfly of her competitors. The shrill cheers of the little Santalucias could be heard over the general hubbub. When the winner climbed out, she glowered at Iantha and said to Connaught: "Louie, if you ever put me in a meet wit' moimaids again, I no swim for you again, never. Now I go home." With which she marched off to the shower room.

Ritchey was just about to announce the final event, the 300-yard free style, when Connaught plucked his sleeve. "Jack," he said, "wait a second. One of my swimmers is gonna be delayed a coupla minutes." He went out a door.

Laird said to Vining: "Wonder what Louie's grinning about. He's got something nasty, I bet. He was phoning earlier, you remember."

"We'll soon see— What's that?" A hoarse bark wafted in from somewhere and rebounded from the walls.

Connaught reappeared carrying two buckets. Behind him was a little round man in three sweaters. Behind the little round man galumphed a glossy California sea lion. At the sight of the gently rippling, jade-green pool the animal barked joyously and skidded the water, swam swiftly about, and popped out onto the landing-platform, barking. The bark had a peculiarly nerve-racking effect in the echoing pool room.

Ogden Wambach seized two handfuls of his sleek gray hair and tugged. "Connaught!" he shouted. "What is that?"

"Oh, that's just one of my swimmers, Mr. Wambach."

"Hey, listen!" rumbled Laird. "We're going to protest this time. Miss Delfoiros is at least a woman, even if she's a kind of peculiar one. But you can't call *that* a woman."

Connaught grinned like Satan looking over a new shipment of sinners. "Didn't you just say to go ahead and enter a sea lion if I wanted to?"

"I don't remember saying—"

"Yes, Herbert," said Wambach, looking haggard. "You did say it. There didn't used to be any trouble in deciding whether a swimmer was a woman or not. But now that you've brought in Miss Delfoiros, there doesn't seem to be any place we can draw a line."

"But look here, Ogden, there is such a thing as going too far—"

"That's just what I said about you!" shrilled Connaught.

Wambach took a deep breath. "Let's not shout, please. Herbert, technically you may have an argument. But after we allowed Miss Delfoiros to enter, I think it would be only sporting to let Louis have his sea lion. Especially after you told him to get one if he could."

Vining spoke up. "Oh, we're always glad to do the sporting thing. But I'm afraid the sea lion wasn't entered at the beginning of the meet as is required by the rules. We don't want to catch hell from the Committee—"

"Oh, yes, she was," said Connaught. "See!" He pointed to one of Horowitz's sheets. "Her name's Alice Black, and there it is.

"But," protested Vining, "I thought *that* was Alice Black." He pointed to a slim dark girl in a bathing suit who was sitting on a window ledge.

"It is," grinned Connaught. "It's just a coincidence that they both got the same name."

"You don't expect us to believe *that?*"

"I don't care whether you believe or not. It's so. Ain't the sea lion's name Alice Black?" He turned to the little fat man, who nodded.

"Let it pass," moaned Wambach. "We can't take time off to get this animal's birth certificate."

"Well, then," said Vining, "how about the regulation suit? Maybe you'd like to try to put a suit on your sea lion?"

"Don't have to. She's got one already. It grows on her. Yah, yah, yah, gotcha that time."

"I suppose," said Wambach, "that you *could* consider a natural sealskin pelt as equivalent to a bathing suit."

"Sure you could. That's the pernt. Anyway the idea of suits is to be modest, and nobody gives a care about a sea lion's modesty."

Vining made a final point. "You refer to the animal as 'her,' but how do we know it's a female? Even Mr. Wambach wouldn't let you enter a male sea lion in a women's meet."

Wambach spoke: "How do you tell on a sea lion?"

Connaught looked at the little fat man. "Well, maybe we had better not go into that here. How would it be if I put up a ten-dollar bond that Alice is a female, and you checked on her sex later?"

"That seems fair," said Wambach.

Vining and Laird looked at each other. "Shall we let 'em get away with that, Mark?" asked the latter.

Vining rocked on his heels for a few seconds. Then he said, "I think we might as well. Can I see you outside a minute, Herb? You people don't mind holding up the race a couple of minutes more, do you? We'll be right back."

Connaught started to protest about further delay, but thought better of it. Laird presently reappeared looking unwontedly cheerful.

"'Erbert!" said Iantha.

"Yes?" he put his head down.

"I'm afraid—"

"You're afraid Alice might bite you in the water? Well, I wouldn't want that—"

"Oh, no, not afraid that way. Alice, poof! If she gets nasty I give her one with the tail. But I am afraid she can swim faster than me."

"Listen, Iantha, you just go ahead and swim the best you can. Twelve legs, remember. And don't be surprised, no matter what happens."

"What you two saying?" asked Connaught suspiciously.

"None of your business, Louie. Whatcha got in that pail? *Fish?* I see how you're going to work this. Wanta give up and concede the meet now?"

Connaught merely snorted.

The only competitors in the 300-yard free style race were Iantha Delfoiros and the sea lion, allegedly named Alice. The normal members of both clubs declared that nothing would induce them to get into the pool with the animal. Not even the importance of collecting a third-place point would move them.

Iantha got into her usual starting position. Beside her the little round man maneuvered Alice, holding her by an improvised leash made of a length of rope. At the far end, Connaught had placed himself and one of the buckets.

Ritchey fired his gun; the little man slipped the leash and said: "Go get 'em, Alice!" Connaught took a fish out of his bucket and waved it. But Alice, frightened by the shot, set up a furious barking and stayed where she was. Not till Iantha had almost reached the far end of the pool did Alice sight the fish at the other end. Then she slid off and shot down the water like a streak. Those who have seen sea lions merely loafing about a pool in a zoo or aquarium have no conception of how fast they can go when they try. Fast as the mermaid was, the sea lion was faster. She made two bucking jumps out of water before she arrived and oozed out onto the concrete. One gulp and the fish had vanished.

Alice spotted the bucket and tried to get her head into it. Connaught fended her off as best he could with his feet. At the starting end, the little round man had taken a fish out of the other bucket and was waving it, calling: "Here, Alice!" Alice didn't get the idea until Iantha had finished her second leg. Then she went like the proverbial bat from hell.

The same trouble occurred at the starting end of the pool; Alice didn't see why she should swim twenty-five yards for a fish when there were plenty of them a few feet away. The result was that at the halfway mark Iantha was two legs ahead. But then Alice, who was no dope as sea lions go, caught on. She caught up with and passed Iantha in the middle of her eighth leg, droozling out of the water at each end long enough to gulp a fish and then speeding down to the other end. In the middle of the tenth leg she was ten yards ahead of the mermaid.

At that point Mark Vining appeared through the door, running. In each hand he held a bowl of goldfish by the edge. Behind him came Miss Havranek and Miss Tufts, also of the Knickerbockers, both similarly burdened. The guests of the Hotel Creston had been mildly curious when a dark, severe-looking young man and two girls in bathing suits had dashed into the lobby and made off with the six bowls. But they had been too well-bred to inquire directly about the rape of the goldfish.

Vining ran down the side of the pool to a point near the far end. There he extended his arms and inverted the bowls. Water and fish cascaded into the pool. Miss Havranek and Miss Tufts did likewise at other points along the edge of the pool.

Results were immediate. The bowls had been large, and each had contained about six or eight fair-sized goldfish. The forty-odd bright-colored fish, terrified by their rough handling, darted hither and thither about the pool, or at least went as fast as their inefficient build would permit them. Alice, in the middle of her ninth leg, angled off sharply. Nobody saw her snatch the fish; one second it was there, and the next it wasn't. Alice doubled with a swirl of flippers and shot diagonally across the pool. Another fish vanished. Forgotten were her master and Louis Connaught and their buckets.

This was much more fun. Meanwhile, Iantha finished her race, narrowly avoiding a collision with the sea lion on her last leg.

Connaught hurled the fish he was holding as far as he could. Alice snapped it up and went on hunting. Connaught ran toward the starting-platform, yelling: "Foul! Foul! Protest! Protest! Foul! Foul!"

He arrived to find the timekeepers comparing watches on Iantha's swim, Laird and Vining doing a kind of war dance, and Ogden Wambach looking like the March Hare on the twenty-eighth of February. "Stop!" cried the referee. "Stop, Louie! If you shout like that you'll drive me mad! I'm almost mad now! I know what you're going to say."

"Well . . . well . . . why don't you do something, then? Why don't you tell these crooks where to head in? Why don't you have 'em expelled from the Union? Why don't you—"

"Relax, Louie," said Vining. "We haven't done anything illegal."

"*What*? Why, you dirty—"

"Easy, easy." Vining looked speculatively at his fist. The little man followed his glance and quieted somewhat. "There's nothing in the rules about putting fish into a pool. Intelligent swimmers, like Miss Delfoiros, know enough to ignore them when they're swimming a race."

"But . . . what . . . why you—"

Vining walked off, leaving the two coaches and the referee to fight it out. He looked for Iantha. She was sitting on the edge of pool, paddling in the water with her flukes. Beside her were four feebly flopping goldfish laid out in a row on the tiles. As he approached, she picked one up and put the front end of it in her mouth. There was a flash of pearly teeth and a spasmodic flutter of the fish's tail, and the front half of the fish was gone. The other half followed immediately.

At that instant Alice spotted the three remaining fish. The sea lion had cleaned out the pool, and was now slithering around on the concrete, barking and looking for more prey. She galumphed past Vining toward the mermaid.

Iantha saw her coming. The mermaid hoisted her tail out of water, pivoted where she sat, swung the tail up in a curve, brought the flukes down on the sea lion's head with a loud *spat*. Vining, who was twenty feet off, could have sworn he felt the wind of the blow.

Alice gave a squawk of pain and astonishment and slithered away, shaking her head. She darted past Vining again, and for reasons best known to herself hobbled over to the center of the argument and bit Ogden Wambach in the leg. The referee screeched and climbed up on Horowitz's table.

"Hey," said the scorekeeper. "You're scattering my papers!"

"I still say they're publicity-hunting crooks!" yelled Connaught, waving his copy of the rule book at Wambach.

"Bunk!" bellowed Laird. "He's just sore because we can think up more stunts than he can. He started it, with his web-fingered woman."

"I'm going mad!" screamed Wambach. "You hear? Mad, mad, mad! One more word out of either of you and I'll have you suspended from the Union!"

"Ow, ow, ow!" barked Alice.

Iantha had finished her fish. She started to pull the bathing suit down again; changed her mind, pulled it off over her head, rolled it up, and threw it across the pool. Halfway across it unfolded and floated down onto the water. The mermaid then cleared her throat, took a deep breath, and, in a clear singing soprano, launched into the heart-wrenching strains of:

> *"Rheingold!*
> *Reines Gold,*
> *Wie lauter und hell*
> *Leuchtest hold du uns!*
> *Um dich, du klares—"*

"Iantha!"

"What is it, Markee?" she giggled.

"I said, it's getting time to go home!"

"Oh, but I do not want to go home. I am having much fun.

> *"Nun wir klagen!*
> *Gebt uns das Gold—"*

"No, really, Iantha, we've got to go." He laid a hand on her shoulder. The touch made his blood tingle. At the same time it was plain that the remains of Iantha's carefully husbanded sobriety had gone where the woodbine twineth. The last race in fresh water had been like three oversized Manhattans. Through Vining's head ran an absurd but apt paraphrase of an old song:

> *"What shall we do with a drunken mermaid*
> *At three o'clock in the morning?"*

"Oh, Markee, always you are so serious when people are 'aving fun. But if you say 'please' I will come."

"Very well, please come. Here, put your arm around my neck, and I'll carry you to your chair."

Such, indeed was Mark Vining's intention. He got one hand around her waist and another under her tail. Then he tried to straighten up. He had forgotten that Iantha's tail was a good deal heavier than it looked. In fact, that long and powerful structure of bone, muscle, and cartilage ran the mermaid's total weight up to the surprising figure of over two hundred and fifty pounds. The result of his attempt was to send himself and his burden headlong into the pool. To the spectators it looked as though he picked Iantha up and then deliberately dived in with her.

He came up and shook the water out of his head. Iantha popped up in front of him.

"So!" she gurgled. "You are 'aving fun with Iantha! I think you are serious, but you want to play games! All right, I show you! She brought her palm down smartly, filling Vining's mouth and nose with water. He struck out blindly for the edge of the pool. He was a powerful swimmer, but his street clothes hampered him. Another splash cascaded over his luckless head. He got his eyes clear in time to see Iantha's head go down and her flukes up.

"Markeeee!" The voice was behind him. He turned, and saw Iantha holding a large black block of soft rubber. This object was a plaything for users of the Hotel Creston's pool, and it had been left lying on the bottom during the meet.

"Catch!" cried Iantha gaily, and let drive. The block took Vining neatly between the eyes.

The next thing he knew he was lying on the wet concrete. He sat up and sneezed. His head seemed to be full of ammonia. Louis Connaught put away the smelling-salts bottle, and Laird shoved a glass containing a snort of whiskey at him. Beside him was Iantha, sitting on her curled-up tail. She was actually crying.

"Oh, Markee, you are not dead? You are all right? Oh, I am so sorry! I did not mean to 'it you."

"I'm all right, I guess," he said thickly. "Just an accident. Don't worry."

"Oh, I am so glad!" She grabbed his neck and gave it a hug that made its vertebrae creak alarmingly.

"Now," he said, "if I could dry out my clothes. Louie, could you . . . uh—"

"Sure," said Connaught, helping him up. "We'll put your clothes on the radiator in the men's shower room, and I can lend you a pair of pants and a sweatshirt while they're drying."

When Vining came out in his borrowed garments, he had to push his way through the throng that crowded the starting end of pool room. He was relieved to note that Alice had disappeared. In the crowd Iantha in her wheel chair was holding court. In front of her stood a large man in a dinner jacket and a black coat, with his back to the pool.

"Permit me," he was saying. "I am Joseph Clement. Under my management nothing you wished in the way of a dramatic or musical career would be beyond you. I heard you sing, and I know that with but little training even the doors of the Metropolitan would fly open at your approach."

"No, Mr. Clement. It would be nice, but tomorrow I 'ave to leave for 'ome." She giggled.

"But my dear Miss Delfoiros—where is your home, if I may presume to ask?"

"Cyprus."

"Cyprus? Hm-m-m—let's see, where's that?"

"You do not know where Cyprus is? You are not a nice man. I do not like you. Go away."

"Oh, but my dear, dear Miss Del—"

"Go away I said. Scram."

"But—"

Iantha's tail came up and lashed out, catching the cloaked man in the solar plexus.

Little Miss Havranck looked at her teammate, Miss Tufts, as she prepared to make her third rescue of the evening. "Poisonally," she said, "I am getting sick of pulling dopes out of this pool."

The sky was just turning gray the next morning when Laird drove his huge old town car out into the driveway of his house in the Bronx. Although he always drove himself, he couldn't resist the dirt-cheap prices at which second-hand town cars can be obtained. Now the car had the detachable top over the driver's seat in place, with good reason; the wind was driving a heavy rain almost horizontally.

He got out and helped Vining carry Iantha into the car. Vining got in the back with the mermaid. He spoke into the voice tube: "Jones Beach, Chauncey."

"Aye, aye, sir," came the reply. "Listen, Mark, you sure we remembered everything?"

"I made a list and checked it." He paused. "I could have done with some more sleep last night. Are you sure you won't fall asleep at the wheel?"

"Listen, Mark, with all the coffee I got sloshing around in me, I won't get to sleep for a week."

"We certainly picked a nice time to leave."

"I know we did. In a coupla hours the place'll be covered six deep with reporters. If it weren't for the weather, they might be arriving now. When they do, they'll find the horse has stolen the stable door—that isn't what I mean, but you get the idea. Listen, you better pull down some of those curtains until we get out on Long Island."

"Righto, Herb."

Iantha spoke up in a small voice. "Was I very bad last night when I was drunk, Mark?"

"Not very. At least, not worse than I'd be if I went swimming in a tank of sherry."

"I am so sorry—always I try to be nice, but the fresh water gets me out of my head. And that poor Mr. Clement, that I pushed into the water—"

"Oh, he's used to temperamental people. That's his business. But I don't know that it was such a good idea on the way home to stick your tail out of the car and biff that cop under the chin with it."

She giggled. "But he looked so surprised!"

"I'll say he did! But a surprised cop is sometimes a tough customer."

"Will that make trouble for you?"

"I don't think so. If he's a wise cop, he won't report it at all. You know how the report would read: 'Attacked by mermaid at corner Broadway and Ninety-eighth Street, 11:45 P.M.' And *where* did you learn the unexpurgated version of 'Barnacle Bill the Sailor'?"

"Greek sponge diver I met in Florida told me. 'E is a friend of us mer-folk, and he taught me my first English. 'E used to joke about my Cypriot accent when we talked Greek. It is a pretty song, is it not?"

"I don't think 'pretty' is exactly the word I'd use."

"'Oo won the meet? I never die 'ear."

"Oh, Louie and Herb talked it over, and decided they'd both get so much publicity out of it that it didn't much matter. They're leaving it up to the A.A.U., who will get a first-class headache. For instance, we'll claim we didn't foul Alice, because Louie had already disqualified her by his calling and fish-waving. You see, that's coaching, and coaching a competitor during an event is illegal. But, look here, Iantha, why do you have to leave so abruptly?"

She shrugged. "My business with 'Erbert is over, and I promised to get back to Cyprus before my sister's baby was born."

"You don't lay eggs? But of course you don't. Didn't I just prove last night you were mammals?"

"Markee, what an idea! Anyway, I do not want to stay around. I like you and I like 'Erbert, but I do not like living on land. You just imagine living in water for yourself, and you get an idea. And if I stay, the newspapers come, and soon all New York knows about me. We mer-folk do not believe in letting the land men know about us."

"Why?"

"We used to be friends with them sometimes, and always it made trouble. And now they 'ave guns and go around shooting things a mile away, to collect them, my great-uncle was shot in the tail last year by some aviator man who thought he was a porpoise or something. We don't like being collected. So when we see a boat or an airplane coming, we duck down and swim away quick."

"I suppose," said Vining slowly, "that that's why there were plenty of reports of mer-folks up to a few centuries ago, and then they stopped, so that now people don't believe they exist."

"Yes. We are smart, and we can see as far as the land men can. So you do not catch us very often. That is why this business with 'Erbert, to buy ten thousand caps for the mer-folk, 'as to be secret. Not even his company will know about it. But they will not care if they get their money. And we shall not 'ave to sit on rocks drying our 'air so much. Maybe later we can arrange to buy some good knives and spears the same way. They would be better than the shell things we use now."

"I suppose you get all these old coins out of wrecks?"

"Yes. I know of one just off . . . no, I must not tell you. If the land men know about a wreck, they come with divers. Of course, the very deep ones we do not care about, because we cannot dive down that far. We 'ave to come up for air, like a whale."

"How did Herb happen to sack you in on that swimming meet?"

"Oh, I promised him when he asked—when I did not know 'ow much what-you-call-it fuss there would be. When I found out he would not let me go back on my promise. I think he 'as a conscience about that, and that is why he gave me that nice fish spear."

"Do you ever expect to get back this way?"

"No, I do not think so. We 'ad a committee to see about the caps, and they chose me to represent them. But now that is arranged, and there is no more reason for me going out on land again."

He was silent for a while. Then he burst out: "Iantha, I just can't believe that you're starting off this morning to swim the Atlantic, and I'll never see you again."

She patted his hand. "Maybe you cannot, but that is so. Remember, friendships between my folks and yours always make people un'appy. I shall remember you a long time, but that is all there will ever be to it."

He growled something in his throat, looking straight in front of him.

She said: "Mark, you know I like you, and I think you like me.

'Erbert 'as a moving-picture machine in his house, and he showed me some pictures of 'ow the land folk live.

"These pictures showed a custom of the people in this country, when they like each other. It is called—kissing, I think. I should like to learn that custom."

"Huh? You mean *me?*" To a man of Vining's temperament, the shock was almost physically painful. But her arms were already sliding around his neck. Presently twenty firecrackers, six Roman candles, and a skyrocket seemed to go off inside him.

"Here we are, folks," called Laird. Getting no response, he repeated the statement more loudly. A faint and unenthusiastic "Yeah" came through the voice tube.

Jones Beach was bleak under the lowering March clouds. The wind drove the rain against the car windows.

They drove down the beach road a way, till the tall tower was lost in the rain. Nobody was in sight.

The men carried Iantha down onto the beach and brought the things she was taking. These consisted of a boxful of cans of sardines, with a trap to go over the shoulders; a similar but smaller container with her personal belongings; and the fish spear, with which she might be able to pick up lunch on the way.

Iantha peeled off her land-woman's clothes and pulled on the emerald bathing cap. Vining, watching her with the skirt of his overcoat whipping about his legs, felt as if his heart were running out of his damp shoes onto the sand.

They shook hands, and Iantha kissed them both. She squirmed down the sand and into the water. Then she was gone. Vining thought he saw her wave back from the crest of a wave, but in that visibility he couldn't be sure.

They walked back to the car, squinting against the drops. Laird said: "Listen, Mark, you look as if you'd just taken a right to the button."

Vining merely grunted. He had got in front with Laird, and was drying his glasses with his handkerchief, as if that were an important and delicate operation.

"Don't tell me you're hooked?"

"So what?"

"Well, I suppose you know there's absolutely nothing you can do about it."

"Herb!" Vining snapped angrily. "Do you have to point out the obvious?"

Laird, sympathizing with his friend's feelings, did not take offense. After they had driven awhile, Vining spoke on his own initiative. "That," he said, "is the only woman I've ever known that made me feel at ease. I could talk to her."

Later, he said, "I never felt so mixed up in my life. I doubt whether anybody else ever did, either. Maybe I ought to feel relieved it's over. But I don't."

Pause. Then: "You'll drop me in Manhattan on your way back, won't you?"

"Sure, anywhere you say. Your apartment?"

"Anywhere near Times Square will do. There's a bar there I like."

So, thought Laird, at least the normal male's instincts were functioning correctly in the crisis.

When he let Vining out on Forty-sixth Street, the young lawyer walked off into the rain whistling. The whistle surprised Laird. Then he recognized the tune as one that was written for one of Kipling's poems. But he couldn't, at the moment, think which one.

Fruit of Knowledge

C. L. Moore

C. L. Moore (1911–1987) never gained the critical or popular acclaim she deserved as one of the earliest female science fiction writers. She was often an uncredited coauthor with Henry Kuttner, collaborating on books that crossed the boundary between science fiction and fantasy, such as Valley of the Flame *and* Well of the Worlds. *However, the short fiction she wrote alone deserves recognition on its own merits of strong character development and psychological motivation. The two stories she's best known for are her first published tale, "Shambleau," which introduced her hero Northwest Smith, and "Vintage Season," which details a group of tourists from the future watching the past unobserved, the latter considered a classic tale of speculative fiction.*

It was the first Sabbath. Down the open glades of Eden a breeze stirred softly. Nothing else in sight moved except a small winged head that fluttered, yawning, across the glade and vanished among leaves that drew back to receive it. The air quivered behind it like a wake left in water of incomparable clarity. From far away and far above a faint drift of singing echoed, "Hosannah . . . hosannah . . . hosannah—" The seraphim were singing about the Throne.

A pool at the edge of the glade gave back light and color like a great, dim jewel. It gave back reflections, too. The woman who bent over it had just discovered that. She was leaning above the water until her cloudy dark hair almost dipped into the surface. There was a curious shadow all about her, like a thin garment which did not quite conceal how lovely she was, and though no breeze stirred just now, that shadow garment moved uneasily upon her and her hair lifted a little as if upon a breeze that did not blow.

She was so quiet that a passing cherub-head paused above the water to look, too, hanging like a hummingbird motionless over its own reflection in the pool.

"Pretty!" approved the cherub in a small, piping voice. "New here, aren't you?"

The woman looked up with a slow smile, putting back the veil of her hair.

"Yes, I am," she answered softly. Her voice did not sound quite sure of itself. She had never spoken aloud before until this moment.

"You'll like the Garden," said the cherub in a slightly patronizing tone, giving his rainbow wings a shake. "Anything I can do for you? I'm not busy just now. Be glad to show you around."

"Thank you," smiled the woman, her voice sounding a little more confident. "I'll find my way."

The cherub shrugged his colored wings. "Just as you say. By the way, I suppose they warned you about the Tree?"

The woman glanced up at him rather quickly, her shadowy eyes narrowing.

"The Tree? Is there danger?"

"Oh, no. You mustn't touch it, that's all. It's the one in the middle of the Garden, the Tree of the Knowledge of Good and Evil— you can't miss it. I saw the Man looking at it yesterday for quite a while. That reminds me, have you met the Man?"

The woman bent her head so that the hair swung forward to veil her face. From behind it, in a voice that sounded as if she might be smiling, she said:

"He's waiting for me now."

"Oh?" said the cherub, impressed. "Well, you'll find him over by the orange grove east of the Tree. He's resting. It's the Day of Rest, you know." The cherub tilted an intimate eyebrow heavenward and added, "He's resting, too. Hear the singing? He made the Man only yesterday, right out of this very earth you're standing on. We were all watching. It was wonderful— Afterward, He called the man Adam, and then Adam named the animals— By the way, what's your name?"

The woman smiled down at her own veiled reflection in the water. After a moment—

"Lilith," she said.

The cherub stared, his eyes widening into two blue circles of surprise. He was speechless for an instant. Then he pursed his pink mouth to whistle softly.

"Why," he stammered, "you . . . you're the Queen of Air and Darkness!"

Smiling up at him from the corners of her eyes, the woman nodded. The cherub stared at her big-eyed for a moment longer, too overcome for speech. Then, suddenly, he beat his rainbow pinions together and darted off through the trees without another word, the translucent air rippling in a lazy, half-visible wake behind him.

Lilith looked after him with a shadowy smile on her face. He was going to warn Adam. The smile deepened. Let him.

Lilith turned for one last glance into the mirror of the pool at the strange new shape she had just put on. It was the newest thing in creation—not even God knew about it. And rather surprisingly, she thought she was going to like it. She did not feel nearly as stifled and heavy as she had expected to feel, and there was something distinctly pleasant in the softness of the breeze pouring caressingly about her body, the fragrance of springtime sweet in her nostrils, the grass under her bare feet. The Garden was beautiful with a beauty she had not realized until she saw it through human eyes. Everything she saw through them, indeed, was curiously different now. Here in this flesh all her faculties seemed refocused, as if she, who had always seen with such crystal clarity, now looked through rainbows at everything she saw. But it was a pleasant refocusing. She wished she had longer to enjoy her tenancy in this five-sensed flesh she shared with Adam.

But she had very little time. She glanced up toward the bright, unchanging glory above the trees as if she could pierce the floor of heaven and see God resting on the unimaginable splendor of the Throne while the seraphim chanted in long, shining rows about him. At any moment He might stir and lean forward over Eden, looking down. Lilith instinctively shrugged her shadowy garment closer about her. If He did not look too closely, He might not pierce that shadow. But if He did— A little thrill of excitement, like forked lightning, went through the strange new flesh she wore. She liked danger.

She bent over the pool for one last look at herself, and the pool was a great dim eye looking back at her, almost sentient, almost aware of her. This was a living Garden. The translucent air quivered with a rhythmic pulsing through the trees; the ground was resilient under her feet; vines drew back to let her pass beneath them. Lilith, turning away through the swimming air after the cherub, puzzled a little as she walked through the parting trees. The relation was very close between flesh and earth—perhaps her body was so responsive to the beauty of the Garden because it aped so closely flesh that had been a part of the Garden yesterday. And if even she felt that kinship, what must Adam feel, who was himself earth only yesterday?

The Garden was like a vast, half-sentient entity all around her, pulsing subtly with the pulse of the lucent air. Had God drawn from this immense and throbbing fecundity all the life which peopled Eden? Was Adam merely an extension of it, a focus and intensification of the same life which pulsed through the Garden? Creation was too new; she could only guess.

She thought, too, of the Tree of Knowledge as she walked smoothly through the trees. That Tree, tempting and forbidden. Why? Was God testing Man somehow? Was Man then, not quite finished, after all? Was there any flaw in Eden? Suddenly she knew that there must be. Her very presence here was proof of it, for she, above all others, had no right to intrude into this magical closed sphere which was God's greatest work. Yet here she walked through the heart of it, and not even God knew, yet—

Lilith slanted a smile up through the leaves toward the choruses of the seraphim whose singing swelled and sank and swelled again, unutterably sweet high above the trees. The animals watched her pass with wide, bewildered eyes, somehow not quite at ease, although no such thing as fear had yet stirred through the Garden. Lilith glanced at them curiously as she passed. They were pretty things. She liked Eden.

Presently a swooning fragrance came drifting to her through the trees, almost too sweet to enjoy, and she heard a small voice piping excitedly: "Lilith . . . Air and Darkness— He won't like it! Michael ought to know—"

Lilith smiled and stepped clear of the trees into the full, soft glow of Eden's sun. It did not touch the shadow that dimly veiled the pale contours of this newest shape in Eden. Once or twice that intangible breeze lifted her hair in a great, dim cloud about her, though no leaves moved. She stood quiet, staring across the glade, and as she stared she felt the first small tremor of distrust in this new flesh she wore.

For on a grassy bank in the sunlight, under the blossoming orange trees, lay Adam. And the trees and the flowers of Eden had seemed beautiful to the eyes of this body Lilith wore, and the breezes and the perfumes had delighted it—but here was flawless perfection newly shaped out of the warm red earth of Eden into the image of its Maker, and the sight of him frightened Lilith because it pleased her so. She did not trust a beauty that brought her to a standstill under the trees, not quite certain why she had stopped.

He sprawled in long-limbed magnificence on the grass, laughing up at the cherub with his curly yellow head thrown back. Every line of him and every motion had a splendid male beauty as perfect as Omnipotence could make it. Though he wore no clothing he was no more naked than she, for there was a curious glow all about him, a garment of subtle glory that clothed him as if with an all-enveloping halo.

The cherub danced excitedly up and down in the air above him, shrilling:

"She shouldn't be here! You know she shouldn't! She's evil, that's what she is! God won't like it! She—" Then above Adam's head he caught Lilith's eye, gulped a time or two, piped one last admonishing, "Better watch out!" and fluttered away among the leaves, looking back over one wing as he flew.

Adam's gaze followed the cherub's. The laughter faded from his face and he got up slowly, the long, smooth muscles sliding beautifully under his garment of subtle glory as he moved. He was utter perfection in everything he did, flawless, new-made at the hands of God. He came toward her slowly, a shining wonder on his face.

Lilith stared at him distrustfully. The other glories of the Garden had pleased her abstractly, in a way that left her mistress of herself. But here was something she did not understand at all. The eternal Lilith looked out, bewildered, through the eyes of a body that found something strange and wonderful in Adam. She laid a hand on the upper part of that body which rose and fell with her breathing, and felt something beating strongly beneath the smooth, curved surface of the stuff called flesh.

Adam came toward her slowly. They met in the middle of the glade, and for a long moment neither spoke. Then Adam said in a marveling voice, resonant and deep:

"You . . . you're just as I knew you'd be— I knew you'd be somewhere, if I could only find you. Where were you hiding?"

With an effort Lilith mastered this odd, swimming warmth in her which she did not understand. After all, he was nothing but a certain limited awareness housed in newly shaped flesh, and it made no real difference at all what shape that flesh wore. Her business was too dangerous for her to linger here admiring him because by some accident he was pleasing to the eyes of her newly acquired body. She made her voice like honey in her throat and looked up at him under her lashes, crooning:

"I wasn't here at all, until you thought of me."

"Until I—" Adam's golden brows met.

"God made you in His image," said Lilith, fluttering the lashes. "There's so much of God in you still—didn't you know you could create, too, if you desired strongly enough?"

She remembered that deep need of his pulsing out and out in great, demanding waves from the Garden, and how it had seemed a call addressed to her alone. She had delighted as she yielded to it, deliberately subordinating her will to the will of the unseen caller in the Garden. She had let it draw her down out of the swimming void, let it mold flesh around her in the shape it chose, until all her being

was encased in the strange, soft, yielding substance which was proving so treacherously responsive to the things she was encountering
in Eden.

Adam shook his curly head uncomprehendingly. "You weren't
here. I couldn't find you," he repeated, as if he had not heard her.
"I watched all day among the animals, and they were all in twos but
Man. I knew you must be somewhere. I knew just how you'd look. I
thought I'd call you Eve when I found you—Eve, the Mother of All
Living. Do you like it?"

"It's a good name," murmured Lilith, coming nearer to him, "but
not for me. I'm Lilith, who came out of the dark because you
needed me." She smiled a heady smile at him, and the shadowy garment drew thin across her shoulders as she lifted her arms. Adam
seemed a little uncertain about what to do with his own arms as she
clasped her hands behind his neck and tiptoed a little, lifting her
face.

"Lilith?" he echoed in a bemused voice. "I like the sound. What
does it mean?"

"Never mind," she crooned in her sweetest voice. "I came
because you wanted me." And then, in a murmur: "Bend your head,
Adam. I want to show you something—"

It was the first kiss in Eden. When it was over, Lilith opened her eyes
and looked up at Adam aghast, so deeply moved by the pleasant-
ness of that kiss that she could scarcely remember the purpose that
had prompted it. Adam blinked dizzily down at her. He had found
what to with his arms. He stammered, still in that bemused voice:

"Thank God, you did come! I wish He could have sent you
sooner. We—"

Lilith recovered herself enough to murmur gently: "Don't you
understand, dear? God didn't send me. It was you, yourself, waiting
and wanting me, that let me take shape out of . . . never mind . . .
and come to you in the body you pictured for me, because I knew
what wonderful things we could accomplish here in Eden, together.
You're God's own image, and you have greater powers than you
know, Adam." The tremendous idea that had come to her in the
ether when she first heard his soundless call glowed in her voice.
"There's no limit to what we could do here, together! Greater
things than even God ever dreamed—"

"You're so pretty," interrupted Adam, smiling down at her with
his disarming, empty smile. "I'm so glad you came—"

Lilith let the rest of her eagerness run out in a long sigh. It was
no use trying to talk to him now. He was too new. Powerful with a
godlike power, yes, but unaware of it—unaware even of himself as

an individual being. He had not tasted the Fruit of Knowledge and his innocence was as flawless as his beauty. Nothing was in his mind, or could be, that God had not put there at his shaping from the warm earth of Eden.

And perhaps it was best, after all. Adam was too close to godhood to see eye to eye with her in all she might want to do. If he never tasted knowledge, then he would ask no questions—and so he must never touch the Tree.

The Tree— It reminded her that Eden was still a testing ground, not a finished creation. She thought she knew now what the flaw in Man had been which made it possible for Lilith, of all the creatures of ether, to stand here at the very focus of all the power and beauty and innocence in Eden. Lilith, who was evil incarnate and knew it very well. God had made Adam incomplete, and not, perhaps, realized the flaw. And out of Adam's need Adam himself had created woman—who was not complete either. Lilith realized it suddenly, and began to understand the depth of her reaction to this magnificent creature who still held her in his arms.

There was an idea somewhere of all this which was immensely important, but her mind would not pursue it. Her mind kept sliding off the question to dwell cloudily on the Man upon whose shoulder she was leaning. What curious stuff this flesh was! While she wore it, not even the absorbing question of God's purpose, not even her own peril here, could quite obliterate the knowledge of Adam's presence, his arm about her. Values had changed in a frightening way, and the most frightening thing of all was that she did not care. She laid her head back on his shoulder and inhaled the honeyed perfume of the orange blossoms, futilely reminding herself that she was dangerously wasting time. At any moment God might look down and see her, and there was so much to be done before that happened. She must master this delicious fogging of the senses whenever Adam's arm tightened about her. The Garden must be fortified, and she must begin now.

Sighing, she laced her fingers through Adam's and crooned in the softest voice.

"I want to see the Garden. Won't you show it to me?"

His voice was warm as he answered:

"I want to! I hoped you'd ask me that. It's such a wonderful place."

A cherub fluttered across the valley as they strolled eastward, and paused on beating wings to frown down at them.

"Wait till *He* looks down," he piped. "Just wait, that's all!" Adam laughed and the cherub clucked disapprovingly and fluttered off, shaking his head.

Lilith, leaning on Adam's shoulder, laughed, too. She was glad that he could not understand the cherub's warnings, deaf in the perfection of his innocence. So long as she could prevent it he would never taste that Fruit. The knowledge of evil was not in him and it must never be. For she was herself, as she realized well, the essence of abstract evil as opposed to abstract good—balancing it, making it possible. Her part was necessary as God's in the scheme of creation, for light cannot exist without dark, nor positive without negative, nor good without evil.

Yet she did not feel in the least evil just now. There was no antagonism at all between her negation and the strong positive innocence of the Man beside her.

"Look," said Adam, sweeping a long-armed gesture. A low hillside lay before them, starry with flowers except for a scar in its side where the raw, bare earth of Eden showed through. The scar was already healing over with a faint mist of green. "That's where I was made," said Adam softly. "Right out of that hillside. Does it seem rather . . . rather wonderful to you, Lilith?"

"If it does to you," she crooned, and meant it. "Why?"

"The animals don't seem to understand. I hoped you would. It's as if the . . . the whole Garden were part of me. If there are other men, do you suppose they'll love the earth like this, Lilith, for its own sake? Do you think they'll have this same feeling about the place where they were born? Will one certain hill or valley be almost one flesh with theirs, so that they'd sicken away from it and fight and die if they had to, to keep it—as I think I would? Do you feel it, too?"

The air went pulsing past them, sweet with the music of the seraphim, while Lilith looked out over the valley that had brought Adam to birth. She was trying hard, but she could not quite grasp that passionate identification with the earth of Eden which beat like blood through Adam's veins.

"Eden is you," she murmured. "I can understand that. You mustn't ever leave it."

"Leave it?" laughed Adam. "Where else is there? Eden belongs to us forever—and you belong to me."

Lilith let herself relax delightfully against his shoulder, knowing suddenly that she loved this irresponsible, dangerous flesh even while she distrusted it. And—

Something was wrong. The sudden awareness of it chilled her and she glanced uneasily about, but it was several minutes before her fleshbound senses located the wrongness. Then she put her head back and stared up through the trees with puckered brows.

"What is it?" Adam smiled down at her. "Angels? They go over quite often, you know."

Lilith did not answer. She was listening hard. Until now all Eden had echoed faintly and sweetly with the chanting of seraphim about the Throne. But now the sounds that sifted down through the bright, translucent air were not carols of praise. There was trouble in heaven. She could hear faraway shouts in great, ringing, golden voices from infinitely high above, the clash and hiss of flaming swords, and now and again a crash as if part of the very walls of heaven had crumbled inward under some unimaginable onslaught.

It was hard to believe—but there was war in heaven.

A wave of relief went delightfully through Lilith. Good—let them fight. She smiled to herself and snuggled closer to Adam's side. The trouble, whatever it might be, would keep God's attention distracted a while longer from what went on in Eden, and she was devoutly grateful for that. She needed this respite. She had awhile longer, then, to accustom herself to the vagaries of this strange body, and to the strange reaction Adam was causing, before the war was over in heaven and war began in Eden between Lilith and God.

A shudder of terror and anticipation went over her again as she thought of that. She was not sure God could destroy her if He would, for she was a creature of the darkness beyond His light and her existence was necessary to the structure He was rearing in heaven and upon earth. Without the existence of such as Lilith, the balance of creation might tip over. No, God would not—perhaps could not—destroy her, but He could punish very terribly.

This flesh, for instance. It was so soft, so perishable. She was aware of a definite cleavage between the mind and the body that housed it. Perhaps God had been wise in choosing this fragile container instead of some imperishable substance into which to pour all the innocence, the power that was Adam. It was dangerous to trust such power in an independent body—as Lilith meant to prove to God if her plan went well. But it was no part of that plan—now—to have an angered God destroy His fleshy image.

She must think of some way to prevent it. Presently she would waken out of this warm, delightful fog that persisted so long as Adam's arm was about her, but there was no hurry yet. Not while war raged in heaven. She had never known a mood like this before, when cloudy emotions moved like smoke through her mind and nothing in creation had real significance except this magnificent male upon whose shoulder she leaned.

Then Adam looked down at her and smiled, and all the noises of war above blanked out as if they had never been. The Garden, half sentient, stirred uneasily from grass roots to treetops in response to those ringing battle shouts from above; but the Man and the woman did not even hear.

Time was nothing. Imperceptibly it passed, and presently a soft green twilight deepened over Eden. Adam and Lilith paused after a while on a mossy bank above a stream that tinkled over stones. Sitting with her head on Adam's shoulder and listening to the sound of the water, Lilith remembered how lightly life was rooted in this flesh of theirs.

"Adam," she murmured, "a while ago you mentioned dying. Do you know about death?"

"Death?" said Adam comfortably. "I don't remember. I think I never heard of it."

"I hope," she said, "that you never will. It would mean leaving, Eden, you know."

His arm went rigid around her. "I couldn't! I wouldn't!"

"You're not immortal, dear. It could happen, unless—"

"Unless what? Tell me!"

"If there were a Tree of Life," she said slowly, measuring her words, "a Tree whose fruit would give you immortality as the fruit of that other Tree would give you knowledge, then I think not even God could drive you out of Eden."

"A Tree of Life—" he echoed softly. "What would it be like?"

Lilith closed her eyes. "A dark Tree, I think," she answered, almost in a whisper. "Dark limbs, dark leaves—pale, shining fruit hanging among them like lanterns. Can't you see it?"

Adam was silent. She glanced up at him. His eyes were shut and a look of intense longing was on his face in the twilight. There was silence about them for a long while. Presently she felt the tenseness of his body slacken beside her. He breathed out in a long sigh.

"I think there is a Tree of Life," he said. "I think it's in the center of the Garden near the other Tree. I'm sure it's there. The fruit are pale, just as you thought. They send out a light like moonlight in the dark. Tomorrow we'll taste them."

And Lilith relaxed against his shoulder with a sigh of her own. Tomorrow he would be immortal, like herself. She listened anxiously, and still heard the faraway battle cries of the seraphim echoing through the sky. War in heaven and peace on earth—

Through the deepening twilight of Eden no sound came except the music of the water and, somewhere off through the trees, a crooning lullaby in a tiny, piping voice as some cherub sang himself to sleep. Somewhere nearer other small voices squabbled drowsily a while, then fell silent. The most delightful lassitude was stealing over Lilith's body. She turned her cheek against Adam's shoulder and felt that cloudy fogging of the senses which she was coming to know so well—close like water above her head.

And the evening and the morning were the eighth day.

Lilith woke first. Birds were singing gloriously, and as she lay there on Adam's shoulder a cherub flashed across the stream on dazzling wings, caroling at the top of his piping voice. He did not see them. The pleasant delirium of a spring morning filled the whole wakening Garden, and Lilith sat up with a smile. Adam scarcely stirred. Lilith looked down at him with a glow of tenderness that alarmed her. She was coming to identify herself with Adam, as Adam was one with the Garden—this flesh was a treacherous thing.

Suddenly, blindingly, she knew that. Terror of what it was doing to the entity which was Lilith rolled over her in a great wave, and without thinking, almost without realizing what she did, she sprang up and out of the flesh that was betraying her. Up, up through the crystal morning she sprang, impalpable as the air around her. Up and up until the Adam that flesh had valued too highly was invisible, and the very treetops that hid him were a feathery green blur and she could see the walls that closed the Garden in, the rivers running out of it like four great blades of silver in the morning sun.

Beside the sleeping Adam nothing was left but the faintest blur of a woman shape, wrapped in shadow that made it almost invisible against the moss. The eye could scarcely have made it out there under the trees.

Lilith swam delightfully through the bright, still emptiness of the early morning. From here she could hear quite clearly the strong hosannahs of the seraphim pouring out in mighty golden choruses over the jasper walls. Whatever trouble had raged in heaven yesterday, today it was resolved. She scarcely troubled her mind about it.

She was free—free of the flesh and the terrifying weakness that had gone with it. She could see clearly now, no longer deluded by the distortions of value that had made life in the flesh so confusing. Her thoughts were not colored by it anymore. Adam was nothing but a superb vessel now, brimmed with the power of God. Her perspective had been too warped down there in Eden to realize how little that magnificent body of his mattered in comparison to the power inherent in it.

She let the cold, clear ether bathe her of illusions while the timeless time of the void swam motionless around her. She had been in greater danger than she knew; it had taken this morning dip in the luminous heights to cleanse her mind of Adam. Refreshed, fortified against that perilous weakness, she could return now and take up her mission again. And she must do it quickly, before God noticed her. *Or was He watching already?*

She swooped luxuriously in a long, airy curve and plummeted toward Eden.

Adam still slept timelessly upon the moss. Lilith dropped closer, shrugging herself together in anticipation of entering and filling out into life the body she had thrown off. And then—then a shock like the shock of lightning jolted her in midair until the Garden reeled beneath her. For where she had left only the faint, ephemeral husk of a woman beside Adam, a woman of firm, pale flesh lay now, asleep on the Man's shoulder. Golden hair spilled in a long skein across the moss, and the woman's head moved a little to the rhythm of Adam's breathing.

Lilith recovered herself and hovered near, incandescent with such jealousy and rage as she had never dreamed could touch her. The woman was clothed in a softly glowing halo as Adam was clothed. But it was Lilith's own shape she wore beneath that halo.

A sick dismay shook Lilith bodilessly in the air. God *had* been watching, then—waiting, perhaps, to strike. He had been here—it might have been no longer than a moment ago. She knew it by the very silence of the place. Everything was still hushed and awed by the recent Presence. God had passed by, and God had seen that tenantless garment of flesh she had cast off to swim in the ether, and God had known her whole scheme in one flash of His all-seeing eye.

He had taken the flesh she had worn, then, and used it for His own purposes—her precious, responsive flesh that had glowed at the touch of Adam's hand belonged now to another woman, slept in her place on Adam's shoulder. Lilith shook with intolerable emotion at the thought of it. She would not—

Adam was waking. Lilith hovered closer, watching jealously as he yawned, blinked, smiled, turned his curly head to look down at the woman beside him. Then he sat up so abruptly that the golden creature at his side cried out in a sweet, high voice and opened eyes bluer than a cherub's to stare at him reproachfully. Lilith, hating her, still saw that she had beauty of a sort comparable to Adam's, exquisite, brimming with the glorious emptiness of utter innocence. There was a roundness and an appealing softness to her that was new in Eden, but the shape she wore was Lilith's and none other.

Adam stared down at her in amazement.

"L-Lilith—" he stammered. "Who are you? Where's Lilith? I—"

"Who is Lilith?" demanded the golden girl in a soft, hurt voice, sitting up and pushing the glowing hair back with both hands in a lovely, smooth gesture. "I don't know. I can't remember—" She let the words die and stared about the Garden with a blue gaze luminous with wonder. Then the eyes came back to Adam and she smiled very sweetly.

Adam had put a hand to his side, a pucker of the first pain in Eden drawing his golden brows together. For no reason at all he was remembering the scarred bank from which the earth that shaped him had been taken. He opened his mouth to speak.

And then out of the glow of the morning a vast, bodiless Voice spoke quietly.

"I have taken a rib from your side, Man," said the Voice. The whole glade trembled at the sound; the brook ceased its tinkling, the leaves stood still upon the trees. Not a bird sang. Filling the whole morning, the whole Garden, the Voice went on: "Out of the flesh of your flesh I have made a helpmate and a wife for you. Forsaking all others, cleave unto her. *Forsaking all others—*"

The Voice ceased not suddenly, but by echoing degrees that made the leaves shiver upon the trees in rhythm to Its fading syllables, "Forsaking all others . . . all others . . . all others—"

And then it was as if a light ceased to glow in the Garden which, until it went out, no one had perceived. The air dimmed a little, and thickened and dulled, so that one blinked in the aftermath when the presence of God was withdrawn.

The woman drew closer to Adam's side, putting out uncertain hands to him, frightened by the quiet, tremendous Voice and the silence of the Garden. Adam dropped an arm automatically about her, stilling her fright against his shoulder. He bent his head as the Voice ceased to echo through the shaken air.

"Yes, Lord," he said obediently. There was an instant more of silence everywhere. Then timidly the brook sent a tentative ripple of sound into the air, a bird piped once, a breeze began to blow. God had withdrawn.

Bodiless, trembling with emotions she had no name for, Lilith watched the Man and the woman alone on the moss bank she had shared last night with Adam. He looked down at the frightened girl huddling against him.

"I suppose you're Eve," he said, a certain gentleness in his voice that made Lilith writhe.

"If you say so," murmured the girl, glancing up at him under a flutter of lashes. Lilith hated him. Over her fair head Adam looked out across the quiet glade.

"Lilith?" he said. "Lilith—"

A warm rush of answer focused all Lilith's being into one responding cry.

"Yes, Adam . . . yes! I'm here!"

He might have heard her bodiless reply, it was so passionate an answer to his call, but at that instant Eve said with childish petulance:

"Who is this Lilith, Adam? Why do you keep calling her? Won't I do?"

Adam looked down uncertainly. While he hesitated, Eve deliberately snuggled against him with a warm little wiggle that was Lilith's alone. By that, if by no other sign, Lilith knew it was her very flesh God had taken to mold this pale girl from Adam's rib, using the same pattern which Adam had designed for Lilith. Eve wore it now, and in that shape knew, without learning them, all the subtle tricks that Lilith's age-old wisdom had evolved during the brief while she dwelt in the body. Lilith's lost flesh, Lilith's delightful use of it, Lilith's Adam—all were Eve's now.

Fury and wild despair and an intolerable ache that made the world turn black around her blinded Lilith to the two beneath the tree. She could not bear to watch them any longer. With a soundless wail of despair she turned and flung herself up again into the limitless heights above Eden.

But this time the ether was no anodyne for her grief. It had been no true anodyne before, she knew now. For a disease was upon her that had its seed, perhaps, in the flesh she wore briefly—but too long. God had made Adam incomplete, and Adam to assuage his need had flung out a net to trap some unwary creature for his own. Shame burned in her. The Queen of Air and Darkness, like some mindless elemental, had fallen into his trap; he had used her as she had meant to use him. She was a part of him, trapped in the flesh that was incomplete without him, and her need for him was so deep that she could not escape, even though that body was no longer hers. The roots of her disease had been in the flesh, but the virulence had spread into the very essence of the being which was Lilith and no bath in the deeps of space could cleanse her now. In the flesh or out of it, on earth or in ether, an insatiable need was upon her that could never be slaked.

And a dreadful suspicion was taking shape in her mind. Adam in his innocence could never have planned this. Had God known, all along? Had it been no error, after all, that Adam was created incomplete? And was this a punishment designed by God for tampering with his plan? Suddenly she thought that it must be. There would be no awe-inspiring struggle between light and dark such as she had half expected when God recognized her presence. There would be no struggle at all. She was vanquished, judged, and punished all at a blow. No glory was in it, only this unbearable longing, a spiritual hunger more insatiable than any hunger the flesh could feel for the Man she would never have again. She clove the airy heights above Eden for what might have been a thousand years, or a moment, had time existed in the void, knowing only that Adam was lost to her forever.

Forever? She writhed around in mid-ether, checking the wild, aimless upward flight. Forever? Adam still looked out across the Garden and called her name, even while he held that pale usurper in his arms. Perhaps God had not realized the strength of the strange unity between the man and the first woman in Eden. Perhaps God had not thought that she would fight. Perhaps there was a chance left, after all—

Downward through the luminous gulfs she plunged, down and down until Eden expanded like a bubble beneath her and the strong choruses of the seraphim were sweet again above the Garden. Adam and Eve were still beside the brook where she had left them. Eve on a rock was splashing her small feet and flashing blue-eyed glances over her shoulder that made Adam smile when he met them. Lilith hated her.

"Adam!" squealed Eve as the plunging Lilith came into hearing. "Look out—I'm slipping! Catch me! Quick!" It was the same croon Lilith had put into the throat of the body she had lost. Remembering how roundly and softly it had come swelling up in her throat, she writhed with a vitriolic helplessness that made the Garden dance in waves like heat around her.

"Catch me!" cried Eve again in the most appealing voice in the world. Adam sprang to clasp her as she slid. She threw both pale arms about his neck and crowed with laughter so infectious that two passing cherubs paused in midair to rock with answering mirth and beat each other over the shoulders with their wings.

"*Adam . . . Adam . . . Adam*—" wailed Lilith voicelessly. It was a silent wail, but all her heartbreak and despair and intolerable longing went into it, and above Eve's golden head Adam looked up, the laughter dying on his face. "*Adam!*" cried Lilith again. And this time he heard.

But he did not answer directly. Association with women was beginning to teach him tact. Instead he beckoned to the reeling cherubs. Rosy with mirth, they fluttered nearer. Eve looked up in big-eyed surprise as the plump little heads balanced on rainbow wings swooped laughing toward her and poised to await Adam's pleasure.

"These are a couple of our cherubs," said Adam. "Dan and Bethuel, from over toward the Tree. They have a nest there. Tell her about the Tree, will you, boys? Eve dear, I'll be getting you some fruit for breakfast. Wait for me here."

She obeyed with only a wistful glance after him as the cherubs burst into eager chatter, squabbling a little as they spoke.

"Well, there's this Tree in the middle of the Garden—"

"Tell her about the Fruit, Dan. You mustn't—"

"Yes, you mustn't touch—"

"No, that's not right, Dan. Michael says you can touch it, you just can't eat—"

"Don't interrupt me! Now it's like this. You see, there's a Tree—"

Adam went slowly off down to the brook. A lie had never yet been spoken in Eden. He was hunting fruit. But Lilith saw him searching the dappled spaces between the trees, too, a certain wistfulness on his face, and she came down with a rustle of invisibility through the leaves.

"Adam . . . Adam!"

"Lilith! Where are you?"

With a tremendous effort Lilith focused her whole being into an intensity so strong that although she remained bodiless, voiceless, intangible, yet the strength of her desire was enough to make Adam hear her dimly, see her remotely in a wavering outline against the leaves, in the shape he had created for her. She held it with difficulty, shimmering before his eyes.

"Lilith!" he cried, and reached her in two long strides, putting out his arms. She leaned into them. But the muscular, light-sheathed arms closed about her and through her and met in empty air.

She called his name miserably, quivering against him through all her bodiless body. But she could feel him no more than he could touch her, and the old ache she had known in mid-ether came back with a rush. Even here in his arms, then, she was forbidden to touch the Man. She could never be more than a wraith of the air to him, while Eve—while Eve, in her stolen body—

"Adam!" cried Lilith again. "You were mine first! Can you hear me? Adam, you could bring me back if you tried! You did it once— you could again. Try, try!"

He stared down at her dim face, the flowers on the hillside beyond visible through it.

"What's wrong, Lilith? I can hardly see you!"

"You wanted me once badly enough to bring me out of nowhere into the flesh," she cried desperately. "Adam, Adam—want me again!"

He stared down at her. "I do," he said, his voice unexpectedly shaken. And then, more strongly, "Come back, Lilith! What's happened to you? Come back!"

Lilith closed her eyes, feeling reality pour marvelously along her bodiless limbs. Faintly now she could feel grass underfoot, Adam's chest against her anxious hands; his arms were around her and in his embrace she was taking shape out of nothingness, summoned into flesh again by the godhood in this image of God. And then—

"Adam . . . Adam!" Eve's sweet, clear voice rang lightly among the leaves. "Adam, where are you? I want to go look at the Tree, Adam. Where are you, dear?"

"Hurry!" urged Lilith desperately, beating her half-tangible hands against his chest.

Adam's arms loosed a little about her. He glanced across his shoulder, his handsome, empty face clouded. He was remembering.

"Forsaking all others—" he murmured, in a voice not entirely his own. Lilith shuddered a little against him, recognizing the timbre of that Voice which had spoken in the silence. *"Forsaking all others—"* God had said that. "Forsaking all others but Eve—"

His arms dropped from about Lilith. "I . . . I'll . . . will you wait for me?" he said hesitantly, stepping back from her half-real shape, lovely and shadow-veiled under the shadow of the trees. "I'll be back—"

"Adam!" called Eve again, nearer and very sweetly. "Adam, I'm lost! Adam! Adam, where are you?"

"Coming," said Adam. He looked once more at Lilith, a long look. Then he turned and ran lightly off through trees that parted to receive him, the glow of his half-divinity shining upon the leaves as he passed. Lilith watched the beautiful, light-glowing figure as far as she could see it.

Then she put her half-real hands to her face and her knees loosened beneath her and she doubled down in a heap upon the grass, her shadowy hair billowing out around her on a breeze that blew from nowhere, not touching the leaves. She was half-flesh now. She had tears. She found a certain relief in the discovery that she could weep.

The next sound she heard—it seemed a long while after—was a faint hiss. Cloaked in the tented shadow of her hair, she considered it a while, hiccupping now and then with receding sobs. Presently she looked up. Then she gasped and got to her feet with the effortless ease of the half-material.

The serpent looked at her sidewise out of slanted eyes, grinning. In the green gloom under the trees he was so handsome that even she, who had seen Adam, was aware of a little thrill of admiration. In those days the serpent went upright like a man, nor was he exactly non-human in shape, but his beauty was as different from man's as day is from night. He was lithe and gorgeously scaled and by any standards a supremely handsome, supremely male creature.

All about him in shadowy outline a radiance stood out that was vaguely an angel shape, winged, tremendous. It invested the serpent body with a glow that was not its own. Out of that celestial radiance the serpent said in a cool voice:

"The Queen of Air and Darkness! I didn't expect you here. What are you doing in that body?"

Lilith collected herself, hiccupped once more and stood up, the cloudy hair moving uneasily about her. She said with a grim composure:

"The same thing I suspect you're doing in that one, only you'll have to do better if you want to deceive anybody. What brings you to Eden—Lucifer?"

The serpent glanced down at himself and sent one or two long, sliding ripples gliding along his iridescent body. The angel shape that hung in the air about him gradually faded, and the beauty deepened as it focused itself more strongly in the flesh he wore. After a moment he glanced up.

"How's that—better? Oh, I came down for a purpose. I have—business with Adam." His cool voice took on a note of grimness. "You may have heard a little trouble in heaven yesterday. That was me."

"Trouble?" echoed Lilith. She had almost forgotten the sounds of combat and the great battle cries of the seraphim in the depths of her own grief.

"It was a fine fight while it lasted," Lucifer grinned. "Blood running like water down the golden streets! I tell you, it was a relief to hear something beside 'hosannah' in heaven for a change! Well"— he shrugged—"they won. Too many of them were fools and stood by Jehovah. But we gave them a good fight, and we took part of the jasper walls with us when they hurled us over." He gave her a satisfied nod. "God won, but he'll think twice before He insults me again."

"Insults you?" echoed Lilith. "How?"

Lucifer drew himself up to a magnificent height. Radiance glowed along his scaled and gleaming body. "God made me of fire! Shall I bow down before this . . . this lump of clay they call Adam? He may be good enough for the other angels to worship when God points a finger, but he isn't good enough for me!"

"Is that why you're here?"

"Isn't it reason enough? I have a quarrel with this Adam!"

"You couldn't touch him," said Lilith desperately. "He's God's image, and remember, you were no match for God."

Lucifer stretched his magnificent, gleaming height and glared down at her.

"The creature's made of clay. He must have a flaw somewhere. What is it? You know him."

Lilith looked up at him speechless, a great excitement beginning to swell so tremendously in her that her half-formed body could hardly contain it. There was a chance! God himself had put a weapon straight into her hands!

"Yes, there is a flaw," she said. "I'll tell you . . . if you'll give me a promise."

"All right, I give it," said Lucifer carelessly. "Tell me."

She hesitated, choosing her words. "Your feud isn't with Adam. He never asked you to worship him. God did that. Your quarrel is with God, not Adam. The Man himself you can't touch, but God had given him a . . . a wife," she choked when she said it. "I think there's a weakness in her, and through her you could spoil God's plan. But you must spare the Man—for me."

Lucifer whistled soundlessly, lifting his brows. "Oh—?"

"I saw him first," said Lilith defensively. "I want him."

The serpent looked at her narrowly. "Why? No . . . never mind. I won't quarrel with you. I may have an idea to suggest to you later, if a plan of mine works out. You and I together could make quite a thing of hell."

Lilith winced a little. She and Adam together had had great prospects, once, too. Perhaps they still had—if God were not listening.

"You promise not to touch him, then?"

"Yes, I won't hurt your precious clod. You're right—my quarrel's with God, not that animated lump of clay named Adam. What's the secret?"

"Eden," said Lilith slowly, "is a testing ground. There are flaws in it, there must be, or neither of us would be here. God planted a Tree in the middle of the Garden and forbade anyone to touch it. That's the test . . . I think I see it now. It's a test of obedience. God doesn't trust Man—he made him too strong. The Tree is the knowledge of Good and Evil, and God doesn't dare let that knowledge exist in the Garden, because He controls Man only by Man's ignorance of his own power. If either of them eats, then God will have to destroy that one quickly. You tempt the woman to eat, Lucifer, and leave Adam and Eden to me!"

The serpent eyed her sidelong. He laughed.

"If either of them fails in this test you're talking about, then God will know neither can be trusted, won't he? He'll know their present form's imperfect, and he'll destroy them both and work out some other plan for the world."

Lilith drew a deep breath. Excitement was rising like a tide in her, and the wind from nowhere swirled the dark hair in a cloud about her shoulders.

"Let him try!" she cried exultantly. "I can save Adam. God made a mistake when he put such power in the Garden. He shouldn't have left it living, half-conscious of itself. He shouldn't have let Adam know how close he is to the earth he was taken from. Adam and the Garden are one flesh, and the power of God is in them both. God can't destroy one without the other, and together they are very strong— If they defied God together, and I helped them—"

Lucifer looked at her, a trace of compassion on his handsome, reptilian face.

"God defeated *me*," he reminded her. "Do you think He couldn't you?"

She gave him a proud glance. "I am the Queen of Air and Darkness. I have secrets of my own, and powers not even God can control. If I join them with Adam's, and the Garden's . . . God made the Garden alive and powerful, and Adam is one flesh with it, each incomplete without the other as Man is without woman. Adam has Eve now—but when Eve's gone he'll remember Lilith. I'll see that he remembers! And I'll see that he understands his danger. With my help, perhaps he can avert it."

"If God destroys Eve," said Lucifer, "he'll destroy Adam, too. They're one pattern."

"But he may not destroy them at the same time. I'll gamble on that. I'd kill her myself if I could, but I can't touch anything in the Garden without its own consent . . . No, I'll have to wait until Eve proves to God her unfitness to wear flesh, and while he punishes her I must seize that moment to rouse the Garden. It's almost aware of itself already. I think I could awaken it—through Adam, perhaps. Adam and Eden are almost one, as Adam and I will be again if we can get rid of Eve. None of us separately has the power to defy God, but Eden and Adam and I together might do it!" She tossed back her head and the wild dark hair swirled like a fog around her. "Eden is an entity of its own— I think I could close a shell of space around us, and there are places in my Darkness where we could hide even from God!"

Lucifer narrowed his eyes at her. "It might work," he nodded slowly. "You're mad—but it might work, with my help. The woman is beautiful, in her way—" He laughed. "And what a revenge on God!"

"The woman," mused Lilith, "is in my body, and I am evil . . . I think enough evil remains there that Eve will find you—interesting. Good luck, Lucifer!"

In a hollow, velvety cup in the Garden's very center the two Trees stood. One at the edge of the clearing was a dark Tree, the leaves folded like a cloak about a pale glow from within where the Fruit of Life hung hidden. But in the center of the hollow the Tree of

Knowledge flaunted its scarlet fruit that burned with a flame almost of their own among the green and glossy leaves. Here was the heart of the Garden. Out of the Tree of the Knowledge of Good and Evil the beat went pulsing that shook the air of Eden.

Eve set one small, bare foot upon the downward slope and looked back timidly over her shoulder. The serpent flicked a forked red tongue at her. His voice was cool and clear, and sweet as honey.

"Eva," he said softly. *"Eva—"*

She smiled and went on, he rippling after her with an unearthly beauty to his gait that is lost forever now. No one knows today how the serpent walked before the Fall. Of all human creatures only Eve knows that, and there were things Eve never told Adam.

They paused under the shadow of the Tree. In long, slow rhythms the air went pulsing past them. Eve's fair hair stirred a little, so strong was the rhythm here. All the Fruit of the Tree pushed out among the leaves to see her, and the nearer branches bent caressingly toward this woman who was of the flesh of Adam.

The nearest branch stooped down enticingly. Eve reached for a scarlet apple that dipped into her hand. Almost of itself it snapped free of the twig that held it. Eve stared at the apple in her palm, and her hand began to shake. She drew back against the serpent, a little whimper of terror rising in her throat.

The serpent dropped a coiled embrace about the lovely, light-clothed pallor of her body and bent his handsome, slanted head to hers, whispering at her ear in a voice so cool and sweet that the terror faded from her face. She smiled a little, and her hand steadied.

She lifted the Fruit of Knowledge to her lips. There was a hush all through the Garden as she hesitated for a long moment, the red fruit at her red mouth, her teeth denting the scarlet cheek of Knowledge. The last few timeless moments stood still while innocence yet reigned over Eden.

Then the serpent whispered again, urgently: *"Eva—"* he said.

Lilith stood shivering in Adam's arms.

"You were mine first," she was whispering fiercely. "You and I and the Garden—don't you remember? I was your wife before her, and you belong to me!"

Adam could see his own arms through the ephemeral stuff of Lilith's body. He was shaken by the violence in her voice, but his mind was too fogged with the unthinking blank of innocence to understand very clearly. He tried hard.

The rhythm that pulsed through Eden was curiously uneven now. Lilith knew what it meant, and excitement choked her. She cried more desperately:

"Adam . . . Adam! Don't let anything separate us, you and the Garden and I! You can hold us together if you try! I know you can! You—"

One great, annihilating throb shook through the air like thunder. The whole Garden reeled with it and every tree in Eden bowed as if before a tremendous wind. Adam looked up, aghast. But Lilith laughed a wild, excited laugh and cried, "This is it! Oh, hurry, Adam, hurry!"

She slipped through his arms that were still clasped about her and went fluttering effortlessly off through branches that did not impede her passage, Adam following half stunned with the stunned Garden. All Eden was still reeling from the violence of what had just happened beneath the Tree.

Lilith watched the sky as she ran. Would a great bolt of lightning come ravening down out of heaven to blast the woman out of being before they reached the Tree? "Wait, wait!" she panted voicelessly to God. "Give me a moment longer—" Would a bolt strike Adam, too, as he slipped through the parting trees beside her? "Hurry!" she gasped again.

Breathless, they paused at the edge of the hollow where the Tree stood. Looking down, they could see Eve just clear of the shadow of it, the fruit in her hand with one white bite flawing its scarlet cheek. She was staring about the Garden as if she had never seen it before. *Where was God? Why had He not blasted her as she stood there?*

Lilith in her first wild glance could not see the serpent except for a glitter of iridescence back in the shadow of the Tree. Even in her terrible excitement she smiled wryly. Lucifer was taking no chances with God.

But she had no time to waste now on Lucifer or on Eve. For some inexplicable reason God was staying His hand, and she must make the most of the respite. For when God was finished with Eve He would turn to Adam, and before that much had to be done. Adam was her business now, and the living Eden, and all eternity waited on what the next few moments held.

She stood out on the lip of the hollow and a great dark wind from nowhere swelled monstrously about her, tossing out her hair until it was a cloud that shut her from sight. Out of the cloud her voice came rolling in tremendous rhythms paced to the rhythm at which Eden breathed—and Adam.

"Garden!" she called. "Eden—hear me! I am Lilith, the wife of Adam—"

She could feel a vast, dim awareness stirring around her. All through Eden the wakening motion ran, drawing closer, welling up deeply from the earth underfoot, monstrously, wonderfully, a world coming alive at her call.

"Adam!" she cried. "Adam do you hear me? You and Eden are one flesh, and Eve has destroyed you both. She has just brought knowledge into Eden, where God dares not let it exist. God will destroy you all, because of Eve . . . unless you listen to me—"

She felt Adam's attention torn away from Eve and focusing upon herself in fear and wonder. She felt the Garden's wakening awareness draw around him with growing intensity, until it was as if the earth of Eden and the flesh of Man quickened into one, married by the same need for one another as the thought of parting and destruction shuddered through each.

Was this what God had planned as an ending for His divine scheme, as it was the beginning of Lilith's? She had no time to wonder, but the thought crossed her mind awesomely even as she wooed the Garden in a voice as sweet and coaxing as the voice she used to Adam.

And the whole great Garden shuddered ponderously around her, awareness thrilling down every tendril and branch and blade, pulsing up out of the very hill on which she stood. And all of it was Adam. The Garden heard and hung upon her words, and Adam heard, and they three together were all that existed. Success was in her hands. She could feel it. And then—

"Adam . . . Adam!" screamed Eve beneath the Tree.

Lilith's sonorous voice paused in its invocation; the Garden hesitated around her.

"Adam!" cried Eve again, terror flattening all the sweetness out of her voice.

And behind Lilith, in a drugged voice, Adam said: "Eve—?"

"God . . . God, destroy her now!" prayed Lilith soundlessly. And aloud, "Eve has no part in Eden! Don't listen to her, Adam! She'll destroy you and the Garden together!"

"Adam, Adam! Where are you?"

"Coming—" said Adam, still in that thick, drugged voice.

Lilith whirled in the mist of her cloudy hair. Where was God! Why had He stayed His hand? Now was the time to strike, if her hope were not to fail. Now, now! Surely the lightning would come ravening down from heaven if she could hold Adam a moment longer—

"Adam, wait!" she cried desperately. "Adam, you know you love me! If you leave—"

Her voice faltered as he peered at her as blindly as if he had never seen her before. The haloed light was like fire all around him, and her words had been a drug to him as they had been to the Garden, until the earth that loved and listened to her had been one with his own earth-formed flesh; a moment ago there had been nothing in creation for Adam or for Eden but this one woman speaking out of the dark. But now—

"Adam!" screamed Eve again in the flat, frightened voice.

"Don't listen!" cried Lilith frantically. "She doesn't belong here! You can't save her now! God will destroy her, and He'll destroy you, too, if you leave me! Stay here and let her die! You and I will be alone again, in the Garden . . . Adam, don't listen!"

"I . . . I have to listen," he stammered almost stupidly. "Get out of my way, Lilith. Don't you understand? She's my own flesh—I have to go."

Lilith stared at him dumbly. His own flesh! She had forgotten that. She had leaned too heavily on his oneness with the Garden— she had forgotten he was one with Eve, too. The prospect of defeat was suddenly like lead in her. If God would only strike now— She swayed forward in one last desperate effort to hold him back from Eve while the Garden stirred uneasily around them, frightened with Lilith's terror, torn with Adam's distress. She wavered between Adam and the valley as if her ephemeral body could hold him, but he went through her as if through a cloud and stumbled blindly downhill toward the terrified Eve beneath the Tree with the fruit in her hand and a dreadful knowledge on her face.

From here Lilith could see what Adam had not yet. She laughed suddenly, wildly, and cried:

"Look at her, Adam! Look!" And Adam blinked and looked.

Eve stood naked beneath the Tree. That burning beauty which had clothed her like a garment was gone with her divine innocence and she was no longer the flawless goddess who had wakened on Adam's shoulder that morning. She stood shivering a little, looking forlorn and somehow pinched and thin, almost a caricature of the perfect beauty that had gone down the hill with the serpent an hour ago. But she did not know that. She looked up at Adam as he hesitated above her, and smiled uncertainly with a sort of leer in her smile.

"Oh, there you are," she said, and even her voice was harsher now. "Everything looked so . . . so queer, for a minute. Look." She held up the fruit. "It's good. Better than anything *you* ever gave me. Try it."

Lilith stared at her from the hilltop with a horror that for a moment blanked out her growing terror because of God's delay. Was knowledge, then, as ugly as this? Why had it destroyed Eve's beauty as if it were some evil thing? Perfect knowledge should have increased her strength and loveliness in the instant before God struck her down, if— Suddenly Lilith understood. Perfect knowledge! But Eve had only tasted the fruit, and she had only a warped half-knowledge from that single taste. The beauty of her innocence was lost, but she had not yet gained the beauty of perfect knowledge. Was this why God delayed? So long as her knowledge was imperfect perhaps she was no menace to God's power in Eden. And yet she had disobeyed, she had proved herself unworthy of the trust of God—Then why did He hesitate? Why had He not blasted her as she stood there with the apple at her lips? A panic was rising in Lilith's throat. *Could it be that He was laughing, even now?* Was He giving her the respite she had prayed for, and watching her fail in spite of it?

"Taste the apple," said Eve again, holding it out.

"Adam!" cried Lilith despairingly from the edge of the hill. "Adam, look at me! You loved me first—don't you remember? Look at me, Adam!"

And Adam turned to look. The wind, which had clouded her from sight in the darkness of her hair, had calmed. She stood now, luminous on the hilltop, the darkness parted like a river by the whiteness of her shoulders. And she was beautiful with a beauty that no mortal woman will ever wear again.

"I was first!" cried Lilith. "You loved me before her—come back to me now, before God strikes you both! Come back, Adam!"

He stared up at her miserably. He looked back at the flawed, shivering creature at his side, knowledge curiously horrible in her eyes. He stared at Eve, too, a long stare. And then he reached for the apple.

"Adam—no!" shrieked Lilith. "See what knowledge did to Eve! You'll be ugly and naked, like her! Don't taste it, Adam! You don't know what you're doing!"

Over the poised red fruit he looked up at her. The light quivered gloriously all around him. He stood like a god beneath the Tree, radiant, perfect.

"Yes, I know," he said, in a clearer voice than she had ever heard him use before.

"God will destroy you!" wailed Lilith, and rolled her eyes up to look for the falling thunderbolt that might be hurtling downward even now.

"I know," said Adam again. And then, after a pause, "You don't understand, Lilith. Eve is my own flesh, closer than Eden—closer than you. Don't you remember what God said? *Forsaking all others—*"

"Eve!" screamed Lilith hopelessly. "Stop him! Your punishment's certain—are you going to drag him down, too?"

Eve looked up, knowledge dark in her blue eyes. She laughed a thin laugh and the last vestige of her beauty went with it.

"Leave him to you?" she sneered. "Oh no! He and I are one flesh—we'll go together. Taste the apple, Adam!"

He turned it obediently in his hand: his teeth crunched through scarlet skin into the sweet white flesh inside. There was a tremendous silence all through the Garden; nothing stirred in Eden while Adam chewed and swallowed the Fruit of Knowledge. And then he turned to stare down into Eve's lifted eyes while awareness of himself as an individual, free-willed being dawned gradually across his awakening mind.

And then the burning glory that clothed him paled, shimmered, went out along his limbs. He, too, was naked. The queer, pinched look of humanity shivered over that magnificent body, and he was no longer magnificent, no longer Adam.

Lilith had forgotten to look for God. Sickness of the heart was swelling terribly in her, and for a moment she no longer cared about God, or Eden, or the future. This was not Adam any more—It would never be Adam again—

"Listen," said Eve in a small, intimate voice to Adam. "How quiet it is! Why, it's the music. The seraphim aren't singing any more around the Throne!"

Lilith glanced up apathetically. That meant, then, that God was coming— But even as she looked up a great golden chorus resounded serenely from high over Eden. Adam tipped his tarnished head to listen.

"You're right," he agreed. "They've stopped their song."

Lilith did not hear him. That dreadful sickness in her was swelling and changing, and she knew now what it was—hatred. Hatred of Adam and Eve and the thing they had done to her. Hatred of these naked caricatures, who had been the magnificent half-god she had loved and the shape she had put on to delight him. True, they might finish the eating of knowledge and grow perfect again, but it would be a perfection that shut her out. They were one flesh together, and even God had failed her now. Looking down, she loathed them both. Eve's very existence was an insult to the unflawed perfection which Lilith still wore, and Adam—Adam shivering beneath the Tree with a warped, imperfect knowledge leering in his eyes—

A sob swelled in her throat. He had been flawless once—she would never forget that. Almost she loved the memory still as it lingered about this shivering human creature beneath the Tree. So long as he was alive she knew now she would never be free of it; this weakness would torment her still for the flesh that had once been

Adam. The prospect of an eternity of longing for him, who would never exist again, was suddenly unbearable to her.

She tipped her head back and looked up through the glory above Eden where golden voices chanted that neither Adam nor Eve would ever hear again.

"Jehovah!" she sobbed. "Jehovah! Come down and destroy us all! You were right—they are both too flawed to bring anything but misery to all who know them. God, come down and give us peace!"

Eve squealed in terror at Adam's side. "Listen!" she cried. "Adam, listen to her!"

Answering human terror dawned across the pinched features that had once been Adam's handsome, immortal face. "The Tree of Life!" he shouted. "No one can touch us if we eat that fruit!"

He whirled to scramble up the slope toward the dark Tree, and Lilith's heart ached to watch how heavily he moved. Yesterday's wonderful, easy litheness was gone with his beauty, and his body was a burden to him now.

But he was not to reach the Tree of Life. For suddenly glory brightened unbearably over the Garden. A silence was in the sky, and the breeze ceased to blow through Eden.

"Adam," said a Voice in the great silence of the Garden, "hast thou eaten of the Tree?"

Adam glanced up the slope at Lilith, standing despairingly against the sky. He looked at Eve beside him, a clumsy caricature of the loveliness he had dreamed of. There was bitterness in his voice.

"The woman thou gavest me—" he began reproachfully, and then hesitated, meeting Eve's eyes. The old godlike goodness was lost to him now, but he had not fallen low enough yet to let Eve know what he was thinking. He could not say, "The woman Thou gavest me has ruined us both—but I had a woman of my own before her and she never did me any harm." No, he could not hurt this flesh of his flesh so deeply, but he was human now and he could not let her go unrebuked. He went on sulkily, "—she gave me the apple, and I ate."

The Voice said awfully, "Eve—?"

Perhaps Eve was remembering that other voice, cool and sweet, murmuring, "Eva—" In the cool, green dimness of the Garden, the voice that had whispered secrets she would never share with Adam. Perhaps if he had been beside her now—but he was not, and her resentment bubbled to her lips in speech.

"The serpent beguiled me," she told God sullenly, "and I ate."

There was silence for a moment in the Garden. Then the Voice said, "Lucifer—" with a sorrow in the sound that had not stirred for the man's plight, or the woman's. "Lucifer, my enemy, come forth from the Tree." There was a divine compassion in the Voice even as

It pronounced sentence. "Upon thy belly shalt thou go, and dust shalt thou eat all the days of thy life—"

Out from beneath the shadow of the Tree a flat and shining length came pouring through the grass. This was the hour for the shedding of beauty: the serpent had lost the fire-bright splendor that had been his while Lucifer dwelt in his flesh, but traces lingered yet in the unearthly fluidness of his motion, in his shining iridescence. He lifted a wedged head toward Eve, flickered his tongue at her once and then dropped back into the grass. Its ripple above him marked his course away. Eve drew one long, sobbing breath for that green twilight hour in the Garden, that Adam would never guess, as she watched him ripple away.

"Adam, Eve," went on the Voice quietly, "the Garden is not for you." There was a passionless pity in It as the Garden stood still to listen. "I made your flesh too weak, because your godhood was too strong to trust. You are not to blame for that—the fault was Mine. But Adam . . . Eve . . . what power did I put in you, that the very elements of fire and darkness find kinship with you? What flaw is in you, that though you are the only two human things alive, yet you cannot keep faith with one another?"

Adam glanced miserably up toward Lilith standing motionless on the hill's edge, clothed in the flawless beauty he had dreamed for her and would never see again. Eve's eyes followed the serpent through the grass that was blurred for her because of the first tears of Eden. Neither of them answered.

"You are not fit yet to put forth your hand to the Tree of Life, and eat, and live forever," went on the Voice after a moment.

"Man . . . woman . . . you are not yet fit for perfect knowledge or immortality. You are not yet fit for trust. But for Lilith the tale would have spun itself out here in the walls of Eden, but now you must go beyond temptation and work your own salvation out in the sweat of your brow, in the lands beyond the Garden. Adam, I dare not trust you any longer in your kinship with the earth I shaped you from. Cursed is the ground for your sake. Adam—it shall be one with you no longer. But I promise this . . . in the end you shall return to it—" The Voice fell silent, and there was from far above the flash of a flaming sword over the gate of Eden.

"Deal with me now," Lilith said in an empty voice. "I have no desire to exist any longer in a world that has no Adam—destroy me, Jehovah."

The Voice said emotionlessly, "You are punished already, by the fruit of what you did."

"Punished enough!" wailed Lilith in sudden despair. "Make an end of it, Jehovah!"

"With Man's end," said God quietly. "No sooner. You four among you have shattered a plan in Eden that you must shape anew before your travail ends. Let the four of you build a new plan with the elements of your being—Adam is Earth, Lucifer is Fire, Lilith is Air and Darkness, and Eve the Mother of All Living, the fertile seas from which all living springs. Earth, Air, Fire and Water—you thought your plan was better than Mine. Work it out for yourselves!"

"What is our part to be, Lord?" asked Adam in a small, humbled voice.

"Earth and water," said the Voice. "The kingdom of earth for you and the woman and your children after you."

"I was Adam's wife before her," wailed Lilith jealously. "What of me . . . and mine?"

The Voice fell silent for a while. Then it said quietly: "Make your own choice, Queen of Air and Darkness."

"Let my children and Adam's haunt hers to their graves, then!" decided Lilith instantly. "Mine are the disinherited—let them take vengeance! Let her and hers beware of my children who wail in the night, and know she deserves their wrath. Let them remind her always that Adam was mine before her!"

"So be it," said the Voice. And for an instant there was silence in Eden while the shadow of times to come brooded inscrutably in the mind of God. Lilith caught flashes of it in the glory so bright over Eden that every grass blade had a splendor which hurt the eyes. She saw Man loving his birthplace upon earth with a deep-rooted love that made it as dear as his very flesh to him, so that dimly he might remember the hour when all earth was as close to him as his newly created body. She saw Man cleaving to one woman as dear as the flesh of his flesh, yet remembering the unattainable and the lost— Lilith, perfect in Eden. She looked down from the hilltop and met Adam's eyes, and voicelessly between them a long farewell went flashing.

No one was watching Eve. She was blinking through tears, remembering a twilight hour and a fire-bright beauty that the dust had quenched a moment ago at God's command. And then . . . then there was the faintest rustling in the air around her, and a cool, clear voice was murmuring:

"Eva—" against her cheek.

She stared. There was nothing. But—

"Eva," said the voice again. "Give me my vengeance, too—upon the Man. Pretty Eva, do you hear me? Call your first child Kayn . . . Eva, will you do as I say? Call him Kayn the Spear of my vengeance, for he shall set murder loose among Adam's sons. Remember, Eva—"

And Eve echoed in a small, obedient whisper, "Cain . . . Cain."

Tlön, Uqbar, Orbis Tertius

Jorge Luis Borges

Jorge Luis Borges (1899–1986) was a professor and lecturer from Argentina who gained worldwide renown for his study and critical analysis of literature. His theory about fantastic fiction was that a universe created by an author should be able to stand independently of any ideas or concepts we know today—it should be a completely new world free of our reality. In "Tlön, Uqbar, Orbis Tertius," he shows how this idea can be accomplished. His short fiction was collected in the anthology Ficciones.

I OWE THE DISCOVERY OF UQBAR TO THE CONJUNCTION OF A MIRROR AND an encyclopedia. The unnerving mirror hung at the end of a corridor in a villa on Calle Goana, in Ramos Mejía; the misleading encyclopedia goes by the name of *The Anglo-American Cyclopaedia* (New York, 1917), and is a literal if inadequate reprint of the 1902 *Encyclopaedia Britannica.* The whole affair happened some five years ago. Bioy Casares had dined with me that night and talked to us at length about a great scheme for writing a novel in the first person, using a narrator who omitted or corrupted what happened and who ran into various contradictions, so that only a handful of readers, a very small handful, would be able to decipher the horrible or banal reality behind the novel. From the far end of the corridor, the mirror was watching us; and we discovered, with the inevitability of discoveries made late at night, that mirrors have something grotesque about them. Then Bioy Casares recalled that one of the heresiarchs of Uqbar had stated that mirrors and copulation are abominable, since they both multiply the numbers of man. I asked him the source of that memorable sentence, and he replied that it was recorded in *The Anglo-American Cyclopaedia,* in its article on Uqbar. It so happened that the villa (which we had rented furnished) possessed a copy of that work. In the final pages of Volume XLVI, we ran across an article on Upsala; in the beginning of Volume XLVII, we found one on Ural-Altaic languages; but not one word on Uqbar. A little put out, Bioy consulted the index volumes. In vain he tried every possible spelling—Ukbar, Ucbar, Ooqbar,

Ookbar, Oukbahr. . . . Before leaving, he informed me it was a region in either Iraq or Asia Minor. I must say that I acknowledged this a little uneasily. I supposed that this undocumented country and its anonymous heresiarch had been deliberately invented by Bioy out of modesty, to substantiate a phrase. A futile examination of one of the atlases of Justus Perthes strengthened my doubt.

On the following day, Bioy telephoned me from Buenos Aires. He told me that he had in front of him the article on Uqbar, in Volume XLVI of the encyclopedia. It did not specify the name of the heresiarch, but it did note his doctrine, in words almost identical to the ones he had repeated to me, though, I would say, inferior from a literary point of view. He had remembered: "Copulation and mirrors are abominable." The text of the encyclopedia read: "For one of those gnostics, the visible universe was an illusion or, more precisely, a sophism. Mirrors and fatherhood are abominable because they multiply it and extend it." I said, in all sincerity, that I would like to see that article. A few days later, he brought it. This surprised me, because the scrupulous cartographic index of Ritter's *Erdkunde* completely failed to mention the name of Uqbar.

The volume which Bioy brought was indeed Volume XLVI of *The Anglo-American Cyclopaedia*. On the title page and spine, the alphabetical key was the same as in our copy, but instead of 917 pages, it had 921. These four additional pages consisted of the article on Uqbar—not accounted for by the alphabetical cipher, as the reader will have noticed. We ascertained afterwards that there was no other difference between the two volumes. Both, as I think I pointed out, are reprints of the tenth *Encyclopaedia Britannica*. Bioy had acquired his copy in one of a number of book sales.

We read the article with some care. The passage remembered by Bioy was perhaps the only startling one. The rest seemed probable enough, very much in keeping with the general tone of the work and, naturally, a little dull. Reading it over, we discovered, beneath the superficial authority of the prose, a fundamental vagueness. Of the fourteen names mentioned in the geographical section, we recognized only three—Khurasan, Armenia, and Erzurum—and they were dragged into the text in a strangely ambiguous way. Among the historical names, we recognized only one, that of the imposter, Smerdis the Magian, and it was invoked in a rather metaphorical sense. The notes appeared to fix precisely the frontiers of Uqbar, but the points of reference were all, vaguely enough, rivers and craters and mountain chains in that same region. We read, for instance, that the southern frontier is defined by the lowlands of Tsai Haldun and the Axa delta, and that wild horses flourish in the islands of that delta. This, at the top of page 918. In the historical section (page 920), we gathered that, just after the religious persecutions of the thirteenth century, the orthodox sought refuge in the islands, where their obelisks have survived, and where it is a common enough occurrence to dig up one of their stone mirrors. The language and literature section was brief. There was one notable characteristic: it remarked that the literature of Uqbar was fantastic in character, and that its epics and legends never referred to reality, but to the two imaginary regions of Mlejnas and Tlön. . . . The bibliography listed four volumes, which we have not yet come across, even although the third—Silas Haslam: *History of the Land Called Uqbar,* 1874—appears in the library catalogues of Bernard Quaritch.* The first, *Lesbare und lesenswerthe Bemerkungen über das Land Ukkbar in Klein-Asien,* is dated 1641, and is a work of Johann Valentin Andreä. The fact is significant; a couple of years later I ran across that name accidentally in the thirteenth volume of De Quincey's *Writings,* and I knew that it was the name of a German theologian who, at the beginning of the seventeenth century, described the imaginary community of Rosae Crucis—the community which was later founded by others in imitation of the one he had preconceived.

That night, we visited the National Library. Fruitlessly we exhausted atlases, catalogues, yearbooks of geographical societies, memoirs of travelers and historians—nobody had ever been in Uqbar. Neither did the general index of Bioy's encyclopedia show the name. The following day, Carlos Mastronardi, to whom I had referred the whole business, caught sight, in a Corrientes and Talcahuano bookshop, of the black and gold bindings of *The Anglo-American Cyclopaedia.* . . . He went in and looked up Volume XLVI. Naturally, there was not the slightest mention of Uqbar.

II

Some small fading memory of one Herbert Ashe, an engineer for the southern railroads, hangs on in the hotel in Androgué, between the luscious honeysuckle and the illusory depths of the mirrors. In life, he suffered from a sense of unreality, as do so many Englishmen; dead, he is not even the ghostly creature he was then. He was tall and languid; his limp squared beard had once been red. He was, I understand, a widower, and childless. Every so many years, he went to England to visit—judging by the photographs he showed us—a sundial and some oak trees. My father and he had cemented

*Haslam has also published *A General History of Labyrinths.*

(the verb is excessive) one of those English friendships which begin by avoiding intimacies and eventually eliminate speech altogether. They used to exchange books and periodicals; they would beat one another at chess, without saying a word. . . . I remember him in the corridor of the hotel, a mathematics textbook in his hand, gazing now and again at the passing colors of the sky. One afternoon, we discussed the duodecimal numerical system (in which twelve is written 10). Ashe said that as a matter of fact, he was transcribing some duodecimal tables, I forget which, into sexagesimals (in which sixty is written 10), adding that this work had been commissioned by a Norwegian in Rio Grande do Sul. We had known him for eight years and he had never mentioned having stayed in that part of the country. . . . We spoke of rural life, of *capangas,* of the Brazilian etymology of the word *gaucho* (which some old people in the east still pronounce *gaúcho*), and nothing more was said—God forgive me— of duodecimal functions. In September, 1937 (we ourselves were not at the hotel at the time), Herbert Ashe died of an aneurysmal rupture. Some days before, he had received from Brazil a stamped, registered package. It was a book, an octavo volume. Ashe left it in the bar where, months later, I found it. I began to leaf through it and felt a sudden curious lightheadedness, which I will not go into, since this is the story, not of my particular emotions, but of Uqbar and Tlön and Orbis Tertius. In the Islamic world, there is one night, called the Night of Nights, on which the secret gates of the sky open wide and the water in the water jugs tastes sweeter; if those gates were to open, I would not feel what I felt that afternoon. The book was written in English, and had 1001 pages. On the yellow leather spine, and again on the title page, I read these words: *A First Encyclopaedia of Tlön*. Volume XI. Hlaer to Jangr. There was nothing to indicate either date or place of origin. On the first page and on a sheet of silk paper covering one of the colored engravings there was a blue oval stamp with the inscription: ORBIS TERTIUS. It was two years since I had discovered, in a volume of a pirated encyclopedia, a brief description of a false country; now, chance was showing me something much more valuable, something to be reckoned with. Now, I had in my hands a substantial fragment of the complete history of an unknown planet, with its architecture and its playing cards, its mythological terrors and the sound of its dialects, its emperors and its oceans, its minerals, its birds, and its fishes, its algebra and its fire, its theological and metaphysical arguments, all clearly stated, coherent, without any apparent dogmatic intention or parodic undertone.

The eleventh volume of which I speak refers to both subsequent and preceding volumes. Néstor Ibarra, in an article (in the *N.R.F.*), now a classic, has denied the existence of those corollary volumes; Ezequiel Martínez Estrada and Drieu La Rochelle have, I think, succeeded in refuting this doubt. The fact is that, up until now, the most patient investigations have proved fruitless. We have turned the libraries of Europe, North and South America upside down—in vain. Alfonso Reyes, bored with the tedium of this minor detective work, proposes that we all take on the task of reconstructing the missing volumes, many and vast as they were: *ex ungue leonem*. He calculates, half seriously, that one generation of Tlönists would be enough. This bold estimate brings us back to the basic problem: who were the people who had invented Tlön? The plural is unavoidable, because we have unanimously rejected the idea of a single creator, some transcendental Leibnitz working in modest obscurity. We conjecture that this "brave new world" was the work of a secret society of astronomers, biologists, engineers, metaphysicians, poets, chemists, mathematicians, moralists, painters, and geometricians, all under the supervision of an unknown genius. There are plenty of individuals who have mastered these various disciplines without having any facility for invention, far less for submitting that inventiveness to a strict, systematic plan. This plan is so vast that each individual contribution to it is infinitesimal. To begin with, Tlön was thought to be nothing more than a chaos, a free and irresponsible work of the imagination; now it was clear that it is a complete cosmos, and that the strict laws which govern it have been carefully formulated, albeit provisionally. It is enough to note that the apparent contradictions in the eleventh volume are the basis for proving the existence of the others, so lucid and clear is the scheme maintained in it. The popular magazines have publicized, with pardonable zeal, the zoology and topography of Tlön. I think, however, that its transparent tigers and its towers of blood scarcely deserve the unwavering attention of *all* men. I should like to take some little time to deal with its conception of the universe.

Hume remarked once and for all that the arguments of Berkeley were not only thoroughly unanswerable but thoroughly unconvincing. This dictum is emphatically true as it applies to our world; but it falls down completely in Tlön. The nations of that planet are congenitally idealist. Their language, with its derivatives—religion, literature, and metaphysics—presupposes idealism. For them, the world is not a concurrence of objects in space, but a heterogeneous series of independent acts. It is serial and temporal, but not spatial. There are no nouns in the hypothetical *Ursprache* of Tlön, which is the source of the living language and the dialects; there are impersonal verbs qualified by monosyllabic suffixes or prefixes which have the force of adverbs. For example, there is no word corresponding to the noun *moon,* but there is a verb *to moon* or *to moondle. The moon rose over the sea* would be written *hlör u fang axaxaxas mlö,* or, to put it in order: *upward beyond the constant flow there was moondling.* (Xul Solar translates it succinctly: *upward, behind the onstreaming it mooned.*)

The previous passage refers to the languages of the southern hemisphere. In those of the northern hemisphere (the eleventh volume has little information on its *Ursprache*), the basic unit is not the verb, but the monosyllabic adjective. Nouns are formed by an accumulation of adjectives. One does not say moon; one says *airy-clear over dark-round* or *orange-faint-of-sky* or some other accumulation. In the chosen example, the mass of adjectives corresponds to a real object. The happening is completely fortuitous. In the literature of this hemisphere (as in the lesser world of Meinong), ideal objects abound, invoked and dissolved momentarily, according to poetic necessity. Sometimes, the faintest simultaneousness brings them about. There are objects made up of two sense elements, one visual, the other auditory—the color of a sunrise and the distant call of a bird. Other objects are made up of many elements—the sun, the water against the swimmer's chest, the vague quivering pink which one sees when the eyes are closed, the feeling of being swept away by a river or by sleep. These second degree objects can be combined with others; using certain abbreviations, the process is practically an infinite one. There are famous poems made up of one enormous word, a word which in truth forms a poetic *object,* the creation of the writer. The fact that no one believes that nouns refer to an actual reality means, paradoxically enough, that there is no limit to the numbers of them. The languages of the northern hemisphere of Tlön include all the names in Indo-European languages— plus a great many others.

It is no exaggeration to state that in the classical culture of Tlön, there is only one discipline, that of psychology. All others are subordinated to it. I have remarked that the men of that planet conceive of the universe as a series of mental processes, whose unfolding is to be understood only as a time sequence. Spinoza attributes to the inexhaustibly divine in man the qualities of extension and of thinking. In Tlön, nobody would understand the juxtaposition of the first, which is only characteristic of certain states of being, with the second, which is a perfect synonym for the cosmos. To put it another way—they do not conceive of the spatial as everlasting in time. The perception of a cloud of smoke on the horizon and, later, of the countryside on fire and, later, of a half-extinguished cigar which caused the conflagration would be considered an example of the association of ideas.

This monism, or extreme idealism, completely invalidates science. To explain or to judge an event is to identify or unite it with another one. In Tlön, such connection is a later stage in the mind of the observer, which can in no way affect or illuminate the earlier stage. Each state of mind is irreducible. The mere act of giving it a name, that is of classifying it, implies a falsification of it. From all this, it would be possible to deduce that there is no science in Tlön, let alone rational thought. The paradox, however, is that sciences exist, in countless number. In philosophy, the same thing happens as happens with the nouns in the northern hemisphere. The fact that any philosophical system is bound in advance to be a dialectical game, a *Philosophie des Als Ob,* means that systems abound, unbelievable systems, beautifully constructed or else sensational in effect. The metaphysicians of Tlön are not looking for truth, nor even for an approximation of it; they are after a kind of amazement. They consider metaphysics a branch of fantastic literature. They know that a system is nothing more than the subordination of all the aspects of the universe to some one of them. Even the phrase "all the aspects" can be rejected, since it presupposes the impossible inclusion of the present moment, and of past moments. Even so, the plural, "past moments" is inadmissable, since it supposes another impossible operation. . . . One of the schools in Tlön has reached the point of denying time. It reasons that the present is undefined, that the future has no other reality than as present hope, that the past is no more than present memory.* Another school declares that the *whole of time* has already happened and that our life is a vague memory or dim reflection, doubtless false and fragmented, of an irrevocable process. Another school has it that the history of the universe, which contains the history of our lives and the most tenuous details of them, is the handwriting produced by a minor god in order to communicate with a demon. Another maintains that the universe is comparable to those code systems in which not all the symbols have meaning, and in which only that which happens every three hundredth night is true. Another believes that, while we are asleep here, we are awake somewhere else, and that thus every man is two men.

Among the doctrines of Tlön, none has occasioned greater scandal than the doctrine of materialism. Some thinkers have formulated it with less clarity than zeal, as one might put forward a paradox. To clarify the general understanding of this unlikely thesis, one eleventh

---

*Russell (*The Analysis of Mind,* 1921, page 159) conjectures that our planet was created a few moments ago, and provided with a humanity which "remembers" an illusory past.

century* heresiarch offered the parable of nine copper coins, which enjoyed in Tlön the same noisy reputation as did the Eleatic paradoxes of Zeno in their day. There are many versions of this "feat of specious reasoning" which vary the number of coins and the number of discoveries. Here is the commonest:

> On Tuesday, X ventures along a deserted road and loses nine copper coins. On Thursday, Y finds on the road four coins, somewhat rusted by Wednesday's rain. On Friday, Z comes across three coins on the road. On Friday morning, X finds two coins in the corridor of his house. [The heresiarch is trying to deduce from this story the reality, that is, the continuity, of the nine recovered coins.] It is absurd, he states, to suppose that four of the coins have not existed between Tuesday and Thursday, three between Tuesday and Friday afternoon, and two between Tuesday and Friday morning. It is logical to assume that they have existed, albeit in some secret way, in a manner whose understanding is concealed from men, in every moment, in all three places.

The language of Tlön is by its nature resistant to the formulation of this paradox; most people do not understand it. At first, the defenders of common sense confined themselves to denying the truth of the anecdote. They declared that it was a verbal fallacy, based on the reckless use of two neological expressions, not substantiated by common usage, and contrary to the laws of strict thought—the verbs *to find* and *to lose* entail a *petitio principii*, since they presuppose that the first nine coins and the second are identical. They recalled that any noun—*man, money, Thursday, Wednesday, rain*—has only metaphorical value. They denied the misleading detail "somewhat rusted by Wednesday's rain," since it assumes what must be demonstrated—the continuing existence of the four coins between Thursday and Tuesday. They explained that equality is one thing and identity another, and formulated a kind of *reductio ad absurdum*, the hypothetical case of nine men who, on nine successive nights, suffer a violent pain. Would it not be ridiculous, they asked, to claim that this pain is the same one each time?[†] They said

---

*A century, in accordance with the duodecimal system, signifies a period of one hundred and forty-four years

†Nowadays, one of the churches of Tlön maintains platonically that such and such a pain, such and such a greenish-yellow color, such and such a temperature, such and such a sound etc., make up the only reality there is. All men, in the climatic instant of coitus, are the same man. All men who repeat one line of Shakespeare *are* William Shakespeare.

that the heresiarch was motivated mainly by the blasphemous intention of attributing the divine category of *being* to some ordinary coins; and that sometimes he was denying plurality, at other times not. They argued thus: that if equality entails identity, it would have to be admitted at the same time that the nine coins are only one coin.

Amazingly enough, these refutations were not conclusive. After the problem had been stated and restated for a hundred years, one thinker no less brilliant than the heresiarch himself, but in the orthodox tradition, advanced a most daring hypothesis. This felicitous supposition declared that there is only one Individual, and that this indivisible Individual is every one of the separate beings in the universe, and that those beings are the instruments and masks of divinity itself. X is Y and is Z. Z finds three coins because he remembers that X lost them. X finds only two in the corridor because he remembers that the others have been recovered. . . . The eleventh volume gives us to understand that there were three principal reasons which led to the complete victory of this pantheistic idealism. First, it repudiated solipsism. Second, it made possible the retention of a psychological basis for the sciences. Third, it permitted the cult of the gods to be retained. Schopenhauer, the passionate and clear-headed Schopenhauer, advanced a very similar theory in the first volume of his *Parerga und Paralipomena*.

The geometry of Tlön has two somewhat distinct systems, a visual one and a tactile one. The latter system corresponds to our geometry; they consider it inferior to the former. The foundation of visual geometry is the surface, not the point. This system rejects the principle of parallelism, and states that, as man moves about, he alters the forms which surround him. The arithmetical system is based on the idea of indefinite numbers. It emphasizes the importance of the concepts *greater* and *lesser,* which our mathematicians symbolize as $>$ and $<$. It states that the operation of counting modifies quantities and changes them from indefinites into definites. The fact that several individuals counting the same quantity arrive at the same result is, say their pyschologists, an example of the association of ideas or the good use of memory. We already know that in Tlön the source of all-knowing is single and eternal.

In literary matters too, the dominant notion is that everything is the work of one single author. Books are rarely signed. The concept of plagiarism does not exist; it has been established that all books are the work of one single writer, who is timeless and anonymous. Criticism is prone to invent authors. A critic will choose two dissimilar works—the *Tao Tê Ching* and *The Thousand and One Nights*, let us say—and attribute them to the same writer, and then with all probity explore the psychology of this interesting *homme de lettres*. . . .

The books themselves are also odd. Works of fiction are based on a single plot, which runs through every imaginable permutation. Works of natural philosophy invariably include thesis and antithesis, the strict pro and con of a theory. A book which does not include its opposite, or "counter-book," is considered incomplete.

Centuries and centuries of idealism have not failed to influence reality. In the very oldest regions of Tlön, it is not an uncommon occurrence for lost objects to be duplicated. Two people are looking for a pencil; the first one finds it and says nothing; the second finds a second pencil, no less real, but more in keeping with his expectation. These secondary objects are called *hrönir* and, even though awkward in form, are a little larger than the originals. Until recently, the *hrönir* were the accidental children of absent-mindedness and forgetfulness. It seems improbable that the methodical production of them has been going on for almost a hundred years, but so it is stated in the eleventh volume. The first attempts were fruitless. Nevertheless, the *modus operandi* is worthy of note. The director of one of the state prisons announced to the convicts that in an ancient river bed certain tombs were to be found, and promised freedom to any prisoner who made an important discovery. In the months preceding the excavation, printed photographs of what was to be found were shown the prisoners. The first attempt proved that hope and zeal could be inhibiting; a week of work with shovel and pick succeeded in unearthing no *hrön* other than a rusty wheel, postdating the experiment. This was kept a secret, and the experiment was later repeated in four colleges. In three of them the failure was almost complete; in the fourth (the director of which died by chance during the initial excavation), the students dug up—or produced—a gold mask, an archaic sword, two or three earthenware urns, and the moldered mutilated torso of a king with an inscription on his breast which has so far not been deciphered. Thus was discovered the unfitness of witnesses who were aware of the experimental nature of the search. . . . Mass investigations produced objects which contradicted one another; now, individual projects, as far as possible spontaneous, are preferred. The methodical development of *hrönir*, states the eleventh volume, has been of enormous service to archaeologists. It has allowed them to question and even to modify the past, which nowadays is no less malleable or obedient than the future. One curious fact: the *hrönir* of the second and third degree—that is, the *hrönir* derived from another *hrön*, and the *hrönir* derived from the *hrön* of a *hrön*—exaggerate the flaws of the original; those of the fifth degree are almost uniform; those of the ninth can be confused with those of the second; and those of the eleventh degree have a purity of form which the originals do not possess. The process is a recurrent one; a *hrön* of the twelfth degree begins to deteriorate in quality. Stranger and more perfect than any *hrön* is sometimes the *ur*, which is a thing produced by suggestion, an object brought into being by hope. The great gold mask I mentioned previously is a distinguished example.

Things duplicate themselves in Tlön. They tend at the same time to efface themselves, to lose their detail when people forget them. The classic example is that of a stone threshold which lasted as long as it was visited by a beggar, and which faded from sight on his death. Occasionally, a few birds, a horse perhaps, have saved the ruins of an amphitheater. (1940. *Salto Oriental.*)

Postscript. 1947. I reprint the foregoing article just as it appeared in the *Anthology of Fantastic Literature, 1940,* omitting no more than some figures of speech, and a kind of burlesque summing up, which now strikes me as frivolous. So many things have happened since that date. . . . I will confine myself to putting them down.

In March, 1941, a manuscript letter by Gunnar Erfjord came to light in a volume of Hinton, which had belonged to Herbert Ashe. The envelope bore the postmark of Ouro Preto. The letter cleared up entirely the mystery of Tlön. The text of it confirmed Martínez Estrada's thesis. The elaborate story began one night in Lucerne or London, in the early seventeenth century. A benevolent secret society (which counted Dalgarno and, later, George Berkeley among its members) came together to invent a country. The first tentative plan gave prominence to "hermetic studies," philanthropy, and the cabala. Andreä's curious book dates from that first period. At the end of some years of conventicles and premature syntheses, they realized that a single generation was not long enough in which to define a country. They made a resolution that each one of the master-scholars involved should elect a disciple to carry on the work. The hereditary arrangement prevailed; and after a hiatus of two centuries, the persecuted brotherhood reappeared in America. About 1824, in Memphis, Tennessee, one of the members had a conversation with the millionaire ascetic, Ezra Buckley. Buckley listened with some disdain as the other man talked, and then burst out laughing at the modesty of the project. He declared that in America it was absurd to invent a country, and proposed the invention of a whole planet. To this gigantic idea, he added another, born of his own nihilism*—that of keeping the enormous project a secret. The twenty volumes of the *Encyclopaedia Britannica* were then in circulation; Buckley suggested a systematic encyclopedia of the imaginary planet. He would leave the society his mountain ranges with their gold fields, his navigable rivers, his prairies where bull and bison roamed, his Negroes, his brothels, and his dollars, on one condition: "The work will have no truck with the imposter Jesus Christ." Buckley did not believe in God, but nevertheless wished to demonstrate to the nonexistent God that mortal men were capable of conceiving a world. Buckley was poisoned in Baton Rouge in 1828; in 1914, the society forwarded to its collaborators, three hundred in number, the final volume of the *First Encyclopaedia of Tlön*. The edition was secret; the forty volumes which comprised it (the work was vaster than any previously undertaken by men) were to be the basis for another work, more detailed, and this time written, not in English, but in some one of the languages of Tlön. This review of an illusory world was called, provisionally, *Orbis Tertius*, and one of its minor demiurges was Herbert Ashe, whether as an agent of Gunnar Erfjord, or as a full associate, I do not know. The fact that he received a copy of the eleventh volume would favor the second view. But what about the others? About 1942, events began to speed up. I recall with distinct clarity one of the first, and I seem to have felt something of its premonitory character. It occurred in an apartment on the Calle Laprida, facing a high open balcony which looked to the west. From Poitiers, the Princess of Faucigny Lucinge had received her silver table service. Out of the recesses of a crate, stamped all over with international markings, fine immobile pieces were emerging—silver plate from Utrecht and Paris, with hard heraldic fauna, a samovar. Amongst them, trembling faintly, just perceptibly, like a sleeping bird, was a magnetic compass. It shivered mysteriously. The princess did not recognize it. The blue needle longed for magnetic north. The metal case was concave. The letters on the dial corresponded to those of one of the alphabets of Tlön. Such was the first intrusion of the fantastic world into the real one. A disturbing accident brought it about that I was also witness to the second. It happened some months afterward, in a grocery store belonging to a Brazilian, in Cuchilla Negra. Amorim and I were on our way back from Sant'Anna. A sudden rising of the Tacuarembó river compelled us to test (and to suffer patiently) the rudimentary hospitality of the general store. The grocer set up some creaking cots for us in a large room, cluttered with

---

*Buckley was a freethinker, a fatalist, and an apologist for slavery.

barrels and wineskins. We went to bed, but were kept from sleeping until dawn by the drunkenness of an invisible neighbor, who alternated between shouting indecipherable abuse and singing snatches of *milongas,* or rather, snatches of the same *milonga.* As might be supposed, we attributed this insistent uproar to the fiery rum of the proprietor. . . . At dawn, the man lay dead in the corridor. The coarseness of his voice had deceived us; he was a young boy. In his delirium, he had spilled a few coins and a shining metal cone, of the diameter of a die, from his heavy gaucho belt. A serving lad tried to pick up this cone—in vain. It was scarcely possible for a man to lift it. I held it in my hand for some minutes. I remember that it was intolerably heavy, and that after putting it down, its oppression remained. I also remember the precise circle it marked in my flesh. This manifestation of an object which was so tiny and at the same time so heavy left me with an unpleasant sense of abhorrence and fear. A countryman proposed that it be thrown into the rushing river. Amorim acquired it for a few pesos. No one knew anything of the dead man, only that "he came from the frontier." Those small and extremely heavy cones, made of a metal which does not exist in this world, are images of divinity in certain religions in Tlön.

Here I conclude the personal part of my narrative. The rest, when it is not in their hopes or their fears, is at least in the memories of all my readers. It is enough to recall or to mention subsequent events, in as few words as possible; that concave basin which is the collective memory will furnish the wherewithal to enrich or amplify them. About 1944, a reporter from the Nashville, Tennessee, *American* uncovered, in a Memphis library, the forty volumes of the *First Encyclopaedia of Tlön.* Even now it is uncertain whether this discovery was accidental, or whether the directors of the still nebulous *Orbis Tertius* condoned it. The second alternative is more likely. Some of the more improbable features of the eleventh volume (for example, the multiplying of the *hrönir*) had been either removed or modified in the Memphis copy. It is reasonable to suppose that these erasures were in keeping with the plan of projecting a world which would not be too incompatible with the real world. The dissemination of objects from Tlön throughout various countries would complement that plan. . . .* The fact is that the international press overwhelmingly hailed the "find." Manuals, anthologies, summaries, literal versions, authorized reprints, and pirated editions of the Master Work of Man poured and continue to

---

*There remains, naturally, the problem of the *matter* of which some of these objects consisted.

pour out into the world. Almost immediately, reality gave ground on more than one point. The truth is that it hankered to give ground. Ten years ago, any symmetrical system whatsoever which gave the appearance of order—dialectical materialism, anti-Semitism, Nazism—was enough to fascinate men. Why not fall under the spell of Tlön and submit to the minute and vast evidence of an ordered planet? Useless to reply that reality, too, is ordered. It may be so, but in accordance with divine laws—I translate: inhuman laws—which we will never completely perceive. Tlön may be a labyrinth, but it is a labyrinth plotted by men, a labyrinth destined to be deciphered by men.

Contact with Tlön and the ways of Tlön have disintegrated this world. Captivated by its discipline, humanity forgets and goes on forgetting that it is the discipline of chess players, not of angels. Now, the conjectural "primitive language" of Tlön has found its way into the schools. Now, the teaching of its harmonious history, full of stirring episodes, has obliterated the history which dominated my childhood. Now, in all memories, a fictitious past occupies the place of any other. We know nothing about it with any certainty, not even that it is false. Numismatics, pharmacology and archaeology have been revised. I gather that biology and mathematics are awaiting their avatar. . . . A scattered dynasty of solitaries has changed the face of the world. Its task continues. If our foresight is not mistaken, a hundred years from now someone will discover the hundred volumes of the *Second Encyclopaedia of Tlön*.

Then, English, French, and mere Spanish will disappear from this planet. The world will be Tlön. I take no notice. I go on revising, in the quiet of the days in the hotel at Androgué, a tentative translation into Spanish, in the style of Quevedo, which I do not intend to see published, of Sir Thomas Browne's *Urn Burial*.

Translated by Alastair Reid

The Compleat Werewolf

Anthony Boucher

Anthony Boucher (1911–1968) was an author, book reviewer, and editor whose contributions to the field in one aspect of his career overwhelms all others. In his case, it was his excellent criticism of the mystery field in general, which led to an annual convention, Bouchercon, being named after him. His work editing The Magazine of Fantasy and Science Fiction *in its early years firmly established him as a man who left his mark on not just one but two fiction genres. His novels were mainly mysteries, but his short fantasy and science fiction were often nearly perfect examples of the genres, with ordinary characters encountering comic, often supernatural occurrences.*

AUTHOR'S NOTE: IN MY CRIMINOLOGICAL RESEARCHES, I HAVE OCCAsionally come across references to an agent of the Federal Bureau of Investigation who bids fair to become as a great a figure of American legend as Paul Bunyan or John Henry. This man is invulnerable to bullets. He strikes such terror into criminals as to drive them to suicide or madness. He sometimes vanishes from human ken entirely, and at other times he is reported to have appeared with equal suddenness stark naked. And perhaps the most curious touch of all, he engages in a never ceasing quest, of Arthurian intensity, for someone who can perform the Indian rope trick.

Only recently, after intensive probings in Berkeley, where I have certain fortunate connections particularly with the department of German, and a few grudging confidences from my old friend Fergus O'Breen, have I been able to piece together the facts behind this legend.

Here, then, is the story, with only one important detail suppressed, and that, I assure you, strictly for your own good.

———

THE PROFESSOR GLANCED AT THE NOTE:

Don't be silly—Gloria.

Wolfe Wolf crumpled the sheet of paper into a yellow ball and hurled it out the window into the sunshine of the bright campus spring. He made several choice and profane remarks in fluent Middle High German.

Emily looked up from typing the proposed budget for the departmental library. "I'm afraid I didn't understand that, Professor Wolf. I'm weak on Middle High."

"Just improvising," said Wolf, and sent a copy of the *Journal of English and Germanic Philology* to follow the telegram.

Emily rose from the typewriter. "There's something the matter. Did the committee reject your monograph on Hager?"

"That monumental contribution to human knowledge? Oh, no. Nothing so important as that."

"But you're so upset . . ."

"The office wife!" Wolf snorted. "And pretty polyandrous at that, with the whole department on your hands. Go 'way."

Emily's dark little face lit up with a flame of righteous anger that removed any trace of plainness. "Don't talk to me like that, Mr. Wolf. I'm simply trying to help you. And it isn't the whole department. It's . . ."

Professor Wolf picked up an inkwell, looked after the telegram and the *Journal,* then set the glass pot down again. "No. There are better ways of going to pieces. Sorrows drown easier than they smash . . . Get Herbrecht to take my two o'clock, will you?"

"Where are you going?"

"To hell in sectors. So long."

"Wait. Maybe I can help you. Remember when the dean jumped you for serving drinks to students? Maybe I can . . ."

Wolf stood in the doorway and extended one arm impressively, pointing with that curious index which was as long as the middle finger. "Madam, academically you are indispensable. You are the prop and stay of the existence of this department. But at the moment this department can go to hell, where it will doubtless continue to need your invaluable services."

"But don't you see . . ." Emily's voice shook. "No. Of course not. You wouldn't see. You're just a man—no, not even a man. You're just Professor Wolf. You're Woof-woof."

Wolf staggered. "I'm what?"

"Woof-woof. That's what everybody calls you because your name's Wolfe Wolf. All your students, everybody. But you wouldn't notice a thing like that. Oh, no. Woof-woof, that's what you are."

"This," said Wolfe Wolf, "is the crowning blow. My heart is breaking, my world is shattered, I've got to walk a mile from the campus to find a bar; but all this isn't enough. I've got to be called Woof-woof. Good-bye!"

He turned, and in the doorway caromed into a vast and yielding bulk, which gave out with a noise that might have been either a greeting of "Wolf!" or probably an inevitable grunt of "Oof!"

Wolf backed into the room and admitted Professor Fearing, paunch, pince-nez, cane and all. The older man waddled over to his desk, plumped himself down, and exhaled a long breath. "My dear boy," he gasped. "Such impetuosity."

"Sorry, Oscar."

"Ah, youth . . ." Professor Fearing fumbled about for a handkerchief, found none, and proceeded to polish his pince-nez on his somewhat stringy necktie. "But why such haste to depart? And why is Emily crying?"

"Is she?"

"You see?" said Emily hopelessly, and muttered "Woof-woof" into her damp handkerchief.

"And why do copies of the *JEGP* fly about my head as I harmlessly cross the campus? Do we have teleportation on our hands?"

"Sorry," Wolf repeated curtly. "Temper. Couldn't stand that ridiculous argument of Glocke's. Good-bye."

"One moment." Professor Fearing fished into one of his unnumbered handkerchiefless pockets and produced a sheet of yellow paper. "I believe this is yours?"

Wolf snatched at it and quickly converted it into confetti.

Fearing chuckled. "How well I remember when Gloria was a student here! I was thinking of it only last night when I saw her in *Moonbeams and Melody*. How she did upset this whole department! Heavens, my boy, if I'd been a younger man myself . . ."

"I'm going. You'll see about Herbrecht, Emily?"

Emily sniffled and nodded.

"Come, Wolfe." Fearing's voice had grown more serious. "I didn't mean to plague you. But you mustn't take these things too hard. There are better ways of finding consolation than in losing your temper or getting drunk."

"Who said anything about . . ."

"Did you need to say it? No, my boy, if you were to . . . You're not a religious man, are you?"

"Good God, no," said Wolf contradictorily.

"If only you were . . . If I might make a suggestion, Wolf, why don't you come over to the Temple tonight? We're having very special services. They might take your mind off Glo—off your troubles."

"Thanks, no. I've always meant to visit your Temple—I've heard rumors about it—but not tonight. Some other time."

"Tonight would be especially interesting."

"Why? What's so special about April thirtieth?"

Fearing shook his gray head. "It is shocking how ignorant a scholar can be outside of his chosen field . . . But you know the place, Wolfe; I'll hope to see you there tonight."

"Thanks. But my troubles don't need any supernatural solutions. A couple of zombies will do nicely, and I do *not* mean serviceable stiffs. Good-bye, Oscar." He was halfway through the door before he added as an afterthought, "'Bye, Emily."

"Such rashness," Fearing murmured. "Such impetuosity. Youth is a wonderful thing to enjoy, is it not, Emily?"

Emily said nothing, but plunged into typing the proposed budget as though all the fiends of hell were after her, as indeed many of them were.

The sun was setting, and Wolf's tragic account of his troubles had laid an egg, too. The bartender had polished every glass in the joint and still the repetitive tale kept pouring forth. He was torn between a boredom new even in his experience and a professional admiration for a customer who could consume zombies indefinitely.

"Did I tell you about the time she flunked the midterm?" Wolf demanded truculently.

"Only three times," said the bartender.

"All right, then; I'll tell you. Yunnerstand, I don't do things like this. Profeshical ethons, that's what's I've got. But this was different. This wasn't like somebody that doesn't know just because she doesn't know; this was a girl that didn't know because she wasn't the kind of girl that has to know the kind of things a girl has to know if she's the kind of girl that ought to know that kind of things. Yunnerstand?"

The bartender cast a calculating glance at the plump little man who sat alone at the end of the deserted bar, carefully nursing his gin and tonic.

"She made me see that. She made me see lossa things and I can still see the things she made me see the things. It wasn't just like a professor falls for a coed, yunnerstand? This was different. This was wunnaful. This was like a whole new life like."

The bartender sidled down to the end of the bar. "Brother," he whispered softly.

The little man with the odd beard looked up from his gin and tonic. "Yes, colleague?"

"If I listen to that potted professor another five minutes, I'm going to start smashing up the joint. How's about slipping down there and standing in for me, huh?"

The little man looked Wolf over and fixed his gaze especially on the hand that clenched the tall zombie glass. "Gladly, colleague," he nodded.

The bartender sighed a gust of relief.

"She was Youth," Wolf was saying intently to where the bartender had stood. "But it wasn't just that. This was different. She was Life and Excitement and Joy and Ecstasy and Stuff. Yunner . . ." He broke off and stared at the empty space. *"Uh-mazing!"* he observed. "Right before my very eyes. *Uh-mazing!"*

"You were saying, colleague?" the plump little man prompted from the adjacent stool.

Wolf turned. "So there you are. Did I tell you about the time I went to her house to check her term paper?"

"No. But I have a feeling you will."

"Howja know? Well, this night . . ."

The little man drank slowly; but his glass was empty by the time Wolf had finished the account of an evening of pointlessly tentative flirtation. Other customers were drifting in, and the bar was now about a third full.

"—and ever since then—" Wolf broke off sharply. "That isn't you," he objected.

"I think it is, colleague."

"But you're a bartender and *you* aren't a bartender."

"No. I'm a magician."

"Oh. That explains it. Now like I was telling you . . . Hey! Your bald is beard."

"I beg your pardon?"

"Your bald is beard. Just like your head. It's all jussa fringe running around."

"I like it that way."

"And your glass is empty."

"That's all right, too."

"Oh, no, it isn't. It isn't every night you get to drink with a man that proposed to Gloria Garton and got turned down. This is an occasion for celebration." Wolf thumped loudly on the bar and held up his first two fingers.

The little man regarded their equal length. "No," he said softly. "I think I'd better not. I know my capacity. If I have another—well, things might start happening."

"Lettemappen!"

"No. Please, colleague. I'd rather . . ."

The bartender brought the drinks. "Go on, brother," he whispered. "Keep him quiet. I'll do you a favor sometime."

Reluctantly the little man sipped at his fresh gin and tonic.

The professor took a gulp of his nth zombie. "My name's Woof-woof," he proclaimed "Lots of people call me Wolfe Wolf. They think that's funny. But it's really Woof-woof. Wazoors?"

The other paused a moment to decipher that Arabic-sounding word, then said, Mine's Ozymandias the Great."

"That's a funny name."

"I told you I'm a magician. Only I haven't worked for a long time. Theatrical managers are peculiar, colleague. They don't want a real magician. They won't even let me show 'em my best stuff. Why, I remember one night in Darjeeling . . ."

"Glad to meet you, Mr. . . . Mr. . . ."

"You can call me Ozzy. Most people do."

"Glad to meet you, Ozzy. Now about this girl. This Glória. Yunnerstand, donya?"

"Sure, colleague."

"She thinks being a professor of German is nothing. She wants something glamorous. She says if I was an actor now or a G-man . . . Yunnerstand?"

Ozymandias the Great nodded.

"Awright then! So yunnerstand. Fine. But whatddayou want to keep talking about it for? Yunnerstand. That's that. To hell with it."

Ozymandias's round and fringed face brightened. "Sure," he said, and added recklessly, "let's drink to that."

They clinked glasses and drank. Wolf carelessly tossed off a toast in Old Low Frankish, with an unpardonable error in the use of the genitive.

The two men next to them began singing "My Wild Irish Rose," but trailed off disconsolately. "What we need," said the one with the derby, "is a tenor."

"What I need," Wolf muttered, "is a cigarette."

"Sure," said Ozymandias the Great. The bartender was drawing beer directly in front of them. Ozymandias reached across the bar, removed a lighted cigarette from the barkeep's ear, and handed it to his companion.

"Where'd that come from?"

"I don't quite know. All I know is how to get them. I told you I was a magician."

"Oh. I see. Pressajijijation."

"No. Not a prestidigitator; I said a magician. Oh, blast it! I've done it again. More than one gin and tonic and I start showing off."

"I don't believe you," said Wolf flatly. "No such thing as magicians. That's just as silly as Oscar Fearing and his Temple and what's so special about April thirtieth, anyway?"

The bearded man frowned. "Please, colleague. Let's forget it."

"No. I don't believe you. You pressajijijated that cigarette. You didn't magic it." His voice began to rise. "You're a fake."

"Please, brother," the barkeep whispered. "Keep him quiet."

"All right," said Ozymandias wearily. "I'll show you something that can't be prestidigitation." The couple adjoining had begun to sing again. "They need a tenor. All right: listen!"

And the sweetest, most ineffably Irish tenor ever heard joined in on the duet. The singers didn't worry about the source; they simply accepted the new voice gladly and were spurred on to their very best, with the result that the bar knew the finest harmony it had heard since the night the Glee Club was suspended en masse.

Wolf looked impressed, but shook his head. "That's not magic, either. That's ventriloquism."

"As a matter of strict fact, that was a street singer who was killed in the Easter Rebellion. Fine fellow, too; never heard a better voice unless it was that night in Darjeeling when . . ."

"Fake!" said Wolfe Wolf loudly and belligerently.

Ozymandias once more contemplated that long index finger. He looked at the professor's dark brows that met in a straight line over his nose. He picked his companion's limpish hand off the bar and scrutinized the palm. The growth of hair was not marked, but it was perceptible.

The magician chortled. "And you sneer at magic!"

"Whasso funny about me sneering at magic?"

Ozymandias lowered his voice. "Because, my fine furry friend, you are a werewolf."

The Irish martyr had begun "Rose of Tralee" and the two mortals were joining in valiantly.

"I'm what?"

"A werewolf."

"But there isn't any such thing. Any fool knows that."

"Fools," said Ozymandias, "know a great deal which the wise do not. There are werewolves. There always have been, and quite probably always will be." He spoke as calmly and assuredly as though he were mentioning that the earth was round. "And there are three infallible physical signs; the meeting eyebrows, the long index finger, the hairy palms. You have all three. And even your name is an indication. Family names do not come from nowhere. Every Smith has an ancestor somewhere who was a Smith. Every Fisher comes from a family that once fished. And your name is Wolf."

The statement was so quiet, so plausible, that Wolf faltered. "But a werewolf is a man that changes into a wolf. I've never done that. Honest I haven't."

"A mammal," said Ozymandias, "is an animal that bears its young alive and suckles them. A virgin is nonetheless a mammal. Because you have never changed does not make you any the less a werewolf."

"But a werewolf . . ." Suddenly Wolf's eyes lit up. "A werewolf! But that's even better than a G-man! Now I can show Gloria!"

"What on earth do you mean, colleague?"

Wolf was climbing down from his stool. The intense excitement of this brilliant new idea seemed to have sobered him. He grabbed the little man by the sleeve. "Come on. We're going to find a nice quiet place. And you're going to prove you're a magician."

"But how?"

"You're going to show me how to change!"

Ozymandias finished his gin and tonic, and with it drowned his last regretful hesitation. "Colleague," he announced, "you're on!"

Professor Oscar Fearing, standing behind the curiously carved lectern of the Temple of the Dark Truth, concluded the reading of the prayer with mumbling sonority. "And on this night of all nights, in the name of the black light that glows in the darkness, we give thanks!" He closed the parchment-bound book and faced the small congregation, calling out with fierce intensity, "Who wishes to give his thanks to the Lower Lord?"

A cushioned dowager rose. "I give thanks!" she shrilled excitedly. "My Ming Choy was sick, even unto death. I took of her blood and offered it to the Lower Lord, and he had mercy and restored her to me!"

Behind the altar an electrician checked his switches and spat disgustedly. "Bugs! Every last one of 'em!"

The man who was struggling into a grotesque and terrible costume paused and shrugged. "They pay good money. What's it to us if they're bugs?"

A tall, thin, old man had risen uncertainly to his feet. "I give thanks!" he cried. "I give thanks to the Lower Lord that I have finished my great work. My protective screen against magnetic bombs is a tried and proven success, to the glory of our country and science and the Lord."

"Crackpot," the electrician muttered.

The man in costume peered around the altar. "Crackpot, hell! That's Chiswick from the physics department. Think of a man like that falling for this stuff! And listen to him: He's even telling about the government's plans for installation. You know, I'll bet you one of these fifth columnists could pick up something around here."

There was silence in the Temple when the congregation had finished its thanksgiving. Professor Fearing leaned over the lectern and spoke quietly and impressively. "As you know, brothers in Darkness, tonight is May Eve, the thirtieth of April, the night consecrated by the Church to that martyr missionary St. Walpurgis, and by us to other and deeper purposes. It is on this night, and this night only, that we may directly give our thanks to the Lower Lord himself. Not in wanton orgy and obscenity, as the Middle Ages misconceived his desires, but in praise and in deep, dark joy that issues forth from Blackness."

"Hold your hats, boys," said the man in the costume. "Here I go again."

"Eka!" Fearing thundered. *"Dva tri chatur! Pancha! Shas sapta! Ashta nava dasha ekadasha!"* He paused. There was always the danger that at this moment some scholar in this university town might recognize that the invocation, though perfect Sanskrit, consisted solely of the numbers from one to eleven. But no one stirred, and he launched forth in more apposite Latin: *"Per vota nostra ipse nunc surgat nobls dicatus Baal Zebub!"*

"Baal Zebub!" the congregation chorused.

"Cue," said the electrician, and pulled a switch.

The lights flickered and went out. Lightning played across the sanctuary. Suddenly out of the darkness came a sharp bark, a yelp of pain, and a long-drawn howl of triumph.

A blue light now began to glow dimly. In the faint reflection of this, the electrician was amazed to see his costumed friend at his side, nursing his bleeding hand.

"What the . . ." the electrician whispered.

"Hanged if I know. I go out there on cue, all ready to make my terrifying appearance, and what happens? Great big dog up and nips my hand. Why didn't they tell me they'd switched the script?"

In the glow of the blue light the congregation reverently contemplated the plump little man with the fringe of beard and the splendid gray wolf that stood beside him. "Hail, O Lower Lord!" resounded the chorus, drowning out one spinster's murmur of "But my *dear,* I *swear* he was *much* handsomer last year."

"Colleagues!" said Ozymandias the Great, and there was utter silence, a dread hush awaiting the momentous words of the Lower Lord. Ozymandias took one step forward, placed his tongue carefully between his lips, uttered the ripest, juiciest raspberry of his career, and vanished, wolf and all.

Wolfe Wolf opened his eyes and shut them again hastily. He had never expected the quiet and sedate Berkeley Inn to install centrifugal rooms. It wasn't fair. He lay in darkness, waiting for the whirling to stop and trying to reconstruct the past night.

He remembered the bar all right, and the zombies. And the bartender. Very sympathetic chap that, up until he suddenly changed into a little man with a fringe of beard. That was where things began getting strange. There was something about a cigarette and an Irish tenor and a werewolf. Fantastic idea, that. Any fool knows . . .

Wolf sat up suddenly. He *was* the werewolf. He threw back the bedclothes and stared down at his legs. Then he sighed relief. They were long legs. They were hairy enough. They were brown from much tennis. But they were indisputably human.

He got up, resolutely stifling his qualms, and began to pick up the clothing that was scattered nonchalantly about the floor. A crew of gnomes was excavating his skull, but he hoped they might go away if he didn't pay too much attention to them. One thing was certain; he was going to be good from now on. Gloria or no Gloria, heartbreak or no heartbreak, drowning your sorrows wasn't good enough. If you felt like this and could imagine you'd been a werewolf . . .

But why should he have imagined it in such detail? So many fragmentary memories seemed to come back as he dressed. Going up Strawberry Canyon with the fringed beard, finding a desolate and isolated spot for magic, learning the words . . . He could even remember the words. The word that changed you and the one that changed you back.

Had he made up those words, too, in his drunken imaginings? And had he made up what he could only barely recall—the wonderful, magical freedom of changing, the single sharp pang of alteration and then the boundless happiness of being lithe and fleet and free?

He surveyed himself in the mirror. He looked exactly what he was, save for the unwonted wrinkles in his conservative single-breasted gray suit: a quiet academician, a little better built, a little more impulsive, a little more romantic than most, perhaps, but still just that—Professor Wolf.

The rest was nonsense. But there was, that impulsive side of him suggested, only one way of proving the fact. And that was to say The Word.

"All right," said Wolfe Wolf to his reflection. "I'll show you." And he said it.

The pang was sharper and stronger than he'd remembered. Alcohol numbs you to pain. It tore him for a moment with an anguish like the descriptions of childbirth. Then it was gone, and he flexed his limbs in happy amazement. But he was not a lithe, fleet, free beast. He was a helplessly trapped wolf, irrevocably entangled in a conservative, single-breasted gray suit.

He tried to rise and walk, but the long sleeves and legs tripped him over flat on his muzzle. He kicked with his paws, trying to tear his way out, and then stopped. Werewolf or no werewolf, he was likewise still Professor Wolf, and this suit had cost thirty-five dollars. There must be some cheaper way of securing freedom than tearing the suit to shreds.

He used several good, round, Low German expletives. This was a complication that wasn't in any of the werewolf legends he'd ever read. There, people—boom!—became wolves or—bang!—became men again. When they were men, they wore clothes; when they were wolves, they wore fur. Just like Hyperman becoming Bark Lent again on top of the Empire State Building and finding his street clothes right there. Most misleading. He began to remember now how Ozymandias the Great had made him strip before teaching him the words . . .

The words! That was it. All he had to do was say the word that changed you back—*Absarka!*—and he'd be a man again, comfortably fitted inside his suit. Then he could strip and start all over again. You see? Reason solves all. *"Absarka!"* he said.

Or thought he said. He went through all the proper mental processes for saying *Absarka!* but all that came of his muzzle was a sort of clicking whine. And he was still a conservatively dressed and helpless wolf.

This was worse than the clothes problem. If he could be released only by saying *Absarka!* and if, being a wolf, he could say nothing, why, there he was, Indefinitely. He could go find Ozzy and ask—but how could a wolf wrapped up in a gray suit get safely out of a hotel and set out hunting for an unknown address?

He was trapped. He was lost. He was . . .

"Absarka!"

Professor Wolfe Wolf stood up in his grievously rumpled gray suit and beamed on the beard-fringed face of Ozymandias the Great.

"You see, colleague," the little magician explained, "I figured you'd want to try it again as soon you got up, and I knew darned well you'd have your troubles. Thought I'd come over and straighten things for you."

Wolf lit a cigarette in silence and handed the pack to Ozymandias. "When you came in just now," he said at last, "what did you see?"

"You as a wolf."

"Then it really . . . I actually . . ."

"Sure. You're a full-fledged werewolf, all right."

Wolf sat down on the rumpled bed. "I guess," he ventured slowly, "I've got to believe it. And if I believe that . . . But it means I've got to believe everything I've always scorned. I've got to believe in gods and devils and hells and . . ."

"You needn't be so pluralistic. But there is a God." Ozymandias said this as calmly and convincingly as he had stated last night that there were werewolves.

"And if there's a God, then I've got a soul?"

"Sure."

"And if I'm a werewolf . . . Hey!"

"What's the trouble, colleague?"

"All right, Ozzy. You know everything. Tell me this: Am I damned?"

"For what? Just for being a werewolf? Shucks, no; let me explain. There's two kinds of werewolves. There's the cursed kind that can't help themselves, that just go turning into wolves without any say in the matter; and there's the voluntary kind like you. Now most of the voluntary kind are damned, sure, because they're wicked men who lust for blood and eat innocent people. But they aren't damnably wicked because they're werewolves; they became werewolves because they are damnably wicked. Now you changed yourself just for the fun of it and because it looked like a good way to impress a gal; that's an innocent enough motive, and being a werewolf doesn't make it any less so. Werewolves don't have to be monsters; it's just that we only hear about the ones that are."

"But how can I be voluntary when you told me I was a werewolf before ever I changed?"

"Not everybody can change. It's like being able to roll your tongue or wiggle your ears. You can, or you can't; and that's that. And, like those abilities, there's probably a genetic factor involved, though nobody's done any serious research on it. You were a werewolf *in posse;* now you're one *in esse.*"

"Then it's all right? I can be a werewolf just for having fun and it's safe?"

"Absolutely."

Wolf chortled. "Will I show Gloria! Dull and unglamorous, indeed! Anybody can marry an actor or a G-man; but a werewolf . . ."

"Your children probably will be, too," said Ozymandias cheerfully.

Wolf shut his eyes dreamily, then opened them with a start. "You know what?"

"What?"

"I haven't got a hangover any more! This is marvelous. That is . . . Why, this is practical. At last the perfect hangover cure. Shuffle yourself into a wolf and back and . . . Oh, that reminds me. How do I get back?"

"Absarka."

"I know. But when I'm a wolf I can't say it."

"That," said Ozymandias sadly, "is the curse of being a white magician. You keep having to use the second-best form of spells, because the best would be black. Sure, a black-magic werebeast can turn himself back whenever he wants to. I remember in Darjeeling . . ."

"But how about me?"

"That's the trouble. You have to have somebody to *Absarka!* for you. That's what I did last night, or you remember? After we broke up the party at your friend's Temple . . . Tell you what. I'm retired now, and I've got enough to live on modestly because I can always magic up a little . . . Are you going to take up werewolfing seriously?"

"For a while, anyway. Till I get Gloria."

"Then why shouldn't I come and live here in your hotel? Then I'll always be handy to *Absarka!* you. After you get the girl, you can teach her."

Wolf extended his hand. "Noble of you. Shake." And then his eye caught his wrist watch. "I've missed two classes this morning. Werewolfing's all very well, but a man's got to work for his living."

"Most men." Ozymandias calmly reached his hand into the air and plucked a coin. He looked at it ruefully; it was a gold moidore. "Hang these spirits; I simply cannot explain to them about gold being illegal."

"From Los Angeles," Wolf thought, with the habitual contempt of the northern Californian, as he surveyed the careless sport coat and the bright-yellow shirt of his visitor.

This young man rose politely as the professor entered the office. His green eyes gleamed cordially and his red hair glowed in the spring sunlight. "Professor Wolf?" he asked.

Wolf glanced impatiently at his desk. "Yes."

"O'Breen's the name. I'd like to talk to you a minute."

"My office hours are from three to four Tuesdays and Thursdays. I'm afraid I'm rather busy now."

"This isn't faculty business. And it's important." The young man's attitude was affable and casual, but he managed none the less to convey a sense of urgency that piqued Wolf's curiosity. The all-important letter to Gloria had waited while he took two classes; it could wait another five minutes.

"Very well, Mr. O'Breen."

"And alone, if you please."

Wolf himself hadn't noticed that Emily was in the room. He now turned to the secretary and said, "All right. If you don't mind, Emily . . ."

Emily shrugged and went out.

"Now, sir. What is this important and secret business?"

"Just a question or two. To start with, how well do you know Gloria Garton?"

Wolf paused. You could hardly say, "Young man, I am about to repropose to her in view of my becoming a werewolf." Instead he simply said—the truth if not whole truth—"She was a pupil of mine a few years ago."

"I said *do,* not *did.* How well do you know her now?"

"And why should I bother to answer such a question?"

The young man handed over a card. Wolf read:

FERGUS O'BREEN

PRIVATE INQUIRY AGENT

Licensed by the State of California

Wolf smiled. "And what does this mean? Divorce Evidence? Isn't that the usual field of private inquiry agents?"

"Miss Garton isn't married, as you probably know very well. I'm just asking you if you've been in touch with her much lately?"

"And I'm simply asking why you should want to know?"

O'Breen rose and began to pace around the office. "We don't seem to be getting very far, do we? I'm to take it that you refuse to state the nature of your relations with Gloria Garton?"

"I see no reason why I should do otherwise." Wolf was beginning to be annoyed.

To his surprise, the detective relaxed into a broad grin. "O.K. Let it ride. Tell me about your department: How long have the various faculty members been here?"

"Instructors and all?"

"Just the professors."

"I've been here for seven years. All the others at least a good ten, probably more. If you want exact figures, you can probably get them from the dean, unless, as I hope"—Wolf smiled cordially—"he throws you out flat on your red pate."

O'Breen laughed. "Professor, I think we could get on. One more question, and you can do some pate-tossing yourself. Are you an American citizen?"

"Of course."

"And the rest of the department?"

"All of them. And now would you have the common decency to give me some explanation of this fantastic farrago of questions?"

"No," said O'Breen casually. "Good-bye, Professor." His alert, green eyes had been roaming about the room, sharply noticing everything. Now, as he left, they rested on Wolf's long index finger, moved up to his heavy meeting eyebrows, and returned to the finger. There was a suspicion of a startled realization in those eyes as he left the office.

But that was nonsense, Wolf told himself. A private detective, no matter how shrewd his eyes, no matter how apparently meaningless his inquiries, would surely be the last man on earth to notice the signs of lycanthropy.

Funny. Werewolf was a word you could accept. You could say, "I am a werewolf," and it was all right. But say, "I am a lycanthrope," and your flesh crawled. Odd. Possibly material for a paper on the influence of etymology on connotation for one of the learned periodicals.

But, hell! Wolfe Wolf was no longer primarily a scholar. He was a werewolf now, a white-magic werewolf, a werewolf-for-fun; and fun he was going to have. He lit his pipe, stared at the blank paper on his desk, and tried desperately to draft a letter to Gloria. It should hint at just enough to fascinate her and hold her interest until he could go south when the term ended and reveal to her the whole wonderful new truth. It . . .

Professor Oscar Fearing grunted his ponderous way into the office. "Good afternoon, Wolfe. Hard at it, my boy?"

"Afternoon," Wolf replied distractedly, and continued to stare at the paper.

"Great events coming, eh? Are you looking forward to seeing the glorious Gloria?"

Wolf started. "How . . . What do you mean?"

Fearing handed him a folded newspaper. "You hadn't heard?"

Wolf read with growing amazement and delight:

GLORIA GARTON TO ARRIVE FRIDAY
Local Girl Returns to Berkeley

As part of the most spectacular talent hunt since the search for Scarlett O'Hara, Gloria Garton, glamorous Metropolis starlet, will visit Berkeley Friday.

Friday afternoon at the Campus Theater, Berkeley canines will have their chance to compete in the nation-wide quest for a dog to play Tookah the wolf dog in the great Metropolis epic, *Fangs of the Forest,* and Gloria Garton herself will be present at the auditions.

"I owe so much to Berkeley," Miss Garton said. "It will mean so much to me to see the campus and the city again." Miss Garton has the starring human role in *Fangs of the Forest.*

Miss Garton was a student at the University of California when she received her first chance in films. She is a member of Mask and Dagger, honorary dramatic society, and Rho Rho Rho Sorority.

Wolfe Wolf glowed. This was perfect. No need now wait till term was over. He could see Gloria now and claim her in all his wolfish vigor. Friday—today was Wednesday—that gave him two nights to practice and perfect the technique of werewolfry. And then / . .

He noticed the dejected look on the older professor's face, and a small remorse smote him. "How did things go last night, Oscar?" he asked sympathetically. "How were your big Walpurgis night services?"

Fearing regarded him oddly. "You know that now? Yesterday April thirtieth meant nothing to you."

"I got curious and looked it up. But how did it go?"

"Well enough," Fearing lied feebly. "Do you know, Wolfe," he demanded after a moment's silence, "what is the real curse of every man interested in the occult?"

"No. What?"

"That true power is never enough. Enough for yourself, perhaps, but never enough for others. So that no matter what your true abilities, you must forge on beyond them into charlatanry to convince the others. Look at St. Germain. Look at Francis Stuart. Look at Cagliostro. But the worst tragedy is the next stage; when you realize that your powers were greater than you supposed and that the charlatanry was needless. When you realize that you have no notion of the extent of your powers. Then . . ."

"Then, Oscar?"

"Then, my boy, you are a badly frightened man."

Wolf wanted to say something consoling. He wanted to say, "Look, Oscar. It was just me. Go back to your half-hearted charlatanry and be happy." But he couldn't do that. Only Ozzy could know the truth of that splendid gray wolf. Only Ozzy and Gloria.

The moon was bright on that hidden spot in the canyon. The night was still. And Wolfe Wolf had a severe case of stage fright. Now that it came to the real thing—for this morning's clothes-complicated fiasco hardly counted and last night he could not truly remember— he was afraid to plunge cleanly into wolfdom and anxious to stall and talk as long as possible.

"Do you think," he asked the magician nervously, "that I could teach Gloria to change, too?"

Ozymandias pondered. "Maybe, colleague. It'd depend. She might have the natural ability, and she might not. And, of course, there's no telling what she might change into."

"You mean she wouldn't necessarily be a wolf?"

"Of course not. The people who can change, change into all sorts of things. And every folk knows best the kind that most interests it. We've got an English and Central European tradition; so we know mostly about werewolves. But take Scandinavia, and you'll hear chiefly about werebears, only they call 'em berserkers. And Orientals, now, they're apt to know about weretigers. Trouble is, we've thought so much about were*wolves* that that's all we know the signs for; I wouldn't know how to spot a weretiger just offhand."

"Then there's no telling what might happen if I taught her The Word?"

"Not the least. Of course, there's some werethings that just aren't much use being. Take like being a wereant. You change and somebody steps on you and that's that. Or like a fellow I knew once in Madagascar. Taught him The Word, and know what? Hanged if he wasn't a werediplodocus. Shattered the whole house into little pieces when he changed and almost trampled me under hoof before I could say *Absarka!* He decided not to make a career of it. Or then there was that time in Darjeeling . . . But, look colleague, are you going to stand around here naked all night?"

"No," said Wolf. "I'm going to change now. You'll take my clothes back to the hotel?"

"Sure. They'll be there for you. And I've put a very small spell on the night clerk, just enough for him not to notice wolves wandering in. Oh, and by the way—anything missing from your room?"

"Not that I noticed. Why?"

"Because I thought I saw somebody come out of it this afternoon. Couldn't be sure, but I think he came from there. Young fella with red hair and Hollywood clothes."

Wolfe Wolf frowned. That didn't make sense. Pointless questions from a detective were bad enough, but searching your hotel room . . . But what were detectives to a full-fledged werewolf? He grinned, nodded a friendly good-bye to Ozymandias the Great, and said The Word.

The pain wasn't so sharp as this morning, though still quite bad enough. But it passed almost at once, and his whole body filled with a sense of limitless freedom. He lifted his snout and sniffed deep at the keen freshness of this night air. A whole new realm of pleasure opened up for him through this acute new nose alone. He wagged his tail amicably at Ozzy and set up off the canyon on a long, easy lope.

For hours loping was enough—simply and purely enjoying one's wolfness was the finest pleasure one could ask. Wolf left the canyon and turned up into the hills, past the Big C and on into noble wildness that seemed far remote from all campus civilization. His brave new legs were stanch and tireless, his wind seemingly inexhaustible. Every turning brought fresh and vivid scents of soil and leaves and air, and life was shimmering and beautiful.

But a few hours of this, and Wolf realized that he was lonely. All this grand exhilaration was very well, but if his mate Gloria were loping by his side . . . And what fun was it to be something as splendid as a wolf if no one admired you? He began to want people, and he turned back to the city.

Berkeley goes to bed early. The streets were deserted. Here and there a light burned in a rooming house where some solid grind was plodding on his almost due term paper. Wolf had done that himself. He couldn't laugh in this shape, but his tail twitched with amusement at the thought.

He paused along the tree-lined street. There was a fresh human scent here, though the street seemed empty. Then he heard a soft whimpering, and trotted off toward the noise.

Behind the shrubbery fronting an apartment house sat a disconsolate two-year-old, shivering in his sunsuit and obviously lost for hours on hours. Wolf put a paw on the child's shoulder and shook him gently.

The boy looked around and was not in the least afraid. "He'o," he said brightening up.

Wolf growled a cordial greeting, and wagged his tail and pawed at the ground to indicate that he'd take the lost infant wherever it wanted to go.

The child stood up and wiped away its tears with a dirty fist which left wide, black smudges. "Tootootootoo!" he said.

Games, thought Wolf. He wants to play choo-choo. He took the child by the sleeve and tugged gently.

"Tootootootoo!" the boy repeated firmly. "Die way."

The sound of a railway whistle, to be sure, does die away; but this seemed a poetic expression for such a toddler, Wolf thought, and then abruptly would have snapped his fingers if he'd had them. The child was saying "2222 Dwight Way," having been carefully brought up to tell its address when lost. Wolf glanced up at the street sign. Bowditch and Hillegas—2222 Dwight would be just a couple of blocks.

Wolf tried to nod his head, but the muscles didn't seem to work that way. Instead he wagged his tail in what he hoped indicated comprehension, and started off leading the child.

The infant beamed and said, "Nice woof-woof."

For an instant Wolf felt like a spy suddenly addressed by his right name, then realized that if some say "bow-wow" others might well say "woof-woof."

He led the child for two blocks without event. It felt good, having an innocent human being put his whole life and trust in your charge like this. There was someing about children; he hoped Gloria felt the same. He wondered what would happen if he could teach this confiding infant The Word. It would be swell to have a pup that would . . .

He paused. His nose twitched and the hair on the back of his neck rose. Ahead of them stood a dog, a huge mongrel, seemingly a mixture of St. Bernard and Husky. But the growl that issued from his throat indicated that carrying brandy kegs or rushing serum was not for him. He was a bandit, an outlaw, an enemy of man and dog. And they had to pass him.

Wolf had no desire to fight. He was as big as this monster and certainly, with his human brain, much cleverer; but scars from a dog fight would not look well on the human body of Professor Wolf, and there was, moreover, the danger of hurting the toddler in the fracas. It would be wiser to cross the street. But before he could steer the child that way, the mongrel brute had charged at them, yapping and snarling.

Wolf placed himself in front of the boy, poised and ready to leap in defense. The scar problem was secondary to the fact that this baby had trusted him. He was ready to face this cur and teach him a lesson, at whatever cost to his own human body. But halfway to him the huge dog stopped. His growls died away to a piteous whimper. His great flanks trembled in the moonlight. His tail curled craven between his legs. And abruptly he turned and fled.

The child crowed delightedly. "Bad woof-woof go way." He put his little arms around Wolf's neck, *"Nice woof-woof."* Then he straightened up and said insistently, "Tootootootoo. Die way," and Wolf led on, his strong wolf's heart pounding as it had never pounded at the embrace of a woman.

"Tootootootoo" was a small frame house set back from the street in a large yard. The lights were still on, and even from the sidewalk Wolf could hear a woman's shrill voice.

"—since five o'clock this afternoon, and you've got to find him, officer. You simply must. We've hunted all over the neighborhood and—"

Wolf stood up against the wall on his hindlegs and rang the door-bell with his front right paw.

"Oh! Maybe that's somebody now. The neighbors said they'd . . . Come, officer, and let's see . . . Oh!"

At the same moment Wolf barked politely, the toddler yelled "Mamma!" and his thin and worn-looking young mother let out a scream half delight at finding her child and half terror of this large, gray canine shape that loomed behind him. She snatched up the infant protectively and turned to the large man in uniform. Officer! Look! That big dreadful thing! It stole my Robby!"

"No," Robby protested firmly. "Nice woof-woof."

The officer laughed. "The lad's probably right, ma'am. It *is* a nice woof-woof. Found your boy wandering around and helped him home. You haven't maybe got a bone for him?"

"Let that big nasty brute into my home? Never! Come on, Robby."

"Want my nice woof-woof."

"I'll woof-woof you, staying out till all hours and giving your father and me the fright of our lives. Just wait till your father sees you, young man; he'll . . . Oh, good night, officer!" And she shut the door on the yowls of Robby.

The policeman patted Wolf's head. "Never mind about the bone, Rover. She didn't so much as offer me a glass of beer, either. My, you're a husky specimen, aren't you, boy? Look almost like a wolf. Who do you belong to, and what you are doing wandering about alone? Huh?" He turned on his flash and bent over to look at the nonexistent collar.

He straightened up and whistled. "No license. Rover, that's bad. You know what I ought to do? I ought to turn you in. If you weren't a hero that just got cheated out of his bone, I'd . . . I ought to do it, anyway. Laws are laws, even for heroes. Come on, Rover. We're going for a walk."

Wolf thought quickly. The pound was the last place on earth he wanted to wind up. Even Ozzy would never think of looking for him there. Nobody'd claim him, nobody'd say *Absarka!* and in the end a dose of chloform . . . He wrenched loose from the officer's grasp on his hair, and with one prodigious leap cleared the yard, landed on the sidewalk, and started up the street. But the instant he was out of the officer's sight he stopped dead and slipped behind a hedge.

He scented the policeman's approach even before he heard it. The man was running with the lumbering haste of two hundred pounds. But opposite the hedge he, too, stopped. For a moment

Wolf wondered if his ruse had failed; but the officer had paused only to scratch his head and mutter, "Say! There's something screwy here. *Who rang that doorbell?* The kid couldn't reach it, and the dog . . . Oh, well," he concluded. "Nuts," and seemed to find in that monosyllabic summation the solution to all his problems.

As his footsteps and smell died away, Wolf became aware of another scent. He had only just identified it as cat when someone said, "You're were, aren't you?"

Wolf started up, lips drawn back and muscles tense. There was nothing human in sight, but someone had spoken to him. Unthinkingly, he tried to say, "Where are you?" but all that came out was a growl.

"Right behind you. Here in the shadows. You can scent me, can't you?"

"But you're a cat," Wolf thought in his snarls. "And you're talking."

"Of course. But I'm not talking human language. It's just your brain that takes it that way. If you had your human body, you'd just think I was going *meowrr.* But you are were, aren't you?"

"How do you . . . Why did you think so?"

"Because you didn't try to jump me, as any normal dog would have. And besides, unless Confucius taught me all wrong, you're a wolf, not a dog; and we don't have wolves around here unless they're were."

"How do you know all this? Are you . . ."

"Oh, no. I'm just a cat. But I used to live next door to a werechow named Confucius. He taught me things."

Wolf was amazed. "You mean he was a man who changed to chow and stayed that way? Lived as a pet?"

"Certainly. This was back at the worst of the Depression. He said a dog was more apt to be fed and looked after than a man. I thought it was a smart idea."

"But how terrible! Could a man so debase himself as . . ."

"Men don't debase themselves. They debase each other. That's the way of most weres. Some change to keep from being debased, others to do a little more effective debasing. Which are you?"

"Why, you see, I . . ."

"*Sh!* Look. This is going to be fun. Holdup."

Wolf peered around the hedge. A well-dressed, middle-aged man was waking along briskly, apparently enjoying a night constitutional. Behind him moved a thin, silent figure. Even as Wolf watched, the figure caught up with him and whispered harshly, "Up, with 'em, buddy!"

The quiet pomposity of the stroller melted away. He was ashen and aspen, as the figure slipped a hand around into his breast pocket and removed an impressive wallet.

And what, thought Wolf, was the good of his fine, vigorous body if it merely crouched behind hedges as a spectator? In one fine bound, to the shocked amazement of the were-wise cat, he had crossed the hedge and landed with his forepaws full in the figure's face. It went over backward with him on top and then there was a loud noise, a flash of light, and a frightful sharp smell. For a moment Wolf felt an acute pang in his shoulder, like the jab of a long needle, and then the pain was gone.

But his momentary recoil had been enough to let the figure get to its feet. "Missed you, huh?" it muttered. "Let's see how you like a slug in the belly, you interfering . . ." and he applied an epithet which would have been purely literal description if Wolf had not been were.

There were three quick shots in succession even as Wolf sprang. For a second he experienced the most acute stomach-ache of his life. Then he landed again. The figure's head hit the concrete sidewalk and he was still.

Lights were leaping into brightness everywhere. Among all the confused noises, Wolf could hear the shrill complaints of Robby's mother, and among all the compounded smells, he could distinguish scent of the policeman who wanted to impound him. That meant getting out, and quick.

The city meant trouble, Wolf decided as he loped off. He could endure loneliness while he practiced his wolfry, until he had Gloria. Though just as a precaution he must arrange with Ozzy about a plausible-looking collar, and . . .

The most astounding realization yet suddenly struck him! He had received four bullets, three of them square in the stomach, and he hadn't a wound to show for it! Being a werewolf certainly offered its practical advantages. Think what a criminal could do with such bulletproofing. Or . . . But no. He was a werewolf for fun, and that was that.

But even for a werewolf, being shot, though relatively painless, is tiring. A great deal of nervous energy is absorbed in the magical and instantaneous knitting of those wounds. And when Wolfe Wolf reached the peace and calm of the uncivilized hills, he no longer felt like reveling in freedom. Instead he stretched out to his full length, nuzzled his head down between his forepaws, and slept.

"Now the essence of magic," said Heliophagus of Smyrna, "is deceit; and that deceit is of two kinds. By magic, the magician deceives others; but magic deceives the magician himself."

So far the lycanthropic magic of Wolfe Wolf had worked smoothly and pleasantly, but now it was to show him the second trickery that lurks behind every magic trick. And the first step was that he slept.

He woke in confusion. His dreams had been human—and of Gloria—despite the body in which he dreamed them, and it took several full minutes for him to reconstruct just how he happened to be in that body. For a moment the dream, even that episode in which he and Gloria had been eating blueberry waffles on a roller coaster, seemed more sanely plausible than the reality.

But he readjusted quickly, and glanced up at the sky. The sun looked as though it had been up at least an hour, which meant that the time was somewhere between six and seven. Today was Thursday, which meant that he was saddled with an eight-o'clock class. That left plenty of time to change back, shave, dress, breakfast, and resume the normal life of Professor Wolf, which was, after all, important if he intended to support a wife.

He tried, as he trotted through the streets, to look as tame and unwolflike as possible, and apparently succeeded. No one paid him any mind save children, who wanted to play, and dogs, who began by snarling and ended by cowering away terrified. His friend the cat might be curiously tolerant of weres, but not so dogs.

He trotted up the steps of the Berkeley Inn confidently. The clerk was under a slight spell and would not notice wolves. There was nothing to do but rouse Ozzy, be *absarka'd,* and . . .

"Hey! Where you going? Get out of here! Shoo!"

It was the clerk, a stanch and brawny young man, who straddled the stairway and vigorously waved him off.

"No dogs in here! Go on now. Scoot!"

Quite obviously this man was under no spell, and equally obviously there was no way of getting up that staircase short of using a wolf's strength to tear the clerk apart. For a second Wolf hesitated. He had to get changed back. It would be a pity to use his powers to injure another human being—if only he had not slept and arrived before this unmagicked day clerk came on duty—but necessity knows no . . .

Then the solution hit him. Wolf turned and loped off just as the clerk hurled an ash tray at him. Bullets may be relatively painless, but even a werewolf's rump, he learned promptly, is sensitive to flying glass.

The solution was foolproof. The only trouble was that it meant an hour's wait, and he was hungry. He found himself even displaying a certain shocking interest in the plump occupant of a baby carriage. You do get different appetites with a different body. He could understand how some originally well-intentioned werewolves might in time become monsters. But he was stronger in will, and much smarter. His stomach could hold out until this plan worked.

The janitor had already opened the front door of Wheeler Hall, but the building was deserted. Wolf had no trouble reaching the second floor unnoticed or finding his classroom. He had a little more trouble holding the chalk between his teeth and a slight tendency to gag on the dust; but by balancing his forepaws on the eraser trough, he could manage quite nicely. It took three springs to catch the ring of the chart in his teeth, but once that was pulled down there was nothing to do but crouch under the desk and pray that he would not starve quite to death.

The students of German 31B, as they assembled reluctantly for their eight o'clock, were a little puzzled at being confronted by a chart dealing with the influence of the gold standard on world economy, but they decided simply that the janitor had been forgetful.

The wolf under the desk listened unseen to their gathering murmurs, overheard that cute blonde in the front row make dates with three different men for the same night, and finally decided that enough had assembled to make his chances plausible. He slipped out from under the desk far enough to reach the ring of the chart, tugged at it, and let go.

The chart flew up with a rolling crash. The students broke off their chatter, looked up at the blackboard, and beheld in a huge and shaky scrawl the mysterious letters

A B S A R K A

It worked. With enough people, it was an almost mathematical certainty that one of them in his puzzlement—for the race of subtitle readers, though handicapped by the talkies, still exists—would read the mysterious word aloud. It was the much-bedated blonde who did it.

"*Absarka,*" she said wonderingly.

And there was Professor Wolfe Wolf, beaming cordially at his class.

The only flaw was this: He had forgotten that he was only a werewolf, and not Hyperman. His clothes were still at the Berkeley Inn, and here on the lecture platform he was stark naked.

Two of his best pupils screamed and one fainted. The blonde only giggled appreciatively.

Emily was incredulous but pitying.

Professor Fearing was sympathetic but reserved.

The chairman of the department was cool.

The dean of letters was chilly.

The president of the university was frigid.

Wolfe Wolf was unemployed.

And Heliophagus of Smyrna was right. "The essence of magic is deceit."

"But what can I do?" Wolf moaned into his zombie glass. "I'm stuck. I'm stymied. Gloria arrives in Berkeley tomorrow, and here I am— nothing. Nothing but a futile, worthless werewolf. You can't support a wife on that. You can't raise a family. You can't . . . you can't even propose . . . I want another. Sure you won't have one?"

Ozymandias the Great shook his round, fringed head. "The last time I took two drinks I started all this. I've got to behave if I want to stop it. But you're an able-bodied, strapping, young man; surely, colleague, you can get work?"

"Where? All I'm trained for is academic work, and this scandal has put the kibosh on that forever. What university is going to hire a man who showed up naked in front of his class without even the excuse of being drunk? And supposing I try something else, I'd have to give references, say something about what I'd been doing with my thirty-odd years. And once these references were checked . . . Ozzy, I'm a lost man."

"Never despair, colleague. I've learned that magic gets you into some tight squeezes, but there's always a way of getting out. Now take that time in Darjeeling . . . "

"But what can I do? I'll wind up like Confucius the werechow and live off charity, if you'll find me somebody who wants a pet wolf."

"You know," Ozymandias reflected, "you may have something there, colleague."

"Nuts! That was a gag. I can at least retain my self-respect, even if I go on relief doing it. And I'll bet they don't like naked men on relief, either."

"No. I don't mean just being a pet wolf. But look at it this way: What are your assets? You have only two outstanding abilities. One of them is to teach German, and that is now completely out."

"Check."

"And the other is to change yourself into a wolf. All right, colleague. There must be some commercial possibilities in that. Let's look into them."

"Nonsense."

"Not quite. For every merchandise there's a market. The trick is to find it. And you, colleague, are going to be the first practical commercial werewolf on record."

"I could ... They say Ripley's Odditorium pays good money. Supposing I changed six times a day regular for delighted audiences?"

Ozymandias shook his head sorrowfully. "It's no good. People don't want to see real magic. It makes 'em uncomfortable—starts 'em wondering what else might be loose in the world. They've got to feel sure it's all done with mirrors. I know. I had to quit vaudeville because I wasn't smart enough at faking it; all I could do was the real thing."

"I could be a Seeing Eye dog, maybe?"

"They have to be female."

"When I'm changed I can understand animal language. Maybe I could be a dog trainer and ... No, that's out. I forgot; they're scared to death of me."

But Ozymandias's pale-blue eyes had lit up at the suggestion. "Colleague, you're warm. Oh, are you warm! Tell me: Why did you say your fabulous Gloria was coming to Berkeley?"

"Publicity for a talent hunt."

"For what?"

"A dog to star in *Fangs of the Forest*."

"And what kind of a dog?"

"A ..." Wolf's eyes widened and his jaw sagged. "A wolf dog," he said softly.

And the two men looked at each other with a wild surmise—silent, beside a bar in Berkeley.

"It's all the fault of that Disney dog," the trainer complained. "Pluto does anything. Everything. So our poor mutts are expected to do likewise. Listen to that dope! 'The dog should come into the room, give one paw to the baby, indicate that he recognizes the hero in his Eskimo disguise, go over to the table, find the bone, and clap his paws gleefully!' Now who's got a set of signals to cover stuff like that? Pluto!" he snorted.

Gloria Garton said, "Oh." By that one sound she managed to convey that she sympathized deeply, that the trainer was a nice-looking young man whom she'd just as soon see again, and that no dog star was going to steal *Fangs of the Forest* from her. She adjusted her skirt slightly, leaned back, and made the plain wooden chair on the bare theater stage seem more than ever like a throne.

"All right." The man in the violet beret waved away the last unsuccessful applicant and read from a card: "Dog: Wopsy. Owner: Mrs. Channing Galbraith. Trainer: Luther Newby. Bring it in."

An assistant scurried offstage, and there was a sound of whines and whimpers as a door opened.

"What's got into those dogs today?" the man in the violet beret demanded. "They all seem scared to death and beyond."

"I think," said Fergus O'Breen, "that it's that big gray wolf dog. Somehow, the others just don't like him."

Gloria Garton lowered her bepurpled lids and cast a queenly stare of suspicion on the young detective. There was nothing wrong with his being there. His sister was head of publicity for Metropolis, and he'd handled several confidential cases for the studio, even one for her, that time her chauffeur had decided to try his hand at blackmail. Fergus O'Breen was a Metropolis fixture; but still it bothered her.

The assistant brought in Mrs. Galbraith's Wopsy. The man in the violet beret took one look and screamed. The scream bounced back from every wall of the theater in the ensuing minute of silence. At last he found words. "A wolf dog! Tookah is the greatest role ever written for a wolf dog! And what do they bring us! A terrier yet! So if we wanted a terrier we could cast Asta!"

"But if you'd only let us show you . . ." Wopsy's tall young trainer started to protest.

"Get out!" the man in the violet beret shrieked. "Get out before I lose my temper!"

Wopsy and her trainer slunk off.

"In El Paso," the casting director lamented, "they bring me a Mexican hairless. In St. Louis it's a Pekinese yet! And if I do find a wolf dog, it sits in a corner and waits for somebody to bring in a sled to pull."

"Maybe," said Fergus, "you should try a real wolf."

"Wolf, *schmolf!*" He picked up the next card. "Dog: Yoggoth. Owner and trainer: Mr. O. Z. Manders. Bring it in."

The whining noise offstage ceased as Yoggoth was brought out to be tested. The man in the violet beret hardly glanced at the fringe-bearded owner and trainer. He had eyes only for that splendid gray wolf. "If you can only act . . ." he prayed, with the same fervor with which many a man has thought, "If you could only cook . . ."

He pulled the beret to an even more unlikely angle and snapped, "All right, Mr. Manders. The dog should come into the room, give one paw to the baby, indicate that he recognizes the hero in his Eskimo disguise, go over to the table, find the bone, and clap his paws joyfully. Baby here, here, here, table here. Got that?"

Mr. Manders looked at his wolf dog and repeated, "Got that?"

Yoggoth wagged his tail.

"Very well, colleague," said Mr. Manders. "Do it." Yoggoth did it.

The violet beret sailed into the flies, on the wings of its owner's triumphal scream of joy. "He did it!" he kept burbling. "He did it!"

"Of course, colleague," said Mr. Manders calmly. The trainer who hated Pluto had a face as blank as a vampire's mirror. Fergus O'Breen was speechless with wonderment. Even Gloria Garton permitted surprise and interest to cross her regal mask.

"You mean he can do anything?" gurgled the man who used to have a violet beret.

"Anything," said Mr. Manders.

"Can he . . . Let's see, in the dance-hall sequnce—can he knock a man down, roll him over, and frisk his back pocket?"

Even before Mr. Manders could say, "Of course," Yoggoth had demonstrated, using Fergus O'Breen as convenient dummy.

"Peace!" the casting director sighed. "Peace—Charley!" he yelled to his assistant. "Send 'em all away. No more try-outs. We've found Tookah! It's wonderful."

The trainer stepped up to Mr. Manders. "It's more than that, sir. It's positively superhuman. I'll swear I couldn't detect the slightest signal, and for such complicated operations, too. Tell me, Mr. Manders, what system do you use?"

Mr. Manders made a Hoopleish *kaff-kaff* noise. "Professional secret, you understand, young man. I'm planning on opening a school when I retire, but obviously until then . . ."

"Of course, sir. I understand. But I've never seen anything like it in all my born days."

"I wonder," Fergus O'Breen observed from the floor, "if your marvel dog can get off of people, too?"

Mr. Manders stifled a grin. "Of course! Yoggoth!"

Fergus picked himself up and dusted from his clothes the grime of the stage, which is the most clinging grime on earth. "I'd swear," he muttered, "that beast of yours enjoyed that."

"No hard feelings, I trust, Mr. . . ."

"O'Breen. None at all. In fact, I'd suggest a little celebration in honor of this great event. I know you can't buy a drink this near the campus, so I brought along a bottle just in case."

"Oh," said Gloria Garton, implying that carousals were ordinarily beneath her, that this, however, was a special occasion, and that possibly there was something to be said for the green-eyed detective, after all.

This was all too easy, Wolfe Wolf-Yoggoth kept thinking. There was a catch to it somewhere. This was certainly the ideal solution to the problem of how to earn money as a werewolf. Bring an understanding of human speech and instructions into a fine animal body, and you are the answer to a director's prayer. It was perfect as long as it lasted; and if *Fangs of the Forest* was a smash hit, there were bound to be other Yoggoth pictures. Look at Rin-tin-tin. But it was too easy . . .

His ears caught a familiar "Oh" and his attention reverted to Gloria. This "Oh" had meant that she really shouldn't have another drink, but since liquor didn't affect her anyway and this was a special occasion, she might as well.

She was even more beautiful than he had remembered. Her golden hair was shoulder-length now, and flowed with such rippling perfection that it was all he could do to keep from reaching out a paw to it. Her body had ripened, too, was even more warm and promising than his memories of her. And in his new shape he found her greatest charm in something he had not been able to appreciate fully as a human being, the deep, heady scent of her flesh.

"To *Fangs of the Forest!*" Fergus O'Breen was toasting. "And may that pretty-boy hero of yours get a worse mauling than I did."

Wolf-Yoggoth grinned to himself. That had been fun. That'd teach the detective to go crawling around hotel rooms.

And while we're celebrating, colleagues," said Ozymandias the Great, "why should we neglect our star? Here, Yoggoth." And he held out the bottle.

"He drinks yet!" the casting director exclaimed delightedly.

"Sure. He was weaned on it."

Wolf took a sizable gulp. It felt good. Warm and rich—almost the way Gloria smelled.

"But how about you, Mr. Manders?" the detective insisted for the fifth time. "It's your celebration really. The poor beast won't get the four-figure checks from Metropolis. And you've taken only one drink."

"Never take two, colleague. I know my danger point. Two drinks in me and things start happening."

"More should happen yet than training miracle dogs? Go on, O'Breen. Make him drink. We should see what happens."

Fergus took another long drink himself. "Go on. There's another bottle in the car, and I've gone far enough to be resolved not to leave here sober. And I don't want sober companions, either." His green eyes were already beginning to glow with a new wildness.

"No, thank you, colleague."

Gloria Garton left her throne, walked over to the plump man, and stood close, her soft hand resting on his arm. "Oh," she said, implying that dogs were dogs, but still that the party was inevitably in her honor his refusal to drink was a personal insult.

Ozymandias the Great looked at Gloria, sighed, shrugged, resigned himself to fate, and drank.

"Have you trained many dogs?" the casting director asked.

"Sorry, colleague. This is my first."

"All the more wonderful! But what's your profession otherwise?"

"Well, you see, I'm a magician."

"Oh," said Gloria Garton, implying delight, and went so far as to add, "I have a friend who does black magic."

"I'm afraid, ma'am, mine's simply white. That's tricky enough. With the black you're in for some real dangers."

"Hold on!" Fergus interposed. "You mean really a magician? Not just presti . . . sleight of hand?"

"Of course, colleague."

"Good theater," said the casting director. "Never let 'em see the mirrors."

"Uh-huh." Fergus nodded. "But look, Mr. Manders. What can you do, for instance?"

"Well, I can change . . ."

Yoggoth barked loudly.

"Oh, no," Ozymandias covered hastily, "that's really a little beyond me. But I can . . ."

"Can you do the Indian rope trick?" Gloria asked languidly. "My friend says that's terribly hard."

"Hard? Why, ma'am, there's nothing to it. I can remember that time in Darjeeling . . ."

Fergus took another long drink. "I," he announced defiantly, "want to see the Indian rope trick. I have met people who've met people who've met people who've seen it, but that's as close as I ever get. And I don't believe it."

"But, colleague, it's so simple."

"I don't believe it."

Ozymandias the Great drew himself up to his full lack of height. "Colleague, you are about to see it!" Yoggoth tugged warningly at his coat tails. "Leave me alone, Wolf. An aspersion has been cast!"

Fergus returned from the wings dragging a soiled length of rope. "This do?"

"Admirably."

"What goes?" the casting director demanded.

"Shh!" said Gloria. "Oh . . ."

She beamed worshipfully on Ozymandias, whose chest swelled to the point of threatening the security of his buttons. "Ladies and gentlemen!" he announced, in the manner of one prepared to fill a vast amphitheater with his voice. "You are about to behold Ozymandias the Great in—The Indian Rope Trick! Of course," he added conversationally, "I haven't got a small boy to chop into mincemeat, unless perhaps one of you . . . No? Well, we'll try it without. Not quite so impressive, though. And will you stop yapping, Wolf?"

"I thought his name was Yogi," said Fergus.

"Yoggoth. But since he's part wolf on his mother's side . . . Now quiet, all of you!"

He had been coiling the rope as he spoke. Now he placed the coil in the center of the stage, where it lurked like a threatening rattler. He stood beside it and deftly, professionally, went through a series of passes and mumblings so rapidly that even the superhumanly sharp eyes and ears of Wolf-Yoggoth could not follow them.

The end of the rope detached itself from the coil, reared in the air, turned for a moment like a head uncertain where to strike, then shot straight up until all the rope was uncoiled. The lower end rested a good inch above the stage.

Gloria gasped. The casting director drank hurriedly. Fergus, for some reason, stared curiously at the wolf.

"And now, ladies and gentlemen—oh, hang it, I do wish I had a boy to carve—Ozymandias the Great will ascend this rope into that land which only the users of the rope may know. Onward and upward! Be right back," he added reassuringly to Wolf.

His plump hands grasped the rope above his head and gave a little jerk. His knees swung up and clasped about the hempen pillar. And up he went, like a monkey on a stick, up and up and up—

—until suddenly he was gone.

Just gone. That was all there was to it. Gloria was beyond even saying "Oh." The casting director sat his beautiful flannels down on the filthy floor and gaped. Fergus swore softly and melodiously. And Wolf felt a premonitory prickling in his spine.

The stage door opened, admitting two men in denim pants and work shirts. "Hey!" said the first. "Where do you think you are?"

"We're from Metropolis Pictures," the casting director started to explain, scrambling to his feet.

"I don't care if you're from Washington, we gotta clear this stage. There's movies here tonight. Come on, Joe, help me get 'em out. And that pooch, too."

"You can't, Fred," said Joe reverently, and pointed. His voice sank to an awed whisper. "That's Gloria Garton . . ."

"So it is. Hi, Miss Garton, wasn't that last one of yours a stinkeroo!"

"Your public, darling," Fergus murmured.

"Come on!" Fred shouted. "Out of here. We gotta clean up. And you, Joe! Strike that rope!"

Before Fergus could move, before Wolf could leap to the rescue, the efficient stage hand had struck the rope and was coiling it up.

Wolf stared up into the flies. There was nothing up there. Nothing at all. Some place beyond the end of that rope was the only man on earth he could trust to say *Absarka!* for him; and the way down was cut off forever.

Wolfe Wolf sprawled on the floor of Gloria Garton's boudoir and watched that vision of volupty change into her most fetching negligee.

The situation was perfect. It was the fulfillment of his dearest dreams. The only flaw was that he was still in a wolf's body.

Gloria turned, leaned over, and chucked him under the snout. "Wuzzum a cute wolf dog, wuzzum?"

Wolf could not restrain a snarl.

"Doesn't um like Gloria to talk baby talk? Um was a naughty wolf, yes, um was."

It was torture. Here you are in your best beloved's hotel room, all her beauty revealed to your hungry eyes and she talks baby talk to you! Wolf had been happy at first when Gloria suggested that she might take over the care of her co-star pending the reappearance of his trainer—for none of them was quite willing to admit that "Mr. O. Z. Manders" might truly and definitely have vanished—but he was beginning to realize that the situation might bring on more torment than pleasure.

"Wolves are funny," Gloria observed. She was more talkative when alone, with no need to be cryptically fascinating. "I knew a Wolf once, only that was his name. He was a man. And he was a funny one."

Wolf felt his heart beating fast under his gray fur. To hear his own name on Gloria's warm lips— But before she could go on to tell her pet how funny Wolf was, her maid rapped on the door.

"Mr. O'Breen to see you, madam."

"Tell him to go 'way."

"He says it's important, and he does look, madam, as though he might make trouble."

"Oh, all right." Gloria rose and wrapped her negligee more respectably about her. "Come on, Yog— No, that's a silly name. I'm going to call you Wolfie. That's cute. Come on, Wolfie, and protect me from big, bad detective."

Fergus O'Breen was pacing the sitting room with a certain vicious deliberateness in his strides. He broke off and stood still as Gloria and the wolf entered.

"So?" he observed tersely. "Reinforcements?"

"Will I need them?" Gloria cooed.

"Look, light of my love life." The glint in the green eyes was cold and deadly. "You've been playing games, and whatever their nature, there's one thing they're not. And that's cricket."

Gloria gave him her slow, languid smile. "You're amusing, Fergus."

"Thanks. I doubt, however, if your activities are."

"You're still a little boy playing cops and robbers. And what boogyman are you after now?"

"Ha-ha," said Fergus politely. "And you know the answer to that question better than I do. That's why I'm here."

Wolf was puzzled. This conversation meant nothing to him. And yet he sensed a tension of danger in the air as clearly as though he could smell it.

"Go on," Gloria snapped impatiently. "And remember how dearly Metropolis Pictures will thank you for annoying one of its best box-office attractions."

"Some things, my sweet, are more important than pictures, though you mightn't think it where you come from. One of them is a certain federation of forty-eight units. Another is an abstract concept called democracy."

"And so?"

"And so I want to ask you one question: Why did you come to Berkeley?"

"For publicity on *Fangs,* of course. It was your sister's idea."

"You've gone temperamental and turned down better ones. Why leap at this?"

"You don't haunt publicity stunts yourself, Fergus, Why are you here?"

Fergus was pacing again. "And why was your first act in Berkeley a visit to the office of the German department?"

"Isn't that natural enough? I used to be a student here."

"Majoring in dramatics, and you didn't go near the Little Theater. Why the German department?" He paused and stood straight in front of her, fixing her with his green gaze.

Gloria assumed the attitude of a captured queen defying the barbarian conqueror. "Very well. If you must know—I went to the German department to see the man I love."

Wolf held his breath, and tried to keep his tail from trashing.

"Yes," she went on impassionedly, "you strip the last veil from me, and force me to confess to you what he alone should have heard first. This man proposed to me by mail. I foolishly rejected his proposal. But I thought and thought—and at last I knew. When I came to Berkeley I had to see him . . ."

"And did you?"

"The little mouse of a secretary told me he wasn't there. But I shall see him yet. And when I do . . ."

Fergus bowed stiffly. "My congratulations to you both, my sweet. And the name of this more than fortunate gentleman?"

"Professor Wolfe Wolf."

"Who is doubtless the individual referred to in this?" He whipped a piece of paper from his sport coat and thrust it at Gloria. She paled and was silent. But Wolfe Wolf did not wait for her reply. He did not care. He knew the solution to his problem now, and he was streaking unobserved for her boudoir.

Gloria Garton entered the boudoir a minute later, a shaken and wretched woman. She unstoppered one of the delicate perfume bottles on her dresser and poured herself a stiff drink of whiskey. Then her eyebrows lifted in surprise as she stared at her mirror. Scrawlingly lettered across the glass in her own deep-crimson lipstick was the mysterious word

ABSARKA

Frowning, she said it aloud. *"Absarka . . ."*
From behind a screen stepped Professor Wolfe Wolf, incongruously wrapped in one of Gloria's lushest dressing robes. "Gloria dearest . . ." he cried.
"Wolfe!" she exclaimed. "What on earth are you doing here in my room?"
"I love you. I've always loved you since you couldn't tell a strong from a weak verb. And now that I know that you love me . . ."
"This is terrible. Please get out of here!"
"Gloria . . ."
"Get out of here, or I'll sick my dog on you. Wolfie—Here, nice Wolfie!"
"I'm sorry, Gloria. But Wolfie won't answer you."
"Oh, you beast! Have you hurt Wolfie? Have you . . ."
"I wouldn't touch a hair on his pelt. Because, you see, Gloria darling, I am Wolfie."
"What on earth do you—" Gloria stared around the room. It was undeniable that there was no trace of the presence of a wolf dog. And here was a man dressed only in one of her robes and no sign of his own clothes. And after that funny little man and the rope . . .
"You thought I was drab and dull," Wolf went on. "You thought I'd sunk into an academic rut. You'd sooner have an actor or a G-man. But I, Gloria, am something more exciting than you've ever dreamed of. There's not another soul on earth I'd tell this to; but I, Gloria, am a werewolf."
Gloria gasped. "That isn't possible! But it all fits in. What I heard about you on the campus, and your friend with the funny beard and how he vanished, and, of course, it explains how you did tricks that any real dog couldn't possibly do . . ."

"Don't you believe me, darling?"

Gloria rose from the dresser chair and went into his arms. "I believe you, dear. And it's wonderful! I'll bet there's not another woman in all Hollywood that was ever married to a werewolf!"

"Then you will . . ."

"But of course, dear. We can work it out beautifully. We'll hire a stooge to be your trainer on the lot. You can work daytimes, and come home at night and I'll say *Absarka!* for you. It'll be perfect."

"Gloria . . ." Wolf murmured with tender reverence.

"One thing, dear. Just a little thing. Would you do Gloria a favor?"

"Anything!"

"Show me how you change. Change for me now. Then I'll *Absarka!* you back right away."

Wolf said The Word. He was in such ecstatic bliss that he hardly felt the pang this time. He capered about the room with all the litheness of his fine wolfish legs, and ended up before Gloria, wagging his tail and looking for approval.

Gloria patted his head. "Good boy, Wolfie. And now, darling, you can just stay that way."

Wolf let out a yelp of amazement.

"You heard me, Wolfie. You're staying that way. You didn't happen to believe any of that guff I was feeding the detective, did you? Love you? I should waste my time! But this way you can be very useful to me. With your trainer gone, I can take charge of you and pick up an extra thousand a week or so. I won't mind that. And Professor Wolfe Wolf will have vanished forever, which fits right in with my plans."

Wolf snarled.

"Now don't try to get nasty, Wolfie darling. Um wouldn't threaten ums darling Gloria, would ums? Remember what I can do for you. I'm the only person who can turn you into a man again. You wouldn't dare teach anyone else that. You wouldn't dare let people know what you really are. An ignorant person would kill you. A smart one would have you locked up as a lunatic."

Wolf still advanced threateningly.

"Oh, no. You can't hurt me. Because all I'd have to do would be to say the word on the mirror. Then you wouldn't be a dangerous wolf any more. You'd just be a man here in my room, and I'd scream. And after what happened on the campus yesterday, how long do you think you'd stay out of the madhouse?"

Wolf backed away and let his tail droop.

"You see, Wolfie darling? Gloria has ums just where she wants ums. And ums is going to be a good boy."

There was a rap on the boudoir door, and Gloria called, "Come in."

"A gentleman to see you, madam," the maid announced. "A Professor Fearing."

Gloria smiled her best cruel and queenly smile, "Come along, Wolfie. This may interest you."

Professor Oscar Fearing, overflowing one of the graceful chairs of the sitting room, beamed benevolently as Gloria and the wolf entered. "Ah, my dear! A new pet. Touching."

"And what a pet, Oscar. Wait till you hear."

Professor Fearing buffed his pince-nez against his sleeve. "And wait, my dear, until you hear all that I have learned. Chiswick has perfected his protective screen against magnetic bombs, and the official trial is set for next week. And Farnsworth has all but completed his researches on a new process for obtaining osmium. Gas warfare may start any day, and the power that can command a plentiful supply of . . ."

"Fine, Oscar," Gloria broke in. "But we can go over all this later. We've got other worries right now."

"What do you mean, my dear?"

"Have you run onto a red-headed young Irishman in a yellow shirt?"

"No, I . . . Why, yes. I did see such an individual leaving the office yesterday. I believe he had been to see Wolf."

"He's on to us. He's a detective from Los Angeles, and he's tracking us down. Some place he got hold of a scrap of record that should have been destroyed. He knows I'm in it, and he knows I'm tied up with somebody here in the German department."

Professor Fearing scrutinized his pince-nez, approved of their cleanness, and set them on his nose. "Not so much excitement, my dear. No hysteria. Let us approach this calmly. Does he know about the Temple of the Dark Truth?"

"Not yet. Nor about you. He just knows it's somebody in the department."

"Then what could be simpler? You have heard of the strange conduct of Wolfe Wolf?"

"Have I?" Gloria laughed harshly.

"Everyone knows of Wolfe's infatuation with you. Throw the blame onto him. It should be easy to clear yourself and make you appear an innocent tool. Direct attention to him and the organization will be safe. The Temple of the Dark Truth can go its mystic way and extract even more invaluable information from weary scientists who need the emotional release of a false religion."

"That's what I've tried to do. I gave O'Breen a long song and dance about my devotion to Wolf, so obviously phony he'd be bound to think it was a cover-up for something else. And I think he bit. But the situation is trickier than you guess. Do you know where Wolfe Wolf is?"

"No one knows. After the president . . . ah . . . rebuked him, he seems to have vanished."

Gloria laughed again. "He's right here. In this room."

"My dear! Secret panels and such? You take your espionage too seriously. Where?"

"There!"

Professor Fearing gaped. "Are you serious?"

"As serious as you are about the future of Fascism. That is Wolfe Wolf."

Fearing approached the wolf incredulously and extended his hand.

"He might bite," Gloria warned him a second too late.

Fearing stared at his bleeding hand. "That, at least," he observed, "is undeniably true." And he raised his foot to deliver a sharp kick.

"No, Oscar! Don't! Leave him alone. And you'll have to take my word for it—it's way too complicated. But the wolf is Wolfe Wolf, and I've got him completely under control. He's absolutely in our hands. We'll switch suspicion to him, and I'll keep him this way while Fergus and his friends the G-men go off hotfoot on his trail."

"My dear!" Fearing ejaculated. "You're mad. You're more hopelessly mad than the devout members of the Temple." He took off his pince-nez and stared again at the wolf. "And yet Tuesday night . . . Tell me one thing: From whom did you get this . . . this wolf dog?"

"From a funny plump little man with a fringy beard."

Fearing gasped. Obviously he remembered the furor in the Temple, and the wolf and the fringe-beard. "Very well, my dear. I believe you. Don't ask me why, but I believe you. And now . . ."

"Now it's all set, isn't it? We keep him here helpless, and we use him to . . ."

"The wolf as scapegoat. Yes. Very pretty."

"Oh! One thing . . ." She was suddenly frightened.

Wolfe Wolf was considering the possibilities of a sudden attack on Fearing. He could probably get out of the room before Gloria could say *Absarka!* And after that? Whom could he trust to restore him? Especially if G-men were to be set on his trail . . .

"What is it?" Fearing asked.

"That secretary. That little mouse in the department office. She knows it was you I asked for, not Wolf. Fergus can't have talked to her yet, because he swallowed my story; but he will. He's thorough."

"Hm-m-m. Then, in that case . . ."

"Yes, Oscar?"

"She must be attended to." Professor Oscar Fearing beamed genially and reached for the phone.

Wolf acted instantly, on inspiration and impulse. His teeth were strong, quite strong enough to jerk the phone cord from the wall. That took only a second, and in the next second he was out of the room and into the hall before Gloria could open her mouth to speak that word that would convert him from a powerful and dangerous wolf to a futile man.

There were shrill screams and a shout or two of "Mad dog!" as he dashed through the lobby, but he did no heed to them. The main thing was to reach Emily's house before she could be "attended to." Her evidence was essential. That could swing the balance, show Fergus and his G-men where the true guilt lay. And, besides, he admitted to himself, Emily was a nice kid . . .

His rate of collision was about 1.66 per block, and the curses heaped upon him, if theogically valid, would have been more than enough to damn him forever. But he was making time, and that was all that counted. He dashed through traffic signals, cut into the path of trucks, swerved from under street cars, and once even leaped over a stalled car which obstructed him. Everything was going fine, he was halfway there, when two hundred pounds of human flesh landed on him in a flying tackle.

He looked up through the brilliant lighting effects of smashing his head on the sidewalk and saw his old Nemesis, the policeman who had been cheated of his beer.

"So, Rover!" said that officer. "Got you at last, did I? Now we'll see if you'll wear a proper license tag. Didn't know I used to play football, did you?"

The officer's grip on his hair was painfully tight. A gleeful crowd was gathering and heckling the policeman with fantastic advice.

"Get along, boys," he admonished. "This is a private matter between me and Rover here. Come on," and he tugged even harder.

Wolf left a large tuft of fur and skin in the officer's grasp and felt the blood ooze out of the bare patch on his neck. He heard an oath and a pistol shot simultaneously, and felt the needlelike sting drive through his shoulder. The awestruck crowd thawed before him. Two more bullets hied after him, but he was gone, leaving the most dazed policeman in Berkeley.

"I hit him," the officer kept muttering blankly. "I hit the . . ."

Wolfe Wolf coursed along Dwight Way. Two more blocks and he'd be at the little bungalow that Emily shared with a teaching assistant in something or other. That telephone gag had stopped Fearing only momentarily; the orders would have been given by now, the henchmen would be on their way. But he was almost there . . .

"He'o!" a child's light voice called to him. "Nice woof-woof came back!"

Across the street was the modest frame dwelling of Robby and his shrewish mother. The child had been playing on the sidewalk. Now he saw his idol and deliverer and started across the street at a lurching toddle. "Nice woof-woof!" he kept calling. "Wait for Robby!"

Wolf kept on. This was no time for playing games with even the most delightful of cubs. And then he saw the car. It was an ancient jalopy, plastered with wisecracks even older than itself; and the high-school youth driving was obviously showing his girl friend how it could make time on this deserted residential street. The girl was a cute dish, and who could be bothered watching out for children?

Robby was directly in front of the car. Wolf leaped straight as a bullet. His trajectory carried him so close to the car that he could feel the heat of the radiator on his flank. His forepaws struck Robby and thrust him out of danger. They fell to the ground together, just as the car ground over the last of Wolf's caudal vertebrae.

The cute dish screamed. "Homer! Did we hit them?"

Homer said nothing, and the jalopy zoomed on.

Robby's screams were louder. "You hurt me! You hurt me! *Baaaaad* woof-woof!"

His mother appeared on the porch and joined in with her own howls of rage. The cacophony was terrific. Wolf let out one wailing yelp of his own, to make it perfect and to lament his crushed tail, and dashed on. This was no time to clear up misunderstandings.

But the two delays had been enough. Robby and the policeman had proved the perfect unwitting tools of Oscar Fearing. As Wolf approached Emily's little bunglow, he saw a gray sedan drive off. In the rear was a small, slim girl, and she was struggling.

Even a werewolf's lithe speed cannot equal a motor car. After a block of pursuit, Wolf gave up and sat back in his haunches panting. It felt funny, he thought even in that tense moment, not to be able to sweat, to have to open your mouth and stick out your tongue and . . .

"Trouble?" inquired a solicitous voice.

This time Wolf recognized the cat. "Heavens, yes," he assented wholeheartedly. "More than you ever dreamed of."

"Food shortage?" the cat asked. "But that toddler back there is nice and plump."

"Shut up," Wolf snarled.

"Sorry; I was just judging from what Confucius told me about werewolves. You don't mean to tell me that you're an altruistic were?"

"I guess I am. I know werewolves are supposed to go around slaughtering, but right now I've got to save a life."

"You expect me to believe that?"

"It's the truth."

"Ah," the cat reflected philosophically. "Truth is a dark and deceitful thing."

Wolfe Wolf was on his feet. "Thanks," he barked. "You've done it."

"Done what?"

"See you later." And Wolf was off at top speed for the Temple of the Dark Truth.

That was the best chance. That was Fearing's headquarters. The odds were at least even that when it wasn't being used for services it was the hang-out of his ring, especially since the consulate had been closed in San Francisco. Again the wild running and leaping, the narrow escapes; and where Wolf had not taken these too seriously before, he knew now that he might be immune to bullets, but certainly not to being run over. His tail still stung and ached tormentingly. But he had to get there. He had to clear his own reputation, he kept reminding himself; but what he really thought was, *I have to save Emily.*

A block from the Temple he heard the crackle of gunfire. Pistol shots and, he'd swear, machine guns, too. He couldn't figure what it meant, but he pressed on. Then a bright yellow roadster passed him and a vivid flash came from its window. Instinctively he ducked. You might be immune to bullets, but you still didn't just stand still for them.

The roadster was gone and he was about to follow when a glint of bright metal caught his eye. The bullet which had missed him had hit a brick wall and ricocheted back onto the sidewalk. It glittered there in front of him—pure silver.

This, he realized abruptly, meant the end of his immunity. Fearing had believed Gloria's story, and with his smattering of occult lore he had known the successful counterweapon. A bullet, from now on, might mean no more needle sting, but instant death.

And so Wolfe Wolf went straight on.

He approached the Temple cautiously, lurking behind shrubbery. And he was not the only lurker. Before the Temple, crouching in the shelter of a car every window of which was shattered, were Fergus O'Breen and a moonfaced giant. Each held an automatic, and they were taking pot shots at the steeple.

Wolf's keen, lupine hearing could catch their words even above the firing. "Gabe's around back," Moonface was explaining. "But it's no use. Know what that steeple is? It's a revolving machine-gun turret. They've been ready for something like this. Only two men in there, far as we can tell, but that turret covers all the approaches."

"Only two?" Fergus muttered.

"And the girl. They brought a girl here with them. If she's still alive."

Fergus took careful aim at the steeple, fired, and ducked back behind the car as a bullet missed him by millimeters. "Missed him again! By all the kings that ever ruled Tara, Moon, there's got to be a way in there. How about tear gas?"

Moon snorted. "Think you can reach the firing gap in that armored turret at this angle?"

"That girl . . ." said Fergus.

Wolf waited no longer. As he sprang forward, the gunner noticed him and shifted his fire. It was like a needle shower in which all the spray is solid steel. Wolf's nerves ached with the pain of reknitting. But at least machine guns apparently didn't fire silver.

The front door was locked, but the force of his drive carried him through and added a throbbing ache in his shoulder to his other discomforts. The lower-floor guard, a pasty-faced individual with a jutting Adam's apple, sprang up, pistol in hand. Behind him, in the midst of the litter of the cult, ceremonial robes, incense burners, curious books, even a Ouija board, lay Emily.

Pasty-face fired. The bullets struck Wolf full in the chest and for an instant he expected death. But this, too, was lead, and he jumped forward. It was not his usual powerful leap. His strength was almost spent by now. He needed to lie on cool earth and let his nerves knit. And this spring was only enough to grapple with his foe, not to throw him.

The man reversed his useless automatic and brought its butt thudding down on the beast's skull. Wolf reeled back, lost his balance, and fell to the floor. For a moment he could not rise. The temptation was so strong just to lie there and . . .

The girl moved. Her bound hands grasped a corner of the Ouija board. Somehow, she stumbled to her rope-tied feet and raised her arms. Just as Pasty-face rushed for the prostrate wolf, she brought the heavy board down.

Wolf was on his feet now. There was an instant of temptation. His eyes fixed themselves to the jut of that Adam's apple, and his long tongue licked his jowls. Then he heard the machine-gun fire from the turret, and tore himself from Pasty-face's unconscious form.

Ladders are hard on a wolf, almost impossible. But if you use your jaws to grasp the rung above you and pull up, it can be done.

He was halfway up the ladder when the gunner heard him. The firing stopped, and Wolf heard a rich German oath in what he automatically recognized as an East Prussian dialect with possible Lithuanian influences. Then he saw the man himself, a broken-nosed blond, staring down the ladder well.

The other man's bullets had been lead. So this must be the one with the silver. But it was too late to turn back now. Wolf bit the next rung and hauled up as the bullet struck his snout and stung through. The blond's eyes widened as he fired again and Wolf climbed another round. After the third shot he withdrew precipitately from the opening.

Shots still sounded from below, but the gunner did not return them. He stood frozen against the wall of the turret watching in horror as the wolf emerged from the well. Wolf halted and tried to get his breath. He was dead with fatigue and stress, but this man must be vanquished.

The blond raised his pistol, sighted carefully, and fired once more. He stood for one terrible instant, gazing at this deathless wolf and knowing from his grandmother's stories what it must be. Then deliberately he clamped his teeth on the muzzle of the automatic and fired again.

Wolf had not yet eaten in his wolf's body, but food must have been transferred from the human stomach to the lupine. There was at least enough for him to be extensively sick.

Getting down the ladder was impossible. He jumped. He had never heard anything about a wolf's landing on his feet, but it seemed to work. He dragged his weary and bruised body along to where Emily sat by the still unconscious Pasty-face, his discarded pistol in her hand. She wavered as the wolf approached her, as though uncertain yet as to whether he was friend or foe.

Time was short. With the machine gun dead, Fergus and his companions would be invading the Temple at any minute. Wolf hurriedly nosed about and found the planchette of the Ouija board. He pushed the heart-shaped bit of wood onto the board and began to shove it around with his paw.

Emily watched, intent and puzzled. "A," she said aloud. "B—S—"

Wolf finished the word and edged around so that he stood directly beside one of the ceremonial robes. "Are you trying to say something?" Emily frowned.

Wolf wagged his tail in vehement affirmation and began again.

"A—" Emily repeated. "B—S—A—R— "

He could already hear approaching footsteps.

"—K—A—What on earth does that mean? *Absarka* . . ."

Ex-professor Wolfe Wolf hastily wrapped his naked human body in the cloak of the Dark Truth. Before either he or Emily knew quite what was happening, he had folded her in his arms, kissed her in a most thorough expression of gratitude, and fainted.

Even Wolf's human nose could tell, when he awakened, that he was in a hospital. His body was still limp and exhausted. The bare patch on his neck, where the policeman had pulled out the hair, still stung, and there was a lump where the butt of the automatic had connected. His tail, or where his tail had been, sent twinges through him if he moved. But the sheets were cool and he was at rest and Emily was safe.

"I don't know how you got in there, Mr. Wolf, or what you did; but I want you to know you've done your country a signal service." It was the moonfaced giant speaking.

Fergus O'Breen was sitting beside the bed, too. "Congratulations, Wolf. And I don't know if the doctor would approve, but here."

Wolfe Wolf drank the whiskey gratefully and looked a question at the huge man.

"This is Moon Lafferty," said Fergus. "F.B.I. man. He's been helping me track down this ring of spies ever since I first got wind of them."

"You got them—all?" Wolf asked. "Picked up Fearing and Garton at the hotel," Lafferty rumbled.

"But how . . . I thought . . ."

"You thought we were out for you?" Fergus answered. "That was Garton's idea, but I didn't quite tumble. You see, I'd already talked to your secretary. I knew it was Fearing she'd wanted to see. And when I asked around about Fearing, and learned of the Temple and the defense researches of some of its members, the whole picture cleared up."

"Wonderful work, Mr. Wolf," said Lafferty. "Any time we can do anything for you . . . And how you got into that machine-gun turret . . . Well, O'Breen, I'll see you later. Got to check up on the rest of this round-up. Pleasant convalescence to you, Wolf."

Fergus waited until the G-man had left the room. Then he leaned over the bed and asked confidentially, "How about it, Wolf? Going back to your acting career?"

Wolf gasped. "What acting career?"

"Still going to play Tookah? If Metropolis makes *Fangs* with Miss Garton in a Federal prison."

Wolf fumbled for words. "What sort of nonsense . . ."

"Come on, Wolf. It's pretty clear I know that much. Might as well tell me the whole story."

Still dazed, Wolf told it. "But how did you know it?" he concluded.

Fergus grinned. "Look, Dorothy Sayers said some place that in a detective story the supernatural may be introduced only to be dispelled. Sure, that's swell. Only in real life there come times when it won't be dispelled. And this was one. There was too much. There were your eyebrows and fingers, there were the obviously real magical powers of your friend, there were the tricks which no dog could possibly do without signals, there was the way the other dogs whimpered and cringed . . . I'm pretty hard-headed, Wolf, but I'm Irish. I'll string along only so far with the materialistic, but too much coincidence is too much."

"Fearing believed it, too," Wolf reflected. "But one thing that worries me—if they used a silver bullet on me once, why were all the rest of them lead? Why was I safe from then on?"

"Well," said Fergus, "I'll tell you. Because it wasn't 'they' who fired the silver bullet. You see, Wolf, up till the last minute I thought you were on 'their' side. I, somehow, didn't associate good will with a werewolf. So I got a mold from a gunsmith and paid a visit to a jeweler and . . . I'm glad I missed," he added sincerely.

"*You're* glad!"

"But look. Previous question stands. Are you going back to acting? Because if not, I've got a suggestion."

"Which is?"

"You say you fretted about how to be a practical, commercial werewolf. All right. You're strong and fast. You can terrify people even to committing suicide. You can overhear conversations that no human being could get in on. You're invulnerable to bullets. Can you tell me better qualifications for a G-man?"

Wolf goggled. "Me? A G-man?"

"Moon's been telling me how badly they need new men. They've changed the qualifications lately so that your language knowledge'll do instead of the law or accounting they used to require. And, after what you did today, there won't be any trouble about a little academic scandal in your past. Moon's pretty sold on you."

Wolf was speechless. Only three days ago he had been in torment because he was not an actor or a G-man. Now . . .

"Think it over," said Fergus.

"I will. Indeed I will. Oh, and one other thing. Has there been any trace of Ozzy?"

"Nary a sign."

"I like that man. I've got to try to find him and . . ."

"If he's the magician I think he is, he's staying up there only because he decided he likes it."

"I don't know. Magic's tricky. Heaven knows I've learned that. I'm going to do all I can for that fringe-bearded old colleague."

"Wish you luck. Shall I send in your other guest?"

"Who's that?"

"Your secretary. Here on business, no doubt."

Fergus disappeared discreetly as he admitted Emily. She walked over to the bed and took Wolf's hand. His eyes drank in her quiet, charming simplicity, and his mind wondered what freak of belated adolescence had made him succumb to the blatant glamour of Gloria.

They were silent for a long time. Then at once they both said, "How can I thank you? You saved my life."

Wolf laughed. "Let's not argue. Let's say we saved our life."

"You mean that?" Emily asked gravely.

Wolf pressed her hand. "Aren't you tired of being an office wife?"

In the bazaar of Darjeeling, Chulundra Lingasuta stared at his rope in numb amazement. Young Ali had climbed up only five minutes ago, but now as he descended he was a hundred pounds heavier and wore a curious fringe of beard.

The Small Assassin

Ray Bradbury

Ray Bradbury has remained at the forefront of speculative fiction for the last half century, writing hundreds of short stories that deal with man's ambitions and shortcomings. Space exploration and extrapolations of what future societies might be like are major themes in his work. Among his many collections are The Martian Chronicles, The Illustrated Man, *and* Dark Carnival. *His novel* Fahrenheit 451 *is his best known novel, depicting a repressive government where firemen start fires instead of fighting them. He has also written screenplays, poetry, and mystery novels, and has won several awards for his work, including the Grand Master Nebula award in 1988.*

JUST WHEN THE IDEA OCCURRED TO HER THAT SHE WAS BEING MURDERED she could not tell. There had been little subtle signs, little suspicions for the past month; things as deep as sea tides in her, like looking at a perfectly calm stretch of tropic water, wanting to bathe in it and finding, just as the tide takes your body, that monsters dwell just under the surface, things unseen, bloated, many-amed, sharp-finned, malignant, and inescapable.

A room floated around her in an effluvium of hysteria. Sharp instruments hovered, and there were voices and people in sterile white masks.

My name, she thought, what is it?

Alice Leiber. It came to her. David Leiber's wife. But it gave her no comfort. She was alone with these silent, whispering white people and there was great pain and nausea and death-fear in her.

I am being murdered before their eyes. These doctors, these nurses, don't realize what hidden thing has happened to me. David doesn't know. Nobody knows except me and—the killer, the little murderer, the small assassin.

I am dying and I can't tell them now. They'd laugh and call me one in delirium. They'll see the murderer and hold him and never think him responsible for my death. But here I am, in front of God and man, dying, no one to believe my story, everyone to doubt me, comfort me with lies, bury me in ignorance, mourn me, and salvage my destroyer.

Where is David? she wondered. In the waiting room, smoking one cigarette after another, listening to the long tickings of the very slow clock?

Sweat exploded from all of her body at once, and with it an agonized cry. Now. Now! Try and kill me, she screamed. Try, try, but I won't die! I won't!

There was a hollowness. A vacuum. Suddenly the pain fell away. Exhaustion, and dusk came around. It was over. Oh, God! She plummeted down and struck a black nothingness which gave way to nothingness and nothingness and another and still another. . . .

Footsteps. Gentle, approaching footsteps.

Far away, a voice said, "She's asleep. Don't disturb her."

An odor of tweeds, a pipe, a certain shaving lotion. David was standing over her. And beyond him the immaculate smell of Dr. Jeffers.

She did not open her eyes. "I'm awake," she said quietly. It was a surprise, a relief, to be able to speak, not to be dead.

"Alice," someone said, and it was David beyond her closed eyes, holding her tired hands.

Would you like to meet the murderer, David? she thought. I hear your voice asking to see him, so there's nothing but for me to point him out to you.

David stood over her. She opened her eyes. The room came into focus. Moving a weak hand, she pulled aside a coverlet.

The murderer looked up at David Leiber with a small, red-faced, blue-eyed calm. Its eyes were deep and sparkling.

"Why!" cried David Leiber, smiling, "He's a *fine* baby!"

Dr. Jeffers was waiting for David Leiber the day he came to take his wife and new child home. He motioned Leiber to a chair in his office, gave him a cigar, lit one for himself, sat on the edge of his desk, puffing solemnly for a long moment. Then he cleared his throat, looked David Leiber straight on, and said, "Your wife doesn't like her child, Dave."

"What!"

"It's been a hard thing for her. She'll need a lot of love this next year. I didn't say much at the time, but she was hysterical in the delivery room. The strange things she said—I won't repeat them. All I'll say is that she feels alien to the child. Now, this may simply be a thing we can clear up with one or two questions." He sucked on his cigar another moment, then said, "Is this child a 'wanted' child, Dave?"

"Why do you ask?"

"It's vital."

"Yes, Yes, it is a 'wanted' child. We planned it together. Alice was so happy, a year ago, when—"

"Mmmm—that makes it more difficult. Because if the child was unplanned, it would be a simple case of a woman hating the idea of motherhood. That doesn't fit Alice." Dr. Jeffers took his cigar from his lips, rubbed his hand across his jaw. "It must be something else, then. Perhaps something buried in her childhood that's coming out now. Or it might be the simple temporary doubt and distrust of any mother who's gone through the unusual pain and near death that Alice has. If so, then a little time should heal that. I thought I'd tell you, though, Dave. It'll help you be easy and tolerant with her if she says anything about—well—about wishing the child had been born dead. And if things don't go well, the three of you drop in on me. I'm always glad to see old friends, eh? Here, take another cigar along for—ah—for the baby."

It was a bright spring afternoon. Their car hummed along wide, tree-lined boulevards. Blue sky, flowers, a warm wind. Dave talked a lot, lit his cigar, talked some more. Alice answered directly, softly, relaxing a bit more as the trip progressed. But she held the baby not tightly or warmly or motherly enough to satisfy the queer ache in Dave's mind. She seemed to be merely carrying a porcelain figurine.

"Well," he said at last, smiling. "What'll we name him?"

Alice Leiber watched green trees slide by. "Let's not decide yet. I'd rather wait until we get an exceptional name for him. Don't blow smoke in his face." Her sentences ran together with no change of tone. The last statement held no motherly reproof, no interest, no irritation. She just mouthed it and it was said.

The husband, disquieted, dropped the cigar from the window. "Sorry," he said.

The baby rested in the crook of his mother's arm, shadows of sun and trees changing his face. His blue eyes opened like fresh blue spring flowers. Moist noises came from the tiny pink, elastic mouth.

Alice gave her baby a quick glance. Her husband felt her shiver against him.

"Cold?" he asked.

"A chill. Better raise the window, David."

It was more than a chill. He rolled the window slowly up.

Suppertime.

Dave had brought the child from the nursery, propped him at a tiny, bewildered angle, supported by many pillows, in a newly purchased high chair.

Alice watched her knife and fork move. "He's not high-chair size," she said.

"Fun having him here, anyway," said Dave, feeling fine. "Everything's fun. At the office too. Orders up to my nose. If I don't watch myself I'll make another fifteen thousand this year. Hey, look at Junior, will you? Drooling all down his chin!" He reached over to wipe the baby's mouth with his napkin. From the corner of his eye he realized that Alice wasn't even watching. He finished the job.

"I guess it wasn't very interesting," he said, back again at his food. "But one would think a mother'd take some interest in her own child!"

Alice jerked her chin up. "Don't speak that way! Not in front of him! Later, if you must."

"Later?" he cried. "In front of, in back of, what's the difference?" He quieted suddenly, swallowed, was sorry. "All right. Okay. I know how it is."

After dinner she let him carry the baby upstairs. She didn't tell him to; she *let* him.

Coming down, he found her standing by the radio, listening to music she didn't hear. Her eyes were closed, her whole attitude one of wondering, self-questioning. She started when he appeared.

Suddenly she was at him, against him, soft, quick; the same. Her lips found him, kept him. He was stunned. Now that the baby was gone, upstairs, out of the room, she began to breathe again, live again. She was free. She was whispering, rapidly, endlessly.

"Thank you, thank you, darling. For being yourself, always. Dependable, so very dependable!"

He had to laugh. "My father told me, 'Son, provide for your family!' "

Wearily, she rested her dark, shining hair against his neck.

"You've overdone it. Sometimes I wish we were just the way we were when we were first married. No responsibilities, nothing but ourselves. No—no babies."

She crushed his hand in hers, a supernatural whiteness in her face.

"Oh, Dave, once it was just you and me. We protected each other, and now we protect the baby, but get no protection from it. Do you understand? Lying in the hospital I had time to think a lot of things. The world is evil—"

"Is it?"

"Yes. It is. But laws protect us from it. And when there aren't laws, then love does the protecting. You're protected from my hurting you, by my love. You're vulnerable to me, of all people, but love shields you. I feel no fear of you, because love cushions all your irritations, unnatural instincts, hatreds, and immaturities. But—what about the baby? It's too young to know love, or a law of love, or anything, until we teach it. And in the meantime we're vulnerable to it."

"Vulnerable to a baby?" He held her away and laughed gently.

"Does a baby know the difference between right and wrong?" she asked.

"No. But it'll learn."

"But a baby is so new, so amoral, so conscience-free." She stopped. Her arms dropped from him and she turned swiftly.

"That noise? What was it?"

Leiber looked around the room. "I didn't hear—"

She stared at the library door. "In there," she said slowly.

Leiber crossed the room, opened the door, and switched the library lights on and off. "Not a thing." He came back to her. "You're worn out. To bed with you—right now."

Turning out the lights together they walked slowly up the soundless hall stairs, not speaking. At the top she apologized. "My wild talk, darling. Forgive me. I'm exhausted."

He understood, and said so.

She paused, undecided, by the nursery door. Then she fingered the brass knob sharply, walked in. He watched her approach the crib much too carefully, look down, and stiffen as if she'd been struck in the face. "David!"

Leiber stepped forward, reached the crib.

The baby's face was bright red and very moist; his small pink mouth opened and shut, opened and shut; his eyes were a fiery blue. His hands flew about in the air.

"Oh," said Dave, "he's just been crying."

"Has he?" Alice Leiber seized the crib railing to balance herself. "I didn't hear him."

"The door was closed."

"Is that why he breathes so hard, why his face is red?"

"Sure. Poor little guy. Crying all alone in the dark. He can sleep in our room tonight, just in case he cries."

"You'll spoil him," his wife said.

Leiber felt her eyes follow as he rolled the crib into their bedroom. He undressed silently, sat on the edge of the bed. Suddenly he lifted his head, swore under his breath, snapped his fingers. "Damn it! Forgot to tell you. I must fly to Chicago Friday."

"Oh, David." Her voice was lost in the room.

"I've put this trip off for two months, and now it's so critical I just *have* to go."

"I'm afraid to be alone."

"We'll have the new cook by Friday. She'll be here all the time. I'll only be gone a few days."

"I'm afraid. I don't know of what. You wouldn't believe me if I told you. I guess I'm crazy."

He was in bed now. She darkened the room; he heard her walk around the bed, throw back the cover, slide in. He smelled the warm woman-smell of her next to him. He said, "If you want me to wait a few days, perhaps I could—"

"No," she said, unconvinced. "You go. I know it's important. It's just that I keep thinking about what I told you. Laws and love and protection. Love protects you from me. But the baby—" She took a breath. "What protects you from him, David?"

Before he could answer, before he could tell her how silly it was, speaking of infants, she switched on the bed light abruptly.

"Look," she said, pointing.

The baby lay wide-awake in its crib, staring straight at him, with deep, sharp blue eyes.

The lights went out again. She trembled against him.

"It's not nice being afraid of the thing you birthed." Her whisper lowered, became harsh, fierce, swift. "He tried to kill me! He lies there, listens to us talking, waiting for you to go away so he can try to kill me again! I swear it!" Sobs broke from her.

"Please," he kept saying, soothing her. "Stop it, stop it. Please."

She cried in the dark for a long time. Very late she relaxed, shakingly, against him. Her breathing came soft, warm, regular, her body twitched its worn reflexes, and she slept.

He drowsed.

And just before his eyes lidded wearily down, sinking him into deeper and deeper tides, he heard a strange little sound of awareness and awakeness in the room.

The sound of small, moist, pinkly elastic lips.

The baby.

And then—sleep.

In the morning the sun blazed. Alice smiled.

David Leiber dangled his watch over the crib. "See, baby? Something bright. Something pretty. Sure. Sure. Something bright. Something pretty."

Alice smiled. She told him to go ahead, fly to Chicago, she'd be very brave, no need to worry. She'd take care of baby. Oh, yes, she'd take care of him, all right.

The airplane went east. There was a lot of sky, a lot of sun and clouds and Chicago running over the horizon. Dave was dropped into the rush of ordering, planning, banqueting, telephoning, arguing in conference. But he wrote letters each day and sent telegrams to Alice and the baby.

On the evening of his sixth day away from home he received the long-distance phone call. Los Angeles.

"Alice?"

"No, Dave. This is Jeffers speaking."

"Doctor!"

"Hold on to yourself, son. Alice is sick. You'd better get the next plane home. It's pneumonia. I'll do everything I can, boy. If only it wasn't so soon after the baby. She needs strength."

Leiber dropped the phone into its cradle. He got up, with no feet under him, and no hands and no body. The hotel room blurred and fell apart.

"Alice," he said, blindly starting for the door.

The propellers spun about, whirled, fluttered, stopped; time and space were put behind. Under his hand David felt the doorknob turn, under his feet the floor assumed reality, around him flowed the walls of a bedroom, and in the late afternoon sunlight Dr. Jeffers stood, turning from a window, as Alice lay waiting in her bed, something carved from a fall of winter snow. Then Dr. Jeffers was talking, talking continuously, gently, the sound rising and falling through the lamplight, a soft flutter, a white murmur of voice.

"You wife's too good a mother, Dave. She worried more about the baby than herself. . . ."

Somewhere in the paleness of Alice's face there was a sudden constriction that smoothed itself out before it was realized. Then, slowly, half-smiling, she began to talk, and she talked as a mother should about this, that, and the other thing, the telling detail, the minute-by-minute and hour-by-hour report of a mother concerned with a dollhouse world and the miniature life of that world. But she could not stop; the spring was wound tight, and her voice rushed on to anger, fear, and the faintest touch of revulsion, which did not change Dr. Jeffers's expression, but caused Dave's heart to match the rhythm of this talk that quickened and could not stop:

"The baby wouldn't sleep. I thought he was sick. He just lay, staring, in his crib, and late at night he'd cry. So loud, he'd cry, and he'd cry all night and all night. I couldn't quiet him, and I couldn't rest."

Dr. Jeffers's head nodded slowly, slowly. "Tired herself right into pneumonia. But she's full of sulfa now and on the safe side of the whole damn thing."

David felt ill. "The baby, what about the baby?"

"Fit as a fiddle; cock of the walk!"

"Thanks, Doctor."

The doctor walked off away and down the stairs, opened the front door faintly, and was gone.

"David!"

He turned to her frightened whisper.

"It was the baby again." She clutched his hand. "I try to lie to myself and say that I'm a fool, but the baby knew I was weak from the hospital, so he cried all night every night, and when he wasn't crying he'd be much too quiet. I knew if I switched on the light he'd be there, staring up at me."

David felt his body close in on itself like a fist. He remembered seeing the baby, feeling the baby, awake in the dark, awake very late at night when babies should be asleep. Awake and lying there, silent as thought, not crying, but watching from its crib. He thrust the thought aside. It was insane.

Alice went on. "I was going to kill the baby. Yes, I was. When you'd been gone only a day on your trip I went to his room and put my hands about his neck; and I stood there, for a long time, thinking, afraid. Then I put the covers up over his face and turned him over on his face and pressed him down and left him that way and ran out of the room."

He tried to stop her.

"No, let me finish," she said hoarsely, looking at the wall. "When I left his room I thought, It's simple. Babies smother every day. No one'll ever know. But when I came back to see him dead, David, he was alive! Yes, alive, turned over on his back, alive and smiling and breathing. And I couldn't touch him again after that. I left him there and I didn't come back, not to feed him or look at him or do anything. Perhaps the cook tended to him. I don't know. All I know is that his crying kept me awake, and I thought all through the night, and walked around the rooms, and now I'm sick." She was almost finished now. "The baby lies there and thinks of ways to kill me. Simple ways. Because he knows I know so much about him. I have no love for him; there is no protection between us; there never will be."

She was through. She collapsed inward on herself and finally slept. David Leiber stood for a long time over her, not able to move. His blood was frozen in his body; not a cell stirred anywhere, anywhere at all.

The next morning there was only one thing to do. He did it.

He walked into Dr. Jeffers's office and told him the whole thing, and listened to Jeffers's tolerant replies:

"Let's take this thing slowly, son. It's quite natural for mothers to hate their children, sometimes. We have a label for it—ambiva-lence. The ability to hate while loving. Lovers hate each other, fre-quently. Children detest their mothers—"

Leiber interrupted. "I never hated my mother."

"You won't admit it, naturally. People don't enjoy admitting hatred for their loved ones."

"So Alice hates her baby."

"Better say she has an obsession. She's gone a step further than plain, ordinary ambivalence. A cesarean operation brought the child into the world and almost took Alice out of it. She blames the child for her near death and her pneumonia. She's projecting her troubles, blaming them on the handiest object she can use as a source of blame. We *all* do it. We stumble into a chair and curse the furniture, not our own clumsiness. We miss a golf stroke and damn the turf or our club, or the make of ball. If our business fails we blame the gods, the weather, our luck. All I can tell you is what I told you before. Love her. Finest medicine in the world. Find little ways of showing your affection, give her security. Find ways of show-ing her how harmless and innocent the child is. Make her feel that the baby was worth the risk. After a while, she'll settle down, forget about death, and begin to love the child. If she doesn't come around in the next month or so, ask me. I'll recommend a good psychiatrist. Go on along now, and take that look off your face."

When summer came, things seemed to settle, become easier. Dave worked, immersed himself in office detail, but found much time for his wife. She in turn took long walks, gained strength, played an occasional light game of badminton. She rarely burst out anymore. She seemed to have rid herself of her fears.

Except on one certain midnight when a sudden summer wind swept around the house, warm and swift, shaking the trees like so many shining tambourines. Alice wakened, trembling, and slid over into her husband's arms, and let him console her and ask her what was wrong.

She said, "Something's here in the room, watching us."

He switched on the light. "Dreaming again," he said. "You're bet-ter, though. Haven't been troubled for a long time."

She sighed as he clicked off the light again, and suddenly she slept. Her held her, considering what a sweet, weird creature she was, for about half an hour.

He heard the bedroom door sway open a few inches.

There was nobody at the door. No reason for it to come open. The wind had died.

He waited. It seemed like an hour he lay silently in the dark.

Then, far away, wailing like some small meteor dying in the vast inky gulf of space, the baby began to cry in his nursery.

It was a small, lonely sound in the middle of the stars and the dark and the breathing of this woman in his arms and the wind beginning to sweep through the trees again.

Leiber counted to one hundred slowly. The crying continued.

Carefully disengaging Alice's arm he slipped from bed, put on his slippers, robe, and moved quietly from the room.

He'd go downstairs, he thought, fix some warm milk, bring it up, and—

The blackness dropped out from under him. His foot slipped and plunged. Slipped on something soft. Plunged into nothingness.

He thrust his hands out, caught frantically at the railing. His body stopped falling. He held. He cursed.

The "something soft" that had caused his feet to slip rustled and thumped down a few steps. His head rang. His heart hammered at the base of his throat, thick and shot with pain.

Why do careless people leave things strewn about a house? He groped carefully with his fingers for the object that had almost spilled him headlong down the stairs.

His hand froze, startled. His breath went in. His heart held one or two beats.

The thing he held in his hand was a toy. A large, cumbersome patchwork doll he had bought as a joke, for—

For the baby.

Alice drove him to work the next day.

She slowed the car halfway downtown, pulled to the curb, and stopped it. Then she turned on the seat and looked at her husband.

"I want to go away on a vacation. I don't know if you can make it now, darling, but if not, please let me go alone. We can get someone to take care of the baby, I'm sure. But I just have to get away. I thought I was growing out of this—this *feeling*. But I haven't. I can't stand being in the room with him. He looks up at me as if he hates me too. I can't put my finger on it; all I know is I want to get away before something happens."

He got out on his side of the car, came around, motioned to her to move over, got in. "The only thing you're going to do is see a good psychiatrist. And if he suggests a vacation, well, okay. But this can't go on; my stomach's in knots all the time." He started the car. "I'll drive the rest of the way."

Her head was down; she was trying to keep back tears. She looked up when they reached his office building. "All right. Make the appointment. I'll go talk to anyone you want, David."

He kissed her. "Now you're talking sense, lady. Think you can drive home okay?"

"Of course, silly."

"See you at supper, then. Drive carefully."

"Don't I always? Bye."

He stood on the curb, watching her drive off, the wind taking hold of her long, dark, shining hair. Upstairs, a minute later, he phone Jeffers and arranged an appointment with a reliable neuro-psychiatrist.

The day's work went uneasily. Things fogged over, and in the fog he kept seeing Alice lost and calling his name. So much of her fear had come over to him. She actually had him convinced that the child was in some ways not quite natural.

He dictated long, uninspired letters. He checked some shipments downstairs. Assistants had to be questioned and kept going. At the end of the day he was exhausted, his head throbbed, and he was very glad to go home.

On the way down in the elevator he wondered, What if I told Alice about the toy—that patchwork doll—I slipped on on the stairs last night? Lord, wouldn't *that* back her off? No, I won't ever tell her. Accidents are, after all, accidents.

Daylight lingered in the sky as he drove home in a taxi. In front of the house he paid the driver and walked slowly up the concrete walk, enjoying the light that was still in the sky and the trees. The white colonial front of the house looked unnaturally silent and uninhabited, and then he remembered this was Thursday and the hired help they were able to obtain from time to time were all gone for the day.

He took a deep breath of air. A bird sang behind the house. Traffic moved on the boulevard a block away. He twisted the key in the door. The knob turned under his fingers, oiled, silent.

The door opened. He stepped in, put his hat on the chair with his briefcase, started to shrug out of his coat, when he looked up.

Late sunlight streamed down the stairwell from the window near the top of the hall. Where the sunlight touched it took on the bright color of the patchwork doll sprawled at the bottom of the stairs.

But he paid no attention to the toy.

He could only look, and not move, and look again at Alice.

Alice lay in a broken, grotesque, pallid gesturing and angling of her thin body at the bottom of the stairs, like a crumpled doll that doesn't want to play anymore, ever.

Alice was dead.

The house remained quiet, except for the sound of his heart.

She was dead.

He held her head in his hands, he felt her fingers. He held her body. But she wouldn't live. She wouldn't even try to live. He said her name, out loud, many times, and he tried, once again, by holding her to him, to give her back some of the warmth she had lost, but that didn't help.

He stood up. He must have made a phone call. He didn't remember. He found himself suddenly upstairs. He opened the nursery door and walked inside and stared blankly at the crib. His stomach was sick. He couldn't see very well.

The baby's eyes were closed, but his face was red, moist with perspiration, as if he'd been crying long and hard.

"She's dead," said Leiber to the baby. "She's dead."

Then he started laughing low and soft and continuously for a long time until Dr. Jeffers walked in out of the night and slapped him again and again across his face.

"Snap out of it! Pull yourself together!"

"She fell down the stairs, Doctor. She tripped on a patchwork doll and fell. I almost slipped on it the other night myself. And now—"

The doctor shook him.

"Doc, Doc, Doc," said Dave hazily. "Funny thing. Funny, I—I finally thought of a name for the baby."

The doctor said nothing.

Leiber put his head back in his trembling hands and spoke the words. "I'm going to have him christened next Sunday. Know what name I'm giving him? I'm going to call him Lucifer."

It was eleven at night. A lot of strange people had come and gone through the house, taking the essential flame with them—Alice.

David Leiber sat across from the doctor in the library.

"Alice wasn't crazy," he said slowly. "She had good reason to fear the baby."

Jeffers exhaled. "Don't follow after her! She blamed the child for her sickness, now you blame it for her death. She stumbled on a toy, remember that. You can't blame the child."

"You mean Lucifer?"

"Stop calling him that!"

Leiber shook his head. "Alice heard things at night, moving in the halls. You want to know what made those noises, Doctor? They were made by the baby. Four months old, moving in the dark, listening to us talk. Listening to every word!" He held to the sides of the chair. "And if I turned the lights on, a baby is so small. It can hide behind furniture, a door, against a wall—below eye level."

"I want you to stop this!" said Jeffers.

"Let me say what I think or I'll go crazy. When I went to Chicago, who was it kept Alice awake, tiring her into pneumonia? The baby! And when Alice didn't die, then he tried killing me. It was simple; leave a toy on the stairs, cry in the night until your father goes downstairs to fetch your milk and stumbles. A crude trick, but effective. It didn't get me. But it killed Alice dead."

David Leiber stopped long enough to light a cigarette. "I should have caught on. I'd turn on the lights in the middle of the night, many nights, and the baby'd be lying there, eyes wide. Most babies sleep all the time. Not this one. He stayed awake, thinking."

"Babies don't think."

"He stayed awake doing whatever he *could* do with his brain, then. What in hell do we know about a baby's mind? He had every reason to hate Alice; she suspected him for what he was—certainly not a normal child. Something—different. What do you know of babies, Doctor? The general run, yes. You know, of course, how babies kill their mothers at birth. Why? Could it be resentment at being forced into a lousy world like this one?"

Leiber leaned toward the doctor tiredly. "It all ties up. Suppose that a few babies out of all the millions born are instantaneously able to move, see, hear, think, like many animals and insects can. Insects are born self-sufficient. In a few weeks most mammals and birds adjust. But children take years to speak and to learn to stumble around on their weak legs.

"But suppose one child in a billion is—strange? Born perfectly aware, able to think, instinctively. Wouldn't it be a perfect setup, a perfect blind for anything the baby might want to do? He could pretend to be ordinary, weak, crying, ignorant. With just a *little* expenditure of energy he could crawl about a darkened house, listening. And how easy to place obstacles at the top of stairs. How easy to cry all night and tire a mother into pneumonia. How easy, right at birth, to be so close to the mother that *a few deft maneuvers might cause peritonitis!*"

"For God's sake!" Jeffers was on his feet. "That's a repulsive thing to say!"

"It's a repulsive thing I'm speaking of. How many mothers have died at the birth of their children? How many have suckled strange little improbabilities who cause death one way or another? Strange, red little creatures with brains that work in a bloody darkness we can't even guess at. Elemental little brains, warm with racial memory, hatred, and raw cruelty, with no more thought than self-preservation.

And self-preservation in this case consisted of eliminating a mother who realized what a horror she had birthed. I ask you, Doctor, what is there in the world more selfish than a baby? Nothing!"

Jeffers scowled and shook his head helplessly.

Leiber dropped his cigarette down. "I'm not claiming any great strength for the child. Just enough to crawl around a little, a few months ahead of schedule. Just enough to listen all the time. Just enough to cry late at night. That's enough, more than enough."

Jeffers tried ridicule. "Call it murder, then. But murder must be motivated. What motive had the child?"

Leiber was ready with the answer. "What is more at peace, more dreamfully content, at ease, at rest, fed, comforted, unbothered, than an unborn child? Nothing. It floats in a sleepy, timeless wonder of nourishment and silence. Then suddenly it is asked to give up its berth, is forced to vacate, rushed out into a noisy, uncaring, selfish world where it is asked to shift for itself, to hunt, to feed from the hunting, to seek after a vanishing love that once was its unquestionable right, to meet confusion instead of inner silence and conservative slumber! And the child *resents* it! Resents the cold air, the huge spaces, the sudden departure from familiar things. And in the tiny filament of brain the only thing the child knows is selfishness and hatred because the spell has been rudely shattered. Who is responsible for this disenchantment, this rude breaking of the spell? The mother. So here the new child has someone to hate with all its unreasoning mind. The mother has cast it out, rejected it. And the father is no better; kill him too! He's responsible in *his* way!"

Jeffers interrupted. "If what you say is true, then every woman in the world would have to look on her baby as something to dread, something to wonder about."

"And why not? Hasn't the child a perfect alibi? A thousand years of accepted medical belief protects him. By all natural accounts he is helpless, not responsible. The child is born hating. And things grow worse instead of better. At first the baby gets a certain amount of attention and mothering. But then as time passes, things change. When very new, a baby has the power to make parents do silly things when it cries or sneezes, jump when it makes a noise. As the years pass, the baby feels even that small power slip rapidly, forever away, never to return. Why shouldn't it grasp all the power it can have? Why shouldn't it jockey for position while it has all the advantages? In later years it would be too late to express its hatred. *Now* would be the time to strike."

Leiber's voice was very soft, very low.

"My little boy baby, lying in his crib nights, his face moist and red and out of breath. From crying? No. From climbing slowly out of his crib, from crawling long distances through darkened hallways. My little boy baby. I want to kill him."

The doctor handed him a water glass and some pills. "You're not killing anyone. You're going to sleep for twenty-four hours. Sleep'll change your mind. Take this."

Leiber drank down the pills and let himself be led upstairs to his bedroom, crying, and felt himself being put to bed. The doctor waited until he was moving into sleep, then left the house.

Leiber, alone, drifted down, down.

He heard a noise. "What's—what's *that?*" he demanded feebly.

Something moved in the hall.

David Leiber slept.

Very early the next morning Dr. Jeffers drove up to the house. It was a good morning, and he was here to drive Leiber to the country for a rest. Leiber would still be asleep upstairs. Jeffers had given him enough sedative to knock him out for at least fifteen hours.

He rang the doorbell. No answer. The servants were probably not up. Jeffers tried the front door, found it open, stepped in. He put his medical kit on the nearest chair.

Something white moved out of sight at the top of the stairs. Just a suggestion of a movement. Jeffers hardly noticed it.

The smell of gas was in the house.

Jeffers ran upstairs, crashed into Leiber's bedroom.

Leiber lay motionless on the bed, and the room billowed with gas, which hissed from a released jet at the base of the wall near the door. Jeffers twisted it off, then forced up all the windows and ran back to Leiber's body.

The body was cold. It had been dead quite a few hours.

Coughing violently, the doctor hurried from the room, eyes watering. Leiber hadn't turned on the gas himself. He *couldn't* have. Those sedatives had knocked him out, he wouldn't have wakened until noon. It wasn't suicide. Or was there the faintest possibility?

Jeffers stood in the hall for five minutes. Then he walked to the door of the nursery. It was shut. He opened it. He walked inside and to the crib.

The crib was empty.

He stood swaying by the crib for half a minute, then he said something to nobody in particular.

"The nursery door blew shut. You couldn't get back into your crib where it was safe. You didn't plan on the door blowing shut. A little thing like a slammed door can ruin the best of plans. I'll find you somewhere in the house, hiding, pretending to be something you are not." The doctor looked dazed. He put his hand to his head and smiled palely. "Now I'm talking like Alice and David talked. But I can't take any chances. I'm not sure of anything, but I can't take chances."

He walked downstairs, opened his medical bag on the chair, took something out of it, and held it in his hands.

Something rustled down the hall. Something very small and very quiet. Jeffers turned rapidly.

I had to operate to bring you into this world, he thought. Now I guess I can operate to take you out of it. . . .

He took half a dozen slow, sure steps forward into the hall. He raised his hand into the sunlight.

"See, baby! Something bright—something pretty!"

A scalpel.

The Lottery

Shirley Jackson

Shirley Jackson (1919–1965) attended Syracuse University before turning to writing and creating such classic novels as The Haunting of Hill House *and* We Have Always Lived in the Castle. *Her fiction combines the bleak trappings of gothic literature with a thorough examination of the dark nature of man, his fear of the unknown, and desperate clinging to rituals and order. Her work has a timeless quality and reads as well today as it did when it was first written.*

THE MORNING OF JUNE 27TH WAS CLEAR AND SUNNY, WITH THE FRESH warmth of a full-summer day; the flowers were blossoming profusely and the grass was richly green. The people of the village began to gather in the square, between the post office and the bank, around ten o'clock; in some towns there were so many people that the lottery took two days and had to be started on June 26th, but in this village, where there were only about three hundred people, the whole lottery took less than two hours, so it could begin at ten o'clock in the morning and still be through in time to allow the villagers to get home for noon dinner.

The children assembled first, of course. School was recently over for the summer, and the feeling of liberty sat uneasily on most of them; they tended to gather together quietly for a while before they broke into boisterous play, and their talk was still of the classroom and the teacher, of books and reprimands. Bobby Martin had already stuffed his pockets full of stones, and the other boys soon followed his example, selecting the smoothest and roundest stones; Bobby and Harry Jones and Dickie Delacroix—the villagers pronounced this name "Dellacroy"—eventually made a great pile of stones in one corner of the square and guarded it against the raids of the other boys. The girls stood aside, talking among themselves, looking over their shoulders at the boys, and the very small children rolled in the dust or clung to the hands of their older brothers or sisters.

Soon the men began to gather, surveying their own children, speaking of planting and rain, tractors and taxes. They stood together, away from the pile of stones in the corner, and their jokes were quiet and they smiled rather than laughed. The women, wearing faded house dresses and sweaters, came shortly after their menfolk. They greeted one another and exchanged bits of gossip as they went to join their husbands. Soon the women, standing by their husbands, began to call to their children, and the children came reluctantly, having to be called four or five times. Bobby Martin ducked under his mother's grasping hand and ran, laughing, back to the pile of stones. His father spoke up sharply, and Bobby came quickly and took his place between his father and his oldest brother.

The lottery was conducted—as were the square dances, the teenage club, the Halloween program—by Mr. Summers, who had time and energy to devote to civic activities. He was a round-faced, jovial man and he ran the coal business, and people were sorry for him, because he had no children and his wife was a scold. When he arrived in the square, carrying the black wooden box, there was a murmur of conversation among the villagers, and he waved and called, "Little late today, folks." The postmaster, Mr. Graves, followed him, carrying a three-legged stool, and the stool was put in the center of the square and Mr. Summers set the black box down on it. The villagers kept their distance, leaving a space between themselves and the stool, and when Mr. Summers said, "Some of you fellows want to give me a hand?" there was a hesitation before two men, Mr. Martin and his oldest son, Baxter, came forward to hold the box steady on the stool while Mr. Summers stirred up the papers inside it.

The original paraphernalia for the lottery had been lost long ago, and the black box now resting on the stool had been put into use even before Old Man Warner, the oldest man in town, was born. Mr. Summers spoke frequently to the villagers about making a new box, but no one liked to upset even as much tradition as was represented by the black box. There was a story that the present box had been made with some pieces of the box that had preceded it, the one that had been constructed when the first people settled down to make a village here. Every year, after the lottery, Mr. Summers began talking again about a hew box, but every year the subject was allowed to fade off without anything's being done. The black box grew shabbier each year; by now it was no longer completely black but splintered badly along one side to show the original wood color, and in some places faded or stained.

Mr. Martin and his oldest son, Baxter, held the black box securely on the stool until Mr. Summers had stirred the papers thoroughly with his hand. Because so much of the ritual had been forgotten or discarded, Mr. Summers had been successful in having slips of paper substituted for the chips of wood that had been used for generations. Chips of wood, Mr. Summers had argued, had been all very well when the village was tiny, but now that the population was more than three hundred and likely to keep on growing, it was necessary to use something that would fit more easily into the black box. The night before the lottery, Mr. Summers and Mr. Graves made up the slips of paper and put them in the box, and it was then taken to the safe of Mr. Summers's coal company and locked up until Mr. Summers was ready to take it to the square next morning. The rest of the year, the box was put away, sometimes one place, sometimes another; it had spent one year in Mr. Graves's barn and another year underfoot in the post office, and sometimes it was set on a shelf in the Martin grocery and left there.

There was a great deal of fussing to be done before Mr. Summers declared the lottery open. There were the lists to make up—of heads of families, heads of households in each family, members of each household in each family. There was the proper swearing-in of Mr. Summers by the postmaster, as the official of the lottery; at one time, some people remembered, there had been a recital of some sort, performed by the official of the lottery, a perfunctory, tuneless chant that had been rattled off duly each year; some people believed that the official of the lottery used to stand just so when he said or sang it, others believed that he was supposed to walk among the people, but years and years ago this part of the ritual had been allowed to lapse. There had been, also, a ritual salute, which the official of the lottery had had to use in addressing each person who came up to draw from the box, but this also had changed with time, until now it was felt necessary only for the official to speak to each person approaching. Mr. Summers was very good at all this; in his clean white shirt and blue jeans, with one hand resting carelessly on the black box, he seemed very proper and important as he talked interminably to Mr. Graves and the Martins.

Just as Mr. Summers finally left off talking and turned to the assembled villagers, Mrs. Hutchinson came hurriedly along the path to the square, her sweater thrown over her shoulders, and slid into place in the back of the crowd. "Clean forgot what day it was," she said to Mrs. Delacroix, who stood next to her, and they both laughed softly. "Thought my old man was out back stacking wood," Mrs. Hutchinson went on, "and then I looked out the window and the kids was gone, and then I remembered it was the twenty-seventh and came a-running." She dried her hands on her apron, and Mrs. Delacroix said, "You're in time, though. They're still talking away up there."

Mrs. Hutchinson craned her neck to see through the crowd and found her husband and children standing near the front. She tapped

Mrs. Delacroix on the arm as a farewell and began to make her way through the crowd. The people separated good-humoredly to let her through; two or three people said, in voices just loud enough to be heard across the crowd, "Here comes your Missus, Hutchinson," and "Bill, she made it after all." Mrs. Hutchinson reached her husband, and Mr. Summers, who had been waiting, said cheerfully, "Thought we were going to have to get on without you, Tessie." Mrs. Hutchinson said, grinning, "Wouldn't have me leave m'dishes in the sink, now, would you, Joe?" and soft laughter ran through the crowd as the people stirred back into position after Mrs. Hutchinson's arrival.

"Well, now," Mr. Summers said soberly, "guess we better get started, get this over with, so's we can go back to work. Anybody ain't here?"

"Dunbar," several people said. "Dunbar, Dunbar."

Mr. Summers consulted his list. "Clyde Dunbar," he said. "That's right. He's broke his leg, hasn't he? Who's drawing for him?"

"Me, I guess," a woman said, and Mr. Summers turned to look at her. "Wife draws for her husband," Mr. Summers said. "Don't you have a grown boy to do it for you, Janey?" Although Mr. Summers and everyone else in the village knew the answer perfectly well, it was the business of the official of the lottery to ask such questions formally. Mr. Summers waited with an expression of polite interest while Mrs. Dunbar answered.

"Horace's not but sixteen yet," Mrs. Dunbar said regretfully. "Guess I gotta fill in for the old man this year."

"Right," Mr. Summers said. He made a note on the list he was holding. Then he asked, "Watson boy drawing this year?"

A tall boy in the crowd raised his hand. "Here," he said. "I'm drawing for m'mother and me." He blinked his eyes nervously and ducked his head as several voices in the crowd said things like "Good fellow, Jack," and "Glad to see your mother's got a man to do it."

"Well," Mr. Summers said, "guess that's everyone. Old Man Warner make it?"

"Here," a voice said, and Mr. Summers nodded.

A sudden hush fell on the crowd as Mr. Summers cleared his throat and looked at the list. "All ready?" he called. "Now, I'll read the names—heads of families first—and the men come up and take a paper out of the box. Keep the paper folded in your hand without looking at it until everyone has had a turn. Everything clear?"

The people had done it so many times that they only half listened to the directions; most of them were quiet, wetting their lips, not looking around. Then Mr. Summers raised one hand high and said, "Adams." A man disengaged himself from the crowd and came forward. "Hi, Steve," Mr. Summers said, and Mr. Adams said, "Hi, Joe." They grinned at one another humorlessly and nervously. Then Mr. Adams reached into the black box and took out a folded paper. He held it firmly by one corner as he turned and went hastily back to his place in the crowd, where he stood a little apart from his family, not looking down at his hand.

"Allen," Mr. Summers said. "Anderson . . . Bentham."

"Seems like there's no time at all between lotteries any more," Mrs. Delacroix said to Mrs. Graves in the back row. "Seems like we got through with the last one only last week."

"Time sure goes fast," Mrs. Graves said.

"Clark . . . Delacroix."

"There goes my old man," Mrs. Delacroix said. She held her breath while her husband went forward.

"Dunbar," Mr. Summers said, and Mrs. Dunbar went steadily to the box while one of the women said, "Go on, Janey," and another said, "There she goes."

"We're next," Mrs. Graves said. She watched while Mr. Graves came around from the side of the box, greeted Mr. Summers gravely, and selected a slip of paper from the box. By now, all through the crowd there were men holding the small folded papers in their large hands, turning them over and over nervously. Mrs. Dunbar and her two sons stood together, Mrs. Dunbar holding the slip of paper.

"Harburt . . . Hutchinson."

"Get up there, Bill," Mrs. Hutchinson said, and the people near her laughed.

"Jones."

"They do say," Mr. Adams said to Old Man Warner, who stood next to him, "that over in the north village they're talking of giving up the lottery."

Old Man Warner snorted. "Pack of crazy fools," he said. "Listening to the young folks, nothing's good enough for *them*. Next thing you know, they'll be wanting to go back to living in caves, nobody work any more, live *that* way for a while. Used to be a saying about 'Lottery in June, corn be heavy soon.' First thing you know, we'd all be eating stewed chickweed and acorns. There's *always* been a lottery," he added petulantly. "Bad enough to see young Joe Summers up there joking with everybody."

"Some places have already quit lotteries," Mrs. Adams said.

"Nothing but trouble in *that*," Old Man Warner said stoutly. "Pack of young fools."

"Martin." And Bobby Martin watched his father go forward. "Overdyke . . . Percy."

"I wish they'd hurry," Mrs. Dunbar said to her older son. "I wish they'd hurry."

"They're almost through," her son said.

"You get ready to run tell Dad," Mrs. Dunbar said.

Mr. Summers called his own name and then stepped forward precisely and selected a slip from the box. Then he called, "Warner."

"Seventy-seventh year I been in the lottery," Old Man Warner said as he went through the crowd. "Seventy-seventh time."

"Watson." The tall boy came awkwardly through the crowd. Someone said, "Don't be nervous, Jack," and Mr. Summers said, "Take your time, son."

"Zanini."

After that, there was a long pause, a breathless pause, until Mr. Summers, holding his slip of paper in the air, said, "All right, fellows." For a minute, no one moved, and then all the slips of paper were opened. Suddenly, all the women began to speak at once, saying, "Who is it?," "Who's got it?," "Is it the Dunbars?," "Is it the Watsons?" Then the voices began to say, "It's Hutchinson. It's Bill," "Bill Hutchinson's got it."

"Go tell your father," Mrs. Dunbar said to her older son.

People began to look around to see the Hutchinsons. Bill Hutchinson was standing quiet, staring down at the paper in his hand. Suddenly, Tessie Hutchinson shouted to Mr. Summers, "You didn't give him time enough to take any paper he wanted. I saw you. It wasn't fair!"

"Be a good sport, Tessie," Mrs. Delacroix called, and Mrs. Graves said, "All of us took the same chance."

"Shut up, Tessie," Bill Hutchinson said.

"Well, everyone," Mr. Summers said, "that was done pretty fast, and now we've got to be hurrying a little more to get done in time." He consulted his next list. "Bill," he said, "you draw for the Hutchinson family. You got any other households in the Hutchinsons?"

"There's Don and Eva," Mrs. Hutchinson yelled. "Make *them* take their chance!"

"Daughters draw with their husbands' families, Tessie," Mr. Summers said gently. "You know that as well as anyone else."

"It wasn't *fair*," Tessie said.

"I guess not, Joe," Bill Hutchinson said regretfully. "My daughter draws with her husband's family, that's only fair. And I've got no other family except the kids."

"Then, as far as drawing for families is concerned, it's you," Mr.

Summers said in explanation, "and as far as drawing for households is concerned, that's you, too. Right?"

"Right," Bill Hutchinson said.

"How many kids, Bill?" Mr. Summers asked formally.

"Three," Bill Hutchinson said. "There's Bill, Jr., and Nancy, and little Dave. And Tessie and me."

"All right, then," Mr. Summers said. "Harry, you got their tickets back?"

Mr. Graves nodded and held up the slips of paper. "Put them in the box, then," Mr. Summers directed. "Take Bill's and put it in."

"I think we ought to start over," Mrs. Hutchinson said, as quietly as she could. "I tell you it wasn't *fair.* You didn't give him time enough to choose. *Every*body saw that."

Mr. Graves had selected the five slips and put them in the box, and he dropped all the papers but those onto the ground, where the breeze caught them and lifted them off.

"Listen, everybody," Mrs. Hutchinson was saying to the people around her.

"Ready, Bill?" Mr. Summers asked, and Bill Hutchinson, with one quick glance around at his wife and children, nodded.

"Remember," Mr. Summers said, "take the slips and keep them folded until each person has taken one. Harry, you help little Dave." Mr. Graves took the hand of the little boy, who came willingly with him up to the box. "Take a paper out of the box, Davy," Mr. Summers said. Davy put his hand into the box and laughed. "Take just *one* paper," Mr. Summers said. "Harry, you hold it for him." Mr. Graves took the child's hand and removed the folded paper from the tight fist and held it while little Dave stood next to him and looked up at him wonderingly.

"Nancy next," Mr. Summers said. Nancy was twelve, and her school friends breathed heavily as she went forward, switching her skirt, and took a slip daintily from the box. "Bill, Jr.," Mr. Summers said, and Billy, his face red and his feet overlarge, nearly knocked the box over as he got a paper out. "Tessie," Mr. Summers said. She hesitated for a minute, looking around defiantly, and then set her lips and went up to the box. She snatched a paper out and held it behind her.

"Bill," Mr. Summers said, and Bill Hutchinson reached into the box and felt around, bringing his hand out at last with the slip of paper in it.

The crowd was quiet. A girl whispered, "I hope it's not Nancy," and the sound of the whisper reached the edges of the crowd.

"It's not the way it used to be," Old Man Warner said clearly. "People ain't the way they used to be."

"All right," Mr. Summers said. "Open the papers. Harry, you open little Dave's."

Mr. Graves opened the slip of paper and there was a general sigh through the crowd as he held it up and everyone could see that it was blank. Nancy and Bill, Jr., opened theirs at the same time, and both beamed and laughed, turning around to the crowd and holding their slips of paper above their heads.

"Tessie," Mr. Summers said. There was a pause, and then Mr. Summers looked at Bill Hutchinson, and Bill unfolded his paper and showed it. It was blank.

"It's Tessie," Mr. Summers said, and his voice was hushed. "Show us her paper, Bill."

Bill Hutchinson went over to his wife and forced the slip of paper out of her hand. It had a black spot on it, the black spot Mr. Summers had made the night before with the heavy pencil in the coal-company office. Bill Hutchinson held it up, and there was a stir in the crowd.

"All right, folks," Mr. Summers said. "Let's finish quickly."

Although the villagers had forgotten the ritual and lost the original black box, they still remembered to use stones. The pile of stones the boys had made earlier was ready; there were stones on the ground with the blowing scraps of paper that had come out of the box. Mrs. Delacroix selected a stone so large she had to pick it up with both hands and turned to Mrs. Dunbar. "Come on," she said. "Hurry up."

Mrs. Dunbar had small stones in both hands, and she said, gasping for breath, "I can't run at all. You'll have to go ahead and I'll catch up with you."

The children had stones already, and someone gave little Davy Hutchinson a few pebbles.

Tessie Hutchinson was in the center of a cleared space by now, and she held her hands out desperately as the villagers moved in on her. "It isn't fair," she said. A stone hit her on the side of the head.

Old Man Warner was saying, "Come on, come on, everyone." Steve Adams was in the front of the crowd of villagers, with Mrs. Graves beside him.

"It isn't fair, it isn't right," Mrs. Hutchinson screamed, and then they were upon her.

Our Fair City

Robert A. Heinlein

Robert A. Heinlein (1907–1988) produced a staggering body of work during his lifetime, including some of the best science fiction novels ever written. Stranger in a Strange Land, The Moon Is a Harsh Mistress, *and* Starship Troopers *in one way or another reflected his fascination with the concept of time's effect on mankind's lifespan. This theme was a recurring thread in many of his works, with* Time Enough for Love *and* Number of the Beast *being two other prime examples from later in his career. A four-time recipient of the Hugo award, he was awarded the Grand Master Nebula award in 1974.*

PETE PERKINS TURNED INTO THE ALL-NITE PARKING LOT AND CALLED out, "Hi, Pappy!"

The old parking lot attendant looked up and answered, "Be with you in a moment, Pete." He was tearing a Sunday comic sheet in narrow strips. A little whirlwind waltzed near him, picking up pieces of old newspaper and bits of dirt and flinging them in the faces of passing pedestrians. The old man held out to it a long streamer of the brightly colored funny-paper. "Here, Kitten," he coaxed. "Come, Kitten . . ."

The whirlwind hesitated, then drew itself up until it was quite tall, jumped two parked cars, and landed right near him.

It seemed to sniff at the offering.

"Take it, Kitten," the old man called softly and let the gay streamer slip from his fingers. The whirlwind whipped it up and wound it around its middle. He tore off another and yet another; the whirlwind wound them in a corkscrew through the loose mass of dirty paper and trash that constituted its visible body. Renewed by cold gusts that poured down the canyon of tall buildings, it swirled faster and ever taller, while it lifted the colored paper ribbons in a fantastic upswept hair-do. The old man turned, smiling. "Kitten does like new clothes."

"Take it easy, Pappy, or you'll have me believing in it."

"Eh? You don't have to believe in Kitten—you can *see* her."

"Yeah, sure—but you act as if she—I mean 'it'—could understand what you say."

"You still don't think so?" His voice was gently tolerant.

"Now, Pappy!"

"Hmm . . . Lend me your hat." Pappy reached up and took it. "Here, Kitten," he called. "Come back, Kitten!" The whirlwind was playing around over their heads, several stories high. It dipped down.

"Hey! Where you going with that chapeau?" demanded Perkins.

"Just a moment . . . Here, Kitten!" The whirlwind sat down suddenly, spilling its load. The old man handed it the hat. The whirlwind snatched it and started it up a fast, long spiral.

"Hey!" yelped Perkins. "What do you think you're doing? That's not funny—that hat cost me six bucks only three years ago."

"Don't worry," the old man soothed. "Kitten will bring it back."

"She will, huh? More likely she'll dump it in the river."

"Oh, no! Kitten never drops anything she doesn't want to drop. Watch." The old man looked up to where the hat was dancing near the penthouse of the hotel across the street. "Kitten! Oh, Kitten! Bring it back."

The whirlwind hesitated, the hat fell a couple of stories. It swooped, caught it, and juggled it reluctantly. "Bring it *here*, Kitten."

The hat commenced a downward spiral, finishing in a long curving swoop. It hit Perkins full in the face. "She was trying to put it on your head," the attendant explained. "Usually she's more accurate."

"She is, eh?" Perkins picked up his hat and stood looking at the whirlwind, mouth open.

"Convinced?" asked the old man.

"'Convinced?' Oh, sho' sho'." He looked back at his hat, then again at the whirlwind. "Pappy, this calls for a drink."

They went inside the lot's little shelter shack; Pappy found glasses; Perkins produced a pint, nearly full, and poured two generous slugs. He tossed his down, poured another, and sat down. "The first was in honor of Kitten," he announced. "This one is to fortify me for the Mayor's banquet."

Pappy cluck-clucked sympathetically. "You have to cover that?"

"Have to write a column about *something*, Pappy. 'Last night Hizzoner the Mayor, surrounded by a glittering galaxy of highbinders, grifters, sycophants, and ballot thieves, was the recipient of a testimonial dinner celebrating . . .' Got to write something, Pappy; the cash customers expect it. Why don't I brace up like a man and go on relief?"

"Today's column was good, Pete," the old man comforted him. He picked up a copy of the *Daily Forum;* Perkins took it from him and ran his eye down his own column.

"'Our Fair City, by Peter Perkins,'" he read, and below that, "'What, No Horsecars? It is the tradition of our civic paradise that what was good enough for the founding fathers is good enough for us. We stumble over the very chuckhole in which great-uncle Tozier broke his leg in '09. It is good to know that the bath water, running out, is not gone forever, but will return through the kitchen faucet, thicker and disguised with chlorine, but the same. (Memo— Hizzoner uses bottled spring water. Must look into this.)

"'But I must report a dismaying change. Someone has done away with the horsecars!

"'You may not believe this. Our public conveyances run so seldom and slowly that you may not have noticed it; nevertheless I swear that I saw one wobbling down Grand A venue with no horses of any sort. It seemed to be propelled by some newfangled electrical device.

"'Even in the atomic age some changes are too much. I urge all citizens . . .'" Perkins gave a snort of disgust. "It's tackling a pillbox with a beanshooter, Pappy. This town is corrupt; it'll stay corrupt. Why should I beat out my brains on such piffle? Hand me the bottle."

"Don't be discouraged, Pete. The tyrant fears the laugh more than the assassin's bullet."

"Where'd you pick that up? Okay, so I'm not funny. I've tried laughing them out of office and it hasn't worked. My efforts are as pointless as the activities of your friend the whirling dervish."

The windows rattled under a gusty impact. "Don't talk that way about Kitten," the old man cautioned. "She's sensitive."

"I apologize." He stood up and bowed toward the door. "Kitten, I apologize. Your activities are *more* useful than mine." He turned to his host. Let's go out and talk to her, Pappy. I'd rather do that than go to the Mayor's banquet, if I had my druthers."

They went outside, Perkins bearing with him the remains of the colored comic sheet. He began tearing off streamers. "Here, Kitty! Here, Kitty! Soup's on!"

The whirlwind bent down and accepted the strips as fast as he tore them. "She's still got the ones you gave her."

"Certainly," agreed Pappy. "Kitten is a pack rat. When she likes something she'll keep it indefinitely."

"Doesn't she ever get tired? There must be some calm days."

"It's never really calm here. It's the arrangement of the buildings and the way Third Avenue leads up from the river. But I think she hides her pet playthings on tops of buildings."

The newspaperman peered into the swirling trash. "I'll bet she's got newspapers from months back. Say, Pappy, I see a column in this, one about our trash collection service and how we don't clean our streets. I'll dig up some papers a couple of years old and claim that they have been blowing around town since publication."

"Why fake it?" answered Pappy. "Let's see what Kitten has." He whistled softly. "Come, baby—let Pappy see your playthings." The whirlwind bulged out; its contents moved less rapidly. The attendant plucked a piece of old newspaper from it in passing. "Here's one three months old."

"We'll have to do better than that."

"I'll try again." He reached out and snatched another. "Last June."

"That's better."

A car honked for service and the old man hurried away. When he returned Perkins was still watching the hovering column. "Any luck?" asked Pappy.

"She won't let me have them. Snatches them away."

"Naughty Kitten," the old man said. "Pete is a friend of ours. You be nice to him." The whirlwind fidgeted uncertainly.

"It's all right," said Perkins. "She didn't know. But look, Pappy— see that piece up there? A front page."

"You want it?"

"Yes. Look closely—the headline reads 'Dewey' something. You don't suppose she's been hoarding it since the '44 campaign?"

"Could be. Kitten has been around here as long as I can remember. And she does hoard things. Wait a second." He called out softly. Shortly the paper was in his hands. "Now we'll see."

Perkins peered at it. "I'll be a short-term Senator! Can you top that, Pappy?"

The headline read: DEWEY CAPTURES MANILA; the date was 1898.

Twenty minutes later they were still considering it over the last of Perkins's bottle. The newspaperman stared at the yellowed, filthy sheet. "Don't tell me this has been blowing around town for the last half century."

"Why not?"

"'Why not?' Well, I'll concede that the streets haven't been cleaned in that time, but this paper wouldn't last. Sun and rain and so forth."

"Kitten is very careful of her toys. She probably put it under cover during bad weather."

"For the love of Mike, Pappy, you don't really believe . . . But you do. Frankly, I don't care where she got it; the official theory is going to be that this particular piece of paper has been kicking around our dirty streets, unnoticed and uncollected, for the past fifty years. Boy, am I going to have fun!" He rolled the fragment carefully and started to put it in his pocket.

"Say, don't do that!" his host protested.

"Why not? I'm going to take it down and get a pic of it."

"You mustn't! It belongs to Kitten—I just borrowed it."

"Huh? Are you nuts?"

"She'll be upset if she doesn't get it back. Please, Pete—she'll let you look at it any time you want to."

The old man was so earnest that Perkins was stopped. "Suppose we never see it again? My story hangs on it."

"It's no good to *you*—*she* has to keep it, to make your story stand up. Don't worry—I'll tell her that she mustn't lose it under any circumstances."

"Well—okay." They stepped outside and Pappy talked earnestly to Kitten, then gave her the 1898 fragment. She promptly tucked it into the top of her column. Perkins said good-bye to Pappy, and started to leave the lot. He paused and turned around, looking a little befuddled. "Say, Pappy . . ."

"Yes, Pete?"

"You don't really think that whirlwind is alive, do you?"

"Why not?"

"Why not? Why not, the man says?"

"Well," said Pappy reasonably, "How do you know *you* are alive?"

"But . . . Why, because I—well, now, if you put it . . ." He stopped. "I don't know. You got me, pal."

Pappy smiled. "You see?"

"Uh, I guess so. G'night, Pappy. G'night, Kitten." He tipped his hat to the whirlwind. The column bowed.

The managing editor sent for Perkins. "Look, Pete," he said, chucking a sheaf of gray copy paper at him, "whimsy is all right, but I'd like to see some copy that wasn't dashed off in a gin mill."

Perkins looked over the pages shoved at him.

OUR FAIR CITY, by Peter Perkins. *Whistle Up the Wind*. Walking our streets always is a piquant, even adventurous, experience. We pick our way through the assorted trash, bits of old garbage, cigarette butts, and other less appetizing items that stud our sidewalks while our faces are assaulted by more buoyant souvenirs, the confetti of last Halloween, shreds of dead leaves, and other items too weather-beaten to be identified. However, I had always assumed that a constant turnover in the riches of our streets caused them to renew themselves at least every seven years . . .

The column then told of the whirlwind that contained the fifty-year-old newspaper and challenged any other city in the country to match it.

"'Smatter with it?" demanded Perkins.

"Beating the drum about the filth in the streets is fine, Pete, but give it a factual approach."

Perkins leaned over the desk. "Boss, this *is* factual."

"Huh? Don't be silly, Pete."

"Silly, he says. Look . . ." Perkins gave him a circumstantial account of Kitten and the 1898 newspaper.

"Pete, you must have been drinking."

"Only java and tomato juice. Cross my heart and hope to die."

"How about yesterday? I'll bet the whirlwind came right up to the bar with you."

"I was cold, stone . . ." Perkins stopped himself and stood on his dignity. "That's my story. Print it, or fire me."

"Don't be like that, Pete. I don't want your job; I just want a column with some meat. Dig up some facts on man-hours and costs for street cleaning, compared with other cities."

"Who'd read that junk? Come down the street with me. I'll *show* you the facts. Wait a moment—I'll pick up a photographer."

A few minutes later Perkins was introducing the managing editor and Clarence V. Weems to Pappy. Clarence unlimbered his camera. "Take a pic of him?"

"Not yet, Clarence. Pappy, can you get Kitten to give us back the museum piece?"

"Why, sure." The old man looked up and whistled. "Oh, Kitten! Come to Pappy." Above their heads a tiny gust took shape, picked up bits of paper and stray leaves, and settled on the lot. Perkins peered into it.

"She hasn't got it," he said in aggrieved tones.

"She'll get it." Pappy stepped forward until the whirlwind enfolded him. They could see his lips move, but the words did not reach them.

"Now?" said Clarence.

"Not yet." The whirlwind bounded up and leapt over an adjoining building. The managing editor opened his mouth, closed it again.

Kitten was soon back. She dropped everything else and had just one piece of paper—*the* paper. "Now!" said Perkins. "Can you get a shot of that paper, Clarence—while it's in the air?"

"Natch," said Clarence, and raised his Speed Graphic. "Back a little, and hold it," he ordered, speaking to the whirlwind.

Kitten hesitated and seemed about to skitter away. "Bring it around slow and easy, Kitten," Pappy supplemented, "and turn it over—no, no! Not that way—the other edge up." The paper flattened out and sailed slowly past them, the headline showing.

"Did you get it?" Perkins demanded.

"Natch," said Clarence. "Is that all?" he asked the editor.

"Natc—I mean, that's all."

"Okay," said Clarence, picked up his case, and left.

The editor sighed. "Gentlemen," he said, "let's have a drink."

Four drinks later Perkins and his boss were still arguing. Pappy had left. "Be reasonable, Boss," Pete was saying, "you can't print an item about a live whirlwind. They'd laugh you out of town."

Managing Editor Gaines straightened himself.

"It's the policy of the *Forum* to print all the news, and print it straight. This is news—we print it." He relaxed. "Hey! Waiter! More of the same—and not so much soda."

"But it's scientifically impossible."

"You saw it, didn't you?"

"Yes, but . . ."

Gaines stopped him. "We'll ask the Smithsonian Institution to investigate it."

"They'll laugh at you," Perkins insisted. "Ever hear of mass hypnotism?"

"Huh? No, that's no explanation—Clarence saw it, too."

"What does that prove?"

"Obvious—to be hypnotized you have to have a mind, *Ipso facto.*"

"You mean *Ipse dixit.*"

"Quit hiccuping. Perkins, you shouldn't drink in the daytime. Now start over and say it slowly."

"How do you know Clarence doesn't have a mind?"

"Prove it."

"Well, he's alive—he must have some sort of a mind, then."

"That's just what I was saying. The whirlwind is alive; therefore it has a mind. Perkins, if those long beards from the Smithsonian are going to persist in their unscientific attitude, I for one will not stand for it. The *Forum* will not stand for it. You will not stand for it."

"Won't I?"

"Not for one minute. I want you to know the *Forum* is behind you, Pete. You go back to the parking lot and get an interview with that whirlwind."

"But I've got one. You wouldn't let me print it."

"Who wouldn't let you print it? I'll fire him! Come on, Pete. We're going to blow this town sky high. Stop the run. Hold the front page. Get busy!" He put on Pete's hat and strode rapidly into the men's room.

Pete settled himself at his desk with a container of coffee, a can of tomato juice, and the Midnight Final (late afternoon) edition. Under a four-column cut of Kitten's toy was his column, boxed and

moved to the front page. Eighteen-point boldface ordered SEE EDI-
TORIAL PAGE TWELVE. On page twelve another black line enjoined
him to SEE OUR FAIR CITY PAGE ONE. He ignored this and read: MR.
MAYOR—RESIGN!!!!

Pete read it and chuckled. "An ill wind—" "—symbolic of the
spiritual filth lurking in the dark corners of the city hall." "—will
grow to cyclonic proportions and sweep a corrupt and shameless
administration from office." The editorial pointed out that the contract for street cleaning and trash removal was held by the Mayor's
brother-in-law, and then suggested that the whirlwind could give
better service cheaper.

The telephone jingled. He picked it up and said, "Okay—you
started it."

"Pete—is that you?" Pappy's voice demanded. "They got me
down at the station house."

"What for?"

"They claim Kitten is a public nuisance."

"I'll be right over." He stopped by the Art Department, snagged
Clarence, and left. Pappy was seated in the station lieutenant's
office, looking stubborn. Perkins shoved his way in. "What's he here
for?" he demanded, jerking a thumb at Pappy.

The lieutenant looked sour. "What are you butting in for, Perkins?
You're not his lawyer."

"Now?" said Clarence.

"Not yet, Clarence. For news, Dumbrosky—I work for a newspaper, remember? I repeat—what's he in for?"

"Obstructing an officer in the performance of his duty."

"That right, Pappy?"

The old man looked disgusted. "This character—" he indicated
one of the policemen "—comes up to my lot and tries to snatch the
Manila-Bay paper away from Kitten. I tell her to keep it up out of his
way. Then he waves his stick at me and orders me to take it away
from her. I tell him what he can do with his stick." He shrugged. "So
here we are."

"I get it," Perkins told him, and turned to Dumbrosky. "You got a
call from the city hall, didn't you? So you sent Dugan down to do
the dirty work. What I don't get is why you sent Dugan. I hear he's
so dumb you don't even let him collect the pay-off on his own beat."

"That's a lie!" put in Dugan. "I do so . . . ."

"Shut up, Dugan!" his boss thundered. "Now, see here, Perkins—
you clear out. There ain't no story here."

"No story?" Perkins said softly. "The police force tries to arrest a
whirlwind and you say there's no story?"

"Now?" said Clarence.

"Nobody tried to arrest no whirlwind! Now scram."

"Then how come you're charging Pappy with obstructing an officer? What was Dugan doing—flying a kite?"

"He's not charged with obstructing an officer."

"He's not, eh? Just what have you booked him for?"

"He's not booked. We're holding him for questioning."

"So? not booked, no warrant, no crime alleged, just pick up a citizen and roust him around, Gestapo style." Perkins turned to Pappy. "You're not under arrest. My advice is to get up and walk out that door."

Pappy started to get up. "Hey!" Lieutenant Dumbrosky bounded out of his chair, grabbed Pappy by the shoulder and pushed him down. "I'm giving the orders around here. You stay . . ."

Now!" yelled Perkins. Clarence's flashbulb froze them. Then Dumbrosky started up again.

"Who let him in here? Dugan—get that camera."

Nyannh!" said Clarence and held it away from the cop. They started doing a little Maypole dance, with Clarence as the Maypole.

"Hold it!" yelled Perkins. "Go ahead and grab the camera, Dugan—I'm just aching to write the story. 'Police Lieutenant Destroys Evidence of Police Brutality.'"

"What do you want I should do, Lieutenant?" pleaded Dugan.

Dumbrosky looked disgusted. "Siddown and close your face. Don't use that picture, Perkins—I'm warning you."

"Of what? Going to make me dance with Dugan? Come on, Pappy. Come on, Clarence." They left.

"Our Fair City" read the next day:

City Hall Starts Clean Up. While the city street cleaners were enjoying their usual siesta, Lieutenant Dumbrosky, acting on orders of Hizzoner's office, raided our Third Avenue whirlwind. It went sour, as Patrolman Dugan could not entice the whirlwind into the paddy wagon. Dauntless Dugan was undeterred; he took a citizen standing nearby, one James Metcalfe, parking-lot attendant, into custody as an accomplice of the whirlwind. An accomplice in what, Dugan didn't say—everybody knows that an accomplice is something pretty awful. Lieutenant Dumbrosky questioned the accomplice. See cut. Lieutenant Dumbrosky weighs 215 pounds, without his shoes. The accomplice weighs 119.

Moral: Don't get underfoot when the police department is playing games with the wind.

P.S. As we go to press, the whirlwind is still holding the 1898 museum piece. Stop by Third and Main and take a look. Better hurry—Dumbrosky is expected to make an arrest momentarily.

Pete's column continued needling the administration the following day:

> *Those Missing Files.* It is annoying to know that any document needed by the Grand Jury is sure to be mislaid before it can be introduced in evidence. We suggest that Kitten, our Third Avenue Whirlwind, be hired by the city as file clerk extraordinary and entrusted with any item which is likely to be needed later. She could take the special civil exam used to reward the faithful—the one nobody ever flunks.
>
> Indeed, why limit Kitten to a lowly clerical job? She is persistent—and she hangs on to what she gets. No one will argue that she is less qualified than some city officials we have had.
>
> Let's run Kitten for Mayor! She's an ideal candidate—she has the common touch, she doesn't mind hurly-burly, she runs around in circles, she knows how to throw dirt, and the opposition can't pin anything on her.
>
> As to the sort of Mayor she would make, there is an old story—Aesop told it—about King Log and King Stork. We're fed up with King Stork; King Log would be welcome relief.
>
> Memo to Hizzoner—what *did* become of those Grand Avenue paving bids?
>
> P.S. Kitten still has the 1898 newspaper on exhibit. Stop by and see it before our police department figures out some way to intimidate a whirlwind.

Pete snagged Clarence and drifted down to the parking lot. The lot was fenced now; a man at a gate handed them two tickets but waved away their money. Inside he found a large circle chained off for Kitten and Pappy inside it. They pushed their way through the crowd to the old man. "Looks like you're coining money, Pappy."

"Should be, but I'm not. They tried to close me up this morning, Pete. Wanted me to pay the $50-a-day circus-and-carnival fee and post a bond besides. So I quit charging for the tickets—but I'm keeping track of them. I'll sue 'em, by gee."

"You won't collect, not in this town. Never mind, we'll make 'em squirm till they let up."

"That's not all. They tried to capture Kitten this morning."

"Huh? Who? How?"

"The cops. They showed up with one of those blower machines used to ventilate manholes, rigged to run backwards and take a suction. The idea was to suck Kitten down into it, or anyhow to grab what she was carrying."

Pete whistled. "You should have called me."

"Wasn't necessary. I warned Kitten and she stashed the Spanish-War paper someplace, then came back. She loved it. She went through that machine about six times, like a merry-go-round. She'd zip through and come out more full of pep than ever. Last time through she took Sergeant Yancel's cap with her and it clogged the machine and ruined his cap. They got disgusted and left."

Peter chortled. "You still should have called me. Clarence should have gotten a picture of that."

"Got it," said Clarence.

"Huh? I didn't know you were here this morning, Clarence."

"You didn't ask me."

Pete looked at him. "Clarence, darling—the idea of a news picture is to print it, not to hide it in the Art Department."

"On your desk," said Clarence.

"Oh. Well, let's move on to a less confusing subject. Pappy, I'd like to put up a big sign here."

"Why not! What do you want to say?"

"Kitten-for-Mayor—Whirlwind Campaign Headquarters. Stick a 24-sheet across the corner of the lot, where they can see it both ways. It fits in with—oh, oh! Company, girls!" He jerked his head toward the entrance.

Sergeant Yancel was back. "All right, all right!" he was saying. "Move on! Clear out of here." He and three cohorts were urging the spectators out of the lot. Pete went to him.

"What goes on, Yancel?"

Yancel looked around. "Oh, it's you, huh? Well, you, too—we got to clear this place out. Emergency."

Pete looked back over his shoulder. "Better get Kitten out of the way, Pappy!" he called out. "*Now,* Clarence."

"Got it," said Clarence.

"Okay," Pete answered. "Now, Yancel, you might tell me what it is we just took a picture of, so we can title it properly."

"Smart guy. You and your stooge had better scram if you don't want your heads blown off. We're setting up a bazooka."

"You're setting up a *what?*" Pete looked toward the squad car, unbelievingly. Sure enough, two of the cops were unloading a bazooka. "Keep shooting, kid," he said to Clarence.

"Natch," said Clarence.

"And quit popping your bubble gum. Now, look, Yancel—I'm just a newsboy. What in the world is the idea?"

"Stick around and find out, wise guy." Yancel turned away. "Okay there! Start doing it—commence firing!"

One of the cops looked up. "At what, Sergeant?"

"I thought you used to be a marine—at the whirlwind, of course."

Pappy leaned over Pete's shoulder. "What are they doing?"

"I'm beginning to get a glimmering. Pappy, keep Kitten out of range—I think they mean to put a rocket shell through her gizzard. It might bust up dynamic stability or something."

"Kitten's safe. I told her to hide. But this is crazy, Pete. They must be absolute, complete and teetotal nuts."

"Any law says a cop has to be sane to be on the force?"

"What whirlwind, Sergeant?" the bazooka man was asking. Yancel started to tell him, forcefully, then deflated when he realized that no whirlwind was available.

"You wait," he told him, and turned to Pappy. "You!" he yelled. "You chased away that whirlwind. Get it back here."

Pete took out his notebook. "This is interesting, Yancel. Is it your professional opinion that a whirlwind can be ordered around like a trained dog? Is that the official position of the police department?"

"I . . . No comment! You button up, or I'll run you in."

"By all means. But you have that Buck-Rogers cannon pointed so that, after the shell passes through the whirlwind, if any, it should end up just about at the city hall. Is this a plot to assassinate Hizzoner?"

Yancel looked around suddenly, then let his gaze travel an imaginary trajectory.

"Hey, you lugs!" he shouted. "Point that thing the other way. You want to knock off the Mayor?"

"That's better," Pete told the Sergeant. "Now they have it trained on the First National Bank. I can't wait."

Yancel looked over the situation again. "Point it where it won't hurt nobody," he ordered. "Do I have to do all your thinking?"

"But, Sergeant . . ."

"Well?"

"You *point* it. We'll fire it."

Pete watched them. "Clarence," he sighed, "you stick around and get a pic of them loading it back into the car. That will be in about five minutes. Pappy and I will be in the Happy Hour Bar-Grill. Get a nice picture, with Yancel's features."

"Natch," said Clarence.

The next installment of "Our Fair City" featured three cuts and was headed "Police Declare War on Whirlwind." Pete took a copy and set out for the parking lot, intending to show it to Pappy.

Pappy wasn't there. Nor was Kitten. He looked around the neighborhood, poking his nose in lunchrooms and bars. No luck.

He headed back toward the *Forum* building, telling himself that Pappy might be shopping, or at a movie. He returned to his desk, made a couple of false starts on a column for the morrow, crumpled them up and went to the Art Department. "Hey! Clarence! Have you been down to the parking lot today?"

"Nah."

"Pappy's missing."

"So what?"

"Well, come along. We got to find him."

"Why?" But he came, lugging his camera.

The lot was still deserted, no Pappy, no Kitten—not even a stray breeze. Pete turned away. "Come on, Clarence—say, what are you shooting now?"

Clarence had his camera turned up toward the sky. "Not shooting," said Clarence. "Light is no good."

"What was it?"

"Whirlwind."

"Huh? Kitten?"

"Maybe."

"Here, Kitten—come Kitten." The whirlwind came back near him, spun faster, and picked up a piece of cardboard it had dropped. It whipped it around, then let him have it in the face.

"That's not funny, Kitten," Pete complained. "Where's Pappy?"

The whirlwind sidled back toward him. He saw it reach again for the cardboard. "No, you don't!" he yelped and reached for it, too.

The whirlwind beat him to it. It carried it up some hundred feet and sailed it back. The card caught him edgewise on the bridge of the nose. "Kitten!" Pete yelled. "Quit the horsing around."

It was a printed notice, about six by eight inches. Evidently it had been tacked up; there were small tears at all four corners. It read: "THE RITZ—CLASSIC" and under that, "Room 2013, Single Occupancy $6.00, Double Occupancy $8.00." There followed a printed list of the house rules.

Pete stared at it and frowned. Suddenly he chucked it back at the whirlwind. Kitten immediately tossed it back in his face.

"Come on, Clarence," he said briskly. "We're going to the Ritz-Classic—room 2013."

"Natch." said Clarence.

The Ritz-Classic was a colossal fleabag, favored by the bookie-and-madame set, three blocks away. Pete avoided the desk by using the basement entrance. The elevator boy looked at Clarence's camera and said, "No, you don't, Doc. No divorce cases in this hotel."

"Relax," Pete told him. "That's not a real camera. We peddle marijuana—that's the hay mow."

"Whyn't you say so? You hadn't ought to carry it in a camera. You make people nervous. What floor?"

"Twenty-one."

The elevator operator took them up nonstop, ignoring other calls. "That'll be two bucks. Special service."

"What do you pay for the concession?" inquired Pete.

"You gotta nerve to beef—with your racket."

They went back down a floor by stair and looked up room 2013. Pete tried the knob cautiously; the door was locked. He knocked on it—no answer. He pressed an ear to it and thought he could hear movement inside. He stepped back, frowning.

Clarence said, "I just remembered something," and trotted away. He returned quickly, with a red fire ax. "Now?" he asked Pete.

"A lovely thought, Clarence! Not yet." Pete pounded and yelled, "Pappy! Oh, Pappy!"

A large woman in a pink coolie coat opened the door behind them. "How do you expect a party to sleep?" she demanded.

Pete said, "Quiet, madame! We're on the air." He listened. This time there were sounds of struggling and then, "Pete! Pe—"

"Now!" said Pete. Clarence started swinging.

The lock gave up on the third swing. Pete poured in, with Clarence after him. He collided with someone coming out and sat down abruptly. When he got up he saw Pappy on a bed. The old man was busily trying to get rid of a towel tied around his mouth.

Pete snatched it away. "Get 'em!" yelled Pappy.

"Soon as I get you untied."

"I ain't tied. They took my pants. Boy, I thought you'd never come!"

"Took Kitten a while to make me understand."

"I got 'em," announced Clarence. "Both of 'em."

"Where?" demanded Pete.

"Here," said Clarence proudly, and patted his camera.

Pete restrained his answer and ran to the door. "They went thataway," said the large woman, pointing. He took out, skidded around the corner and saw an elevator door just closing.

Pete stopped, bewildered by the crowd just outside the hotel. He was looking uncertainly around when Pappy grabbed him. "There! That touring car!" The car Pappy pointed out was even then swinging out from the curb just beyond the rank of cabs in front of the hotel; with a deep growl it picked up speed, and headed away. Pete yanked open the door of the nearest cab.

"Follow that car!" he yelled. They all piled in.

"Why?" asked the hackie.

Clarence lifted the fire ax. "Now?" he asked.

The driver ducked. "Forget it," he said. "It was just a yak." He let in his clutch.

The hack driver's skill helped them in the downtown streets, but the driver of the touring car swung right on Third and headed for the river. They streamed across it, fifty yards apart, with traffic snarled behind them, and then were on the no-speed-limit freeway. The cabbie turned his head. "Is the camera truck keeping up?"

"What camera truck?"

"Ain't this a movie?"

"Good grief, no! That car is filled with kidnappers. Faster!"

"A snatch? I don't want no part of it." He braked suddenly.

Pete took the ax and prodded the driver. "You catch 'em!"

The hack speeded up again but the driver protested, "Not in this wreck. They got more power than me."

Pappy grabbed Pete's arm. "There's Kitten!"

"Where? Oh, never mind that now!"

"Slow down!" yelled Pappy. "Kitten, oh, Kitten—over here!"

The whirlwind swooped down and kept pace with them. Pappy called to it. "Here, baby! Go get that car! Up ahead—*get it!*"

Kitten seemed confused, uncertain. Pappy repeated it and she took off—like a whirlwind. She dipped and gathered a load of paper and trash as she flew.

·They saw her dip and strike the car ahead, throwing paper in the face of the driver. The car wobbled. She struck again. The car veered, climbed the curb, ricocheted against the crash rail, and fetched up against a lamp post.

Five minutes later Pete, having left Kitten, Clarence, and the fire ax to hold the fort over two hoodlums suffering from abrasion, multiple contusions and shock, was feeding a dime into a pay phone at the nearest filling station. He dialed long distance. "Gimme the F.B.I.'s kidnap number," he demanded. "You know—the Washington, D.C., snatch number."

"My goodness," said the operator, "do you mind if I listen in?"

"Get me that number!"

"Right away!"

Presently a voice answered. "Federal Bureau of Investigation."

"Lemme talk to Hoover! Huh? Okay, okay—I'll talk to you. Listen, this is a snatch case. I've got 'em on ice, for the moment, but unless you get one of your boys from your local office here pronto there won't be any snatch case—not if the city cops get here first. What?" Pete quieted down and explained who he was, where he was, and the more believable aspects of the events that had led up to the present situation. The government man cut in on him as he was urging speed and more speed and more speed and assured him that the local office was already being notified.

Pete got back to the wreck just as Lieutenant Dumbrosky climbed out of a squad car. Pete hurried up. "Don't do it, Dumbrosky," he yelled.

The big cop hesitated. "Don't do what?"

"Don't do anything. The F.B.I. are on their way now—and you're already implicated. Don't make it any worse."

Pete pointed to the two gunsels; Clarence was sitting on one and resting the spike of the ax against the back of the other. "These birds have already sung. This town is about to fall apart. If you hurry, you might be able to get a plane for Mexico."

Dumbrosky looked at him. "Wise guy," he said doubtfully.

"Ask them. They confessed."

One of the hoods raised his head. "We was threatened," he announced. "Take 'em in, Lieutenant. They assaulted us."

"Go ahead," Pete said cheerfully. "Take us all in—together. Then you won't be able to lose that pair before the F.B.I. can question them. Maybe you can cop a plea."

"Now?" asked Clarence.

Dumbrosky swung around. "Put that ax down!"

"Do as he says, Clarence. Get your camera ready to get a picture as the G-men arrive."

"You didn't send for no G-men."

"Look behind you!"

A dark blue sedan slid quietly to a stop and four lean, brisk men got out. The first of them said, "Is there someone here named Peter Perkins?"

"Me," said Pete. "Do you mind if I kiss you?"

It was after dark but the parking lot was crowded and noisy. A stand for the new Mayor and distinguished visitors had been erected on one side, opposite it was a bandstand; across the front was a large illuminated sign: HOME OF KITTEN—HONORARY CITIZEN OF OUR FAIR CITY.

In the fenced-off circle in the middle Kitten herself bounced and spun and swayed and danced. Pete stood on one side of the circle with Pappy opposite him; at four-foot intervals around it children were posted. "All set?" called out Pete.

"All set," answered Pappy. Together, Pete, Pappy and the kids started throwing serpentine into the ring. Kitten swooped, gathered the ribbons up and wrapped them around herself.

"Confetti!" yelled Pete. Each of the kids dumped a sackful toward the whirlwind—little of it reached the ground.

"Balloons!" yelled Pete. "Lights!" Each of the children started blowing up toy balloons; each had a dozen different colors. As fast as they were inflated they fed them to Kitten. Floodlights and searchlights came on; Kitten was transformed into a fountain of boiling, bubbling color, several stories high.

"Now?" said Clarence.

"Now!"

There Shall Be No Darkness

James Blish

James Blish (1921–1975) spent his career writing stories about certain aspects of science fiction—psychic powers, miniature humans, and antigravity, for example—and then expanded those stories into longer pieces with the broader scope of a novel. The finished pieces The Seedling Stars, A Case of Conscience, *and* Jack of Eagles *are prime examples. He also wrote excellent television novelizations, most notably the* Star Trek *logs 1–12 and the classic novel* Spock Must Die!

IT WAS ABOUT 10:00 P.M. WHEN PAUL FOOTE DECIDED THAT THERE WAS A monster at Newcliffe's house party.

Foote was tight at the time—tighter than he like to be ever. He sprawled in a too-easy chair in the front room on the end of his spine, his arms resting on the high arms of the chair. A half-empty glass depended laxly from his right hand. A darker spot on one gray trouser-leg showed where some of the drink had gone. Through half-shut eyes he watched Jarmoskowski at the piano.

The pianist was playing, finally, the Scriabin sonata for which the rest of the gathering had been waiting, but for Foote, who was a painter with a tin ear, it wasn't music at all. It was a cantrap, whose implications were secret and horrible.

The room was stuffy and was only half as large as it had been during the afternoon and Foote was afraid that he was the only living man in it except for Jan Jarmoskowski. The rest were wax figures, pretending to be humans in an aesthetic trance.

Of Jarmoskowski's vitality there could be no question. He was not handsome but there was in him a pure brute force that had its own beauty—that and the beauty of precision with which the force was controlled. When his big hairy hands came down it seemed that the piano should fall into flinders. But the impact of fingers on keys was calculated to the single dyne.

It was odd to see such delicacy behind such a face. Jarmoskowski's hair grew too low on his rounded head despite the fact that he had avoided carefully any suggestion of Musician's Haircut. His brows were straight, rectangular, so shaggy that they seemed to meet.

From where Foote sat he noticed for the first time the odd way the Pole's ears were placed—tilted forward as if in animal attention, so that the vestigial "point" really was in the uppermost position.

They were cocked directly toward the keyboard, reminding Foote irresistibly of the dog on the His Master's Voice trademark.

Where had he seen that head before? In Matthias Grünewald, perhaps—in that panel on the Isenheim Altar that showed the Temptation of St. Anthony. Or was it one of the illustrations in the *Red Grimoire,* those odd old woodcuts that Chris Lundgren called "Rorschach tests of the mediaeval mind"?

Jarmoskowski finished the Scriabin, paused, touched his hands together reflectively, began a work of his own, the *Galliard Fantasque.*

The wax figures did not stir, but a soft eerie sigh of recognition came from their frozen lips. There was another person in the room but Foote could not tell who it was. When he turned his unfocused eyes to count, his mind went back on him and he never managed to reach a total. But somehow there was the impression of another presence that had not been of the party before.

Jarmoskowski was not the presence. He had been there before. But he had something to do with it. There was an eighth presence now and it had something to do with Jarmoskowski.

What was it?

For it was there—there was no doubt about that. The energy which the rest of Foote's senses ordinarily would have consumed was flowing into his instincts now because his senses were numbed. Acutely, poignantly, his instincts told him of the Monster. It hovered around the piano, sat next to Jarmoskowski as he caressed the musical beast's teeth, blended with the long body and the serpentine fingers.

Foote had never had the horrors from drinking before and he knew he did not have them now. A part of his mind which was not drunk had recognized real horror somewhere in this room. And the whole of his mind, its skeptical barriers down, believed and trembled within itself.

The batlike circling of the frantic notes was stilled abruptly. Foote blinked, startled. "Already?" he said stupidly.

"Already?" Jarmoskowski echoed. "But that's a long piece, Paul. Your fascination speaks well for my writing."

His eyes flashed redly as he looked directly at the painter. Foote tried frantically to remember whether or not his eyes had been red during the afternoon. Or whether it was possible for any man's eyes to be as red at any time as this man's were now.

"The writing?" he said, condensing the far-flung diffusion of his brain. Newcliffe's highballs were damn strong. "Hardly the writing, Jan. Such fingers as those could put fascination into *Three Blind Mice.*"

He laughed inside at the parade of emotions which marched across Jarmoskowski's face. Startlement at a compliment from Foote—for there had been an inexplicable antagonism between the two since the pianist had first arrived—then puzzled reflection—then finally veiled anger as the hidden slur bared its fangs in his mind. Nevertheless the man could laugh at it.

"They are long, aren't they?" he said to the rest of the group, unrolling them like the party noisemakers which turn from snail to snake when blown through. "But it's a mistake to suppose that they assist my playing, I assure you. Mostly they stumble over each other. Especially over this one."

He held up his hands for inspection. Suddenly Foote was trembling. On both hands, the index fingers and the middle fingers were exactly the same length.

"I suppose Lundgren would call me a mutation. It's a nuisance at the piano."

Doris Gilmore, once a student of Jarmoskowski in Prague, and still obviously, painfully, in love with him, shook coppery hair back from her shoulders and held up her own hands.

"My fingers are so stubby," she said ruefully. "Hardly pianist's hands at all."

"The hands of a master pianist," Jarmoskowski said. He smiled, scratching his palms abstractedly, and Foote found himself in a universe of brilliant perfectly-even teeth. No, not perfectly even. The polished rows were bounded almost mathematically by slightly longer cuspids. They reminded him of that idiotic Poe story—was it *Berenice?* Obviously Jarmoskowski would not die a natural death. He would be killed by a dentist for possession of those teeth.

"Three fourths of the greatest pianists I know have hands like truck drivers," Jarmoskowski was saying. "Surgeons too, as Lundgren will tell you. Long fingers tend to be clumsy."

"You seem to manage to make tremendous music, all the same," Newcliffe said, getting up.

"Thank you, Tom." Jarmoskowski seemed to take his host's rising as a signal that he was not going to be required to play any more. He lifted his feet from the pedals and swung them around to the end of the bench. Several of the others rose also. Foote struggled up to numb feet from the infernal depths of the armchair. He set his glass cautiously on the side table and picked his way over to Christian Lundgren.

"I read your paper, the one you read to the Stockholm Congress," he said, controlling his tongue with difficulty. "Jarmoskowski's hands are—"

"Yes," the psychiatrist said, looking at Foote with sharp, troubled eyes. Suddenly Foote was aware of Lundgren's chain of thought. The gray, chubby little man was assessing his drunkenness, and wondering whether or not Foote would have forgotten the whole business in the morning.

Lundgren made a gesture of dismissal. "I saw them," he said, his tone flat. "A mutation probably, as he himself suggests. This is the twentieth century. I'm going to bed and forget it. Which you may take for advice as well as information."

He stalked out of the room, leaving Foote standing alone, wondering whether to be reassured or more alarmed than before. Lundgren should know. Still, if Jarmoskowski was what he seemed—

The party appeared to be surviving quite nicely without Foote. Conversations were starting up about the big room. Jarmoskowski and Doris shared the piano bench and were talking in low tones, punctuated now and then by brilliant arpeggios as the Pole showed her easier ways of handling the work she had played before dinner.

James and Bennington, the American critic, were dissecting James's most recent novel for a fascinated Newcliffe. Blandly innocent Caroline Newcliffe was talking to the air about nothing at all. Nobody missed Lundgren and it seemed unlikely that Foote would be missed.

He walked with wobbly nonchalance into the dining room, where the butler was still clearing the table.

"'Scuse me," he said. "Little experiment. Return in the morning." He snatched a knife from the table, looked for the door which led from the dining room into the foyer, propelled himself through it. The hallway was dim but intelligible.

As he closed the door to his room he paused for a moment to listen to Jarmoskowski's technical exhibition on the keys. It might be that at midnight Jarmoskowski would give another sort of exhibition. If he did Foote would be glad to have the knife. He shrugged uneasily, closed the door all the way and walked over to his bedroom window.

At 11:30, Jarmoskowski stood alone on the terrace of Newcliffe's country house. Although there was no wind the night was frozen with a piercing cold—but he did not seem to notice it. He stood motionless, like a black statue, with only the long streamers of his breathing, like twin jets of steam from the nostrils of a dragon, to show that he was alive.

Through the haze of lace that curtained Foote's window Jarmoskowski was an heroic pillar of black stone—but a pillar above a fumarole.

The front of the house was entirely dark and the moonlight gleamed dully on the snow. In the dim light the heavy tower which was the central structure was like some ancient donjon-keep. Thin slits of embrasures watched the landscape with a dark vacuity and each of the crowning merlons wore a helmet of snow.

The house huddled against the malice of the white night. A sense of age vested it. The curtains smelt of dust and antiquity. It seemed impossible that anyone but Foote and Jarmoskowski could be alive in it. After a long moment Foote moved the curtain very slightly and drew it back.

His face was drenched in moonlight and he drew back into the dark again, leaving the curtains parted.

If Jarmoskowski saw the furtive motion he gave no sign. He remained engrossed in the acerb beauty of the night. Almost the whole of Newcliffe's estate was visible from where he stood. Even the black border of the forest, beyond the golf course to the right, could be seen through the dry frigid air. A few isolated trees stood nearer the house, casting grotesque shadows on the snow, shadows that flowed and changed shape with infinite slowness as the moon moved.

Jarmoskowski sighed and scratched his left palm. His lips moved soundlessly.

A wandering cloud floated idly toward the moon, its shadow preceding it, gliding in a rush of darkness toward the house. The gentle ripples of the snowbanks contorted in the vast umbra, assumed demon shapes, twisted bodies half-rising from the earth, sinking back, rising again, whirling closer. A damp frigid wind rose briefly, whipping crystalline showers of snow from the terrace flagstones.

The wind died as the shadow engulfed the house. For a long instant the darkness and silence persisted. Then, from somewhere among the stables behind the house, a dog raised his voice in a faint sustained throbbing howl. Others joined him.

Jarmoskowski's teeth gleamed dimly in the occluded moonlight. He stood a moment longer—then his head turned with startling quickness and his eyes flashed a feral scarlet at the dark window where Foote hovered. Foote released the curtains hastily. Even through them he could see the pianist's grim phosphorescent smile. Jarmoskowski went back into the house.

There was a single small light burning in the corridor. Jarmoskowski's room was at the end of the hall next to Foote's. As he walked reflectively toward it the door of the room across from Foote's swung open and Doris Gilmore came out, clad in a housecoat, a towel over her arm and a toothbrush in her hand.

"Oh!" she said. Jarmoskowski turned toward her. Foote slipped behind his back and into Jarmoskowski's room. He did not propose to have Doris a witness to the thing he expected from Jarmoskowski.

In a quieter voice Doris said, "Oh, it's you, Jan. You startled me."

"So I see," Jarmoskowski's voice said. Foote canted one eye around the edge of the door. "It appears that we are the night-owls of the party."

"The rest are tight. Especially that horrible painter. I've been reading the magazines Tom left by my bed and I finally decided to go to sleep too. What have you been doing?"

"Oh, I was just out on the terrace, getting a breath of air. I like the winter night—it bites."

"The dogs are restless too," she said. "Did you hear them?"

"Yes," Jarmoskowski said and smiled. "Why does a full moon make a dog feel so sorry for himself?"

"Maybe there's a banshee about."

"I doubt it," Jarmoskowski said. "This house isn't old enough to have any family psychopomps. As far as I know none of Tom's or Caroline's relatives have had the privilege of dying in it."

"You talk as if you almost believed it." There was a shiver in her voice. She wrapped the housecoat more tightly about her slim waist.

"I come from a country where belief in such things is common. In Poland most of the skeptics are imported."

"I wish you'd pretend to be an exception," she said. "You give me the creeps."

He nodded seriously. They looked at each other. Then he stepped forward and look her hands in his.

Foote felt a belated flicker of embarrassment. If he were wrong he'd speedily find himself in a position for which no apology would be possible.

The girl was looking up at Jarmoskowski, smiling uncertainly. "Jan," she said.

"No," Jarmoskowski said. "Wait. It has been a long time since Prague."

"I see," she said. She tried to release her hands.

Jarmoskowski said sharply, "You don't see. I was eighteen then. You were—what was it?—eleven, I think. In those days I was proud of your schoolgirl crush but of course infinitely too old for you; I am not so old any more and you are so lovely—no, no, hear me out, please! Doris, I love you now, as I can see you love me, but—"

In the brief pause Foote could hear the sharp indrawn breaths that Doris Gilmore was trying to control. He writhed with shame for himself. He had no business being—

"But we must wait, Doris—until I warn you of something neither of us could have dreamed in the old days."

"Warn me?"

"Yes," Jarmoskowski paused again. Then he said, "You will find it hard to believe. But if you do we may yet be happy. Doris, I cannot be a skeptic. I am—"

He stopped. He had looked down abstractedly at her hands as if searching for precisely the right words. Then, slowly, he turned her hands over until they rested palms up upon his. An expression of inexpressible shock crossed his face and Foote saw his grip tighten spasmodically.

In that silent moment, Foote knew that he had been right about Jarmoskowski and despite his pleasure he was frightened.

For an instant Jarmoskowski shut his eyes. The muscles along his jaw stood out with the violence with which he was clenching his teeth. Then, deliberately, he folded Doris's hands together and his curious fingers made a fist about them. When his eyes opened again they were red as flame in the weak light.

Doris jerked her hands free and crossed them over her breasts. "Jan—what is it? What's the matter?"

His face, that should have been flying into flinders under the force of the thing behind it, came under control muscle by muscle.

"Nothing," he said. "There's really no point in what I was going to say. Nice to have seen you again, Doris. Good night."

He brushed past her, walked the rest of the way down the corridor, wrenched back the doorknob of his own room. Foote barely managed to get out of his way.

Behind the house a dog howled and was silent again.

II

In Jarmoskowski's room the moonlight played in through the open window upon a carefully turned-down bed and the cold air had penetrated every cranny. He shut the door and went directly across the room to the table beside his bed. As he crossed the path of silvery light his shadow was oddly foreshortened, so that it looked as if it were walking on all fours. There was a lamp on the side table and he reached for it.

Then he stopped dead still, his hand halfway to the switch. He seemed to be listening. Finally, he turned and looked back across the room, directly at the spot behind the door where Foote was standing.

It was the blackest spot of all, for it had its back to the moon. But Jarmoskowski said immediately, "Hello, Paul. Aren't you up rather late?"

Foote did not reply for a while. His senses were still a little alcohol-numbed and he was overwhelmed by the thing he knew to be. He stood silently in the darkness, watching the Pole's barely visible figure beside the fresh bed, and the sound of his own breathing was loud in his ears. The broad flat streamer of moonlight lay between them like a metallic river.

"I'm going to bed shortly," he said at last. His voice sounded flat and dead and faraway, as if belonging to someone else entirely. "I just came to issue a little warning."

"Well, well," said Jarmoskowski pleasantly. "Warnings seem to be all the vogue this evening. Do you customarily pay your social calls with a knife in your hand?"

"That's the warning, Jarmoskowski. The knife is a—*silver* knife."

"You must be drunker than ever," said the pianist. "Why don't you just go to bed? We can talk about it in the morning."

"Don't give me that," Foote snapped savagely. "You can't fool me. I know you for what you are."

"All right. I'll bite, as Bennington would say."

"Yes, you'd bite," Foote said and his voice shook a little despite himself. "Shall I give it a name, Jarmoskowski? In Poland they called you *Vrolok,* didn't they? And in France it was *loup-garou.* In the Carpathians it was *stregoica* or *strega* or *Vlkoslak.*"

"Your command of languages is greater than your common sense. But you interest me strangely. Isn't it a little out of season for such things? The aconites do not bloom in the dead of winter. And perhaps the thing you call so many fluent names is also out of the season in nineteen sixty-two."

"The dogs hate you," Foote said softly. "That was a fine display Brucey put on when Tom brought him in from his run and he found you here. Walked sidewise through the room, growling, watching you with every step until Tom dragged him out. He's howling now. And that shock you got from the table silver at dinner—I heard your excuse about rubber-soled shoes.

"I looked under the table, if you recall, and your shoes turned out to be leather-soled. But it was a pretty feeble excuse anyhow, for anybody knows that you can't get an electric shock from an ungrounded piece of tableware, no matter how long you've been scuffing rubber. It was the silver that hurt you the first time you touched it. Silver's deadly, isn't it?

"And those fingers—the index fingers as long as the middle ones—you *were* clever about those. You were careful to call everybody's attention to them. It's supposed to be the obvious that everybody misses. But Jarmoskowski, that 'Purloined Letter' gag has been worked too often in detective stories. It didn't fool Lundgren and it didn't fool me."

"Ah," Jarmoskowski said. "Quite a catalogue."

"There's more. How does it happen that your eyes were gray all afternoon and turned red as soon as the moon rose? And the palms of your hands—there was some hair growing there, but you shaved it off, didn't you, Jarmoskowski? I've been watching you scratch them. Everything about you, the way you look, the way you act— everything you say screams your nature in a dozen languages to anyone who knows the signs."

After a long silence Jarmoskowski said, "I see. You've been most attentive, Paul—I see you are what people call the suspicious drunk. But I appreciate your warning, Paul. Let us suppose that what you say of me is true. Have you thought that, knowing that you know, I would have no choice any more? That the first word you said to me about it all might brand *your* palm with the pentagram?"

Foote had not thought about it. He had spent too much time trying to convince himself that it was all a pipe dream. A shock of blinding terror convulsed him. The silver knife clattered to the floor. He snatched up his hands and stared frantically at them, straining his eyes through the blackness. The full horror implicit in Jarmoskowski's suggestion struck him all at once with paralyzing force.

From the other side of his moonlit room, Jarmoskowski's voice came mockingly. "So—you hadn't thought. *Better never* than late, Paul!"

The dim figure of Jarmoskowski began to writhe and ripple in the reflected moonlight. It foreshortened, twisting obscenely, sinking toward the floor, flesh and clothing alike *changing* into something not yet describable.

A cry ripped from Foote's throat and he willed his legs to move with frantic, nightmarish urgency. His clutching hand grasped the doorknob. Tearing his eyes from the hypnotic fascination of the thing that was going on across from him he leaped from his corner and out into the corridor.

A bare second after he had slammed the door, something struck it a frightful blow from the inside. The paneling split. He held it shut with all the strength in his body.

A dim white shape drifted down upon him through the dark corridor and a fresh spasm of fear sent rivers of sweat down on his back, his sides, into his eyes. But it was only the girl.

"Paul! What on earth! What's the *matter!*"

"Quick!" he choked out. "Get something silver—something heavy made out of silver—quick, *quick!*"

Despite her astonishment the frantic urgency in his voice was enough. She darted back into her room.

To Foote it seemed an eternity before she returned—an eternity while he listened with abnormally sensitized ears for a sound inside the room. Once he thought he heard a low growl but he was not sure. The sealike hissing and sighing of his blood, rushing through the channels of the inner ear, seemed very loud to him. He couldn't imagine why it was not arousing the whole countryside. He clung to the doorknob and panted.

Then the girl was back, bearing a silver candlestick nearly three feet in length—a weapon that was almost too good, for his fright-weakened muscles had some difficulty in lifting it. He shifted his grip on the knob to his left hand, hefted the candlestick awkwardly.

"All right," he said, in what he hoped was a grim voice. "Now let him come."

"What in heaven's name is this all about?" Doris said. "You're waking everybody in the house with this racket. Look—even one of the dogs is in to see—"

"The dog!"

He swung around, releasing the doorknob. Not ten paces from them, an enormous coal-black animal, nearly five feet in length, grinned at them with polished fangs. As soon as it saw Foote move it snarled. Its eyes gleamed red in the single bulb.

It sprang.

Foote lifted the candlestick high and brought it down—but the animal was not there. Somehow the leap was never completed. There was a brief flash of movement at the open end of the corridor, then darkness and silence.

"He saw the candlestick," Foote panted. "Must have jumped out the window and come around through the front door. Saw the silver and beat it."

"Paul!" Doris cried. "What—how did you know that thing would jump? It was so big! Silver—"

He chuckled, surprising even himself. He had a mental picture of what the truth would sound like to Doris. "That," he said, "was a wolf and a whopping one. Even the usual kind of wolf isn't very friendly and—"

Footsteps sounded on the floor above and the voice of Newcliffe, grumbling loudly, came down the stairs. Newcliffe liked his evenings noisy and his nights quiet. The whole house seemed to have heard the commotion, for in a moment a number of half-clad figures were elbowing out into the corridor, wanting to know what was up.

Abruptly the lights went on, revealing blinking faces and pajama-clad forms struggling into robes. Newcliffe came down the stairs. Caroline was with him, impeccable even in disarray, her face openly and honestly ignorant and unashamedly beautiful. She made an excellent foil for Tom. She was no lion-hunter but she loved parties. Evidently she was pleased that the party was starting again.

"What's all this?" Newcliffe demanded in a gravelly voice. "Foote, are you the center of this whirlpool? Why all the noise?"

"Werewolf," said Foote, suddenly very conscious of how meaningless the word would be here. "We've got a werewolf here. And somebody's marked out for him."

How else could you put it? Let it stand.

There was a chorus of "What's" as the group jostled about him. "Eh? What was that? . . . Werewolf, I thought he said . . . What's this all about? . . . Somebody's been a wolf . . . Is that new? What an uproar!"

"Paul." Lundgren's voice cut through. "Details, please."

"Jarmoskowski's a werewolf," Foote said grimly, making his tone as emotionless and factual as he could. "I suspected it earlier tonight and went into his room and accused him of it. He changed shape, right on the spot while I was watching."

The sweat started out afresh at the recollection of that horrible, half-seen mutation. "He came around into the hall and went for us and I scared him off with a silver candlestick for a club." He realized suddenly that he still held the candlestick, brandished it as proof. "Doris saw the wolf—she'll vouch for that."

"I saw a big doglike thing, all right," Doris admitted. "And it did jump at us. It was black and had huge teeth. But—Paul, was that supposed to be Jan? Why, that's ridiculous!"

"It certainly is," Newcliffe said feelingly. "Getting us all up for a practical joke. Probably one of the dogs is loose."

"Do you have any coal-black dogs five feet long?" Foote demanded desperately. "And where's Jarmoskowski now. Why isn't he here? Answer me that!"

Bennington gave a skeptical grunt from the background and opened Jarmoskowski's door. The party tried to jam itself into the room. Foote forced his way through the jam.

"See? He isn't here, either. And the bed's not been slept in. Doris, you saw him go in there. Did you see him come out?"

The girl looked startled. "No, but I was in my room—"

"All right. Here. Look at this." Foote led the way over to the window and pointed. "See? The prints on the snow?"

One by one the others leaned out. There was no arguing it. A set of animal prints, like large dogtracks, led away from a spot just beneath Jarmoskowski's window—a spot where the disturbed snow indicated the landing of some heavy body.

"Follow them around," Foote said. "They lead around to the front door, and in."

"Have you traced them?" James asked.

"I don't have to. I saw the thing, James."

"Maybe he just went for a walk," Caroline suggested.

"Barefoot? There are his shoes."

Bennington vaulted over the windowsill with an agility astonishing for so round a man and plowed away with slippered feet along the line of racks. A little while later he entered the room behind their backs.

"Paul's right," he said, above the hub-bub of excited conversation. "The tracks go around to the front door, then come out again and go away around the side of the house toward the golf course." He rolled up his wet pajama-cuffs awkwardly.

"This is crazy," Newcliffe declared angrily. "This is the twentieth century. We're like a lot of little children, panicked by darkness. There's no such thing as a werewolf!"

"I wouldn't place any wagers on that," James said. "Millions of people have thought so for hundreds of years. That's a lot of people."

Newcliffe turned sharply to Lundgren. "Chris, I can depend upon you at east to have your wits about you."

The psychiatrist smiled wanly. "You didn't read my Stockholm paper, did you, Tom? I mean my paper on mental diseases. Most of it dealt with lycanthropy—werewolfism."

"You mean—you believe this idiot story?"

"I spotted Jarmoskowski early in the evening," Lundgren said. "He must have shaved the hair on his palms but he has all the other signs—eyes bloodshot with moonrise, first and second fingers of equal length, pointed ears, domed prefrontal bones, elongated upper cuspids or fangs—in short, the typical hyperpineal type—a lycanthrope."

"Why didn't you say something?"

"I have a natural horror of being laughed at," Lundgren said drily.

"And *I didn't want to draw Jarmoskowski's attention to me*. These endocrine-imbalance cases have a way of making enemies very easily."

Foote grinned ruefully. If he had thought of that part of it before accusing Jarmoskowski he would have kept his big mouth shut.

"Lycanthropy is quite common," Lundgren droned, "but seldom mentioned. It is the little-known aberration of a little-known ductless gland. It appears to enable the victim to control his body."

"I'm still leery of this whole business," Bennington growled, from somewhere deep in his pigeon's chest. "I've known Jan for years. Nice fella—did a lot for me once. And I think there's enough discord in this house so that I won't add to it much if I say I wouldn't trust Paul Foote as far as I could throw him. By heaven, Paul, if this does turn out to be some practical joke of yours—"

"Ask Lundgren," Foote said.

There was dead silence, broken only by heavy breathing. Lundgren was known to every one of them as the world's ultimate authority on hormone-created insanity. Nobody seemed to want to ask him.

"Paul's right," Lundgren said at last. "Take it or leave it. Jarmoskowski is a lycanthrope. A hyperpineal. No other gland could affect the blood-vessels of the eyes like that or make such a reorganization of the cells possible. Jarmoskowski is inarguably a werewolf."

Bennington sagged, the light of righteous incredulity dying from his eyes. "I'll be damned!" he muttered.

"We've got to get him tonight," Foote said. "He's seen the pentagram on somebody's palm—somebody in the party."

"What's that?" asked James.

"Common illusion of lycanthropic seizures," Lundgren said. "Hallucination, I should say. A five-pointed star inscribed in a circle— you find it in all the old mystical books, right back to the so-called fourth and fifth Books of Moses. The werewolf sees it on the palm of his next victim."

There was a gasping little scream from Doris. "So that's it!" she cried. "Dear God, I'm the one! He saw something on my hand tonight while we were talking in the hall. He was awfully startled and went away without another word. He said he was going to warn me about something and then he—"

"Steady," Bennington said in a soft voice that had all the penetrating power of a thunderclap. "There's safety in numbers. We're all here." Nevertheless, he could not keep himself from glancing surreptitiously over his shoulder.

"Well, that settles it," James said in earnest squeaky tones. "We've got to trail the—the beast and kill him. It should be easy to follow his trail in the snow. We must kill him before he kills Doris or somebody else. Even if he misses us it would be just as bad to have him roaming the countryside."

"What are you going to kill him with?" asked Lundgren matter-of-factly.

"Eh?"

"I said, what are you going to kill him with? With that pineal hormone in his blood he can laugh at any ordinary bullet. And since there are no chapels dedicated to St. Hubert around here you can't scare him to death with a church-blessed bullet."

"Silver will do," Foote said.

"Yes, silver will do. It poisons the pinearin-catalysis. But are you going out to hunt a full-grown wolf, a giant wolf, armed with table silver and candlesticks? Or is somebody here metallurgist enough to cast a decent silver bullet?"

Foote sighed. With the burden of proof lifted from him, completely sobered up by shock, he felt a little more like his old self, despite the pall of horror which hung over them.

"Like I always tell my friends," he said, "there's never a dull moment at a Newcliffe house party."

III

The clock struck one-thirty. Foote picked up one of Newcliffe's rifles and hefted it. It felt—useless. He said, "How are you coming?"

The group by the kitchen stove shook their heads in comical unison. One of the gas burners had been jury-rigged as a giant Bunsen burner and they were trying to melt down some soft unalloyed silver articles, mostly of Mexican manufacture.

They were using a small earthenware bowl, also Mexican, for a crucible. It was lidded with the bottom of a flower pot, the hole in which had been plugged with a mixture of garden clay and rock wool yanked forcibly out of the insulation in the attic. The awkward flame leapt uncertainly and sent fantastic shadows flickering over their intent faces.

"We've got it melted, all right," Bennington said, lifting the lid cautiously with a pair of kitchen tongs and peering in. "But what do we do now? Drop it from the top of the tower?"

"You can't kill a wolf with buckshot," Newcliffe pointed out. Now that the problem had been reduced temporarily from a hypernatural one to ordinary hunting he was in his element. "And I haven't got a decent shotgun here anyhow. But we ought to be able to whack together a mold. The bullet should be soft enough so that it won't ruin the rifling of my guns."

He opened the door to the cellar stairs and disappeared, carrying several ordinary cartridges in one hand. Faintly the dogs renewed their howling and Doris began to tremble. Foote put his arm around her.

"It's all right," he said. "We'll get him. You're safe enough."

She swallowed. "I know," she agreed in a small voice. "But every time I think of the way he looked at my hands and how red his eyes were— You don't suppose he's prowling around the house? That that's what the dogs are howling about?"

"I don't know," Foote said carefully. "But dogs are funny that way.

They can sense things at great distances. I suppose a man with pineearin in his blood would have a strong odor to them. But he probably knows that we're after his scalp, so he won't be hanging around if he's smart."

She managed a tremulous smile. "All right," she said. "I'll try not to be frightened." He gave her an awkward reassuring pat, feeling a little absurd.

"Do you suppose we can use the dogs?" James wanted to know.

"Certainly," said Lundgren. "Dogs have always been our greatest allies against the abnormal. You saw what a rage Jarmoskowski's very presence put Brucey in this afternoon. He must have smelled the incipient seizure. Ah, Tom—what did you manage?"

Newcliffe set a wooden box on the table. "I pried the slug out of one shell for each gun," he said, "and made impressions in clay. The cold has made the stuff pretty hard, so it's a passable mold. Bring the silver over here."

Bennington lifted his improvised crucible from the burner, which immediately shot up a tall blue flame. James carefully turned it off.

"All right, pour," Newcliffe said. "Lundgren, you don't suppose it might help to chant a blessing or something?"

"Not unless Jarmoskowski overheard it—probably not even then since we haven't a priest among us."

"Okay. Pour, Bennington, before the goo hardens."

Bennington decanted sluggishly molten silver into each depression in the clay and Newcliffe cleaned away the oozy residue from the casts before it had time to thicken. At any other time the whole scene would have been funny—now it was grimly grotesque. Newcliffe picked up the box and carried it back down to the cellar, where the emasculated cartridges awaited their new slugs.

"Who's going to carry these things, now?" Foote asked. "There are five rifles. James, how about you?"

"I couldn't hit an elephant's rump at three paces. Tom's an expert shot. So is Bennington here, with a shotgun anyhow."

"I can use a rifle," Bennington said diffidently.

"I've done some shooting," Foote said. "During the Battle of the Bulge I even hit something."

"I," Lundgren said, "am an honorary member of the Swiss Militia."

Nobody laughed. Most of them were aware that Lundgren in his own obscure way was bragging, that he had something to brag about. Newcliffe appeared abruptly from the cellar.

"I pried 'em loose, cooled 'em with snow and rolled 'em out with a file. They're probably badly crystallized but we needn't let that worry us."

He put one cartridge in the chamber of each rifle and shot the bolts home. "There's no sense in loading these any more thoroughly—ordinary bullets are no good anyhow, Chris says. Just make your first shots count. Who's elected?"

Foote, Lundgren and Bennington each took a rifle. Newcliffe took the fourth and handed the last one to his wife.

"I say, wait a minute," James objected. "Do you think that's wise, Tom? I mean, taking Caroline along?"

"Why certainly," Newcliffe said, looking surprised. "She shoots like a fiend—she's snatched prizes away from me a couple of times. I thought *everybody* was going along."

"That isn't right," Foote said. "Especially not Doris, since the wolf—that is, I don't think she ought to go."

"Are you going to leave her here by herself?"

"Oh, no!" Doris cried. "Not here! I've got to go! I don't want to wait all alone in this house. He might come back, and there'd be nobody here. I couldn't stand it!"

"We're *all* going," Newcliffe concluded. "We can't leave Doris here unprotected and we need Caroline's marksmanship. Let's get going. It's two now."

He put on his heavy coat and, with the heavy-eyed butler, went out to get the dogs. The rest of the company got out their own heavy clothes. Doris and Caroline climbed into ski-suits. They assembled one by one in the living room. Lundgren's eyes swung on a vase of irislike flowers.

"Hello, what's this?" he said.

"Monkshood," Caroline informed him. "We grow it in the greenhouse. It's pretty, isn't it? Though the gardener says it's poisonous."

"Chris," Foote said. "That isn't wolfsbane, is it?"

The psychiatrist shook his head. "I'm no botanist. I can't tell one aconite from the other. But it hardly matters. Hyperpineals are allergic to the whole group. The pollen, you see. As in hay fever your hyperpineal breathes the pollen, anaphylaxis sets in and—"

"The last twist of the knife," James murmured.

A clamoring of dogs outside announced that Newcliffe was ready. With somber faces the party filed out through the front door. For some reason all of them avoided stepping on the wolf's prints in the snow. Their mien was that of condemned prisoners on the way to the tumbrels. Lundgren took one of the sprigs of flowers from the vase.

The moon had passed its zenith and was almost half-way down the sky, projecting the Bastille-like shadow of the house before it. But there was still plenty of light and the house itself was glowing from basement to tower room. Lundgren located Brucey in the milling yapping pack and abruptly thrust the sprig of flowers under his muzzle. The animal sniffed once, then crouched back and snarled softly.

"Wolfsbane," Lundgren said. "Dogs don't react to the other aconites—basis of the legend, no doubt. Better fire your gardener, Caroline. In the end he's to blame for all this in the dead of winter. Lycanthropy normally is an autumn affliction."

James said,

"Even a man who says his prayers
Before he sleeps each night
May turn to wolf when the wolfsbane blooms
And the moon is high and bright."

"Stop it, you give me the horrors," Foote snapped angrily.

"Well, the dog knows now," said Newcliffe. "Good. It would have been hard for them to pick up the spoor from cold snow but Brucey can lead them. Let's go."

The tracks of the wolf were clear and sharp in the snow. It had formed a hard crust from which fine, powdery showers of tiny ice-crystals were shipped by a fitful wind. The tracks led around the side of the house and out across the golf course. The little group plodded grimly along beside them. The spoor was cold for the dogs but every so often they would pick up a faint trace and go bounding ahead, yanking their master after them. For the most part however the party had to depend upon its eyes.

A heavy mass of clouds had gathered in the west. The moon dipped lower. Foote's shadow, grotesquely lengthened, marched on before him and the crusted snow crunched and crackled beneath his feet. There was a watchful unnaturally still atmosphere to the night and they all moved in tense silence except for a few subdued growls and barks from the dogs.

Once the marks of the werewolf doubled back a short distance, then doubled again as if the monster had turned for a moment to look back at the house before continuing his prowling. For the most part however the trail led directly toward the dark boundary of the woods.

As the brush began to rise about them they stopped by mutual consent and peered warily ahead, rifles held ready for instant action. Far out across the countryside behind them, the great cloud-shadow once more began its sailing. The brilliantly lit house stood out fantastically in the gloom.

"Should have turned those out," Newcliffe muttered, looking back. Outlines us."

The dogs strained at their leashes. In the black west was an inaudible muttering as of winter thunder. Brucey pointed a quivering nose at the woods and growled.

"He's in there, all right."

"We'd better step on it," Bennington said, whispering. "Going to be plenty dark in about five minutes. Storm."

Still they hesitated, regarding the menacing darkness of the forest. Then Newcliffe waved his gun hand in the conventional deploy-as-skirmishers signal and plowed forward. The rest spread out in a loosely spaced line and followed and Foote's finger trembled over his trigger.

The forest in the shrouded darkness was a place of clutching brittle claws, contorted bodies, and the briefly glimpsed demon-faces of ambushed horrors. It was Dante's jungle, the woods of Purgatory, where each tree was a body frozen in agony and branches were gnarled arms and fingers which groaned in the wind or gave sharp tiny tinkling screams as they were broken off.

The underbrush grasped at Foote's legs. His feet broke jarringly through the crust of snow or were supported by it when he least expected support. His shoulders struck unseen tree-trunks. Imagined things sniffed frightfully at his heels or slunk about him just beyond his range of vision. The touch of a hand was enough to make him jump and smother an involuntary outcry. The dogs strained and panted, weaving, no longer snarling, silent with a vicious intentness.

"They've picked up something, all right," Bennington whispered. "Turn 'em loose, Tom?"

Newcliffe bent and snapped the leashes free. Without a sound the animals shot ahead and disappeared.

Over the forest the oncoming storm-clouds crawled across the moon. Total blackness engulfed them. The beam of a powerful flashlight lanced from Newcliffe's free hand, picking out a path of tracks on the brush-littered snow. The rest of the night drew in closer about the blue-white ray.

"Hate to do this," Newcliffe said. "It gives us away. But he knows we're— Hello, it's snowing."

"Let's go then," Foote said. "The tracks will be blotted out shortly."

A terrible clamorous baying rolled suddenly through the woods. "That's *it!*" Newcliffe shouted. "*Listen* to them! Go get him, Brucey!"

They crashed ahead. Foote's heart was beating wildly, his nerves at an impossible pitch. The bellowing cry of the dogs echoed all around him, filling the universe with noise.

"They must have sighted him," he panted. "What a racket! They'll raise the whole countryside."

They plowed blindly through the snow-filled woods. Then, without any interval, they stumbled into a small clearing. Snowflakes flocculated the air. Something dashed between Foote's legs, snapping savagely, and he tripped and fell into a drift.

A voice shouted something indistinguishable. Foote's mouth was full of snow. He jerked his head up—and looked straight into the red rage-glowing eyes of the wolf.

It was standing on the other side of the clearing, facing him, the dogs leaping about it, snapping furiously at its legs. It made no sound at all but crouched tiger-fashion, its lips drawn back in a grinning travesty of Jarmoskowski's smile. It lashed at the dogs as they came closer. One of the dogs already lay writhing on the ground, a dark pool spreading from it, staining the snow.

"Shoot, for heaven's sake!" somebody screamed.

Newcliffe clapped his rifle to his shoulder, then lowered it indecisively. "I can't," he said. "The dogs are in the way."

"The heck with the dogs!" James shouted. "This is no fox-hunt! Shoot, Tom, you're the only one of us that's clear."

It was Foote who fired first. The rifle's flat crack echoed through the woods and snow pulled up in a little explosion by the wolf's left hind pad. A concerted groan arose from the party and Newcliffe's voice thundered above it, ordering his dogs back. Bennington aimed with inexorable care.

The werewolf did not wait. With a screaming snarl he burst through the ring of dogs and charged.

Foote jumped in front of Doris, throwing one arm across his throat. The world dissolved into rolling, twisting pandemonium, filled with screaming and shouting and the frantic hatred of dogs. The snow flew thick. Newcliffe's flashlight rolled away and lay on the snow, regarding the tree-tops with an idiot stare.

Then there was the sound of a heavy body moving swiftly away. The shouting died gradually.

"Anybody hurt?" James's voice asked. There was a general chorus of no's. Newcliffe retrieved his flashlight and played it about but the snowfall had reached blizzard proportions and the light showed nothing but shadows and cold confetti.

"He got away," Bennington said. "And the snow will cover his tracks. Better call your dogs back, Tom."

"They're back," Newcliffe said. "When I call them off they come off."

He bent over the body of the injured animal, which was still twitching feebly. "So—so," he said softly. "So—Brucey. Easy—easy. So, Brucey—so."

Still murmuring, he brought his rifle into position with one arm. The dog's tail beat feebly against the snow.

"So, Brucey."

The rifle crashed.

Newcliffe arose, and looked away. "It looks as if we lose round one," he said tonelessly.

IV

It seemed to become daylight very quickly. The butler went phlegmatically around the house, snapping off the lights. If he knew what was going on he gave no sign of it.

"Cappy?" Newcliffe said into the phone. "Listen and get this straight—it's important. Send a cable to Consolidated Warfare Service—no, no, not the Zurich office, they've offices in London—and place an order for a case of .44 caliber rifle cartridges.

"Listen to me, dammit, I'm not through yet—with *silver slugs*. Yes, that's right—silver—and it had better be the pure stuff too. No, not sterling, that's too hard. Tell them I want them flown over, and that they've got to arrive here tomorrow. Yes, I know it's impossible but if you offer them enough—yes, of course I'll cover it. Got that?"

"Garlic," Lundgren said to Caroline. She wrote it dutifully on her marketing list. "How many windows does this place have? All right, make it one clove for each and get half a dozen boxes of rosemary too."

He turned to Foote. "We must cover every angle," he said somberly. "As soon as Tom gets off the phone I'll try to raise the local priest and get him out here with a truckload of silver crucifixes. Understand, Paul, there is a strong physiological basis behind all the mediaeval mumbo-jumbo.

"The herbs are anti-spasmodics—they act rather as ephedrine does in hay fever to reduce the violence of the seizure. It's possible that Jan may not be able to maintain the wolf shape if he gets a good enough sniff. As for the religious trappings, that's all psychological.

"If Jan happens to be a skeptic in such matters they won't bother him but I suspect he's—" Lundgren's English abruptly gave out. The word he wanted obviously was not in his vocabulary. *"Aberglaeubig,"* he said. *"Criandre."*

"Superstitious?" Foote suggested, smiling grimly.

"Yes. Yes, certainly. Who has better reason, may I ask?"

"But how does he maintain the wolf shape at all?"

"Oh, that's the easiest part. You know how water takes the shape of a vessel it sits in? Well, protoplasm is a liquid. This pineal hormone lowers the surface tension of the cells and at the same time short-circuits the sympathetic nervous system directly to the cerebral cortex.

"Result, a plastic, malleable body within limits. A wolf is easiest because the skeletons are similar—not much pinearin can do with bone, you see. An ape would be easier, but apes don't eat people."

"And vampires? Are they just advanced cases of the same thing?"

"Vampires," said Lundgren pontifically, "are people we put in padded cells. It's impossible to change the bony structure *that* much. They just think they're bats. But yes, it's advanced hyper-pinealism. In the last stages it is quite something to see.

"The surface tension is lowered so much that the cells begin to boil away. Pretty soon there is just a mess. The process is arrested when the vascular system can no longer circulate the hormone but of course the victim is dead long before that."

"No cure?"

"None yet. Someday perhaps, but until then— We will be doing Jan a favor."

"Also," Newcliffe was saying, "drive over and pick me up six Browning automatic rifles. Never mind the bipods, just the rifles themselves. What? Well, you might call it a siege. All right, Cappy. No, I won't be in today. Pay everybody off and send them home until further notice."

"It's a good thing," Foote said, "that Newcliffe has money."

"It's a good thing," said Lundgren, "that he has me—and you. We'll see how twentieth century methods can cope with this Dark-Age disease."

Newcliffe hung up and Lundgren took possession of the phone. "As soon as my man gets back from the village I'm going to set out traps. He may be able to detect hidden metal. I've known dogs that could do it by smell in wet weather but it's worth a try."

"What's to prevent his just going away?" Doris asked. Somehow the shadows of exhaustion and fear around her eyes made her lovelier than ever.

"As I understand it he thinks he's bound by the pentagram," Foote said. At the telephone, where Lundgren evidently was listening to a different conversation with each ear, there was an energetic nod.

"In the old books, the figure is supposed to be a sure trap for demons and such if you can lure them into it. And the werewolf feels compelled to go only for the person whom he thinks is marked with it."

Lundgren said, "Excuse me," and put his hand over the mouthpiece. "Only lasts seven days," he said.

"The compulsion? Then we'll have to get him before then."

"Well, maybe we'll sleep tonight anyhow," Doris said dubiously.

Lundgren hung up and rejoined them. "I didn't have much

difficulty selling the good Father the idea," he said. "But he only has crucifixes enough for our ground floor windows. By the way, he wants a picture of Jan in case he should turn up in the village."

"There are no existing photographs of Jarmoskowski," Newcliffe said positively. "He never allowed any to be taken. It was a headache to his concert manager."

"That's understandable," Lundgren said. "With his cell radiogens under constant stimulation any picture of him would turn out over-exposed anyhow—probably a total blank. And that in turn would expose Jan."

"Well, that's too bad but it's not irreparable," Foote said. He was glad to be of some use again. He opened Newcliffe's desk and took out a sheet of stationery and a pencil. In ten minutes he had produced a head of Jarmoskowski in three-quarter profile as he had seen him at the piano that last night so many centuries ago. Lundgren studied it.

"To the life," he said. "I'll send this over by messenger. You draw well, Paul."

Bennington laughed. "You're not telling him anything he doesn't know," he said. Nevertheless, Foote thought, there was considerably less animosity in the critic's manner.

"What now?" James asked.

"We wait," Newcliffe said. "Bennington's gun was ruined by that one handmade slug. We can't afford to have our weapons taken out of action. If I know Consolidated they'll have the machine-made jobs here tomorrow. Then we'll have some hope of getting him. Right now he's shown us he's more than a match for us in open country."

The group looked at each other. Some little understanding of what it would mean to wait through nervous days and fear-stalked nights, helpless and inactive, already showed on their faces. But there were necessities before which the demands of merely human feelings were forced to yield.

The conference broke up in silence.

For Foote, as for the rest, that night was instilled with dread, pregnant every instant with terror of the outcry that the next moment might bring. The waning moon, greenish and sickly, reeled over the house through a sky troubled with fulgurous clouds. An insistent wind made distant wolf-howls, shook from the trees soft sounds like the padding of stealthy paws, rattled windows with the scrape of claws trying for a hold.

The atmosphere of the house, hot and stuffy because of the closed windows and reeking of garlic, was stretched to an impossible tautness with waiting. In the empty room next to Foote there was the imagined coming and going of thin ghosts and the crouched expectancy of a turned-down bed—awaiting an occupant who might depress the sheets in a shocking pattern, perhaps regardless of the tiny pitiful glint of the crucifix upon the pillow. Above him, other sleepers turned restlessly, or groaned and started up from chilling nightmares.

The boundary between the real and the unreal had been let down in his mind and in the flickering shadows of the moon and the dark errands of the ghosts there was no way of making any selection. He had entered the cobwebby blackness of the border-land between the human and the demon, where nothing is ever more than half true—or half untruth.

After a while, on the threshold of this darkness, the blasphemous voices of the hidden evil things beyond it began to seep through. The wind, abandoning the trees and gables, whispered and echoed the voices, counting the victims slowly as death stalked through the house.

One.

Two.

Three—closer now!

Four—the fourth sleeper struggled a little. Foote could hear a muffled creak of springs over his head.

Five.

Six—who was Six? Who is next? When?

Seven— Oh, Lord, I'm next . . . I'm next . . . I'm next.

He curled into a ball, trembling. The wind died away and there was silence, tremendous silence. After a long while he uncurled, swearing at himself but not aloud—because he was afraid to hear his own voice. Cut that out, now. Foote, you bloody fool. You're like a kid hiding from the goblins. You're perfectly safe. Lundgren says so.

Mamma says so.

How the heck does Lundgren know?

He's an expert. He wrote a paper. Go ahead, be a kid. Remember your childhood faith in the printed word? All right then. Go to sleep, will you?

There goes that damned counting again.

But after a while his worn-down nerves would be denied no longer. He slept a little but fitfully, falling in his dreams through such deep pits of evil that he awoke fighting the covers and gasping for the vitiated garlic-heavy air. There was a fetid foulness in his mouth and his heart pounded. He threw off the covers and sat up, lighting a cigarette with trembling hands and trying not to see the shadows the flame threw.

He was no longer waiting for the night to end. He had forgotten that there ever was such a thing as daylight, was waiting only for the inevitable growl that would herald the last horror. Thus it was a shock almost beyond bearing to look out the window and see the brightening of dawn over the forest.

After staring incredulously at it for a moment he snubbed out his cigarette in the candlestick—which he had been carrying around the house as if it had grown to him—and collapsed. With a sigh he was instantly in deep and dreamless sleep.

When he finally came to consciousness he was being shaken and Bennington's voice was in his ear. "Get up, man," the critic was saying. No, you needn't reach for the candlestick—everything's okay thus far."

Foote grinned. "It's a pleasure to see a friendly expression on your face, Bennington," he said with a faint glow of general relief.

Bennington looked a little abashed. "I misjudged you," he admitted. "I guess it takes a crisis to bring out what's really in a man so that blunt brains like mine can see it. You don't mind if I continue to dislike your latest abstractions, I trust?"

"That's your function," Foote said cheerfully. "To be a gadfly. Now what's happened?"

"Newcliffe got up early and made the rounds of the traps. We got a good-sized rabbit out of one of them and made a stew—very good—you'll see. The other one was empty but there was blood on it and on the snow. Lundgren isn't up yet but we've saved scrapings for him."

James poked his head around the door jamb, then came in. "Hope it cripples him," he said, dextrously snaffling a cigarette from Foote's shirt pocket. "Pardon me. All the servants have deserted us but the butler, and nobody will bring cigarettes up from the village."

"My, my," said Foote. "Everyone feels so chipper. Boy, I never thought I'd be as glad to see any sunrise as I was today's."

"If you—"

There was a sound outside. It sounded like the world's biggest tea-kettle. Something flitted through the sky, wheeled and came back.

"Cripes," Foote said, shading his eyes. "A big jet job. What's he doing here?"

The plane circled silently, jets cut. It lost flying speed and glided in over the golf course, struck and rolled at breakneck speed straight for the forest. At the last minute the pilot spun to a stop expertly.

"By heaven, I'll bet that's Newcliffe's bullets!"

They pounded downstairs. By the time they reached the front room the pilot was coming in with Newcliffe. A heavy case was slung between them.

Newcliffe pried the case open. Then he sighed. "Look at 'em," he said. "Nice, shiny brass cartridges, and dull-silver heads machined for perfect accuracy—yum, yum. I could just stand here and pet them. Where are you from?"

"Croydon," said the pilot. "If you don't mind, Mr. Newcliffe, the company said I was to collect from you. That's a hundred pounds for the cartridges and five hundred for me."

"Cheap enough. Hold on. I'll write you a check."

Foote whistled. He didn't know whether to be more awed by the trans-Atlantic express service or the vast sum it had cost.

The pilot took the check and shortly thereafter the tea-kettle began to whistle again. From another huge wooden crate Newcliffe was handing out brand-new Brownings.

"Now let him come," he said grimly. "Don't worry about wasting shots—there's a full case of clips. As soon as you see him, blaze away like mad. Use it like a hose if you have to."

"Somebody go wake Chris," Bennington said. "He should have lessons too. Doris, go knock on his door like a good girl."

Doris nodded and went upstairs. "Now this stud here," Newcliffe said, "is the fire-control button. You put it in this position and the gun will fire one shot and reload. Put it here and you have to reload it yourself like any rifle. Put it here and it goes into automatic operation, firing every shell in the clip, one after the other."

"*Thunder!*" James said admiringly. "We could stand off an army."

"Wait a minute—there seem to be two missing."

"Those are all you unpacked," Bennington said.

"Yes but there were two older models of my own. I never used 'em because it didn't seem right to hunt with such a cannon. But I got 'em out last night on account of this trouble."

"Oh," Bennington said with an air of sudden enlightenment. "I thought that thing I had looked odd. I slept with one last night. I think Lundgren has another."

"Where is Lundgren? Doris should have had him up by now. Go see, Bennington, and get that gun."

"Isn't there a lot of recoil?" Foote asked.

"Sure. These are really meant to operate from bipods. Hold the gun at your hip, not your shoulder—what's *that?*"

"Bennington's voice," Foote said, suddenly tense. "Something must be wrong with Doris." The four of them clattered for the stairs.

They found Doris at Bennington's feet in front of Lundgren's open door. Evidently she had fainted without a sound. The critic was in the process of being very sick. On Lundgren's bed lay a crimson horror.

The throat was ripped out and the face and all the soft parts of the body had been eaten away. The right leg had been gnawed in one place all the way to the bone, which gleamed white and polished in the reassuring sunlight.

V

Foote stood in the living room by the piano in the full glare of all the electric lights. He hefted the B. A. R. and surveyed the remainder of his companions, who were standing in a puzzled group before him.

"No," he said, "I don't like that. I don't want you all bunched together. String out in a line, in front of me, so I can see everybody."

He grinned briefly. "Got the drop on you, didn't I? Not a rifle in sight. Of course, there's the big candlestick behind you, Newcliffe, but I can shoot quicker than you can club me." His voice grew ugly. "*And I will*, if you make it necessary. So I would advise everybody—including the women—not to make any sudden moves."

"What is this all about, Paul?" Bennington demanded angrily. "As if things aren't bad enough!"

"You'll see directly. Now line up the way I told you. *Quick!*" He moved the gun suggestively. "And remember what I said about sudden moves. It may be dark outside but I didn't turn on all the lights for nothing."

Quietly the line formed and the eyes that looked at Foote were narrowed with suspicion of madness—or worse.

"Good. Now we can talk comfortably. You see, after what happened to Chris I'm not taking any chances. That was partly his fault and partly mine. But the gods allow no one to err twice in matters like this. He paid a ghastly price for his second error—a price I don't intend to pay or to see anyone else here pay."

"Would you honor us with an explanation of this error?" Newcliffe said icily.

"Yes. I don't blame you for being angry, Tom, since I'm your guest. But you see I'm forced to treat you all alike for the moment. I was fond of Lundgren."

There was silence for a moment, then a thin indrawing of breath from Bennington. "You were fond—my Lord!" he whispered raggedly. "What do you mean?"

"I mean that Lundgren was not killed by Jarmoskowski," Foote said coldly and deliberately. "He was killed by someone else. Another werewolf. *One who is standing before me at this moment.*"

A concerted gasp went up.

"Surprised? But it's true. The error for which Chris paid so dearly, which I made too, was this—we forgot to examine everybody for injuries after the encounter with Jan. We forgot one of the cardinal laws of lycanthropy.

"A man who survives being bitten by a werewolf himself becomes a werewolf. That's how the disease is passed on. The pinearin in the saliva gets in the bloodstream, stimulates the victim's own pineal gland and—"

"But nobody was bitten, Paul," Doris said in a reasonable voice.

"Somebody was, lightly. None of you but Chris and myself could know about the bite-infection. Evidently somebody got a few small scratches, didn't think them worth mentioning, put iodine on them and forgot them—until it was too late."

There were slow movements in the line—heads turning surreptitiously, eyes glancing nervously at persons to left and right.

"Once the attack occurred," Foote said relentlessly, "Chris was the logical first victim. The expert, hence the most dangerous enemy. I wish I had thought of this before lunch. I might have seen which one of you was uninterested in his lunch. In any event Chris's safeguards against letting Jarmoskowski in also keep you from getting out. You won't leave this room ever again."

He gritted his teeth and brought himself back into control. "All right," he said. "This is the showdown. Everybody hold up both hands in plain view."

Almost instantly there was a ravening wolf in the room.

Only Foote, who could see at a glance the order of the people in the line, knew who it was. The frightful tragedy of it struck him such a blow that the gun dropped nervelessly from his hands. He wept convulsively. The monster lunged for his throat like a reddish projectile.

Newcliffe's hand darted back, grasped the candlestick. He leapt forward in a swift, catlike motion and brought it down across the werewolf's side. Ribs burst with a horrible splintering sound. The beast spun, snarling with agony. Newcliffe hit it again across the backbone. It fell, screaming, fangs slashing the air.

Three times, with concentrated viciousness, Newcliffe struck at its head. Then it cried out once in an almost familiar voice—and died.

Slowly the cells of its body groped back toward their natural positions. The awful crawling metamorphosis was never completed. But the hairy-haunched thing with the crushed skull which sprawled at Newcliffe's feet was recognizable.

It had been Caroline Newcliffe.

There was a frozen tableau of wax figures in the yellow lamplight. Tears coursed along Foote's palms, dropped from under them, fell silently to the carpet. After a while he dropped his hands. Bennington's face was gray with illness but rigidly expressionless like a granite statue. James's back was against the wall. He watched the anomalous corpse as if waiting for some new movement.

As for Newcliffe he had no expression at all. He merely stood where he was, the bloody candlestick held loosely in a limp hand.

His eyes were quite empty.

After a moment Doris walked over to Newcliffe and touched his shoulder compassionately. The contact seemed to let something out of him. He shrank visibly into himself, shoulders slumping, his whole body withering visibly into a dry husk.

The candlestick thumped against the floor, rocked wildly on its base, toppled across the body. As it struck, Foote's cigarette butt, which had somehow remained in it all day, tumbled out and rolled crazily along the carpet.

"Tom," Doris said softly. "Come away now. There's nothing you can do."

"Blood," he said emptily. "She had a cut. On her hand. Handled the scrapings from the trap—my trap. I did it. Just a breadknife cut from making canapes. I did it."

"No you didn't, Tom. Let's get some rest." She took his hand. He followed her obediently, stumbling a little as his blood-spattered shoes scuffed over the thick rug, his breath expelling from his lungs with a soft whisper. The two disappeared up the stairs.

Bennington bolted for the kitchen sink.

Foote sat down on the piano bench, his worn face taut with dried tears, and picked at the dusty keys. The lightly struck notes aroused James. He crossed the room and looked down at Foote.

"You did well," the novelist said shakily. "Don't condemn yourself, Paul."

Foote nodded. He felt—nothing. Nothing at all.

"The body?"

"Yes. I suppose so." He got up from the bench. Together they carried the tragic corpse out through the house to the greenhouse.

"We should leave her here," Foote said with a faint return of his old irony. "Here's where the wolfsbane bloomed and started the whole business."

"Poetic justice, I suppose," James said. "But I don't think it's wise. Tom has a toolshed at the other end that isn't steam heated. It should be cold enough."

Gently they placed the body on the cement floor, laying some gunnysacks under it. "In the morning," Foote said, "we can have someone come for her."

"How about legal trouble?" James said frowning. "Here's a woman whose skull has been crushed with a blunt instrument—"

"I think I can get Lundgren's priest to help us there," Foote said somberly. "They have some authority to make death certificates in this state. Besides, James—is that a woman? Inarguably it isn't Caroline."

James looked sidewise at the hairy, contorted haunches. "Yes. It's—legally it's nothing. I see your point."

Together they went back into the house. "Jarmoskowski?" James said.

"Not tonight. We're all too tired and sick. And we do seem to be safe enough in here. Chris saw to that."

Whatever James had to say in reply was lost in the roar of an automatic rifle somewhere over their heads, exhausting its shots in a quick stream. After a moment there was another burst of ten. Footsteps echoed. Then Bennington came bouncing down the stairs.

"Watch out tonight," he panted. "He's around. I saw him come out of the woods in wolf form. I emptied the clip but missed and he went back again. I sprayed another ten rounds around where I saw him go in but I don't think I hit him."

"Where were you shooting from?"

"The top of the tower." His face was very grim. "Went up for a last look around and there he was. I hope he comes tonight, I want to be the one who kills him."

"How is Tom?"

"Bad. Doesn't seem to know where he is or what he's doing. Well, good night. Keep your eyes peeled."

James nodded and followed him upstairs. Foote remained in the empty room a few minutes longer, looking thoughtfully at the splotch of blood on the priceless Persian carpet. Then he felt of his face and throat, looked at his hands, arms and legs, inside his shirt. Not so much as a scratch—Tom had seen to that.

So hard not to hate these afflicted people, so impossible to remember that lycanthropy was a disease like any other! Caroline, like the man in *The Red Laugh*, had been noble-hearted and gentle and had wished no one evil. Yet—

Maybe God is on the side of the werewolves.

The blasphemy of an exhausted mind. Yet he could not put it from him. Suppose Jarmoskowski should conquer his compulsion and lie out of sight until the seven days were over. Then he could disappear. It was a big country. It would not be necessary for him to kill all his victims—just those he actually needed for food. But he could nip a good many. Every other one, say.

And from wherever he lived the circle of lycanthropy would grow and widen and engulf—

Maybe God had decided that proper humans had made a mess of running the world, had decided to give the *nosferatu,* the undead, a chance at it. Perhaps the human race was on the threshold of that darkness into which he had looked throughout last night.

He ground his teeth and made an exasperated noise. Shock and exhaustion would drive him as crazy as Newcliffe if he kept this up.

He went around the room, making sure that all the windows were tightly closed and the crucifixes in place, turning out the lights as he went. The garlic was getting rancid—it smelled like mercaptan—but he was too tired to replace it. He clicked out the last light, picked up the candlestick and went out into the hall.

As he passed Doris's room, he noticed that the door was ajar. Inside, two voices murmured. Remembering what he had heard before he stopped to eavesdrop.

It was years later that Foote found out exactly what had happened at the very beginning. Doris, physically exhausted by the hideous events of the day, emotionally drained by tending the childlike Newcliffe, feeding him from a spoon and seeing him into bed, had fallen asleep almost immediately.

It was a sleep dreamless except for a vague, dull undercurrent of despair. When the light tapping against the window-panes finally reached her consciousness she had no idea how long she had slumbered.

She struggled to a sitting position and forced her eyelids up. Across the room the moonlight, gleaming in patches against the rotting snow outside, glared through the window. Silhouetted against it was a tall human figure. She could not see its face but there was no mistaking the red glint of the eyes. She clutched for the rifle and brought it awkwardly into position.

Jarmoskowski did not dodge. He moved his arms out a little way away from his body, palms forward in a gesture that looked almost supplicating, and waited. Indecisively she lowered the gun again. Was he inviting death?

As she lowered the weapon she saw that the stud was in the continuous-fire position and carefully she shifted it to *repeat.* She was afraid of the recoil Newcliffe had mentioned, felt surer of her target if she could throw one shot at a time at it.

Jarmoskowski tapped again and motioned with his finger. Reasoning that he would come in if he were able, she took time out to get into her housecoat. Then, holding her finger against the trigger, she went to the window. It was closed tightly and a crucifix, suspended from a silk thread, hung exactly in the center of it. She checked it, and then opened one of the small panes directly above Jarmoskowski's head.

"Hello, Doris," he said softly.

"Hello." She was more uncertain than afraid. Was this actually happening or just the recurrent nightmare? "What do you want? I should shoot you. Can you tell me why I shouldn't?"

"Yes I can. Otherwise I wouldn't have risked exposing myself. That's a nasty-looking weapon."

"There are ten silver bullets in it."

"I know it. I've seen Brownings before. I would be a good target for you too, so I have no hope of escape—my nostrils are full of rosemary." He smiled ruefully. "And Lundgren and Caroline are dead and I am responsible. I deserve to die. That is why I am here."

"You'll get your wish, Jan," she said. "You have some other reason, I know. I will back my wits against yours. I want to ask you questions."

"Ask."

"You have your evening clothes on. Paul said they changed with you. How is that possible?"

"But a wolf has clothes," Jarmoskowski said. "He is not naked like a man. And surely Chris must have spoken of the effect of the pineal upon the cell radiogens. These little bodies act upon any organic matter, including wool or cotton. When I change my clothes change with me. I can hardly say how, for it is in the blood, like musicianship. Either you can or you can't. But they change."

His voice took on a darkly somber tone. "Lundgren was right throughout. This werewolfery is now nothing but a disease. It is not prosurvival. Long ago there must have been a number of mutations which brought the pineal gland into use.

"None of them survived but the werewolves and these are dying. Someday the pineal will come into better use and all men will be able to modify their forms without this terrible madness as a penalty. For us, the lycanthropes, the failures, nothing is left.

"It is not good for a man to wander from country to country, knowing that he is a monster to his fellow-men and cursed eternally by his God—if he can claim a God. I went through Europe, playing the piano and giving pleasure, meeting people, making friends— and always, sooner or later, there were whisperings, and strange looks and dawning horror.

"And whether I was hunted down for the beast I was or whether there was merely a vague gradually growing revulsion, they drove me out. Hatred, silver bullets, crucifixes—they are all the same in the end.

"Sometimes, I could spend several months without incident in some one place and my life would take on a veneer of normality. I could attend to my music and have people about me that I liked and be—human. Then the wolfsbane bloomed and the pollen freighted the air and when the moon shone down on that flower my blood surged with the thing I have within me.

"And then I made apologies to my friends and went north to Sweden, where Lundgren was and where spring was much later. I loved him and I think he missed the truth about me until night before last. I was careful.

"Once or twice I did *not* go north and then the people who had been my friends would be hammering silver behind my back and waiting for me in dark corners. After years of this few places in Europe would have me. With my reputation as a musician spread darker rumors.

"Towns I had never visited closed their gates to me without a word. Concert halls were booked up too many months in advance for me to use them, inns and hotels were filled indefinitely, people were too busy to talk to me, to listen to my playing, to write me any letters.

"I have been in love. That—I cannot describe.

"And then I came to this country. Here no one believes in the werewolf. I sought scientific help—not from Lundgren, because I was afraid I should do him some harm. But here I thought someone would know enough to deal with what I had become.

"It was not so. The primitive hatred of my kind lies at the heart of the human as it lies at the heart of the dog. There was no help for me.

"I am here to ask for an end to it."

Slow tears rolled over Doris's cheeks. The voice faded away indefinitely. It did not seem to end at all but rather to retreat into some limbo where men could not hear it. Jarmoskowski stood silently in the moonlight, his eyes burning bloodily, a somber sullen scarlet.

Doris said, "Jan—Jan, I am sorry, I am so sorry. What can I do?"

"Shoot."

"I—can't!"

"Please, Doris."

The girl was crying uncontrollably. "Jan, don't. I can't. You know I can't. Go away, *please* go away."

Jarmoskowski said, "Then come with me, Doris. Open the window and come with me."

"Where?"

"Does it matter? You have denied me the death I ask. Would you deny me this last desperate love, would you deny your own love, your own last and deepest desire? It is too late now, too late for you to pretend revulsion. Come with me."

He held out his hands.

"Say goodbye," he said. "Goodbye to these self-righteous humans. I will give you of my blood and we will range the world, wild and uncontrollable, the last of our race. They will remember us, I promise you."

"Jan—"

"I am here. Come now."

Like a somnambulist she swung the panes out. Jarmoskowski did not move but looked first at her, then at the crucifix. She lifted one end of the thread and let the little thing tinkle to the floor.

"After us there shall be no darkness comparable to our darkness," Jarmoskowski said. "Let them rest—let the world rest."

He sprang into the room with so sudden, so feral a motion that he seemed hardly to have moved at all. From the doorway the automatic rifle yammered with demoniac ferocity. The impact of the slugs hurled Jarmoskowski back against the wall. Foote lowered the smoking muzzle and took one step into the room.

"Too late, Jan," he said stonily.

Doris wailed like a little girl awakened from a dream. Jarmoskowski's lips moved but there was not enough left of his lungs. The effort to speak brought a bloody froth to his mouth. He stood for an instant, stretched out a hand toward the girl. Then the fingers clenched convulsively and the long body folded.

He smiled, put aside that last of all his purposes and died.

The Loom of Darkness

Jack Vance

Jack Vance's work combines elements of the mystery, fantasy, and science fiction genres into a adventure-filled style that is all his own. His strengths lie in creating detailed, imaginative, yet plausible societies, complete with a noticeable lack of altruism. Along the way to garnering accolades such as the Edgar, Hugo, and Nebula awards, he has examined such far ranging topics as the power of language and the concept and price of freedom and independence. Notable novels include The Languages of Pao, The Dragon Masters, *and* To Live Forever.

THROUGH THE DIM FOREST CAME LIANE THE WAYFARER, PASSING ALONG the shadowed glades with a prancing light-footed gait. He whistled, he caroled, he was plainly in high spirits. Around his finger he twirled a bit of wrought bronze—a circlet graved with angular crabbed characters, now stained black.

By excellent chance he had found it, banded around the root of an ancient yew. Hacking it free, he had seen the characters on the inner surface—rude forceful symbols, doubtless the cast of a powerful antique rune. . . . Best take it to a magician and have it tested for sorcery.

Liane made a wry mouth. There were objections to the course. Sometimes it seemed as if all living creatures conspired to exasperate him. Only this morning, the spice merchant—what a tumult he had made dying! How carelessly he had spewed blood on Liane's cockscomb sandals! Still, thought Liane, every unpleasantness carried with it compensation. While digging the grave he had found the bronze ring.

And Liane's spirits soared; he laughed in pure joy. He bounded, he leapt. His green cape flapped behind him, the red feather in his cap winked and blinked. . . . But still—Liane slowed his step—he was no whit closer to the mystery of the magic, if magic the ring possessed.

Experiment, that was the word!

He stopped where the ruby sunlight slanted down without

hindrance from the high foliage, examined the ring, traced the glyphs with his fingernail. He peered through. A faint film, a flicker? He held it at arm's length. It was clearly a coronet. He whipped off his cap, set the band on his brow, rolled his great golden eyes, preened himself. . . . Odd. It slipped down on his ears. It tipped across his eyes. Darkness. Frantically Liane clawed it off. . . . A bronze ring, a hand's-breadth in diameter. Queer.

He tried again. It slipped down over his head, his shoulders. His head was in the darkness of a strange separate space. Looking down, he saw the level of the outside light dropping as he dropped the ring.

Slowly down . . . Now it was around his ankles—and in sudden panic, Liane snatched the ring up over his body, emerged blinking into the maroon light of the forest.

He saw a blue-white, green-white flicker against the foliage. It was a Twk-man, mounted on a dragon-fly, and light glinted from the dragon-fly's wings.

Liane called sharply, "Here, sir! Here, sir!"

The Twk-man perched his mount on a twig. "Well, Liane, what do you wish?"

"Watch now, and remember what you see." Liane pulled the ring over his head, dropped it to his feet, lifted it back. He looked up to the Twk-man, who was chewing a leaf. "And what did you see?"

"I saw Liane vanish from mortal sight—except for the red curled toes of his sandals. All else was as air."

"Ha!" cried Liane. "Think of it! Have you ever seen the like?"

The Twk-man asked carelessly, "Do you have salt? I would have salt."

Liane cut his exultations short, eyed the Twk-man closely.

"What news do you bring me?"

"Three erbs killed Florejin the Dream-builder, and burst all his bubbles. The air above the manse was colored for many minutes with the flitting fragments."

"A gram."

"Lord Kandive the Golden has built a barge of carven mo-wood ten lengths high, and it floats on the River Scaum for the Regatta, full of treasure."

"Two grams."

"A golden witch named Lith has come to live on Thamber Meadow. She is quiet and very beautiful."

"Three grams."

"Enough," said the Twk-man, and leaned forward to watch while Liane weighed out the salt in a tiny balance. He packed it in small panniers hanging on each side of the ribbed thorax, then twitched the insect into the air and flicked off through the forest vaults.

Once more Liane tried his bronze ring, and this time brought it entirely past his feet, stepped out of it and brought the ring up into the darkness beside him. What a wonderful sanctuary! A hole whose opening could be hidden inside the hole itself! Down with the ring to his feet, step through, bring it up his slender frame and over his shoulders, out into the forest with a small bronze ring in his hand.

Ho! and off to Thamber Meadow to see the beautiful golden witch.

Her hut was a simple affair of woven reeds—a low dome with two round windows and a low door. He saw Lith at the pond bare-legged among the water shoots, catching frogs for her supper. A white kirtle was gathered up tight around her thighs; stock-still she stood and the dark water rippled rings away from her slender knees.

She was more beautiful than Liane could have imagined, as if one of Florejin's wasted bubbles had burst here on the water. Her skin was pale creamed stirred gold, her hair a denser, wetter gold. Her eyes were like Liane's own, great golden orbs, and hers were wide apart, tilted slightly.

Liane strode forward and planted himself on the bank.

She looked up startled, her ripe mouth half-open.

"Behold, golden witch, here is Liane. He has come to welcome you to Thamber; and he offers you his friendship, his love. . . ."

Lith bent, scooped a handful of slime from the bank and flung it into his face.

Shouting the most violent curses, Liane wiped his eyes free, but the door to the hut had slammed shut.

Liane strode to the door and pounded it with his fist.

"Open and show your witch's face, or I burn the hut!"

The door opened, and the girl looked forth, smiling. "What now?"

Liane entered the hut and lunged for the girl, but twenty thin shafts darted out, twenty points pricking his chest. He halted, eyebrows raised, mouth twitching.

"Down, steel," said Lith. The blades snapped from view. "So easily could I seek your vitality," said Lith, "had I willed."

Liane frowned and rubbed his chin as if pondering. "You understand," he said earnestly, "what a witless thing you do. Liane is feared by those who fear fear, loved by those who love love. And you—" his eyes swam the golden glory of her body "—you are ripe as a sweet fruit, you are eager, you glisten and tremble with love. You please Liane, and he will spend much warmness on you."

"No, no," said Lith, with a slow smile. "You are too hasty."

Liane looked at her in surprise. "Indeed?"

"I am Lith," said she. "I am what you say I am. I ferment, I burn, I seethe. Yet I may have no lover but him who has served me. He must be brave, swift, cunning."

"I am he," said Liane. He chewed at his lip. "It is not usually thus. I detest this indecision." He took a step forward. "Come, let us—"

She backed away. "No, no. You forget. How have you served me, how have you gained the right to my love?"

"Absurdity!" stormed Liane. "Look at me! Note my perfect grace, the beauty of my form and feature, my great eyes, as golden as your own, my manifest will and power. . . . It is you who should serve me. That is how I will have it." He sank upon a low divan. "Woman, give me wine."

She shook her head. "In my small domed hut I cannot be forced. Perhaps outside on Thamber Meadow—but in here, among my blue and red tassels, with twenty blades of steel at my call, you must obey me. . . . So choose. Either arise and go, never to return, or else agree to serve me on one small mission, and then have me and all my ardor."

Liane sat straight and stiff. An odd creature, the golden witch. But, indeed, she was worth some exertion, and he would make her pay for her impudence.

"Very well, then," he said blandly. "I will serve you. What do you wish? Jewels? I can suffocate you in pearls, blind you with diamonds. I have two emeralds the size of your fist, and they are green oceans, where the gaze is trapped and wanders forever among vertical green prisms. . . ."

"No, no jewels—"

"An enemy, perhaps. Ah, so simple. Liane will kill you ten men. Two steps forward, thrust—*thus!*" He lunged. "And souls go thrilling up like bubbles in a beaker of mead."

"No. I want no killing."

He sat back, frowning. "What, then?"

She stepped to the back of the room and pulled at a drape. It swung aside, displaying a golden tapestry. The scene was a valley bounded by two steep mountains, a broad valley where a placid river ran, past a quiet village and so into a grove of trees. Golden was the river, golden the mountains, golden the trees—golds so various, so rich, so subtle that the effect was like a many-colored landscape. But the tapestry had been rudely hacked in half.

Liane was entranced. "Exquisite, exquisite . . ."

Lith said, "It is the Magic Valley of Ariventa so depicted. The other half has been stolen from me, and its recovery is the service I wish of you."

"Where is the other half?" demanded Liane. "Who is the dastard?"

Now she watched him closely. "Have you ever heard of Chun? Chun the Unavoidable?"

Liane considered. "No."

"He stole the half to my tapestry, and hung it in a marble hall, and this half is in the ruins to the north of Kaiin."

"Ha!" muttered Liane.

"The hall is by the Place of Whispers, and is marked by a leaning column with a black medallion of a phoenix and a two-headed lizard."

"I go," said Liane. He rose. "One day to Kaiin, one day to steal, one day to return. Three days."

Lith followed him to the door. "Beware of Chun the Unavoidable," she whispered.

And Liane strode away whistling, the red feather bobbing in his green cap. Lith watched him, then turned and slowly approached the golden tapestry. "Golden Ariventa," she whispered, "my heart cries and hurts with longing for you. . . ."

The Derna is a swifter, thinner river than the Scaum, its bosomy sister to the south. And where the Scaum wallows through a broad dale, purple with horse-blossom, pocked white and gray with crumbling castles, the Derna has sheered a steep canyon, overhung by forested bluffs.

An ancient flint road long ago followed the course of the Derna, but now the exaggeration of the meandering has cut into the pavement, so that Liane, treading the road to Kaiin, was occasionally forced to leave the road and make a detour through banks of thorn and the tube-grass which whistled in the breeze.

The red sun, drifting across the universe like an old man creeping to his death-bed, hung low to the horizon when Liane breasted Porphiron Scar, looked across white-walled Kaiin and the blue bay of Sanreale beyond.

Directly below was the market-place, a medley of stalls selling fruits, slabs of pale meat, molluscs from the slime banks, dull flagons of wine. And the quiet people of Kaiin moved among the stalls, buying their sustenance, carrying it loosely to their stone chambers.

Beyond the market-place rose a bank of ruined columns, like broken teeth—legs to the arena built two hundred feet from the ground by Mad King Shin; beyond, in a grove of bay trees, the glassy dome of the palace was visible, where Kandive the Golden ruled Kaiin and as much of Ascolais as one could see from a vantage on Porphiron Scar.

The Derna, no longer a flow of clear water, poured through a network of dank canals and subterranean tubes, and finally seeped past rotting wharves into the Bay of Sanreale.

A bed for the night, thought Liane; then to his business in the morning.

He leapt down the zig-zag steps—back, forth, back, forth—and came into the market-place. And now he put on a grave demeanor. Liane the Wayfarer was not unknown in Kaiin, and many were ill-minded enough to work him harm.

He moved sedately in the shade of the Pannone Wall, turned through a narrow cobbled street, bordered by old wooden houses glowing the rich brown of old stump-water in the rays of the setting sun, and so came to a small square and the high stone face of the Magician's Inn.

The host, a small fat man, sad of eye, with a small fat nose the identical shape of his body, was scraping ashes from the hearth. He straightened his back and hurried behind the counter of his little alcove.

Liane said, "A chamber, well-aired, and a supper of mushrooms, wine and oysters."

The innkeeper bowed humbly.

"Indeed, sir—and how will you pay?"

Liane flung down a leather sack, taken this very morning. The innkeeper raised his eyebrows in pleasure at the fragrance.

"The ground buds of the spase-bush, brought from a far land," said Liane.

"Excellent, excellent . . . Your chamber, sir, and your supper at once."

As Liane ate, several other guests of the house appeared and sat before the fire with wine, and the talk grew large, and dwelt on wizards of the past and the great days of magic.

"Great Phandaal knew a lore now forgot," said one old man with hair dyed orange. "He tied white and black strings to the legs of sparrows and sent them veering to his direction. And where they wove their magic woof, great trees appeared, laden with flowers, fruits, nuts, or bulbs of rare liqueurs. It is said that thus he wove Great Da Forest on the shores of Sanra Water."

"Ha," said a dour man in a garment of dark blue, brown and black, "this I can do." He brought forth a bit of string, flicked it, whirled it, spoke a quiet word, and the vitality of the pattern fused the string into a tongue of red and yellow fire, which danced, curled, darted back and forth along the table till the dour man killed it with a gesture.

"And this I can do," said a hooded figure in a black cape sprinkled with silver circles. He brought forth a small tray, laid it on the table and sprinkled therein a pinch of ashes from the hearth. He brought forth a whistle and blew a clear tone, and up from the tray came glittering motes, flashing the prismatic colors red, blue, green, yellow. They floated up a foot and burst in coruscations of brilliant colors, each a beautiful star-shaped pattern, and each burst sounded a tiny repetition of the original tone—the clearest, purest sound in the world. The motes became fewer, the magician blew a different tone, and again the motes floated up to burst in glorious ornamental spangles. Another time—another swarm of motes. At last the magician replaced his whistle, wiped off the tray, tucked it inside his cloak and lapsed back to silence.

Now the other wizards surged forward, and soon the air above the table swarmed with visions, quivered with spells. One showed the group nine new colors of ineffable charm and radiance; another caused a mouth to form on the landlord's forehead and revile the crowd, much to the landlord's discomfiture, since it was his own voice. Another displayed a green glass bottle from which the face of a demon peered and grimaced; another a ball of pure crystal which rolled back and forward to the command of the sorcerer who owned it, and who claimed it to be an earring of the fabled master Sankaferrin.

Liane had attentively watched all, crowing in delight at the bottled imp, and trying to cozen the obedient crystal from its owner, without success.

And Liane became pettish, complaining that the world was full of rock-hearted men, but the sorcerer with the crystal earring remained indifferent, and even when Liane spread out twelve packets of rare spice he refused to part with his toy.

Liane pleaded, "I wish only to please the witch Lith."

"Please her with the spice, then."

Liane said ingenuously, "Indeed, she has but one wish, a bit of tapestry which I must steal from Chun the Unavoidable."

And he looked from face to suddenly silent face.

"What causes such immediate sobriety? Ho, Landlord, more wine!"

The sorcerer with the earring said, "If the floor swam ankle-deep with wine—the rich red wine of Tanvilkat—the leaden print of that name would still ride the air."

"Ha," laughed Liane, "let only a taste of that wine pass your lips, and the fumes would erase all memory."

"See his eyes," came a whisper. "Great and golden."

"And quick to see," spoke Liane. "And these legs—quick to run, fleet as starlight on the waves. And this arm—quick to stab with steel. And my magic—which will set me to a refuge that is out of all cognizance." He gulped wine from a beaker. "Now behold. This is magic from antique days." He set the bronze band over his head, stepped through, brought it up inside the darkness. When he deemed that sufficient time had elapsed, he stepped through once more.

The fire glowed, the landlord stood in his alcove, Liane's wine was at hand. But of the assembled magicians, there was no trace.

Liane looked about in puzzlement. "And where are my wizardly friends?"

The landlord turned his head: "They took to their chambers; the name you spoke weighed on their souls."

And Liane drank his wine in frowning silence.

Next morning he left the inn and picked a roundabout way to the Old Town—a gray wilderness of tumbled pillars, weathered blocks of sandstone, slumped pediments with crumbled inscriptions, flagged terraces overgrown with rusty moss. Lizards, snakes, insects crawled the ruins; no other life did he see.

Threading a way through the rubble, he almost stumbled on a corpse—the body of a youth, one who stared at the sky with empty eye-sockets.

Liane felt a presence. He leapt back, rapier half-bared. A stooped old man stood watching him. He spoke in a feeble, quavering voice: "And what will you have in the Old Town?"

Liane replaced his rapier. "I seek the Place of Whispers. Perhaps you will direct me."

The old man made a croaking sound at the back of his throat. "Another? Another? When will it cease? . . ." He motioned to the corpse. "This one came yesterday seeking the Place of Whispers. He would steal from Chun the Unavoidable. See him now." He turned away. "Come with me." He disappeared over a tumble of rock.

Liane followed. The old man stood by another corpse with eye-sockets bereft and bloody. "This one came four days ago, and he met Chun the Unavoidable. . . . And over there behind the arch is still another, a great warrior in cloison armor. And there—and there—" he pointed, pointed. "And there—and there—like crushed flies."

He turned his watery blue gaze back to Liane. "Return, young man, return—lest your body lie here in its green cloak to rot on the flagstones."

Liane drew his rapier and flourished it. "I am Liane the Wayfarer; let them who offend me have fear. And where is the Place of Whispers?"

"If you must know," said the old man, "it is beyond that broken obelisk. But you go to your peril."

"I am Liane the Wayfarer. Peril goes with me."

The old man stood like a piece of weathered statuary as Liane strode off.

And Liane asked himself, suppose this old man were an agent of Chun, and at this minute were on his way to warn him? . . . Best to take all precautions. He leapt up on a high entablature and ran crouching back to where he had left the ancient.

Here he came, muttering to himself, leaning on his staff. Liane dropped a block of granite as large as his head. A thud, a croak, a gasp—and Liane went his way.

He strode past the broken obelisk, into a wide court—the Place of Whispers. Directly opposite was a long wide hall, marked by a leaning column with a big black medallion, the sign of a phoenix and a two-headed lizard.

Liane merged himself with the shadow of a wall, and stood watching like a wolf, alert for any flicker of motion.

All was quiet. The sunlight invested the ruins with dreary splendor. To all sides, as far as the eye could reach, was broken stone, a wasteland leached by a thousand rains until now the sense of man had departed and the stone was one with the natural earth.

The sun moved across the dark-blue sky. Liane presently stole from his vantage-point and circled the hall. No sight nor sign did he see.

He approached the building from the rear and pressed his ear to the stone. It was dead, without vibration. Around the side—watching up, down, to all sides; a breach in the wall. Liane peered inside. At the back hung half a golden tapestry. Otherwise the hall was empty.

Liane looked up, down, this side, that. There was nothing in sight. He continued around the hall.

He came to another broken place. He looked within. To the rear hung the golden tapestry. Nothing else, to right or left, no sight or sound.

Liane continued to the front of the hall and sought into the eaves; dead as dust.

He had a clear view of the room. Bare, barren, except for the bit of golden tapestry.

Liane entered, striding with long soft steps. He halted in the middle of the floor. Light came to him from all sides except the rear wall. There were a dozen openings from which to flee and no sound except the dull thudding of his heart.

He took two steps forward. The tapestry was almost at his fingertips.

He stepped forward and swiftly jerked the tapestry down from the wall.

And behind was Chun the Unavoidable.

Liane screamed. He turned on paralyzed legs and they were leaden, like legs in a dream which refused to run.

Chun dropped out of the wall and advanced. Over his shiny black back he wore a robe of eyeballs threaded on silk.

Liane was running, fleetly now. He sprang, he soared. The tips of his toes scarcely touched the ground. Out the hall, across the square, into the wilderness of broken statues and fallen columns. And behind came Chun, running like a dog.

Liane sped along the crest of a wall and sprang a great gap to a shattered fountain. Behind came Chun.

Liane darted up a narrow alley, climbed over a pile of refuse, over a roof, down into a court. Behind came Chun.

Liane sped down a wide avenue lined with a few stunted old cypress trees, and he heard Chun close at his heels. He turned into an archway, pulled his bronze ring over his head, down to his feet. He stepped through, brought the ring up inside the darkness. Sanctuary. He was alone in a dark magic space, vanished from earthly gaze and knowledge. Brooding silence, dead space . . .

He felt a stir behind him, a breath of air. At his elbow a voice said, "I am Chun the Unavoidable."

Lith sat on her couch near the candles, weaving a cap from frogskins. The door to her hut was barred, the windows shuttered. Outside, Thamber Meadow dwelled in darkness.

A scrape at her door, a creak as the lock was tested. Lith became rigid and stared at the door.

A voice said, "Tonight, O Lith, tonight it is two long bright threads for you. Two because the eyes were so great, so large, so golden. . . ."

Lith sat quiet. She waited an hour; then, creeping to the door, she listened. The sense of presence was absent. A frog croaked nearby.

She eased the door ajar, found the threads and closed the door. She ran to her golden tapestry and fitted the threads into the ravelled warp.

And she stared at the golden valley, sick with longing for Ariventa, and tears blurred out the peaceful river, the quiet golden forest. "The cloth slowly grows wider. . . . One day it will be done, and I will come home. . . ."

The Man Who Sold Rope to the Gnoles

Margaret St. Clair

Margaret St. Clair was known for her novels of distant futures both adventurous and beautiful. Particularly noteworthy are Vulcan's Dolls *and* The Shadow People. *Before she became a writer, she attended college at the University of California and worked in horticulture for several years.*

THE GNOLES HAVE A BAD REPUTATION, AND MORTENSEN WAS QUITE AWARE of this. But he reasoned, correctly enough, that cordage must be something for which the gnoles had a long unsatisfied want, and he saw no reason why he should not be the one to sell it to them. What a triumph such a sale would be! The district sales manager might single out Mortensen for special mention at the annual sales-force dinner. It would help his sales quota enormously. And, after all, it was none of his business what the gnoles used cordage for.

Mortensen decided to call on the gnoles on Thursday morning. On Wednesday night he went through his *Manual of Modern Salesmanship,* underscoring things.

"The mental states through which the mind passes in making a purchase," he read, "have been catalogued as; 1) arousal of interest 2) increase of knowledge 3) adjustment to needs ..." There were seven mental states listed, and Mortensen underscored all of them. Then he went back and double-scored No. 1, arousal of interest, No. 4, appreciation of suitability, and No. 7, decision to purchase. He turned the page.

"Two qualities are of exceptional importance to a salesman," he read. "They are adaptability and knowledge of merchandise." Mortensen underlined the qualities. "Other highly desirable attributes are physical fitness, a high ethical standard, charm of manner, a dogged persistence, and unfailing courtesy." Mortensen underlined these too. But he read on to the end of the paragraph without underscoring anything more, and it may be that his failure to put "tact and keen power of observation" on a footing with the other attributes of a salesman was responsible for what happened to him.

The gnoles live on the very edge of Terra Cognita, on the far side of a wood which all authorities unite in describing as dubious. Their house is narrow and high, in architecture a blend of Victorian Gothic and Swiss chalet. Though the house needs paint, it is kept in good repair. Thither on Thursday morning, sample case in hand, Mortensen took his way.

No path leads to the house of the gnoles, and it is always dark in that dubious wood. But Mortensen, remembering what he had learned at his mother's knee concerning the odor of gnoles, found the house quite easily. For a moment he stood hesitating before it. His lips moved as he repeated, "Good morning, I have come to supply your cordage requirements," to himself. The words were the beginning of his sales talk. Then he went up and rapped on the door.

The gnoles were watching him through holes they had bored in the trunks of trees; it is an artful custom of theirs to which the prime authority on gnoles attests. Mortensen's knock almost threw them into confusion, it was so long since anyone had knocked at their door. Then the senior gnole, the one who never leaves the house, went flitting up from the cellars and opened it.

The senior gnole is a little like a Jerusalem artichoke made of India rubber, and he has small red eyes which are faceted in the same way that gemstones are. Mortensen had been expecting something unusual, and when the gnole opened the door he bowed politely, took off his hat, and smiled. He had got past the sentence about cordage requirements and into an enumeration of the different types of cordage his firm manufactured when the gnole, by turning his head to the side, showed him that he had no ears. Nor was there anything on his head which could take their place in the conduction of sound. Then the gnole opened his little fanged mouth and let Mortensen look at his narrow, ribbony tongue. As a tongue it was no more fit for human speech than was a serpent's. Judging from his appearance, the gnole could not safely be assigned to any of the four physio-characterological types mentioned in the *Manual;* and for the first time Mortensen felt a definite qualm.

Nonetheless, he followed the gnole unhesitatingly when the creature motioned him within. Adaptability, he told himself, adaptability must be his watchword. Enough adaptability, and his knees might even lose their tendency to shakiness.

It was the parlor the gnole led him to. Mortensen's eyes widened as he looked around it. There were whatnots in the corners, and cabinets of curiosities, and on the fretwork table an album with gilded hasps; who knows whose pictures were in it? All around the walls in brackets, where in lesser houses the people display ornamental plates, were emeralds as big as your head. The gnoles set great store by their emeralds. All the light in the dim room came from them.

Mortensen went through the phrases of his sales talk mentally. It distressed him that that was the only way he could go through them. Still, adaptability! The gnole's interest was already aroused, or he would never have asked Mortensen into the parlor; and as soon as the gnole saw the various cordages the sample case contained he would no doubt proceed of his own accord through "appreciation of suitability" to "desire to possess."

Mortensen sat down in the chair the gnole indicated and opened his sample case. He got out henequen cable-laid rope, an assortment of ply and yarn goods, and some superlative slender abaca fiber rope. He even showed the gnole a few soft yarns and twines made of cotton and jute.

On the back of an envelope he wrote prices for hanks and cheeses of the twines, and for 550-foot lengths of the ropes. Laboriously he added details about the strength, durability, and resistance to climatic conditions of each sort of cord. The senior gnole watched him intently, putting his little feet on the top rung of his chair and poking at the facets of his left eye now and then with a tentacle. In the cellars from time to time someone would scream.

Mortensen began to demonstrate his wares. He showed the gnole the slip and resilience of one rope, the tenacity and stubborn strength of another. He cut a tarred hemp rope in two and laid a five-foot piece on the parlor floor to show the gnole how absolutely "neutral" it was, with no tendency to untwist of its own accord. He even showed the gnole how nicely some of the cotton twines made up in square knotwork.

They settled at last on two ropes of abaca fiber, $3/16$ and $5/8$ inch in diameter. The gnole wanted an enormous quantity. Mortensen's comment on these ropes' "unlimited strength and durability," seemed to have attracted him.

Soberly Mortensen wrote the particulars down in his order book, but ambition was setting his brain on fire. The gnoles, it seemed, would be regular customers; and after the gnoles, why should he not try the Gibbelins? They too must have a need for rope.

Mortensen closed his order book. On the back of the same envelope he wrote, for the gnole to see, that delivery would be made within ten days. Terms were 30 percent with order, balance upon receipt of goods.

The senior gnole hesitated. Slyly he looked at Mortensen with his little red eyes. Then he got down the smallest of the emeralds from the wall and handed it to him.

The sales representative stood weighing it in his hands. It was the smallest of the gnoles' emeralds, but it was as clear as water, as green as grass. In the outside world it would have ransomed a Rockefeller or a whole family of Guggenheims; a legitimate profit from a transaction was one thing, but this was another; "a high ethical standard"—any kind of ethical standard—would forbid Mortensen to keep it. He weighed it a moment longer. Then with a deep, deep sigh he gave the emerald back.

He cast a glance around the room to see if he could find something which would be more negotiable. And in an evil moment he fixed on the senior gnole's auxiliary eyes.

The senior gnole keeps his extra pair of optics on the third shelf of the curiosity cabinet with the glass doors. They look like fine dark emeralds about the size of the end of your thumb. And if the gnoles in general set store by their gems, it is nothing at all compared to the senior gnole's emotions about his extra eyes. The concern good Christian folk should feel for their soul's welfare is a shadow, a figment, a nothing, compared to what the thoroughly heathen gnole feels for those eyes. He would rather, I think, choose to be a mere miserable human being than that some vandal should lay hands upon them.

If Mortensen had not been elated by his success to the point of anaesthesia, he would have seen the gnole stiffen, he would have heard him hiss, when he went over to the cabinet. All innocent, Mortensen opened the glass door, took the twin eyes out, and juggled them sacrilegiously in his hand; the gnole could feel them clink. Smiling to evince the charm of manner advised in the *Manual,* and raising his brows as one who says, "Thank you, these will do nicely," Mortensen dropped the eyes into his pocket.

The gnole growled.

The growl awoke Mortensen from his trance of euphoria. It was a growl whose meaning no one could mistake. This was clearly no time to be doggedly persistent. Mortensen made a break for the door.

The senior gnole was there before him, his network of tentacles outstretched. He caught Mortensen in them easily and wound them, flat as bandages, around his ankles and his hands. The best abaca fiber is no stronger than those tentacles; though the gnoles would find rope a convenience, they get along very well without it. Would you, dear reader, go naked if zippers should cease to be made? Growling indignantly, the gnole fished his ravished eyes from Mortensen's pockets, and then carried him down to the cellar to the fattening pens.

But great are the virtues of legitimate commerce. Though they fattened Mortensen sedulously, and, later, roasted and sauced him and ate him with real appetite, the gnoles slaughtered him in quite a humane manner and never once thought of torturing him. That is unusual, for gnoles. And they ornamented the plank on which they served him with a beautiful border of fancy knotwork made out of cotton cord from his own sample case.

The Silken-Swift

Theodore Sturgeon

Theodore Sturgeon (1918–1985) influenced many authors with his penetrating insight into the psychology of human behavior. Among his best-known works are the novels More Than Human *and* The Dreaming Jewels, *and dozens of superb short stories. He was the Guest of Honor at the twentieth World Science Fiction Convention, and was awarded the Life Achievement Award by the World Fantasy Association in 1985.*

THERE'S A VILLAGE BY THE BOGS, AND IN THE VILLAGE IS A GREAT HOUSE. In the Great House lived a squire who had land and treasures and, for a daughter, Rita.

In the village lived Del, whose voice was a thunder in the inn when he drank there; whose corded, cabled body was golden-skinned, and whose hair flung challenges back to the sun.

Deep in the Bogs, which were brackish, there was a pool of purest water, shaded by willows and wide-wondering aspen, cupped by banks of a moss most marvelously blue. Here grew mandrake, and there were strange pipings in midsummer. No one ever heard them but a quiet girl whose beauty was so very contained that none of it showed. Her name was Barbara.

There was a green evening, breathless with growth, when Del took his usual way down the lane beside the manor and saw a white shadow adrift inside the tall iron pickets. He stopped, and the shadow approached, and became Rita. "Slip around to the gate," she said, "and I'll open it for you."

She wore a gown like a cloud and a silver circlet round her head. Night was caught in her hair, moonlight in her face, and in her great eyes, secrets swam.

Del said, "I have no business with the squire."

"He's gone," she said. "I've sent the servants away. Come to the gate."

"I need no gate." He leapt and caught the top bar of the fence, and in a continuous fluid motion went high and across and down beside her. She looked at his arms, one, the other; then up at his hair. She pressed her small hands tight together and made a little laugh, and then she was gone through the tailored trees, lightly, swiftly, not looking back. He followed, one step for three of hers, keeping pace with a new pounding in the sides of his neck. They crossed a flower bed and a wide marble terrace. There was an open door, and when he passed through it he stopped, for she was nowhere in sight. Then the door clicked shut behind him and he whirled. She was there, her back to the panel, laughing up at him in the dimness. He thought she would come to him then, but instead she twisted by, close, her eyes on his. She smelt of violets and sandalwood. He followed her into the great hall, quite dark but full of the subdued lights of polished wood, cloisonné, tooled leather and gold-threaded tapestry. She flung open another door, and they were in a small room with a carpet made of rosy silences, and a candle-lit table. Two places were set, each with five different crystal glasses and old silver as prodigally used as the iron pickets outside. Six teakwood steps rose to a great oval window. "The moon," she said, "will rise for us there."

She motioned him to a chair and crossed to a sideboard, where there was a rack of decanters—ruby wine and white; one with a strange brown bead; pink, and amber. She took down the first and poured. Then she lifted the silver domes from the salvers on the table, and a magic of fragrance filled the air. There were smoking sweets and savories, rare seafood and slivers of fowl, and morsels of strange meat wrapped in flower petals, spitted with foreign fruits and tiny soft seashells. All about were spices, each like a separate voice in the distant murmur of a crowd: saffron and sesame, cumin and marjoram and mace.

And all the while Del watched her in wonder, seeing how the candles left the moonlight in her face, and how completely she trusted her hands, which did such deftness without supervision—so composed she was, for all the silent secret laughter that tugged at her lips, for all the bright dark mysteries that swirled and swam within her.

They ate, and the oval window yellowed and darkened while the candlelight grew bright. She poured another wine, and another, and with the courses of the meal they were as May to the crocus and as frost to the apple.

Del knew it was alchemy and he yielded to it without questions. That which was purposely oversweet would be piquantly cut; this induced thirst would, with exquisite timing, be quenched. He knew she was watching him; he knew she was aware of the heat in his cheeks and the tingle at his fingertips. His wonder grew, but he was not afraid.

In all this time she spoke hardly a word; but at last the feast was over and they rose. She touched a silken rope on the wall, and paneling slid aside. The table rolled silently into some ingenious recess and the panel returned. She waved him to an L-shaped couch in one corner, and as he sat close to her, she turned and took down the lute which hung on the wall behind her. He had his moment of confusion; his arms were ready for her, but not for the instrument as well. Her eyes sparkled, but her composure was unshaken.

Now she spoke, while her fingers strolled and danced on the lute, and her words marched and wandered in and about the music. She had a thousand voices, so that he wondered which of them was truly hers. Sometimes she sang; sometimes it was a wordless crooning. She seemed at times remote from him, puzzled at the turn the music was taking, and at other times she seemed to hear the pulsing roar in his eardrums, and she played laughing syncopations to it. She sang words which he almost understood:

> *"Bee to blossom, honey dew,*
> *Claw to mouse, and rain to tree,*
> *Moon to midnight, I to you;*
> *Sun to starlight, you to me . . ."*

and she sang something wordless:

> *"Ake ya rundefle, rundefle fye,*
> *Orel ya rundefle kown,*
> *En yea, en yea, ya bunderbee bye*
> *En sor, en see, en sown."*

which he also almost understood.

In still another voice she told him the story of a great hairy spider and a little pink girl who found it between the leaves of a half-open book; and at first he was all fright and pity for the girl, but then she went on to tell of what the spider suffered, with his home disrupted by this yawping giant, and so vividly did she tell of it that at the end he was laughing at himself and all but crying for the poor spider.

So the hours slipped by, and suddenly, between songs, she was in his arms; and in the instant she had twisted up and away from him, leaving him gasping. She said, in still a new voice, sober and low, "No, Del. We must wait for the moon."

His thighs ached and he realized that he had half-risen, arms out, hands clutching and feeling the extraordinary fabric of her gown though it was gone from them; and he sank back to the couch with an odd, faint sound that was wrong for the room. He flexed his fingers and, reluctantly, the sensation of white gossamer left them. At last he looked across at her and she laughed and leapt high lightly, and it was as if she stopped in midair to stretch for a moment before she alighted beside him, bent and kissed his mouth, and leapt away.

The roaring in his ears was greater, and at this it seemed to acquire a tangible weight. His head bowed; he tucked his knuckles into the upper curve of his eye sockets and rested his elbows on his knees. He could hear the sweet susurrus of Rita's gown as she moved about the room; he could sense the violets and sandalwood. She was dancing, immersed in the joy of movement and of his nearness. She made her own music, humming, sometimes whispering to the melodies in her mind.

And at length he became aware that she had stopped; he could hear nothing, though he knew she was still near. Heavily he raised his head. She was in the center of the room, balanced like a huge white moth, her eyes quite dark now with their secrets quiet. She was staring at the window, poised, waiting.

He followed her gaze. The big oval was black no longer, but dusted over with silver light. Del rose slowly. The dust was a mist, a loom, and then, at one edge, there was a shard of the moon itself creeping and growing.

Because Del stopped breathing, he could hear her breathe; it was rapid and so deep it faintly strummed her versatile vocal cords.

"Rita . . ."

Without answering she ran to the sideboard and filled two small glasses. She gave him one, then, "Wait," she breathed, "oh, wait!"

Spellbound, he waited while the white stain crept across the window. He understood suddenly that he must be still until the great oval was completely filled with direct moonlight, and this helped him, because it set a foreseeable limit to his waiting; and it hurt him, because nothing in life, he thought, had ever moved so slowly. He had a moment of rebellion, in which he damned himself for falling in with her complex pacing; but with it he realized that now the darker silver was wasting away, now it was a finger's breadth, and now a thread, and now, and *now*—

She made a brittle feline cry and sprang up the dark steps to the window. So bright was the light that her body was a jet cameo against it. So delicately wrought was her gown that he could see the epaulettes of silver light the moon gave her. She was so beautiful his eyes stung.

"Drink," she whispered. "Drink with me, darling, darling . . ."

For an instant he did not understand her at all, and only gradually did he become aware of the little glass he held. He raised it toward her and drank. And of all the twists and titillations of taste he had had this night, this was the most startling; for it had no taste at all, almost no substance, and a temperature almost exactly that of blood. He looked stupidly down at the glass and back up at the girl. He thought that she had turned about and was watching him, though he could not be sure, since her silhouette was the same.

And then he had his second of unbearable shock, for the light went out.

The moon was gone, the window, the room. Rita was gone.

For a stunned instant he stood tautly, stretching his eyes wide. He made a sound that was not a word. He dropped the glass and pressed his palms to his eyes, feeling them blink, feeling the stiff silk of his lashes against them. Then he snatched the hands away, and it was still dark, and more than dark; this was not a blackness. This was like trying to see with an elbow or with a tongue; it was not black; it was *Nothingness*.

He fell to his kness.

Rita laughed.

An odd, alert part of his mind seized on the laugh and understood it, and horror and fury spread through his whole being; for this was the laugh which had been tugging at her lips all evening, and it was a hard, cruel, self-assured laugh. And at the same time, because of the anger or in spite of it, desire exploded whitely within him. He moved toward the sound, groping, mouthing. There was a quick, faint series of rustling sounds from the steps, and then a light, strong web fell around him. He struck out at it, and recognized it for the unforgettable thing it was—her robe. He caught at it, ripped it, stamped upon it. He heard her bare feet run lightly down and past him, and lunged, and caught nothing. He stood, gasping painfully.

She laughed again.

"I'm blind," he said hoarsely. "Rita, I'm blind!"

"I know," she said coolly, close beside him. And again she laughed.

"What have you done to me?"

"I've watched you be a dirty animal of a man," she said.

He grunted and lunged again. His knees struck something—a chair, a cabinet—and he fell heavily. He thought he touched her foot.

"Here, lover, here!" she taunted.

He fumbled about for the thing which had tripped him, found it, used it to help him upright again. He peered uselessly about.

"Here, lover!"

He leapt, and crashed into the doorjamb: cheekbone, collarbone, hipbone, ankle were one straight blaze of pain. He clung to the polished wood.

After a time he said, in agony, "Why?"

"No man has ever touched me and none ever will," she sang. Her breath was on his cheek. He reached and touched nothing, and then he heard her leap from her perch on a statue's pedestal by the door, where she had stood high and leaned over to speak.

No pain, no blindness, not even the understanding that it was her witch's brew working in him could quell the wild desire he felt at her nearness. Nothing could tame the fury that shook him as she laughed. He staggered after her, bellowing.

She danced around him, laughing. Once she pushed him into a clattering rack of fire-irons. Once she caught his elbow from behind and spun him. And once, incredibly, she sprang past him and, in midair, kissed him again on the mouth.

He descended into Hell, surrounded by the small, sure patter of bare feet and sweet cool laughter. He rushed and crashed, he crouched and bled and whimpered like a hound. His roaring and blundering took an echo, and that must have been the great hall. Then there were walls that seemed more than unyielding; they struck back. And there were panels to lean against, gasping, which became opening doors as he leaned. And always the black nothing-ness, the writhing temptation of the pat-pat of firm flesh on smooth stones, and the ravening fury.

It was cooler, and there was no echo. He became aware of the whis-per of the wind through trees. The balcony, he thought; and then, right in his ear, so that he felt her warm breath, "Come, lover . . ." and he sprang. He sprang and missed, and instead of sprawling on the terrace, there was nothing, and nothing, and nothing, and then, when he least expected it, a shower of cruel thumps as he rolled down the marble steps.

He must have had a shred of consciousness left, for he was vaguely aware of the approach of her bare feet, and of the small, cautious hand that touched his shoulder and moved to his mouth, and then his chest. Then it was withdrawn, and either she laughed or the sound was still in his mind.

Deep in the Bogs, which were brackish, there was a pool of purest water, shaded by willows and wide-wondering aspens, cupped by banks of a moss most marvelously blue. Here grew mandrake, and there were strange pipings in midsummer. No one ever heard them but a quiet girl whose beauty was so very contained that none of it showed. Her name was Barbara.

No one noticed Barbara, no one lived with her, no one cared. And Barbara's life was very full, for she was born to receive. Others are born wishing to receive, so they wear bright masks and make attractive sounds like cicadas and operettas, so others will be forced, one way or another, to give to them. But Barbara's receptors were wide open, and always had been, so that she needed no substitute for sunlight through a tulip petal, or the sound of morning glories climbing, or the tangy sweet smell of formic acid which is the only death cry possible to an ant, or any other of the thousand things overlooked by folk who can only wish to receive. Barbara had a garden and an orchard, and took things in to market when she cared to, and the rest of the time she spent in taking what was given. Weeds grew in her garden, but since they were welcomed, they grew only where they could keep the watermelons from being sunburned. The rabbits were welcome, so they kept to the two rows of carrots, the one of lettuce, and the one of tomato vines which were planted for them, and they left the rest alone. Goldenrod shot up beside the bean hills to lend a hand upward, and the birds ate only the figs and peaches from the waviest top branches, and in return patrolled the lower ones for caterpillars and egglaying flies. And if a fruit stayed green for two weeks longer until Barbara had time to go to market, or if a mole could channel moisture to the roots of the corn, why it was the least they could do.

For a brace of years Barbara had wandered more and more, impelled by a thing she could not name—if indeed she was aware of it at all. She knew only that over-the-rise was a strange and friendly place, and that it was a fine thing on arriving there to find another rise to go over. It may very well be that she now needed someone to love, for loving is a most receiving thing, as anyone can attest who has been loved without returning it. It is the one who is loved who must give and give. And she found her love, not in her wandering, but at the market. The shape of her love, his colors and sounds, were so much with her that when she saw him first it was without surprise; and thereafter, for a very long while, it was quite enough that he lived. He gave to her by being alive, by setting the air athrum with his mighty voice, by his stride, which was, for a man afoot, the exact analog of what the horseman calls a "perfect seat."

After seeing him, of course, she received twice and twice again as much as ever before. A tree was straight and tall for the magnificent sake of being straight and tall, but wasn't straightness a part of him, and being tall? The oriole gave more now than song, and the hawk more than walking the wind, for had they not hearts like his, warm blood and his same striving to keep it so for tomorrow? And more and more, over-the-rise was the place for her, for only there could there be more and still more things like him.

But when she found the pure pool in the brackish Bogs, there was no more over-the-rise for her. It was a place without hardness or hate, where the aspens trembled only for wonder, and where all contentment was rewarded. Every single rabbit there was *the* champion nose-twinkler, and every waterbird could stand on one leg the longest, and proud of it. Shelf-fungi hung to the willow-trunks, making that certain, single purple of which the sunset is incapable, and a tanager and a cardinal gravely granted one another his definition of "red."

Here Barbara brought a heart light with happiness, large with love, and set it down on the blue moss. And since the loving heart can receive more than anything else, so it is most needed, and Barbara took the best bird songs, and the richest colors, and the deepest peace, and all the other things which are most worth giving. The chipmunks brought her nuts when she was hungry and the prettiest stones when she was not. A green snake explained to her, in pantomime, how a river of jewels may flow uphill, and three mad otters described how a bundle of joy may slip and slide down and down and be all the more joyful for it. And there was the magic moment when a midge hovered, and then a honeybee, and then a bumblebee, and at last a hummingbird; and there they hung, playing a chord in A sharp minor.

Then one day the pool fell silent, and Barbara learned why the water was pure.

The aspens stopped trembling.

The rabbits all came out of the thicket and clustered on the blue bank, backs straight, ears up, and all their noses as still as coral.

The waterbirds stepped backwards, like courtiers, and stopped on the brink with their heads turned sidewise, one eye closed the better to see with the other.

The chipmunks respectfully emptied their cheek pouches, scrubbed their paws together and tucked them out of sight; then stood still as tent pegs.

The pressure of growth around the pool ceased: the very grass waited.

The last sound of all to be heard—and by then it was very quiet—was the soft *whick!* of an owl's eyelids as it awoke to watch.

He came like a cloud, the earth cupping itself to take each of his golden hooves. He stopped on the bank and lowered his head, and for a brief moment his eyes met Barbara's, and she looked into a second universe of wisdom and compassion. Then there was the arch of the magnificent neck, the blinding flash of his golden horn.

And he drank, and he was gone. Everyone knows the water is pure, where the unicorn drinks.

How long had he been there? How long gone? Did time wait too, like the grass?

"And couldn't he stay?" she wept. "Couldn't he stay?"

To have seen the unicorn is a sad thing; one might never see him more. But then—to have seen the unicorn!

She began to make a song.

It was late when Barbara came in from the Bogs, so late the moon was bleached with cold and fleeing to the horizon. She struck the highroad just below the Great House and turned to pass it and go out to her garden house.

Near the locked main gate an animal was barking. A sick animal, a big animal . . .

Barbara could see in the dark better than most, and soon saw the creature clinging to the gate, climbing, uttering that coughing moan as it went. At the top it slipped, fell outward, dangled; then there was a ripping sound, and it fell heavily to the ground and lay still and quiet.

She ran to it, and it began to make the sound again. It was a man, and he was weeping.

It was her love, her love, who was tall and straight and so very alive—her love, battered and bleeding, puffy, broken, his clothes torn, crying.

Now of all times was the time for a lover to receive, to take from the loved one his pain, his trouble, his fear. "Oh, hush, hush," she whispered, her hands touching his bruised face like swift feathers. "It's all over now. It's all over."

She turned him over on his back and knelt to bring him up sitting. She lifted one of his thick arms around her shoulder. He was very heavy, but she was very strong. When he was upright, gasping weakly, she looked up and down the road in the waning moonlight. Nothing, no one. The Great House was dark. Across the road, though, was a meadow with high hedgerows which might break the wind a little.

"Come, my love, my dear love," she whispered. He trembled violently.

All but carrying him, she got him across the road, over the shallow ditch, and through a gap in the hedge. She almost fell with him there. She gritted her teeth and set him down gently. She let him lean against the hedge, and then ran and swept up great armfuls of sweet broom. She made a tight springy bundle of it and set it on the ground beside him, and put a corner of her cloak over it, and gently lowered his head until it was pillowed. She folded the rest of the cloak about him. He was very cold.

There was no water near, and she dared not leave him. With her kerchief she cleaned some of the blood from his face. He was still very cold. He said, "You devil. You rotten little devil."

"Shh." She crept in beside him and cradled his head. "You'll be warm in a minute."

"Stand still," he growled. "Keep running away."

"I won't run away," she whispered. "Oh, my darling, you've been hurt, so hurt. I won't leave you. I promise I won't leave you."

He lay very still. He made the growling sound again.

"I'll tell you a lovely thing," she said softly. "Listen to me, think about the lovely thing," she crooned.

"There's a place in the bog, a pool of pure water, where the trees live beautifully, willow and aspen and birch, where everything is peaceful, my darling, and the flowers grow without tearing their petals. The moss is blue and the water is like diamonds."

"You tell me stories in a thousand voices," he muttered.

"Shh. Listen, my darling. This isn't a story, it's a real place. Four miles north and a little west, and you can see the trees from the ridge with the two dwarf oaks. And I know why the water is pure!" she cried gladly. "I know why!"

He said nothing. He took a deep breath and it hurt him, for he shuddered painfully.

"The unicorn drinks there," she whispered. "I *saw* him!"

Still he said nothing. She said, "I made a song about it. Listen, this is the song I made:

"And He—suddenly gleamed! My dazzled eyes
Coming from outer sunshine to this green
And secret gloaming, met without surprise
The vision. Only after, when the sheen
And Splendor of his going fled away,
I knew amazement, wonder and despair,
That he should come—and pass—and would not stay,
The Silken-swift—the gloriously Fair!
That he should come—and pass—and would not stay,
So that, forever after, I must go,
Take the long road that mounts against the day,
Traveling in the hope that I shall know
Again that lifted moment, high and sweet,
Somewhere—on purple moor or windy hill—
Remembering still his wild and delicate feet,
The magic and the dream—remembering still!"

His breathing was more regular. She said, "I truly *saw* him!"

"I'm blind," he said. "Blind, I'm blind."

"Oh, my dear . . ."

He fumbled for her hand, found it. For a long moment he held it. Then, slowly, he brought up his other hand and with them both he felt her hand, turned it about, squeezed it. Suddenly he grunted, half sitting. "You're here."

"Of course, darling. Of course I'm here."

"Why?" he shouted. "Why? *Why?* Why all of this? Why blind me?" He sat up, mouthing, and put his great hand on her throat. "Why do all that if . . ." The words ran together into an animal noise. Wine and witchery, anger and agony boiled in his veins.

Once she cried out.

Once she sobbed.

"Now," he said, "you'll catch no unicorns. Get away from me." He cuffed her.

"You're mad. You're sick," she cried.

"Get away," he said ominously.

Terrified, she rose. He took the cloak and hurled it after her. It almost toppled her as she ran away, crying silently.

After a long time, from behind the hedge, the sick, coughing sobs began again.

Three weeks later Rita was in the market when a hard hand took her upper arm and pressed her into the angle of a cottage wall. She did not start. She flashed her eyes upward and recognized him, and then said composedly, "Don't touch me."

"I need you to tell me something," he said. "And tell me you *will!*" His voice was as hard as his hand.

"I'll tell you anything you like," she said. "But don't touch me."

He hesitated, then released her. She turned to him casually. "What is it?" Her gaze darted across his face and its almost-healed scars. The small smile tugged at one corner of her mouth.

His eyes were slits. "I have to know this: why did you make up all that . . . prettiness, that food, that poison . . . just for me? You could have had me for less."

She smiled. "Just for you? It was your turn, that's all."

He was genuinely surprised. "It's happened before?"

She nodded. "Whenever it's the full of the moon—and the squire's away."

"You're lying!"

"You forget yourself!" she said sharply. Then, smiling, "It is the truth, though."

"I'd've heard talk—"

"Would you now? And tell me—how many of your friends know about your humiliating adventure?"

He hung his head.

She nodded. "You see? They go away until they're healed, and they come back and say nothing. And they always will."

"You're a devil . . . why do you do it? Why?"

"I told you," she said openly. "I'm a woman and I act like a woman in my own way. No man will ever touch me, though. I am virgin and shall remain so."

"You're *what?*" he roared.

She held up a restraining, ladylike glove. "Please," she said, pained.

"Listen," he said, quietly now, but with such intensity that for once she stepped back a pace. He closed his eyes, thinking hard: "You told me—the pool, the pool of the unicorn, and a song, wait. 'The Silken-swift, the gloriously Fair . . .' Remember? And then I—I saw to it that *you'd* never catch a unicorn!"

She shook her head, complete candor in her face. "I like that, 'the Silken-swift.' Pretty. But believe me—no! That isn't mine."

He put his face close to hers, and though it was barely a whisper, it came out like bullets. "Liar! Liar! I couldn't forget. I was sick, I was hurt, I was poisoned, but I know what I did!" He turned on his heel and strode away.

She put the thumb of her glove against her upper teeth for a second, then ran after him. "Del!"

He stopped but, rudely, would not turn. She rounded him, faced him. "I'll not have you believing that of me—it's the one thing I have left," she said tremulously.

He made no attempt to conceal his surprise. She controlled her expression with a visible effort, and said, "Please. Tell me a little more—just about the pool, the song, whatever it was."

"You don't remember?"

"I don't *know!*" she flashed. She was deeply agitated.

He said with mock patience. "You told me of a unicorn pool out on the Bogs. You said you had seen *him* drink there. You made a song about it. And then I—"

"Where? Where was this?"

"You forget so soon?"

"Where? Where did it happen?"

"In the meadow, across the road from your gate, where you followed me," he said. "Where my sight came back to me, when the sun came up."

She looked at him blankly, and slowly her face changed. First the imprisoned smile struggling to be free, and then—she was herself again, and she laughed. She laughed a great ringing peal of the laughter that had plagued him so, and she did not stop until he put one hand behind his back, then the other, and she saw his shoulders swell with the effort to keep from striking her dead.

"You animal!" she said, good-humoredly. "Do you know what you've done? Oh, you . . . you *animal!*" She glanced around to see that there were no ears to hear her. "I left you at the foot of the terrace steps," she told him. Her eyes sparkled. "Inside the gates, you understand? And you . . ."

"Don't laugh," he said quietly.

She did not laugh. "That was someone else out there. Who, I can't imagine. But it wasn't I."

He paled. "You followed me out."

"On my soul I did not," she said soberly. Then she quelled another laugh.

"That can't be," he said. "I couldn't have . . ."

"But you were blind, blind and crazy, Del-my-lover!"

"Squire's daughter, take care," he hissed. Then he pulled his big hand through his hair. "It can't be. It's three weeks; I'd have been accused . . ."

"There are those who wouldn't." She smiled. "Or—perhaps she will, in time."

"There has never been a woman so foul," he said evenly, looking her straight in the eye. "You're lying—you know you're lying."

"What must I do to prove it—aside from that which I'll have no man do?"

His lip curled. "Catch the unicorn," he said.

"If I did, you'd believe I was a virgin?"

"I must," he admitted. He turned away, then said, over his shoulder. "But—*you*?"

She watched him thoughtfully until he left the marketplace. Her eyes sparkled; then she walked briskly to the goldsmith's, where she ordered a bridle of woven gold.

If the unicorn pool lay in the Bogs nearby, Rita reasoned, someone who was familiar with that brackish wasteland must know of it. And when she made a list in her mind of those few who traveled the Bogs, she knew whom to ask. With that, the other deduction came readily. Her laughter drew stares as she moved through the marketplace.

By the vegetable stall she stopped. The girl looked up patiently.

Rita stood swinging one expensive glove against the other wrist, half-smiling. "So you're the one." She studied the plain, inward-turning, peaceful face until Barbara had to turn her eyes away. Rita said, without further preamble, "I want you to show me the unicorn pool in two weeks."

Barbara looked up again, and now it was Rita who dropped her eyes. Rita said, "I can have someone else find it, of course. If you'd rather not." She spoke very clearly, and people turned to listen. They looked from Barbara to Rita and back again, and they waited.

"I don't mind," said Barbara faintly. As soon as Rita had left, smiling, she packed up her things and went silently back to her house.

The goldsmith, of course, made no secret of such an extraordinary commission; and that, plus the gossips who had overheard Rita talking to Barbara, made the expedition into a cavalcade. The whole village turned out to see; the boys kept firmly in check so that Rita might lead the way; the young bloods ranged behind her (some a little less carefree than they might be) and others snickering behind their hands. Behind them the girls, one or two a little pale, others eager as cats to see the squire's daughter fail, and perhaps even . . . but then, only she had the golden bridle.

She carried it casually, but casualness could not hide it, for it was not wrapped, and it swung and blazed in the sun. She wore a flowing white robe, trimmed a little short so that she might negotiate the rough bogland; she had on a golden girdle and little gold sandals, and a gold chain bound her head and hair like a coronet.

Barbara walked quietly a little behind Rita, closed in with her own thoughts. Not once did she look at Del, who strode somberly by himself.

Rita halted a moment and let Barbara catch up, then walked beside her. "Tell me," she said quietly, "why did you come? It needn't have been you."

"I'm his friend," Barbara said. She quickly touched the bridle with her finger. "The unicorn."

"Oh," said Rita. "The unicorn." She looked archly at the other girl. "You wouldn't betray all your friends, would you?"

Barbara looked at her thoughtfully, without anger. "If—when you catch the unicorn," she said carefully, "what will do you with him?"

"What an amazing question! I shall keep him, of course!"

"I thought I might persuade you to let him go."

Rita smiled, and hung the bridle on the other arm. "You could never do that."

"I know," said Barbara. "But I thought I might, so that's why I came." And before Rita could answer, she dropped behind again.

The last ridge, the one which overlooked the unicorn pool, saw a series of gasps as the ranks of villagers topped it, one after the other, and saw what lay below; and it was indeed beautiful.

Surprisingly, it was Del who took it upon himself to call out, in his great voice, "Everyone wait here!" And everyone did; the top of the ridge filled slowly, from one side to the other, with craning, murmuring people. And then Del bounded after Rita and Barbara.

Barbara said, "I'll stop here."

"Wait," said Rita, imperiously. Of Del she demanded, "What are you coming for?"

"To see fair play," he growled. "The little I know of witchcraft makes me like none of it."

"Very well," she said calmly. Then she smiled her very own smile. "Since you insist, I'd rather enjoy Barbara's company too."

Barbara hesitated. "Come, he won't hurt you, girl," said Rita. "He doesn't know you exist."

"Oh," said Barbara, wonderingly.

Del said gruffly, "I do so. She has the vegetable stall."

Rita smiled at Barbara, the secrets bright in her eyes. Barbara said nothing, but came with them.

"You should go back, you know," Rita said silkily to Del, when she could. "Haven't you been humiliated enough yet?"

He did not answer.

She said, "Stubborn animal! Do you think I'd have come this far if I weren't sure?"

"Yes," said Del, "I think perhaps you would."

They reached the blue moss. Rita shuffled it about with her feet and then sank gracefully down to it. Barbara stood alone in the shadows of the willow grove. Del thumped gently at an aspen with his fist. Rita, smiling, arranged the bridle to cast, and laid it across her lap.

The rabbits stayed hid. There was an uneasiness about the grove. Barbara sank to her knees, and put out her hand. A chipmunk ran to nestle in it.

This time there was a difference. This time it was not the slow silencing of living things that warned of his approach, but a sudden babble from the people on the ridge.

Rita gathered her legs under her like a sprinter, and held the bridle poised. Her eyes were round and bright, and the tip of her tongue showed between her white teeth. Barbara was a statue. Del put his back against his tree, and became as still as Barbara.

Then from the ridge came a single, simultaneous intake of breath, and silence. One knew without looking that some stared speechless, that some buried their faces or threw an arm over their eyes.

He came.

He came slowly this time, his golden hooves choosing his paces like so many embroidery needles. He held his splendid head high. He regarded the three on the bank gravely, and then turned to look at the ridge for a moment. At last he turned, and came round the pond by the willow grove. Just on the blue moss, he stopped to look down into the pond. It seemed that he drew one deep clear breath. He bent his head then, and drank, and lifted his head to shake away the shining drops.

He turned toward the three spellbound humans and looked at them each in turn. And it was not Rita he went to, at last, nor Barbara. He came to Del, and he drank of Del's eyes with his own just as he had partaken of the pool—deeply and at leisure. The beauty and wisdom were there, and the compassion, and what looked like a bright white point of anger. Del knew that the creature had read everything then, and that he knew all three of them in ways unknown to human beings.

There was a majestic sadness in the way he turned then, and dropped his shining head, and stepped daintily to Rita. She sighed, and rose up a little, lifting the bridle. The unicorn lowered his horn to receive it—

—and tossed his head, tore the bridle out of her grasp, sent the golden thing high in the air. It turned there in the sun, and fell into the pond.

And the instant it touched the water, the pond was a bog and the birds rose mourning from the trees. The unicorn looked up at them, and shook himself. Then he trotted to Barbara and knelt, and put his smooth, stainless head in her lap.

Barbara's hands stayed on the ground by her sides. Her gaze moved over the warm white beauty, up to the tip of the golden horn and back.

The scream was frightening. Rita's hands were up like claws, and she had bitten her tongue; there was blood on her mouth. She screamed again. She threw herself off the now withered moss toward the unicorn and Barbara. "She can't be!" Rita shrieked. She collided with Del's broad right hand. "It's wrong, I tell you, she, you, I . . ."

"I'm satisfied," said Del, low in his throat. "Keep away, squire's daughter."

She recoiled from him, made as if to try to circle him. He stepped forward. She ground her chin into one shoulder, then the other, in a gesture of sheer frustration, turned suddenly and ran toward the ridge. "It's mine, it's mine," she screamed. "I tell you it can't be hers, don't you understand? I never once, I never did, but she, but she—"

She slowed and stopped, then, and fell silent at the sound that rose from the ridge. It began like the first patter of rain on oak leaves, and it gathered voice until it was a rumble and then a roar. She stood looking up, her face working, the sound washing over her. She shrank from it.

It was laughter.

She turned once, a pleading just beginning to form on her face. Del regarded her stonily. She faced the ridge then, and squared her shoulders, and walked up the hill, to go into the laughter, to go through it, to have it follow her all the way home and all the days of her life.

Del turned to Barbara just as she bent over the beautiful head. She said, "Silken-swift . . . go free."

The unicorn raised its head and looked up at Del. Del's mouth opened. He took a clumsy step forward, stopped again. *"You!"*

Barbara's face was set. "You weren't to know," she choked. "You weren't ever to know . . . I was so glad you were blind, because I thought you'd never know."

He fell on his knees beside her. And when he did, the unicorn touched her face with his satin nose, and all the girl's pent-up beauty flooded outward. The unicorn rose from his kneeling, and whickered softly. Del looked at her, and only the unicorn was more beautiful. He put out his hand to the shining neck, and for a moment felt the incredible silk of the mane flowing across his fingers. The unicorn reared then, and wheeled, and in a great leap was across the bog, and in two more was on the crest of the farther ridge. He paused there briefly, with the sun on him, and then was gone.

Barbara said, "For us, he lost his pool, his beautiful pool."

And Del said, "He will get another. He must." With difficulty he added, "He couldn't be . . . punished . . . for being so gloriously Fair."

The Golem

Avram Davidson

Avram Davidson (1923–1993), like many of the authors included here, wrote in several genres. Getting his start in speculative fiction in the 1950s, he wrote several classic stories such as "All the Seas with Oysters," and "Dagon." At the urging of the editor for Ellery Queen's Mystery Magazine, *he turned to writing mysteries, and he won the Ellery Queen award as well as the Edgar Allan Poe award. When he began writing novels, he went back to the form in which he had started, science fiction and fantasy. Notable works include* The Phoenix and the Mirror *and* The Island Under the Earth.

THE GRAY-FACED PERSON CAME ALONG THE STREET WHERE OLD MR. AND Mrs. Gumbeiner lived. It was afternoon, it was autumn, the sun was warm and soothing to their ancient bones. Anyone who attended the movies in the twenties or the early thirties has seen that street a thousand times. Past these bungalows with their half-double roofs Edmund Lowe walked arm-in-arm with Leatrice Joy and Harold Lloyd was chased by Chinamen waving hatchets. Under these squamous palm trees Laurel kicked Hardy and Woolsey beat Wheeler upon the head with a codfish. Across these pocket-handkerchief-sized lawns the juveniles of the Our Gang Comedies pursued one another and were pursued by angry fat men in golf knickers. On this same street—or perhaps on some other one of five hundred streets exactly like it.

Mrs. Gumbeiner indicated the gray-faced person to her husband.

"You think maybe he's got something the matter?" she asked. "He walks kind of funny, to me."

"Walks like a *golem*," Mr. Gumbeiner said indifferently.

The old woman was nettled.

"Oh, I don't know," she said. "*I* think he walks like your cousin Mendel."

The old man pursed his mouth angrily and chewed on his pipestem. The gray-faced person turned up the concrete path, walked up the steps to the porch, sat down in a chair. Old Mr. Gumbeiner ignored him. His wife stared at the stranger.

"Man comes in without a hello, goodbye, or howareyou, sits himself down and right away he's at home. . . . The chair is comfortable?" she asked. "Would you like maybe a glass tea?"

She turned to her husband.

"Say something, Gumbeiner!" she demanded. "What are you, made of wood?"

The old man smiled a slow, wicked, triumphant smile.

"Why should *I* say anything?" he asked the air. "Who am I? Nothing, that's who."

The stranger spoke. His voice was harsh and monotonous.

"When you learn who—or, rather, what—I am, the flesh will melt from your bones in terror." He bared porcelain teeth.

"Never mind about my bones!" the old woman cried. "You've got a lot of nerve talking about my bones!"

"You will quake with fear," said the stranger. Old Mrs. Gumbeiner said that she hoped he would live so long. She turned to her husband once again.

"Gumbeiner, when are you going to mow the lawn?"

"All mankind—" the stranger began.

"*Shah!* I'm talking to my husband. . . . He talks *eppis* kind of funny, Gumbeiner, no?"

"Probably a foreigner," Mr. Gumbeiner said, complacently.

"You think so?" Mrs. Gumbeiner glanced fleetingly at the stranger. "He's got a very bad color in his face, *nebbich,* I suppose he came to California for his health."

"Disease, pain, sorrow, love, grief—all are nought to—"

Mr. Gumbeiner cut in on the stranger's statement.

"Gall bladder," the old man said. "Guinzburg down at the *shule* looked exactly the same before his operation. Two professors they had in for him, and a private nurse day and night."

"I am not a human being!" the stranger said loudly.

"Three thousand seven hundred fifty dollars it cost his son, Guinzburg told me. 'For you, Poppa, nothing is too expensive— only get well,' the son told him."

"*I am not a human being!*"

"Ai, is that a son for you!" the old woman said, rocking her head. "A heart of gold, pure gold." She looked at the stranger. "All right, all right, I heard you the first time. Gumbeiner! I asked you a question. When are you going to cut the lawn?"

"On Wednesday, *odder* maybe Thursday, comes the Japaneser to the neighborhood. To cut lawns is *his* profession. *My* profession is to be a glazier—retired."

"Between me and all mankind is an inevitable hatred," the stranger said. "When I tell you what I am, the flesh will melt—"

"You said, you said already," Mr. Gumbeiner interrupted.

"In Chicago where the winters were as cold and bitter as the Czar of Russia's heart," the old woman intoned, "you had strength to carry the frames with the glass together day in and day out. But in California with the golden sun to mow the lawn when your wife asks, for this you have no strength. Do I call in the Japaneser to cook for you supper?"

"Thirty years Professor Allardyce spent perfecting his theories. Electronics, neuronics—"

"Listen, how educated he talks," Mr. Gumbeiner said, admiringly. "Maybe he goes to the University here?"

"If he goes to the University, maybe he knows Bud?" his wife suggested.

"Probably they're in the same class and he came to see him about the homework, no?"

"Certainly he must be in the same class. How many classes are there? Five *in ganzen:* Bud showed me on his program card." She counted off on her fingers. "Television Appreciation and Criticism, Small Boat Building, Social Adjustment, The American Dance . . . The American Dance—*nu,* Gumbeiner—"

"Contemporary Ceramics," her husband said, relishing the syllables. "A fine boy, Bud. A pleasure to have him for a boarder."

"After thirty years spent in these studies," the stranger, who had continued to speak unnoticed, went on, "he turned from the theoretical to the pragmatic. In ten years' time he had made the most titanic discovery in history: he made mankind, *all* mankind, superfluous; he made *me.*"

"What did Tillie write in her last letter?" asked the old man.

The old woman shrugged.

"What should she write? The same thing. Sidney was home from the Army, Naomi has a new boy friend—"

"He made ME!"

"Listen, Mr. Whatever-your-name-is," the old woman said, maybe where you came from is different, but in *this* country you don't interrupt people the while they're talking. . . . Hey. Listen—what do you mean, he *made* you? What kind of talk is that?"

The stranger bared all his teeth again, exposing the too-pink gums.

"In his library, to which I had a more complete access after his sudden and as yet undiscovered death from entirely natural causes, I found a complete collection of stories about androids, from Shelley's *Frankenstein* through Capek's *R.U.R.* to Asimov's—"

"Frankenstein?" said the old man, with interest. "There used to be a Frankenstein who had the soda-*wasser* place on Haltead Street—a Litvack, *nebbich.*"

"What are you talking?" Mrs. Gumbeiner demanded. "His name was Frankenthal, and it wasn't on Halstead, it was on Roosevelt."

"—clearly shown that all mankind has an instinctive antipathy towards androids and there will be an inevitable struggle between them—"

"Of course, of course!" Old Mr. Gumbeiner clicked his teeth against his pipe. "I am always wrong, you are always right. How could you stand to be married to such a stupid person all this time?"

"I don't know," the old woman said. "Sometimes I wonder, myself. I think it must be his good looks." She began to laugh. Old Mr. Gumbeiner blinked, then began to smile, then took his wife's hand.

"Foolish old woman," the stranger said. "Why do you laugh? Do you not know I have come to destroy you?"

"What?" old Mr. Gumbeiner shouted. "Close your mouth, you!" He darted from his chair and struck the stranger with the flat of his hand. The stranger's head struck against the porch pillar and bounced back.

"When you talk to my wife, talk respectable, you hear?"

Old Mrs. Gumbeiner, cheeks very pink, pushed her husband back to his chair. Then she leaned forward and examined the stranger's head. She clicked her tongue as she pulled aside a flap of gray, skinlike material.

"Gumbeiner, look! He's all springs and wires inside!"

"I *told* you he was a *golem*, but no, you wouldn't listen," the old man said.

"You said he *walked* like a *golem*."

"How could he walk like a *golem* unless he was one?"

"All right, all right . . . You broke him, so now fix him."

"My grandfather, his light shines from Paradise, told me that when MoHaRaL—Moreyne Ha-Rav Löw—his memory for a blessing, made the *golem* in Prague, three hundred? four hundred years ago? he wrote on his forehead the Holy Name."

Smiling reminiscently, the old woman continued, "And the *golem* cut the rabbi's wood and brought his water and guarded the ghetto."

"And one time only he disobeyed the Rabbi Löw, and Rabbi Löw erased the *Shem Ha-Mephorash* from the *golem*'s forehead and the *golem* fell down like a dead one. And they put him up in the attic of the *shule* and he's still there today if the Communisten haven't sent him to Moscow. . . . This is not just a story," he said.

"*Avadda* not!" said the old woman.

"I myself have seen both the *shule and* the rabbi's grave," her husband said, conclusively.

"But I think this must be a different kind of *golem*, Gumbeiner. See, on his forehead; nothing written."

"What's the matter, there's a law I can't write something there? Where is that lump clay Bud brought us from his class?"

The old man washed his hands, adjusted his little black skullcap, and slowly and carefully wrote four Hebrew letters on the gray forehead.

"Ezra the Scribe himself couldn't do better," the old woman said, admiringly. "Nothing happens," she observed, looking at the lifeless figure sprawled in the chair.

"Well, after all, am I Rabbi Löw?" her husband asked, deprecatingly. "No," he answered. He leaned over and examined the exposed mechanism. "This spring goes here . . . this wire comes with this one. . . ." The figure moved. "But this one goes where? And this one?"

"Let be," said his wife. The figure sat up slowly and rolled its eyes loosely.

"Listen, Reb *Golem*," the old man said, wagging his finger. Pay attention to what I say—you understand?"

"Understand . . ."

"If you want to stay here, you got to do like Mr. Gumbeiner says."

"Do-like—Mr.-Gumbeiner-says . . ."

"*That's* the way I like to hear a *golem* talk. Malka, give here the mirror from the pocketbook. Look, you see your face? You see on the forehead, what's written? If you don't do like Mr. Gumbeiner says, he'll wipe out what's written and you'll be no more alive."

"No-more-alive . . ."

"*That's* right. Now, listen. Under the porch you'll find a lawn-mower. Take it. And cut the lawn. Then come back. Go."

"Go . . ." The figure shambled down the stairs. Presently the sound of the lawnmower whirred through the quiet air in the street just like the street where Jackie Cooper shed huge tears on Wallace Beery's shirt and Chester Conklin rolled his eyes at Marie Dressler.

"So what will you write to Tillie?" old Mr. Gumbeiner asked.

"What should I write?" old Mrs. Gumbeiner shrugged. "I'll write that the weather is lovely out here and that we are both, Blessed be the Name, in good health."

The old man nodded his head slowly, and they sat together on the front porch in the warm afternoon sun.

Operation Afreet

Poul Anderson

Mention the name Poul Anderson and instantly dozens of excellent science fiction novels and short stories spring to mind. However, like many authors, he has also tried his hand at fantasy fiction, with equally impressive results. Two of his novels that deserve mention are Three Hearts and Three Lions *and* The Broken Sword, *the latter based on the Norse elven myths. He has also written in universes as diverse as Shakespeare's comedies and Robert E. Howard's Conan mythos. A seven-time winner of the Hugo award, he has also been awarded three Nebulas and the Tolkien Memorial award.*

I

IT WAS SHEER BAD LUCK, OR MAYBE THEIR INTELLIGENCE WAS BETTER THAN we knew, but the last raid, breaking past our air defenses, had spattered the Weather Corps tent from here to hell. Supply problems being what they were, we couldn't get replacements for weeks, and meanwhile the enemy had control of the weather. Our only surviving Corpsman, Major Jackson, had to save what was left of his elementals to protect us against thunderbolts; so otherwise we took whatever they chose to throw at us. At the moment, it was rain.

There's nothing so discouraging as a steady week of cold rain. The ground turns liquid and runs up into your boots, which get so heavy you can barely lift them. Your uniform is a drenched rag around your shivering skin, the rations are soggy, the rifles have to have extra care, and always the rain drums down on your helmet till you hear it in dreams. You'll never forget that endless gray washing and beating; ten years later a rainstorm will make you feel depressed.

The one consolation, I thought, was that they couldn't very well attack us from the air while it went on. Doubtless they'd yank the cloud cover away when they were ready to strafe us, but our broomsticks could scramble as fast as their carpets could arrive. Meanwhile, we slogged ahead, a whole division of us with auxiliaries—the 45th, the Lightning Busters, pride of the United States Army, turned into a wet misery of men and dragons hunting through the Oregon hills for the invader.

I made a slow way through the camp. Water ran off tents and gurgled in slit trenches. Our sentries were, of course, wearing Tarnkappen, but I could see their footprints form in the mud and hear the boots squelch and the tired monotonous cursing.

I passed by the Air Force strip; they were bivouacked with us, to give support as needed. A couple of men stood on guard outside the knockdown hangar, not bothering with invisibility. Their blue uniforms were as mucked and bedraggled as my OD's, but they had shaved and their insignia—the winged broomstick and the anti–Evil Eye beads—were polished. They saluted me, and I returned the gesture idly. *Esprit de corps*, wild blue yonder, nuts.

Beyond was the armor. The boys had erected portable shelters for their beasts, so I only saw steam rising out of the cracks and caught the rank reptile smell. Dragons hate rain, and their drivers were having a hell of a time controlling them.

Nearby lay Petrological Warfare, with a pen full of hooded basilisks writhing and hissing and striking out with their crowned heads at the men feeding them. Personally, I doubted the practicality of that whole corps. You have to get a basilisk quite close to a man, and looking straight at him, for petrifaction; and the aluminum-foil suit and helmet you must wear to deflect the influence of your pets is an invitation to snipers. Then, too, when human carbon is turned to silicon, you have a radioactive isotope, and maybe get such a dose of radiation yourself that the medics have to give you St. John's Wort plucked from a graveyard in the dark of the moon.

So, in case you didn't know, cremation hasn't simply died out as a custom; it's become illegal under the National Defense Act. We have to have plenty of old-fashioned cemeteries. Thus does the age of science pare down our liberties.

I went on past the engineers, who were directing a gang of zombies carving another drainage ditch, and on to General Vanbrugh's big tent. When the guard saw my Tetragramaton insigne, for the Intelligence Corps, and the bars on my shoulders, he saluted and let me in. I came to a halt before the desk and brought my own hand up.

"Captain Matuchek reporting, sir," I said.

Vanbrugh looked at me from beneath shaggy gray brows. He was a large man with a face like weathered rock, 103 percent Regular Army, but we liked him as well as you can like a buck general. "At ease," he said. "Sit down. This'll take a while."

I found a folding chair and lowered myself into it. Two others were already seated whom I didn't know. One was a plump man with a round red face and a fluffy white beard, a major bearing the crystal-ball emblem of the Signal Corps. The other was a young woman. In spite of my weariness, I blinked and looked twice at her. She was worth it—a tall green-eyed redhead with straight high-cheeked features and a figure too good for the WAC clothes or any other. Captain's bars, Cavalry spider . . . or Sleipnir, if you want to be official about it.

"Major Harrigan," grumbled the general. "Captain Graylock. Captain Matuchek. Let's get down to business."

He spread a map out before us. I leaned over and looked at it. Positions were indicated, ours and the enemy's. They still held the Pacific seaboard from Alaska halfway down through Oregon, though that was considerable improvement from a year ago, when the Battle of the Mississippi had turned the tide.

"Now then," said Vanbrugh, "I'll tell you the overall situation. This is a dangerous mission, you don't have to volunteer, but I want you to know how important it is."

What I knew, just then, was that I'd been told to volunteer or else. That was the Army, at least in a major war like this, and in principle I couldn't object. I'd been a reasonably contented Hollywood actor when the Saracen Caliphate attacked us. I wanted to go back to more of the same, but that meant finishing the war.

"You can see we're driving them back," said the general, "and the occupied countries are primed and cocked to revolt as soon as they get a fighting chance. The British have been organizing the underground and arming them while readying for a cross-Channel jump. The Russians are set to advance from the north. But we have to give the enemy a decisive blow, break this whole front and roll 'em up. That'll be the signal. If we succeed, the war will be over this year. Otherwise it might drag on for another three."

I knew it. The whole Army knew it. Official word hadn't been passed yet, but somehow you feel when a big push is impending.

His stumpy finger traced along the map. "The 9th Armored Division is here, the 12th Broomborne here, the 14th Cavalry here, the Salamanders here where we know they've concentrated their fire-breathers. The Marines are ready to establish a beachhead and retake Seattle, now that the Navy's bred enough Krakens. One good goose, and we'll have 'em running."

Major Harrigan snuffled into his beard and stared gloomily at a crystal ball. It was clouded and vague; the enemy had been jamming our crystals till they were no use whatsoever, though naturally we'd retaliated. Captain Graylock tapped impatiently on the desk with a perfectly manicured nail. She was so clean and crisp and efficient, I decided I didn't like her looks after all. Not while I had three days' beard bristling from my chin.

"But apparently something's gone wrong, sir," I ventured.

"Correct, damn it," said Vanbrugh. "In Trollburg."

I nodded. The Saracens held that town: a key position, sitting as it did on U.S. Highway 20 and guarding the approach to Salem and Portland.

"I take it we're supposed to seize Trollburg, sir," I murmured.

Vanbrugh scowled. "That's the job for the 45th," he grunted. "If we muff it, the enemy can sally out against the 9th, cut them off, and throw the whole operation akilter. But now Major Harrigan and Captain Graylock come from the 14th to tell me the Trollburg garrison has an afreet."

I whistled, and a chill crawled along my spine. The Caliphate had exploited the Powers recklessly—that was one reason why the rest of the Moslem world regarded them as heretics and hated them as much as we did—but I never thought they'd go as far as breaking Solomon's seal. An afreet getting out of hand could destroy more than anybody cared to estimate.

"I hope they haven't but one," I whispered.

"No, they don't," said the Graylock woman. Her voice was low and could have been pleasant if it weren't so brisk. "They've been dredging the Red Sea in hopes of finding another Solly bottle, but this seems to be the last one left."

"Bad enough," I said. The effort to keep my tone steady helped calm me down. "How'd you find out?"

"We're with the 14th," said Graylock unnecessarily. Her Cavalry badge had surprised me, however. Normally, the only recruits the Army can dig up to ride unicorns are picklefaced schoolteachers and the like.

"I'm simply a liaison officer," said Major Harrigan in haste. "I go by broomstick myself." I grinned at that. No American male, unless he's in holy orders, likes to admit he's qualified to control a unicorn. He saw me and flushed angrily.

Graylock went on, as if dictating. She kept her tone flat, though little else. "We had the luck to capture a bimbashi in a commando attack. I questioned him."

"They're pretty close-mouthed, those noble sons of . . . um . . . the desert," I said. I'd bent the Geneva Convention myself, occasionally, but didn't relish the idea of breaking it completely—even if the enemy had no such scruples.

"Oh, we practiced no brutality," said Graylock. "We housed him and fed him very well. But the moment a bite of food was in his throat, I'd turn it into pork. He broke pretty fast, and spilled everything he knew."

I had to laugh aloud, and Vanbrugh himself chuckled; but she sat perfectly deadpan. Organic-organic transformation, which merely shuffles molecules around without changing atoms, has no radiation hazards but naturally requires a good knowledge of chemistry. That's the real reason the average dogface hates the technical corps: pure envy of a man who can turn K rations into steak and French fries. The quartermasters have enough trouble conjuring up the rations themselves, without branching into fancy dishes.

"Okay, you learned they have an afreet in Trollburg," said the general. "What about their strength otherwise?"

"A small division, sir. You can take the place handily, if that demon can be immobilized," said Harrigan.

"Yes. I know." Vanbrugh swiveled his eyes around to me. "Well, Captain, are you game? If you can carry the stunt off, it'll mean a Silver Star at least—pardon me, a Bronze."

"Uh—" I paused, fumbling after words. I was more interested in promotion and ultimate discharge, but that might follow, too. Nevertheless . . . quite apart from my own neck, there was a practical objection. "Sir, I don't know a damn thing about the job. I nearly flunked Demonology 1 in college."

"That'll be my part," said Graylock.

"You!" I picked my jaw off the floor again, but couldn't find anything else to say.

"I was head witch of the Arcane Agency in New York before the war," she said coldly. Now I knew where she got that personality: the typical big-city career girl. I can't stand them. "I know as much about handling demons as anyone on this coast. Your task will be to escort me safely to the place and back."

"Yeah," I said weakly. "Yeah, that's all."

Vanbrugh cleared his throat. He didn't like sending a woman on such a mission, but time was too short for him to have any choice. "Captain Matuchek is one of the best werewolves in the business," he complimented me.

Ave, Caesar, morituri te salutant, I thought. No, that isn't what I mean, but never mind. I can figure out a better phrasing at my leisure after I'm dead.

I wasn't afraid, exactly. Besides the spell laid on me to prevent that, I had reason to believe my personal chances were no worse than those of any infantryman headed into a firefight. Nor would Vanbrugh sacrifice personnel on a mission he himself considered hopeless. But I did feel less optimistic about the prospects than he.

"I think two adepts can get past their guards," the general proceeded. "From then on, you'll have to improvise. If you can put that monster out of action, we attack at noon tomorrow." Grimly: "If I haven't got word to that effect by dawn, we'll have to regroup, start retreating, and save what we can. Okay, here's a geodetic survey map of the town and approaches—"

He didn't waste time asking me if I had really volunteered.

II

I guided Captain Graylock back to the tent I shared with two brother officers. Darkness was creeping across the long chill slant of rain. We plodded through the muck in silence until we were under canvas. My tentmates were out on picket duty, so we had the place to ourselves. I lit the saint-elmo and sat down on the sodden plank floor.

"Have a chair," I said, pointing to our one camp stool. It was an animated job we'd bought in San Francisco: not especially bright, but it would carry our duffel and come when called. It shifted uneasily at the unfamiliar weight, then went back to sleep.

Graylock took out a pack of Wings and raised her brows. I nodded my thanks, and the cigaret flapped over to my mouth. Personally, I smoke Luckies in the field: self-striking tobacco is convenient when your matches may be wet. When I was a civilian and could afford it, my brand was Philip Morris, because the little red-coated smoke sprite can also mix you a drink.

We puffed for a bit in silence, listening to the rain. "Well," I said at last, "I suppose you have transportation."

"My personal broomstick," she said. "I don't like this GI Willys. Give me a Cadillac anytime. I've souped it up, too."

"And you have your grimoires and powders and whatnot?"

"Just some chalk. No material agency is much use against a powerful demon."

"Yeah? What about the sealing wax on the Solly bottle?"

"It isn't the wax that holds an afreet in, but the seal. The spells are symbolic; in fact, it's believed their effect is purely psychosomatic." She hollowed the flat planes of her cheeks, sucking in smoke, and I saw what a good bony structure she had. "We may have a chance to test that theory tonight."

"Well, then, you'll want a light pistol loaded with silver slugs; they have weres of their own, you know. I'll take a grease gun and a forty-five and a few grenades."

"How about a squirter?"

I frowned. The notion of using holy water as a weapon has always struck me as blasphemous, though the chaplain said it was permissible against Low World critters. "No good to us," I said. "The Moslems don't have that ritual, so of course they don't use any beings that can be controlled by it. Let's see, I'll want my Polaroid flash, too. And that's about it."

Ike Abrams stuck his big nose in the tent flap. "Would you and the lady captain like some eats, sir?" he asked.

"Why, sure," I said. Inwardly, I thought: Hate to spend my last night on Midgard standing in a chow line. When he had gone, I explained to the girl: "Ike's only a private, but we were friends in Hollywood—he was a prop man when I played in *Call of the Wild* and *Silver Chief*—and he's kind of appointed himself my orderly. He'll bring us some food here."

"You know," she remarked, "that's one good thing about the technological age. Did you know there used to be widespread anti-Semitism in this country? Not just among a few Johannine cranks; no, among ordinary respectable citizens."

"Fact?"

"Fact. Especially a false belief that Jews were cowards and never found in the front lines. Now, when religion forbids most of them to originate spells, and the Orthodox don't use goetics at all, the proportion of them who serve as dogfaces and Rangers is simply too high to ignore."

I myself had gotten tired of comic-strip supermen and pulp-magazine heroes having such monotonously Yiddish names—don't Anglo-Saxons belong to our culture, too?—but she'd made a good point. And it showed she was a trifle more than a money machine. A bare trifle.

"What'd you do in civilian life?" I asked, chiefly to drown out the incessant noise of the rain.

"I told you," she snapped, irritable again. "I was with the Arcane Agency. Advertising, public relations, and so on."

"Oh, well," I said. "Hollywood is at least as phony, so I shouldn't sneer."

I couldn't help it, however. Those Madison Avenue characters gave me a pain in the rear end. Using the good Art to puff some self-important nobody, or to sell a product whose main virtue is its total similarity to other brands of the same. The SPCA has cracked down on training nixies to make fountains spell out words, or cramming young salamanders into glass tubes to light up Broadway, but I can still think of better uses for slick paper than trumpeting Ma Chère perfume. Which is actually a love potion anyway, though you know what postal regulations are.

"You don't understand," she said. "It's part of our economy—part of our whole society. Do you think the average backyard warlock is capable of repairing, oh, say a lawn sprinkler? Hell, no! He'd probably let loose the water elementals and flood half a township if it weren't for the inhibitory spells. And we, Arcane, undertook the campaign to convince the Hydros they had to respect our symbols. I told you it's psychosomatic when you're dealing with these really potent beings. For that job, I had to go down in an aqualung!"

I stared at her with more respect. Ever since mankind found how to degauss the ruinous effects of cold iron, and the goetic age began, the world had needed some pretty bold people. Apparently she was one of them.

Abrams brought in two plates of rations. He looked wistful, and I would have invited him to join us except that our mission was secret and we had to thresh out the details.

Captain Graylock 'chanted the coffee into martinis—not quite dry enough—and the dog food into steaks—a turn too well done; but you can't expect the finer sensibilities in a woman, and it was the best chow I'd had in a month. She relaxed a bit over the brandy, and I learned that her repellent crispness was simply armor against the slick types she dealt with, and we found out that our first names were Steven and Virginia. But then dusk had become dark outside, and we must be going.

III

You may think it was sheer lunacy, sending two people, one of them a woman, into an enemy division on a task like this. It would seem to call for a Ranger brigade, at least. But present-day science had transformed war as well as industry, medicine, and ordinary life. Our mission was desperate in any event, and we wouldn't have gained enough by numbers to make reinforcements worthwhile.

You see, while practically anyone can learn a few simple cantrips, to operate a presensitized broomstick or vacuum cleaner or turret lathe or whatever, only a small minority of the human race can qualify as adepts. Besides years of study and practice, that takes inborn talent. It's kind of like therianthropy: if you're one of the rare persons with chromosomes for that, you can change into your characteristic animal almost by instinct; otherwise you need a transformation performed on you by powerful outside forces.

My scientific friends tell me that the Art involves regarding the universe as a set of Cantorian infinities. Within any given class, the part is equal to the whole and so on. One good witch could do all the running we were likely to need; a larger party would simply be more liable to detection, and would risk valuable personnel. So Vanbrugh had very rightly sent us two alone.

The trouble with sound military principles is that sometimes you personally get caught in them.

Virginia and I turned our backs on each other while we changed clothes. She got into an outfit of slacks and combat jacket, I into the elastic knit garment which would fit me as well in wolf-shape. We put on our helmets, hung our equipment around us, and turned about. Even in the baggy green battle garb she looked good.

"Well," I said tonelessly, "shall we go?"

I wasn't afraid, of course. Every recruit is immunized against fear when they put the geas on him. But I didn't like the prospect.

"The sooner the better, I suppose," she answered. Stepping to the entrance, she whistled.

Her stick swooped down and landed just outside. It had been stripped of the fancy chrome, but was still a neat job. The foam-rubber seats had good shock absorbers and well-designed back rests, unlike Army transport. Her familiar was a gigantic tomcat, black as a furry midnight, with two malevolent yellow eyes. He arched his back and spat indignantly. The weatherproofing spell kept rain off him, but he didn't like this damp air.

Virginia chucked him under the chin. "Oh, so, Svartalf," she murmured. "Good cat, rare sprite, prince of darkness, if we outlive this night you shall sleep on cloudy cushions and lap cream from a golden bowl." He cocked his ears and raced his motor.

I climbed into the rear seat, snugged my feet in the stirrups, and leaned back. The girl mounted in front of me and crooned to the stick. It swished upward, the ground fell away and the camp was hidden in gloom. Both of us had been given witch-sight—infrared vision, actually—so we didn't need lights.

When we got above the clouds, we saw a giant vault of stars overhead and a swirling dim whiteness below. I also glimpsed a couple of P-56s circling on patrol, fast jobs with six brooms each to lift their weight of armor and machine guns. We left them behind and streaked northward. I rested the BAR on my lap and sat listening to the air whine past. Underneath us, in the rough-edged murk of the hills, I spied occasional flashes, an artillery duel. So far no one had been able to cast a spell fast enough to turn or implode a shell. I'd heard rumors that General Electric was developing a gadget which could recite the formula in microseconds, but meanwhile the big guns went on talking.

Trollburg was a mere few miles from our position. I saw it as a vague sprawling mass, blacked out against our cannon and bombers. It would have been nice to have an atomic weapon just then, but as long as the Tibetans keep those antinuclear warfare prayer wheels turning, such thoughts must remain merely science-fictional. I felt my belly muscles tighten. The cat bottled out his tail and swore. Virginia sent the broomstick slanting down.

We landed in a clump of trees and she turned to me. "Their outposts must be somewhere near," she whispered. "I didn't dare try landing on a rooftop; we could have been seen too easily. We'll have to go in from here."

I nodded. "Okay. Gimme a minute."

I turned the flash on myself. How hard to believe that transforming had depended on a bright full moon till only ten years ago! Then Wiener showed that the process was simply one of polarized light of the right wavelengths, triggering the pineal gland, and the Polaroid Corporation made another million dollars or so from its WereWish Lens. It's not easy to keep up with this fearful and wonderful age we live in, but I wouldn't trade.

The usual rippling, twisting sensations, the brief drunken dizziness and half-ecstatic pain, went through me. Atoms reshuffled into whole new molecules, nerves grew some endings and lost others, bone was briefly fluid and muscles like stretched rubber. Then I stabilized, shook myself, stuck my tail out the flap of the skin-tight pants, and nuzzled Virginia's hand.

She stroked my neck, behind the helmet. "Good boy," she whispered. "Go get 'em."

I turned and faded into the brush.

A lot of writers have tried to describe how it feels to be were, and every one of them has failed, because human language doesn't have the words. My vision was no longer acute, the stars were blurred above me and the world took on a colorless flatness. But I heard with a clarity that made the night almost a roar, way into the supersonic; and a universe of smells roiled in my nostrils, wet grass and teeming dirt, the hot sweet little odor of a scampering field mouse, the clean tang of oil and guns, a faint harshness of smoke— Poor stupefied humanity, half-dead to such earthy glories!

The psychological part is the hardest to convey. I was a wolf, with a wolf's nerves and glands and instincts, a wolf's sharp but limited intelligence. I had a man's memories and a man's purposes, but they were unreal, dreamlike. I must make an effort of trained will to hold to them and not go hallooing off after the nearest jackrabbit. No wonder weres had a bad name in the old days, before they themselves understood the mental changes involved and got the right habits drilled into them from babyhood.

I weigh a hundred and eighty pounds, and the conservation of mass holds good like any other law of nature, so I was a pretty big wolf. But it was easy to flow through the bushes and meadows and gullies, another drifting shadow. I was almost inside the town when I caught a near smell of man.

I flattened, the gray fur bristling along my spine, and waited. The sentry came by. He was a tall bearded fellow with gold earrings that glimmered wanly under the stars. The turban wrapped around his helmet bulked monstrous against the Milky Way.

I let him go and followed his path until I saw the next one. They were placed around Trollburg, each pacing a hundred-yard arc and meeting his opposite number at either end of it. No simple task to—

Something murmured in my ears. I crouched. One of their aircraft ghosted overhead. I saw two men and a couple of machine guns squatting on top of the carpet. It circled low and lazily, above the ring of sentries. Trollburg was well guarded.

Somehow, Virginia and I had to get through that picket. I wished the transformation had left me with full human reasoning powers. My wolf-impulse was simply to jump on the nearest man, but that would bring the whole garrison down on my hairy ears.

Wait—maybe that was what was needed!

I loped back to the thicket. The Svartalf cat scratched at me and zoomed up a tree. Virginia Graylock started, her pistol sprang into her hand, then she relaxed and laughed a bit nervously. I could work the flash hung about my neck, even as I was, but it went more quickly with her fingers.

"Well?" she asked when I was human again. "What'd you find out?"

I described the situation, and saw her frown and bite her lip. It was really too shapely a lip for such purposes. "Not so good," she reflected. "I was afraid of something like this."

"Look," I said, "can you locate that afreet in a hurry?"

"Oh, yes. I've studied at Congo U. and did quite well at witch-smelling. What of it?"

"If I attack one of those guards, and make a racket doing it, their main attention will be turned that way. You should have an even chance to fly across the line unobserved, and once you're in the town your Tarnkappe—"

She shook her red head. "I didn't bring one. Their detection systems are as good as ours. Invisibility is actually obsolete."

"Mmm—yeah, I suppose you're right. Well, anyhow, you can take advantage of the darkness to get to the afreet house. From there on, you'll have to play by ear."

"I suspected we'd have to do something like this," she replied. With a softness that astonished me: "But Steve, that's a long chance for you to take."

"Not unless they hit me with silver, and most of their cartridges are plain lead. They use a tracer principle like us; every tenth round is argent. I've got a ninety percent probability of getting home free."

"You're a liar," she said. "But a brave liar."

I wasn't brave at all. It's inspiring to think of Valley Forge, or the Alamo, or San Juan Hill, or Casablanca where our outnumbered Army stopped three Panther divisions of von Ogerhaus's Afrika Korps—but only when you're safe and comfortable yourself. Down underneath the antipanic geas, a cold knot was in my guts. Still, I couldn't see any other way to do the job, and failure to attempt it would mean court-martial.

"I'll run their legs off once they start chasing me," I told her. "When I've shaken 'em, I'll try to circle back and join you."

"Okay." Suddenly she rose on tiptoe and kissed me. The impact was explosive.

I stood for a moment, looking at her. "What are you doing Saturday night?" I asked, a mite shakily.

She laughed. "Don't get ideas, Steve. I'm in the Cavalry."

"Yeah, but the war won't last forever." I grinned at her, a reckless fighting grin that made her eyes linger. Acting experience is often useful.

We settled the details as well as we could. She herself had no soft touch: the afreet would be well guarded, and was plenty dangerous in itself. The chances of us both seeing daylight were nothing to feel complacent about.

I turned back to wolf-shape and licked her hand. She rumpled my fur. I slipped off into the darkness.

I had chosen a sentry well off the highway, across which there would surely be barriers. A man could be seen to either side of my victim, tramping slowly back and forth. I glided behind a stump near the middle of his beat and waited for him.

When he came, I sprang. I caught a dark brief vision of eyes and teeth in the bearded face, I heard him yelp and smelled the upward spurt of his fear, then we shocked together. He went down on his back, threshing, and I snapped for the throat. My jaws closed on his arm, and blood was hot and salty on my tongue.

He screamed again. I sensed the call going down the line. The two nearest Saracens ran to help. I tore out the gullet of the first man and bunched myself for a leap at the next.

He fired. The bullet went through me in a jag of pain and the impact sent me staggering. But he didn't know how to deal with a were. He should have dropped on one knee and fired steadily till he got to the silver bullet; if necessary, he should have fended me off, even pinned me with his bayonet, while he shot. This one kept running toward me, calling on the Allah of his heretical sect.

My tissues knitted as I plunged to meet him. I got past the bayonet and gun muzzle, hitting him hard enough to knock the weapon
loose but not to bowl him over. He braced his legs, grabbed my
neck, and hung on.

I swung my left hind leg back of his ankle and shoved. He fell
with me on top, the position an infighting werewolf always tries for.
My head swiveled; I gashed open his arm and broke his grip.

Before I could settle the business, three others had piled on me.
Their trench scimitars went up and down, in between my ribs and
out again. Lousy training they'd had. I snapped my way free of the
heap—half a dozen by then—and broke loose.

Through sweat and blood I caught the faintest whiff of Channel
No. 5, and something in me laughed. Virginia had sped past the
confusion, riding her stick a foot above ground, and was inside
Trollburg. My next task was to lead a chase and not stop a silver slug
while doing so.

I howled, to taunt the men spilling from outlying houses, and let
them have a good look at me before making off across the fields.
My pace was easy, not to lose them at once; I relied on zigzags to
keep me unpunctured. They followed, stumbling and shouting.

As far as they knew, this had been a mere commando raid. Their
pickets would have re-formed and the whole garrison been alerted.
But surely none except a few chosen officers knew about the afreet,
and none of those knew we'd acquired the information. So they
had no way of telling what we really planned. Maybe we *would* pull
this operation off—

Something swooped overhead, one of their damned carpets. It
rushed down on me like a hawk, guns spitting. I made for the nearest patch of woods.

Into the trees! Given half a break, I could—

They didn't give it. I heard a bounding behind me, caught the
acrid smell and whimpered. A weretiger could go as fast as I.

For a moment I remembered an old guide I'd had in Alaska, and
wished to blazes he were here. He was a were–Kodiak bear. Then I
whirled and met the tiger before he could pounce.

He was a big one, five hundred pounds at least. His eyes smoldered above the great fangs, and he lifted a paw that could crack
my spine like a dry twig. I rushed in, snapping, and danced back
before he could strike.

Part of me heard the enemy, blundering around in the underbrush trying to find us. The tiger leaped. I evaded him and bolted
for the nearest thicket. Maybe I could go where he couldn't. He
ramped through the woods behind me, roaring.

I saw a narrow space between a pair of giant oaks, too small for

him, and hurried that way. But it was too small for me also. In the
half second that I was stuck, he caught up. The lights exploded and
went out.

IV

I was nowhere and nowhen. My very body had departed from me,
or I from it. How could I think of infinite eternal dark and cold and
emptiness when I had no senses? How could I despair when I was
nothing but a point in spacetime? . . . No, not even that, for there
was nothing else, nothing to find or love or hate or fear or be
related to in any way whatsoever. The dead were less alone than I,
for I was all which existed.

This was my despair.

But on the instant, or after a quadrillion years, or both or neither, I
came to know otherwise. I was under the regard of the Solipsist.
Helpless in unconsciousness, I could but share that egotism so ultimate that it would yield no room even to hope. I swirled in the tides
and storms of thoughts too remote, too alien, too vast for me to take
in save as I might brokenly hear the polar ocean while it drowned me.

*—danger, this one—he and those two—somehow they can be a terrible
danger—not now* (scornfully) *when they merely help complete the ruin of a
plan already bungled into wreck—no, later, when the next plan is ripening,
the great one of which this war was naught but an early leaf—something
about them warns thinly of danger—could I only scan more clearly into
time!—they must be diverted, destroyed, somehow dealt with before their
potential has grown—but I cannot originate anything yet—maybe they will
be slain by the normal chances of war—if not, I must remember them and try
later—now I have too much else to do, saving those seeds I planted in the
world—the birds of the enemy fly thick across my fields, hungry crows and
eagles to guard them—*(with ever wilder hate) *my snares shall take you
yet, birds—and the One Who loosed you!*

So huge was the force of that final malevolence that I was cast
free.

V

I opened my eyes. For a while I was aware entirely of the horror.
Physical misery rescued me, driving those memories back to where
half-forgotten nightmares dwell. The thought flitted by me that
shock must have made me briefly delirious.

A natural therianthrope in his beast shape isn't quite as invulnerable as most people believe. Aside from things like silver—biochem-
ical poisons to a metabolism in that semifluid state—damage which

stops a vital organ will stop life; amputations are permanent unless a surgeon is near to sew the part back on before its cells die; and so on and so on, no pun intended. We are a hardy sort, however. I'd taken a blow that probably broke my neck. The spinal cord not being totally severed, the damage had healed at standard therio speed.

The trouble was, they'd arrived and used my flash to make me human before the incidental hurts had quite gone away. My head drummed and I retched.

"Get up." Someone stuck a boot in my ribs.

I lurched erect. They'd removed my gear, including the flash. A score of them trained their guns on me. Tiger Boy stood close. In man-shape he was almost seven feet tall and monstrously fat. Squinting through the headache, I saw he wore the insignia of an emir—which was a military rank these days rather than a title, but pretty important nevertheless.

"Come," he said. He led the way, and I was hustled along behind.

I saw their carpets in the sky and heard the howling of their own weres looking for spoor of other Americans. I was still too groggy to care very much.

We entered the town, its pavement sounding hollow under the boots, and went toward the center. Trollburg wasn't big, maybe five thousand population once. Most of the streets were empty. I saw a few Saracen troops, antiaircraft guns poking into the sky, a dragon lumbering past with flames flickering around its jaws and cannon projecting from the armored howdah. No trace of the civilians, but I knew what had happened to them. The attractive young women were in the officers' harems, the rest dead or locked away pending shipment to the slave markets.

By the time we got to the hotel where the enemy headquartered, my aches had subsided and my brain was clear. That was a mixed blessing under the circumstances. I was taken upstairs to a suite and told to stand before a table. The emir sat down behind it, half a dozen guards lined the walls, and a young pasha of Intelligence seated himself nearby.

The emir's big face turned to that one, and he spoke a few words—I suppose to the effect of "I'll handle this, you take notes." He looked back at me. His eyes were the pale tigergreen.

"Now then," he said in good English, "we shall have some questions. Identify yourself, please."

I told him mechanically that I was called Sherrinford Mycroft, Captain, AUS, and gave him my serial number.

"That is not your real name, is it?" he asked.

"Of course not!" I replied. "I know the Geneva Convention, and you're not going to cast name-spells on me. Sherrinford Mycroft is my official johnsmith."

"The Caliphate has not subscribed to the Geneva Convention," said the emir quietly, "and stringent measures are sometimes necessary in a jehad. What was the purpose of this raid?"

"I am not required to answer that," I said. Silence would have served the same end, delay to gain time for Virginia, but not as well.

"You may be persuaded to do so," he said.

If this had been a movie, I'd have told him I was picking daisies, and kept on wisecracking while they brought out the thumbscrews. In practice it would have fallen a little flat.

"All right," I said. "I was scouting."

"A single one of you?"

"A few others. I hope they got away." That might keep his boys busy hunting for a while.

"You lie," he said dispassionately.

"I can't help it if you don't believe me." I shrugged.

His eyes narrowed. "I shall soon know if you speak truth," he said. "If not, may Eblis have mercy on you."

I couldn't help it, I jerked where I stood and sweat pearled out on my skin. The emir laughed. He had an unpleasant laugh, a sort of whining growl deep in his fat throat, like a tiger playing with its kill.

"Think over your decision," he advised, and turned to some papers on the table.

It grew most quiet in that room. The guards stood as if cast in bronze. The young shavetail dozed beneath his turban. Behind the emir's back, a window looked out on a blankness of night. The sole sounds were the loud ticking of a clock and the rustle of papers. They seemed to deepen the silence.

I was tired, my head ached, my mouth tasted foul and thirsty. The sheer physical weariness of having to stand was meant to help wear me down. It occurred to me that the emir must be getting scared of us, to take this much trouble with a lone prisoner. That was kudos for the American cause, but small consolation to me.

My eyes flickered, studying the tableau. There wasn't much to see, standard hotel furnishings. The emir had cluttered his desk with a number of objects: a crystal ball useless because of our own jamming, a fine cut-glass bowl looted from somebody's house, a set of nice crystal wineglasses, a cigar humidor of quartz glass, a decanter full of what looked like good Scotch. I guess he just liked crystal.

He helped himself to a cigar, waving his hand to make the humidor open and a Havana fly into his mouth and light itself. As the minutes crawled by, an ashtray soared up from time to time to receive from him. I guessed that everything he had was 'chanted so it would rise and move easily. A man that fat, paying the price of being a really big werebeast, needed such conveniences.

It was very quiet. The light glared down on us. It was somehow hideously wrong to see a good ordinary GE saint-elmo shining on those turbaned heads.

I began to get the forlorn glimmerings of an idea. How to put it into effect I didn't yet know, but just to pass the time I began composing some spells.

Maybe half an hour had passed, though it seemed more like half a century, when the door opened and a fennec, the small fox of the African desert, trotted in. The emir looked up as it went into a closet, to find darkness to use its flash. The fellow who came out was, naturally, a dwarf barely one foot high. He prostrated himself and spoke rapidly in a high thready voice.

"So." The emir's chins turned slowly around to me. "The report is that no trace was found of other tracks than yours. You have lied."

"Didn't I tell you?" I asked. My throat felt stiff and strange. "We used owls and bats. I was the lone wolf."

"Be still," he said tonelessly. "I know as well as you that the only werebats are vampires, and that vampires are—what you say—4-F in all armies."

That was true. Every so often, some armchair general asks why we don't raise a force of Draculas. The answer is routine: they're too light and flimsy; they can't endure sunshine; if they don't get a steady blood ration they're apt to turn on their comrades; and you can't possibly use them around Italian troops. I swore at myself, but my mind had been too numb to think straight.

"I believe you are concealing something," went on the emir. He gestured at his glasses and decanter, which supplied him with a shot of Scotch, and sipped judiciously. The Caliphate sect was also heretical with respect to strong drink; they maintained that while the Prophet forbade wine, he said nothing about beer, gin, whisky, brandy, rum, or akvavit.

"We shall have to use stronger measures," the emir said at last. "I was hoping to avoid them." He nodded at his guards.

Two held my arms. The pasha worked me over. He was good at that. The werefennec watched avidly, the emir puffed his cigar and went on with his paperwork. After a long few minutes, he gave an order. They let me go, and even set forth a chair for me, which I needed badly.

I sat breathing hard. The emir regarded me with a certain gentleness. "I regret this," he said. "It is not enjoyable." Oddly, I believed him. "Let us hope you will be reasonable before we have to inflict permanent injuries. Meanwhile, would you like a cigar?"

The old third degree procedure. Knock a man around for a while, then show him kindness. You'd be surprised how often that makes him blubber and break.

"We desire information about your troops and their plans," said the emir. "If you will cooperate and accept the true faith, you can have an honored position with us. We like good men in the Caliphate." He smiled. "After the war, you could select your harem out of Hollywood if you desired."

"And if I don't squeal—" I murmured.

He spread his hands. "You will have no further wish for a harem. The choice is yours."

"Let me think," I begged. "This isn't easy."

"Please do," he answered urbanely, and returned to his papers.

I sat as relaxed as possible, drawing the smoke into my throat and letting strength flow back. The Army geas could be broken by their technicians only if I gave my free consent, and I didn't want to. I considered the window behind the emir. It was a two-story drop to the street.

Most likely, I'd just get myself killed. But that was preferable to any other offer I'd had.

I went over the spells I'd haywired. A real technician has to know at least one arcane language—Latin, Greek, classical Arabic, Sanskrit, Old Norse, or the like—for the standard reasons of sympathetic science. Paranatural phenomena are not strongly influenced by ordinary speech. But except for the usual tag-ends of incantations, the minimum to operate the gadgets of daily life, I was no scholar.

However, I knew one slightly esoteric dialect quite well. I didn't know if it would work, but I could try.

My muscles tautened as I moved. It was a shuddersome effort to be casual. I knocked the end of ash off my cigar. As I lifted the thing again, it collected some ash from the emir's.

I got the rhyme straight in my mind, put the cigar to my lips, and subvocalized the spell.

"Ashes-way of the urningbay,
upward-way ownay eturningray.
as-way the arksspay do yflay,
ikestray imhay in the eye-way!"

I closed my right eye and brought the glowing cigar end almost against the lid.

The emir's El Fumo leaped up and ground itself into *his* right eye.

He screamed and fell backward. I soared to my feet. I'd marked the werefennec, and one stride brought me over to him. I broke his

vile little neck with a backhanded cuff and yanked off the flash that
hung from it.

The guards howled and plunged for me. I went over the table
and down on top of the emir, snatching his decanter en route. He
clawed at me, wild with pain, I saw the ghastliness in his eye socket,
and meanwhile I was hanging on to the vessel and shouting:

"Ingthay of ystalcray,
ebay a istralmay!
As-way I-way owthray,
yflay ouyay osay!"

As I finished, I broke free and hurled the decanter at the guards.
It was lousy poetics, and might not have worked if the fat man hadn't
already sensitized his stuff. As it was, the ball, the ashtray, the bowl,
the glasses, the humidor, and the windowpanes all took off after the
decanter. The air was full of flying glass.

I didn't stay to watch the results, but went out that window like an
exorcised devil. I landed in a ball on the sidewalk, bounced up, and
began running.

VI

Soldiers were around. Bullets sleeted after me. I set a record reaching the nearest alley. My witch-sight showed me a broken window,
and I wriggled through that. Crouching beneath the sill, I heard
the pursuit go by.

This was the back room of a looted grocery store, plenty dark for
my purposes. I hung the flash around my neck, turned it on myself,
and made the changeover. They'd return in a minute, and I didn't
want to be vulnerable to lead.

Wolf, I snuffled around after another exit. A rear door stood half
open. I slipped through into a courtyard full of ancient packing cases.
They made a good hideout. I lay there, striving to control my lupine
nature which wanted to pant, while they swarmed through the area.

When they were gone again, I tried to consider my situation. The
temptation was to hightail out of this poor, damned place. I could
probably make it, and had technically fulfilled my share of the mission. But the job wasn't really complete, and Virginia was alone with
the afreet—if she still lived—and—

When I tried to recall her, the image came as a she-wolf and a
furry aroma. I shook my head angrily. Weariness and desperation
were submerging my reason and letting the animal instincts take
over. I'd better do whatever had to be done fast.

I cast about. The town smells were confusing, but I caught the faintest sulfurous whiff and trotted cautiously in that direction. I kept to the shadows, and was seen twice but not challenged. They must have supposed I was one of theirs. The brimstone reek grew stronger.

They kept the afreet in the courthouse, a good solid building. I went through the small park in front of it, snuffed the wind carefully, and dashed over street and steps. Four enemy soldiers sprawled on top, throats cut open, and the broomstick was parked by the door. It had a twelve-inch switchblade in the handle, and Virginia had used it like a flying lance.

The man side of me, which had been entertaining stray romantic thoughts, backed up in a cold sweat; but the wolf grinned. I poked at the door. She'd 'chanted the lock open and left it that way. I stuck my nose in, and almost had it clawed off before Svartalf recognized me. He jerked his tail curtly, and I passed by and across the lobby. The stinging smell was coming from upstairs. I followed it through a thick darkness.

Light glowed in a second-floor office. I thrust the door ajar and peered in. Virginia was there. She had drawn the curtains and lit the elmos to see by. She was still busy with her precautions, started a little on spying me but went on with the chant. I parked my shaggy behind near the door and watched.

She'd chalked the usual figure, same as the Pentagon in Washington, and a Star of David inside that. The Solly bottle was at the center. It didn't look impressive, an old flask of hard-baked clay with its hollow handle bent over and returning inside—merely a Klein bottle, with Solomon's seal in red wax at the mouth. She'd loosened her hair, and it floated in a ruddy cloud about the pale beautiful face.

The wolf of me wondered why we didn't just make off with this crock of It. The man reminded him that undoubtedly the emir had taken precautions and would have sympathetic means to uncork it from afar. We had to out the demon out of action . . . somehow . . . but nobody on our side knew a great deal about his race.

Virginia finished her spell, drew the bung, and sprang outside the pentacle as smoke boiled from the flask. She almost didn't make it, the afreet came out in such a hurry. I stuck my tail between my legs and snarled. She was scared, too, trying hard not to show that but I caught the adrenaline odor.

The afreet must bend almost double under the ceiling. He was a monstrous gray thing, nude, more or less anthropoid but with wings and horns and long ears, a mouthful of fangs and eyes like hot embers. His assets were strength, speed, and physical near-invulnerability. Turned loose, he could break any attack of Vanbrugh's, and inflict frightful casualties on the most well-dug-in defense. Controlling him afterward, before he laid the countryside waste, would be a problem. But why should the Saracens care? They'd have exacted a geas from him, that he remain their ally, as the price of his freedom.

He roared something in Arabic. Smoke swirled from his mouth. Virginia looked tiny under those half-unfurled bat membranes. Her voice was less cool than she would have preferred: "Speak English, Marid. Or are you too ignorant?"

The demon huffed indignantly. "O spawn of a thousand baboons!" My eardrums flinched from the volume. "O thou white and gutless infidel thing, which I could break with my least finger, come in to me if thou darest!"

I was frightened, less by the chance of his breaking loose than by the racket he was making. It could be heard for a quarter mile.

"Be still, accursed of God!" Virginia answered. That shook him a smidgen. Like most of the hell-breed, he was allergic to holy names, though only seriously so under conditions that we couldn't reproduce here. She stood hands on hips, head tilted, to meet the gaze that smoldered down upon her. "Suleiman bin-Daoud, on whom be peace, didn't jug you for nothing, I see. Back to your prison and never come forth again, lest the anger of Heaven smite you!"

The afreet fleered. "Know that Suleiman the Wise is dead these three thousand years," he retorted. "Long and long have I brooded in my narrow cell, I who once raged free through earth and sky and will now at last be released to work my vengeance on the puny sons of Adam." He shoved at the invisible barrier, but one of that type has a rated strength of several million p.s.i. It would hold firm—till some adept dissolved it. "O thou shameless unveiled harlot with hair of hell, know that I am Rashid the Mighty, the glorious in power, the smiter of rocs! Come in here and fight like a man!"

I moved close to the girl, my hackles raised. The hand that touched my head was cold. "Paranoid type," she whispered. "A lot of these harmful Low Worlders are psycho. Stupid, though. Trickery's our single chance. I don't have any spells to compel him directly. But—" Aloud, to him, she said: "Shut up, Rashid, and listen to me. I also am of your race, and to be respected as such."

"Thou?" He hooted with fake laughter. "Thou of the Marid race? Why, thou fish-faced antling, if thou'dst come in here I'd show thee thou'rt not even fit to—" The rest was graphic but not for any gentlewere to repeat.

"No, hear me," said the girl. "Look and hearken well." She made signs and uttered a formula. I recognized the self-geas against telling a falsehood in the particular conversation. Our courts still haven't adopted it—Fifth Amendment—but I'd seen it used in trials abroad.

The demon recognized it, too. I imagine the Saracen adept who pumped a knowledge of English into him, to make him effective in this war, had added other bits of information about the modern world. He grew more quiet and attentive.

Virginia intoned impressively: "I can speak nothing to you except the truth. Do you agree that the name is the thing?"

"Y-y-yes," the afreet rumbled. "That is common knowledge."

I scented her relief. First hurdle passed! He had *not* been educated in scientific goetics. Though the name is, of course, in sympathy with the object, which is the principle of nymic spells and the like—nevertheless, only in this century has Korzybski demonstrated that the word and its referent are not identical.

"Very well," she said. "My name is Ginny."

He started in astonishment. "Art thou indeed?"

"Yes. Now will you listen to me? I came to offer you advice, as one jinni to another. I have powers of my own, you know, albeit I employ them in the service of Allah, the Omnipotent, the Omniscient, the Compassionate."

He glowered, but supposing her to be one of his species, he was ready to put on a crude show of courtesy. She couldn't be lying about her advice. It did not occur to him that she hadn't said the counsel would be good.

"Go on, then, if thou wilst," he growled. "Knowest thou that tomorrow I fare forth to destroy the infidel host?" He got caught up in his dreams of glory. "Aye, well will I rip them, and trample them, and break and gut and flay them. Well will they learn the power of Rashid the bright-winged, the fiery, the merciless, the wise, the . . ."

Virginia waited out his adjectives, then said gently: "But Rashid, why must you wreak harm? You earn nothing thereby except hate."

A whine crept into his bass. "Aye, thou speakest sooth. The whole world hates me. Everybody conspires against me. Had he not had the aid of traitors, Suleiman had never locked me away. All which I have sought to do has been thwarted by envious ill-wishers— Aye, but tomorrow comes the day of reckoning!"

Virginia lit a cigaret with a steady hand and blew smoke at him. "How can you trust the emir and his cohorts?" she asked. "He, too, is your enemy. He only wants to make a cat's-paw of you. Afterward, back in the bottle!"

"Why . . . why . . ." The afreet swelled till the spacewarp barrier creaked. Lighting crackled from his nostrils. It hadn't occurred to him before; his race isn't bright; but of course a trained psychologist would understand how to follow out paranoid logic.

"Have you not known enmity throughout your long days?" continued Virginia quickly. "Think back, Rashid. Was not the very first thing you remember the cruel act of a spitefully envious world?"

"Aye—it was." The maned head nodded, and the voice dropped very low. "On the day I was hatched . . . aye, my mother's wingtip smote me so I reeled."

"Perhaps that was accidental," said Virginia.

"Nay. Ever she favored my older brother—the lout!"

Virginia sat down cross-legged. "Tell me about it," she urged. Her tone dripped sympathy.

I felt a lessening of the great forces that surged within the barrier. The afreet squatted on his hams, eyes half-shut, going back down a memory trail of millennia. Virginia guided him, a hint here and there. I didn't know what she was driving at, surely you couldn't psychoanalyze the monster in half a night, but—

"—Aye, and I was scarce turned three centuries when I fell into a pit my foes must have dug for me."

"Surely you could fly out of it," she murmured.

The afreet's eyes rolled. His face twisted into still more gruesome furrows. "It was a pit, I say!"

"Not by any chance a lake?" she inquired.

"Nay!" His wings thundered. "No such damnable thing . . . 'twas dark, and wet, but—nay, not wet either, a cold which burned . . ."

I saw dimly that the girl had a lead. She dropped long lashes to hide the sudden gleam in her gaze. Even as a wolf, I could realize what a shock it must have been to an aerial demon, nearly drowning, his fires hissing into steam, and how he must ever after deny to himself that it had happened. But what use could she make of—

Svartalf the cat streaked in and skidded to a halt. Every hair on him stood straight, and his eyes blistered me. He spat something and went out again with me in his van.

Down in the lobby I heard voices. Looking through the door, I saw a few soldiers milling about. They'd come by, perhaps to investigate the noise, seen the dead guards, and now they must have sent after reinforcements.

Whatever Ginny was trying to do, she needed time for it. I went out that door in one gray leap and tangled with the Saracens. We boiled into a clamorous pile. I was almost pinned flat by their numbers, but kept my jaws free and used them. Then Svartalf rode that broomstick above the fight, stabbing.

We carried a few of their weapons back into the lobby in our jaws, and sat down to wait. I figured I'd do better to remain wolf and be immune to most things than have the convenience of hands. Svartalf regarded a tommy gun thoughtfully, propped it along a wall, and crouched over it.

I was in no hurry. Every minute we were left alone, or held off the coming attack, was a minute gained for Ginny. I laid my head on my forepaws and dozed off. Much too soon I heard hobnails rattle on pavement.

The detachment must have been a good hundred. I saw their dark mass, and the gleam of starlight off their weapons. They hovered for a while around the squad we'd liquidated. Abruptly they whooped and charged up the steps.

Svartalf braced himself and worked the tommy gun. The recoil sent him skating back across the lobby, swearing, but he got a couple. I met the rest in the doorway.

Slash, snap, leap in, leap out, rip them and gash them and howl in their faces! They were jammed together in the entrance, slow and clumsy. After a brief whirl of teeth they retreated. They left half a dozen dead and wounded.

I peered through the glass in the door and saw my friend the emir. He had a bandage over his eye, but lumbered around exhorting his men with more energy than I'd expected. Groups of them broke from the main bunch and ran to either side. They'd be coming in the windows and the other doors.

I whined as I realized we'd left the broomstick outside. There could be no escape now, not even for Ginny. The protest became a snarl when I heard glass breaking and rifles blowing off locks.

That Svartalf was a smart cat. He found the tommy gun again and somehow, clumsy though paws are, managed to shoot out the lights. He and I retreated to the stairway.

They came at us in the dark, blind as most men are. I let them fumble around, and the first one who groped to the stairs was killed quietly. The second had time to yell. The whole gang of them crowded after him.

They couldn't shoot in the gloom and press without potting their own people. Excited to mindlessness, they attacked me with scimitars, which I didn't object to. Svartalf raked their legs and I tore them apart—whick, snap, clash, Allah Akbar and teeth in the night!

The stair was narrow enough for me to hold, and their own casualties hampered them, but the sheer weight of a hundred brave men forced me back a tread at a time. Otherwise one could have tackled me and a dozen more have piled on top. As things were, we gave the houris a few fresh customers for every foot we lost.

I have no clear memory of the fight. You seldom do. But it must have been about twenty minutes before they fell back at an angry growl. The emir himself stood at the foot of the stairs, lashing his tail and rippling his gorgeously striped hide.

I shook myself wearily and braced my feet for the last round. The one-eyed tiger climbed slowly toward us. Svartalf spat. Suddenly he zipped down the banister past the larger cat and disappeared in the gloom. Well, he had his own neck to think about—

We were almost nose to nose when the emir lifted a paw full of swords and brought it down. I dodged somehow and flew for his throat. All I got was a mouthful of baggy skin, but I hung on and tried to work my way inward.

He roared and shook his head till I swung like a bell clapper. I shut my eyes and clamped on tight. He raked my ribs with those long claws. I skipped away but kept my teeth where they were. Lunging, he fell on me. His jaws clashed shut. Pain jagged through my tail. I let go to howl.

He pinned me down with one paw, raising the other to break my spine. Somehow, crazed with the hurt, I writhed free and struck upward. His remaining eye was glaring at me, and I bit it out of his head.

He screamed! A sweep of one paw sent me kiting up to slam against the banister. I lay with the wind knocked from me while the blind tiger rolled over in his agony. The beast drowned the man, and he went down the stairs and wrought havoc among his own soldiers.

A broomstick whizzed above the melee. Good old Svartalf! He'd only gone to fetch our transportation. I saw him ride toward the door of the afreet, and rose groggily to meet the next wave of Saracens.

They were still trying to control their boss. I gulped for breath and stood watching and smelling and listening. My tail seemed ablaze. Half of it was gone.

A tommy gun began stuttering. I heard blood rattle in the emir's lungs. He was hard to kill. *That's the end of you, Steve Matuchek,* thought the man of me. *They'll do what they should have done in the first place, stand beneath you and sweep you with their fire, every tenth round argent.*

The emir fell and lay gasping out his life. I waited for his men to collect their wits and remember me.

Ginny appeared on the landing, astride the broomstick. Her voice seemed to come from very far away. "Steve! Quick! Here!"

I shook my head dazedly, trying to understand. I was too tired, too canine. She stuck her fingers in her mouth and whistled. That fetched me.

She slung me across her lap and hung on tight as Svartalf piloted the stick. A gun fired blindly from below. We went out a second-story window and into the sky.

A carpet swooped near. Svartalf arched his back and poured on the Power. That Cadillac had legs! We left the enemy sitting there, and I passed out.

VII

When I came to, I was prone on a cot in a hospital tent. Daylight was bright outside; the earth lay wet and steaming. A medic looked around as I groaned. "Hello, hero," he said. "Better stay in that position for a while. How're you feeling?"

I waited till full consciousness returned before I accepted a cup of bouillon. "How am I?" I whispered; they'd humanized me, of course.

"Not too bad, considering. You had some infection of your wounds—a staphylococcus that can switch species for a human or canine host—but we cleaned the bugs out with a new antibiotic technique. Otherwise, loss of blood, shock, and plain old exhaustion. You should be fine in a week or two."

I lay thinking, my mind draggy, most of my attention on how delicious the bouillon tasted. A field hospital can't lug around the equipment to stick pins in model bacteria. Often it doesn't even have the enlarged anatomical dummies on which the surgeon can do a sympathetic operation. "What technique do you mean?" I asked.

"One of our boys has the Evil Eye. He looks at the germs through a microscope."

I didn't inquire further, knowing that *Reader's Digest* would be waxing lyrical about it in a few months. Something else nagged at me. "The attack . . . have they begun?"

"The— Oh. That! That was two days ago, Rin-Tin-Tin. You've been kept under asphodel. We mopped 'em up along the entire line. Last I heard, they were across the Washington border and still running."

I sighed and went back to sleep. Even the noise as the medic dictated a report to his typewriter couldn't hold me awake.

Ginny came in the next day, with Svartalf riding her shoulder. Sunlight striking through the tent flap turned her hair to hot copper. "Hello, Captain Matuchek," she said. "I came to see how you were, soon as I could get leave."

I raised myself on my elbows, and whistled at the cigaret she offered. When it was between my lips, I said slowly: "Come off it, Ginny. We didn't exactly go on a date that night, but I think we're properly introduced."

"Yes." She sat down on the cot and stroked my hair. That felt good. Svartalf purred at me, and I wished I could respond.

"How about the afreet?" I asked after a while.

"Still in his bottle." She grinned. "I doubt if anybody'll ever be able to get him out again, assuming anybody would want to."

"But what did you *do*?"

"A simple application of Papa Freud's principles. If it's ever written up, I'll have every Jungian in the country on my neck, but it worked. I got him to spinning out his memories and illusions, and soon found he had a hydrophobic complex—which is fear of water, Rover, not rabies—"

"You can call me Rover," I growled, "but if you call me Fido, gives a paddling."

She didn't ask why I assumed I'd be sufficiently close in future for such laying on of hands. That encouraged me. Indeed, she blushed, but went on: "Having gotten the key to his personality, I found it simple to play on his phobia. I pointed out how common a substance water is and how difficult total dehydration is. He got more and more scared. When I showed him that all animal tissue, including his own, is about eighty percent water, that was that. He crept back into his bottle and went catatonic."

After a moment, she added thoughtfully: "I'd like to have him for my mantelpiece, but I suppose he'll wind up in the Smithsonian. So I'll simply write a little treatise on the military uses of psychiatry."

"Aren't bombs and dragons and elfshot gruesome enough?" I demanded with a shudder.

Poor simple elementals! They think they're fiendish, but ought to take lessons from the human race.

As for me, I could imagine certain drawbacks to getting hitched with a witch, but— "C'mere, youse."

She did.

I don't have many souvenirs of the war. It was an ugly time and best forgotten. But one keepsake will always be with me, in spite of the plastic surgeons' best efforts. As a wolf, I've got a stumpy tail, and as a man I don't like to sit down in wet weather.

That's a hell of a thing to receive a Purple Heart for.

That Hell-Bound Train

Robert Bloch

Robert Bloch (1917–1994) is remembered as the writer of the book Psycho, *the basis for Alfred Hitchcock's famous film of the same name. He got his start writing stories for pulp magazines such as* Weird Tales, Fantastic Adventures, *and* Unknown. *Later in his career he wrote the novels* American Gothic, Firebug, *and* Fear and Trembling, *among many others. He also edited several anthologies, including* Psycho-paths *and* Monsters in Our Midst.

WHEN MARTIN WAS A LITTLE BOY, HIS DADDY WAS A RAILROAD MAN. Daddy never rode the high iron, but he walked the tracks for the *CB&Q,* and he was proud of his job. And every night when he got drunk, he sang this old song about *That Hell-Bound Train.*

Martin didn't quite remember any of the words, but he couldn't forget the way his Daddy sang them out. And when Daddy made the mistake of getting drunk in the afternoon and got squeezed between a Pennsy tank-car and an *AT&SF* gondola, Martin sort of wondered why the Brotherhood didn't sing the song at his funeral.

After that, things didn't go so good for Martin, but somehow he always recalled Daddy's song. When Mom up and ran off with a traveling salesman from Keokuk (Daddy must have turned over in his grave, knowing she'd done such a thing, and with a *passenger,* too!) Martin hummed the tune to himself every night in the Orphan Home. And after Martin himself ran away, he used to whistle the song softly at night in the jungles, after the other bindlestiffs were asleep.

Martin was on the road for four-five years before he realized he wasn't getting anyplace. Of course he'd tried his hand at a lot of things—picking fruit in Oregon, washing dishes in a Montana hash-house, stealing hubcaps in Denver and tires in Oklahoma City—but by the time he'd put in six months on the chain-gang down in Alabama he knew he had no future drifting around this way on his own.

So he tried to get on the railroad like his Daddy had and they told him that times were bad.

But Martin couldn't keep away from the railroads. Wherever he traveled, he rode the rods; he'd rather hop a freight heading north in sub-zero weather than lift his thumb to hitch a ride with a Cadillac headed for Florida. Whenever he managed to get hold of a can of Sterno, he'd sit there under a nice warm culvert, think about the old days, and often as not he'd hum the song about *That Hell-Bound Train*. That was the train the drunks and the sinners rode— the gambling men and the grifters, the big-time spenders, the skirt-chasers, and all the jolly crew. It would be really fine to take a trip in such good company, but Martin didn't like to think of what happened when that train finally pulled into the Depot Way Down Yonder. He didn't figure on spending eternity stoking boilers in Hell, without even Company Union to protect him. Still, it would be a lovely ride. If there was *such* a thing as a Hell-Bound Train. Which, of course, there wasn't.

At least Martin didn't *think* there was, until that evening when he found himself walking the tracks heading south, just outside of Appleton Junction. The night was cold and dark, the way November nights are in the Fox River Valley, and he knew he'd have to work his way down to New Orleans for the winter, or maybe even Texas. Somehow he didn't much feel like going, even though he'd heard tell that a lot of those Texas automobiles had solid gold hub-caps.

No sir, he just wasn't cut out for petty larceny. It was worse than a sin—it was unprofitable, too. Bad enough to do the Devil's work, but then to get such miserable pay on top of it! Maybe he'd better let the Salvation Army convert him.

Martin trudged along humming Daddy's song, waiting for a rattler to pull out of the Junction behind him. He'd have to catch it— there was nothing else for him to do.

But the first train to come along came from the other direction, roaring towards him along the track from the south.

Martin peered ahead, but his eyes couldn't match his ears, and so far all could recognize was the sound. It *was* a train, though; he felt the steel shudder and sing beneath his feet.

And yet, how could it be? The next station was Neenah-Menasha, and there was nothing due out of there for hours.

The clouds were thick overhead, and the field-mists rolled like a cold fog in a November midnight. Even so, Martin should have been able to see the headlight as the train rushed on. But there was only the whistle, screaming out of the black throat of the night. Martin could recognize the equipment of just about any locomotive ever built, but he'd never heard a whistle that sounded like this one. It wasn't signalling; it was screaming like a lost soul.

He stepped to one side, for the train was almost on top of him now. And suddenly there it was, looming along the tracks and grinding to a stop in less time than he'd believed possible. The wheels hadn't been oiled, because they screamed, too, screamed like the damned. But the train slid to halt and the screams died away into a series of low, groaning sounds, and Martin looked up and saw that this was a passenger train. It was big and black, without a single light shining in the engine cab or any of the long string of cars; Martin couldn't read any lettering on the sides, but he was pretty sure this train didn't belong on the Northwestern Road.

He was even more sure when he saw the man clamber down out of the forward car. There was something wrong about the way he walked, as though one of his feet dragged, and about the lantern he carried. The lantern was dark, and the man held it up to his mouth and blew, and instantly it glowed redly. You don't have to be a member of the Railway Brotherhood to know that this is a mighty peculiar way of lighting a lantern.

As the figure approached, Martin recognized the conductor's cap perched on his head, and this made him feel a little better for a moment—until he noticed that it was worn a bit too high, as though there might be something sticking up on the forehead underneath it.

Still, Martin knew his manners, and when the man smiled at him, he said, "Good evening, Mr. Conductor."

"Good evening, Martin."

"How did you know my name?"

The man shrugged. "How did you know I was the Conductor?"

"You *are*, aren't you?"

"To you, yes. Although other people, in other walks of life, may recognize me in different roles. For instance, you ought to see what I look like to the folks out in Hollywood." The man grinned. "I travel a great deal," he explained.

"What brings you here?" Martin asked.

"Why, you ought to know the answer to that, Martin. I came because you needed me. Tonight, I suddenly realized you were backsliding. Thinking of joining the Salvation Army, weren't you?"

"Well—" Martin hesitated.

"Don't be ashamed. To err is human, as somebody-or-other once said. *Reader's Digest*, wasn't it? Never mind. The point is, I felt you needed me. So I switched over and came your way."

"What for?"

"Why, to offer you a ride, of course. Isn't it better to travel comfortably by train than to march along the cold streets behind a Salvation Army band? Hard on the feet, they tell me, and even harder on the eardrums."

"I'm not sure I'd care to ride your train, sir," Martin said. "Considering where I'm likely to end up."

"Ah, yes. The old argument." The Conductor sighed. "I suppose you'd prefer some sort of bargain, is that it?"

"Exactly," Martin answered.

"Well, I'm afraid I'm all through with that sort of thing. There's no shortage of prospective passengers any more. Why should I offer you any special inducements?"

"You must want me, or else you wouldn't have bothered to go out of your way to find me."

The Conductor sighed again. "There you have a point. Pride was always my besetting weakness, I admit. And somehow I'd hate to lose you to the competition, after thinking of you as my own all these years." He hesitated. "Yes, I'm prepared to deal with you on your own terms, if you insist."

"The terms?" Martin asked.

"Standard proposition. Anything you want."

"Ah," said Martin.

"But I warn you in advance, there'll be no tricks. I'll grant you any wish you can name—but in return, you must promise to ride the train when the time comes."

"Suppose it never comes?"

"It will."

"Suppose I've got the kind of a wish that will keep me off for-ever?"

"There is no such wish."

"Don't be too sure."

"Let me worry about that," the conductor told him. "No matter what you have in mind, I warn you that I'll collect in the end. And there'll be none of this last-minute hocus-pocus, either. No last-hour repentances, no blonde *frauleins* or fancy lawyers showing up to get you off. I offer a clean deal. That is to say, you'll get what you want, and I'll get what I want."

"I've heard you trick people. They say you're worse than a used-car salesman."

"Now, wait a minute—"

"I apologize," Martin said, hastily. "But it *is* supposed to be a fact that you can't be trusted."

"I admit it. On the other hand, you seem to think you have found a way."

"A sure-fire proposition."

"Sure-fire? Very funny!" The man began to chuckle, then halted. "But we waste valuable time, Martin. Let's get down to cases. What do you want from me?"

Martin took a deep breath. "I want to be able to stop Time."

"Right now?"

"No. Not yet. And not for everybody. I realize that would be impossible, of course. But I want to be able to stop Time for myself. Just once, in the future. Whenever I get to a point where I know I'm happy and contented, that's where I'd like to stop. So I can just keep on being happy forever."

"That's quite a proposition," the Conductor mused. "I've got to admit I've never heard anything just like it before—and believe me, I've listened to some lulus in my day." He grinned at Martin. "You've really been thinking about this, haven't you?"

"For years," Martin admitted. Then he coughed. "Well, what do you say?"

"It's not impossible, in terms of your own *subjective* time-sense," the Conductor murmured. "Yes, I think it could be arranged."

"But I mean *really* to stop. Nor for me just to *imagine* it."

"I understand. And it can be done."

"Then you'll agree?"

"Why not? I promised you, didn't I? Give me your hand."

Martin hesitated. "Will it hurt very much? I mean, I don't like the sight of blood, and—"

"Nonsense! You've been listening to a lot of poppycock. We already have made our bargain, my boy. I merely intend to put something into your hand. The ways and means of fulfilling your wish. After all, there's no telling at just what moment you may decide to exercise the agreement, and I can't drop everything and come running. So it's better if you can regulate matters for yourself."

"You're going to give me a Time-stopper?"

"That's the general idea. As soon as I can decide what would be practical." The Conductor hesitated. "Ah, the very thing! Here, take my watch."

He pulled it out of his vest-pocket; a railroad watch in a silver case. He opened the back and made a delicate adjustment; Martin tried to see just exactly what he was doing, but the fingers moved in a blinding blur.

"There we are." The Conductor smiled. "It's all set, now. When you finally decide where you'd like to call a halt, merely turn the stem in reverse and unwind the watch until it stops. When it stops, Time stops, for you. Simple enough?" And the Conductor dropped the watch into Martin's hand.

The young man closed his fingers tightly around the case. "That's all there is to it, eh?"

"Absolutely. But remember—you can stop the watch only once. So you'd better make sure that you're satisfied with the moment you choose to prolong. I caution you in all fairness; make very certain of your choice."

"I will." Martin grinned. "And since you've been so fair about it, I'll be fair, too. There's one thing you seem to have forgotten. It doesn't really matter *what* moment I choose. Because once I stop Time for myself, that means I stay where I am forever. I'll never have to get any older. And if I don't get any older, I'll never die. And if I never die, then I'll never have to take a ride on your train."

The Conductor turned away. His shoulders shook convulsively, and he may have been crying. "And you said *I* was worse than a used-car salesman," he gasped, in a strangled voice.

Then he wandered off into the fog, and the train-whistle gave an impatient shriek, and all at once it was moving swiftly down the track, rumbling out of sight in the darkness.

Martin stood there, blinking down at the silver watch in his hand. If it wasn't that he could actually see it and feel it there, and if he couldn't smell that peculiar odor, he might have thought he'd imagined the whole thing from start to finish—train, Conductor, bargain, and all.

But he had the watch, and he could recognize the scent left by the train as it departed, even though there aren't many locomotives around that use sulphur and brimstone as fuel.

And he had no doubts about his bargain. That's what came of thinking things through to a logical conclusion. Some fools would have settled for wealth, or power, or Kim Novak. Daddy might have sold out for a fifth of whiskey.

Martin knew that he'd made a better deal. Better? It was foolproof. All he needed to do now was choose his moment.

He put the watch in his pocket and started back down the railroad track. He hadn't really had a destination in mind before, but he did now. He was going to find a moment of happiness. . . .

Now young Martin wasn't altogether a ninny. He realized perfectly well that happiness is a relative thing; there are conditions and degrees of contentment, and they vary with one's lot in life. As a hobo, he was often satisfied with a warm handout, a double-length bench in the park, or a can of Sterno made in 1957 (a vintage year). Many a time he had reached a state of momentary bliss through such simple agencies, but he was aware that there were better things. Martin determined to seek them out.

Within two days he was in the great city of Chicago. Quite naturally, he drifted over to West Madison Street, and there he took steps to elevate his role in life. He became a city bum, a panhandler, a moocher. Within a week he had risen to the point where happiness was a meal in a regular one-arm luncheon joint, a two-bit flop on a real army cot in a real flophouse, and a full fifth of muscatel.

There was a night, after enjoying all three of these luxuries to the full, when Martin thought of unwinding his watch at the pinnacle of intoxication. But he also thought of the faces of the honest johns he'd braced for a handout today. Sure, they were squares, but they were prosperous. They wore good clothes, held good jobs, drove nice cars. And for them, happiness was even more ecstatic—they ate dinner in fine hotels, they slept on innerspring mattresses, they drank blended whiskey.

Squares or no, they had something there. Martin fingered his watch, put aside the temptation to hock it for another bottle of muscatel, and went to sleep determined to get himself a job and improve his happiness-quotient.

When he awoke he had a hangover, but the determination was still with him. Before the month was out Martin was working for a general contractor over on the South Side, at one of the big reha-bilitation projects. He hated the grind, but the pay was good, and pretty soon he got himself a one-room apartment out on Blue Island Avenue. He was accustomed to eating in decent restaurants now, and he bought himself a comfortable bed, and every Saturday night he went down to the corner tavern. It was all very pleasant, but—

The foreman liked his work and promised him a raise in a month. If he waited around, the raise would mean that he could afford a secondhand car. With a car, he could even start picking up a girl for a date now and then. Other fellows on the job did, and they seemed pretty happy.

So Martin kept on working, and the raise came through and the car came through and pretty soon a couple of girls came through.

The first time it happened, he wanted to unwind his watch imme-diately. Until he got to thinking about what some of the older men always said. There was a guy named Charlie, for example, who worked alongside him on the hoist. "When you're young and don't know the score, maybe you get a kick out of running around with those pigs. But after a while, you want something better. A nice girl of your own. That's the ticket."

Martin felt he owed it to himself to find out. If he didn't like it better, he could always go back to what he had.

Almost six months went by before Martin met Lillian Gillis. By that time he'd had another promotion and was working inside, in the office. They made him go to night school to learn how to do simple bookkeeping, but it meant another fifteen bucks extra a week, and it was nicer working indoors.

And Lillian *was* a lot of fun. When she told him she'd marry him, Martin was almost sure that the time was now. Except that she was sort of—well, she was a *nice* girl, and she said they'd have to wait until they were married. Of course, Martin couldn't expect to marry her until he had a little more money saved up, and another raise would help, too.

That took a year. Martin was patient, because he knew it was going to be worth it. Every time he had any doubts, he took out his watch and looked at it. But he never showed it to Lillian, or anybody else. Most of the other men wore expensive wristwatches and the old silver railroad watch looked just a little cheap.

Martin smiled as he gazed at the stem. Just a few twists and he'd have something none of these other poor working slobs would ever have. Permanent satisfaction, with his blushing bride—

Only getting married turned out to be just the beginning. Sure, it was wonderful, but Lillian told him how much better things would be if they could move into a new place and fix it up. Martin wanted decent furniture, a TV set, a nice car.

So he started taking night courses and got a promotion to the front office. With the baby coming, he wanted to stick around and see his son arrive. And when it came, he realized he'd have to wait until it got a little older, started to walk and talk and develop a personality of its own.

About this time the company sent him out on the road as a troubleshooter on some of those other jobs, and now he *was* eating at those good hotels, living high on the hog and the expense-account. More than once he was tempted to unwind his watch. This was the good life. . . . Of course, it would be even better if he just didn't have to *work*. Sooner or later, if he could cut in on one of the company deals, he could make a pile and retire. Then everything would be ideal.

It happened, but it took time. Martin's son was going to high school before he really got up there into the chips. Martin got a strong hunch that it was now or never, because he wasn't exactly a kid any more.

But right about then he met Sherry Westcott, and she didn't seem to think he was middle-aged at all, in spite of the way he was losing hair and adding stomach. She taught him that a *toupee* would cover the bald spot and a cummerbund could cover the potgut. In fact, she taught him quite a lot and he so enjoyed learning that he actually took out his watch and prepared to unwind it.

Unfortunately, he chose the very moment that the private detectives broke down the door of the hotel room, and then there was a long stretch of time when Martin was so busy fighting the divorce action that he couldn't honestly say he was enjoying any given moment.

When he made the final settlement with Lil he was broke again, and Sherry didn't seem to think he was so young, after all. So he squared his shoulders and went back to work.

He made his pile, eventually, but it took longer this time, and there wasn't much chance to have fun along the way. The fancy dames in the fancy cocktail lounges didn't seem to interest him any more, and neither did the liquor. Besides, the Doc had warned him off that.

But there were other pleasures for a rich man to investigate. Travel, for instance—and not riding the rods from one hick burg to another, either. Martin went around the world by plane and luxury liner. For a while it seemed as though he would find his moment after all, visiting the Taj Mahal by moonlight. Martin pulled out the battered old watchcase, and got ready to unwind it. Nobody else was there to watch him—

And that's why he hesitated. Sure, this was an enjoyable moment, but he was alone. Lil and the kid were gone, Sherry was gone, and somehow he'd never had time to make any friends. Maybe if he found new congenial people, he'd have the ultimate happiness. That must be the answer—it wasn't just money or power or sex or seeing beautiful things. The real satisfaction lay in friendship.

So on the boat trip home, Martin tried to strike up a few acquaintances at the ship's bar. But all these people were much younger, and Martin had nothing in common with them. Also they wanted to dance and drink, and Martin wasn't in condition to appreciate such pastimes. Nevertheless, he tried.

Perhaps that's why he had the little accident the day before they docked in San Francisco. "Little accident" was the ship's doctor's way of describing it, but Martin noticed he looked very grave when he told him to stay in bed, and he'd called an ambulance to meet the liner at the dock and take the patient right to the hospital.

At the hospital, all the expensive treatment and the expensive smiles and the expensive words didn't fool Martin any. He was an old man with a bad heart, and they thought he was going to die.

But he could fool them. He still had the watch. He found it in his coat when he put on his clothes and sneaked out of the hospital.

He didn't have to die. He could cheat death with a single gesture—and he intended to do it as a free man, out there under a free sky.

That was the real secret of happiness. He understood it now. Not even friendship meant as much as freedom. This was the best thing of all—to be free of friends or family or the furies of the flesh.

Martin walked slowly beside the embankment under the night sky. Come to think of it, he was just about back where he'd started, so many years ago. But the moment was good, good enough to prolong forever. Once a bum, always a bum.

He smiled as he thought about it, and then the smile twisted sharply and suddenly, like the pain twisting sharply and suddenly in his chest. The world began to spin and he fell down on the side of the embankment.

He couldn't see very well, but he was still conscious, and he knew what had happened. Another stroke, and a bad one. Maybe this was it. Except that he wouldn't be a fool any longer. He wouldn't wait to see what was around the corner.

Right now was his chance to use his power and save his life. And he was going to do it. He could still move, nothing could stop him.

He groped in his pocket and pulled out the old silver watch, fumbling with the stem. A few twists and he'd cheat death, he'd never have to ride that Hell-Bound Train. He could go on forever.

Forever.

Martin had never really considered the word before. To go on forever—but *how?* Did he *want* to go on forever, like this; a sick old man, lying helplessly here in the grass?

No. He couldn't do it. He wouldn't do it. And suddenly he wanted very much to cry, because he knew that somewhere along the line he'd outsmarted himself. And now it was too late. His eyes dimmed, there was a roaring in his ears. . . .

He recognized the roaring, of course, and he wasn't at all surprised to see the train come rushing out of the fog up there on the embankment. He wasn't surprised when it stopped, either, or when the Conductor climbed off and walked slowly towards him.

The Conductor hadn't changed a bit. Even his grin was still the same.

"Hello, Martin," he said. "All aboard."

"I know," Martin whispered. "But you'll have to carry me. I can't walk. I'm not even really talking any more, am I?"

"Yes you are," the Conductor said. "I can hear you fine. And you can walk, too." He leaned down and placed his hand on Martin's chest. There was a moment of icy numbness, and then, sure enough, Martin could walk after all.

He got up and followed the Conductor along the slope, moving to the side of the train.

"In here?" he asked.

"No, the next car," the Conductor murmured. "I guess you're entitled to ride Pullman. After all, you're quite a successful man. You've tasted the joys of wealth and position and prestige. You've known the pleasures of marriage and fatherhood. You've sampled the delights of dining and drinking and debauchery, too, and you traveled high, wide and handsome. So let's not have any last-minute recriminations."

"All right," Martin sighed. "I can't blame you for my mistakes. On the other hand, you can't take credit for what happened, either. I worked for everything I got. I did it all on my own. I didn't even need your watch."

"So you didn't," the Conductor said, smiling. "But would you mind giving it back to me now?"

"Need it for the next sucker, eh?" Martin muttered.

"Perhaps."

Something about the way he said it made Martin look up. He tried to see the Conductor's eyes, but the brim of his cap cast a shadow. So Martin looked down at the watch instead.

"Tell me something," he said, softly. "If I give you the watch, what will you do with it?"

"Why, throw it into the ditch," the Conductor told him. "That's all I'll do with it." And he held out his hand.

"What if somebody comes along and finds it? And twists the stem backwards, and stops Time?"

"Nobody would do that," the Conductor murmured. "Even if they knew."

"You mean, it was all a trick? This is only an ordinary, cheap watch?"

"I didn't say that," whispered the Conductor. "I only said that no one has ever twisted the stem backwards. They've all been like you, Martin—looking ahead to find that perfect happiness. Waiting for the moment that never comes."

The Conductor held out his hand again.

Martin sighed and shook his head. "You cheated me after all."

"You cheated yourself, Martin. And now you're going to ride that Hell-Bound Train."

He pushed Martin up the steps and into the car ahead. As he entered, the train began to move and the whistle screamed. And Martin stood there in the swaying Pullman, gazing down the aisle at the other passengers. He could see them sitting there, and somehow it didn't seem strange at all.

Here they were; the drunks and the sinners, the gambling men and the grifters, the big-time spenders, the skirt-chasers, and all the jolly crew. They knew where they were going, of course, but they didn't seem to give a damn. The blinds were drawn on the windows, yet it was light inside, and they were all living it up—singing and passing the bottle and roaring with laughter, throwing the dice and telling their jokes and bragging their big brags, just the way Daddy used to sing about them in the old song.

"Mighty nice traveling companions," Martin said. "Why, I've never seen such a pleasant bunch of people. I mean, they seem to be really enjoying themselves!"

The Conductor shrugged. "I'm afraid things won't be quite so jazzy when we pull into that Depot Way Down Yonder."

For the third time, he held out his hand. "Now, before you sit down, if you'll just give me that watch. A bargain's a bargain—"

Martin smiled. "A bargain's a bargain," he echoed. "I agreed to ride your train if I could stop Time when I found the right moment of happiness. And I think I'm about as happy right here as I've ever been."

Very slowly, Martin took hold of the silver watch-stem.

"No!" gasped the Conductor. "No!"

But the watch-stem turned.

"Do you realize what you've done?" the Conductor yelled. "Now we'll never reach the Depot! We'll just go on riding, all of us—forever!"

Martin grinned. "I know," he said. "But the fun is in the trip, not the destination. You taught me that. And I'm looking forward to a wonderful trip. Look, maybe I can even help. If you were to find me another one of those caps, now, and let me keep this watch—"

And that's the way it finally worked out. Wearing his cap and carrying his battered old silver watch, there's no happier person in or out of this world—now and forever—than Martin. Martin, the new Brakeman on That Hell-Bound Train.

The Bazaar of the Bizarre

Fritz Leiber

Fritz Leiber (1910–1992) is widely considered one of the founding fathers of sword and sorcery fiction, with his elegantly witty tales of Fafhrd and the Grey Mouser ranking beside Robert Howard's Conan tales for their impact. His science fiction is no less memorable, having won the Hugo award for the novels The Wanderer *and* The Big Time. *Other novels include* Conjure Wife, *a tale of modern day witchcraft and the uses it has in the world of academia, and* Our Lady of Darkness, *which won the World Fantasy award. A fifty-year retrospective of his short fiction,* The Leiber Chronicles, *was published by Dark Harvest Press.*

THE STRANGE STARS OF THE WORLD OF NEHWON GLINTED THICKLY ABOVE the black-roofed city of Lankhmar, where swords clink almost as often as coins. For once there was no fog.

In the Plaza of Dark Delights, which lies seven blocks south of the Marsh Gale and extends from the Fountain of Dark Abundance to the Shrine of the Black Virgin, the shop-lights glinted upward no more brightly than the stars glinted down. For there the vendors of drugs and the peddlers of curiosa and the hawkers of assignations light their stalls and crouching places with foxfire, glowworms, and firepots with tiny single windows, and they conduct their business almost as silently as the stars conduct theirs.

There are plenty of raucous spots a-glare with torches in nocturnal Lankhmar, but by immemorial tradition soft whispers and a pleasant dimness are the rule in the Plaza of Dark Delights. Philosophers often go there solely to mediate, students to dream, and fanatic-eyed theologians to spin like spiders abstruse new theories of the Devil and of the other dark forces ruling the universe. And if any of these find a little illicit fun by the way, their theories and dreams and theologies and demonologies are undoubtedly the better for it.

Tonight, however, there was a glaring exception to the darkness rule. From a low doorway with a trefoil arch new-struck through an ancient wall, light spilled into the Plaza. Rising above the horizon of the pavement like some monstrous moon a-shine with the ray of a murderous sun, the new doorway dimmed almost to extinction the stars of the other merchants of mystery.

Eerie and unearthly objects for sale spilled out of the doorway a little way with the light, while beside the doorway crouched an avid-faced figure clad in garments never before seen on land or sea . . . in the World of Nehwon. He wore a hat like a small red pail, baggy trousers, and outlandish red boots with upturned toes. His eyes were as predatory as a hawk's, but his smile as cynically and lascivi-ously cajoling as an ancient satyr's.

Now and again he sprang up and pranced about, sweeping and re-sweeping with a rough long broom the flagstones as if to clean path for the entry of some fantastic emperor, and he often paused in his dance to blow low and loutingly, but always with upglancing eyes, to the crowd gathering in the darkness cross from the doorway and to swing his hand from them toward the interior of the new shop in a gesture of invitation at once servile and sinister.

No one of the crowd had yet plucked up courage to step forward into the glare and enter the shop, or even inspect the rarities set out so carelessly yet temptingly before it. But the number of fasci-nated peerers increased momently. There were mutterings of cen-sure at the dazzling new method of merchandising—the infraction of the Plaza's custom of darkness—but on the whole the complaints were outweighed by the gasps and murmurings of wonder, admira-tion, and curiosity kindling even hotter.

The Gray Mouser slipped into the Plaza at the Fountain end as silently as if he had come to slit a throat or spy on the spies of the Overlord. His ratskin moccasins were soundless. His sword Scalpel in its mouseskin sheath did not swish ever so faintly against either his tunic or cloak, both of gray silk curiously coarse of weave. The glances he shot about him from under his gray silk hood half thrown back were freighted with menace and a freezing sense of superiority.

Inwardly the Mouser was feeling very much like a schoolboy—a schoolboy in dread of rebuke and a crushing assignment of home-work. For in the Mouser's pouch of ratskin was a note scrawled in dark brown squid-ink on silvery fish-skin by Sheelba of the Eyeless Face, inviting the Mouser to be at this spot at this time.

Sheelba was the Mouser's supernatural tutor and—when the whim struck Sheelba—guardian, and it never did to ignore his invi-tations, for Sheelba had eyes to track down the unsociable though he did not carry them between his cheeks and forehead.

But the tasks Sheelba would set the Mouser at times like these were apt to be peculiarly onerous and even noisome—such as procuring nine white cats with never a black hair among them, or stealing five copies of the same book of magic runes from five widely separated sorcerous libraries or obtaining specimens of the dung of four kings living or dead—so the Mouser had come early, to get the bad news as soon as possible, and he had come alone, for he certainly did not want his comrade Fafhrd to stand snickering by while Sheelba delivered his little wizardly homilies to a dutiful Mouser . . . and perchance thought of extra assignments.

Sheelba's note, invisible graven somewhere inside the Mouser's skull, read merely, *When the star Akul bedizens the Spire of Rhan, be you by the Fountain of Dark Abundance,* and the note was signed only with the little featureless oval which is Sheelba's sigil.

The Mouser glided now through the darkness to the Fountain, which was a squat black pillar from the rough rounded top of which a single black drop welled and dripped every twenty elephant's heartbeats.

The Mouser stood beside the Fountain and, extending a bent hand, measured the altitude of the green star Akul. It had still to drop down the sky seven finger widths more before it would touch the needle-point of the slim star-silhouetted distant minaret of Rhan.

The Mouser crouched doubled-up by the black pillar and then vaulted lightly atop it to see if that would make any great difference in Akul's attitude. It did not.

He scanned the nearby darkness for motionless figures . . . especially that of one robed and cowled like a monk—cowled so deeply that one might wonder how he saw to walk. There were no figures at all.

The Mouser's mood changed. If Sheelba chose not to come courteously beforehand, why he could be boorish too! He strode off to investigate the new bright arch-doored shop, of whose infractious glow he had become inquisitively aware at least a block before he had entered the Plaza of Dark Delights.

Fafhrd the Northerner opened one wine-heavy eye and without moving his head scanned half the small firelit room in which he slept naked. He shut that eye, opened the other, and scanned the other half.

There was no sign of the Mouser anywhere. So far so good! If his luck held, he would be able to get through tonight's embarrassing business without being jeered at by the small gray rogue.

He drew from under his stubbly check a square of violet serpent-hide pocked with tiny pores so that when he held it between his eyes and the dancing fire it made stars. Studied for a time, these stars spelled out obscurely the message: *When Rhan-dagger stabs the darkness in Akul-heart, seek you the Source of the Black Drops.*

Drawn boldly across the prickholes in an orange-brown like dried blood—in fact spanning the violet square—was a seven-armed swastika, which is one of the sigils of Ningauble of the Seven Eyes.

Fafhrd had no difficulty in interpreting the Source of the Black Drops as the Fountain of Dark Abundance. He had become wearily familiar with such cryptic poetic language during his boyhood as a scholar of the singing skalds.

Ningauble stood to Fafhrd very much as Sheelba stood to the Mouser except that the Seven-Eyed One was a somewhat more pretentious archimage, whose taste in the thaumaturgical tasks he set Fafhrd ran in larger directions, such as the slaying of dragons, the sinking of four-masted magic ships, and the kidnapping of ogre-guarded enchanted queens.

Also, Ningauble was given to quiet realistic boasting, especially about the grandeur of his vast cavern-home, whose stony serpent-twisting back corridors led, he often averred, to all spots in space and time—provided Ningauble instructed one beforehand exactly how to step those rocky crooked low-ceilinged passageways.

Fafhrd was driven by no great desire to learn Ningauble's formulas and enchantments, as the Mouser was driven to learn Sheelba's, but the Septinocular One had enough holds on the Northerner, based on the latter's weaknesses and past misdeeds, so that Fafhrd had always to listen patiently to Ningauble's wizardly admonishments and vaunting sorcerous chit-chat—but *not,* if humanly or inhumanly possible, while the Gray Mouser was present to snigger and grin.

Meanwhile, Fafhrd standing before the fire, had been whipping, slapping, and belting various garments and weapons and ornaments onto his huge brawny body with its generous stretches of thick short curling red-gold hairs. When he opened the outer door and, also booted and helmeted now, glanced down the darkling alleyway preparatory to leaving and noted only the hunch-backed chestnut vendor a-squat by his brazier at the next corner, one would have sworn that when he did stride forth toward the Plaza of Dark Delights it would be with the clankings and thunderous tread of a siege-tower approaching a thick-walled city.

Instead the lynx-eared old chestnut vendor, who was also a spy of the Overlord, had to swallow down his heart when it came sliding crookedly up his throat as Fafhrd rushed past him, tall as a pine tree, swift as the wind, and silent as a ghost.

———

The Mouser elbowed aside two gawkers with shrewd taps on the floating rib and strode across the dark flagstones toward the garishly bright shop with its doorway like an upended heart. It occurred to him they must have had masons working like fiends to have cut and plastered that archway so swiftly. He had been past here this afternoon and noted nothing but blank wall.

The outlandish porter with the red cylinder hat and twisty red shoe-toes came frisking out to the Mouser with his broom and then went curtsying back as he reswept a path for this first customer with many an obsequious bow and smirk.

But the Mouser's visage was set in an expression of grim and all-skeptical disdain. He paused at the heaping of objects in front of the door and scanned it with disapproval. He drew Scalpel from its thin gray sheath and with the tip of the long blade flipped back the cover on the topmost of a pile of musty books. Without going any closer he briefly scanned the first page, shook his head, rapidly turned a half dozen more pages with Scalpel's tip, using the sword as if it were a teacher's wand to point out words here and there—because they were ill-chosen, to judge from his expression—and then abruptly closed the book with another sword-flip.

Next he used Scalpel's tip to lift a red cloth hanging from a table behind the books and peer under it suspiciously, to rap contemptuously a glass jar with a human head floating in it, to touch disparagingly several other objects and to waggle reprovingly at a foot-chained owl which hooted at him solemnly from its high perch.

He sheathed Scalpel and turned toward the porter with a sour, lifted-eyebrow look which said—nay, shouted—plainly, "Is *this* all you have to offer? Is this garbage your excuse for defiling the Dark Plaza with glare?"

Actually the Mouser was mightily interested by every least item which he had glimpsed. The book, incidentally, had been in a script which he not only did not understand, but did not even recognize.

Three things were very clear to the Mouser: first, that this stuff offered here for sale did not come from anywhere in the World of Nehwon, no, not even from Nehwon's farthest outback; second, that all this stuff was, in some way which he could not yet define, extremely dangerous; third, that all this stuff was monstrously fascinating and that he, the Mouser, did not intend to stir from this place until he had personally scanned, studied, and if need be tested, every last intriguing item and scrap.

At the Mouser's sour grimace, the porter went into a convulsion of wheedling and fawning caperings, seemingly torn between a desire to kiss the Mouser's foot and to point out with flamboyant caressing gestures every object in his shop.

He ended by bowing so low that his chin brushed the pavement, sweeping an ape-long arm toward the interior of the shop, and gibbering in atrocious Lankhmarese, "Every object to pleasure the flesh and senses and imagination of man. Wonders undreamed. Very cheap, very cheap! Yours for a penny! The Bazaar of the Bizarre. Please to inspect, oh king!"

The Mouser yawned a very long yawn with the back of his hand to his mouth, next he looked around him again with the weary, patient, worldly smile of a duke who knows he must put up with many boredoms to encourage business in his demesne, finally he shrugged faintly and entered the shop.

Behind him the porter went into a jigging delirium of glee and began to re-sweep the flagstones like a man maddened with delight.

Inside, the first thing the Mouser saw was a stack of slim books bound in gold-lined fine-grained red and violet leather.

The second was a rack of gleaming lenses and slim brass tubes calling to be peered through.

The third was a slim dark-haired girl smiling at him mysteriously from a gold-barred cage that swung from the ceiling.

Beyond that cage hung others with bars of silver and strange green, ruby, orange, ultramarine, and purple metals.

Fafhrd saw the Mouser vanish into the shop just as his left hand touched the rough chill pate of the Fountain of Dark Abundance and as Akul pointed precisely on Rhan-top as if it were that needle-spire's green-lensed pinnacle-lantern.

He might have followed the Mouser, he might have done no such thing, he certainly would have pondered the briefly glimpsed event, but just then there came from behind him a long low "Hssssst!"

Fafhrd turned like a giant dancer and his longsword Graywand came out of its sheath swiftly and rather more silently than a snake emerges from its hole.

Ten arm lengths behind him, in the mouth of an alleyway darker than the Dark Plaza would have been without its new commercial moon, Fafhrd dimly made out two robed and deeply cowled figures poised side by side.

One cowl held darkness absolute. Even the face of a Negro of Klesh might have been expected to shoot ghostly bronze gleams. But here there were none.

In the other cowl there nested seven very faint pale greenish glows. They moved about restlessly, sometimes circling each other, swinging mazily. Sometimes one of the seven horizontally oval gleams would grow a little brighter, seemingly as it moved forward toward the mouth of the cowl—or a little darker, as it drew back.

Fafhrd sheathed Graywand and advanced toward the figures. Still facing him, they retreated slowly and silently down the alley.

Fafhrd followed as they receded. He felt a stirring of interest . . . and of other feelings. To meet his own supernatural mentor alone might be only a bore and a mild nervous strain; but it would be hard for anyone entirely to repress a shiver of awe at encountering at one and the same time both Ningauble of the Seven Eyes and Sheelba of the Eyeless Face.

Moreover, that those two bitter wizardly rivals would have joined forces, that they should apparently be operating together in amity . . . Something of great note must be afoot! There was no doubting that.

The Mouser meantime was experiencing the smuggest, most mind-teasing, most exotic enjoyments imaginable. The sleekly leather-bound gold-stamped books turned out to contain scripts stranger far than that in the book whose pages he had flipped outside— scripts that looked like skeletal beasts, cloud swirls, and twisty-branched bushes and trees—but for a wonder he could read them all without the least difficulty.

The books dealt in the fullest detail with such matters as the private life of devils, the secret histories of murderous cults, and— these were illustrated—the proper dueling techniques to employ against sword-armed demons and the crotic tricks of lamias, succubi, bacchantes, and hamadryads.

The lenses and brass tubes, some of the latter of which were as fantastically crooked as if they were periscopes for seeing over the walls and through the barred windows of other universes, showed at first only delightful jeweled patterns, but after a bit the Mouser was able to see through them into all sorts of interesting places: the treasure-room of dead kings, the bedchambers of living queens, council-crypts of rebel angels, and the closets in which the gods hid plans for worlds too frighteningly fantastic to risk creating.

As for the quaintly clad slim girls in their playfully widely-barred cages, well, they were pleasant pillows on which to rest eyes momentarily fatigued by book-scanning and tube-peering.

Ever and anon one of the girls would whistle softly at the Mouser and then point cajolingly or imploringly or with languorous hintings at a jeweled crank set in the wall whereby her cage, suspended on a gleaming chain running through gleaming pulleys, could be lowered to the floor.

At these invitations the Mouser would smile with a bland amorousness and nod and softly wave a hand from the fingerhinge as if to whisper, "Later . . . later. Be patient."

After all, girls had a way of blotting out all lesser, but not thereby despicable, delights. Girls were for dessert.

Ningauble and Sheelba receded down the dark alleyway with Fafhrd following them until the latter lost patience and, somewhat conquering his unwilling awe, called out nervously, "Well, are you going to keep on fleeing me backward until we all pitch into the Great Salt Marsh? What do you want of me? What's it all about?"

But the two cowled figures had already stopped, as he could perceive by the starlight and the glow of a few high windows, and now it seemed to Fafhrd that they had stopped a moment before he had called out. A typical sorcerers' trick for making one feel awkward! He gnawed his lip in the darkness. It was ever thus!

"Oh My Gentle Son . . ." Ningauble began in his most sugary-priestly tones, the dim puffs of his seven eyes now hanging in his cowl as steadily and glowing as mildly as the Pleiades seen late on a summer night through a greenish mist rising from a lake freighted with blue vitriol and corrosive gas of salt.

"I asked what it's all about!" Fafhrd interrupted harshly. Already convicted of impatience, he might as well go the whole hog.

"Let me put it as a hypothetical case," Ningauble replied imperturbably. "Let us suppose, My Gentle Son, that there is a man in a universe and that a most evil force comes to this universe from another universe, or perhaps from a congeries of universes, and that this man is a brave man who wants to defend his universe and who counts his life as a trifle and that moreover he has to counsel him a very wise and prudent and public-spirited uncle who knows all about these matters which I have been hypothecating—"

"The Devourers menace Lankhmar!" Sheelba rapped out in a voice as harsh as a tree cracking and so suddenly that Fafhrd almost started—and for all we know, Ningauble too.

Fafhrd waited a moment to avoid giving false impressions and then switched his gaze to Sheelba. His eyes had been growing accustomed to the darkness and he saw much more now than he had seen at the alley's mouth, yet he still saw not one jot more than absolute blackness inside Sheelba's cowl.

"Who are the Devourers?" he asked.

It was Ningauble, however, who replied, "The Devourers are the most accomplished merchants in all the many universes—so accomplished, indeed, that they sell only trash. There is a deep necessity in this, for the Devourers must occupy all their cunning in perfecting their methods of selling and so have not an instant to spare in considering the worth of what they sell. Indeed, they dare not concern themselves with such matters for a moment, for fear of losing their golden touch—and yet such are their skills that their wares are utterly irresistible, indeed the finest wares in all the many universes—if you follow me?"

Fafhrd looked hopefully toward Sheelba, but since the latter did not this time interrupt with some pithy summation, he nodded to Ningauble.

Ningauble continued, his seven eyes beginning to weave a bit, judging from the movements of the seven green glows, "As you might readily deduce, the Devourers possess all the mightiest magics garnered from the many universes, whilst their assault groups are led by the most aggressive wizards imaginable, supremely skilled in all methods of battling, whether it be with the wits, or the feelings, or with the beweaponed body.

"The method of the Devourers is to set up shop in a new world and first entice the bravest and the most adventuresome and the supplest-minded of its people—who have so much imagination that with just a touch of suggestion they themselves do most of the work of selling themselves.

"When these are safely ensnared, the Devourers proceed to deal with the remainder of the population: meaning simply that they sell and sell and sell!—sell trash and take good money and even finer things in exchange."

Ningauble sighed windily and a shade piously. "All this is very bad, My Gentle Son," he continued, his eye-glows weaving hypnotically in his cowl, "but natural enough in universes administered by such gods as we have—natural enough and perhaps endurable. However"—he paused—"there is worse to come! The Devourers want not only the patronage of all beings in all universes, but—doubtless because they are afraid someone will some day raise the ever-unpleasant question of the true worth of things—they want all their customers reduced to a state of slavish and submissive suggestibility, so that they are fit for nothing whatever but to gawk at and buy the trash the Devourers offer for sale. This means of course that eventually the Devourers' customers will have nothing wherewith to pay the Devourers for their trash, but the Devourers do not seem to be concerned with this eventuality. Perhaps they feel that there is always a new universe to exploit. And perhaps there is!"

"Monstrous!" Fafhrd commented. "But what do the Devourers gain from all these furious commercial sorties, all this mad merchandising? What do they really want?"

Ningauble replied, "The Devourers want only to amass cash and to raise little ones like themselves to amass more cash and they want to compete with each other at cash-amassing. (Is that coincidentally a city, do you think, Fafhrd? Cashamash?) And the Devourers want to brood about their great service to the many universes—it is their claim that servile customers make the most obedient subjects for the gods—and to complain about how the work of amassing cash tortures their minds and upsets their digestions. Beyond this, each of the Devourers also secretly collects and hides away forever, to delight no eyes but his own, all the finest objects and thoughts created by true men and women (and true wizards and true demons) and bought by the Devourers at bankruptcy prices and paid for with trash or—this is their ultimate preference—with nothing at all."

"Monstrous indeed!" Fafhrd repeated. "Merchants are ever an evil mystery and these sound the worst. But what has all this to do with me?"

"Oh My Gentle Son," Ningauble responded, the piety in his voice now tinged with a certain clement disappointment, "you force me once again to resort to hypothecating. Let us return to the supposition of this brave man whose whole universe is direly menaced and who counts his life a trifle and to the related supposition of this brave man's wise uncle, whose advice the brave man invariably follows—"

"The Devourers have set up shop in the Plaza of Dark Delights!" Sheelba interjected so abruptly in such iron-harsh syllables that this time Fafhrd actually did start. "You must obliterate this outpost tonight!"

Fafhrd considered that for a bit, then said, in a tentative sort of voice, "You will both accompany me, I presume, to aid me with your wizardly sendings and castings in what I can see must be a most perilous operation, to serve me as a sort of sorcerous artillery and archery corps while I play assault battalion—"

"Oh My Gentle Son . . ." Ningauble interrupted in tones of deepest disappointment, shaking his head so that his eye-glows jogged in his cowl.

"You must do it alone!" Sheelba rasped.

"Without any help at all?" Fafhrd demanded. "No! Get someone else. Get this doltish brave man who always follows his scheming uncle's advice as slavishly as you tell me the Devourers' customers respond to their merchandising. Get *him!* But as for me—No, I say!"

"Then leave us, coward!" Sheelba decreed dourly, but Ningauble only sighed and said quite apologetically, "It was intended that you have a comrade in this quest, a fellow soldier against noisome evil— to wit, the Gray Mouser. But unfortunately he came early to his appointment with my colleague here and was enticed into the shop of the Devourers and is doubtless now deep in their snares, if not already extinct. So you can see that we do take thought for your welfare and have no wish to overburden you with solo quests. However, My Gentle Son, if it still be your firm resolve . . ."

Fafhrd let out a sigh more profound than Ningauble's. "Very well," he said in gruff tones admitting defeat, "I'll do it for you. Someone will have to pull that poor little gray fool out of the pretty-pretty fire—or the twinkly-twinkly water!—that tempted him. But how do I go about it?" He shook a big finger at Ningauble. "And no more Gentle-Sonning!"

Ningauble paused. Then he said only, "Use your own judgment."

Sheelba said, "Beware the Black Wall!"

Ningauble said to Fafhrd, "Hold, I have a gift for you," and held out to him a ragged ribbon a yard long, pinched between the cloth of the wizard's long sleeve so that it was impossible to see the manner of hand that pinched. Fafhrd took the tatter with a snort, crumpled it into a ball, and thrust it into his pouch.

"Have a greater care with it," Ningauble warned. "It is the Cloak of Invisibility, somewhat worn by many magic usings. Do not put it on until you near the Bazaar of the Devourers. It has two minor weaknesses: it will not make you altogether invisible to a master sorcerer if he senses your presence and takes certain steps. Also, see to it that you do not bleed during this exploit, for the cloak will not hide blood."

"I've a gift too!" Sheelba said, drawing from out of his black cowl-hole—with sleeve-masked hand, as Ningauble had done—something that shimmered faintly in the dark like . . .

Like a spiderweb.

Sheelba shook it, as if to dislodge a spider, or perhaps two.

"The Blindfold of True Seeing," he said as he reached it toward Fafhrd. "It shows all things as they really are! Do not lay it across your eyes until you enter the Bazaar. On no account, as you value your life or your sanity, wear it now!"

Fafhrd took it from him most gingerly, the flesh of his fingers crawling. He was inclined to obey the taciturn wizard's instructions. At this moment he truly did not much care to see the true visage of Sheelba of the Eyeless Face.

The Gray Mouser was reading the most interesting book of them all, a great compendium of secret knowledge written in a script of astrologic and geomantic signs, the meanings of which fairly leaped off the page into his mind.

To rest his eyes from that—or rather to keep from gobbling the book too fast—he peered through a nine-elbowed brass tube at a scene that could only be the blue heaven-pinnacle of the universe where angels flew shimmeringly like dragonflies and where a few choice heroes rested from their great mountain-climb and spied down critically on the antlike labors of the gods many levels below.

To rest his eye from *that,* he looked up between the scarlet (bloodmetal?) bars of the inmost cage at the most winsome, slim, fair, jet-eyed girl of them all. She knelt, sitting on her heels, with her upper body leaned back a little. She wore a red velvet tunic and had a mop of golden hair so thick and pliant that she could sweep it in a neat curtain over her upper face, down almost to her pouting lips. With the slim fingers of one hand she would slightly part these silky golden drapes to peer at the Mouser playfully, while with those of the other she rattled golden castanets in a most languorously slow rhythm, though with occasional swift staccato bursts.

The Mouser was considering whether it might not be as well to try a turn or two on the ruby-crusted golden crank next to his elbow, when he spied for the first time the glimmering wall at the back of the shop. What could its material be? he asked himself. Tiny diamonds countless as the sand set in smoky glass? Black opal? Black pearl? Black moonshine?

Whatever it was, it was wholly fascinating, for the Mouser quickly set down his book, using the nine-crooked spy-tube to mark his place—a most engrossing pair of pages on dueling where were revealed the Universal Parry and its five false variants and also the three true forms of the Secret Thrust—and with only a finger-wave to the ensorceling blonde in red velvet he walked quickly toward the back of the shop.

As he approached the Black Wall he thought for an instant that he glimpsed a silver wraith, or perhaps a silver skeleton, walking toward him out of it, but then he saw that it was only his own darkly handsome reflection, pleasantly flattered by the lustrous material. What had momentarily suggested silver ribs was the reflection of the silver lacings on his tunic.

He smirked at his image and reached out a finger to touch *its* lustrous finger when—Lo, a wonder!—his hand went into the wall with never a sensation at all save a faint tingling coolth promising comfort like the sheets of a fresh-made bed.

He looked at his hand inside the wall and—Lo, another wonder—it was all a beautiful silver faintly patterned with tiny scales. And though his own hand indubitably, as he could tell by clenching it, it was scarless now and a mite slimmer and longer fingered—altogether a more handsome hand than it had been a moment ago.

He wriggled his fingers and it was like watching small silver fish dart about—fingerlings!

What a droll conceit, he thought, to have a dark fishpond or rather swimming pool set on its side indoors, so that one could walk into the fracious erect fluid quietly and gracefully, instead of all the noisy, bouncingly athletic business of diving!

And how charming that the pool should be filled not with wet soppy cold water, but with a sort of moon-dark essence of sleep! An essence with beautifying cosmetic properties too—a sort of mud-bath without the mud. The Mouser decided he must have a swim in this wonder pool at once, but just then his gaze lit on a long high black couch toward the other end of the dark liquid wall, and beyond the couch a small high table set with viands and a crystal pitcher and goblet.

He walked along the wall to inspect these, his handsome reflection taking step for step with him.

He trailed his hand in the wall for a space and then withdrew it, the scales instantly vanishing and the familiar old scars returning.

The couch turned out to be a narrow high-sided black coffin lined with quilted black satin and piled at one end with little black satin pillows. It looked most invitingly comfortable and restful—not quite as inviting as the Black Wall, but very attractive just the same; there was even a rack of tiny black books nested in the black satin for the occupant's diversion and also a black candle, unlit.

The collation on the little ebony table beyond the coffin consisted entirely of black foods. By sight and then by nibbling and sipping the Mouser discovered their nature: thin slices of a very dark rye bread crusted with poppy seeds and dripped with black butter; slivers of charcoal-seared steak; similarly broiled tiny thin slices of calf's liver sprinkled with dark spices and liberally pricked with capers; the darkest grape jellies; truffles cut paper thin and mushrooms fried black; pickled chestnuts; and of course, ripe olives and black fish eggs—caviar. The black drink, which foamed when he poured it, turned out to be stout laced with the bubbly wine of Ilthmar.

He decided to refresh the inner Mouser—the Mouser who lived a sort of blind soft greedy undulating surface-life between his lips and his belly—before taking a dip in the Black Wall.

Fafhrd re-entered the Plaza of Dark Delights walking warily and with the long tatter that was the Cloak of Invisibility trailing from between left forefinger and thumb and with the glimmering cobweb that was the Blindfold of True Seeing pinched even more delicately by its edge between the same digits of his right hand. He was not yet altogether certain that the trailing gossamer hexagon was completely free of spiders.

Across the Plaza he spotted the bright-mouthed shop—the shop he had been told was an outpost of the deadly Devourers—through a ragged gather of folk moving about restlessly and commenting and speculating to one another in harsh excited undertones.

The only feature of the shop Fafhrd could make out at all clearly at this distance was the red-capped red-footed baggy-trousered porter, not capering now but leaning on his long broom beside the trefoil-arched doorway.

With a looping swing of his left arm Fafhrd hung the Cloak of Invisibility around his neck. The ragged ribband hung to either side down his chest in its wolfskin jetkin only halfway to his wide belt which supported longsword and short-axe. It did not vanish his body to the slightest degree that he could see and he doubted it worked at all. Like many another thaumaturge, Ningauble never hesitated to give one useless charms, not for any treacherous reason, necessarily, but simply to improve one's morals. Fathrd strode boldly toward the shop.

The Northerner was a tall, broad-shouldered, formidable-looking man—doubly formidable by his barbaric dress and weaponing in supercivilized Lankhmar—and so he took it for granted that the ordinary run of city folk stepped out of his way; indeed it had never occurred to him that they should not.

He got a shock. All the clerks, seedy bravos, scullery folk, students, slaves, second-rate merchants and second-class courtesans who would automatically have moved aside for him (though the last with a saucy swing of the hips) now came straight at him, so that he had to dodge and twist and stop and even sometimes dart back to avoid being toe-tramped and bumped. Indeed one fat pushy proud-stomached fellow almost carried away his cobweb, which he could see now by the light of the shop was free of spiders—or if there were any spiders still on it, they must be very small.

He had so much to do dodging Fafhrd-blind Lankhmarians that he could not spare one more glance for the shop until he was almost at the door. And then before he took his first close look, he found that he was tilting his head so that his left ear touched the shoulder below it and that he was laying Sheelba's spiderweb across his eyes.

The touch of it was simply like the touch of any cobweb when one runs face into it walking between close-set bushes at dawn. Everything shimmered a bit as if seen through a fine crystal grating. Then the least shimmering vanished, and with it the delicate clinging sensation, and Fafhrd's vision returned to normal—as far as he could tell.

It turned out that the doorway to the Devourers' shop was piled with garbage—garbage of a particularly offensive sort: old bones, dead fish, butcher's offal, moldering gracecloths folded in uneven squares like badly bound uncut books, broken glass and potsherds, splintered boxes, large stinking dead leaves orange-spotted with blight, bloody rags, tattered discarded loincloths, large worms nosing about, centipedes a-scuttle, cockroaches a-stagger, maggots a-crawl—and less agreeable things.

Atop all perched a vulture which had lost most of its feathers and seemed to have expired of some avian eczema. At least Fafhrd took it for dead, but then it opened one white-filmed eye.

The only conceivably salable object outside the shop—but it was a most notable exception—was the tall black iron statue, somewhat larger than life-size, of a lean swordsman of dire yet melancholy visage. Standing on its square pedestal beside the door, the statue leaned forward just a little on its long two-handed sword and regarded the Plaza dolefully.

The statue almost teased awake a recollection in Fafhrd's mind—a recent recollection, he fancied—but then there was a blank in his thoughts and he instantly dropped the puzzle. On raids like this one, relentlessly swift action was paramount. He loosened his axe in its loop, noiselessly whipped out Graywand and, shrinking away from the piled and crawling garbage just a little, entered the Bazaar of the Bizarre.

The Mouser, pleasantly replete with tasty black food and heady black drink, drifted to the Black Wall and thrust in his right arm to the shoulder. He waved it about, luxuriating in the softly flowing coolth and balm—admiring its fine silver scales and more than human handsomeness. He did the same with his right leg, swinging it like a dancer exercising at the bar. Then he took a gently deep breath and drifted farther in.

Fafhrd on entering the Bazaar saw the same piles of gloriously bound books and racks of gleaming brass spy-tubes and crystal lenses as had the Mouser—a circumstance which seemed to overset Ningauble's theory that the Devourers sold only trash.

He also saw the eight beautiful cages of jewel-gleaming metals and the gleaming chains that hung them from the ceiling and went to the jeweled wall cranks.

Each cage held a gleaming, gloriously hued, black-or light-haired spider big as a rather small person and occasionally waving a long jointed claw-handed leg, or softly opening a little and then closing a pair of fanged down-swinging mandibles, while staring steadily at Fafhrd with eight watchful eyes set in two jewel-like rows of four.

Set a spider to catch a spider, Fafhrd thought, thinking of his cobweb, and then wondered what the thought meant.

He quickly switched to more practical questions then, but he had barely asked himself whether before proceeding further he should kill the very expensive-looking spiders, fit to be the coursing beasts of some jungle empress—another count against Ning's trash-theory!—when he heard a faint splashing from the back of the shop. It reminded him of the Mouser taking a bath—the Mouser loved baths, slow luxurious ones in hot soapy scented oil-dripped water, the small gray sybarite!—and so Fafhrd hurried off in that direction with many a swift upward overshoulder glance.

He was detouring the last cage, a scarlet-metaled one holding the handsomest spider yet, when he noted a book set down with a crooked spy-tube in it—exactly as the Mouser would keep his place in a book by closing it on a dagger.

Fafhrd paused to open the book. Its lustrous white pages were blank. He put his impalpably cobwebbed eye to the spy-tube. He glimpsed a scene that could only be the smoky red hell-nadir of the universe, where dark devils scuttled about like centipedes and where chained folk gazing yearningly upward and the damned writhed in the grip of black serpents whose eyes shone and whose fangs dripped and whose nostrils breathed fire.

As he dropped tube and book, he heard the faint sonorous quick dull report of bubbles being expelled from a fluid at its surface. Staring instantly toward the dim back of the shop, he saw at last the pearl-shimmering Black Wall and a silver skeleton eyed with great diamonds receding into it. However, this costly bone-man—once more Ning's trash-theory disproved!—still had one arm sticking partway out of the wall and this arm was not bone, whether silver, white, brownish, or pink, but live-looking flesh covered with proper skin.

As the arm sank into the wall, Fafhrd sprang forward as fast as he ever had in his life and grabbed the hand just before it vanished. He knew then he had hold of his friend, for he would recognize anywhere the Mouser's grip, no matter how enfeebled. He tugged, but it was as if the Mouser were mired in black quicksand. He laid Graywand down and grasped the Mouser by the wrist too and braced his feet against the rough black flags and gave a tremendous heave.

The silver skeleton came out of the wall with a black splash, meta-morphosing as it did into a vacant-eyed Gray Mouser who without a look at his friend and rescuer went staggering off in a curve and pitched head over heels into the black coffin.

But before Fafhrd could hoist his comrade from this new gloomy predicament, there was a swift clash of footsteps and there came racing into the shop, somewhat to Fafhrd's surprise, the tall black iron statue. It had forgotten or simply stepped off its pedestal, but it had remembered its two-handed sword, which it brandished about most fiercely while shooting searching black glances like iron darts at every shadow and corner and nook.

The black gaze passed Fafhrd without pausing, but halted at Gray-wand lying on the floor. At the sight of that longsword the statue started visibly, snarled its iron lips, narrowed its black eyes. It shot glances more ironly stabbing than before, and it began to move about the shop in sudden zigzag rushes, sweeping its darkly flashing sword in low scythe-strokes.

At that moment the Mouser peeped moon-eyed over the edge of the coffin, lifted a limp hand and waved it at the statue, and in a soft sly foolish voice cried, "Yoo-hoo!"

The statue paused in its searchings and scythings to glare at the Mouser in mixed contempt and puzzlement.

The Mouser rose to his feet in the black coffin, swaying drunk-enly, and dug in his pouch.

"Ho, slave!" he cried to the statue with maudlin gaiety, "your wares are passing passable. I'll take the girl in red velvet." He pulled a coin from his pouch, goggled at it closely, then pitched it at the statue. "That's one penny. And the nine-crooked spy-tube. That's another penny." He pitched it. "And *Gron's Grand Compendium of Exotic Lore*—another penny for you! Yes, and here's one more for supper—very tasty, 'twas. Oh and I almost forgot—here's for tonight's lodging!" He pitched a fifth large copper coin at the demonic black statue and, smiling blissfully, flopped back out of sight. The black quilted satin could be heard to sigh as he sank in it.

Four-fifths of the way through the Mouser's penny-pitching Fafhrd decided it was useless to try to unriddle his comrade's non-sensical behavior and that it would be far more to the point to make use of this diversion to snatch up Graywand. He did so on the instant, but by that time the black statue was fully alert again, if it had ever been otherwise. Its gaze switched to Graywand the instant Fafhrd touched the longsword and it stamped its foot, which rang against the stone, and cried a harsh metallic "Ha!"

Apparently the sword became invisible as Fafhrd grasped it, for the black statue did not follow him with its iron eyes as he shifted position across the room. Instead it swiftly laid down its own mighty blade and caught up a long narrow silver trumpet and set it to its lips.

Fafhrd thought it wise to attack before the statue summoned rein-forcements. He rushed straight at the thing, swinging back Gray-wand for a great stroke at the neck—and steeling himself for an arm-numbing impact.

The statue blew and instead of the alarm blare Fafhrd had expected, there silently puffed out straight at him a great cloud of white powder that momentarily blotted out everything, as if it were the thickest of fogs from Illal the River.

Fafhrd retreated, choking and coughing. The demon-blown fog cleared quickly, the white powder falling to the stony floor with unnatural swiftness, and he could see again to attack, but now the statue apparently could see him too, for it squinted straight at him and cried its metallic "Ha!" again and whirled its sword around its iron head preparatory to the charge—rather as if winding itself up.

Fafhrd saw that his own hands and arms were thickly filmed with the white powder, which apparently clung to him everywhere except his eyes, doubtless protected by Sheelba's cobweb.

The iron statue came thrusting and slashing in. Fafhrd took the great sword on his, chopped back, and was parried in return. And now the combat assumed the noisy deadly aspects of a conventional longsword duel, except that Graywand was notched whenever it caught the chief force of a stroke, while the statue's somewhat longer weapon remained unmarked. Also, whenever Fafhrd got through the other's guard with a thrust—it was almost impossible to reach him with a slash—it turned out that the other had slipped his lean body or head aside with unbelievably swift and infallible anticipations.

It seemed to Fafhrd—at least at the time—the most fell, frustrating, and certainly the most wearisome combat in which he had ever engaged, so he suffered some feelings of hurt and irritation when the Mouser reeled up in his coffin again and leaned an elbow on the black-satin-quilted side and rested chin on fist and grinned hugely at the battlers and from time to time laughed wildly and shouted such enraging nonsense as, "Use Secret Thrust Two-and-a-Half, Fafhrd—it's all in the book!" or "Jump in the oven!—there'd be a master stroke of strategy!" or—this to the statue—"Remember to sweep under his feet, you rogue!"

Backing away from one of Fafhrd's sudden attacks, the statue bumped the table holding the remains of the Mouser's repast—evidently its anticipatory abilities did not extend to its rear—and scraps of black food and white potsherds and jags of crystal scattered across the floor.

The Mouser leaned out of his coffin and waved a finger waggishly. "You'll have to sweep that up!" he cried and went off into a gale of laughter.

Backing away again, the statue bumped the black coffin. The Mouser only clapped the demonic figure comradely on the shoulder and called, "Set to it again, clown! Brush him down! Dust him off!"

But the worst was perhaps when, during a brief pause while the combatants gasped and eyed each other dizzily, the Mouser waved coyly to the nearest giant spider and called his inane "Yoo-hoo!" again, following it with, "I'll see you, dear, after the circus."

Fafhrd, parrying with weary desperation a fifteenth or a fiftieth cut at his head, thought bitterly, *This comes of trying to rescue small heartless madmen who would howl at their grandmothers hugged by bears. Sheelba's cobweb has shown me the Gray One in his true idiot nature.*

The Mouser had first been furious when the sword-skirling clashed him awake from his black satin dreams, but as soon as he saw what was going on he became enchanted at the wildly comic scene.

For, lacking Sheelba's cobweb, what the Mouser saw was only the zany red-capped porter prancing about in his ridiculous tip-curled red shoes and aiming at Fafhrd, who looked exactly as if he had climbed a moment ago out of a barrel of meal. The only part of the Northerner not whitely dusted was a shadowy dark masklike stretch across his eyes.

What made the whole thing fantastically droll was that miller-white Fafhrd was going through all the motions—and emotions!—of a genuine combat with excruciating precision, parrying the broom as if it were some great jolting scimitar or two-handed broadsword even. The broom would go sweeping up and Fafhrd would gawk at it, giving a marvelous interpretation of apprehensive goggling despite his strangely shadowed eyes. Then the broom would come sweeping down and Fafhrd would brace himself and seem to catch it on his sword only with the most prodigious effort— and then pretend to be jolted back by it!

The Mouser had never suspected Fafhrd had such a perfected theatric talent, even if it were acting of a rather mechanical sort, lacking the broad sweeps of true dramatic genius, and he whooped with laughter.

Then the broom brushed Fafhrd's shoulder and blood sprang out.

Fafhrd, wounded at last and thereby knowing himself unlikely to outendure the black statue—although the latter's iron chest was working now like a bellows—decided on swifter measures. He loosened his hand-axe again in its loop and at the next pause in the fight, both battlers having outguessed each other by retreating simultaneously, whipped it up and hurled it at his adversary's face.

Instead of seeking to dodge or ward off the missile, the black statue lowered its sword and merely wove its head in a tiny circle.

The axe closely circled the lean black head, like a silver wood-tailed comet whipping around a black sun, and came back straight at Fafhrd like a boomerang—and rather more swiftly than Fafhrd had sent it.

But time slowed for Fafhrd then and he half ducked and caught it left-handed as it went whizzing past his cheek.

His thoughts too went for a moment fast as his actions. He thought of how his adversary, able to dodge every frontal attack, had not avoided the table or the coffin behind him. He thought of how the Mouser had not laughed now for a dozen clashes and he looked at him and saw him, though still dazed-seeming, strangely pale and sober-faced, appearing to stare with horror at the blood running down Fafhrd's arm.

So crying as heartily and merrily as he could, "Amuse yourself! Join in the fun, clown!—here's your slap-stick," Fafhrd tossed the axe toward the Mouser.

Without waiting to see the result of that toss—perhaps not daring to—he summoned up his last reserves of speed and rushed at the black statue in a circling advance that drove it back toward the coffin.

Without shifting his stupid horrified gaze, the Mouser stuck out a hand at the last possible moment and caught the axe by the handle as it spun lazily down.

As the black statue retreated near the coffin and poised for what promised to be a stupendous counterattack, the Mouser leaned out and, now grinning foolishly again, sharply rapped its black pate with the axe.

The iron head split like a coconut, but did not come apart. Fafhrd's hand-axe, wedged in it deeply, seemed to turn all at once to iron like the statue and its black haft was wrenched out of the Mouser's hand as the statue stiffened up straight and tall.

The Mouser stared at the split head woefully, like a child who hadn't known knives cut.

The statue brought its great sword flat against its chest, like a staff on which it might lean but did not, and it fell rigidly forward and hit the floor with a ponderous clank.

At that stony-metallic thundering, white wildfire ran across the Black Wall, lightening the whole shop like a distant levin-bolt, and iron-basalt thundering echoed from deep within it.

Fafhrd sheathed Graywand, dragged the Mouser out of the black coffin—the fight hadn't left him the strength to lift even his small friend—and shouted in his ear, "Come on! Run!"

The Mouser ran for the Black Wall.

Fafhrd snagged his wrist as he went by and plunged toward the arched door, dragging the Mouser after him.

The thunder faded out and there came a low whistle, cajolingly sweet.

Wildfire raced again across the Black Wall behind them—much

more brightly this time, as if a lightning storm were racing toward them.

The white glare striking ahead imprinted one vision indelibly on Fafhrd's brain: the giant spider in the inmost cage pressed against the bloodred bars to gaze down at them. It had pale legs and a velvet red body and a mask of sleek thick golden hair from which eight jet eyes peered, while its fanged jaws hanging down in the manner of the wide blades of a pair of golden scissors rattled together in a wild staccato rhythm like castanets.

That moment the cajoling whistle was repeated. It too seemed to be coming from the red and golden spider.

But strangest of all to Fafhrd was to hear the Mouser, dragged unwillingly along behind him, cry out in answer to the whistling, "Yes, darling, I'm coming. Let me go, Fafhrd! Let me climb to her! Just one kiss! Sweetheart!"

"Stop it, Mouser," Fafhrd growled, his flesh crawling in midplunge. "It's a giant spider!"

"Wipe the cobwebs out of your eyes, Fafhrd," the Mouser retorted pleadingly and most unwittingly to the point. "It's a gorgeous girl! I'll never see her ticklesome like—and I've paid for her! *Sweetheart!*"

Then the booming thunder drowned his voice and any more whistling there might have been, and the wildfire came again, brighter than day, and another great thunderclap right on its heels, and the floor shuddered and the whole shop shook, and Fafhrd dragged the Mouser through the trefoil-arched doorway, and there was another great flash and clap.

The flash showed a semicircle of Lankhmarians peering ashenfaced overshoulder as they retreated across the Plaza of Dark Delights from the remarkable indoor thunderstorm that threatened to come out after them.

Fafhrd spun around. The archway had turned to blank wall.

The Bazaar of the Bizarre was gone from the World of Nehwon.

The Mouser, sitting on the dank flags where Fafhrd had dragged him, babbled wailfully, "The secrets of time and space! The lore of the gods! The mysteries of Hell! Black nirvana! Red and gold Heaven! Five pennies gone forever!"

Fafhrd set his teeth. A mighty resolve, rising from his many recent angers and bewilderments, crystallized in him.

Thus far he had used Sheelba's cobweb—and Ningauble's tatter too—only to serve others. Now he would use them for himself! He would peer at the Mouser more closely and at every person he knew. He would study even his own reflection! But most of all, he would stare Sheelba and Ning to their wizardly cores!

There came from overhead a low "Hssst!"

As he glanced up he felt something snatched from around his neck and, with the faintest tingling sensation, from off his eyes.

For a moment there was a shimmer traveling upward and through it he seemed to glimpse distortedly, as through thick glass, a black face with a cobwebby skin that entirely covered mouth and nostrils and eyes.

Then that dubious flash was gone and there were only two cowled heads peering down at him from over the wall top. There was chuckling laughter.

Then both cowled heads drew back out of sight and there was only the edge of the roof and the sky and the stars and the blank wall.

Come Lady Death

Peter S. Beagle

Peter Beagle is most famous for his fantasy novel The Last Unicorn, *which was a national bestseller when it appeared in 1968. Later he turned to writing screenplays for television and film, including the animated version of Tolkien's* Lord of the Rings. *Recently he published* The Unicorn Sonata, *a sequel to* The Last Unicorn, *and edited an anthology of unicorn stories entitled* The Immortal Unicorn. *His latest project is a collection of short stories,* The Magician of Karakosk and Others.

THIS ALL HAPPENED IN ENGLAND A LONG TIME AGO, WHEN THAT GEORGE who spoke English with a heavy German accent and hated his sons was King. At that time there lived in London a lady who had nothing to do but give parties. Her name was Flora, Lady Neville, and she was a widow and very old. She lived in a great house not far from Buckingham Palace, and she had so many servants that she could not possibly remember all their names; indeed, there were some she had never even seen. She had more food than she could eat, more gowns than she could ever wear; she had wine in her cellars that no one would drink in her lifetime, and her private vaults were filled with great works of art that she did not know she owned. She spent the last years of her life giving parties and balls to which the greatest lords of England—and sometimes the King himself—came, and she was known as the wisest and wittiest woman in all London.

But in time her own parties began to bore her, and though she invited the most famous people in the land and hired the greatest jugglers and acrobats and dancers and magicians to entertain them, still she found her parties duller and duller. Listening to court gossip, which she had always loved, made her yawn. The most marvelous music, the most exciting feats of magic put her to sleep. Watching a beautiful young couple dance by her made her feel sad, and she hated to feel sad.

And so, one summer afternoon she called her closest friends around her and said to them, "More and more I find that my parties

entertain everyone but me. The secret of my long life is that nothing
has ever been dull for me. For all my life, I have been interested in
everything I saw and been anxious to see more. But I cannot stand
to be bored, and I will not go to parties at which I expect to be
bored, especially if they are my own. Therefore, to my next ball I
shall invite the one guest I am sure no one, not even myself, could
possibly find boring. My friends, the guest of honor at my next party
shall be Death himself!"

A young poet thought that this was a wonderful idea, but the rest
of her friends were terrified and drew back from her. They did not
want to die, they pleaded with her. Death would come for them
when he was ready; why should she invite him before the appointed
hour, which would arrive soon enough? But Lady Neville said,
"Precisely. If Death has planned to take any of us on the night of my
party, he will come whether he is invited or not. But if none of us
are to die, then I think it would be charming to have Death among
us—perhaps even to perform some little trick if he is in a good
humor. And think of being able to say that we had been to a party
with Death! All of London will envy us, all of England!"

The idea began to please her friends, but a young lord, very new
to London, suggested timidly, "Death is so busy. Suppose he has
work to do and cannot accept your invitation?"

"No one has ever refused an invitation of mine," said Lady
Neville, "not even the King." And the young lord was not invited to
her party.

She sat down then and there and wrote out the invitation. There
was some dispute among her friends as to how they should address
Death. "His Lordship Death" seemed to place him only on the level
of a viscount or a baron. "His Grace Death" met with more acceptance, but Lady Neville said it sounded hypocritical. And to refer to
Death as "His Majesty" was to make him the equal of the King of
England, which oven Lady Neville would not dare to do. It was
finally decided that all should speak of him as "His Eminence
Death," which pleased nearly everyone.

Captain Compson, known both as England's most dashing cavalry officer and most elegant rake; remarked next, "That's all very
well, but how is the invitation to reach Death? Does anyone here
know where he lives?"

"Death undoubtedly lives in London," said Lady Neville, "like
everyone else of any importance, though he probably goes to
Deauville for the summer. Actually, Death must live fairly near my
own house. This is much the best section of London, and you could
hardly expect a person of Death's importance to live anywhere else.

When I stop to think of it, it's really rather strange that we haven't met before now, on the street."

Most of her friends agreed with her, but the poet, whose name was David Lorimond, cried out, "No, my lady, you are wrong! Death lives among the poor. Death lives in the foulest, darkest alleys of this city, in some vile, rat-ridden hovel that smells of—" He stopped here, partly because Lady Neville had indicated her displeasure, and partly because he had never been inside such a hut or thought of wondering what it smelled like. "Death lives among the poor," he went on, "and comes to visit them every day, for he is their only friend."

Lady Neville answered him as coldly as she had spoken to the young lord. "He may be forced to deal with them, David, but I hardly think that he seeks them out as companions. I am certain that it is as difficult for him to think of the poor as individuals as it is for me. Death is, after all, a nobleman."

There was no real argument among the lords and ladies that Death lived in a neighborhood at least as good as their own, but none of them seemed to know the name of Death's street, and no one had ever seen Death's house.

"If there were a war," Captain Compson said, "Death would be easy to find. I have seen him, you know, even spoken to him, but he has never answered me."

"Quite proper," said Lady Neville. "Death must always speak first. You are not a very correct person, Captain." But she smiled at him, as all women did.

Then an idea came to her. "My hairdresser has a sick child, I understand," she said. "He was telling me about it yesterday, sounding most dull and hopeless. I will send for him and give him the invitation, and he in his turn can give it to Death when he comes to take the brat. A bit unconventional, I admit, but I see no other way."

"If he refuses?" asked a lord who had just been married.

"Why should he?" asked Lady Neville.

Again it was the poet who exclaimed amidst the general approval that this was a cruel and wicked thing to do. But he fell silent when Lady Neville innocently asked him, "Why, David?"

So the hairdresser was sent for, and when he stood before them, smiling nervously and twisting his hands to be in the same room with so many great lords, Lady Neville told him the errand that was required of him. And she was right, as she usually was, for he made no refusal. He merely took the invitation in his hand and asked to be excused.

He did not return for two days, but when he did he presented himself to Lady Neville without being sent for and handed her a small white envelope. Saying, "How very nice of you, thank you very much," she opened it and found therein a plain calling card with nothing on it except these words: *Death will be pleased to attend Lady Neville's ball.*

"Death gave you this?" she asked the hairdresser eagerly. "What was he like?" But the hairdresser stood still, looking past her, and said nothing, and she, not really waiting for an answer, called a dozen servants to her and told them to run and summon her friends. As she paced up and down the room waiting for them, she asked again, "What is Death like?" The hairdresser did not reply.

When her friends came they passed the little card excitedly from hand to hand, until it had gotten quite smudged and bent from their fingers. But they all admitted that, beyond its message, there was nothing particularly unusual about it. It was neither hot nor cold to the touch, and what little odor clung to it was rather pleasant. Everyone said that it was a very familiar smell, but no one could give it a name. The poet said that it reminded him of lilacs but not exactly.

It was Captain Compson, however, who pointed out the one thing that no one else had noticed. "Look at the handwriting itself," he said. "Have you ever seen anything more graceful? The letters seem as light as birds. I think we have wasted our time speaking of Death as His This and His That. A woman wrote this note."

Then there was an uproar and a great babble, and the card had to be handed around again so that everyone could exclaim, "Yes, by God!" over it. The voice of the poet rose out of the hubbub saying, "It is very natural, when you come to think of it. After all, the French say *la mort.* Lady Death. I should much prefer Death to be a woman."

"Death rides a great black horse," said Captain Compson firmly, "and wears armor of the same color. Death is very tall, taller than anyone. It was no woman I saw on the battlefield, striking right and left like any soldier. Perhaps the hairdresser wrote it himself, or the hairdresser's wife."

But the hairdresser refused to speak, though they gathered around him and begged him to say who had given him the note. At first they promised him all sorts of rewards, and later they threatened to do terrible things to him. "Did you write this card?" he was asked, and "Who wrote it, then? Was it a living woman? Was it really Death? Did Death say anything to you? How did you know it was Death? Is Death a woman? Are you trying to make fools of us all?"

Not a word from the hairdresser, not one word, and finally Lady Neville called her servants to have him whipped and thrown into the street. He did not look at her as they took him away, or utter a sound.

Silencing her friends with a wave of her hand, Lady Neville said, "The ball will take place two weeks from tonight. Let Death come as Death pleases, whether as man or woman or strange, sexless creature." She smiled calmly. "Death may well be a woman," she said. "I am less certain of Death's form than I was, but I am also less frightened of Death. I am too old to be afraid of anything that can use a quill pen to write me a letter. Go home now, and as you make your preparations for the ball see that you speak of it to your servants, that they may spread the news all over London. Let it be known that on this one night no one in the world will die, for Death will be dancing at Lady Neville's ball."

For the next two weeks Lady Neville's great house shook and groaned and creaked like an old tree in a gale as the servants hammered and scrubbed, polished and painted, making ready for the ball. Lady Neville had always been very proud of her house, but as the ball drew near she began to be afraid that it would not be nearly grand enough for Death, who was surely accustomed to visiting in the homes of richer, mightier people than herself. Fearing the scorn of Death, she worked night and day supervising her servants' preparations. Curtains and carpets had to be cleaned, goldwork and silverware polished until they gleamed by themselves in the dark. The grand staircase that rushed down into the ballroom like a waterfall was washed and rubbed so often that it was almost impossible to walk on it without slipping. As for the ballroom itself, it took thirty-two servants working at once to clean it properly, not counting those who were polishing the glass chandelier that was taller than a man and the fourteen smaller lamps. And when they were done she made them do it all over, not because she saw any dust or dirt anywhere, but because she was sure that Death would.

As for herself, she chose her finest gown and saw to its laundering personally. She called in another hairdresser and had him put up her hair in the style of an earlier time, wanting to show Death that she was a woman who enjoyed her age and did not find it necessary to ape the young and beautiful. All the day of the ball she sat before her mirror, not making herself up much beyond the normal touches of rouge and eye shadow and fine rice powder, but staring at the lean old face she had been born with, wondering how it would appear to Death. Her steward asked her to approve his wine selection, but she sent him away and stayed at her mirror until it was time to dress and go downstairs to meet her guests.

Everyone arrived early. When she looked out of a window, Lady Neville saw that the driveway of her home was choked with carriages and fine horses. "It all looks like a great funeral procession," she said. The footman cried the names of her guests to the echoing ballroom. "Captain Henry Compson, His Majesty's Household Cavalry! Mr. David Lorimond! Lord and Lady Torrance!" (They were the youngest couple there, having been married only three months before.) "Sir Roger Harbison! The Contessa della Candini!" Lady Neville permitted them all to kiss her hand and made them welcome.

She had engaged the finest musicians she could find to play for the dancing, but though they began to play at her signal not one couple stepped out on the floor, nor did one young lord approach her to request the honor of the first dance, as was proper. They milled together, shining and murmuring, their eyes fixed on the ballroom door. Every time they heard a carriage clatter up the driveway they seemed to flinch a little and draw closer together; every time the footman announced the arrival of another guest, they all sighed softly and swayed a little on their feet with relief.

"Why did they come to my party if they were afraid?" Lady Neville muttered scornfully to herself. "I am not afraid of meeting Death. I ask only that Death may be impressed by the magnificence of my house and the flavor of my wines. I will die sooner than anyone here, but I am not afraid."

Certain that Death would not arrive until midnight, she moved among her guests, attempting to calm them, not with her words, which she knew they would not hear, but with the tone of her voice, as if they were so many frightened horses. But little by little, she herself was infected by their nervousness: whenever she sat down she stood up again immediately, she tasted a dozen glasses of wine without finishing any of them, and she glanced constantly at her jeweled watch, at first wanting to hurry the midnight along and end the waiting, later scratching at the watch face with her forefinger, as if she would push away the night and drag the sun backward into the sky. When midnight came, she was standing with the rest of them, breathing through her mouth, shifting from foot to foot, listening for the sound of carriage wheels turning in gravel.

When the clock began to strike midnight, everyone, even Lady Neville and the brave Captain Compson, gave one startled little cry and then was silent again, listening to the toiling of the clock. The smaller clocks upstairs began to chime. Lady Neville's ears hurt. She caught sight of herself in the ballroom mirror, one gray face turned up toward the ceiling as if she were gasping for air, and she thought, "Death will be a woman, a hideous, filthy old crone as tall and strong as a man. And the most terrible thing of all will be that she will have my face." All the clocks stopped striking, and Lady Neville closed her eyes.

She opened them again only when she heard the whispering around her take on a different tone, one in which fear was fused with relief and a certain chagrin. For no new carriage stood in the driveway. Death had not come.

The noise grew slowly louder; here and there people were beginning to laugh. Near her, Lady Neville heard young Lord Torrance say to his wife, "There, my darling, I told you there was nothing to be afraid of. It was all a joke."

"I am ruined," Lady Neville thought. The laughter was increasing; it pounded against her ears in strokes, like the chiming of the clocks. "I wanted to give a ball so grand that those who were not invited would be shamed in front of the whole city, and this is my reward. I am ruined, and I deserve it."

Turning to the poet Lorimond, she said, "Dance with me, David." She signaled to the musicians, who at once began to play. When Lorimond hesitated, she said, "Dance with me now. You will not have another chance. I shall never give a party again."

Lorimond bowed and led her out onto the dance floor. The guests parted for them, and the laughter died down for a moment, but Lady Neville knew that it would soon begin again. "Well, let them laugh," she thought. "I did not fear Death when they were all trembling. Why should I fear their laughter?" But she could feel a stinging at the thin lids of her eyes, and she closed them once more as she began to dance with Lorimond.

And then, quite suddenly, all the carriage horses outside the house whinnied loudly, just once, as the guests had cried out at midnight. There were a great many horses, and their one salute was so loud that everyone in the room became instantly silent. They heard the heavy steps of the footman as he went to open the door, and they shivered a if they felt the cool breeze that drifted into the house. Then they heard a light voice saying, "Am I late? Oh, I am so sorry. The horses were tired," and before the footman could re-enter to announce her, a lovely young girl in a white dress stepped gracefully into the ballroom doorway and stood there smiling.

She could not have been more than nineteen. Her hair was yellow, and she wore it long. It fell thickly upon her bare shoulders that gleamed warmly through it, two limestone islands rising out of a dark golden sea. Her face was wide at the forehead and cheekbones, and narrow at the chin, and her skin was so clear that many of the ladies there—Lady Neville among them—touched their own faces wonderingly, and instantly drew their hands away as though their own skin had rasped their fingers. Her mouth was pale, where the mouths of the other women were red and orange and even purple. Her eyebrows, thicker and straighter than was fashionable, met over dark, calm eyes that were set so deep in her young face and were so black, so uncompromisingly black, that the middle-aged wife of a middle-aged lord murmured, "Touch of the gypsy there, I think."

"Or something worse," suggested her husband's mistress.

"Be silent!" Lady Neville spoke louder than she had intended, and the girl turned to look at her. She smiled, and Lady Neville tried to smile back, but her mouth seemed very stiff. "Welcome," she said. "Welcome, my lady Death."

A sigh rustled among the lords and ladies as the girl took the old woman's hand and curtsied to her, sinking and rising in one motion, like a wave. "You are Lady Neville," she said. "Thank you so much for inviting me." Her accent was as faint and as almost familiar as her perfume.

"Please excuse me for being late," she said earnestly. "I had to come from a long way off, and my horses are so tired."

"The groom will rub them down," Lady Neville said, "and feed them if you wish." .

"Oh, no," the girl answered quickly. "Tell him not to go near the horses, please. They are not really horses, and they are very fierce."

She accepted a glass of wine from a servant and drank it slowly, sighing softly and contentedly. "What good wine," she said. "And what a beautiful house you have."

"Thank you," said Lady Neville. Without turning, she could feel every woman in the room envying her, sensing it as she could always sense the approach of rain.

"I wish I lived here," Death said in her low, sweet voice. "I will, one day."

Then, seeing Lady Neville become as still as if she had turned to ice, she put her hand on the old woman's arm and said, "Oh, I'm sorry, I'm so sorry. I am so cruel, but I never mean to be. Please forgive me, Lady Neville. I am not used to company, and I do such stupid things. Please forgive me."

Her hand felt as light and warm on Lady Neville's arm as the hand of any other young girl, and her eyes were so appealing that Lady Neville replied, "You have said nothing wrong. While you are my guest, my house is yours."

"Thank you," said Death, and she smiled so radiantly that the musicians began to play quite by themselves, with no sign from Lady Neville. She would have stopped them, but Death said, "Oh, what lovely music! Let them play, please."

So the musicians played a gavotte, and Death, unabashed by eyes that stared at her in greedy terror, sang softly to herself without words, lifted her white gown slightly with both hands, and made hesitant little patting steps with her small feet. "I have not danced in so long," she said wistfully. "I'm quite sure I've forgotten how."

She was shy; she would not look up to embarrass the young lords, not one of whom stepped forward to dance with her. Lady Neville felt a flood of shame and sympathy, emotions she thought had withered in her years ago. "Is she to be humiliated at my own ball?" she thought angrily. "It is because she is Death; if she were the ugliest, foulest hag in all the world they would clamor to dance with her, because they are gentlemen and they know what is expected of them. But no gentleman will dance with Death, no matter how beautiful she is." She glanced sideways at David Lorimond. His face was flushed, and his hands were clasped so tightly as he stared at Death that his fingers were like glass, but when Lady Neville touched his arm he did not turn, and when she hissed, "David!" he pretended not to hear her.

Then Captain Compson, gray-haired and handsome in his uniform, stepped out of the crowd and bowed gracefully before Death. "If I may have the honor," he said.

"Captain Compson," said Death, smiling. She put her arm in his. "I was hoping you would ask me."

This brought a frown from the older women, who did not consider it a proper thing to say, but for that Death cared not a rap. Captain Compson led her to the center of the floor, and there they danced. Death was curiously graceless at first—she was too anxious to please her partner, and she seemed to have no notion of rhythm. The Captain himself moved with the mixture of dignity and humor that Lady Neville had never seen in another man, but when he looked at her over Death's shoulder, she saw something that no one else appeared to notice: that his face and eyes were immobile with fear, and that, though he offered Death his hand with easy gallantry, he flinched slightly when she took it. And yet he danced as well as Lady Neville had ever seen him.

"Ah, that's what comes of having a reputation to maintain," she thought. "Captain Compson too must do what is expected of him. I hope someone else will dance with her soon."

But no one did. Little by little, other couples overcame their fear and slipped hurriedly out on the floor when Death was looking the other way, but nobody sought to relieve Captain Compson of his beautiful partner. They danced every dance together. In time, some of the men present began to look at her with more appreciation than terror, but when she returned their glances and smiled at them, they clung to their partners as if a cold wind were threatening to blow them away.

One of the few who stared at her frankly and with pleasure was young Lord Torrance, who usually danced only with his wife. Another was the poet Lorimond. Dancing with Lady Neville, he remarked to her, "If she is Death, what do these frightened fools think they are? If she is ugliness, what must they be? I hate their fear. It is obscene."

Death and the Captain danced past them at that moment, and they heard him say to her, "But if that was truly you that I saw in the battle, how can you have changed so? How can you have become so lovely?"

Death's laughter was gay and soft. "I thought that among so many beautiful people it might be better to be beautiful. I was afraid of frightening everyone and spoiling the party."

"They all thought she would be ugly," said Lorimond to Lady Neville. "I—*I* knew she would be beautiful."

"Then why have you not danced with her?" Lady Neville asked him. "Are you also afraid?"

"No, oh, no," the poet answered quickly and passionately. "I will ask her to dance very soon. I only want to look at her a little longer."

The musicians played on and on. The dancing wore away the night as slowly as falling water wears down a cliff. It seemed to Lady Neville that no night had ever endured longer, and yet she was neither tired nor bored. She danced with every man there, except with Lord Torrance, who was dancing with his wife as if they had just met that night, and, of course, with Captain Compson. Once he lifted his hand and touched Death's golden hair very lightly. He was a striking man still, a fit partner for so beautiful a girl, but Lady Neville looked at his face each time she passed him and realized that he was older than anyone knew.

Death herself seemed younger than the youngest there. No woman at the ball danced better than she now, though it was hard for Lady Neville to remember at what point her awkwardness had given way to the liquid sweetness of her movements. She smiled and called to everyone who caught her eye—and she knew them all by name; she sang constantly, making up words to the dance tunes, nonsense words, sounds without meaning, and yet everyone strained to hear her soft voice without knowing why. And when, during a waltz, she caught up the trailing end of her gown to give her more freedom as she danced, she seemed to Lady Neville to move like a little sailing boat over a still evening sea.

Lady Neville heard Lady Torrance arguing angrily with the Contessa della Candini. "I don't care if she is Death, she's no older than I am, she can't be!"

"Nonsense," said the Contessa, who could not afford to be generous to any other woman. "She is twenty-eight, thirty, if she is an hour. And that dress, that bridal gown she wears—really!"

"Vile," said the woman who had come to the ball as Captain Compson's freely acknowledged mistress. "Tasteless. But one should know better than to expect taste from Death, I suppose." Lady Torrance looked as if she were going to cry.

"They are jealous of Death," Lady Neville said to herself. "How strange. I am not jealous of her, not in the least. And I do not fear her at all." She was very proud of herself.

Then, as unbiddenly as they had begun to play, the musicians stopped. They began to put away their instruments. In the sudden shrill silence, Death pulled away from Captain Compson and ran to look out of one of the tall windows, pushing the curtains apart with both hands. "Look!" she said, with her back turned to them. "Come and look. The night is almost gone."

The summer sky was still dark, and the eastern horizon was only a shade lighter than the rest of the sky, but the stars had vanished and the trees near the house were gradually becoming distinct. Death pressed her face against the window and said, so softly that the other guests could barely hear her, "I must go now."

"No," Lady Neville said, and was not immediately aware that she had spoken. "You must stay a while longer. The ball was in your honor. Please stay."

Death held out both hands to her, and Lady Neville came and took them in her own. "I've had a wonderful time," she said gently. "You cannot possibly imagine how it feels to be actually invited to such a ball as this, because you have given them and gone to them all your life. One is like another to you, but for me it is different. Do you understand me?" Lady Neville nodded silently. "I will remember this night forever," Death said.

"Stay," Captain Compson said. "Stay just a little longer." He put his hand on Death's shoulder, and she smiled and leaned her cheek against it. "Dear Captain Compson," she said. "My first real gallant. Aren't you tired of me yet?"

"Never," he said. "Please stay."

"Stay," said Lorimond, and he too seemed about to touch her. "Stay, I want to talk to you. I want to look at you. I will dance with you if you stay."

"How many followers I have," Death said in wonder. She stretched one hand toward Lorimond, but he drew back from her, and then flushed in shame. "A soldier and a poet. How wonderful it is to be a woman. But why did you not speak to me earlier, both of you? Now it is too late. I must go."

"Please stay," Lady Torrance whispered. She held on to her

husband's hand for courage. "We think you are so beautiful, both of us do."

"Gracious Lady Torrance," the girl said kindly. She turned back to the window, touched it lightly, and it flew open. The cool dawn air rushed into the ballroom, fresh with rain but already smelling faintly of the London streets over which it had passed. They heard birdsong and the strange, harsh nickering of Death's horses.

"Do you want me to stay?" she asked. The question was put, not to Lady Neville, nor to Captain Compson, nor to any of her admirers, but to the Contessa della Candini, who stood well back from them all, hugging her flowers to herself and humming a little song of irritation. She did not in the least want Death to stay, but she was afraid that all the other women would think her envious of Death's beauty, and so she said, "Yes. Of course I do."

"Ah," said Death. She was almost whispering. "And you," she said to another woman, "do you want me to stay? Do you want me to be one of your friends?"

"Yes," said the woman, "because you are beautiful and a true lady."

"And you," said Death to a man, "and you," to a woman, "and you," to another man, "do you want me to stay?" And they all answered, "Yes, Lady Death, we do."

"Do you want me, then?" she cried at last to all of them. "Do you want me to live among you and to be one of you, and not to be Death anymore? Do you want me to visit your houses and come to all your parties? Do you want me to ride horses like yours instead of mine, do you want me to wear the kind of dresses you wear, and say the things you would say? Would one of you marry me, and would the rest of you dance at my wedding and bring gifts to my children? Is that what you want?"

"Yes," said Lady Neville. "Stay here, stay with me, stay with us."

Death's voice, without becoming louder, had become clearer and older; too old a voice, thought Lady Neville, for such a young girl. "Be sure," said Death. "Be sure of what you want, be very sure. Do all of you want me to stay? For if one of you says to me, no, go away, then I must leave at once and never return. Be sure. Do you all want me?"

And everyone there cried with one voice, "Yes! Yes, you must stay with us. You are so beautiful that we cannot let you go."

"We are tired," said Captain Compson.

"We are blind," said Lorimond, adding, "especially to poetry."

"We are afraid," said Lord Torrance quietly, and his wife took his arm and said, "Both of us."

"We are dull and stupid," said Lady Neville, "and growing old uselessly. Stay with us, Lady Death."

And then Death smiled sweetly and radiantly and took a step forward, and it was as though she had come down among them from a great height. "Very well," she said. "I will stay with you. I will be Death no more. I will be a woman."

The room was full of a deep sigh, although no one was seen to open his mouth. No one moved, for the golden-haired girl was Death still, and her horses still whinnied for her outside. No one could look at her for long, although she was the most beautiful girl anyone there had ever seen.

"There is a price to pay," she said. "There is always a price. Some one of you must become Death in my place, for there must forever be Death in the world. Will anyone choose? Will anyone here become Death of his own free will? For only thus can I become a human girl."

No one spoke, no one spoke at all. But they backed slowly away from her, like waves slipping back down a beach to the sea when you try to catch them. The Contessa della Candini and her friends would have crept quietly out of the door, but Death smiled at them and they stood where they were. Captain Compson opened his mouth as though he were going to declare himself, but he said nothing. Lady Neville did not move.

"No one," said Death. She touched a flower with her finger, and it seemed to crouch and flex itself like a pleased cat. "No one at all," she said. "Then I must choose, and that is just, for that is the way that I became Death. I never wanted to be Death, and it makes me so happy that you want me to become one of yourselves. I have searched a long time for people who would want me. Now I have only to choose someone to replace me and it is done. I will choose very carefully."

"Oh, we were so foolish," Lady Neville said to herself. "We were so foolish." But she said nothing aloud; she merely clasped her hands and stared at the young girl, thinking vaguely that if she had had a daughter she would have been greatly pleased if she resembled the lady Death.

"The Contessa della Candini," said Death thoughtfully, and that woman gave a little squeak of terror because she could not draw her breath for a scream. But Death laughed and said, "No, that would be silly." She said nothing more, but for a long time after that the Contessa burned with humiliation at not having been chosen to be Death.

"Not Captain Compson," murmured Death, "because he is too kind to become Death, and because it would be too cruel to him. He wants to die so badly." The expression on the Captain's face did not change, but his hands began to tremble.

"Not Lorimond," the girl continued, "because he knows so little about life, and because I like him." The poet flushed, and turned white, and then turned pink again. He made as if to kneel clumsily on one knee, but instead he pulled himself erect and stood as much like Captain Compson as he could.

"Not the Torrances," said Death, "never Lord and Lady Torrance, for both of them care too much about another person to take any pride in being Death." But she hesitated over Lady Torrance for a while, staring at her out of her dark and curious eyes. "I was your age when I became Death," she said at last. "I wonder what it will be like to be your age again. I have been Death for so long." Lady Torrance shivered and did not speak.

And at last Death said quietly, "Lady Neville."

"I am here," Lady Neville answered.

"I think you are the only one," said Death. "I choose you, Lady Neville."

Again Lady Neville heard every guest sigh softly, and although her back was to them all she knew that they were sighing in relief that neither themselves nor anyone dear to themselves had been chosen. Lady Torrance gave a little cry of protest, but Lady Neville knew that she would have cried out at whatever choice Death made. She heard herself say calmly, "I am honored. But was there no one more worthy than I?"

"Not one," said Death. "There is no one quite so weary of being human, no one who knows better how meaningless it is to be alive. And there is no one else here with the power to treat life"—and she smiled sweetly and cruelly—"the life of your hairdresser's child, for instance, as the meaningless thing it is. Death has a heart, but it is forever an empty heart, and I think, Lady Neville, that your heart is like a dry riverbed, like a seashell. You will be very content as Death, more so than I, for I was very young when I became Death."

She came toward Lady Neville, light and swaying, her deep eyes wide and full of the light of the red morning sun that was beginning to rise. The guests at the ball moved back from her, although she did not look at them, but Lady Neville clenched her hands tightly and watched Death come toward her with her little dancing steps. "We must kiss each other," Death said. "That is the way I became Death." She shook her head delightedly, so that her soft hair swirled about her shoulders. "Quickly, quickly," she said. "Oh, I cannot wait to be human again."

"You may not like it," Lady Neville said. She felt very calm, though she could hear her old heart pounding in her chest and feel it in the tips of her fingers. "You may not like it after a while," she said.

"Perhaps not." Death's smile was very close to her now. "I will not be as beautiful as I am, and perhaps people will not love me as much as they do now. But I will be human for a while, and at last I will die. I have done my penance."

"What penance?" the old woman asked the beautiful girl. "What was it you did? Why did you become Death?"

"I don't remember," said the lady Death. "And you too will forget in time." She was smaller than Lady Neville, and so much younger. In her white dress she might have been the daughter that Lady Neville had never had, who would have been with her always and held her mother's head lightly in the crook of her arm when she felt old and sad. Now she lifted her head to kiss Lady Neville's cheek, and as she did so she whispered in her ear, "You will still be beautiful when I am ugly. Be kind to me then."

Behind Lady Neville the handsome gentlemen and ladies murmured and sighed, fluttering like moths in their evening dress, in their elegant gowns. "I promise," she said, and then she pursed her dry lips to kiss the soft, sweet-smelling cheek of the young lady Death.

The Drowned Giant

J. G. Ballard

J. G. Ballard is recognized as one of the best authors to come out of the "New Wave" literary movement of the 1960s. His novels and stories constantly bombard both the protagonists and the reader with visceral images of a future everyday life that is often one step away from total breakdown. Stories like "The Terminal Beach" and "The Day of Forever" strand his protagonists in nightmare worlds where nothing can be relied on, not even themselves. Two other reoccurring themes in his work are the power of human sexuality and the changes the nuclear age has brought. Recently his autoerotic novel Crash *was made into a movie.*

ON THE MORNING AFTER THE STORM THE BODY OF A DROWNED GIANT WAS washed ashore on the beach five miles to the northwest of the city. The first news was brought by a nearby farmer and subsequently confirmed by the local newspaper reporters and the police. Despite this the majority of people, myself among them, remained sceptical, but the return of more and more eyewitnesses attesting to the vast size of the giant was finally too much for our curiosity. The library where my colleagues and I were carrying out our research was almost deserted when we set off for the coast shortly after two o'clock, and throughout the day people continued to leave their offices and shops as accounts of the giant circulated around the city.

By the time we reached the dunes above the beach a substantial crowd had gathered, and we could see the body lying in the shallow water two hundred yards away. At first the estimates of its size seemed greatly exaggerated. It was then at low tide, and almost all the giant's body was exposed, but he appeared to be a little larger than a basking shark. He lay on his back with his arms at his sides, in an attitude of repose, as if asleep on the mirror of wet sand, the reflection of his blanched skin fading as the water receded. In the clear sunlight his body glistened like the white plumage of a sea bird.

Puzzled by this spectacle, and dissatisfied with the matter-of-fact explanations of the crowd, my friends and I stepped down from the dunes on to the shingle. Everyone seemed reluctant to approach the giant, but half an hour later two fishermen in wading boots walked out across the sand. As their diminutive figures neared the recumbent body a sudden hubbub of conversation broke out among the spectators. The two men were completely dwarfed by the giant. Although his heels were partly submerged in the sand, the feet rose to at least twice the fishermen's height, and we immediately realized that this drowned leviathan had the mass and dimensions of the largest sperm whale.

Three fishing smacks had arrived on the scene and with keels raised remained a quarter of a mile offshore, the crews watching from the bows. Their discretion deterred the spectators on the shore from wading out across the sand. Impatiently everyone stepped down from the dunes and waited on the shingle slopes, eager for a closer view. Around the margins of the figure the sand had been washed away, forming a hollow, as if the giant had fallen out of the sky. The two fishermen were standing between the immense plinths of the feet, waving to us like tourists among the columns of some water-lapped temple on the Nile. For a moment I feared that the giant was merely asleep and might suddenly stir and clap his heels together, but his glazed eyes stared skyward, unaware of the minuscule replicas of himself between his feet.

The fishermen then began a circuit of the corpse, strolling past the long white flanks of the legs. After a pause to examine the fingers of the supine hand, they disappeared from sight between the arm and chest, then reemerged to survey the head, shielding their eyes as they gazed up at its Grecian profile. The shallow forehead, straight high-bridged nose and curling lips reminded me of a Roman copy of Praxiteles, and the elegantly formed cartouches of the nostrils emphasized the resemblance to monumental sculpture.

Abruptly there was a shout from the crowd, and a hundred arms pointed toward the sea. With a start I saw that one of the fishermen had climbed on to the giant's chest and was now strolling about and signaling to the shore. There was a roar of surprise and triumph from the crowd, lost in a rushing avalanche of shingle as everyone surged forward across the sand.

As we approached the recumbent figure, which was lying in a pool of water the size of a field, our excited chatter fell away again, subdued by the huge physical dimensions of this moribund colossus. He was stretched out at a slight angle to the shore, his legs carried nearer the beach, and this foreshortening had disguised his true length. Despite the two fishermen standing on his abdomen, the crowd formed itself into a wide circle, groups of three or four people tentatively advancing toward the hands and feet.

My companions and I walked around the seaward side of the giant, whose hips and thorax towered above us like the hull of a stranded ship. His pearl-colored skin, distended by immersion in salt water, masked the contours of the enormous muscles and tendons. We passed below the left knee, which was flexed slightly, threads of damp seaweed clinging to its sides. Draped loosely across the midriff, and preserving a tenuous propriety, was a shawl of heavy open-weaved material, bleached to a pale yellow by the water. A strong odor of brine came from the garment as it steamed in the sun, mingled with the sweet but potent scent of the giant's skin.

We stopped by his shoulder and gazed up at the motionless profile. The lips were parted slightly, the open eye cloudy and occluded, as if injected with some blue milky liquid, but the delicate arches of the nostrils and eyebrows invested the face with an ornate charm that belied the brutish power of the chest and shoulders.

The ear was suspended in mid-air over our heads like a sculptured doorway. As I raised my hand to touch the pendulous lobe someone appeared over the edge of the forehead and shouted down at me. Startled by this apparition, I stepped back, and then saw that a group of youths had climbed up on to the face and were jostling each other in and out of the orbits.

People were now clambering all over the giant, whose reclining arms provided a double stairway. From the palms they walked along the forearms to the elbow and then crawled over the distended belly of the biceps to the flat promenade of the pectoral muscles which covered the upper half of the smooth hairless chest. From here they climbed up on to the face, hand over hand along the lips and nose, or forayed down the abdomen to meet others who had straddled the ankles and were patrolling the twin columns of the thighs.

We continued our circuit through the crowd, and stopped to examine the outstretched right hand. A small pool of water lay in the palm, like the residue of another world, now being kicked away by the people ascending the arm. I tried to read the palm-lines that grooved the skin, searching for some clue to the giant's character, but the distension of the tissues had almost obliterated them, carrying away all trace of the giant's identity and his last tragic predicament. The huge muscles and wrist bones of the hand seemed to deny any sensitivity to their owner, but the delicate flexion of the fingers and the well-tended nails, each cut symmetrically to within six inches of the quick, argued a certain refinement of temperament, illustrated in the Grecian features of the face, on which the townsfolk were now sitting like flies.

One youth was even standing, arms wavering at his sides, on the very tip of the nose, shouting down at his companions, but the face of the giant retained its massive composure.

Returning to the shore, we sat down on the shingle, and watched the continuous stream of people arriving from the city. Some six or seven fishing boats had collected offshore, and their crews waded in through the shallow water for a closer look at this enormous storm-catch. Later a party of police appeared and made a half-hearted attempt to cordon off the beach, but after walking up to the recumbent figure any such thoughts left their minds, and they went off together with bemused backward glances.

An hour later there were a thousand people on the beach, at least two hundred of them were standing or sitting on the giant, crowded along his arms and legs or circulating in a ceaseless mele across his chest and stomach. A large gang of youths occupied the head, toppling each other off the cheeks and sliding down the smooth planes of the jaw. Two or three straddled the nose, and another crawled into one of the nostrils, from which he emitted barking noises like a dog.

That afternoon the police returned, and cleared a way through the crowd for a party of scientific experts—authorities on gross anatomy and marine biology—from the university. The gang of youths and most of the people on the giant climbed down, leaving behind a few hardy spirits perched on the tips of the toes and on the forehead. The experts strode around the giant, heads nodding in vigorous consultation, preceded by the policemen who pushed back the press of spectators. When they reached the outstretched hand the senior officer offered to assist them up on the palm, but the experts hastily demurred.

After they returned to the shore, the crowd once more climbed on to the giant, and was in full possession when we left at five o'clock, covering the arms and legs like a dense flock of gulls sitting on the corpse of a large fish.

I next visited the beach three days later. My friends at the library had returned to their work, and delegated to me the task of keeping the giant under observation and preparing a report. Perhaps they sensed my particular interest in the case, and it was certainly true that I was eager to return to the beach. There was nothing necrophilic about this, for to all intents the giant was still alive for me, indeed more alive than many of the people watching him. What I found so fascinating was partly his immense scale, the huge volumes of space occupied the his arms and legs, which seemed to confirm the identity of my own miniature limbs, but above all the mere categorical fact of his existence. Whatever else in our lives might be open to doubt, the giant, dead or alive, existed in an absolute sense, providing a glimpse into a world of similar absolutes of which we spectators on the beach were such imperfect and puny copies.

When I arrived at the beach the crowd was considerably smaller, and some two or three hundred people sat on the shingle, picnicking and watching the groups of visitors who walked out across the sand. The successive tides had carried the giant nearer the shore, swinging his head and shoulders toward the beach, so that he seemed doubly to gain in size, his huge body dwarfing the fishing boats beached beside his feet. The uneven contours of the beach had pushed his spine into a slight arch, expanding his chest and tilting back the head, forcing him into a more expressly heroic posture. The combined effects of seawater and the tumefaction of the tissues had given the face a sleeker and less youthful look. Although the vast proportions of the features made it impossible to assess the age and character of the giant, on my previous visit his classically modeled mouth and nose suggested that he had been a young man of discreet and modest temper. Now, however, he appeared to be at least in early middle age. The puffy cheeks, thicker nose and temples and narrowing eyes gave him a look of well-fed maturity that even now hinted at a growing corruption to come.

This accelerated post-mortem development of the giant's character, as if the latent elements of his personality had gained sufficient momentum during his life to discharge themselves in a brief final résumé, continued to fascinate me. It marked the beginning of the giant's surrender to that all-demanding system of time in which the rest of humanity finds itself, and of which, like the million twisted ripples of a fragmented whirlpool, our finite lives are the concluding products. I took up my position on the shingle directly opposite the giant's head, from where I could see the new arrivals and the children clambering over the legs and arms.

Among the morning's visitors were a number of men in leather jackets and cloth caps, who peered up critically at the giant with a professional eye, pacing out his dimensions and making rough calculations in the sand with spars of driftwood. I assumed them to be from the public works department and other municipal bodies, no doubt wondering how to dispose of this gargantuan piece of jetsam.

Several rather more smartly attired individuals, circus proprietors and the like, also appeared on the scene, and strolled slowly around the giant, hands in the pockets of their long overcoats, saying nothing to one another. Evidently its bulk was too great even for their matchless enterprise. After they had gone the children continued to run up and down the arms and legs, and the youths wrestled with each other over the supine face, the damp sand from their feet covering the white skin.

The following day I deliberately postponed my visit until the late afternoon, and when I arrived there were fewer than fifty or sixty people sitting on the shingle. The giant had been carried still closer to the shore, and was now little more than seventy-five yards away, his feet crushing the palisade of a rotting breakwater. The slope of the firmer sand tilted his body toward the sea, and the bruised face was averted in an almost conscious gesture. I sat down on a large metal winch which had been shackled to a concrete caisson above the shingle, and looked down at the recumbent figure.

His blanched skin had now lost its pearly translucence and was spattered with dirty sand which replaced that washed away by the night tide. Clumps of seaweed filled the intervals between the fingers and a collection of litter and cuttlebones lay in the crevices below the hips and knees. But despite this, and the continuous thickening of his features, the giant still retained his magnificent Homeric stature. The enormous breadth of the shoulders, and the huge columns of the arms and legs, still carried the figure into another dimension, and the giant seemed a more authentic image of one of the drowned Argonauts or heroes of the Odyssey than the conventional human-sized portrait previously in my mind.

I stepped down on to the sand, and walked between the pools of water toward the giant. Two small boys were sitting in the well of the ear, and at the far end a solitary youth stood perched high on one of the toes, surveying me as I approached. As I had hoped when delaying my visit, no one else paid any attention to me, and the people on the shore remained huddled beneath their coats.

The giant's supine right hand was covered with broken shells and sand, in which a score of footprints were visible. The rounded bulk of the hip towered above me, cutting off all sight of the sea. The sweetly acrid odor I had noticed before was now more pungent, and through the opaque skin I could see the serpentine coils of congealed blood vessels. However repellent it seemed, this ceaseless metamorphosis, a visible life in death, alone permitted me to set foot on the corpse.

Using the jutting thumb as a stair rail, I climbed up on to the palm and began my ascent. The skin was harder than I expected, barely yielding to my weight. Quickly I walked up the sloping forearm and the bulging balloon of the biceps. The face of the drowned giant loomed to my right, the cavernous nostrils and huge flanks of the cheeks like the cone of some freakish volcano.

Safely rounding the shoulder, I stepped out on to the broad promenade of the chest, across which the bony ridges of the rib cage lay like huge rafters. The white skin was dappled by the darkening bruises of countless footprints, in which the patterns of individual heel marks were clearly visible. Someone had built a small sandcastle on the center of the sternum, and I climbed on to this partly demolished structure to give myself a better view of the face.

The two children had now scaled the ear and were pulling themselves into the right orbit, whose blue globe, completely occluded by some milk-colored fluid, gazed sightlessly past their miniature forms. Seen obliquely from below, the face was devoid of all grace and repose, the drawn mouth and raised chin propped up by its gigantic slings of muscles resembling the torn prow of a colossal wreck. For the first time I became aware of the extremity of this last physical agony of the giant, no less painful for his unawareness of the collapsing musculature and tissues. The absolute isolation of the ruined figure, cast like an abandoned ship upon the empty shore, almost out of sound of the waves, transformed his face into a mask of exhaustion and helplessness.

As I stepped forward, my foot sank into a trough of soft tissue, and a gust of fetid gas blew through an aperture between the ribs. Retreating from the fouled air, which hung like a cloud over my head, I turned toward the sea to clear my lungs. To my surprise I saw that the giant's left hand had been amputated.

I stared with bewilderment at the blackening stump, while the solitary youth reclining on his aerial perch a hundred feet away surveyed me with a sanguinary eye.

This was only the first of a sequence of depredations. I spent the following two days in the library, for some reason reluctant to visit the shore, aware that I had probably witnessed the approaching end of a magnificent illusion. When I next crossed the dunes and set foot on the shingle the giant was little more than twenty yards away, and with this close proximity to the rough pebbles all traces had vanished of the magic which once surrounded his distant wave-washed form. Despite his immense size, the bruises and dirt that covered his body made him appear merely human in scale, his vast dimensions only increasing his vulnerability.

His right hand and foot had been removed, dragged up the slope and trundled away by cart. After questioning the small group of people huddled by the breakwater, I gathered that a fertilizer company and a cattle food manufacturer were responsible.

The giant's remaining foot rose into the air, a steel hawser fixed to the large toe, evidently in preparation for the following day. The surrounding beach had been disturbed by a score of workmen, and deep ruts marked the ground where the hands and foot had been hauled away. A dark brackish fluid leaked from the stumps, and stained the sand and the white cones of the cuttlefish. As I walked down the shingle I noticed that a number of jocular slogans, swastikas and other signs had been cut into the gray skin, as if the mutilation of this motionless colossus had released a sudden flood of repressed spite. The lobe of one of the ears was pierced by a spear of timber, and a small fire had burned out in the center of the chest, blackening the surrounding skin. The fine wood ash was still being scattered by the wind.

A foul smell enveloped the cadaver, the undisguisable signature of putrefaction, which had at last driven away the usual gathering of youths. I returned to the shingle and climbed up on to the winch. The giant's swollen cheeks had now almost closed his eyes, drawing the lips back in a monumental gape. The once straight Grecian nose had been twisted and flattened, stamped into the ballooning face by countless heels.

When I visited the beach the following day I found, almost with relief, that the head had been removed.

Some weeks elapsed before I made my next journey to the beach, and by then the human likeness I had noticed earlier had vanished again. On close inspection the recumbent thorax and abdomen were unmistakably manlike, but as each of the limbs was chopped off, first at the knee and elbow, and then at shoulder and thigh, the carcass resembled that of any headless sea animal—whale or whaleshark. With this loss of identity, and the few traces of personality that had clung tenuously to the figure, the interest of the spectators expired, and the foreshore was deserted except for an elderly beachcomber and the watchman sitting in the doorway of the contractor's hut.

A loose wooden scaffolding had been erected around the carcass, from which a dozen ladders swung in the wind, and the surrounding sand was littered with coils of rope, long metal-handled knives and grappling irons, the pebbles oily with blood and pieces of bone and skin.

I nodded to the watchman, who regarded me dourly over his brazier of burning coke. The whole area was pervaded by the pungent smell of huge squares of blubber being simmered in a vat behind the hut.

Both the thigh bones had been removed, with the assistance of a small crane draped in the gauzelike fabric which had once covered the waist of the giant, and the open sockets gaped like barn doors.

The upper arms, collar bones and pudenda had likewise been dispatched. What remained of the skin over the thorax and abdomen had been marked out in parallel strips with a tar brush, and the first five or six sections had been pared away from the midriff, revealing the great arch of the rib cage.

As I left a flock of gulls wheeled down from the sky and alighted on the beach, picking at the stained sand with ferocious cries.

Several months later, when the news of his arrival had been generally forgotten, various pieces of the body of the dismembered giant began to reappear all over the city. Most of these were bones, which the fertilizer manufacturers had found too difficult to crush, and their massive size, and the huge tendons and discs of cartilage attached to their joints, immediately identified them. For some reason, these disembodied fragments seemed better to convey the essence of the giant's original magnificence than the bloated appendages that had been subsequently amputated. As I looked across the road at the premises of the largest wholesale merchants in the meat market, I recognized the two enormous thighbones on either side of the doorway. They towered over the porters' heads like the threatening megaliths of some primitive druidical religion, and I had a sudden vision of the giant climbing to his knees upon these bare bones and striding away through the streets of the city, picking up the scattered fragments of himself on his return journey to the sea.

A few days later I saw the left humerus lying in the entrance to one of the shipyards (its twin for several years lay on the mud among the piles below the harbor's principal commercial wharf). In the same week the mummified right hand was exhibited on a carnival float during the annual pageant of the guilds.

The lower jaw, typically, found its way to the museum of natural history. The remainder of the skull has disappeared, but is probably still lurking in the waste grounds or private gardens of the city—quite recently, while sailing down the river, I noticed two ribs of the giant forming a decorative arch in a waterside garden, possibly confused with the jawbones of a whale. A large square of tanned and tattooed skin, the size of an Indian blanket, forms a backcloth to the dolls and masks in a novelty shop near the amusement park, and I have no doubt that elsewhere in the city, in the hotels or golf clubs, the mummified nose or ears of the giant hang from the wall above a fireplace. As for the immense pizzle, this ends its days in the freak museum of a circus which travels up and down the northwest. This monumental apparatus, stunning in its proportions and sometime potency, occupies a complete booth to itself. The irony is that it is wrongly identified as that of a whale, and indeed most people, even those who first saw him cast up on the shore after the storm, now remember the giant, if at all, as a large sea beast.

The remainder of the skeleton, stripped of all flesh, still rests on the sea shore, the clutter of bleached ribs like the timbers of a derelict ship. The contractor's hut, the crane and the scaffolding have been removed, and the sand being driven into the bay along the coast has buried the pelvis and backbone. In the winter the high curved bones are deserted, battered by the breaking waves, but in the summer they provide an excellent perch for the sea-wearying gulls.

Narrow Valley

R. A. Lafferty

Humor and hope for the future are two hallmarks of the stories of R. A. Lafferty. Outrageous yet believable characters, transformation, and elements of the eternal war between Heaven and Hell also appear in his work. He has been writing fiction unlike anyone else for more than twenty-five years, and he has been rewarded with a Hugo award and a World Fantasy Lifetime Achievement award in 1990. He lives in Tulsa, Oklahoma.

IN THE YEAR 1893, LAND ALLOTMENTS IN SEVERALTY WERE MADE TO THE remaining eight hundred and twenty-one Pawnee Indians. Each would receive one hundred and sixty acres of land and no more, and thereafter the Pawnees would be expected to pay taxes on their land, the same as the White-Eyes did.

"Kitkehahke!" Clarence Big-Saddle cussed. "You can't kick a dog around proper on a hundred and sixty acres. And I sure am not hear before about this pay taxes on land."

Clarence Big-Saddle selected a nice green valley for his allotment. It was one of the half dozen plots he had always regarded as his own. He sodded around the summer lodge that he had there and made it an all-season home. But he sure didn't intend to pay taxes on it.

So he burned leaves and bark and made a speech:

"That my valley be always wide and flourish and green and such stuff as that!" he orated in Pawnee chant style. "But that it be narrow if an intruder come."

He didn't have any balsam bark to burn. He threw on a little cedar bark instead. He didn't have any elder leaves. He used a handful of jack-oak leaves. And he forgot the word. How you going to work it if you forget the word?

"Petahauerat!" he howled out with the confidence he hoped would fool the fates.

"That's the same long of a word," he said in a low aside to himself. But he was doubtful. "What am I, a White Man, a burr-tailed jack, a new kind of nut to think it will work?" he asked. "I have to laugh at me. Ah well, we see."

He threw the rest of the bark and the leaves on the fire, and he hollered the wrong word out again.

And he was answered by a dazzling sheet of summer lightning.

"Skidi!" Clarence Big-Saddle swore. "It worked. I didn't think it would."

Clarence Big-Saddle lived on his land for many years, and he paid no taxes. Intruders were unable to come down to his place. The land was sold for taxes three times, but nobody ever came down to claim it. Finally, it was carried as open land on the books. Homesteaders filed on it several times, but none of them fulfilled the qualification of living on the land.

Half a century went by. Clarence Big-Saddle called his son.

"I've had it, boy," he said. "I think I'll just go in the house and die."

"Okay, Dad," the son Clarence Little-Saddle said. "I'm going in to town to shoot a few games of pool with the boys. I'll bury you when I get back this evening."

So the son Clarence Little-Saddle inherited. He also lived on the land for many years without paying taxes.

There was a disturbance in the courthouse one day. The place seemed to be invaded in force, but actually there were but one man, one woman, and five children. "I'm Robert Rampart," said the man, "and we want the Land Office."

"I'm Robert Rampart Junior," said a nine-year-old gangler, "and we want it pretty blamed quick."

"I don't think we have anything like that," the girl at the desk said. "Isn't that something they had a long time ago?"

"Ignorance is no excuse for inefficiency, my dear," said Mary Mabel Rampart, an eight-year-old who could easily pass for eight and a half. "After I make my report, I wonder who will be sitting at your desk tomorrow."

"You people are either in the wrong state or the wrong century," the girl said.

"The Homestead Act still obtains," Robert Rampart insisted. "There is one tract of land carried as open in this county. I want to file on it."

Cecilia Rampart answered the knowing wink of a beefy man at the distant desk. "Hi," she breathed as she slinked over. "I'm Cecilia Rampart but my stage name is Cecilia San Juan. Do you think that seven is too young to play ingenue roles?"

"Not for you," the man said. "Tell your folks to come over here."

"Do you know where the Land Office is?" Cecilia asked.

"Sure. It's the fourth left-hand drawer of my desk. The smallest office we got in the whole courthouse. We don't use it much any more."

The Ramparts gathered around. The beefy man started to make out the papers.

"This is the land description," Robert Rampart began. "Why, you've got it down already. How did you know?"

"I've been around here a long time," the man answered.

They did the paperwork, and Robert Rampart filed on the land.

"You won't be able to come onto the land itself, though," the man said.

"Why won't I?" Rampart demanded. "Isn't the land description accurate?"

"Oh, I suppose so. But nobody's ever been able to get to the land. It's become a sort of joke."

"Well, I intend to get to the bottom of that joke," Rampart insisted. "I will occupy the land, or I will find out why not."

"I'm not sure about that," the beefy man said. "The last man to file on the land, about a dozen years ago, wasn't able to occupy the land. And he wasn't able to say why he couldn't. It's kind of interesting, the look on their faces after they try it for a day or two, and then give it up."

The Ramparts left the courthouse, loaded into their camper, and drove out to find their land. They stopped at the house of a cattle and wheat farmer named Charley Dublin. Dublin met them with a grin which indicated he'd been tipped off.

"Come along if you want to, folks," Dublin said. "The easiest way is on foot across my short pasture here. Your land's directly west of mine."

They walked the short distance to the border.

"My name is Tom Rampart, Mr. Dublin." Six-year-old Tom made conversation as they walked. "But my name is really Ramires, and not Tom. I am the issue of an indiscretion of my mother in Mexico several years ago."

"The boy is a kidder, Mr. Dublin," said the mother, Nina Rampart, defending herself. "I have never been in Mexico, but sometimes I have the urge to disappear there forever."

"Ah yes, Mrs. Rampart. And what is the name of the youngest boy here?" Charley Dublin asked.

"Fatty," said Fatty Rampart.

"But surely that is not your given name?"

"Audifax," said five-year-old Fatty.

"Ah well, Audifax, Fatty, are you a kidder too?"

"He's getting better at it, Mr. Dublin," Mary Mabel said. "He was a twin till last week. His twin was named Skinny. Mama left Skinny unguarded while she was out tippling, and there were wild dogs in the neighborhood. When Mama got back, do you know what was left of Skinny? Two neck bones and an ankle bone. That was all."

"Poor Skinny," Dublin said. "Well, Rampart, this is the fence and the end of my land. Yours is just beyond."

"Is that ditch on my land?" Rampart asked.

"That ditch *is* your land."

"I'll have it filled in. It's a dangerous deep cut even if it is narrow. And the other fence looks like a good one, and I sure have a pretty plot of land beyond it."

"No, Rampart, the land beyond the second fence belongs to Holister Hyde," Charley Dublin said. "That second fence is the *end* of your land."

"Now, just wait a minute, Dublin! There's something wrong here. My land is one hundred and sixty acres, which would be a half mile on a side. Where's my half-mile width?"

"Between the two fences."

"That's not eight feet."

"Doesn't look like it, does it, Rampart? Tell you what—there's plenty of throwing-sized rocks around. Try to throw one across it."

"I'm not interested in any such boys' games," Rampart exploded. "I want my land."

But the Rampart children *were* interested in such games. They got with it with those throwing rocks. They winged them out over the little gully. The stones acted funny. They hung in the air, as it were, and diminished in size. And they were small as pebbles when they dropped down, down into the gully. None of them could throw a stone across that ditch, and they were throwing kids.

"You and your neighbor have conspired to fence open land for your own use," Rampart charged.

"No such thing, Rampart," Dublin said cheerfully. "My land checks perfectly. So does Hyde's. So does yours, if we knew how to check it. It's like one of those trick topological drawings. It really is half a mile from here to there, but the eye gets lost somewhere. It's your land. Crawl through the fence and figure it out."

Rampart crawled through the fence, and drew himself up to jump the gully. Then he hesitated. He got a glimpse of just how deep that gully was. Still, it wasn't five feet across.

There was a heavy fence post on the ground, designed for use as a corner post. Rampart up-ended it with some effort. Then he shoved it to fall and bridge the gully. But it fell short, and it shouldn't have. An eight-foot post should bridge a five-foot gully.

The post fell into the gully, and rolled and rolled and rolled. It spun as though it were rolling outward, but it made no progress except vertically. The post came to rest on a ledge of the gully, so close that Rampart could almost reach out and touch it, but it now appeared no bigger than a match stick.

"There is something wrong with that fence post, or with the world, or with my eyes," Robert Rampart said. "I wish I felt dizzy so I could blame it on that."

"There's a little game that I sometimes play with my neighbor Hyde when we're both out," Dublin said. "I've a heavy rifle and I train it on the middle of his forehead as he stands on the other side of the ditch apparently eight feet away. I fire it off then (I'm a good shot), and I hear it whine across. It'd kill him dead if things were as they seem. But Hyde's in no danger. The shot always bangs into that little scuff of rocks and boulders about thirty feet below him. I can see it kick up the rock dust there, and the sound of it rattling into those little boulders comes back to me in about two and a half seconds."

A bull-bat (poor people call it the night-hawk) raveled around in the air and zoomed out over the narrow ditch, but it did not reach the other side. The bird dropped below ground level and could be seen against the background of the other side of the ditch. It grew smaller and hazier as though at a distance of three or four hundred yards. The white bars on its wings could no longer be discerned; then the bird itself could hardly be discerned; but it was far short of the other side of the five-foot ditch.

A man identified by Charley Dublin as the neighbor Hollister Hyde had appeared on the other side of the little ditch. Hyde grinned and waved. He shouted something, but could not be heard.

"Hyde and I both read mouths," Dublin said, "so we can talk across the ditch easy enough. Which kid wants to play chicken? Hyde will barrel a good-sized rock right at your head, and if you duck or flinch you're chicken."

"Me! Me!" Audifax Rampart challenged. And Hyde, a big man with big hands, did barrel a fearsome jagged rock right at the head of the boy. It would have killed him if things had been as they appeared. But the rock diminished to nothing and disappeared into the ditch. Here was a phenomenon: things seemed real-sized on either side of the ditch, but they diminished coming out over the ditch either way.

"Everybody game for it?" Robert Rampart Junior asked.

"We won't get down there by standing here," Mary Mabel said.

"Nothing wenchered, nothing gained," said Cecilia. "I got that from an ad for a sex comedy."

Then the five Rampart kids ran down into the gully. Ran *down* is right. It was almost as if they ran down the vertical face of a cliff. They couldn't do that. The gully was no wider than the stride of the biggest kids. But the gully diminished those children, it ate them alive. They were doll-sized. They were acorn-sized. They were running for minute after minute across a ditch that was only five feet across. They were going deeper in it, and getting smaller. Robert Rampart was roaring his alarm, and his wife, Nina, was screaming. Then she stopped. "What am I carrying on so loud about?" she asked herself. "It looks like fun. I'll do it too."

She plunged into the gully, diminished in size as the children had done, and ran at a pace to carry her a hundred yards away across a gully only five feet wide.

That Robert Rampart stirred things up for a while then. He got the sheriff there, and the highway patrolmen. A ditch had stolen his wife and five children, he said, and maybe killed them. And if anybody laughs, there may be another killing. He got the colonel of the State National Guard there, and a command post set up. He got a couple of airplane pilots. Robert Rampart had one quality: when he hollered, people came.

He got the newsmen out from T-Town, and the eminent scientists, Dr. Velikof Vonk, Arpad Arkabaranan, and Willy McGilly. That bunch turns up every time you get on a good one. They just happen to be in that part of the country where something interesting is going on.

They attacked the thing from all four sides and the top, and by inner and outer theory. If a thing measures half a mile on each side, and the sides are straight, there just has to be something in the middle of it. They took pictures from the air, and they turned out perfect. They proved that Robert Rampart had the prettiest hundred and sixty acres in the country, the larger part of it being a lush green valley, and all of it being half a mile on a side, and situated just where it should be. They took ground-level photos then, and it showed a beautiful half-mile stretch of land between the boundaries of Charley Dublin and Hollister Hyde. But a man isn't a camera. None of them could see that beautiful spread with the eyes in their heads. Where was it?

Down in the valley itself everything was normal. It really was half a mile wide and no more than eighty feet deep with a very gentle slope. It was warm and sweet, and beautiful with grass and grain.

Nina and the kids loved it, and they rushed to see what squatter had built that little house on their land. A house, or a shack. It had never known paint, but paint would have spoiled it. It was built of split timbers dressed near smooth with ax and draw knife, chinked with white clay, and sodded up to about half its height. And there was an interloper standing by the little lodge.

"Here, here what are you doing on our land?" Robert Rampart

Junior demanded of the man. "Now you just shamble off again wherever you came from. I'll bet you're a thief too, and those cattle are stolen."

"Only the black-and white calf," Clarence Little-Saddle said. "I couldn't resist him, but the rest are mine. I guess I'll just stay around and see that you folks get settled all right."

"Is there any wild Indians around here?" Fatty Rampart asked.

"No, not really. I go on a bender about every three months and get a little bit wild, and there's a couple Osage boys from Gray Horse that get noisy sometimes, but that's about all," Clarence Little-Saddle said.

"You certainly don't intend to palm yourself off on us as an Indian," Mary Mabel challenged. "You'll find us a little too knowledgeable for that."

"Little girl, you might as well tell this cow there's no room for her to be a cow since you're so knowledgeable. She thinks she's a short-horn cow named Sweet Virginia. I think I'm a Pawnee Indian named Clarence. Break it to us real gentle if we're not."

"If you're an Indian where's your war bonnet? There's not a feather on you anywhere."

"How you be sure? There's a story that we got feathers instead of hair on—Aw, I can't tell a joke like that to a little girl! How come you're not wearing the Iron Crown of Lombardy if you're a white girl? How you expect me to believe you're a little white girl and your folks came from Europe a couple hundred years ago if you don't wear it? There are six hundred tribes, and only one of them, the Oglala Sioux, had the war bonnet, and only the big leaders, never more than two or three alive at one time, wore it."

"Your analogy is a little strained," Mary Mabel said. "Those Indians we saw in Florida and the ones at Atlantic City had war bonnets, and they couldn't very well have been the kind of Sioux you said. And just last night on the TV in the motel, those Massachusetts Indians put a war bonnet on the President and called him the Great White Father. You mean to tell me that they were all phonies? Hey, who's laughing at who here?"

"If you're an Indian where's your bow and arrow?" Tom Rampart interrupted. "I bet you can't even shoot one."

"You're sure right there," Clarence admitted. "I never shot one of those things but once in my life. They used to have an archery range in Boulder Park over in T-Town, and you could rent the things and shoot at targets tied to hay bales. Hey, I barked my whole forearm and nearly broke my thumb when the bow-string thwacked home. I couldn't shoot that thing at all. I don't see how anybody ever could shoot one of them."

"Okay, kids," Nina Rampart called to her brood. "Let's start pitching this junk out of the shack so we can move in. Is there any way we can drive our camper down here, Clarence?"

"Sure, there's a pretty good dirt road, and it's a lot wider than it looks from the top. I got a bunch of green bills in an old night charley in the shack. Let me get them, and I'll clear out for a while. The shack hasn't been cleaned out for seven years, since the last time this happened. I'll show you the road to the top, and you can bring your car down it."

"Hey, you old Indian, you lied!" Cecilia Rampart shrilled from the doorway of the shack. "You *do* have a war bonnet. Can I have it?"

"I didn't mean to lie, I forgot about that thing," Clarence Little-Saddle said. "My son, Clarence Bareback, sent that to me from Japan for a joke a long time ago. Sure, you can have it."

All the children were assigned tasks carrying the junk out of the shack and setting fire to it. Nina Rampart and Clarence Little-Saddle ambled up to the rim of the valley by the vehicle road that was wider than it looked from the top.

"Nina, you're back! I thought you were gone forever," Robert Rampart jittered at seeing her again. "What—where are the children?"

"Why, I left them down in the valley, Robert. That is, ah, down in that little ditch right there. Now you've got me worried again. I'm going to drive the camper down there and unload it. You'd better go on down and lend a hand too, Robert, and quit talking to all these funny-looking men here."

And Nina went back to Dublin's place for the camper.

"It would be easier for a camel to go through the eye of a needle than for that intrepid woman to drive a car down into that narrow ditch," the eminent scientist Dr. Velikof Vonk said.

"You know how that camel does it?" Clarence Little-Saddle offered, appearing all of a sudden from nowhere. "He just closes one of his own eyes and flops back his ears and plunges right through. A camel is mighty narrow when he closes one eye and flops back his ears. Besides, they use a big-eyed needle in the act."

"Where'd this crazy man come from?" Robert Rampart demanded, jumping three feet in the air. "Things are coming out of the ground now. I want my land! I want my children! I want my wife! Whoops, here she comes driving it. Nina, you can't drive a loaded camper into a ditch like that! You'll be killed or collapsed!"

Nina Rampart drove the loaded camper into the little ditch at a pretty good rate of speed. The best of belief is that she just closed one eye and plunged right through. The car diminished and dropped, and it was smaller than a toy car. But it raised a pretty good cloud of dust as it bumped for several hundred yards across a ditch that was only five feet wide.

"Rampart, it's akin to the phenomenon known as looming, only in reverse," the eminent scientist Arpad Arkabaranan explained as he attempted to throw a rock across the narrow ditch. The rock rose very high in the air, seemed to hang at its apex while it diminished to the size of a grain of sand, and then fell into the ditch not six inches of the way across. There isn't anybody going to throw across a half-mile valley even if it looks five feet. "Look at a rising moon sometimes, Rampart. It appears very large, as though covering a great sector of the horizon, but it only covers one-half of a degree. It is hard to believe that you could set seven hundred and twenty of such large moons side by side around the horizon, or that it would take one hundred and eighty of the big things to reach from the horizon to a point overhead. It is also hard to believe that your valley is five hundred times as wide as it appears, but it has been surveyed, and it is."

"I want my land. I want my children. I want my wife," Robert chanted dully. "Damn, I let her get away again."

"I'll tell you, Rampy," Clarence Little-Saddle squared on him, "a man that lets his wife get away twice doesn't deserve to keep her. I give you till nightfall; then you forfeit. I've taken a liking to the brood. One of us is going to be down there tonight."

After a while a bunch of them were off in that little tavern on the road between Cleveland and Osage. It was only a half a mile away. If the valley had run in the other direction, it would have been only six feet away.

"It is a psychic nexus in the form of an elongated dome," said the eminent scientist Velikof Vonk. "It is maintained subconsciously by the concatenation of at least two minds, the stronger of them belonging to a man dead for many years. It has apparently existed for a little less than a hundred years, and in another hundred years it will be considerably weakened. We know from our checking out folk tales of Europe as well as Cambodia that these ensorceled areas seldom survive for more than two hundred and fifty years. The person who first set such a thing in being will usually lose interest in it, and in all worldly things, within a hundred years of his own death. This is a simple thanato-psychic limitation. As a short-term device, the thing has been used several times as a military tactic.

"This psychic nexus, as long as it maintains itself, causes group illusion, but it is really a simple thing. It doesn't fool birds or rabbits or cattle or cameras, only humans. There is nothing meteorological about it. It is strictly psychological. I'm glad I was able to give a scientific explanation to it or it would have worried me."

"It is continental fault coinciding with a noospheric fault," said the eminent scientist Arpad Arkabaranan. "The valley really is half a mile wide, and at the same time it really is only five feet wide. If we measured correctly, we would get these dual measurements. Of course it is meteorological! Everything including dreams is meteorological. It is the animals and cameras which are fooled, as lacking a true dimension; it is only humans who see the true duality. The phenomenon should be common along the whole continental fault where the earth gains or loses half a mile that has to go somewhere. Likely it extends through the whole sweep of the Cross Timbers. Many of those trees appear twice, and many do not appear at all. A man in the proper state of mind could farm that land or raise cattle on it, but it doesn't really exist. There is a clear parallel in the Luftspiegelungthal sector in the Black Forest of Germany which exists, or does not exist, according to the circumstances and to the attitude of the beholder. Then we have the case of Mad Mountain in Morgan County, Tennessee, which isn't there all the time, and also the Little Lobo Mirage south of Presidio, Texas, from which twenty thousand barrels of water were pumped in one two-and-a-half-year period before the mirage reverted to a mirage status. I'm glad I was able to give a scientific explanation to this or it would have worried me."

"I just don't understand how he worked it," said the eminent scientist Willy McGilly. "Cedar bark, jack-oak leaves, and the word 'Petahauerat.' The thing's impossible! When I was a boy and we wanted to make a hideout, we used bark from the skunk-spruce tree, the leaves of a box-elder, and the word was 'Boadicea.' All three elements are wrong here. I cannot find a scientific explanation for it, and it does worry me."

They went back to Narrow Valley. Robert Rampart was still chanting dully: "I want my land. I want my children. I want my wife."

Nina Rampart came chugging up out of the narrow ditch in the camper and emerged through that little gate a few yards down the fence row.

"Supper's ready and we're tired of waiting for you, Robert," she said. "A fine homesteader you are! Afraid to come onto your own land! Come along now; I'm tired of waiting for you."

"I want my land! I want my children! I want my wife!" Robert Rampart still chanted. "Oh, there you are, Nina. You stay here this time. I want my land! I want my children! I want an answer to this terrible thing!"

"It is time we decided who wears the pants in this family," Nina said stoutly. She picked up her husband, slung him over her shoulder, carried him to the camper and dumped him in, slammed (as it seemed) a dozen doors at once, and drove furiously into the Narrow Valley, which already seemed wider.

Why, the place was getting normaler and normaler by the minute! Pretty soon it looked almost as wide as it was supposed to be. The psychic nexus in the form of an elongated dome had collapsed. The continental fault that coincided with the noospheric fault had faced facts and decided to conform. The Ramparts were in effective possession of their homestead, and Narrow Valley was as normal as any place anywhere.

"I have lost my land," Clarence Little-Saddle moaned. "It was the land of my father, Clarence Big-Saddle, and I meant it to be the land of my son, Clarence Bareback. It looked so narrow that people did not notice how wide it was, and people did not try to enter it. Now I have lost it."

Clarence Little-Saddle and the eminent scientist Willy McGilly were standing on the edge of Narrow Valley, which now appeared its true half-mile extent. The moon was just rising, so big that it filled a third of the sky. Who would have imagined that it would take a hundred and eight of such monstrous things to reach from the horizon to a point overhead, and yet you could sight it with sighters and figure it so.

"I had a little bear-cat by the tail and I let go," Clarence groaned. "I had a fine valley for free, and I have lost it. I am like that hard-luck guy in the funny-paper or Job in the Bible. Destitution is my lot."

Willy McGilly looked around furtively. They were alone on the edge of the half-mile-wide valley.

"Let's give it a booster shot," Willy McGilly said.

Hey, those two got with it! They started a snapping fire and began to throw the stuff onto it. Bark from the dog-elm tree—how do you know it won't work?

It *was* working! Already the other side of the valley seemed a hundred yards closer, and there were alarmed noises coming up from the people in the valley.

Leaves from a black locust tree—and the valley narrowed still more! There was, moreover, terrified screaming of both children and big people from the depths of Narrow Valley, and the happy voice of Mary Mabel Rampart chanting "Earthquake! Earthquake!"

"That my valley be always wide and flourish and such stuff, and green with money and grass!" Clarence Little-Saddle orated in Pawnee chant style, "but that it be narrow if intruders come, smash them like bugs!"

People, that valley wasn't over a hundred feet wide, now, and the screaming of the people in the bottom of the valley had been joined by the hysterical coughing of the camper car starting up.

Willy and Clarence threw everything that was left on the fire. But the word? The word? Who remembers the word?

"Corsicanatexas!" Clarence Little-Saddle howled out with confidence he hoped would fool the fates.

He was answered not only by a dazzling sheet of summer lightning, but also by thunder and raindrops.

"Chahiksi!" Clarence Little-Saddle swore. "It worked. I didn't think it would. It will be all right now. I can use the rain."

The valley was again a ditch only five feet wide.

The camper car struggled out of Narrow Valley through the little gate. It was smashed flat as a sheet of paper, and the screaming kids and people in it had only one dimension.

"It's closing in! It's closing in!" Robert Rampart roared, and he was no thicker than if he had been made out of cardboard.

"We're smashed like bugs," the Rampart boys intoned. "We're thin like paper."

"*Mort, ruine, ecrasement!*" spoke-acted Cecilia Rampart like the great tragedienne she was.

"Help! Help!" Nina Rampart croaked, but she winked at Willy and Clarence as they rolled by. "This homesteading jag always did leave me a little flat."

"Don't throw those paper dolls away. They might be the Ramparts," Mary Mabel called.

The camper car coughed again and bumped along on level ground. This couldn't last forever. The car was widening out as it bumped along.

"Did we overdo it, Clarence?" Willy McGilly asked. "What did one flat-lander say to the other?"

"Dimension of us never got around," Clarence said. "No, I don't think we overdid it, Willy. That car must be eighteen inches wide already, and they all ought to be normal by the time they reach the main road. The next time I do it, I think I'll throw wood-grain plastic on the fire to see who's kidding who."

Faith of Our Fathers

Philip K. Dick (1928–1982) wrote novels and stories which examined "reality" in all of its myriad forms, letting his protagonists, along with his readers, try to sort out what was real and what wasn't. His novel The Man in the High Castle *won the Hugo award in 1962. His work has also inspired films, most notable the Ridley Scott–directed* Blade Runner.

ON THE STREETS OF HANOI HE FOUND HIMSELF FACING A LEGLESS PEDdler who rode a little wooden cart and called shrilly to every passer-by. Chien slowed, listened, but did not stop; business at the Ministry of Cultural Artifacts cropped into his mind and deflected his attention: it was as if he were alone, and none of those on bicycles and scooters and jet-powered motorcycles remained. And likewise it was as if the legless peddler did not exist.

"Comrade," the peddler called however, and pursued him on his cart; a helium battery operated the drive and sent the cart scuttling expertly after Chien. "I possess a wide spectrum of time-tested herbal remedies complete with testimonials from thousands of loyal users; advise me of your malady and I can assist."

Chien, pausing, said, "Yes, but I have no malady." Except, he thought, for the chronic one of those employed by the Central Committee, that of career opportunism testing constantly the gates of each official position. Including mine.

"I can cure for example radiation sickness," the peddler chanted, still pursuing him. "Or expand, if necessary, the element of sexual prowess. I can reverse carcinomatous progressions, even the dreaded melanomae, what you would call black cancers." Lifting a tray of bottles, small aluminum cans, and assorted powders in plastic jars, the peddler sang, "If a rival persists in trying to usurp your gainful bureaucratic position, I can purvey an ointment which, appearing as a dermal balm, is in actuality a desperately effective toxin. And my prices, comrade, are low. And as a special favor to one so distinguished in bearing as yourself I will accept the postwar inflationary paper dollars reputedly of international exchange but in reality damn near no better than bathroom tissue."

"Go to hell," Chien said, and signaled a passing hovercar taxi; he was already three and one half minutes late for his first appointment of the day, and his various fat-assed superiors at the Ministry would be making quick mental notations—as would, to an even greater degree, his subordinates.

The peddler said quietly, "But, comrade; you *must* buy from me."

"Why?" Chien demanded. Indignation.

"Because, comrade, I am a war veteran. I fought in the Colossal Final War of National Liberation with the People's Democratic United Front against the Imperialists; I lost my pedal extremities at the battle of San Francisco." His tone was triumphant, now, and sly. "*It is the law.* If you refuse to buy wares offered by a veteran you risk a fine and possible jail sentence—and in addition disgrace."

Wearily, Chien nodded the hovercab on. "Admittedly," he said. "Okay, I must buy from you." He glanced summarily over the meager display of herbal remedies, seeking one at random. "That," he decided, pointing to a paper-wrapped parcel in the rear row.

The peddler laughed. "That, comrade, is a spermatocide, bought by women who for political reasons cannot qualify for The Pill. It would be of shallow use to you, in fact none at all, since you are a gentleman."

"The law," Chien said bitingly, "does not require me to purchase anything useful from you; only that I purchase something. I'll take that." He reached into his padded coat for his billfold, huge with the postwar inflationary bills in which, four times a week, he as a government servant was paid.

"Tell me your problems," the peddler said.

Chien stared at him. Appalled by the invasion of privacy—and done by someone outside the government.

"All right, comrade," the peddler said, seeing his expression. "I will not probe; excuse me. But as a doctor—an herbal healer—it is fitting that I know as much as possible." He pondered, his gaunt features somber. "Do you watch television unusually much?" he asked abruptly.

Taken by surprise, Chien said, "Every evening. Except on Friday when I go to my club to practice the esoteric imported art from the defeated West of steer-roping." It was his only indulgence; other than that he had totally devoted himself to Party activities.

The peddler reached, selected a gray paper packet. "Sixty trade dollars," he stated. "With a full guarantee; if it does not do as promised, return the unused portion for a full and cheery refund."

"And what," Chien said cuttingly, "is it guaranteed to do?"

"It will rest eyes fatigued by the countenance of meaningless official monologues," the peddler said. "A soothing preparation; take it
as soon is you find yourself exposed to the usual dry and lengthy
sermons which—"

Chien paid the money, accepted the packet, and strode off. Balls,
he said to himself. It's a racket, he decided, the ordinance setting
up war vets as a privileged class. They prey off us—we, the younger
ones—like raptors.

Forgotten, the gray packet remained deposited in his coat pocket,
as he entered the imposing postwar Ministry of Cultural Artifacts
building, and his own considerable stately office, to begin his workday.

A portly, middle-aged Caucasian male, wearing a brown Hong Kong
silk suit, double-breasted with vest, waited in his office. With the
unfamiliar Caucasian stood his own immediate superior, Ssu-Ma
Tso-pin. Tso-pin introduced the two of them in Cantonese, a dialect
which he used badly.

"Mr. Tung Chien, this is Mr. Darius Pethel. Mr. Pethel will be
headmaster at the new ideological and cultural establishment of
didactic character soon to open at San Fernando, California." He
added, "Mr. Pethel has had a rich and full lifetime supporting the
people's struggle to unseat imperialist-bloc countries via pedagogic
media; therefore this high post."

They shook hands.

"Tea?" Chien asked the two of them; he pressed the switch of his
infrared hibachi and in an instant the water in the highly ornamented ceramic pot—of Japanese origin—began to burble. As he
seated himself at his desk he saw that trustworthy Miss Hsi had laid
out the information poop-sheet (confidential) on Comrade Pethel;
he glanced over it, meanwhile pretending to be doing nothing in
particular.

"The Absolute Benefactor of the People," Tso-pin said, "has personally met Mr. Pethel and trusts him. This is rare. The school in
San Fernando will appear to teach run-of-the-mill Taoist philoso-
phies but will, of course, in actuality maintain for us a channel of
communication to the liberal and intellectual youth segment of
western U.S. There are many of them still alive, from San Diego to
Sacramento; we estimate at least ten thousand. The school will
accept two thousand. Enrollment will be mandatory for those we
select. Your relationship to Mr. Pethel's programing is grave. Ahem;
your tea water is boiling."

"Thank you," Chien murmured, dropping in the bag of Lipton's tea.

Tso-pin continued, "Although Mr. Pethel will supervise the setting
up of the courses of instruction presented by the school to its student

body, all examination papers will oddly enough be relayed here to your office for your own expert, careful, ideological study. In other words, Mr. Chien, you will determine who among the two thousand students is reliable, which are truly responding to the programing and who is not."

"I will now pour my tea," Chien said, doing so ceremoniously.

"What we have to realize," Pethel rumbled in Cantonese even worse than that of Tso-pin, "is that, once having lost the global war to us, the American youth has developed a talent for dissembling." He spoke the last word in English; not understanding it, Chien turned inquiringly to his superior.

"Lying," Tso-pin explained.

Pethel said, "Mouthing the proper slogans for surface appearance, but on the inside believing them false. Test papers by this group will closely resemble those of genuine—"

"You mean that the test papers of *two thousand* students will be passing through my office?" Chien demanded. He could not believe it. "That's a full-time job in itself; I don't have time for anything remotely resembling that." He was appalled. "To give critical, official approval or denial of the astute variety which you're envisioning—" He gestured. "Screw that," he said, in English.

Blinking at the strong, Western vulgarity, Tso-pin said, "You have a staff. Plus also you can requisition several more from the pool; the Ministry's budget, augmented this year, will permit it. And remember: the Absolute Benefactor of the People has hand-picked Mr. Pethel." His tone, now, had become ominous, but only subtly so. Just enough to penetrate Chien's hysteria, and to wither it into submission. At least temporarily. To underline his point, Tso-pin walked to the far end of the office; he stood before the full-length 3-D portrait of the Absolute Benefactor, and after an interval his proximity triggered the tape-transport mounted behind the portrait; the face of the Benefactor moved, and from it came a familiar homily, in more than familiar accents. "Fight for peace, my sons," it intoned gently, firmly.

"Ha," Chien said, still perturbed, but concealing it. Possibly one of the Ministry's computers could sort the examination papers; a yes-no-maybe structure could be employed, in conjunction with a pre-analysis of the pattern of ideological correctness—and incorrectness. The matter could be made routine. Probably.

Darius Pethel said, "I have with me certain material which I would like you to scrutinize, Mr. Chien." He unzipped an unsightly, old-fashioned, plastic briefcase. "Two examination essays," he said as he passed the documents to Chien. "This will tell us if you're qualified." He then glanced at Tso-pin; their gazes met. "I understand," Pethel said, "that if you are successful in this venture you will be made vice-councilor of the Ministry, and His Greatness the Absolute Benefactor of the People will personally confer Kisterigian's medal on you." Both he and Tso-pin smiled in wary unison.

"The Kisterigian medal," Chien echoed; he accepted the examination papers, glanced over them in a show of leisurely indifference. But within him his heart vibrated in ill-concealed tension. "Why these two? By that I mean, what am I looking for, sir?"

"One of them," Pethel said, "is the work of a dedicated progressive, a loyal Party member of thoroughly researched conviction. The other is by a young *stilyagi* whom we suspect of holding petit bourgeois imperialist degenerate crypto-ideas. It is up to you, sir, to determine which is which."

Thanks a lot, Chien thought. But, nodding, he read the title of the top paper.

DOCTRINES OF THE ABSOLUTE BENEFACTOR ANTICIPATED IN THE POETRY OF BAHA AD-DIN ZUHAYR, OF THIRTEENTH-CENTURY ARABIA

Glancing down the initial pages of the essay, Chien saw a quatrain familiar to him; it was called "Death" and he had known it most of his adult, educated life.

Once he will miss, twice he will miss,
    He only chooses one of many hours;
For him nor deep nor hill there is,
    But all's one level plain he hunts for flowers.

"Powerful," Chien said. "This poem."

"He makes use of the poem," Pethel said, observing Chien's lips moving as he reread the quatrain, "to indicate the age-old wisdom, displayed by the Absolute Benefactor in our current lives, that no individual is safe; everyone is mortal, and only the supra-personal, historically essential cause survives. As it should be. Would you agree with him? With this student, I mean? Or—" Pethel paused. "Is he in fact perhaps satirizing the Absolute Benefactor's promulgations?"

Cagily, Chien said, "Give me a chance to inspect the other paper."

"You need no further information; decide."

Haltingly, Chien said, "I—had never thought of this poem that way." He felt irritable. "Anyhow, it isn't by Baha ad-Din Zuhayr; it's part of the *Thousand and One Nights* anthology. It is, however, thirteenth century; I admit that." He quickly read over the text of the paper accompanying the poem. It appeared to be a routine, uninspired rehash of Party clichés, all of them familiar to him from

birth. The blind, imperialist monster who mowed down and
snuffed out (mixed metaphor) human aspiration, the calculations
of the still extant anti-Party group in eastern United States . . . He
felt dully bored, and as uninspired as the student's paper. We must
persevere, the paper declared. Wipe out the Pentagon remnants
in the Catskills, subdue Tennessee and most especially the pocket
of die-hard reaction in the red hills of Oklahoma. He sighed.

"I think," Tso-pin said, "we should allow Mr. Chien the opportunity of observing this difficult material at his leisure." To Chien he
said, "You have permission to take them home to your condominium, this evening, and adjudge them on your own time." He
bowed, half mockingly, half solicitously. In any case, insult or not,
he had gotten Chien off the hook, and for that Chien was grateful.

"You are most kind," he murmured, "to allow me to perform this
new and highly stimulating labor on my own time. Mikoyan, were
he alive today, would approve." You bastard, he said to himself.
Meaning both his superior and the Caucasian Pethel. Handing me
a hot potato like this, and on my own time. Obviously the CP USA is
in trouble; its indoctrination academies aren't managing to do their
job with the notoriously mulish, eccentric Yank youths. And you've
passed that hot potato on and on until it reaches me.

Thanks for nothing, he thought acidly.

That evening in his small but well-appointed condominium apartment he read over the other of the two examination papers, this one
by a Marion Culper, and discovered that it too dealt with poetry.
Obviously this was speciously a poetry class, and he felt ill. It had
always run against his grain, the use of poetry—of any art—for social
purposes. Anyhow, comfortable in his special spine-straightening,
simulated-leather easy chair, he lit a Cuesta Rey Number One
English Market immense corona cigar and began to read.

The writer of the paper, Miss Culper, had selected as her text a
portion of a poem of John Dryden, the seventeenth-century
English poet, final lines from the well-known "A Song for St.
Cecilia's Day."

. . . So when the last and dreadful hour
This crumbling pageant shall devour,
The trumpet shall be heard on high,
The dead shall live, the living die,
And Music shall untune the sky.

Well, that's a hell of a thing, Chien thought to himself bitingly.
Dryden, we're supposed to believe, anticipated the fall of capitalism?

That's what he meant by the "crumbling pageant"? Christ. He leaned over to take hold of his cigar and found that it had gone out. Groping in his pockets for his Japanese-made lighter, he half rose to his feet . . .

Tweeeeeee! the TV set at the far end of the living room said.

Aha, Chien said. We're about to be addressed by the Leader. By the Absolute Benefactor of the People, up there in Peking where he's lived for ninety years now; or is it one hundred? Or, as we sometimes like to think of him, the Ass—

"May the ten thousand blossoms of abject self-assumed poverty flower in your spiritual courtyard," the TV announcer said. With a groan, Chien rose to his feet, bowed the mandatory bow of response; each TV set came equipped with monitoring devices to narrate to the Secpol, the Security Police, whether its owner was bowing and/or watching.

On the screen a clearly defined visage manifested itself, the wide, unlined, healthy features of the one-hundred-and-twenty-year-old leader of CP East, ruler of many—far too many, Chien reflected. Blah to you, he thought, and reseated himself in his simulated-leather easy chair, now facing the TV screen.

"My thoughts," the Absolute Benefactor said in his rich and slow tones, "are on you, my children. And especially on Mr. Tung Chien of Hanoi, who faces a difficult task ahead, a task to enrich the people of Democratic East, plus the American West Coast. We must think in unison about this noble, dedicated man and the chore which he faces, and I have chosen to take several moments of my time to honor him and encourage him. Are you listening, Mr. Chien?"

"Yes, Your Greatness," Chien said, and pondered to himself the odds against the Party Leader singling *him* out this particular evening. The odds caused him to feel uncomradely cynicism; it was unconvincing. Probably this transmission was being beamed to his apartment building alone—or at least this city. It might also be a lip-synch job, done at Hanoi TV, Incorporated. In any case he was required to listen and watch—and absorb. He did so, from a life-time of practice. Outwardly he appeared to be rigidly attentive. Inwardly he was still mulling over the two test papers, wondering which was which; where did devout Party enthusiasm end and sardonic lampoonery begin? Hard to say ... which of course explained why they had dumped the task in his lap.

Again he groped in his pockets for his lighter—and found the small gray envelope which the war-veteran peddler had sold him. Gawd, he thought, remembering what it had cost. Money down the drain and what did this herbal remedy do? Nothing. He turned the packet over and saw, on the back, small printed words. Well, he thought, and began to unfold the packet with care. The words had snared him—as of course they were meant to do.

Failing as a Party member and human? Afraid of becoming obsolete and discarded on the ash heap of history by

He read rapidly through the text, ignoring its claims, seeking to find out what he had purchased.

Meanwhile, the Absolute Benefactor droned on.

Snuff. The package contained snuff. Countless tiny black grains, like gunpowder, which sent up an interesting aromatic to tickle his nose. The title of the particular blend was Princes Special, he discovered. And very pleasing, he decided. At one time he had taken snuff—smoked tobacco for a time having been illegal for reasons of health—back during his student days at Peking U; it had been the fad, especially the amatory mixes prepared in Chungking, made from god knew what. Was this that? Almost any aromatic could be added to snuff, from essence of orange to pulverized babycrap . . . or so some seemed, especially an English mixture called High Dry Toast which had in itself more or less put an end to his yearning for nasal, inhaled tobacco.

On the TV screen the Absolute Benefactor rumbled monotonously on as Chien sniffed cautiously at the powder, read the claims—it cured everything from being late to work to falling in love with a woman of dubious political background. Interesting. But typical of claims—

His doorbell rang.

Rising, he walked to the door, opened it with full knowledge of what he would find. There, sure enough, stood Mou Kuei, the Building Warden, small and hard-eyed and alert to his task; he had his armband and metal helmet on, showing that he meant business. "Mr. Chien, comrade Party worker. I received a call from the television authority. You are failing to watch your screen and are instead fiddling with a packet of doubtful content." He produced a clipboard and ballpoint pen. "Two red marks, and hithertonow you are summarily ordered to repose yourself in a comfortable, stress-free posture before your screen and give the Leader your unexcelled attention. His words, this evening, are directed particularly to you, sir; to you."

"I doubt that," Chien heard himself say.

Blinking, Kuei said, "What do you mean?"

"The Leader rules eight billion comrades. He isn't going to single me out." He felt wrathful; the punctuality of the warden's reprimand irked him.

Kuei said, "But I distinctly heard with my own ears. You were mentioned."

Going over to the TV set, Chien turned the volume up. "But now he's talking about crop failures in People's India; that's of no relevance to me."

"Whatever the Leader expostulates is relevant." Mou Kuei scratched a mark on his clipboard sheet, bowed formally, turned away. "My call to come up here to confront you with your slackness originated at Central. Obviously they regard your attention as important; I must order you to set in motion your automatic transmission recording circuit and replay the earlier portions of the Leader's speech."

Chien farted. And shut the door.

Back to the TV set, he said to himself. Where our leisure hours are spent. And there lay the two student examination papers; he had that weighing him down too. And all on my own time, he thought savagely. The hell with them. Up theirs. He strode to the TV set, started to shut it off; at once a red warning light winked on, informing him that he did not have permission to shut off the set—could not in fact end its tirade and image even if he unplugged it. Mandatory speeches, he thought, will kill us all, bury us; if I could be free of the noise of speeches, free of the din of the Party baying as it hounds mankind . . .

There was no known ordinance, however, preventing him from taking snuff while he watched the Leader. So, opening the small gray packet, he shook out a mound of the black granules onto the back of his left hand. He then, professionally, raised his hand to his nostrils and deeply inhaled, drawing the snuff well up into his sinus cavities. Imagine the old superstition, he thought to himself. That the sinus cavities are connected to the brain, and hence an inhalation of snuff directly affects the cerebral cortex. He smiled, seated himself once more, fixed his gaze on the TV screen and the gesticulating individual known so utterly to them all.

The face dwindled away, disappeared. The sound ceased. He faced an emptiness, a vacuum. The screen, white and blank, confronted him and from the speaker a faint hiss sounded.

The frigging snuff, he said to himself. And inhaled greedily at the remainder of the powder on his hand, drawing it up avidly into his nose, his sinuses, and, or so it felt, into his brain; he plunged into the snuff, absorbing it elatedly.

The screen remained blank and then, by degrees, an image once more formed and established itself. It was not the Leader. Not the Absolute Benefactor of the People, in point of fact not a human figure at all.

He faced a dead mechanical construct, made of solid state circuits, of swiveling pseudopodia, lenses, and a squawk-box. And the box began, in a droning din, to harangue him.

Staring fixedly, he thought, *What is this?* Reality? Hallucination, he thought. The peddler came across some of the psychedelic drugs used during the War of Liberation—he's selling the stuff and I've taken some, taken a whole lot!

Making his way unsteadily to the vidphone he dialed the Secpol station nearest his building. "I wish to report a pusher of hallucinogenic drugs," he said into the receiver.

"Your name, sir, and conapt location?" Efficient, brisk, and impersonal bureaucrat of the police.

He gave them the information, then haltingly made it back to his simulated-leather easy chair, once again to witness the apparition on the TV screen. This is lethal, he said to himself. It must be some preparation developed in Washington, D.C., or London—stronger and stranger than the LSD-25 which they dumped so effectively into our reservoirs. And I thought it was going to relieve me of the burden of the Leader's speeches . . . this is far worse, this electronic, sputtering, swiveling, metal and plastic monstrosity yammering away—this is terrifying.

To have to face *this* the remainder of my life—

It took ten minutes for the Secpol two-man team to come rapping at his door. And by then, in a deteriorating set of stages, the familiar image of the Leader had seeped back into focus on the screen, had supplanted the horrible artificial construct which waved its 'podia and squalled on and on. He let the two cops in shakily, led them to the table on which he had left the remains of the snuff in its packet.

"Psychedelic toxin," he said thickly. "Of short duration. Absorbed into the blood stream directly, through nasal capillaries. I'll give you details as to where I got it, from whom, all that." He took a deep shaky breath; the presence of the police was comforting.

Ballpoint pens ready, the two officers waited. And all the time, in the background, the Leader rattled out his endless speech. As he had done a thousand evenings before in the life of Tung Chien. But, he thought, it'll never be the same again, at least not for me. Not after inhaling that near-toxic snuff.

He wondered, Is that what they intended?

It seemed odd to him, thinking of a *they*. Peculiar—but somehow correct. For an instant he hesitated, not giving out the details, not telling the police enough to find the man. A peddler, he started to say. I don't know where; can't remember. But he did; he remembered the exact street intersection. So, with unexplainable reluctance, he told them.

"Thank you, Comrade Chien." The boss of the team of police carefully gathered up the remaining snuff—most of it remained—and placed it in his uniform—smart, sharp uniform—pocket. "We'll have it analyzed at the first available moment," the cop said, "and inform you immediately in case counter medical measures are indicated for you. Some of the old wartime psychedelics were eventually fatal, as you have no doubt read."

"I've read," he agreed. That had been specifically what he had been thinking.

"Good luck and thanks for notifying us," both cops said, and departed. The affair, for all their efficiency, did not seem to shake them; obviously such a complaint was routine.

The lab report came swiftly—surprisingly so, in view of the vast state bureaucracy. It reached him by vidphone before the Leader had finished his TV speech.

"It's not a hallucinogen," the Secpol lab technician informed him.

"No?" he said, puzzled and, strangely, not relieved. Not at all.

"On the contrary. It's a phenothiazine, which as you doubtless know is anti-hallucinogenic. A strong dose per gram of admixture, but harmless. Might lower your blood pressure or make you sleepy. Probably stolen from a wartime cache of medical supplies. Left by the retreating barbarians. I wouldn't worry."

Pondering, Chien hung up the vidphone in slow motion. And then walked to the window of his conapt—the window with the fine view of other Hanoi high-rise conapts—to think.

The doorbell rang. Feeling as if he were in a trance, he crossed the carpeted living room to answer it.

The girl standing there, in a tan raincoat with a babushka over her dark, shiny, and very long hair, said in a timid little voice, "Um, Comrade Chien? Tung Chien? Of the Ministry of—"

He led her in, reflexively, and shut the door after her. "You've been monitoring my vidphone," he told her; it was a shot in darkness, but something in him, an unvoiced certitude, told him that she had.

"Did—they take the rest of the snuff?" She glanced about. "Oh, I hope not; it's so hard to get these days."

"Snuff," he said, "is easy to get. Phenothiazine isn't. Is that what you mean?"

The girl raised her head, studied him with large, moon-darkened eyes. "Yes. Mr. Chien—" She hesitated, obviously as uncertain as the Secpol cops had been assured. "Tell me what you saw; it's of great importance for us to be certain."

"I had a choice?" he said acutely.

"Y-yes, very much so. That's what confuses us; that's what is not as we planned. We don't understand; it fits nobody's theory." Her eyes even darker and deeper, she said, "Was it the aquatic horror shape? The thing with slime and teeth, the extraterrestrial life form? Please tell me; we have to know." She breathed irregularly, with effort, the tan raincoat rising and falling; he found himself watching its rhythm.

"A machine," he said.

"Oh!" She ducked her head, nodding vigorously. "Yes, I understand; a mechanical organism in no way resembling a human. Not a simulacrum, something constructed to resemble a man."

He said, "This did not look like a man." He added to himself, And it failed—did not try—to talk like a man.

"You understand that it was not a hallucination."

"I've been officially told that what I took was a phenothiazine. That's all I know." He said as little as possible; he did not want to talk but to hear. Hear what the girl had to say.

"Well, Mr. Chien—" She took a deep, unstable breath. "If it was not a hallucination, then what was it? What does that leave? What is called 'extra-consciousness'—could that be it?"

He did not answer; turning his back, he leisurely picked up the two student test papers, glanced over them, ignoring her. Waiting for her next attempt.

At his shoulder she appeared, smelling of spring rain, smelling of sweetness and agitation, beautiful in the way she smelled, and looked, and, he thought, speaks. So different from the harsh plateau speech patterns we hear on the TV—have heard since I was a baby.

"Some of them," she said huskily, "who take the stelazine—it was stelazine you got, Mr. Chien—see one apparition, some another. But distinct categories have emerged; there is not an infinite variety. Some see what you saw; we call it the Clanker. Some the aquatic horror; that's the Gulper. And then there's the Bird, and the Climbing Tube, and—" She broke off. "But other reactions tell you very little. Tell us very little." She hesitated, then plunged on. "Now that this has happened to you, Mr. Chien, we would like you to join our gathering. Join your particular group, those who see what you see. Group Red. We want to know what it really is, and—" She gestured with tapered, wax-smooth fingers. "It can't be all those manifestations." Her tone was poignant, naïvely so. He felt his caution relax—a trifle.

He said, "What do you see? You in particular?"

"I'm a part of Group Yellow. I see—a storm. A whining, vicious whirlwind. That roots everything up, crushes condominium apartments built to last a century." She smiled wanly. "The Crusher. Twelve groups in all, Mr. Chien. Twelve absolutely different experiences, all from the same phenothiazines, all of the Leader as he speaks over TV. As *it* speaks, rather." She smiled up at him, lashes long—probably protracted artificially—and gaze engaging, even trusting. As if she thought he knew something or could do something.

"I should make a citizen's arrest of you," he said presently.

"There is no law, not about this. We studied Soviet juridical writings before we—found people to distribute the stelazine. We don't have much of it; we have to be very careful whom we give it to. It seemed to us that you constituted a likely choice . . . a well-known, postwar, dedicated young career man on his way up." From his fingers she took the examination papers. "They're having you pol-read?" she asked.

"'Pol-read'?" He did not know the term.

"Study something said or written to see if it fits the Party's current world view. You in the hierarchy merely call it 'read,' don't you?" Again she smiled. "When you rise one step higher, up with Mr. Tsopin, you will know that expression." She added somberly, "And with Mr. Pethel. He's very far up. Mr. Chien, there is no ideological school in San Fernando; these are forged exam papers, designed to read back to them a thorough analysis of *your* political ideology. And have you been able to distinguish which paper is orthodox and which is heretical?" Her voice was pixielike, taunting with amused malice. "Choose the wrong one and your budding career stops dead, cold, in its tracks. Choose the proper one—"

"Do you know which is which?" he demanded.

"Yes." She nodded soberly. "We have listening devices in Mr. Tsopin's inner offices; we monitored his conversation with Mr. Pethel—who is not Mr. Pethel but the Higher Secpol Inspector Judd Craine. You have possibly heard mention of him; he acted as chief assistant to Judge Vorlawsky at the '98 war crimes trial in Zurich."

With difficulty he said, "I—see." Well, that explained that.

The girl said, "My name is Tanya Lee."

He said nothing; he merely nodded, too stunned for any cerebration.

"Technically, I am a minor clerk," Miss Lee said, "at your Ministry. You have never run into me, however, that I can at least recall. We try to hold posts wherever we can. As far up as possible. My own boss—"

"Should you be telling me this?" He gestured at the TV set, which remained on. "Aren't they picking this up?"

Tanya Lee said, "We introduced a noise factor in the reception of both vid and aud material from this apartment building; it will take them almost an hour to locate the sheathing. So we have"—she examined the tiny wristwatch on her slender wrist—"fifteen more minutes. And still be safe."

"Tell me," he said, "which paper is orthodox."

"Is that what you care about? Really?"

"What," he said, "should I care about?"

"Don't you see, Mr. Chien? You've learned something. The Leader is not the Leader; he is something else, but we can't tell what. Not yet. Mr. Chien, with all due respect, have you ever had your drinking water analyzed? I know it sounds paranoiac, but have you?"

"No," he said. "Of course not." Knowing what she was going to say.

Miss Lee said briskly, "Our tests show that it's saturated with hallucinogens. It is, has been, will continue to be. Not the ones used during the war; not the disorienting ones, but a synthetic quasi-ergot derivative called Datrox-3. You drink it here in the building from the time you get up; you drink it in restaurants and other apartments that you visit. You drink it at the Ministry; it's all piped from a central, common source." Her tone was bleak and ferocious. "We solved that problem; we knew, as soon as we discovered it, that any good phenothiazine would counter it. What we did not know, of course, was this—a *variety* of authentic experiences; that makes no sense, rationally. It's the hallucination which should differ from person to person, and the reality experience which should be ubiquitous—it's all turned around. We can't even construct an ad hoc theory which accounts for that, and god knows we've tried. Twelve mutually exclusive hallucinations—that would be easily understood. But not one hallucination and twelve realities." She ceased talking, then, and studied the two test papers, her forehead wrinkling. "The one with the Arabic poem is orthodox," she stated. "If you tell them that they'll trust you and give you a higher post. You'll be another notch up in the hierarchy of Party officialdom." Smiling—her teeth were perfect and lovely—she finished, "Look what you received back for your investment this morning. Your career is underwritten for a time. And by us."

He said, "I don't believe you." Instinctively, his caution operated within him, always, the caution of a lifetime lived among the hatchet men of the Hanoi branch of the CP East. They knew an infinitude of ways by which to ax a rival out of contention—some of which he himself had employed; some of which he had seen done to himself and to others. This could be a novel way, one unfamiliar to him. It could always be.

"Tonight," Miss Lee said, "in the speech the Leader singled you out. Didn't this strike you as strange? You, of all people? A minor officeholder in a meager ministry—"

"Admitted," he said. "It struck me that way; yes."

"That was legitimate. His Greatness is grooming an elite cadre of younger men, postwar men, he hopes will infuse new life into the hidebound, moribund hierarchy of old fogies and Party hacks. His Greatness singled you out for the same reason that we singled you out; if pursued properly, your carecr could lead you all the way to the top. At least for a time . . . as we know. That's how it goes."

He thought, So virtually everyone has faith in me. Except myself; and certainly not after this, the experience with the anti-hallucinatory snuff. It had shaken years of confidence, and no doubt rightly so. However, he was beginning to regain his poise; he felt it seeping back, a little at first, then with a rush.

Going to the vidphone, he lifted the receiver and began, for the second time that night, to dial the number of the Hanoi Security Police.

"Turning me in," Miss Lee said, "would be the second most regressive decision you could make. I'll tell them that you brought me here to bribe me; you thought, because of my job at the Ministry, I would know which examination paper to select."

He said, "And what would be my first most regressive decision?"

"Not taking a further dose of phenothiazine," Miss Lee said evenly.

Hanging up the phone, Tung Chien thought to himself, I don't understand what's happening to me. Two forces, the Party and His Greatness on one hand—this girl with her alleged group on the other. One wants me to rise as far as possible in the Party hierarchy; the other—*What did Tanya Lee want?* Underneath the words, inside the membrane of an almost trivial contempt for the Party, the Leader, the ethical standards of the People's Democratic United Front—what was she after in regard to him?

He said curiously, "Are you anti-Party?"

"No."

"But—" He gestured. "That's all there is; Party and anti-Party. You must be Party, then." Bewildered, he stared at her; with composure she returned the stare. "You have an organization," he said, "and you meet. What do you intend to destroy? The regular function of government? Are you like the treasonable college students of the United States during the Vietnam War who stopped troop trains, demonstrated—"

Wearily Miss Lee said, "It wasn't like that. But forget it; that's not the issue. What we want to know is this: who or what is leading us? We must penetrate far enough to enlist someone, some rising young Party theoretician, who could conceivably be invited to a tête-à-tête with the Leader—you see?" Her voice lifted; she consulted her watch, obviously anxious to get away: the fifteen minutes were almost up. "Very few persons actually see the Leader, as you know. I mean really see him."

"Seclusion," he said. "Due to his advanced age."

"We have hope," Miss Lee said, "that if you pass the phony test which they have arranged for you—and with my help you have—you will be invited to one of the stag parties which the Leader has from time to time, which of course the 'papes don't report. Now do you see?" Her voice rose shrilly, in a frenzy of despair. "Then we would know; if you could go in there under the influence of the anti-hallucinogenic drug, could see him face to face as he actually is—"

Thinking aloud, he said, "And end my career of public service. If not my life."

"You owe us something," Tanya Lee snapped, her cheeks white. "If I hadn't told you which exam paper to choose you would have picked the wrong one and your dedicated public service career would be over anyhow; you would have failed—failed at a test you didn't even realize you were taking!"

He said mildly, "I had a fifty-fifty chance."

"No." She shook her head fiercely. "The heretical one is faked up with a lot of Party jargon; they deliberately constructed the two texts to trap you. They *wanted* you to fail!"

Once more he examined the two papers, feeling confused. Was she right? Possibly. Probably. It rang true, knowing the Party functionaries as he did, and Tso-pin, his superior, in particular. He felt weary then. Defeated. After a time he said to the girl, "What you're trying to get out of me is a quid pro quo. You did something for me—you got, or claim you got—the answer to this Party inquiry. But you've already done your part. What's to keep me from tossing you out of here on your head? I don't have to do a goddam thing." He heard his voice, toneless, sounding the poverty of empathic emotionality so usual in Party circles.

Miss Lee said, "There will be other tests, as you continue to ascend. And we will monitor for you with them too." She was calm, at ease; obviously she had forseen his reaction.

"How long do I have to think it over?" he said.

"I'm leaving now. We're in no rush; you're not about to receive an invitation to the Leader's Yellow River villa in the next week or even month." Going to the door, opening it, she paused. "As you're given covert rating tests we'll be in contact, supplying the answers—so you'll see one or more of us on those occasions. Probably it won't be me; it'll be that disabled war veteran who'll sell you the correct response sheets as you leave the Ministry building." She smiled a brief, snuffed-out-candle smile. "But one of these days, no doubt unexpectedly, you'll get an ornate, official, very formal invitation to the villa, and when you go you'll be heavily sedated with stelazine . . . possibly our last dose of our dwindling supply. Good night." The door shut after her; she had gone.

My god, he thought. They can blackmail me. For what I've done. And she didn't even bother to mention it; in view of what they're involved with it was not worth mentioning.

But blackmail for what? He had already told the Secpol squad that he had been given a drug which had proved to be a phenothiazine. *Then they know,* he realized. They'll watch me; they're alert. Technically I haven't broken a law, but—they'll be watching, all right.

However, they always watched anyhow. He relaxed slightly, thinking that. He had, over the years, become virtually accustomed to it, as had everyone.

I will see the Absolute Benfactor of the People as he is, he said to himself. Which possibly no one else has done. What will it be? Which of the subclasses of non-hallucination? Classes which I do not even know about . . . a view which may totally overthrow me. How am I going to be able to get through the evening, to keep my poise, if it's like the shape I saw on the TV screen? The Crusher, the Clanker, the Bird, the Climbing Tube, the Gulper—or worse.

He wondered what some of the other views consisted of . . . and then gave up that line of speculation; it was unprofitable. And too anxiety-inducing.

The next morning Mr. Tso-pin and Mr. Darius Pethel met him in his office, both of them calm but expectant. Wordlessly, he handed them one of the two "exam papers." The orthodox one, with its short and heart-smothering Arabian poem.

"This one," Chien said tightly, "is the product of a dedicated Party member or candidate for membership. The other—" He slapped the remaining sheets. "Reactionary garbage." He felt anger. "In spite of a superficial—"

"All right, Mr. Chien," Pethel said, nodding. "We don't have to explore each and every ramification; your analysis is correct. You heard the mention regarding you in the Leader's speech last night on TV?"

"I certainly did," Chien said.

"So you have undoubtedly inferred," Pethel said, "that there is a good deal involved in what we are attempting, here. The Leader has his eye on you; that's clear. As a matter of fact, he has communicated to myself regarding you." He opened his bulging briefcase and rummaged. "Lost the goddam thing. Anyhow—" He glanced at Tso-pin, who nodded slightly. "His Greatness would like to have you appear for dinner at the Yangtze River Ranch next Thursday night. Mrs. Fletcher in particular appreciates—"

Chien said, "'Mrs. Fletcher'? Who is 'Mrs. Fletcher'?"

After a pause Tso-pin said dryly, "The Absolute Benefactor's wife. His name—which you of course had never heard—is Thomas Fletcher."

"He's a Caucasian," Pethel explained. "Originally from the New Zealand Communist Party; he participated in the difficult take-over there. This news is not in the strict sense secret, but on the other hand it hasn't been noised about." He hesitated, toying with his watchchain. "Probably it would be better if you forgot about that. Of course, as soon as you meet him, see him face to face, you'll realize that, realize that he's a Cauc. As I am. As many of us are."

"Race," Tso-pin pointed out, "has nothing to do with loyalty to the Leader and the Party. As witness Mr. Pethel, here."

But His Greatness, Chien thought, jolted. He did not appear, on the TV screen, to be occidental. "On TV—" he began.

"The image," Tso-pin interrupted, "is subjected to a variegated assortment of skillful refinements. For ideological purposes. Most persons holding higher offices are aware of this." He eyed Chien with hard criticism.

So everyone agrees, Chien thought. What we see every night is not real. The question is, How unreal? Partially? Or—completely?

"I will be prepared," he said tautly. And he thought, There has been a slip-up. They weren't prepared for me—the people that Tanya Lee represents—to gain entry so soon. Where's the anti-hallucinogen? Can they get it to me or not? Probably not on such short notice.

He felt, strangely, relief. He would be going into the presence of His Greatness in a position to see him as a human being, see him as he—and everybody else—saw him on TV. It would be a most stimulating and cheerful dinner party, with some of the most influential Party members in Asia. I think we can do without the phenothiazines, he said to himself. And his sense of relief grew.

"Here it is, finally," Pethel said suddenly, producing a white envelope from his briefcase. "Your card of admission. You will be flown by Sino-rocket to the Leader's villa Thursday morning; there the protocol officer will brief you on your expected behavior. It will be formal dress, white tie and tails, but the atmosphere will be cordial. There are always a great number of toasts." He added, "I have attended two such stag gets-together. Mr. Tso-pin"—he smiled creakily—"has not been honored in such a fashion. But as they say, all things come to him who waits. Ben Franklin said that."

Tso-pin said, "It has come for Mr. Chien rather prematurely, I would say." He shrugged philosophically. "But my opinion has never at any time been asked."

"One thing," Pethel said to Chien. "It is possible that when you see His Greatness in person you will be in some regards disappointed. Be alert that you do not let this make itself apparent, if you should so feel. We have, always, tended—been trained—to regard him as more than a man. But at table he is"—he gestured—"a forked radish. In certain respects like ourselves. He may for instance indulge in moderately human oral-aggressive and -passive activity; he possibly may tell an off-color joke or drink too much . . . To be candid, no one ever knows in advance how these things will work out, but they do generally hold forth until late the following morning. So it would be wise to accept the dosage of amphetamines which the protocol officer will offer you."

"Oh?" Chien said. This was news to him, and interesting.

"For stamina. And to balance the liquor. His Greatness has amazing staying power; he often is still on his feet and raring to go after everyone else has collapsed." ·

"A remarkable man," Tso-pin chimed in. "I think his—indulgences only show that he is a fine fellow. And fully in the round; he is like the ideal Renaissance man; as, for example, Lorenzo de Medici."

"That does come to mind," Pethel said; he studied Chien with such intensity that some of last night's chill returned. Am I being led into one trap after another? Chien wondered. That girl—was she in fact an agent of the Secpol probing me, trying to ferret out a disloyal, anti-Party streak in me?

I think, he decided, I will make sure that the legless peddler of herbal remedies does not snare me when I leave work; I'll take a totally different route back to my conapt.

He was successful. That day he avoided the peddler and the same the next, and so on until Thursday.

On Thursday morning the peddler scooted from beneath a parked truck and blocked his way, confronting him.

"My medication?" the peddler demanded. "It helped? I know it did; the formula goes back to the Sung Dynasty—I can tell it did. Right?"

Chien said, "Let me go."

"Would you be kind enough to answer?" The tone was not the expected, customary whining of a street peddler operating in a marginal fashion, and that tone came across to Chien; he heard loud and clear . . . as the Imperialist puppet troops of long ago phrased it.

"I know what you gave me," Chien said. "And I don't want any more. If I change my mind I can pick it up at a pharmacy. Thanks." He started on, but the cart, with the legless occupant, pursued him.

"Miss Lee was talking to me," the peddler said loudly.

"Hmm," Chien said, and automatically increased his pace; he spotted a hovercab and began signaling for it.

"It's tonight you're going to the stag dinner at the Yangtze River villa," the peddler said, panting for breath in his effort to keep up. "Take the medication—now!" He held out a flat packet, imploringly. "Please, Party Member Chien; for your own sake, for all of us. So we can tell what it is we're up against. Good lord, it may be non-terran; that's our most basic fear. Don't you understand, Chien? What's your goddam career compared with that? If we can't find out—"

The cab bumped to a halt on the pavement; its door slid open. Chien started to board it.

The packet sailed past him, landed on the entrance sill of the cab, then slid into the gutter, damp from earlier rain.

"Please," the peddler said. "And it won't cost you anything; today it's free. Just take it, use it before the stag dinner. And don't use the amphetamines; they're a thalamic stimulant, contra-indicated whenever an adrenal suppressant such as a phenothiazine is—"

The door of the cab closed after Chien. He seated himself.

"Where to, comrade?" the robot drive-mechanism inquired.

He gave the ident tag number of his conapt.

"That half-wit of a peddler managed to infiltrate his seedy wares into my clean interior," the cab said. "Notice; it reposes by your foot."

He saw the packet—no more than an ordinary-looking envelope. I guess, he thought, this is how drugs come to you; all of a sudden they're lying there. For a moment he sat, and then he picked it up.

As before, there was a written enclosure above and beyond the medication, but this time, he saw, it was handwritten. A feminine script: from Miss Lee:

We were surprised at the suddenness. But thank heaven we were ready. Where were you Tuesday and Wednesday? Anyhow, here it is, and good luck. I will approach you later in the week; I don't want you to try to find me.

He ignited the note, burned it up in the cab's disposal ashtray. And kept the dark granules.

All this time, he thought. Hallucinogens in our water supply. Year after year. Decades. And not in wartime but in peacetime. And not to the enemy camp but here in our own. The evil bastards, he said to himself. Maybe I ought to take this; maybe I ought to find out what he or it is and let Tanya's group know.

I will, he decided. And—he was curious.

A bad emotion, he knew. Curiosity was, especially in Party activities, often a terminal state careerwise.

A state which, at the moment, gripped him thoroughly. He wondered if it would last through the evening, if, when it came right down to it, he would actually take the inhalant.

Time would tell. Tell that and everything else. We are blooming flowers, he thought, on the plain, which he picks. As the Arabic poem had put it. He tried to remember the rest of the poem but could not.

That probably was just as well.

The villa protocol officer, a Japanese named Kimo Okubara, tall and husky, obviously a quondam wrestler, surveyed him with innate hostility, even after he presented his engraved invitation and had successfully managed to prove his identity.

"Surprise you bother to come," Okubara muttered. "Why not stay home and watch on TV? Nobody miss you. We got along fine without up to right now."

Chien said tightly, "I've already watched on TV." And anyhow the stag dinners were rarely televised; they were too bawdy.

Okubara's crew double-checked him for weapons, including the possibility of an anal suppository, and then gave him his clothes back. They did not find the phenothiazine, however. Because he had already taken it. The effects of such a drug, he knew, lasted approximately four hours; that would be more than enough. And, as Tanya had said, it was a major dose; he felt sluggish and inept and dizzy, and his tongue moved in spasms of pseudo Parkinsonism—an unpleasant side effect which he had failed to anticipate.

A girl, nude from the waist up, with long coppery hair down her shoulders and back, walked by. Interesting.

Coming the other way, a girl nude from the bottom up made her appearance. Interesting too. Both girls looked vacant and bored, and totally self-possessed.

"You go in like that too," Okubara informed Chien.

Startled, Chien said, "I understood white tie and tails."

"Joke," Okubara said. "At your expense. Only girls wear nude; you even get so you enjoy, unless you homosexual."

Well, Chien thought, I guess I had better like it. He wandered on with the other guests—they, like him, wore white tie and tails or, if women, floor-length gowns—and felt ill at ease, despite the tranquilizing effect of the stelazine. Why am I here? he asked himself. The ambiguity of his situation did not escape him. He was here to advance his career in the Party apparatus, to obtain the intimate and personal nod of approval from His Greatness . . . and in addition he was here to decipher His Greatness as a fraud; he did not know what variety of fraud, but there it was: fraud against the Party, against all the peace-loving democratic peoples of Terra. Ironic, he thought. And continued to mingle.

A girl with small, bright, illuminated breasts approached him for a match; he absent-mindedly got out his lighter. "What makes your breasts glow?" he asked her. "Radioactive injections?"

She shrugged, said nothing, passed on, leaving him alone. Evidently he had responded in the incorrect way.

Maybe it's a wartime mutation, he pondered.

"Drink, sir." A servant graciously held out a tray; he accepted a martini—which was the current fad among the higher Party classes in People's China—and sipped the ice-cold dry flavor. Good English gin, he said to himself. Or possibly the original Holland compound; juniper or whatever they added. Not bad. He strolled on, feeling better; in actuality he found the atmosphere here a pleasant one. The people here were self-assured; they had been successful and now they could relax. It evidently was a myth that proximity to His Greatness produced neurotic anxiety: he saw no evidence here, at least, and felt little himself.

A heavy-set elderly man, bald, halted him by the simple means of holding his drink glass against Chien's chest. "That frably little one who asked you for a match," the elderly man said, and sniggered. "The quig with the Christmas-tree breasts—that was a boy, in drag." He giggled. "You have to be cautious around here."

"Where, if anywhere," Chien said, "do I find authentic women? In the white ties and tails?"

"Darn near," the elderly man said, and departed with a throng of hyperactive guests, leaving Chien alone with his martini.

A handsome, tall woman, well dressed, standing near Chien, suddenly put her hand on his arm; he felt her fingers tense and she said, "Here he comes. His Greatness. This is the first time for me; I'm a little scared. Does my hair look all right?"

"Fine," Chien said reflexively, and followed her gaze, seeking a glimpse—his first—of the Absolute Benefactor.

What crossed the room toward the table in the center was not a man.

And it was not, Chien realized, a mechanical construct either; it was not what he had seen on TV. That evidently was simply a device for speechmaking, as Mussolini had once used an artificial arm to salute long and tedious processions.

God, he thought, and felt ill. Was this what Tanya Lee had called the "aquatic horror" shape? It had no shape. Nor pseudopodia, either flesh or metal. It was, in a sense, not there at all; when he managed to look directly at it, the shape vanished; he saw through it, saw the people on the far side—but not it. Yet if he turned his head, caught it out of a sidelong glance, he could determine its boundaries.

It was terrible; it blasted him with its awfulness. As it moved it drained the life from each person in turn; it ate the people who had assembled, passed on, ate again, ate more with an endless appetite. It hated; he felt its hate. It loathed; he felt its loathing for everyone present—in fact he shared its loathing. All at once he and everyone else in the big villa were each a twisted slug, and over the fallen slug-carcases the creature savored, lingered, but all the time coming directly toward him—or was that an illusion? If this is a hallucination, Chien thought, it is the worst I have ever had; if it is not, then it is evil reality; it's an evil thing that kills and injures. He saw the trail of stepped-on, mashed men and women remnants behind it; he saw them trying to reassemble, to operate their crippled bodies; he heard them attempting speech.

I know who you are, Tung Chien thought to himself. You, the supreme head of the world-wide Party structure. You, who destroy whatever living object you touch; I see that Arabic poem, the searching for the flowers of life to eat them—I see you astride the plain which to you is Earth, plain without hills, without valleys. You go anywhere, appear any time, devour anything; you engineer life and then guzzle it, and you enjoy that.

He thought, You are God.

"Mr. Chien," the voice said, but it came from inside his head, not from the mouthless spirit that fashioned itself directly before him. "It is good to meet you again. You know nothing. Go away. I have no interest in you. Why should I care about slime? Slime; I am mired in it, I must excrete it, and I choose to. I could break you; I can break even myself. Sharp stones are under me; I spread sharp pointed things upon the mire. I make the hiding places, the deep places, boil like a pot; to me the sea is like a pot of ointment. The flakes of my flesh are joined to everything. You are me. I am you. It makes no difference, just as it makes no difference whether the creature with ignited breasts is a girl or boy; you could learn to enjoy either." It laughed.

He could not believe it was speaking to him; he could not imagine—it was too terrible—that it had picked him out.

"I have picked everybody out," it said. "No one is too small; each falls and dies and I am there to watch. I don't need to do anything but watch; it is automatic; it was arranged that way." And then it ceased talking to him; it disjoined itself. But he still saw it; he felt its manifold presence. It was a globe which hung in the room, with fifty thousand eyes, with a million eyes—billions: an eye for each living thing as it waited for each thing to fall, and then stepped on the living thing as it lay in a broken state. Because of this it had created the things, and he knew; he understood. What had seemed in the Arabic poem to be death was not death but God; or rather God was death, it was one force, one hunter, one cannibal thing, and it missed again and again but, having all eternity, it could afford to miss. Both poems, he realized; the Dryden one too. The crumbling; that is our world and you are doing it. Warping it to come out that way; bending us.

But at least, he thought, I still have my dignity. With dignity he set down his drink glass, turned, walked toward the doors of the room. He passed through the doors. He walked down a long carpeted hall. A villa servant dressed in purple opened a door for him; he found himself standing out in the night darkness, on a veranda, alone.

Not alone.

It had followed after him. Or it had already been here before him; yes, it had been expecting. It was not really through with him.

"Here I go," he said, and made a dive for the railing; it was six stories down, and there below gleamed the river, and death, real death, not what the Arabic poem had seen.

As he tumbled over, it put an extension of itself on his shoulder.

"Why?" he said. But, in fact, he paused. Wondering. Not understanding, not at all.

"Don't fall on my account," it said. He could not see it because it had moved behind him. But the piece of it on his shoulder—it had begun to look to him like a human hand.

And then it laughed.

"What's funny?" he demanded, as he teetered on the railing, held back by its pseudo-hand.

"You're doing my task for me," it said. "You aren't waiting; don't you have time to wait? I'll select you out from among the others; you don't need to speed the process up."

"What if I do?" he said. "Out of revulsion for you?"

It laughed. And didn't answer.

"You won't even say," he said.

Again no answer. He started to slide back, onto the veranda. And at once the pressure of its pseudo-hand lifted.

"You founded the Party?" he asked.

"I founded everything. I founded the anti-Party and the Party that isn't a Party, and those who are for it and those who are against, those that you call Yankee Imperialists, those in the camp of reaction, and so on endlessly. I founded it all. As if they were blades of grass."

"And you're here to enjoy it?" he said.

"What I want," it said, "is for you to see me, as I am, as you have seen me, and then trust me."

"What?" he said, quavering. "Trust you to what?"

It said, "Do you believe in me?"

"Yes," he said. "I can see you."

"Then go back to your job at the Ministry. Tell Tanya Lee that you saw an overworked, overweight, elderly man who drinks too much and likes to pinch girls' rear ends."

"Oh, Christ," he said.

"As you live on, unable to stop, I will torment you," it said. "I will deprive you, item by item, of everything you possess or want. And then when you are crushed to death I will unfold a mystery."

"What's the mystery?"

"The dead shall live, the living die. I kill what lives; I save what has died. And I will tell you this: *there are things worse than I.* But you won't meet them because by then I will have killed you. Now walk back into the dining room and prepare for dinner. Don't question what I'm doing; I did it long before there was a Tung Chien and I will do it long after."

He hit it as hard as he could.

And experienced violent pain in his head.

And darkness, with the sense of falling.

After that, darkness again. He thought, I will get you. I will see that you die too. That you suffer; you're going to suffer, just like us, exactly in every way we do. I'll dedicate my life to that; I'll confront you again, and I'll nail you; I swear to god I'll nail you up somewhere. And it will hurt. As much as I hurt now.

He shut his eyes.

Roughly, he was shaken. And heard Mr. Kimo Okubara's voice. "Get to your feet, common drunk. Come on!"

Without opening his eyes he said, "Get me a cab."

"Cab already waiting. You go home. Disgrace. Make a violent scene out of yourself."

Getting shakily to his feet, he opened his eyes, examined himself. Our Leader whom we follow, he thought, is the One True God. And the enemy whom we fight and have fought is God too. They are right; he is everywhere. But I didn't understand what that meant. Staring at the protocol officer, he thought, You are God too. So there is no getting away, probably not even by jumping. As I started, instinctively, to do. He shuddered.

"Mix drinks with drugs," Okubara said witheringly. "Ruin career. I see it happen many times. Get lost."

Unsteadily, he walked toward the great central door of the Yangtze River villa; two servants, dressed like medieval knights, with crested plumes, ceremoniously opened the door for him and one of them said, "Good night, sir."

"Up yours," Chien said, and passed out into the night.

At a quarter to three in the morning, as he sat sleepless in the living room of his conapt, smoking one Cuesta Rey Astoria after another, a knock sounded at the door.

When he opened it he found himself facing Tanya Lee in her trenchcoat, her face pinched with cold. Her eyes blazed, questioningly.

"Don't look at me like that," he said roughly. His cigar had gone out; he relit it. "I've been looked at enough," he said.

"You saw it," she said.

He nodded.

She seated herself on the arm of the couch and after a time she said, "Want to tell me about it?"

"Go as far from here as possible," he said. "Go a long way." And then he remembered; no way was long enough. He remembered reading that too. "Forget it," he said; rising to his feet, he walked clumsily into the kitchen to start up the coffee.

Following after him, Tanya said, "Was—it that bad?"

"We can't win," he said. "You can't win; I don't mean me. I'm not in this; I just want to do my job at the Ministry and forget about it. Forget the whole damned thing."

"Is it non-terrestrial?"

"Yes." He nodded.

"Is it hostile to us?"

"Yes," he said. "No. Both. Mostly hostile."

"Then we have to—"

"Go home," he said, "and go to bed." He looked her over carefully; he had sat a long time and he had done a great deal of thinking. About a lot of things. "Are you married?" he said.

"No. Not now. I used to be."

He said, "Stay with me tonight. The rest of tonight, anyhow. Until the sun comes up." He added, "The night part is awful."

"I'll stay," Tanya said, unbuckling the belt of her raincoat, "but I have to have some answers."

"What did Dryden mean," Chien said, "about music untuning the sky? I don't get that. What does music do to the sky?"

"All the celestial order of the universe ends," she said as she hung her raincoat up in the closet of the bedroom; under it she wore an orange striped sweater and stretchpants.

He said, "And that's bad."

Pausing, she reflected. "I don't know. I guess so."

"It's a lot of power," he said, "to assign to music."

"Well, you know that old Pythagorean business about the 'music of the spheres.'" Matter-of-factly she seated herself on the bed and removed her slipperlike shoes.

"Do you believe in that?" he said. "Or do you believe in God?"

"'God'!" She laughed. "That went out with the donkey steam engine. What are you talking about? God, or god?" She came over close beside him, peering into his face.

"Don't look at me so closely," he said sharply, drawing back. "I don't ever want to be looked at again." He moved away, irritably.

"I think," Tanya said, "that if there is a God He has very little interest in human affairs. That's my theory, anyhow. I mean, He doesn't seem to care if evil triumphs or people and animals get hurt and die. I frankly don't see Him anywhere around. And the Party has always denied any form of—"

"Did you ever see Him?" he asked. "When you were a child?"

"Oh, sure, as a child. But I also believed—"

"Did it ever occur to you," Chien said, "that good and evil are names for the same thing? That God could be both good and evil at the same time?"

"I'll fix you a drink," Tanya said, and padded barefoot into the kitchen.

Chien said, "The Crusher. The Clanker. The Gulper and the Bird and the Climbing Tube—plus other names, forms, I don't know. I had a hallucination. At the stag dinner. A big one. A terrible one."

"But the stelazine—"

"It brought on a worse one," he said.

"Is there any way," Tanya said somberly, "that we can fight this thing you saw? This apparition you call a hallucination but which very obviously was not?"

He said, "Believe in it."

"What will that do?"

"Nothing," he said wearily. "Nothing at all. I'm tired; I don't want a drink—let's just go to bed."

"Okay." She padded back into the bedroom, began pulling her striped sweater over her head. "We'll discuss it more thoroughly later."

"A hallucination," Chien said, "is merciful. I wish I had it; I want mine back. I want to be before your peddler got to me with that phenothiazine."

"Just come to bed. It'll be toasty. All warm and nice."

He removed his tie, his shirt—and saw, on his right shoulder, the mark, the stigma, which it had left when it stopped him from jumping. Livid marks which looked as if they would never go away. He put his pajama top on, then; it hid the marks.

"Anyhow," Tanya said as he got into the bed beside her, "your career is immeasurably advanced. Aren't you glad about that?"

"Sure," he said, nodding sightlessly in the darkness. "Very glad."

"Come over against me," Tanya said, putting her arms around him. "And forget everything else. At least for now."

He tugged her against him, then, doing what she asked and what he wanted to do. She was neat; she was swiftly active; she was successful and she did her part. They did not bother to speak until at last she said, "Oh!" And then she relaxed.

"I wish," he said, "that we could go on forever."

"We did," Tanya said. "It's outside of time; it's boundless, like an ocean. It's the way we were in Cambrian times, before we migrated up onto the land; it's the ancient primary waters. This is the only time we get to go back, when this is done. That's why it means so much. And in those days we weren't separate; it was like a big jelly, like those blobs that float up on the beach."

"Float up," he said, "and are left there to die."

"Could you get me a towel?" Tanya asked. "Or a washcloth? I need it."

He padded into the bathroom for a towel. There—he was naked, now—he once more saw his shoulder, saw where it had seized hold of him and held on, dragged him back, possibly to toy with him a little more.

The marks, unaccountably, were bleeding.

He sponged the blood away. More oozed forth at once and, seeing that, he wondered how much time he had left. Probably only hours.

Returning to bed, he said, "Could you continue?"

"Sure. If you have any energy left; it's up to you." She lay gazing up at him unwinkingly, barely visible in the dim nocturnal light.

"I have," he said. And hugged her to him.

AFTERWORD:

I don't advocate any of the ideas in "Faith of Our Fathers"; I don't, for example, claim that the Iron Curtain countries will win the cold war—or morally ought to. One theme in the story, however, seems compelling to me, in view of recent experiments with hallucinogenic drugs: the theological experience, which so many who have taken LSD have reported. This appears to me to be a true new frontier; to a certain extent the religious experience can now be scientifically studied ... and, what is more, may be viewed as part hallucination but containing other, real components. God, as a topic in science fiction, when it appeared at all, used to be treated polemically, as in "Out of the Silent Planet." But I prefer to treat it as intellectually exciting. What if, through psychedelic drugs, the religious experience becomes commonplace in the life of intellectuals? The old atheism, which seemed to many of us—including me—valid in terms of our experiences, or rather lack of experiences, would have to step momentarily aside. Science fiction, always probing what is about to be thought, become, must eventually tackle without preconceptions a future neo-mystical society in which theology constitutes as major a force as in the medieval period. This is not necessarily a backward step, because now these beliefs can be tested—forced to put up or shut up. I, myself, have no real beliefs about God; only my experience that He is present ... subjectively, of course; but the inner realm is real too. And in a science fiction story one projects what has been a personal inner experience into a milieu; it becomes socially shared, hence discussable. The last word, however, on the subject of God may have already been said: in A.D. 840 by John Scotus Erigena at the court of the Frankish king Charles the Bald. "We do not know what God is. God Himself does not know what He is because He is not anything. Literally God *is not*, because He transcends being." Such a penetrating—and Zen—mystical view, arrived at so long ago, will be hard to top; in my own experiences with psychedelic drugs I have had precious tiny illumination compared with Erigena.

The Ghost of a Model T

Clifford D. Simak

Clifford D. Simak (1904–1988) wrote more than twenty-five novels and dozens of short stories during his writing career. While he was writing science fiction, he was also a newspaper editor and columnist for papers such as the Minneapolis Star Tribune. *He wrote an acclaimed series of nonfiction works as well, including* Prehistoric Man, The Solar System, *and* Trilobite. *His fiction often centered about nonhuman beings; whether they be aliens or animals with enhanced intelligence, these creatures usually contained qualities his human protagonists lacked, such as compassion and honor. His best works include* City, Cosmic Engineers, They Walked Like Men, *and* A Heritage of Stars.

HE WAS WALKING HOME WHEN HE HEARD THE MODEL T AGAIN. IT WAS not a sound that he could well mistake, and it was not the first time he had heard it running, in the distance, on the road. Although it puzzled him considerably, for so far as he knew, no one in the country had a Model T. He'd read somewhere, in a paper more than likely, that old cars, such as Model T's, were fetching a good price, although why this should be, he couldn't figure out. With all the smooth, sleek cars that there were today, who in their right mind would want a Model T? But there was no accounting, in these crazy times, for what people did. It wasn't like the old days, but the old days were long gone, and a man had to get along the best he could with the way that things were now.

Brad had closed up the beer joint early, and there was no place to go but home, although since Old Bounce had died he rather dreaded to go home. He certainly did miss Bounce, he told himself; they'd got along just fine, the two of them, for more than twenty years, but now, with the old dog gone, the house was a lonely place and had an empty sound.

He walked along the dirt road out at the edge of town, his feet scuffing in the dust and kicking at the clods. The night was almost as light as day, with a full moon above the treetops. Lonely cricket noises were heralding summer's end. Walking along, he got to remembering the Model T he'd had when he'd been a young sprout, and how he'd spent hours out in the old machine shed tuning it up, although, God knows, no Model T ever really needed tuning. It was about as simple a piece of mechanism as anyone could want, and despite some technological cantankerousness, about as faithful a car as ever had been built. It got you there and got you back, and that was all, in those days, that anyone could ask. Its fenders rattled, and its hard tires bounced, and it could be balky on a hill, but if you knew how to handle it and mother it along, you never had no trouble.

Those were the days, he told himself, when everything had been as simple as a Model T. There were no income taxes (although, come to think of it, for him, personally, income taxes had never been a problem), no social security that took part of your wages, no licensing this and that, no laws that said a beer joint had to close at a certain hour. It had been easy, then, he thought; a man just fumbled along the best way he could, and there was no one telling him what to do or getting in his way.

The sound of the Model T, he realized, had been getting louder all the time, although he had been so busy with his thinking that he'd paid no real attention to it. But now, from the sound of it, it was right behind him, and although he knew it must be his imagination, the sound was so natural and so close that he jumped to one side of the road so it wouldn't hit him.

It came up beside him and stopped, and there it was, as big as life, and nothing wrong with it. The front-right-hand door (the only door in front, for there was no door on the left-hand side) flapped open—just flapped open by itself, for there was no one in the car to open it. The door flapping open didn't surprise him any, for to his recollection, no one who owned a Model T ever had been able to keep that front door closed. It was held only by a simple latch, and every time the car bounced (and there was seldom a time it wasn't bouncing, considering the condition of the roads in those days, the hardness of the tires, and the construction of the springs)—every time the car bounced, that damn front door came open.

This time, however—after all these years—there seemed to be something special about how the door came open. It seemed to be a sort of invitation, the car coming to a stop and the door not just sagging open, but coming open with a flourish, as if it were inviting him to step inside the car.

So he stepped inside of it and sat down on the right-front seat, and as soon as he was inside, the door closed and the car began rolling down the road. He started moving over to get behind the wheel, for there was no one driving it, and a curve was coming up, and the car needed someone to steer it around the curve. But before he could move over and get his hands upon the wheel, the car began to take the curve as neatly as it would have with someone driving it. He sat astonished and did not touch the wheel, and it went around the curve without even hesitating, and beyond the curve was a long, steep hill, and the engine labored mightily to achieve the speed to attack the hill.

The funny thing about it, he told himself, still half-crouched to take the wheel and still not touching it, was that he knew this road by heart, and there was no curve or hill on it. The road ran straight for almost three miles before it joined the River Road, and there was not a curve or kink in it, and certainly no hill. But there had been a curve, and there was a hill, for the car laboring up it quickly lost its speed and had to shift to low.

Slowly he straightened up and slid over to the right-hand side of the seat, for it was quite apparent that this Model T, for whatever reason, did not need a driver—perhaps did better with no driver. It seemed to know where it was going, and he told himself, this was more than he knew, for the country, while vaguely familiar, was not the country that lay about the little town of Willow Bend. It was rough and hilly country, and Willow Bend lay on a flat, wide flood plain of the river, and there were no hills and no rough ground until you reached the distant bluffs that stood above the valley.

He took off his cap and let the wind blow through his hair, and there was nothing to stop the wind, for the top of the car was down. The car gained the top of the hill and started going down, wheeling carefully back and forth down the switchbacks that followed the contour of the hill. Once it started down, it shut off the ignition somehow, just the way he used to do, he remembered, when he drove his Model T. The cylinders slapped and slobbered prettily, and the engine cooled.

As the car went around a looping bend that curved above a deep, black hollow that ran between the hills, he caught the fresh, sweet scent of fog, and that scent woke old memories in him, and if he'd not known differently, he would have thought he was back in the country of his young manhood. For in the wooded hills where he'd grown up, fog came creeping up a valley of a summer evening, carrying with it the smells of cornfields and of clover pastures and many other intermingled scents abstracted from a fat and fertile land. But it could not be, he knew, the country of his early years, for that country lay far off and was not to be reached in less than an hour of travel. Although he was somewhat puzzled by exactly where he could be, for it did not seem the kind of country that could be found within striking distance of the town of Willow Bend.

The car came down off the hill and ran blithely up a valley road. It passed a farmhouse huddled up against the hill, with two lighted windows gleaming, and off to one side the shadowy shapes of barn and henhouse. A dog came out and barked at them. There had been no other houses, although, far off, on the opposite hills, he had seen a pinpoint of light here and there and was sure that they were farms. Nor had they met any other cars, although, come to think of it, that was not so strange, for out here in the farming country there were late chores to do, and bedtime came early for people who were out at the crack of dawn. Except on weekends, there'd not be much traffic on a country road.

The Model T swung around a curve, and there, up ahead, was a garish splash of light, and as they came closer, music could be heard. There was about it all an old familiarity that nagged at him, but as yet he could not tell why it seemed familiar. The Model T slowed and turned in at the splash of light, and now it was clear that the light came from a dance pavilion. Strings of bulbs ran across its front, and other lights were mounted on tall poles in the parking area. Through the lighted windows he could see the dancers; and the music, he realized, was the kind of music he'd not heard for more than half a century. The Model T ran smoothly into a parking spot beside a Maxwell touring car. A Maxwell touring car, he thought with some surprise. There hadn't been a Maxwell on the road for years. Old Virg once had owned a Maxwell, at the same time he had owned his Model T. Old Virg, he thought. So many years ago. He tried to recall Old Virg's last name, but it wouldn't come to him. Of late, it seemed, names were often hard to come by. His name had been Virgil, but his friends always called him Virg. They'd been together quite a lot, the two of them, he remembered, running off to dances, drinking moonshine whiskey, playing pool, chasing girls—all the things that young sprouts did when they had the time and money.

He opened the door and got out of the car, the crushed gravel of the parking lot crunching underneath his feet; and the crunching of the gravel triggered the recognition of the place, supplied the reason for the familiarity that had first eluded him. He stood stock-still, half-frozen at the knowledge, looking at the ghostly leafiness of the towering elm trees that grew to either side of the dark bulk of the pavilion. His eyes took in the contour of the looming hills, and he recognized the contour, and standing there, straining for the sound, he heard the gurgle of the rushing water that came out of the hill, flowing through a wooden channel into a wayside watering trough that was now falling apart with neglect, no longer needed since the automobile had taken over from the horse-drawn vehicles of some years before.

He turned and sat down weakly on the running board of the Model T. His eyes could not deceive him or his ears betray him. He'd heard the distinctive sound of that running water too often in years long past to mistake it now; and the loom of the elm trees, the contour of the hills, the graveled parking lot, the string of bulbs on the pavilion's front, taken all together, could only mean that somehow he had returned or been returned, to Big Spring Pavilion. But that, he told himself, was fifty years or more ago, when I was lithe and young, when Old Virg had his Maxwell and I my Model T.

He found within himself a growing excitement that surged above the wonder and the sense of absurd impossibility—an excitement that was as puzzling as the place itself and his being there again. He rose and walked across the parking lot, with the coarse gravel rolling and sliding and crunching underneath his feet, and there was a strange lightness in his body, the kind of youthful lightness he had not known for years, and as the music came welling out at him, he found that he was gliding and turning to the music. Not the kind of music the kids played nowadays, with all the racket amplified by electronic contraptions, not the grating, no-rhythm junk that set one's teeth on edge and turned the morons glassy-eyed, but music with a beat to it, music you could dance to with a certain haunting quality that was no longer heard. The saxophone sounded clear, full-throated; and a sax, he told himself, was an instrument all but forgotten now. But it was here, and the music to go with it, and the bulbs above the door swaying in the little breeze that came drifting up the valley.

He was halfway through the door when he suddenly remembered that the pavilion was not free, and he was about to get some change out of his pocket (what little there was left after all those beers he'd had at Brad's) when he noticed the inky marking of the stamp on the back of his right hand. That had been the way, he remembered, that they'd marked you as having paid your way into the pavilion, a stamp placed on your hand. He showed his hand with its inky marking to the man who stood beside the door and went on in. The pavilion was bigger than he'd remembered it. The band sat on a raised platform to one side, and the floor was filled with dancers.

The years fell away, and it all was as he remembered it. The girls wore pretty dresses; there was not a single one who was dressed in jeans. The boys wore ties and jackets, and there was a decorum and a jauntiness that he had forgotten. The man who played the saxophone stood up, and the sax wailed in lonely melody, and there was a magic in the place that he had thought no longer could exist.

He moved out into the magic. Without knowing that he was

about to do it, surprised when he found himself doing it, he was out on the floor, dancing by himself, dancing with all the other dancers, sharing in the magic—after all the lonely years, a part of it again. The beat of the music filled the world, and all the world drew in to center on the dance floor, and although there was no girl and he danced all by himself, he remembered all the girls he had ever danced with.

Someone laid a heavy hand on his arm, and someone else was saying, "Oh, for Christ's sake, leave the old guy be; he's just having fun like all the rest of us." The heavy hand was jerked from his arm, and the owner of the heavy hand went staggering out across the floor, and there was a sudden flurry of activity that could not be described as dancing. A girl grabbed him by the hand. "Come on, Pop," she said, "let's get out of here." Someone else was pushing at his back to force him in the direction that the girl was pulling, and then he was out-of-doors. "You better get on your way, Pop," said a young man. "They'll be calling the police. Say, what is your name? Who are you?"

"I am Hank," he said. "My name is Hank, and I used to come here. Me and Old Virg. We came here a lot. I got a Model T out in the lot if you want a lift."

"Sure, why not," said the girl. "We are coming with you."

He led the way, and they came behind him, and all piled in the car, and there were more of them than he had thought there were. They had to sit on one another's laps to make room in the car. He sat behind the wheel, but he never touched it, for he knew the Model T would know what was expected of it, and of course it did. It started up and wheeled out of the lot and headed for the road.

"Here, Pop," said the boy who sat beside him, "have a snort. It ain't the best there is, but it's got a wallop. It won't poison you; it ain't poisoned any of the rest of us."

Hank took the bottle and put it to his lips. He tilted up his head and let the bottle gurgle. And if there'd been any doubt before of where he was, the liquor settled all the doubt. For the taste of it was a taste that could never be forgotten. Although it could not be remembered, either. A man had to taste it once again to remember it.

He took down the bottle and handed it to the one who had given it to him. "Good stuff," he said.

"Not good," said the young man, "but the best that we could get. These bootleggers don't give a damn what they sell you. Way to do it is to make them take a drink before you buy it, then watch them for a while. If they don't fall down dead or get blind staggers, then it's safe to drink."

Reaching from the back seat of the car, one of them handed him a saxophone. "Pop, you look like a man who could play this thing," said one of the girls, "so give us some music."

"Where'd you get this thing?" asked Hank.

"We got it off the band," said a voice from the back. "That joker who was playing it had no right to have it. He was just abusing it."

Hank put it to his lips and fumbled at the keys, and all at once the instrument was making music. And it was funny, he thought, for until right now he'd never held any kind of horn. He had no music in him. He'd tried a mouth organ once, thinking it might help to pass away the time, but the sounds that had come out of it had set Old Bounce to howling. So he'd put it up on a shelf and had forgotten it till now.

The Model T went tooling down the road, and in a little time the pavilion was left behind. Hank tootled on the saxophone, astonishing himself at how well he played, while the others sang and passed around the bottle. There were no other cars on the road, and soon the Model T climbed a hill out of the valley and ran along a ridgetop, with all the countryside below a silver dream flooded by the moonlight.

Later on, Hank wondered how long this might have lasted, with the car running through the moonlight on the ridgetop, with him playing the saxophone, interrupting the music only when he laid aside the instrument to have another drink of moon. But when he tried to think of it, it seemed it had gone on forever, with the car eternally running in the moonlight, trailing behind it the wailing and the honking of the saxophone.

He woke to night again. The same full moon was shining, although the Model T had pulled off the road and was parked beneath a tree, so that the full strength of the moonlight did not fall upon him. He worried rather feebly if this might be the same night or a different night, and there was no way for him to tell, although, he told himself, it didn't make much difference. So long as the moon was shining and he had the Model T and a road for it to run on, there was nothing more to ask, and which night it was had no consequence.

The young people who had been with him were no longer there, but the saxophone was laid upon the floorboards, and when he pulled himself erect, he heard a gurgle in his pocket, and upon investigation, pulled out the moonshine bottle. It still was better than half-full, and from the amount of drinking there had been done, that seemed rather strange.

He sat quietly behind the wheel, looking at the bottle in his hand, trying to decide if he should have a drink. He decided that he shouldn't, and put the bottle back into his pocket, then reached down and got the saxophone and laid it on the seat beside him.

The Model T stirred to life, coughing and stuttering. It inched forward, somewhat reluctantly, moving from beneath the tree, heading in a broad sweep for the road. It reached the road and went bumping down it. Behind it a thin cloud of dust, kicked up by its wheels, hung silver in the moonlight.

Hank sat proudly behind the wheel, being careful not to touch it. He folded his hands in his lap and leaned back. He felt good—the best he'd ever felt. Well, maybe not the best, he told himself, for back in the time of youth, when he was spry and limber and filled with the juice of hope, there might have been some times when he felt as good as he felt now. His mind went back, searching for the times when he'd felt as good, and out of olden memory came another time, when he'd drunk just enough to give himself an edge, not as yet verging into drunkenness, not really wanting any more to drink, and he'd stood on the gravel of the Big Spring parking lot, listening to the music before going in, with the bottle tucked inside his shirt, cold against his belly. The day had been a scorcher, and he'd been working in the hayfield, but now the night was cool, with fog creeping up the valley, carrying that indefinable scent of the fat and fertile land; and inside, the music playing, and a waiting girl who would have an eye out for the door, waiting for the moment he came in.

It had been good, he thought, that moment snatched out of the maw of time, but no better than this moment, with the car running on the ridgetop road and all the world laid out in moonlight. Different, maybe, in some ways, but no better than this moment.

The road left the ridgetop and went snaking down the bluff face, heading for the valley floor. A rabbit hopped across the road, caught for a second in the feeble headlights. High in the nighttime sky, invisible, a bird cried out, but that was the only sound there was, other than the thumping and the clanking of the Model T.

The car went skittering down the valley, and here the moonlight often was shut out by the woods that came down close against the road.

Then it was turning off the road, and beneath its tires he heard the crunch of gravel, and ahead of him loomed a dark and crouching shape. The car came to a halt, and sitting rigid in the seat, Hank knew where he was.

The Model T had returned to the dance pavilion, but the magic was all gone. There were no lights, and it was deserted. The parking lot was empty. In the silence, as the Model T shut off its engine, he heard the gushing of the water from the hillside spring running into the watering trough.

Suddenly he felt cold and apprehensive. It was lonely here,

lonely as only an old remembered place can be when all its life is gone. He stirred reluctantly and climbed out of the car, standing beside it, with one hand resting on it, wondering why the Model T had come here and why he'd gotten out.

A dark figure moved out from the front of the pavilion, an undistinguishable figure slouching in the darkness.

"That you, Hank?" a voice asked.

"Yes, it's me," said Hank.

"Christ," the voice asked, "where is everybody?"

"I don't know," said Hank. "I was here just the other night. There were a lot of people then."

The figure came closer. "You wouldn't have a drink, would you?" it asked.

"Sure, Virg," he said, for now he recognized the voice. "Sure, I have a drink."

He reached into his pocket and pulled out the bottle. He handed it to Virg. Virg took it and sat down on the running board. He didn't drink right away, but sat there cuddling the bottle.

"How you been, Hank?" he asked. "Christ, it's a long time since I seen you."

"I'm all right," said Hank. "I drifted up to Willow Bend and just sort of stayed there. You know Willow Bend?"

"I was through it once. Just passing through. Never stopped or nothing. Would have if I'd known you were there. I lost all track of you."

There was something that Hank had heard about Old Virg, and felt that maybe he should mention it, but for the life of him he couldn't remember what it was, so he couldn't mention it.

"Things didn't go so good for me," said Virg. "Not what I had expected. Janet up and left me, and I took to drinking after that and lost the filling station. Then I just knocked around from one thing to another. Never could get settled. Never could latch on to anything worthwhile."

He uncorked the bottle and had himself a drink.

"Good stuff," he said, handing the bottle back to Hank.

Hank had a drink, then sat down on the running board alongside Virg and set the bottle down between them.

"I had a Maxwell for a while," said Virg, "but I seem to have lost it. Forgot where I left it, and I've looked everywhere."

"You don't need your Maxwell, Virg," said Hank. "I have got this Model T."

"Christ, it's lonesome here," said Virg. "Don't you think it's lonesome?"

"Yes, it's lonesome. Here, have another drink. We'll figure what to do."

"It ain't good sitting here," said Virg. "We should get out among them."

"We'd better see how much gas we have," said Hank. "I don't know what's in the tank."

He got up and opened the front door and put his hand under the front seat, searching for the measuring stick. He found it and unscrewed the gas-tank cap. He began looking through his pockets for matches so he could make a light.

"Here," said Virg, "don't go lighting any matches near that tank. You'll blow us all to hell. I got a flashlight here in my back pocket. If the damn thing's working."

The batteries were weak, but it made a feeble light. Hank plunged the stick into the tank, pulled it out when it hit bottom, holding his thumb on the point that marked the topside of the tank. The stick was wet up almost to his thumb.

"Almost full," said Virg. "When did you fill it last?"

"I ain't never filled it."

Old Virg was impressed. "That old tin lizard," he said, "sure goes easy on the gas."

Hank screwed the cap back on the tank, and they sat down on the running board again, and each had another drink.

"It seems to me it's been lonesome for a long time now," said Virg. "Awful dark and lonesome. How about you, Hank?"

"I been lonesome," said Hank, "ever since Old Bounce up and died on me. I never did get married. Never got around to it. Bounce and me, we went everywhere together. He'd go up to Brad's bar with me and camp out underneath a table; then, when Brad threw us out, he'd walk home with me."

"We ain't doing ourselves no good," said Virg, "just sitting here and moaning. So let's have another drink, then I'll crank the car for you, and we'll be on our way."

"You don't need to crank the car," said Hank. "You just get into it, and it starts up by itself."

"Well, I be damned," said Virg. "You sure have got it trained."

They had another drink and got into the Model T, which started up and swung out of the parking lot, heading for the road.

"Where do you think we should go?" asked Virg. "You know of any place to go?"

"No, I don't," said Hank. "Let the car take us where it wants to. It will know the way."

Virg lifted the sax off the seat and asked, "Where'd this thing come from? I don't remember you could blow a sax."

"I never could before," said Hank. He took the sax from Virg and put it to his lips, and it wailed in anguish, gurgled with light-heartedness.

"I be damned," said Virg. "You do it pretty good."

The Model T bounced merrily down the road, with its fenders flapping and the windshield jiggling, while the magneto coils mounted on the dashboard clicked and clacked and chattered. All the while, Hank kept blowing on the sax and the music came out loud and true, with startled night birds squawking and swooping down to fly across the narrow swath of light.

The Model T went clanking up the valley road and climbed the hill to come out on a ridge, running through the moonlight on a narrow, dusty road between close pasture fences, with sleepy cows watching them pass by.

"I be damned," cried Virg, "if it isn't just like it used to be. The two of us together, running in the moonlight. Whatever happened to us, Hank? Where did we miss out? It's like this now, and it was like this a long, long time ago. Whatever happened to the years between? Why did there have to be any years between?"

Hank said nothing. He just kept blowing on the sax.

"We never asked for nothing much," said Virg. "We were happy as it was. We didn't ask for change. But the old crowd grew away from us. They got married and got steady jobs, and some of them got important. And that was the worst of all, when they got important. We were left alone. Just the two of us, just you and I, the ones who didn't want to change. It wasn't just being young that we were hanging on to. It was something else. It was a time that went with being young and crazy. I think we knew it somehow. And we were right, of course. It was never quite as good again."

The Model T left the ridge and plunged down a long, steep hill, and below them they could see a massive highway, broad and many-laned, with many car lights moving on it.

"We're coming to a freeway, Hank," said Virg. "Maybe we should sort of veer away from it. This old Model T of yours is a good car, sure, the best there ever was, but that's fast company down there."

"I ain't doing nothing to it," said Hank. "I ain't steering it. It is on its own. It knows what it wants to do."

"Well, all right, what the hell," said Virg, "we'll ride along with it. That's all right with me. I feel safe with it. Comfortable with it. I never felt so comfortable in all my goddamn life. Christ, I don't know what I'd done if you hadn't come along. Why don't you lay down that silly sax and have a drink before I drink it all."

So Hank laid down the sax and had a couple of drinks to make up for lost time, and by the time he handed the bottle back to Virg, the

Model T had gone charging up a ramp, and they were on the free-way. It went running gaily down its lane, and it passed some cars that were far from standing still. Its fenders rattled at a more rapid rate, and the chattering of the magneto coils was like machine-gun fire.

"Boy," said Virg admiringly, "see the old girl go. She's got life left in her yet. Do you have any idea, Hank, where we might be going?"

"Not the least," said Hank, picking up the sax again.

"Well, hell," said Virg, "it don't really matter, just so we're on our way. There was a sign back there a ways that said Chicago. Do you think we could be headed for Chicago?"

Hank took the sax out of his mouth. "Could be," he said. "I ain't worried over it."

"I ain't worried neither," said Old Virg. "Chicago, here we come! Just so the booze holds out. It seems to be holding out. We've been sucking at it regular, and it's still better than half-full."

"You hungry, Virg?" asked Hank.

"Hell, no," said Virg. "Not hungry, and not sleepy, either. I never felt so good in all my life. Just so the booze holds out and this heap hangs together."

The Model T banged and clattered, running with a pack of smooth, sleek cars that did not bang and clatter, with Hank playing on the sax-ophone and Old Virg waving the bottle high and yelling whenever the rattling old machine outdistanced a Lincoln or a Cadillac. The moon hung in the sky and did not seem to move. The freeway became a throughway, and the first toll booth loomed ahead.

"I hope you got change," said Virg. "Myself, I am cleaned out."

But no change was needed, for when the Model T came near, the toll-gate arm moved up and let it go thumping through without payment.

"We got it made," yelled Virg. "The road is free for us, and that's the way it should be. After all you and I been through, we got some-thing coming to us."

Chicago loomed ahead, off to their left, with night lights gleam-ing in the towers that rose along the lakeshore, and they went around it in a long, wide sweep, and New York was just beyond the fishhook bend as they swept around Chicago and the lower curve of the lake.

"I never saw New York," said Virg, "but seen pictures of Manhattan, and that can't be nothing but Manhattan. I never did know, Hank, that Chicago and Manhattan were so close together."

"Neither did I," said Hank, pausing from his tootling on the sax. "The geography's all screwed up for sure, but what the hell do we care? With this rambling wreck, the whole damn world is ours."

He went back to the sax, and the Model T kept rambling on.

They went thundering through the canyons of Manhattan and circumnavigated Boston and went on down to Washington, where the Washington Monument stood up high and Old Abe sat brooding on Potomac's shore.

They went on down to Richmond and skated past Atlanta and skimmed along the moon-drenched sands of Florida. They ran along old roads where trees dripped Spanish moss and saw the lights of Old N'Orleans way off to their left. Now they were heading north again, and the car was galumphing along a ridgetop with neat farming country all spread out below them. The moon still stood where it had been before, hanging at the selfsame spot. They were moving through a world where it was always three A.M.

"You know," said Virg, "I wouldn't mind if this kept on forever. I wouldn't mind if we never got to wherever we are going. It's too much fun getting there to worry where we're headed. Why don't you lay down that horn and have another drink? You must be getting powerful dry."

Hank put down the sax and reached out for the bottle. "You know, Virg," he said, "I feel the same way you do. It just don't seem there's any need for fretting about where we're going or what's about to happen. It don't seem that nothing could be better than right now."

Back there at the dark pavilion he'd remembered that there had been something he'd heard about Old Virg and had thought he should speak to him about, but couldn't, for the life of him, remember what it was. But now he'd remembered it, and it was of such slight importance that it seemed scarcely worth the mention.

The thing that he'd remembered was that good Old Virg was dead.

He put the bottle to his lips and had a drink, and it seemed to him he'd never had a drink that tasted half so good. He handed back the bottle and picked up the sax and tootled on it with high spirit while the ghost of the Model T went on rambling down the moonlit road.

The Demoness

Tanith Lee

Tanith Lee has made her reputation by successfully mixing science fiction, heroic fantasy, and fairy tales, often turning fantasy conventions upside down. Her examination of the ambiguities of moral behavior can be found in her novels Death's Master, Dark Dance, *and* Darkness, I. *A World Fantasy award–winner, she lives in London, England.*

SHE WAITED IN HER HIGH TOWER.

Day in, day out she waited.

The tower was white and stretched beneath her, far, far, to the sweep of the bleached dunes and the gray glister of the sea.

Her world was all gray, all white, half-tones, glitterings, without shape. A world colorless, and abstract. And she too was white, her foamy dress, her feet, her narrow hands—all white as the chalk hills that ran distantly above the sea. But her long, long hair was red, blood red, red as an eruption of magma out of the white volcanic crystal of her flesh. She did not look at her hair; obscurely she feared it. She bound it on her head in braids.

She was waiting, and not certain why she waited, or for whom, or for what.

She did not think of her past or her future, or really of any particular thing. She had no memory, or so it seemed, only an empty page from which words had faded. She watched the gulls dip in on the wind, screaking in their wind voices. She came out of the tower at certain times, and went in again at certain other times. Like a figure on a clock. She had no ambitions or yearnings, nor any hope. She was, in the sense that she existed. She was, but that was all.

Time passed, but time had no meaning. It might have been yesterday or tomorrow when she saw him.

He was riding up the beach in the dawn, a man in gold on a golden horse, its mane like blowing corn, scarlet reins and golden bells on them, its hooves striking up the sand. He dazzled her eyes. He wore a kind of armor that was either too antique or else too recent for her to recognize it. Tassels swung from his shoulders, his hair was ragged and bright like the ripped-out strings of a golden harp.

She felt a quickening as she leaned down from the length of the white tower. *Am I waiting for this man?* He was a burning ant on the beach, but soon he rode under the arch of the tower. An echo came, and then his feet loud on the stairs. She heard him pass through room after room, stopping sometimes. She imagined him examining certain things. But all the while he was drawing nearer. She turned to face the door through which he would come. Her heart beat. Without thinking, she reached up and let down her hair.

He stood still in the doorway looking at her. He was stern; she wanted to make him smile. He stared in her face.

"Where is Golbrant?" he asked her.

She put her hand to her mouth. She shook her head.

"He that passed by here, thirty days gone, riding to Krennok-dol. He that had a harp on his back and a scar like a cross on his brow."

She shook her head once more, and her heart beat fast and she put her hand on her throat and waited.

"Golbrant," he said, his eyes narrow and very bright, "my brother by vow, not blood. He to whom the Sisters said, 'Beware the white woman waiting for death in the tall tower by the sea.'"

He came forward and seized her by the hair, and twisted it around his hand until the pain filled her skull like a silver cloud.

"Where is Golbrant?" he hissed, and then he met her eyes.

This was how it was to her. His eyes were like a summer garden. She wanted to draw from them those vistas of amber shades and yellow darts of sun, she wanted those hopes, those ambitions and yearnings she saw in them to fill her emptiness, her darkness, with their purpose and their light. She was hungry and thirsty for his reflected life as the fish for water, the wings of the bird for air. And her eyes began to breathe, to drink like beasts at a pool, and she put out her hands to his neck and drew herself against the hard armor, and clung to him tight. He spat a curse at her, and tried to shake himself free of her hands, her eyes, but could not. There was a kind of pleasant deathly heaviness in her embrace, her gaze, like sleep, except where it filled and curdled in his loins. She drew him down. She drowned him in her eyes and her body. He swam in the current of her flesh, and the tide took him away, and he was lost in the tunnel of the pleasure she had to give him. Such pleasure it was no woman before or since had been, would be. It was the whole store of her pleasure, held for him. She was the jar that contained the oceans, the fountainhead; he strove to reach the source and cried aloud to reach it.

But at the last his body checked itself. Out of desire came a great numbness, and then a revulsion of the pale thing wriggling beneath him. He understood then what he would have given her along with the life that ran out of him.

And then he twisted aside. He pulled his body free, and he turned his head, shielding his eyes as if from a dreadful and consuming glare.

"So, what they said of you is true, white woman," he muttered in sick cold anger, more to his own self than to her. "You devour the brain's knowledge and the mind's reason with your look and your womb. Yes, I felt it leaving me, and I would be hollow after as the bone of marrow when the wolf has had it. Is this then how you dealt with Golbrant?"

Her gaze was darkening, dimming, going out. She lay on the ground. She did not understand. And yet there was a faint memory, a memory like a dream, of a man on a dark horse, dark-haired, with a harp on his back with a woman's face, and a jagged criss-cross above his eyes. She had waited for him too, she remembered now, and he had come, across the long rooms, up the stairs of the tower. But he had not flinched aside, the light had passed from him to her. She looked up at the man whom she had almost possessed, for she recollected now, abruptly, what it meant when she lay with men. It was neither a shock nor a surprise, and not abhorrent. It seemed natural, for what did she know of the natural order of things to make this one thing that was hers seem strange and dark and evil?

"He is dead," she said softly, an explanation only.

The golden man drew his sword, swung it to lop her head from her shoulders, but it was not the habit of the warriors of Krennok-dol to kill women, however great their anger. So he halted, and after a moment he sheathed the sword again.

"Live, vampire," he said, his eyes now blind with hate, "but never practice on a man again to take his wits, or I'll see your head on a pole yet."

It could make no sense to her; she was not quite human, human values and laws had no meaning. Yet she stared at him, and she loved him, because he had won free from her and had no need of her any more.

He strode from room to room, searching for his vow-brother, Golbrant, but Golbrant had staggered from room to room when his self and his sanity had gone from him, and had fallen down from the high place into the sea. The waves had carried him off like sour green vinegar dogs, and the vulture gulls had picked at him, and the fish, so that now he was ivory on the ocean floor, with no mark on him any more to say who he was, except the gold harp turning green in the sand at his side.

While the warrior searched, the woman followed him. She could not tell him where Golbrant had gone, could not remember, though no doubt he guessed. She stared at his back, stared at his face when he turned. Her love was all-devouring; she would have eaten him if she could. Her love was like that.

But he thrust her aside, and went down the stairs of the tower, away from her and away. He found the horse and rode it off up the sea road into the chalk stacks that margined the shore.

For three days she wandered in the tower. She did not bind up her long, long hair. She did not go out above the bleached strand. She was no longer waiting. Golbrant and all the other men who had sunk like ships in her deadly embrace, lost their wills and their minds in her eyes and her womb, were quite forgotten again, shadows at the back of her thoughts perhaps, no more. But him she remembered, the warrior on the grain-yellow horse, his narrow bright eyes, his flax hair, his anger and his going away.

On the dawn of the fourth day she went down the stairs of the tower, and out, and up the sea road after him.

She had never left the tower before, not in all her years since she had become what she was. There had been no desire before; now there was a compulsion.

The sun cracked open the gray sky, and the sun and her blowing hair were two bright dabs of scarlet in the colorless land she was leaving.

After some days the land changed color. It changed from white to black. Hills like black crouching crows stood guard on either side of the road. The sky was dark with storms. Now her feet were red as her hair because the sharp black tones bit them like snakes. She was one of those who had no need to eat or sleep, so she simply walked day and night. She followed the hoofprints of the horse, and sometimes here were droppings; here and there a piece of his cloak night have caught on brambles, or she would come to the cold ashes of a fire and run her fingers through them and ouch the ash with her tongue because he had lain by them or warmth when they were alive three nights before.

Then there was a black river in the twilight. There was a round blue moon overhead that looked almost transparent, and great clouds beating by like angry birds. And there was an old devil-woman crouched by the rushing water tending a bluish fire and a caldron of death over it. She was wrapped up in something black, only her eyes showed and her skinny hands stuck out, all bone. When she saw the white woman walking along the river bank she screamed out:

"Krennok-dol lies that way! That way! Over the river."

Then the devil-woman left her brew and went up to her, and turned her to look out across the river.

"No way for you to cross. The bridge is down—he did it, knowing you followed after. He was afraid, the horse leaped and struck sparks from its iron feet, knowing the vampire girl came behind them. I gave him a charm to protect him from you, but it will do him no good. Look at you, all hunger. Is this your love then, to follow a man who runs in terror, a man who hates you in his loins and sword arm? Didn't you drive to death his vow-brother, Golbrant the Good?" Here the devil-woman spat. "What is it makes you hurry after the sword stroke which is all he wants to give you?"

But the white woman was already wandering down the bank away from her, searching, searching for a place to cross, though there was none at all, and anyone could see it but her. The devil-woman ran after her, skipping like a ghastly black goat, for she had goat horns on her head, being what she was. She tapped the woman's shoulder.

"Do you know his name even? No. Well, there's too much of him in the world. If you want him, walk into the water and it'll carry you over, unless you're afraid to do it. A long search you will have, but when you find him, he will be yours. Only remember the price he pays for it. Witless he will be then, but what a joy to you—if you keep him from the tall crags and death. Like your child and your man, all in one, for ever and ever."

She heard, and though it was only a shadow on her thoughts, yet she understood. At the brink of the river the devil-woman whispered:

"If you let him go free, you will be dust, for a sword will strike off your head. Let nothing and no one come between. Remember."

Then she thrust with her bony hands, pushing the woman down into the water. The white woman had no fear. Her hair and her dress floated her up, the current bore her downstream, her hands trailed like drowned flowers, and she thought only of him she sought. All night, under the blue-ringed stars, the river pulled her between the hills by silver ropes. Near dawn it cast her up like a white fish-maid on the icy quays that lie below the dol hill.

Six or seven river fishermen found her. They thought she was a suicide and crossed themselves, but before they could run for the priest, she got up and walked away from them up the stone path to the hill, not seeing them.

The hill was green. Things grew on it that were not rank or poisonous in any way, and behind lay a forest. The land of Krennok was a land alive between the dead lands, north, south, east and west. High on the green hill the king's house stood, made of wood, stone and brass. Two hundred pillars upheld the roof in the king's great hall, pillars carved like trees of green marble. Fountains played and pools lay clear as glass, and white birds fluted in the gardens where round fruits grew in clusters under the yellow sky. This was Krennok-dol. At the great gate of bronze hung a bell the size of a warrior, with a tongue the size of a girl-child ten years old.

She had no means to strike the bell; it would take a tall man on a tall horse, striking with his sword, to do it. So she knocked, till her hands bled like her feet, on the bronze door panels.

It was the law in the king's hold that whoever came asking for mercy or justice, or any other kind of boon, should at least get a hearing from him. Consequently the porter came at last and let her in. Her dress and hair were still wet from the river, and she walked over the threshold trailing black river weed from her skirt. She frightened the porter a good deal.

She went up the great stairways into the hall with its forest of pillars. The king and his warriors had come from their dawn prayers, and were sitting eating and drinking at long tables. The king himself sat on his high seat of hammered gold, as he had sat three days before when a warrior came galloping from the sea with red-rimmed eyes and a horse frothing with fear. The king had risen to welcome and embrace him; he loved this warrior perhaps better than the rest, though possibly he had loved Golbrant the Good even more than this his Alondor, that women called the Gold behind their hands.

But Alondor held away from the king.

"There is a curse on me," he said. "God forbid I give it to you like a contagion."

He told them of Golbrant's death in the high tower by the sea. He reminded them of the Sisters, those five dark witches who had come to Krennok-dol five months ago to wail prophecies of death for five warriors. When he spoke of the woman in the tower and what he had done with her, he went white with shame. Later he made confession to the priest. The priest prayed hard, understanding very well what Alondor feared. Having lain with her but given nothing, having failed to kill her when he was able, he had left with her those powers of his pleasure and his hate he had renounced. And she had come after him, still came, relentless as winter with her cold white desire. If again he stood in her presence he knew he, in turn, would have no power. The succubus would entangle him and destroy him, draining his brain of its life. Such was the shadowy magic of her sexual vampirism, the oldest and most terrible of all the demons in the world. He had not known all this till he was three days on the road and sensed, by a prickling of his skin, a coldness and a frenzy in his loins, what followed and with what ability.

Alondor fled out of Krennok-dol a day before she came there.

As she stood in the king's hall, she looked about for him, and her heart beat. When she saw he was not there, a deadly misery made her falter. Yet only for a moment. Then, forgetting it, remembering only him, she turned to leave the king's house the way she had come.

The king sprang up with an oath and three warriors ran into her path. They raised their swords to strike her down, but again the old stigma caught at their hands. They had never killed or harmed a woman. It came hard to do it now. Then she walked by them with her pale blind eyes.

"Go after!" shouted the king. "Do as he should have done. Remember her foulness and her sorcery! Not a woman but a *thing* under your blades."

They followed her out. On the stairway one looked in her face. He shrank back and could do nothing. Farther down another reached her. He swung her about and the sword swung, but at the last instant she seemed so pitiful, only a poor madwoman.

This is some mistake! he cried to himself, and let her go in an agony of bewilderment.

The third ran for his horse. He followed her across the court, out of the gate, grinning with fury. It seemed to him he was out hunting; he heard the dogs snarling ahead and glimpsed the running white deer leaping down from the green dol hill. When he was near enough, he snatched her on the horse, and rode with her limp in one arm into the forest beyond the hill. There he flung her down and himself over her in an unbearable ecstasy of need. The sword he used on her was flesh, and soon she slid from under him and walked away, barely conscious of what he had done or had become. Days later the king's warriors found him, a wandering madman screaming for his hunting dogs under the thick-leafed boughs.

She walked through a year. For a year Alondor the Gold fled before her. He became a mercenary, hiring out his war skills to many kings whose causes seemed good. Never did he stay long in any one place. He dreamed of fear and lust, and of Golbrant, his vow-brother, whom he had loved better than any man or woman.

The seasons changed. Red leaves fell into her red hair and over her scarred, misused, unnoticed feet, also into the bloody battlefields

where he rode. Snows came and went, frost and rain. Beyond the
land of Krennok, in the gray dead lands with their twisted trees and
tall-spired mountains, he ran, she followed, drawn by instinct and
desire, seeing and hearing only him.

In the barren steeples of the north he came at last to the pile of a
solitary hold. It was dark and it was gloomy as were the crags
around it. A green moon watched as he hammered at the gates. He
was sick with the wound a battle two months before had given him,
and he was sick of himself and his compulsion to fly the unknown
thing which followed. He still had his looks; he was a man to be
stared at, but there were white strings in the gold harp hair now, and
his eyes ran back deep into his soul, the eyes of a murderer, a victim,
or a man possessed by devils. Such was the penalty of an unstruck
blow in a tower by the sea.

In a hall where flickering torches burned, he spoke with the lord
of the place, but a ringing noise came and went in his head. Finally,
from the corner of his eye, he saw a pale shape in the arch of a
door. From over the white face to the white shoulders and beyond
fell a bloodred curtain. He thought she had found him, she who
came after, and terror rose up in his belly and choked him, and
struck him, like all enemies, from behind. He fell down in the kind
of faint that is an outpost of death.

Yet the woman in the door was not the one he thought. She was
the daughter of the hold, her name Siandra, and she wore a scarlet
shawl over her head because the hall was cold. She was beautiful as
an icon. Her skin was white but her mouth was red, and her hair as
black as Golbrant's hair when he rode with the harp on his back
toward Krennok-dol. She might have been indeed a sister to Golbrant,
for she resembled him very curiously, but she knew nothing of the
warriors of the green-growing hill. She had her own kind of waiting,
did Sian. When she saw the gold-haired man with nightmares in his
eyes, she felt a quickening too. If he had chosen at that time to win
her love, he could have done nothing better than fall down like a
dead man a few yards from her feet.

She took it on herself to nurse him, and did not find it irksome
in the least. Opening his eyes on her face, he felt life turn for him
like a page.

Love grew up between them as easily as a child will grow.

As the spring drew on, a night came and took her with it into his
chamber. She brought sweetness with her, if not the full draught of
the cup. But then, he had known the pleasure of demons, and it was
almost good that with this human girl it must be less. Towards dawn
he kissed her and said:

"Tomorrow, Sian, I must be gone from you and here."

Tears filled her eyes. She thought the immemorial thought of the discarded.

"No," he said, "not for that. There is a doom on me. I am pursued. If I remain, I die."

"Then let me go with you," Siandra said.

"No. What gift of love is that from me to your sweet self, to make you wander the world homeless at my heels?" His face was pale and he had shut his eyes. "Let me go alone, and have your peace. There's none for me. I have already stayed too long."

If she was sweet, she was strong too, this girl in the north land. She took his hands fast and asked him for the truth, asked him again and again, until he thrust her from him as if he hated her, and told her everything, and then wept on her breast like a child.

"Let her come," Siandra whispered, and her eyes burned.

He was so tired. The year had tired him out. He stayed, for her woman's strength seemed more than any shield or sword in the wide world.

Nights passed. Spring lay on the land, but nothing grew save bright weeds at the door, and birds made nests in the crags of the mountains and the hold. Alondor was the lord's man now. He fought a battle for him and came back with the heads of enemies. The feast ran on into the dark, but for all the wine and meat, he felt a growing cold and uneasiness on him, like a fever coming.

In the close room he paced about while Siandra lay asleep. The moon rose late, the color of yellow bones, and he looked with a turmoil in his belly along the causeway, and saw something standing there, ice-white, holding back its blowing scarlet hair with long white narrow hands on which the nails had grown to talons. She had had no change of garment; her white clothes hung on her like the tatters of a shroud, her feet were carved over with scars. Her face looked up, yearning, her eyes like pools holding only his image. Her love had lasted, was still all-devouring; she would have eaten him if she could. Her love was like that.

Alondor fell on his knees and prayed, but no words came into his mind, only the woman. He felt her draw nearer and nearer across the rocky road, he felt her drift through the gates like white smoke, while the sentries dozed or did not see. He heard her soundless feet on the stairs, and how doors sprang silently wide at her touch.

Siandra woke and sat up in the bed. She looked at him crouching to pray, and heard how his prayers grew weaker and weaker.

She felt terror—*She* is here.

At that instant he got to his feet and the prayers left him altogether. He was a man deprived suddenly of everything—

except that one thing which drew him and drew him. Like an automaton, he turned and crossed the room, went out through the door, and his eyes were very bright, his cheeks flushed. He went cheerfully, eagerly, the blood hot as fire in him, lusting, forgetting, caught up in the spell of the white woman who waited, this time, below.

When he was on the stairs, Siandra slid from the bed. If he looked burning and alive, she looked like his death. She snatched up the sword he had left behind and walked trembling, yet soft as a cat, after him.

She was in the house, the woman from the high tower by the sea. She was in a passage, and sensing that now at last he came to her, she had stopped quite still. Her heart beat. She put up her hands to her hair to let it down; finding it loose, she let down her hands instead. She thought she was in the tower, but it had no meaning for her. She thought she heard the sound of the sea sweeping in against the shale beaches; perhaps it was the sound of her own blood, the tide of her moving in and out. A gull screaked, but it was a stair under his foot. Rounding a corner he came into sight for her. Her heart lifted in her body as if it had no weight or purpose except to lift in her like a bird. A warmth and gladness filled her up like the empty vessel she was, and for the first time since she had become what she was, her lips parted and she smiled. She held out her arms, and he was eager enough to come into them. He had forgotten.

But Siandra was just behind him, holding the sword. She also had the knowledge of old things, old ways—the oldest and most indisputable magic. Even as Alondor reached out to take his own death, Siandra ran between them. She lifted and swung the heavy sword as though it were a grass stem. She knew nothing of Krennok-dol and the warriors, and the chivalry of men who did no harm to a living thing with breasts and a womb, which called itself a woman. She struck for all she held dear and needful, with a selfish, careless, passionate stroke.

What she felt, the woman from the sea, was a long white pain, and then a long scarlet pain. Her head fell from her shoulders in an instant of time, but time had no meaning for her. Her agony lasted many ages. After the passing of these ages, she lay scattered, deaf, dumb, blind and in a million fragments. She knew what it is to be a million separate things, and still to be one.

Siandra shrank back against Alondor, looking away from what she had done, and he held to her, waking from the trance. She had been Golbrant, his vow-brother in that instant, rising out of the sea intact, green-gold harp on back, black hair strings on the strings of the harp, wielding the blow Golbrant had never thought to strike in the tower. This was how Sian finally took his love, more by becoming the past than by ending it.

While they held together, the white woman fell apart like the petals of a blossom. She blew up into their faces like white flour. She was dust as she had been promised she would be by the devil-woman in the blue moonlight. All dust.

The dust circled and pulsed, falling in on itself. Grains disbanded into grains, millions became millions upon millions. Soon there was no more of her to see, neither white nor red.

Yet she was aware. In every minuscule atom her hunger persisted, unassuaged.

Now she is blown here and there, endless varieties of place suck her down and fling her away. She is in everything, her hunger everywhere.

Long after Alondor and his Siandra will be dust of another sort, she will be blown about the world. Into the eyes to cause tears, into the fingernails of murderers, into the crannies of broken hearts to seal up the hurt with more hurting. She has no name. She is in every deed and dream and thought. She is all things and nothing. She is still waiting, and will wait forever, over every inch of the world.

Strangers come and go unharmed up and down the steps of the tall white tower. Gulls build in the ruins. One day every stone will have fallen bit by bit across the sweep of the bleached dunes and into the gray glister of the sea. One day the cliffs too will have fallen. After them, the land. The sea will shrink and drain away, the sky will tumble and the stars go out. And in that last or intermediary dark, she will remain. Still waiting.

Pity her.

Jeffty Is Five

Harlan Ellison

There is little Harlan Ellison has not done in the field of writing. He is the author of over a thousand short stories, essays, criticisms, plays, and tele-plays, and has been a constant force for excellence and experimentation in science fiction and fantasy. His works have pushed and often broken through the borders of what would be considered safe fiction by today's soci-ety. Having won just about every award in the fiction field, including mul-tiple Nebulas, Hugos, and Writer's Guild of America awards, he shows no sign of slowing down. He has also made his mark in the editing field, hav-ing put together the ground-breaking collection Dangerous Visions, *and following that up with* Again, Dangerous Visions, *both books containing stories that at the time were deemed too controversial to publish elsewhere. Currently his entire body of fiction and nonfiction is being published in a twenty-volume set entitled* Edgeworks.

WHEN I WAS FIVE YEARS OLD, THERE WAS A LITTLE KID I PLAYED WITH: Jeffty. His real name was Jeff Kinzer, and everyone who played with him called him Jeffty. We were five years old together, and we had good times playing together.

When I was five, a Clark Bar was as fat around as the gripping end of a Louisville Slugger, and pretty nearly six inches long, and they used real chocolate to coat it, and it crunched very nicely when you bit into the center, and the paper it came wrapped in smelled fresh and good when you peeled off one end to hold the bar so it wouldn't melt onto your fingers. Today, a Clark Bar is as thin as a credit card, they use something artificial and awful-tasting instead of pure choco-late, the thing is soft and soggy, it costs fifteen or twenty cents instead of a decent, correct nickel, and they wrap it so you think it's the same size it was twenty years ago, only it isn't; it's slim and ugly and nasty tasting and not worth a penny, much less fifteen or twenty cents.

When I was that age, five years old, I was sent away to my Aunt Patricia's home in Buffalo, New York, for two years. My father was going through "bad times" and Aunt Patricia was very beautiful, and had married a stockbroker. They took care of me for two years.

When I was seven, I came back home and went to find Jeffty, so we could play together.

I was seven. Jeffty was still five. I didn't notice any difference. I didn't know: I was only seven.

When I was seven years old, I used to lie on my stomach in front of our Atwater-Kent radio and listen to swell stuff. I had tied the ground wire to the radiator, and I would lie there with my coloring books and my Crayolas (when there were only sixteen colors in the big box), and listen to the NBC Red network: Jack Benny on the *Jell-O Program, Amos 'n' Andy*, Edgar Bergen and Charlie McCarthy on the *Chase and Sanborn Program, One Man's Family, First Nighter;* the NBC Blue network: *Easy Aces,* the *Jergens Program* with Walter Winchell, *Information Please, Death Valley Days;* and best of all, the Mutual Network with *The Green Hornet, The Lone Ranger, The Shadow,* and *Quiet, Please.* Today, I turn on my car radio and go from one end of the dial to the other and all I get is 100 strings orchestras, banal housewives and insipid truckers discussing their kinky sex lives with arrogant talk show hosts, country and western drivel and rock music so loud it hurts my ears.

When I was ten, my grandfather died of old age and I was "a troublesome kid," and they sent me off to military school, so I could be "taken in hand."

I came back when I was fourteen. Jeffty was still five.

When I was fourteen years old, I used to go to the movies on Saturday afternoons and a matinee was ten cents and they used real butter on the popcorn and I could always be sure of seeing a western like Lash LaRue, or Wild Bill Elliott as Red Ryder with Bobby Blake as Little Beaver, or Roy Rogers, or Johnny Mack Brown; a scary picture like *House of Horrors* with Rondo Hatton as the Strangler, or *The Cat People,* or *The Mummy,* or *I Married a Witch* with Fredric March and Veronica Lake; plus an episode of a great serial like *The Shadow* with Victor Jory, or *Dick Tracy* or *Flash Gordon;* and three cartoons; a James Fitzpatrick TravelTalk; Movietone News; and a sing-along and, if I stayed on till evening, Bingo or Keeno; and free dishes. Today, I go to movies and see Clint Eastwood blowing people's heads apart like ripe cantaloupes.

At eighteen, I went to college. Jeffty was still five. I came back during the summers, to work at my Uncle Joe's jewelry store. Jeffty hadn't changed. Now I knew there was something different about him, something wrong, something weird. Jeffty was still five years old, not a day older.

At twenty-two, I came home for keeps. To open a Sony television franchise in town, the first one. I saw Jeffty from time to time. He was five.

Things are better in a lot of ways. People don't die from some of the old diseases any more. Cars go faster and get you there more quickly on better roads. Shirts are softer and silkier. We have paperback books even though they cost as much as a good hardcover used to. When I'm running short in the bank I can live off credit cards till things even out. But I still think we've lost a lot of good stuff. Did you know you can't buy linoleum any more, only vinyl floor covering? There's no such thing as oilcloth any more; you'll never again smell that special, sweet smell from your grandmother's kitchen. Furniture isn't made to last thirty years or longer because they took a survey and found that young homemakers like to throw their furniture out and bring in all new, color-coded, borax every seven years. Records don't feel right; they're not thick and solid like the old ones, they're thin and you can bend them . . . that doesn't seem right to me. Restaurants don't serve cream in pitchers any more, just that artificial glop in little plastic tubs, and one is never enough to get coffee the right color. You can make a dent in a car fender with only a sneaker. Everywhere you go, all the towns look the same with Burger Kings and McDonald's and 7-Elevens and Taco Bells and motels and shopping centers. Things may be better, but why do I keep thinking about the past?

What I mean by five years old is not that Jeffty was retarded. I don't think that's what it was. Smart as a whip for five years old; very bright, quick, cute, a funny kid.

But he was three feet tall, small for his age, and perfectly formed: no big head, no strange jaw, none of that. A nice, normal-looking five-year-old kid. Except that he was the same age as I was: twenty-two.

When he spoke it was with the squeaking, soprano voice of a five-year-old; when he walked it was with the little hops and shuffles of a five-year-old; when he talked to you it was about the concerns of a five-year-old . . . comic books, playing soldier, using a clothes pin to attach a stiff piece of cardboard to the front fork of his bike so the sound it made when the spokes hit was like a motorboat, asking questions like *why does that thing do that like that,* how high is up, how old is old, why is grass green, what's an elephant look like? At twenty-two, he was five.

Jeffty's parents were a sad pair. Because I was still a friend of Jeffty's, still let him hang around with me in the store, sometimes took him to the county fair or to the miniature golf or the movies, I wound up spending time with *them.* Not that I much cared for them, because they were so awfully depressing. But then, I suppose one couldn't expect much more from the poor devils. They had an alien thing in their home, a child who had grown no older than five in twenty-two years, who provided the treasure of that special child-like state indefinitely, but who also denied them the joys of watching the child grow into a normal adult.

Five is a wonderful time of life for a little kid . . . or it *can* be, if the child is relatively free of the monstrous beastliness other children indulge in. It is a time when the eyes are wide open and the patterns are not yet set; a time when one has not yet been hammered into accepting everything as immutable and hopeless; a time when the hands cannot do enough, the mind cannot learn enough, the world is infinite and colorful and filled with mysteries. Five is a special time before they take the questing, unquenchable, quixotic soul of the young dreamer and thrust it into dreary schoolroom boxes. A time before they take the trembling hands that want to hold everything, touch everything, figure everything out, and make them lie still on desktops. A time before people begin saying "act your age" and "grow up" or "you're behaving like a baby." It is a time when a child who acts adolescent is still cute and responsive and everyone's pet. A time of delight, of wonder, of innocence.

Jeffty had been stuck in that time, just five, just so.

But for his parents it was an ongoing nightmare from which no one—not social workers, not priests, not child psychologists, not teachers, not friends, not medical wizards, not psychiatrists, no one—could slap or shake them awake. For seventeen years their sorrow had grown through stages of parental dotage to concern, from concern to worry, from worry to fear, from fear to confusion, from confusion to anger, from anger to dislike, from dislike to naked hatred, and finally, from deepest loathing and revulsion to a stolid, depressive acceptance.

John Kinzer was a shift foreman at the Balder Tool & Die plant. He was a thirty-year man. To everyone but the man living it, his was a spectacularly uneventful life. In no way was he remarkable . . . save that he had fathered a twenty-two-year-old five-year-old.

John Kinzer was a small man; soft, with no sharp angles; with pale eyes that never seemed to hold mine for longer than a few seconds. He continually shifted in his chair during conversations, and seemed to see things in the upper corners of the room, things no one else could see . . . or wanted to see. I suppose the word that best suited him was *haunted*. What his life had become . . . well, *haunted* suited him.

Leona Kinzer tried valiantly to compensate. No matter what hour of the day I visited, she always tried to foist food on me. And when Jeffty was in the house she was always at *him* about eating: "Honey, would you like an orange? A nice orange? Or a tangerine? I have tangerines. I could peel a tangerine for you." But there was clearly such fear in her, fear of her own child, that the offers of sustenance always had a faintly ominous tone.

Leona Kinzer had been a tall woman, but the years had bent her. She seemed always to be seeking some area of wallpapered wall or storage niche into which she could fade, adopt some chintz or rose-patterned protective coloration and hide forever in plain sight of the child's big brown eyes, pass her a hundred times a day and never realize she was there, holding her breath, invisible. She always had an apron tied around her waist, and her hands were red from cleaning. As if by maintaining the environment immaculately she could pay off her imagined sin: having given birth to this strange creature.

Neither of them watched television very much. The house was usually dead silent, not even the sibilant whispering of water in the pipes, the creaking of timbers settling, the humming of the refrigerator. Awfully silent, as if time itself had taken a detour around that house.

As for Jeffty, he was inoffensive. He lived in that atmosphere of gentle dread and dulled loathing, and if he understood it, he never remarked in any way. He played, as a child plays, and seemed happy. But he must have sensed, in the way of a five-year-old, just how alien he was in their presence.

Alien. No, that wasn't right. He was *too* human, if anything. But out of phase, out of synch with the world around him, and resonating to a different vibration than his parents, God knows. Nor would other children play with him. As they grew past him, they found him at first childish, then uninteresting, then simply frightening as their perceptions of aging became clear and they could see he was not affected by time as they were. Even the little ones, his own age, who might wander into the neighborhood, quickly came to shy away from him like a dog in the street when a car backfires.

Thus, I remained his only friend. A friend of many years. Five years. Twenty-two years. I liked him; more than I can say. And never knew exactly why. But I did, without reserve.

But because we spent time together, I found I was also—polite society—spending time with John and Leona Kinzer. Dinner, Saturday afternoons sometimes, an hour or so when I'd bring Jeffty back from a movie. They were grateful: slavishly so. It relieved them of the embarrassing chore of going out with him, or having to pretend before the world that they were loving parents with a perfectly normal, happy, attractive child. And their gratitude extended to hosting me. Hideous, every moment of their depression, hideous.

I felt sorry for the poor devils, but I despised them for their inability to love Jeffty, who was eminently lovable.

I never let on, of course, even during the evenings in their company that were awkward beyond belief.

We would sit there in the darkening living room—*always* dark or darkening, as if kept in shadow to hold back what the light might reveal to the world outside through the bright eyes of the house—we would sit and silently stare at one another. They never knew what to say to me.

"So how are things down at the plant?" I'd say to John Kinzer.

He would shrug. Neither conversation nor life suited him with any ease or grace. "Fine, just fine," he would say, finally.

And we would sit in silence again.

"Would you like a nice piece of coffee cake?" Leona would say. "I made it fresh just this morning." Or deep dish green apple pie. Or milk and toll house cookies. Or a brown betty pudding.

"No, no, thank you, Mrs. Kinzer; Jeffty and I grabbed a couple of cheeseburgers on the way home." And again, silence.

Then, when the stillness and the awkwardness became too much even for them (and who knew how long that total silence reigned when they were alone, with that thing they never talked about any more, hanging between them), Leona Kinzer would say, "I think he's asleep."

John Kinzer would say, "I don't hear the radio playing."

Just so, it would go on like that, until I could politely find excuse to bolt away on some flimsy pretext. Yes, that was the way it would go on, every time, just the same . . . except once.

"I don't know what to do any more," Leona said. She began crying. "There's no change, not one day of peace."

Her husband managed to drag himself out of the old easy chair and went to her. He bent and tried to soothe her, but it was clear from the graceless way in which he touched her graying hair that the ability to be compassionate had been stunned in him. "Shhh, Leona, it's all right. Shhh." But she continued crying. Her hands scraped gently at the antimacassars on the arms of the chair.

Then she said, "Sometimes I wish he had been stillborn."

John looked up into the corners of the room. For the nameless shadows that were always watching him? Was it God he was seeking in those spaces? "You don't mean that," he said to her, softly, pathetically, urging her with body tension and trembling in his voice to recant before God took notice of the terrible thought. But she meant it; she meant it very much.

I managed to get away quickly that evening. They didn't want witnesses to their shame. I was glad to go.

———

And for a week I stayed away. From them, from Jeffty, from their street, even from that end of town.

I had my own life. The store, accounts, suppliers' conferences, poker with friends, pretty women I took to well-lit restaurants, my own parents, putting anti-freeze in the car, complaining to the laundry about too much starch in the collars and cuffs, working out at the gym, taxes, catching Jan or David (whichever one it was) stealing from the cash register. I had my own life.

But not even *that* evening could keep me from Jeffty. He called me at the store and asked me to take him to the rodeo. We chummed it up as best a twenty-two-year-old with other interests *could* . . . with a five-year-old. I never dwelled on what bound us together; I always thought it was simply the years. That, and affection for a kid who could have been the little brother I never had. (Except I *remembered* when we had played together, when we had both been the same age; I *remembered* that period, and Jeffty was still the same.)

And then, one Saturday afternoon, I came to take him to a double feature, and things I should have noticed so many times before, I first began to notice only that afternoon.

I came walking up to the Kinzer house, expecting Jeffty to be sitting on the front porch steps, or in the porch glider, waiting for me. But he was nowhere in sight.

Going inside, into that darkness and silence, in the midst of May sunshine, was unthinkable. I stood on the front walk for a few moments, then cupped my hands around my mouth and yelled, "Jeffty? Hey, Jeffty, come on out, let's go. We'll be late."

His voice came faintly, as if from under the ground.

"Here I am, Donny."

I could hear him, but I couldn't see him. It was Jeffty, no question about it: as Donald H. Horton, President and Sole Owner of The Horton TV & Sound Center, no one but Jeffty called me Donny. He had never called me anything else.

(Actually, it isn't a lie. I *am*, as far as the public is concerned, Sole Owner of the Center. The partnership with my Aunt Patricia is only to repay the loan she made me, to supplement the money I came into when I was twenty-one, left to me when I was ten by my grandfather. It wasn't a very big loan, only eighteen thousand, but I asked her to be a silent partner, because of when she had taken care of me as a child.)

"Where are you, Jeffty?"

"Under the porch in my secret place."

I walked around the side of the porch, and stooped down and pulled away the wicker grating. Back in there, on the pressed dirt, Jeffty had built himself a secret place. He had comics in orange crates, he had a little table and some pillows, it was lit by big fat candles, and we used to hide there when we were both . . . five.

"What'cha up to?" I asked, crawling in and pulling the grate closed behind me. It was cool under the porch, and the dirt smelled comfortable, the candles smelled clubby and familiar. Any kid would feel at home in such a secret place: there's never been a kid who didn't spend the happiest, most productive, most deliciously mysterious times of his life in such a secret place.

"Playin'," he said. He was holding something golden and round. It filled the palm of his little hand.

"You forget we were going to the movies?"

"Nope. I was just waitin' for you here."

"Your mom and dad home?"

"Momma."

I understood why he was waiting under the porch. I didn't push it any further. "What've you got there?"

"Captain Midnight Secret Decoder Badge," he said, showing it to me on his flattened palm.

I realized I was looking at it without comprehending what it was for a long time. Then it dawned on me what a miracle Jeffty had in his hand. A miracle that simply could *not* exist.

"Jeffty," I said softly, with wonder in my voice, "where'd you get that?"

"Came in the mail today. I sent away for it."

"It must have cost a lot of money."

"Not so much. Ten cents an' two inner wax seals from two jars of Ovaltine."

"May I see it?" My voice was trembling, and so was the hand I extended. He gave it to me and I held the miracle in the palm of my hand. It was *wonderful*.

You remember. *Captain Midnight* went on the radio nationwide in 1940. It was sponsored by Ovaltine. And every year they issued a Secret Squadron Decoder Badge. And every day at the end of the program, they would give you a clue to the next day's installment in a code that only kids with the official badge could decipher. They stopped making those wonderful Decoder Badges in 1949. I remember the one I had in 1945: it was beautiful. It had a magnifying glass in the center of the code dial. *Captain Midnight* went off the air in 1950, and though I understand it was a short-lived television series in the mid-Fifties, and though they issued Decoder Badges in 1955 and 1956, as far as the *real* badges were concerned, they never made one after 1949.

The Captain Midnight Code-O-Graph I held in my hand, the one Jeffty said he had gotten in the mail for ten cents (*ten cents!!!*) and two Ovaltine labels, was brand new, shiny gold metal, not a dent or a spot of rust on it like the old ones you can find at exorbitant prices in collectible shoppes from time to time . . . it was a *new* Decoder. And the date on it was *this* year.

But *Captain Midnight* no longer existed. Nothing like it existed on the radio. I'd listened to the one or two weak imitations of old-time radio the networks were currently airing, and the stories were dull, the sound effects bland, the whole feel of it wrong, out of date, cornball. Yet I held a *new* Code-O-Graph.

"Jeffty, tell me about this," I said.

"Tell you what, Donny? It's my new Capt'n Midnight Secret Decoder Badge. I use it to figger out what's gonna happen tomorrow."

"Tomorrow how?"

"On the program."

"*What* program?!"

He stared at me as if I was being purposely stupid. "On Capt'n *Mid*night! Boy!" I was being dumb.

I still couldn't get it straight. It was right there, right out in the open, and I still didn't know what was happening. "You mean one of those records they made of the old-time radio programs? Is that what you mean, Jeffty?"

"What records?" he asked. He didn't know what *I* meant.

We stared at each other, there under the porch. And then I said, very slowly, almost afraid of the answer, "Jeffty, how do you hear *Captain Midnight?*"

"Every day. On the radio. On my radio. Every day at five-thirty."

News. Music, dumb music, and news. That's what was on the radio every day at 5:30. Not *Captain Midnight*. The Secret Squadron hadn't been on the air in twenty years.

"Can we hear it tonight?" I asked.

"Boy!" he said. I was being dumb. I knew it from the way he said it; but I didn't know *why*. Then it dawned on me: this was Saturday. *Captain Midnight* was on Monday through Friday. Not on Saturday or Sunday.

"We goin' to the movies?"

He had to repeat himself twice. My mind was somewhere else. Nothing definite. No conclusions. No wild assumptions leapt to. Just off somewhere trying to figure it out, and concluding—as *you* would have concluded, as *any*one would have concluded rather than accepting the truth, the impossible and wonderful truth—just finally concluding there was a simple explanation I didn't yet perceive. Something mundane and dull, like the passage of time that steals all good, old things from us, packratting trinkets and plastic in exchange. And all in the name of Progress.

"We goin' to the movies, Donny?"

"You bet your boots we are, kiddo," I said. And I smiled. And I handed him the Code-O-Graph. And he put it in his side pants pocket. And we crawled out from under the porch. And we went to the movies. And neither of us said anything about *Captain Midnight* all the rest of that day. And there wasn't a ten-minute stretch, all the rest of that day, that I didn't think about it.

It was inventory all that next week. I didn't see Jeffty till late Thursday. I confess I left the store in the hands of Jan and David, told them I had some errands to run, and left early. At 4:00. I got to the Kinzers' right around 4:45. Leona answered the door, looking exhausted and distant. "Is Jeffty around?" She said he was upstairs in his room . . .

. . . listening to the radio.

I climbed the stairs two at a time.

All right, I had finally made that impossible, illogical leap. Had the stretch of belief involved anyone but Jeffty, adult or child, I would have reasoned out more explicable answers. But it *was* Jeffty, clearly another kind of vessel of life, and what he might experience should not be expected to fit into the ordered scheme.

I admit it: I *wanted* to hear what I heard.

Even with the door closed, I recognized the program:

"There he goes, Tennessee! Get him!"

There was the heavy report of a rifle shot and the keening whine of the slug ricocheting, and then the same voice yelled triumphantly, *"Got him! D-e-a-a-a-a-d center!"*

He was listening to the American Broadcasting Company, 790 kilocycles, and he was hearing *Tennessee Jed,* one of my most favorite programs from the Forties, a western adventure I had not heard in twenty years, because it had not existed for twenty years.

I sat down on the top step of the stairs, there in the upstairs hall of the Kinzer home, and I listened to the show. It wasn't a rerun of an old program, because there were occasional references in the body of the drama to current cultural and technological developments, and phrases that had not existed in common usage in the Forties: aerosol spray cans, laserasing of tattoos, Tanzania, the word "uptight."

I could not ignore the fact. Jeffty was listening to a *new* segment of *Tennessee Jed.*

I ran downstairs and out the front door to my car. Leona must have been in the kitchen. I turned the key and punched on the radio and spun the dial to 790 kilocycles. The ABC station. Rock music.

I sat there for a few moments, then ran the dial slowly from one end to the other. Music, news, talk shows. No *Tennessee Jed.* And it was a Blaupunkt, the best radio I could get. I wasn't missing some perimeter station. It simply was not there!

After a few moments I turned off the radio and the ignition and went back upstairs quietly. I sat down on the top step and listened to the entire program. It was *wonderful.*

Exciting, imaginative, filled with everything I remembered as being most innovative about radio drama. But it was modern. It wasn't an antique, re-broadcast to assuage the need of that dwindling listenership who longed for the old days. It was a new show, with all the old voices, but still young and bright. Even the commercials were for currently available products, but they weren't as loud or as insulting as the screamer ads one heard on radio these days.

And when *Tennessee Jed* went off at 5:00, I heard Jeffty spin the dial on his radio till I heard the familiar voice of the announcer Glenn Riggs proclaim, *"Presenting Hop Harrigan! America's ace of the airwaves!"* There was the sound of an airplane in flight. It was a prop plane, *not* a jet! Not the sound kids today have grown up with, but the sound *I* grew up with, the *real* sound of an airplane, the growling, revving, throaty sound of the kind of airplanes G-8 and His Battle Aces flew, the kind Captain Midnight flew, the kind Hop Harrigan flew. And then I heard Hop say, *"CX-4 calling control tower. CX-4 calling control tower. Standing by!"* A pause, then, *"Okay, this is Hop Harrigan . . . coming in!"*

And Jeffty, who had the same problem all of us kids had had in the Forties with programming that pitted equal favorites against one another on different stations, having paid his respects to Hop Harrigan and Tank Tinker, spun the dial and went back to ABC, where I heard the stroke of a gong, the wild cacophony of nonsense Chinese chatter, and the announcer yelled, *"T-e-e-e-rry and the Pirates!"*

I sat there on the top step and listened to Terry and Connie and Flip Corkin and, so help me God, Agnes Moorehead as The Dragon Lady, all of them in a new adventure that took place in a Red China that had not existed in the days of Milton Caniff's 1937 version of the Orient, with river pirates and Chiang Kai-shek and warlords and the naïve Imperialism of American gunboat diplomacy.

Sat, and listened to the whole show, and sat even longer to hear *Superman* and part of *Jack Armstrong, The All American Boy* and part of *Captain Midnight,* and John Kinzer came home and neither he nor Leona came upstairs to find out what had happened to me, or where Jeffty was, and sat longer, and found I had started crying, and could not stop, just sat there with tears running down my face, into the corners of my mouth, sitting and crying until Jeffty heard me and opened his door and saw me and came out and looked at me in childish confusion as I heard the station break for the Mutual Network and they began the theme music of *Tom Mix,* "When It's Round-up Time in Texas and the Bloom Is on the Sage," and Jeffty touched my shoulder and smiled at me, with his mouth and his big brown eyes, and said, "Hi, Donny. Wanna come in an' listen to the radio with me?"

Hume denied the existence of an absolute space, in which each thing has its place; Borges denies the existence of one single time, in which all events are linked.

Jeffty received radio programs from a place that could not, in logic, in the natural scheme of the space-time universe as conceived by Einstein, exist. But that wasn't all he received. He got mail order premiums that no one was manufacturing. He read comic books that had been defunct for three decades. He saw movies with actors who had been dead for twenty years. He was the receiving terminal for endless joys and pleasures of the past that the world had dropped along the way. On its headlong suicidal flight toward New Tomorrows, the world had razed its treasure house of simple happinesses, had poured concrete over its playgrounds, had abandoned its elfin stragglers, and all of it was being impossibly, miraculously shunted back into the present through Jeffty. Revivified, updated, the traditions maintained but contemporaneous. Jeffty was the unbidding Aladdin whose very nature formed the magic lampness of his reality.

And he took me into his world with him.

Because he trusted me.

We had breakfast of Quaker Puffed Wheat Sparkies and warm Ovaltine we drank out of *this* year's Little Orphan Annie Shake-Up Mugs. We went to the movies and while everyone else was seeing a comedy starring Goldie Hawn and Ryan O'Neal, Jeffty and I were enjoying Humphrey Bogart as the professional thief Parker in John Huston's brilliant adaptation of the Donald Westlake novel *Slayground.* The second feature was Spencer Tracy, Carole Lombard and Laird Cregar in the Val Lewton-produced film of *Leiningen Versus the Ants.*

Twice a month we went down to the newsstand and bought the current pulp issues of *The Shadow, Doc Savage* and *Startling Stories.* Jeffty and I sat together and I read to him from the magazines. He particularly liked the new short novel by Henry Kuttner, "The Dreams of Achilles," and the new Stanley G. Weinbaum series of short stories set in the subatomic particle universe of Redurna. In September we enjoyed the first installment of the new Robert E. Howard Conan novel, *Isle of the Black Ones,* in *Weird Tales;* and in

August we were only mildly disappointed by Edgar Rice Burroughs's fourth novella in the Jupiter series featuring John Carter of Barsoom—"Corsairs of Jupiter." But the editor of *Argosy All-Story Weekly* promised there would be two more stories in the series, and it was such an unexpected revelation for Jeffty and me that it dimmed our disappointment at the lessened quality of the current story.

We read comics together, and Jeffty and I both decided—separately, before we came together to discuss it—that our favorite characters were Doll Man, Airboy and The Heap. We also adored the George Carlson strips in *Jingle Jangle Comics,* particularly the Pie-Face Prince of Old Pretzleburg stories, which we read together and laughed over, even though I had to explain some of the esoteric puns to Jeffty, who was too young to have that kind of subtle wit.

How to explain it? I can't. I had enough physics in college to make some offhand guesses, but I'm more likely wrong than right. The laws of the conservation of energy occasionally break. These are laws that physicists call "weakly violated." Perhaps Jeffty was a catalyst for the weak violation of conservation laws we're only now beginning to realize exist. I tried doing some reading in the area—muon decay of the "forbidden" kind: gamma decay that doesn't include the muon neutrino among its products—but nothing I encountered, not even the latest readings from the Swiss Institute for Nuclear Research near Zurich gave me an insight. I was thrown back on a vague acceptance of the philosophy that the real name for "science" is *magic*.

No explanations, but enormous good times.

The happiest time of my life.

I had the "real" world, the world of my store and my friends and my family, the world of profit&loss, of taxes and evenings with young women who talked about going shopping or the United Nations, or the rising cost of coffee and microwave ovens. And I had Jeffty's world, in which I existed only when I was with him. The things of the past he knew as fresh and new, I could experience only when in his company. And the membrane between the two worlds grew ever thinner, more luminous and transparent. I had the best of both worlds. And knew, somehow, that I could carry nothing from one to the other.

Forgetting that, for just a moment, betraying Jeffty by forgetting, brought an end to it all.

Enjoying myself so much, I grew careless and failed to consider how fragile the relationship between Jeffty's world and my world really was. There is a reason why the present begrudges the existence of the past. I never really understood. Nowhere in the beast books, where survival is shown in battles between claw and fang, tentacle and poison sac, is there recognition of the ferocity the present always brings to bear on the past. Nowhere is there a detailed statement of how the present lies in wait for What-Was, waiting for it to become Now-This-Moment so it can shred it with its merciless jaws.

Who could know such a thing . . . at any age . . . and certainly not at my age . . . who could understand such a thing?

I'm trying to exculpate myself. I can't. It was my fault.

It was another Saturday afternoon.

"What's playing today?" I asked him, in the car, on the way downtown.

He looked up at me from the other side of the front seat and smiled one of his best smiles. "Ken Maynard in *Bullwhip Justice* an' *The Demolished Man*." He kept smiling, as if he'd really put one over on me. I looked at him with disbelief.

"You're *kid*ding!" I said, delighted. "Bester's *The Demolished Man*?" He nodded his head, delighted at my being delighted. He knew it was one of my favorite books. "Oh, that's super!"

"Super *duper*," he said.

"Who's in it?"

"Franchot Tone, Evelyn Keyes, Lionel Barrymore and Elisha Cook, Jr." He was much more knowledgeable about movie actors than I'd ever been. He could name the character actors in any movie he'd ever seen. Even the crowd scenes.

"And cartoons?" I asked.

"Three of 'em: a *Little Lulu*, a *Donald Duck* and a *Bugs Bunny*. An' a *Pete Smith Specialty* an' a *Lew Lehr Monkeys is da C-r-r-r-aziest Peoples*."

"Oh boy!" I said. I was grinning from ear to ear. And then I looked down and saw the pad of purchase order forms on the seat. I'd forgotten to drop it off at the store.

"Gotta stop by the Center," I said. "Gotta drop off something. It'll only take a minute."

"Okay," Jeffty said. "But we won't be late, will we?"

"Not on your tintype, kiddo," I said.

When I pulled into the parking lot behind the Center, he decided to come in with me and we'd walk over to the theater. It's not a large town. There are only two movie houses, the Utopia and the Lyric. We were going to the Utopia and it was only three blocks from the Center.

I walked into the store with the pad of forms, and it was bedlam. David and Jan were handling two customers each, and there were people standing around waiting to be helped. Jan turned a look on me and her face was a horror-mask of pleading. David was running from the stockroom to the showroom and all he could murmur as he whipped past was "Help!" and then he was gone.

"Jeffty," I said, crouching down, "listen, give me a few minutes. Jan and David are in trouble with all these people. We won't be late, I promise. Just let me get rid of a couple of these customers." He looked nervous, but nodded okay.

I motioned to a chair and said, "Just sit down for a while and I'll be right with you."

He went to the chair, good as you please, though he knew what was happening, and he sat down.

I started taking care of people who wanted color television sets. This was the first really substantial batch of units we'd gotten in— color television was only now becoming reasonably priced and this was Sony's first promotion—and it was bonanza time for me. I could see paying off the loan and being out in front for the first time with the Center. It was business.

In my world, good business comes first.

Jeffty sat there and stared at the wall. Let me tell you about the wall.

Stanchion and bracket designs had been rigged from floor to within two feet of the ceiling. Television sets had been stacked artfully on the wall. Thirty-three television sets. All playing at the same time. Black and white, color, little ones, big ones, all going at the same time.

Jeffty sat and watched thirty-three television sets, on a Saturday afternoon. We can pick up a total of thirteen channels including the UHF educational stations. Golf was on one channel; baseball was on a second; celebrity bowling was on a third; the fourth channel was a religious seminar; a teenage dance show was on the fifth; the sixth was a rerun of a situation comedy; the seventh was a rerun of a police show; eighth was a nature program showing a man flycasting endlessly; ninth was news and conversation; tenth was a stock car race; eleventh was a man doing logarithms on a blackboard; twelfth was a woman in a leotard doing setting-up exercises; and on the thirteenth channel was a badly animated cartoon show in Spanish. All but six of the shows were repeated on three sets. Jeffty sat and watched that wall of television on a Saturday afternoon while I sold as fast and as hard as I could, to pay back my Aunt Patricia and stay in touch with my world. It was business.

I should have known better. I should have understood about the present and the way it kills the past. But I was selling with both hands. And when I finally glanced over at Jeffty, half an hour later, he looked like another child.

He was sweating. That terrible fever sweat when you have stomach flu. He was pale, as pasty and pale as a worm, and his little hands were gripping the arms of the chair so tightly I could see his knuckles in bold relief. I dashed over to him, excusing myself from the middle-aged couple looking at the new 21" Mediterranean model.

"Jeffty!"

He looked at me, but his eyes didn't track. He was in absolute terror. I pulled him out of the chair and started toward the front door with him, but the customers I'd deserted yelled at me, "Hey!" The middle-aged man said, "You wanna sell me this thing or don't you?"

I looked from him to Jeffty and back again. Jeffty was like a zombie. He had come where I'd pulled him. His legs were rubbery and his feet dragged. The past, being eaten by the present, the sound of something in pain.

I clawed some money out of my pants pocket and jammed it into Jeffty's hand. "Kiddo . . . listen to me . . . get out of here right now!" He still couldn't focus properly. *"Jeffty,"* I said as tightly as I could, "*listen* to me!" The middle-aged customer and his wife were walking toward us. "Listen, kiddo, get out of here right this minute. Walk over to the Utopia and buy the tickets. I'll be right behind you." The middle-aged man and his wife were almost on us. I shoved Jeffty through the door and watched him stumble away in the wrong direction, then stop as if gathering his wits, turn and go back past the front of the Center and in the direction of the Utopia. "Yes sir," I said, straightening up and facing them, "yes, ma'am, that is one terrific set with some sen*sa*tional features! If you'll just step back here with me . . ."

There was a terrible sound of something hurting, but I couldn't tell from which channel, or from which set, it was coming.

Most of it I learned later, from the girl in the ticket booth, and from some people I knew who came to me to tell me what had happened. By the time I got to the Utopia, nearly twenty minutes later, Jeffty was already beaten to a pulp and had been taken to the Manager's office.

"Did you see a very little boy, about five years old, with big brown eyes and straight brown hair . . . he was waiting for me?"

"Oh, I think that's the little boy those kids beat up?"

"What!?! *Where is he?*"

"They took him to the Manager's office. No one knew who he was or where to find his parents—"

A young girl wearing an usher's uniform was kneeling down beside the couch, placing a wet paper towel on his face.

I took the towel away from her and ordered her out of the office.

She looked insulted and snorted something rude, but she left. I sat on the edge of the couch and tried to swab away the blood from the lacerations without opening the wounds where the blood had caked. Both his eyes were swollen shut. His mouth was ripped badly. His hair was matted with dried blood.

He had been standing in line behind two kids in their teens. They started selling tickets at 12:30 and the show started at 1:00. The doors weren't opened till 12:45. He had been waiting, and the kids in front of him had had a portable radio. They were listening to the ball game. Jeffty had wanted to hear some program, God knows what it might have been, *Grand Central Station, Let's Pretend, Land of the Lost,* God only knows which one it might have been.

He had asked if he could borrow their radio to hear the program for a minute, and it had been a commercial break or something, and the kids had given him the radio, probably out of some malicious kind of courtesy that would permit them to take offense and rag the little boy. He had changed the station . . . and they'd been unable to get it to go back to the ball game. It was locked into the past, on a station that was broadcasting a program that didn't exist for anyone but Jeffty.

They had beaten him badly . . . as everyone watched.

And then they had run away.

I had left him alone, left him to fight off the present without sufficient weaponry. I had betrayed him for the sale of a 21" Mediterranean console television, and now his face was pulped meat. He moaned something inaudible and sobbed softly.

"Shhh, it's okay, kiddo, it's Donny. I'm here. I'll get you home, it'll be okay."

I should have taken him straight to the hospital. I don't know why I didn't. I should have. I should have done that.

When I carried him through the door, John and Leona Kinzer just stared at me. They didn't move to take him from my arms. One of his hands was hanging down. He was conscious, but just barely. They stared, there in the semi-darkness of a Saturday afternoon in the present. I looked at them. "A couple of kids beat him up at the theater." I raised him a few inches in my arms and extended him. They stared at me, at both of us, with nothing in their eyes, without movement. "Jesus Christ," I shouted, "he's been beaten! He's your son! Don't you even want to touch him? What the hell kind of people are you?!"

Then Leona moved toward me very slowly. She stood in front of us for a few seconds, and there was a leaden stoicism in her face that was terrible to see. It said, *I have been in this place before, many times, and I cannot bear to be in it again; but I am here now.*

So I gave him to her. God help me, I gave him over to her.

And she took him upstairs to bathe away his blood and his pain.

John Kinzer and I stood in our separate places in the dim living room of their home, and we stared at each other. He had nothing to say to me.

I shoved past him and fell into a chair. I was shaking.

I heard the bath water running upstairs.

After what seemed a very long time Leona came downstairs, wiping her hands on her apron. She sat down on the sofa and after a moment John sat down beside her. I heard the sound of rock music from upstairs.

"Would you like a piece of nice pound cake?" Leona said.

I didn't answer. I was listening to the sound of the music. Rock music. On the radio. There was a table lamp on the end table beside the sofa. It cast a dim and futile light in the shadowed living room. *Rock music from the present, on a radio upstairs?* I started to say something, and then *knew* . . . Oh, God . . . *no!*

I jumped up just as the sound of hideous crackling blotted out the music, and the table lamp dimmed and dimmed and flickered. I screamed something, I don't know what it was, and ran for the stairs.

Jeffty's parents did not move. They sat there with their hands folded, in that place they had been for so many years.

I fell twice rushing up the stairs.

There isn't much on television that can hold my interest. I bought an old cathedral-shaped Philco radio in a second-hand store, and I replaced all the burnt-out parts with the original tubes from old radios I could cannibalize that still worked. I don't use transistors or printed circuits. They wouldn't work. I've sat in front of that set for hours sometimes, running the dial back and forth as slowly as you can imagine, so slowly it doesn't look as if it's moving at all sometimes.

But I can't find *Captain Midnight* or *The Land of the Lost* or *The Shadow* or *Quiet, Please.*

So she did love him, still, a little bit, even after all those years. I can't hate them: they only wanted to live in the present world again. That isn't such a terrible thing.

It's a good world, all things considered. It's much better than it used to be, in a lot of ways. People don't die from the old diseases any more. They die from new ones, but that's Progress, isn't it?

Isn't it?

Tell me.

Somebody please tell me.

The Detective of Dreams

Gene Wolfe

Gene Wolfe is best known for his masterpiece five-volume work The Book of the New Sun, *in which religion, suffering, torture, and rebirth are all combined, along with a classic coming-of-age and quest story, into an allegorical look at Christian symbolism set in the far future. His other series, still in progress, is* The Book of the Long Sun, *where religion also plays a prominent role. However, this is not to say that religion is the only theme in his work. In fact, the complexity of his stories and the experimental viewpoints and characters he uses underscores his excellence as a writer. Other notable works include* Castleview, Soldier of the Mist, *and* Free Live Free.

I WAS WRITING IN MY OFFICE IN THE RUE MADELEINE WHEN ANDRÉE, MY secretary, announced the arrival of Herr D_____. I rose, put away my correspondence, and offered him my hand. He was, I should say, just short of fifty, had the high, clear complexion characteristic of those who in youth (now unhappily past for both of us) have found more pleasure in the company of horses and dogs and the excitement of the chase than in the bottles and bordels of city life, and wore a beard and mustache of the style popularized by the late emperor. Accepting my invitation to a chair, he showed me his papers.

"You see," he said, "I am accustomed to acting as the representative of my government. In this matter I hold no such position, and it is possible that I feel a trifle lost."

"Many people who come here feel lost," I said. "But it is my boast that I find most of them again. Your problem, I take it, is purely a private matter?"

"Not at all. It is a public matter in the truest sense of the words."

"Yet none of the documents before me—admirably stamped, sealed, and beribboned though they are—indicates that you are other than a private gentleman traveling abroad. And you say you do not represent your government. What am I to think? What is this matter?"

"I act in the public interest," Herr D_____ told me. "My fortune is not great, but I can assure you that in the event of your success you will be well recompensed; although you are to take it that I alone am your principal, yet there are substantial resources available to me."

"Perhaps it would be best if you described the problem to me?"

"You are not averse to travel?"

"No."

"Very well then," he said, and so saying launched into one of the most astonishing relations—no, *the* most astonishing relation—I have ever been privileged to hear. Even I, who had at first hand the account of the man who found Paulette Renan with the quince seed still lodged in her throat; who had received Captain Brotte's testimony concerning his finds amid the antarctic ice; who had heard the history of the woman called Joan O'Neil, who lived for two years behind a painting of herself in the Louvre, from her own lips—even I sat like a child while this man spoke.

When he fell silent, I said, "Herr D_____, after all you have told me I would accept this mission though there were not a *sou* to be made from it. Perhaps once in a lifetime one comes across a case that must be pursued for its own sake; I think I have found mine."

He leaned forward and grasped my hand with a warmth of feeling that was, I believe, very foreign to his usual nature. "Find and destroy the Dream-Master," he said, "and you shall sit upon a chair of gold, if that is your wish, and eat from a table of gold as well. When will you come to our country?"

"Tomorrow morning," I said. "There are one or two arrangements I must make here before I go."

"I am returning tonight. You may call upon me at any time, and I will apprise you of new developments." He handed me a card. "I am always to be found at this address—if not I, then one who is to be trusted, acting in my behalf."

"I understand."

"This should be sufficient for your initial expenses. You may call on me should you require more." The cheque he gave me as he turned to leave represented a comfortable fortune.

I waited until he was nearly out the door before saying, "I thank you, Herr Baron." To his credit, he did not turn; but I had the satisfaction of seeing a flush of red rising above the precise white line of his collar before the door closed.

Andrée entered as soon as he had left. "Who was that man? When you spoke to him—just as he was stepping out of your office—he looked as if you had struck him with a whip."

"He will recover," I told her. "He is the Baron H_____, of the secret police of K_____. D_____ was his mother's name. He assumed that because his own desk is a few hundred kilometers from mine, and because he does not permit his likeness to appear in the daily papers, I would not know him; but it was necessary, both for the sake of his opinion of me and my own of myself, that he should discover that I am not so easily deceived. When he recovers from his initial irritation, he will retire tonight with greater confidence in the abilities I will devote to the mission he has entrusted to me."

"It is typical of you, monsieur," Andrée said kindly, "that you are concerned that your clients sleep well."

Her pretty cheek tempted me, and I pinched it. "I am concerned," I replied; "but the Baron will not sleep well."

My train roared out of Paris through meadows sweet with wild flowers, to penetrate mountain passes in which the danger of avalanches was only just past. The glitter of rushing water, sprung from on high, was everywhere; and when the express slowed to climb a grade, the song of water was everywhere too, water running and shouting down the gray rocks of the Alps. I fell asleep that night with the descant of that icy purity sounding through the plainsong of the rails, and I woke in the station of I_____, the old capital of J_____, now a province of K_____.

I engaged a porter to convey my trunk to the hotel where I had made reservations by telegraph the day before, and amused myself for a few hours by strolling about the city. Here I found the Middle Ages might almost be said to have remained rather than lingered. The city wall was complete on three sides, with its merloned towers in repair; and the cobbled streets surely dated from a period when wheeled traffic of any kind was scarce. As for the buildings—Puss in Boots and his friends must have loved them dearly: there were bulging walls and little panes of bull's-eye glass, and overhanging upper floors one above another until the structures seemed unbalanced as tops. Upon one gray old pile with narrow windows and massive doors, I found a plaque informing me that though it had been first built as a church, it had been successively a prison, a customhouse, a private home, and a school. I investigated further, and discovered it was now an arcade, having been divided, I should think at about the time of the first Louis, into a multitude of dank little stalls. Since it was, as it happened, one of the addresses mentioned by Baron H_____, I went in.

Gas flared everywhere, yet the interior could not have been said to be well lit—each jet was sullen and secretive, as if the proprietor in whose cubicle it was located wished it to light none but his own wares. These cubicles were in no order; nor could I find any directory or guide to lead me to the one I sought. A few customers, who seemed to have visited the place for years, so that they understood where everything was, drifted from one display to the next. When they arrived at each, the proprietor came out, silent (so it seemed to me) as a specter, ready to answer questions or accept a payment; but I never heard a question asked, or saw any money tendered—the customer would finger the edge of a kitchen knife, or hold a garment up to her own shoulders, or turn the pages of some moldering book; and then put the thing down again, and go away.

At last, when I had tired of peeping into alcoves lined with booths still gloomier than the ones on the main concourse outside, I stopped at a leather merchant's and asked the man to direct me to Fräulein A_____.

"I do not know her," he said.

"I am told on good authority that her business is conducted in this building, and that she buys and sells antiques."

"We have several antique dealers here. Herr M_____—"

"I am searching for a young woman. Has your Herr M_____ a niece or a cousin?"

"—handles chairs and chests, largely. Herr O_____, near the guildhall—"

"It is within this building."

"—stocks pictures, mostly. A few mirrors. What is it you wish to buy?"

At this point we were interrupted, mercifully, by a woman from the next booth. "He wants Fräulein A_____. Out of here, and to your left; past the wigmaker's, then right to the stationer's, then left again. She sells old lace."

I found the place at last, and sitting at the very back of her booth Fräulein A_____ herself, a pretty, slender, timid-looking young woman. Her merchandise was spread on two tables; I pretended to examine it and found that it was not old lace she sold but old clothing, much of it trimmed with lace. After a few moments she rose and came out to talk to me, saying, "If you could tell me what you require? . . ." She was taller than I had anticipated, and her flaxen hair would have been very attractive if it were ever released from the tight braids coiled round her head.

"I am only looking. Many of these are beautiful—are they expensive?"

"Not for what you get. The one you are holding is only fifty marks."

"That seems like a great deal."

"They are the fine dresses of long ago—for visiting, or going to the ball. The dresses of wealthy women of aristocratic taste. All are like new; I will not handle anything else. Look at the seams in that one you hold, the tiny stitches all done by hand. Those were the work of dressmakers who created only four or five in a year, and worked twelve and fourteen hours a day, sewing at the first light, and continuing under the lamp, past midnight."

I said, "I see that you have been crying, Fräulein. Their lives were indeed miserable, though no doubt there are people today who suffer equally."

"No doubt there are," the young woman said. "I, however, am not one of them." And she turned away so that I should not see her tears.

"I was informed otherwise."

She whirled about to face me. "You know him? Oh, tell him I am not a wealthy woman, but I will pay whatever I can. Do you really know him?"

"No." I shook my head. "I was informed by your own police."

She stared at me. "But you are an outlander. So is he, I think."

"Ah, we progress. Is there another chair in the rear of your booth? Your police are not above going outside your own country for help, you see, and we should have a little talk."

"They are not our police," the young woman said bitterly, "but I will talk to you. The truth is that I would sooner talk to you, though you are French. You will not tell them that?"

I assured her that I would not; we borrowed a chair from the flower stall across the corridor, and she poured forth her story.

"My father died when I was very small. My mother opened this booth to earn our living—old dresses that had belonged to her own mother were the core of her original stock. She died two years ago, and since that time I have taken charge of our business and used it to support myself. Most of my sales are to collectors and theatrical companies. I do not make a great deal of money, but I do not require a great deal, and I have managed to save some. I live alone at Number 877 _____strasse; it is an old house divided into six apartments, and mine is the gable apartment."

"You are young and charming," I said, "and you tell me you have a little money saved. I am surprised you are not married."

"Many others have said the same thing."

"And what did you tell them, Fräulein?"

"To take care of their own affairs. They have called me a man-hater— Frau G_____, who has the confections in the next corridor but two, called me that because I would not receive her son. The truth is that I do not care for people of either sex, young or old. If I want to live by myself and keep my own things to myself, is not it my right to do so?"

"I am sure it is; but undoubtedly it has occurred to you that this person you fear so much may be a rejected suitor who is taking his revenge on you."

"But how could he enter and control my dreams?"

"I do not know, Fräulein. It is you who say that he does these things."

"I should remember him, I think, if he had ever called on me. As it is, I am quite certain I have seen him somewhere, but I cannot recall where. Still . . ."

"Perhaps you had better describe your dream to me. You have the same one again and again, as I understand it?"

"Yes. It is like this. I am walking down a dark road. I am both frightened and pleasurably excited, if you know what I mean. Sometimes I walk for a long time, sometimes for what seems to be only a few moments. I think there is moonlight, and once or twice I have noticed stars. Anyway, there is a high, dark hedge, or perhaps a wall, on my right. There are fields to the left, I believe. Eventually I reach a gate of iron bars, standing open—it's not a large gate for wagons or carriages, but a small one, so narrow I can hardly get through. Have you read the writings of Dr. Freud of Vienna? One of the women here mentioned once that he had written concerning dreams, and so I got them from the library, and if I were a man I am sure he would say that entering that gate meant sexual commerce. Do you think I might have unnatural leanings?" Her voice had dropped to a whisper.

"Have you ever felt such desires?"

"Oh, no. Quite the reverse."

"Then I doubt it very much," I said. "Go on with your dream. How do you feel as you pass through the gate?"

"As I did when walking down the road, but more so—more frightened, and yet happy and excited. Triumphant, in a way."

"Go on."

"I am in the garden now. There are fountains playing, and nightingales singing in the willows. The air smells of lilies, and a cherry tree in blossom looks like a giantess in her bridal gown. I walk on a straight, smooth path; I think it must be paved with marble chips, because it is white in the moonlight. Ahead of me is the *Schloss*—a great building. There is music coming from inside."

"What sort of music?"

"Magnificent—joyous, if you know what I am trying to say, but not the tinklings of a theater orchestra. A great symphony. I have never been to the opera at Bayreuth; but I think it must be like that—yet a happy, quick tune."

She paused, and for an instant her smile recovered the remembered music. "There are pillars, and a grand entrance, with broad steps. I run up—I am so happy to be there—and throw open the door. It is brightly lit inside; a wave of golden light, almost like a wave from the ocean, strikes me. The room is a great hall, with a high ceiling. A long table is set in the middle and there are hundreds of people seated at it, but one place, the one nearest me, is empty. I cross to it and sit down; there are beautiful golden loaves on the table, and bowls of honey with roses floating at their centers, and crystal carafes of wine, and many other good things I cannot remember when I awake. Everyone is eating and drinking and talking, and I begin to eat too."

I said, "It is only a dream, Fräulein. There is no reason to weep."

"I dream this each night—I have dreamed so every night for months."

"Go on."

"Then he comes. I am sure he is the one who is causing me to dream like this because I can see his face clearly, and remember it when the dream is over. Sometimes it is very vivid for an hour or more after I wake—so vivid that I have only to close my eyes to see it before me."

"I will ask you to describe him in detail later. For the present, continue with your dream."

"He is tall, and robed like a king, and there is a strange crown on his head. He stands beside me, and though he says nothing, I know that the etiquette of the place demands that I rise and face him. I do this. Sometimes I am sucking my fingers as I get up from his table."

"He owns the dream palace, then."

"Yes, I am sure of that. It is his castle, his home; he is my host. I stand and face him, and I am conscious of wanting very much to please him, but not knowing what it is I should do."

"That must be painful."

"It is. But as I stand there, I become aware of how I am clothed, and—"

"How are you clothed?"

"As you see me now. In a plain, dark dress—the dress I wear here at the arcade. But the others—all up and down the hall, all up and down the table—are wearing the dresses I sell here. These dresses." She held one up for me to see, a beautiful creation of many layers of lace, with buttons of polished jet. "I know then that I cannot remain; but the king signals to the others, and they seize me and push me toward the door."

"You are humiliated then?"

"Yes, but the worst thing is that I am aware that he knows that I could never drive myself to leave, and he wishes to spare me the struggle. But outside—some terrible beast has entered the garden. I smell it—like the hyena cage at the *Tiergarten*—as the door opens. And then I wake up."

"It is a harrowing dream."

"You have seen the dresses I sell. Would you credit it that for weeks I slept in one, and then another, and then another of them?"

"You reaped no benefit from that?"

"No. In the dream I was clad as now. For a time I wore the dresses always—even here to the stall, and when I bought food at the market. But it did no good."

"Have you tried sleeping somewhere else?"

"With my cousin who lives on the other side of the city. That made no difference. I am certain that this man I see is a real man. He is in my dream, and the cause of it; but he is not sleeping."

"Yet you have never seen him when you are awake?"

She paused, and I saw her bite at her full lower lip. "I am certain I have."

"Ah!"

"But I cannot remember when. Yet I am sure I have seen him— that I have passed him in the street."

"Think! Does his face associate itself in your mind with some particular section of the city?"

She shook her head.

When I left her at last, it was with a description of the Dream-Master less precise than I had hoped, though still detailed. It tallied in almost all respects with the one given me by Baron H_____; but that proved nothing, since the baron's description might have been based largely on Fräulein A_____'s.

The bank of Herr R_____ was a private one, as all the greatest banks in Europe are. It was located in what had once been the town house of some noble family (their arms, overgrown now with ivy, were still visible above the door) and bore no identification other than a small brass plate engraved with the names of Herr R_____ and his partners. Within, the atmosphere was more dignified—even if, perhaps, less tasteful—than it could possibly have been in the noble family's time. Dark pictures in gilded frames lined the walls, and the clerks sat at inlaid tables upon chairs upholstered in tapestry. When I asked for Herr R_____, I was told that it would be impossible to see him that afternoon; I sent in a note with a sidelong allusion to "unquiet dreams," and within five minutes I was ushered into a luxurious office that must once have been the bedroom of the head of the household.

Herr R_____ was a large man—tall, and heavier (I thought) than his physician was likely to have approved. He appeared to be about fifty; there was strength in his wide, fleshy face; his high forehead and capacious cranium suggested intellect; and his small, dark eyes, forever flickering as they took in the appearance of my person, the expression of my face, and the position of my hands and feet, ingenuity.

No pretense was apt to be of service with such a man, and I told him flatly that I had come as the emissary of Baron H_____, that I knew what troubled him, and that if he would cooperate with me I would help him if I could.

"I know you, monsieur," he said, "by reputation. A business with which I am associated employed you three years ago in the matter of a certain mummy." He named the firm. "I should have thought of you myself."

"I did not know that you were connected with them."

"I am not, when you leave this room. I do not know what reward Baron H_____ has offered you should you apprehend the man who is oppressing me, but I will give you, in addition to that, a sum equal to that you were paid for the mummy. You should be able to retire to the south then, should you choose, with the rent of a dozen villas."

"I do not choose," I told him, "and I could have retired long before. But what you just said interests me. You are certain that your persecutor is a living man?"

"I know men." Herr R_____ leaned back in his chair and stared at the painted ceiling. "As a boy I sold stuffed cabbage-leaf rolls in the street—did you know that? My mother cooked them over wood she collected herself where buildings were being demolished, and I sold them from a little cart for her. I lived to see her with half a score of footmen and the finest house in Lindau. I never went to school; I learned to add and subtract in the streets—when I must multiply and divide I have my clerk do it. But I learned men. Do you think that now, after forty years of practice, I could be deceived by a phantom? No, he is a man—let me confess it, a stronger man than I—a man of flesh and blood and brain, a man I have seen somewhere, sometime, here in this city—and more than once."

"Describe him."

"As tall as I. Younger—perhaps thirty or thirty-five. A brown, forked beard, so long." (He held his hand about fifteen centimeters beneath his chin.) "Brown hair. His hair is not yet gray, but I think it may be thinning a little at the temples."

"Don't you remember?"

"In my dream he wears a garland of roses—I cannot be sure."

"Is there anything else? Any scars or identifying marks?"

Herr R_____ nodded. "He has hurt his hand. In my dream, when he holds out his hand for the money, I see blood in it—it is his own, you understand, as though a recent injury has reopened and was beginning to bleed again. His hands are long and slender—like a pianist's."

"Perhaps you had better tell me your dream."

"Of course." He paused, and his face clouded, as though to recount the dream were to return to it. "I am in a great house. I am a person of importance there, almost as though I were the owner; yet I am not the owner—"

"Wait," I interrupted. "Does this house have a banquet hall? Has it a pillared portico, and is it set in a garden?"

For a moment Herr R_____'s eyes widened. "Have you also had such dreams?"

"No," I said. "It is only that I think I have heard of this house before. Please continue."

"There are many servants—some work in the fields beyond the garden. I give instructions to them—the details differ each night, you understand. Sometimes I am concerned with the kitchen, sometimes with the livestock, sometimes with the draining of a field. We grow wheat, principally, it seems; but there is a vineyard too, and a kitchen garden. And of course the house itself must be cleaned and swept and kept in repair. There is no wife; the owner's mother lives with us, I think, but she does not much concern herself with the housekeeping—that is up to me. To tell the truth, I have never actually seen her, though I have the feeling that she is there."

"Does this house resemble the one you bought for your own mother in Lindau?"

"Only as one large house must resemble another."

"I see. Proceed."

"For a long time each night I continue like that, giving orders, and sometimes going over the accounts. Then a servant, usually it is a maid, arrives to tell me that the owner wishes to speak to me. I stand before a mirror—I can see myself there as plainly as I see you now—and arrange my clothing. The maid brings rose-scented water and a cloth, and I wipe my face; then I go in to him.

"He is always in one of the upper rooms, seated at a table with his own account book spread before him. There is an open window behind him, and through it I can see the top of a cherry tree in bloom. For a long time—oh, I suppose ten minutes—I stand before him while he turns over the pages of his ledger."

"You appear somewhat at a loss, Herr R_____—not a common condition for you, I believe. What happens then?"

"He says, 'You owe . . .'" Herr R_____ paused. "This is the problem, monsieur, I can never recall the amount. But it is a large sum. He says, 'And I must require that you make payment at once.'

"I do not have the amount, and I tell him so. He says, 'Then you must leave my employment.' I fall to my knees at this and beg that he will retain me, pointing out that if he dismisses me I will have lost my source of income, and will never be able to make payment. I do not enjoy telling you this, but I weep. Sometimes I beat the floor with my fists."

"Continue. Is the Dream-Master moved by your pleading?"

"No. He again demands that I pay the entire sum. Several times I have told him that I am a wealthy man in this world, and that if only he would permit me to make payment in its currency, I would do so immediately."

"That is interesting—most of us lack your presence of mind in our nightmares. What does he say then?"

"Usually he tells me not to be a fool. But once he said, 'That is a dream—you must know it by now. You cannot expect to pay a real debt with the currency of sleep.' He holds out his hand for the money as he speaks to me. It is then that I see the blood in his palm."

"You are afraid of him?"

"Oh, very much so. I understand that he has the most complete power over me. I weep, and at last I throw myself at his feet—with my head under the table, if you can credit it, crying like an infant.

"Then he stands and pulls me erect, and says, 'You would never be able to pay all you owe, and you are a false and dishonest servant. But your debt is forgiven, forever.' And as I watch, he tears a leaf from his account book and hands it to me."

"Your dream has a happy conclusion, then."

"No. It is not yet over. I thrust the paper into the front of my shirt and go out, wiping my face on my sleeve. I am conscious that if any of the other servants should see me, they will know at once what has happened. I hurry to reach my own counting room; there is a brazier there, and I wish to burn the page from the owner's book."

"I see."

"But just outside the door of my own room, I meet another servant—an upper-servant like myself, I think, since he is well dressed. As it happens, this man owes me a considerable sum of money, and to conceal from him what I have just endured, I demand that he pay at once." Herr R_____ rose from his chair and began to pace the room, looking sometimes at the painted scenes on the walls, sometimes at the Turkish carpet at his feet. "I have had reason to demand money like that often, you understand. Here in this room.

"The man falls to his knees, weeping and begging for additional time; but I reach down, like this, and seize him by the throat."

"And then?"

"And then the door of my counting room opens. But it is not my counting room with my desk and the charcoal brazier, but the owner's own room. He is standing in the doorway, and behind him I can see the open window, and the blossoms of the cherry tree."

"What does he say to you?"

"Nothing. He says nothing to me. I release the other man's throat, and he slinks away."

"You awaken then?"

"How can I explain it? Yes, I wake up. But first we stand here; and while we do I am conscious of . . . certain sounds."

"If it is too painful for you, you need not say more."

Herr R_____ drew a silk handkerchief from his pocket and wiped his face. "How can I explain?" he said again. "When I hear those sounds, I am aware that the owner possesses certain other servants, who have never been under my direction. It is as though I have always known this, but had no reason to think of it before."

"I understand."

"They are quartered in another part of the house—in the vaults beneath the wine cellar, I think sometimes. I have never seen them, but I know—then—that they are hideous, vile and cruel; I know too that he thinks me but little better than they, and that as he permits me to serve him, so he allows them to serve him also. I stand—we stand—and listen to them coming through the house. At last a door at the end of the hall begins to swing open. There is a hand like the paw of some filthy reptile on the latch."

"Is that the end of the dream?"

"Yes." Herr R_____ threw himself into his chair again, mopping his face.

"You have this experience each night?"

"It differs," he said slowly, "in some details."

"You have told me that the orders you give the under-servants vary."

"There is another difference. When the dreams began, I woke when the hinges of the door at the passage-end creaked. Each night now the dream endures a moment longer. Perhaps a tenth of a second. Now I see the arm of the creature who opens that door, nearly to the elbow."

I took the address of his home, which he was glad enough to give me, and leaving the bank made my way to my hotel.

————

When I had eaten my roll and drunk my coffee the next morning, I went to the place indicated by the card given me by Baron H_____, and in a few minutes was sitting with him in a room as bare as those tents from which armies in the field are cast into battle. "You are ready to begin the case this morning?" he asked.

"On the contrary. I have already begun; indeed, I am about to enter a new phase of my investigation. You would not have come to me if your Dream-Master were not torturing someone other than the people whose names you gave me. I wish to know the identity of that person, and to interrogate him."

"I told you that there were many other reports. I—"

"Provided me with a list. They are all of the petite bourgeoisie, when they are not persons still less important. I believed at first that it might be because of the urgings of Herr R_____ that you engaged me; but when I had time to reflect on what I know of your methods, I realized that you would have demanded that he provide my fee had that been the case. So you are sheltering someone of greater importance, and I wish to speak to him."

"The Countess—" Baron H_____ began.

"Ah!"

"The Countess herself has expressed some desire that you should be presented to her. The Count opposes it."

"We are speaking, I take it, of the governor of this province?"

The Baron nodded. "Of Count von V_____. He is responsible, you understand, only to the Queen Regent herself."

"Very well. I wish to hear the Countess, and she wishes to talk with me. I assure you, Baron, that we will meet; the only question is whether it will be under your auspices."

The Countess, to whom I was introduced that afternoon, was a woman in her early twenties, deep-breasted and somber-haired, with skin like milk, and great dark eyes welling with fear and (I thought) pity, set in a perfect oval face.

"I am glad you have come, monsieur. For seven weeks now our good Baron H_____ has sought this man for me, but he has not found him."

"If I had known my presence here would please you, Countess, I would have come long ago, whatever the obstacles. You then, like the others, are certain it is a real man we seek?"

"I seldom go out, monsieur. My husband feels we are in constant danger of assassination."

"I believe he is correct."

"But on state occasions we sometimes ride in a glass coach to the *Rathaus*. There are uhlans all around us to protect us then. I am certain that—before the dreams began—I saw the face of this man in the crowd."

"Very well. Now tell me your dream."

"I am here, at home—"

"In this palace, where we sit now?"

She nodded.

"That is a new feature, then. Continue, please."

"There is to be an execution. In the garden." A fleeting smile crossed the Countess's lovely face. "I need not tell you that that is not where the executions are held; but it does not seem strange to me when I dream.

"I have been away, I think, and have only just heard of what is to take place. I rush into the garden. The man Baron H_____ calls the Dream-Master is there, tied to the trunk of the big cherry tree; a squad of soldiers faces him, holding their rifles; their officer stands beside them with his saber drawn, and my husband is watching from a pace or two away. I call out for them to stop, and my husband turns to look at me. I say: 'You must not do it, Karl. You must not kill this man.' But I see by his expression that he believes that I am only a foolish, tender-hearted child. Karl is . . . several years older than I."

"I am aware of it."

"The Dream-Master turns his head to look at me. People tell me that my eyes are large—do you think them large, monsieur?"

"Very large, and very beautiful."

"In my dream, quite suddenly, his eyes seem far, far larger than mine, and far more beautiful; and in them I see reflected the figure of my husband. Please listen carefully now, because what I am going to say is very important, though it makes very little sense, I am afraid."

"Anything may happen in a dream, Countess."

"When I see my husband reflected in this man's eyes, I know—I cannot say how—that it is this reflection, and not the man who stands near me, who is the real Karl. The man I have thought real is only a reflection of that reflection. Do you follow what I say?"

I nodded. "I believe so."

"I plead again: 'Do not kill him. Nothing good can come of it. . . .' My husband nods to the officer, the soldiers raise their rifles, and . . . and . . ."

"You wake. Would you like my handkerchief, Countess? It is of coarse weave; but it is clean, and much larger than your own."

"Karl is right—I am only a foolish little girl. No, monsieur, I do not wake—not yet. The soldiers fire. The Dream-Master falls forward, though his bonds hold him to the tree. And Karl flies to bloody rags beside me."

On my way back to my hotel, I purchased a map of the city; and when I reached my room I laid it flat on the table there. There could be no question of the route of the Countess's glass coach—straight down the Hauptstrasse, the only street in the city wide enough to take a carriage surrounded by cavalrymen. The most probable route by which Herr R_____ might go from his house to his bank coincided with the Hauptstrasse for several blocks. The path Fräulein A_____ would travel from her flat to the arcade crossed the Hauptstrasse at a point contained by that interval. I needed to know no more.

Very early the next morning I took up my post at the intersection. If my man were still alive after the fusillade Count von V_____ fired at him each night, it seemed certain that he would appear at this spot within a few days, and I am hardened to waiting. I smoked cigarettes while I watched the citizens of I_____ walk up and down before me. When an hour had passed, I bought a newspaper from a vendor, and stole a few glances at its pages when foot traffic was light.

Gradually I became aware that I was watched—we boast of reason, but there are senses over which reasons hold no authority. I did not know where my watcher was, yet I felt his gaze on me, whichever way I turned. So, I thought, you know me, my friend. Will I too dream now? What has attracted your attention to a mere foreigner, a stranger, waiting for who-knows-what at this corner? Have you been talking to Fräulein A_____? Or to someone who has spoken with her?

Without appearing to do so, I looked up and down both streets in search of another lounger like myself. There was no one—not a drowsing grandfather, not a woman or a child, not even a dog. Certainly no tall man with a forked beard and piercing eyes. The windows then—I studied them all, looking for some movement in a dark room behind a seemingly innocent opening. Nothing.

Only the buildings behind me remained. I crossed to the opposite side of the Hauptstrasse and looked once more. Then I laughed.

They must have thought me mad, all those dour burghers, for I fairly doubled over, spitting my cigarette to the sidewalk and clasping my hands to my waist for fear my belt would burst. The presumption, the impudence, the brazen insolence of the fellow! The stupidity, the wonderful stupidity of myself who had not recognized old stories! For the remainder of my life now, I could accept any case with pleasure, pursue the most inept criminal with zest, knowing that there was always a chance he might outwit such an idiot as I.

For the Dream-Master had set up His own picture, and full-length and in the most gorgeous colors, in His window. Choking and sputtering I saluted it, and then, still filled with laughter, I crossed the street once more and went inside, where I knew I would find Him. A man awaited me there—not the one I sought, but one who understood Whom it was I had come for, and knew as well as I that His capture was beyond any thief-taker's power. I knelt, and there, A_____, Herr R_____, and the Count and Countess von V_____, I destroyed the Dream-Master as He has been sacrificed so often, devouring His white, wheaten flesh that we might all possess life without end.

Dear people, dream on.

Unicorn Variations

Roger Zelazny

Roger Zelazny (1937–1995) burst onto the science fiction writing scene as part of the "New Wave" group of writers in the mid to late 1960s. His novels This Immortal *and* Lord of Light *met universal praise, the latter winning a Hugo award for best novel. His work is notable for its lyrical style and innovative use of language both in description and dialogue. His most recognized series is the Amber novels, about a parallel universe which is the one true world, with all others, Earth included, being mere reflections of his created universe. Besides the* Lord of Light *Hugo, he was also awarded three Nebulas, three more Hugos, and two Locus awards.*

A BIZARRERIE OF FIRES, CUNABULUM OF LIGHT, IT MOVED WITH A DEFT, almost dainty deliberation, phasing into and out of existence like a storm-shot piece of evening; or perhaps the darkness between the flares was more akin to its truest nature—swirl of black ashes assembled in prancing cadence to the lowing note of desert wind down the arroyo behind buildings as empty yet filled as the pages of unread books or stillnesses between the notes of a song.

Gone again. Back again. Again.

Power, you said? Yes. It takes considerable force of identity to manifest before or after one's time. Or both.

As it faded and gained it also advanced, moving through the warm afternoon, its tracks erased by the wind. That is, on those occasions when there were tracks.

A reason. There should always be a reason. Or reasons.

It knew why it was there—but not why it was *there*, in that particular locale.

It anticipated learning this shortly, as it approached the desolation-bound line of the old street. However, it knew that the reason may also come before, or after. Yet again, the pull was there and the force of its being was such that it had to be close to something.

The buildings were worn and decayed and some of them fallen and all of them drafty and dusty and empty. Weeds grew among floorboards. Birds nested upon rafters. The droppings of wild things were everywhere, and it knew them all as they would have known it, were they to meet face to face.

It froze, for there had come the tiniest unanticipated sound from somewhere ahead and to the left. At that moment, it was again phasing into existence and it released its outline which faded as quickly as a rainbow in hell, that but the naked presence remained beyond subtraction.

Invisible, yet existing, strong, it moved again. The clue. The cue. Ahead. *A gauche*. Beyond the faded word SALOON on weathered board above. Through the swinging doors. (One of them pinned alop.)

Pause and assess.

Bar to the right, dusty. Cracked mirror behind it. Empty bottles. Broken bottles. Brass rail, black, encrusted. Tables to the left and rear. In various states of repair.

Man seated at the best of the lot. His back to the door. Levi's. Hiking boots. Faded blue shirt. Green backpack leaning against the wall to his left.

Before him, on the tabletop, is the faint, painted outline of a chessboard, stained, scratched, almost obliterated.

The drawer in which he had found the chessmen is still partly open.

He could no more have passed up a chess set without working out a problem or replaying one of his better games than he could have gone without breathing, circulating his blood or maintaining a relatively stable body temperature.

It moved nearer, and perhaps there were fresh prints in dust behind it, but none noted them.

It, too, played chess.

It watched as the man replayed what had perhaps been his finest game, from the world preliminaries of seven years past. He had blown up after that—surprised to have gotten even as far as he had—for he never could perform well under pressure. But he had always been proud of that one game, and he relived it as all sensitive beings do certain turning points in their lives. For perhaps twenty minutes, no one could have touched him. He had been shining and pure and hard and clear. He had felt like the best.

It took up a position across the board from him and stared. The man completed the game, smiling. Then he set he board again, rose and fetched a can of beer from his pack. He popped the top.

When he returned, he discovered that White's King's Pawn had been advanced to K4. His brow furrowed. He turned his head, searching the bar, meeting his own puzzled gaze in the grimy mirror. He looked under the table. He took a drink of beer and seated himself.

He reached out and moved his Pawn to K4. A moment later, he saw White's King's Knight rise slowly into the air and drift forward to settle upon KB3. He stared for a long while into the emptiness across the table before he advanced his own Knight to his KB3.

White's Knight moved to take his Pawn. He dismissed the novelty of the situation and moved his Pawn to Q3. He all but forgot the absence of a tangible opponent as the White Knight dropped back to its KB3. He paused to take a sip of beer, but no sooner had he placed the can upon the tabletop than it rose again, passed across the board and was upended. A gurgling noise followed. Then the can fell to the floor, bouncing, ringing with an empty sound.

"I'm sorry," he said, rising and returning to his pack. "I'd have offered you one if I'd thought you were something that might like it."

He opened two more cans, returned with them, placed one near the far edge of the table, one at his own right hand.

"Thank you," came a soft, precise voice from a point beyond it.

The can was raised, tilted slightly, returned to the tabletop.

"My name is Martin," the man said.

"Call me Tlingel," said the other. "I had thought that perhaps your kind was extinct. I am pleased that you at least have survived to afford me this game."

"Huh?" Martin said. "We were all still around the last time that I looked—a couple of days ago."

"No matter. I can take care of that later," Tlingel replied. "I was misled by the appearance of this place."

"Oh. It's a ghost town. I backpack a lot."

"Not important. I am near the proper point in your career as a species. I can feel that much."

"I am afraid that I do not follow you."

"I am not at all certain that you would wish to. I assume that you intend to capture that pawn?"

"Perhaps. Yes, I do wish to. What are you talking about?"

The beer can rose. The invisible entity took another drink.

"Well," said Tlingel, "to put it simply, your—successors—grow anxious. Your place in the scheme of things being such an important one, I had sufficient power to come and check things out."

" 'Successors'? I do not understand."

"Have you seen any griffins recently?"

Martin chuckled.

"I've heard the stories," he said, "seen the photos of the one supposedly shot in the Rockies. A hoax, of course."

"Of course it must seem so. That is the way with mythical beasts."

"You're trying to say that it was real?"

"Certainly. Your world is in bad shape. When the last grizzly bear died recently, the way was opened for the griffins—just as the death of the last aepyornis brought in the yeti, the dodo the Loch Ness creature, the passenger pigeon the sasquatch, the blue whale the kraken, the American eagle the cockatrice—"

"You can't prove it by me."

"Have another drink."

Martin began to reach for the can, halted his hand and stared.

A creature approximately two inches in length, with a human face, a lion-like body and feathered wings was crouched next to the beer can.

"A mini-sphinx," the voice continued. "They came when you killed off the last smallpox bacillus."

"Are you trying to say that whenever a natural species dies out a mythical one takes its place?" he asked.

"In a word—yes. Now. It was not always so, but you have destroyed the mechanisms of evolution. The balance is now redressed by those others of us, from the morning land—we, who have never truly been endangered. We return, in our time."

"And you—whatever you are, Tlingel—you say that humanity is now endangered?"

"Very much so. But there is nothing that you can do about it, is there? Let us get on with the game."

The sphinx flew off. Martin took a sip of beer and captured the Pawn.

"Who," he asked then, "are to be our successors?"

"Modesty almost forbids," Tlingel replied. "In the case of a species as prominent as your own, it naturally has to be the loveliest, most intelligent, most important of us all."

"And what are you? Is there any way that I can have a look?"

"Well—yes. If I exert myself a trifle."

The beer can rose, was drained, fell to the floor. There followed a series of rapid rattling sounds retreating from the table. The air began to flicker over a large area opposite Martin, darkening within the glowing framework. The outline continued to brighten, its interior growing jet black. The form moved, prancing about the saloon, multitudes of tiny, cloven hoofprints scoring and cracking the floorboards. With a final, near-blinding flash it came into full view and Martin gasped to behold it.

A black unicorn with mocking, yellow eyes sported before him, rising for a moment onto its hind legs to strike a heraldic pose. The fires flared about it a second longer, then vanished.

Martin had drawn back, raising one hand defensively.

"Regard me!" Tlingel announced. "Ancient symbol of wisdom, valor and beauty, I stand before you!"

"I thought your typical unicorn was white," Martin finally said.

"I am archetypical," Tlingel responded, dropping to all fours, "and possessed of virtues beyond the ordinary."

"Such as?"

"Let us continue our game."

"What about the fate of the human race? You said—"

". . . And save the small talk for later."

"I hardly consider the destruction of humanity to be small talk."

"And if you've any more beer . . ."

"All right," Martin said, retreating to his pack as the creature advanced, its eyes like a pair of pale suns. "There's some lager."

Something had gone out of the game. As Martin sat before the ebon horn on Tlingel's bowed head, like an insect about to be pinned, he realized that his playing was off. He had felt the pressure the moment he had seen the beast—and there was all that talk about an imminent doomsday. Any run-of-the-mill pessimist could say it without troubling him, but coming from a source as peculiar as this . . .

His earlier elation had fled. He was no longer in top form. And Tlingel was good. Very good. Martin found himself wondering whether he could manage a stalemate.

After a time, he saw that he could not and resigned.

The unicorn looked at him and smiled.

"You don't really play badly—for a human," it said.

"I've done a lot better."

"It is no shame to lose to me, mortal. Even among mythical creatures there are very few who can give a unicorn a good game."

"I am pleased that you were not wholly bored," Martin said. "Now will you tell me what you were talking about concerning the destruction of my species?"

"Oh, that," Tlingel replied. "In the morning land where those such as I dwell, I felt the possibility of your passing come like a gentle wind to my nostrils, with the promise of clearing the way for us—"

"How is it supposed to happen?"

Tlingel shrugged, horn writing on the air with a toss of the head.

"I really couldn't say. Premonitions are seldom specific. In fact, that is what I came to discover. I should have been about it already, but you diverted me with beer and good sport."

"Could you be wrong about this?"

"I doubt it. That is the other reason I am here."

"Please explain."

"Are there any beers left?"

"Two, I think."

"Please."

Martin rose and fetched them.

"Damn! The tab broke off this one," he said.

"Place it upon the table and hold it firmly."

"All right."

Tlingel's horn dipped forward quickly, piercing the can's top.

". . . Useful for all sorts of things," Tlingel observed, withdrawing it.

"The other reason you're here . . ." Martin prompted.

"It is just that I am special. I can do things that the others cannot."

"Such as?"

"Find your weak spot and influence events to exploit it, to—hasten matters. To turn the possibility into a probability, and then—"

"*You* are going to destroy us? Personally?"

"That is the wrong way to look at it. It is more like a game of chess. It is as much a matter of exploiting your opponent's weaknesses as of exercising your own strengths. If you had not already laid the groundwork I would be powerless. I can only influence that which already exists."

"So what will it be? World War III? An ecological disaster? A mutated disease?"

"I do not really know yet, so I wish you wouldn't ask me in that fashion. I repeat that at the moment I am only observing. I am only an agent—"

"It doesn't sound that way to me."

Tlingel was silent. Martin began gathering up the chessmen.

"Aren't you going to set up the board again?"

"To amuse my destroyer a little more? No thanks."

"That's hardly the way to look at it—"

"Besides, those are the last beers."

"Oh." Tlingel stared wistfully at the vanishing pieces, then remarked, "I would be willing to play you again without additional refreshment . . ."

"No thanks."

"You are angry."

"Wouldn't you be, if our situations were reversed?"

"You are anthropomorphizing."

"Well?"

"Oh, I suppose I would."

"You could give us a break, you know—at least, let us make our own mistakes."

"You've hardly done that yourself, though, with all the creatures my fellows have succeeded."

Martin reddened.

"Okay. You just scored one. But I don't have to like it."

"You are a good player. I know that . . ."

"Tlingel, if I were capable of playing at my best again, I think I could beat you."

The unicorn snorted two tiny wisps of smoke.

"Not *that* good," Tlingel said.

"I guess you'll never know."

"Do I detect a proposal?"

"Possibly. What's another game worth to you?"

Tlingel made a chuckling noise.

"Let me guess: You are going to say that if you beat me you want my promise not to lay my will upon the weakest link in mankind's existence and shatter it."

"Of course."

"And what do I get for winning?"

"The pleasure of the game. That's what you want, isn't it?"

"The terms sound a little lopsided."

"Not if you are going to win anyway. You keep insisting that you will."

"All right. Set up the board."

"There is something else that you have to know about me first."

"Yes?"

"I don't play well under pressure, and this game is going to be a terrific strain. You want my best game, don't you?"

"Yes, but I'm afraid I've no way of adjusting your own reactions to the play."

"I believe I could do that myself if I had more than the usual amount of time between moves."

"Agreed."

"I mean a lot of time."

"Just what do you have in mind?"

"I'll need time to get my mind off it, to relax, to come back to the positions as if they were only problems . . ."

"You mean to go away from here between moves?"

"Yes."

"All right. How long?"

"I don't know. A few weeks, maybe."

"Take a month. Consult your experts, put your computers onto it. It may make for a slightly more interesting game."

"I really didn't have that in mind."

"Then it's time that you're trying to buy."

"I can't deny that. On the other hand, I will need it."

"In that case, I have some terms. I'd like this place cleaned up, fixed up, more lively. It's a mess. I also want beer on tap."

"Okay. I'll see to that."

"Then I agree. Let's see who goes first."

Martin switched a black and a white Pawn from hand to hand beneath the table. He raised his fists then and extended them. Tlingel leaned forward and tapped. The black horn's tip touched Martin's left hand.

"Well, it matches my sleek and glossy hide," the unicorn announced.

Martin smiled, setting up the white for himself, the black pieces for his opponent. As soon as he had finished, he pushed his Pawn to K4.

Tlingel's delicate, ebon hoof moved to advance the Black King's Pawn to K4.

"I take it that you want a month now, to consider your next move?"

Martin did not reply but moved his Knight to KB3. Tlingel immediately moved a Knight to QB3.

Martin took a swallow of beer and then moved his Bishop to N5. The unicorn moved the other Knight to B3. Martin immediately castled and Tlingel moved the Knight to take his Pawn.

"I think we'll make it," Martin said suddenly, "if you'll just let us alone. We do learn from our mistakes, in time."

"Mythical things do not exactly exist in time. Your world is a special case."

"Don't you people ever make mistakes?"

"Whenever we do they're sort of poetic."

Martin snarled and advanced his Pawn to Q4. Tlingel immediately countered by moving the Knight to Q3.

"I've got to stop," Martin said, standing. "I'm getting mad, and it will affect my game."

"You will be going, then?"

"Yes."

He moved to fetch his pack.

"I will see you here in one month's time?"

"Yes."

"Very well."

The unicorn rose and stamped upon the floor and lights began to play across its dark coat. Suddenly, they blazed and shot outward in all directions like a silent explosion. A wave of blackness followed.

Martin found himself leaning against the wall, shaking. When he lowered his hand from his eyes, he saw that he was alone, save for the knights, the bishops, the kings, the queens, their castles and both the kings' men.

He went away.

Three days later Martin returned in a small truck, with a generator, lumber, windows, power tools, paint, stain, cleaning compounds, wax. He dusted and vacuumed and replaced rotted wood. He installed the windows. He polished the old brass until it shone. He stained and rubbed. He waxed the floors and buffed them. He plugged holes and washed glass. He hauled all the trash away.

It took him the better part of a week to turn the old place from a wreck back into a saloon in appearance. Then he drove off, returned all of the equipment he had rented and bought a ticket for the Northwest.

The big, damp forest was another of his favorite places for hiking, for thinking. And he was seeking a complete change of scene, a total revision of outlook. Not that his next move did not seem obvious, standard even. Yet, something nagged . . .

He knew that it was more than just the game. Before that he had been ready to get away again, to walk drowsing among shadows, breathing clean air.

Resting, his back against the bulging root of a giant tree, he withdrew a small chess set from his pack, set it up on a rock he'd moved into position nearby. A fine, mist-like rain was settling, but the tree sheltered him, so far. He reconstructed the opening through Tlingel's withdrawal of the Knight to Q3. The simplest thing would be to take the Knight with the Bishop. But he did not move to do it.

He watched the board for a time, felt his eyelids dropping, closed them and drowsed. It may only have been for a few minutes. He was never certain afterward.

Something aroused him. He did not know what. He blinked several times and closed his eyes again. Then he reopened them hurriedly.

In his nodded position, eyes directed downward, his gaze was fixed upon an enormous pair of hairy, unshod feet—the largest pair of feet that he had ever beheld. They stood unmoving before him, pointed toward his right.

Slowly—very slowly—he raised his eyes. Not very far, as it turned out. The creature was only about four and a half feet in height. As it was looking at the chessboard rather than at him, he took the opportunity to study it.

It was unclothed but very hairy, with a dark brown pelt, obviously masculine, possessed of low brow ridges, deep-set eyes that matched its hair, heavy shoulders, five-fingered hands that sported opposing thumbs.

It turned suddenly and regarded him, flashing a large number of shining teeth.

"White's pawn should take the pawn," it said in a soft, nasal voice.

"Huh? Come on," Martin said. "Bishop takes knight."

"You want to give me black and play it that way? I'll walk all over you."

Martin glanced again at its feet.

". . . Or give me white and let me take that pawn. I'll still do it."

"Take white," Martin said, straightening. "Let's see if you know what you're talking about." He reached for his pack. "Have a beer?"

"What's a beer?"

"A recreational aid. Wait a minute."

Before they had finished the six-pack, the sasquatch—whose name, he had learned, was Grend—had finished Martin. Grend had quickly entered a ferocious midgame, backed him into a position of swindling security and pushed him to the point where he had seen the end and resigned.

"That was one hell of a game," Martin declared, leaning back and considering the ape-like countenance before him.

"Yes, we Bigfeet are pretty good, if I do say it. It's our one big recreation, and we're so damned primitive we don't have much in the way of boards and chessmen. Most of the time, we just play it in our heads. There're not many can come close to us."

"How about unicorns?" Martin asked.

Grend nodded slowly.

"They're about the only ones can really give us a good game. A little dainty, but they're subtle. Awfully sure of themselves, though, I must say. Even when they're wrong. Haven't seen any since we left the morning land, of course. Too bad. Got any more of that beer left?"

"I'm afraid not. But listen, I'll be back this way in a month. I'll bring some more if you'll meet me here and play again."

"Martin, you've got a deal. Sorry. Didn't mean to step on your toes."

He cleaned the saloon again and brought in a keg of beer which he installed under the bar and packed with ice. He moved in some bar stools, chairs and tables which he had obtained at a Goodwill store. He hung red curtains. By then it was evening. He set up the board, ate a light meal, unrolled his sleeping bag behind the bar and camped there that night.

The following day passed quickly. Since Tlingel might show up at any time, he did not leave the vicinity, but took his meals there and sat about working chess problems. When it began to grow dark, he lit a number of oil lamps and candles.

He looked at his watch with increasing frequency. He began to pace. He couldn't have made a mistake. This was the proper day. He—

He heard a chuckle.

Turning about, he saw a black unicorn head floating in the air above the chessboard. As he watched, the rest of Tlingel's body materialized.

"Good evening, Martin." Tlingel turned away from the board. "The place looks a little better. Could use some music . . ."

Martin stepped behind the bar and switched on the transistor radio he had brought along. The sounds of a string quartet filled the air. Tlingel winced.

"Hardly in keeping with the atmosphere of the place."

He changed stations, located a Country & Western show.

"I think not," Tlingel said. "It loses something in transmission."

He turned it off.

"Have we a good supply of beverage?"

Martin drew a gallon stein of beer—the largest mug that he could locate, from a novelty store—and set it upon the bar. He filled a much smaller one for himself. He was determined to get the beast drunk if it were at all possible.

"Ah! Much better than those little cans," said Tlingel whose muzzle dipped for but a moment. "Very good."

The mug was empty. Martin refilled it.

"Will you move it to the table for me?"

"Certainly."

"Have an interesting month?"

"I suppose I did."

"You've decided upon your next move?"

"Yes."

"Then let's get on with it."

Martin seated himself and captured the Pawn.

"Hm. Interesting."

Tlingel stared at the board for a long while, then raised a cloven hoof which parted in reaching for the piece.

"I'll just take that bishop with this little knight. Now I suppose you'll be wanting another month to make up your mind what to do next."

Tlingel leaned to the side and drained the mug.

"Let me consider it," Martin said, "while I get you a refill."

Martin sat and stared at the board through three more refills. Actually, he was not planning. He was waiting. His response to Grend had been Knight takes Bishop, and he had Grend's next move ready.

"Well?" Tlingel finally said. "What do you think?"

Martin took a small sip of beer.

"Almost ready," he said. "You hold your beer awfully well."

Tlingel laughed.

"A unicorn's horn is a detoxicant. Its possession is a universal remedy. I wait until I reach the warm glow stage, then I use my horn to burn off any excess and keep me right there."

"Oh," said Martin. "Neat trick, that."

". . . If you've had too much, just touch my horn for a moment and I'll put you back in business."

"No, thanks. That's all right. I'll just push this little pawn in front of the queen's rook two steps ahead."

"Really . . ." said Tlingel. "That's interesting. You know, what this place really needs is a piano—rinkytink, funky . . . Think you could manage it?"

"I don't play."

"Too bad."

"I suppose I could hire a piano player."

"No. I do not care to be seen by other humans."

"If he's really good, I suppose he could play blindfolded."

"Never mind."

"I'm sorry."

"You are also ingenious. I am certain that you will figure something out by next time."

Martin nodded.

"Also, didn't those old places used to have sawdust all over the floors?"

"I believe so."

"That would be nice."

"Check."

Tlingel searched the board frantically for a moment.

"Yes. I meant 'yes.' I said 'check.' It means 'yes' sometimes, too."

"Oh. Rather. Well, while we're here . . ."

Tlingel advanced the Pawn to Q3.

Martin stared. That was not what Grend had done. For a moment he considered continuing on his own from here. He had tried to think of Grend as a coach up until this point. He had forced away the notion of crudely and crassly pitting one of them against the other. Until P-Q3. Then he recalled the game he had lost to the sasquatch.

"I'll draw the line here," he said, "and take my month."

"All right. Let's have another drink before we say good night. Okay?"

"Sure. Why not?"

They sat for a time and Tlingel told him of the morning land, of primeval forests and rolling plains, of high craggy mountains and purple seas, of magic and mythic beasts.

Martin shook his head.

"I can't quite see why you're so anxious to come here," he said, "with a place like that to call home."

Tlingel sighed.

"I suppose you'd call it keeping up with the griffins. It's the thing to do these days. Well. Till next month . . ."

Tlingel rose and turned away.

"I've got complete control now. Watch!"

The unicorn form faded, jerked out of shape, grew white, faded again, was gone, like an afterimage.

Martin moved to the bar and drew himself another mug. It was a shame to waste what was left. In the morning, he wished the unicorn were there again. Or at least the horn.

It was a gray day in the forest and he held an umbrella over the chessboard upon the rock. The droplets fell from the leaves and made dull, plopping noises as they struck the fabric. The board was set up again through Tlingel's P-Q3. Martin wondered whether Grend had remembered, had kept proper track of the days . . .

"Hello," came the nasal voice from somewhere behind him and to the left.

He turned to see Grend moving about the tree, stepping over the massive roots with massive feet.

"You remembered," Grend said. "How good! I trust you also remembered the beer?"

"I've lugged up a whole case. We can set up the bar right here."

"What's a bar?"

"Well, it's a place where people go to drink—in out of the rain—a bit dark, for atmosphere—and they sit up on stools before a big counter, or else at little tables—and they talk to each other—and sometimes there's music—and they drink."

"We're going to have all that here?"

"No. Just the dark and the drinks. Unless you count the rain as music. I was speaking figuratively."

"Oh. It does sound like a very good place to visit, though."

"Yes. If you will hold this umbrella over the board, I'll set up the best equivalent we can have here."

"All right. Say, this looks like a version of that game we played last time."

"It is. I got to wondering what would happen if it had gone this way rather than the way that it went."

"Hmm. Let me see . . ."

Martin removed four six-packs from his pack and opened the first.

"Here you go."

"Thanks."

Grend accepted the beer, squatted, passed the umbrella back to Martin.

"I'm still white?"

"Yeah."

"Pawn to king six."

"Really?"

"Yep."

"About the best thing for me to do would be to take this pawn with this one."

"I'd say. Then I'll just knock off your knight with this one."

"I guess I'll just pull this knight back to K2."

". . . And I'll take this one over to B3. May I have another beer?"

An hour and a quarter later, Martin resigned. The rain had let up and he had folded the umbrella.

"Another game?" Grend asked.

"Yes."

The afternoon wore on. The pressure was off. This one was just for fun. Martin tried wild combinations, seeing ahead with great clarity, as he had that one day . . .

"Stalemate," Grend announced much later. "That was a good one, though. You picked up considerably."

"I was more relaxed. Want another?"

"Maybe in a little while. Tell me more about bars now."

So he did. Finally, "How is all that beer affecting you?" he asked.

"I'm a bit dizzy. But that's all right. I'll still cream you the third game."

And he did.

"Not bad for a human, though. Not bad at all. You coming back next month?"

"Yes."

"Good. You'll bring more beer?"

"So long as my money holds out."

"Oh. Bring some plaster of paris then. I'll make you some nice footprints and you can take casts of them. I understand they're going for quite a bit."

"I'll remember that."

Martin lurched to his feet and collected the chess set.

"Till then."

"Ciao."

Martin dusted and polished again, moved in the player piano and scattered sawdust upon the floor. He installed a fresh keg. He hung some reproductions of period posters and some atrocious old paintings he had located in a junk shop. He placed cuspidors in strategic locations. When he was finished, he seated himself at the bar and opened a bottle of mineral water. He listened to the New Mexico wind moaning as it passed, to grains of sand striking against the windowpanes. He wondered whether the whole world would have that dry, mournful sound to it if Tlingel found a means of doing away with humanity, or—disturbing thought—whether the successors to his own kind might turn things into something resembling the mythical morning land.

This troubled him for a time. Then he went and set up the board through Black's P-Q3. When he turned back to clear the bar he saw a line of cloven hoofprints advancing across the sawdust.

"Good evening, Tlingel," he said. "What is your pleasure?"

Suddenly, the unicorn was there, without preliminary pyrotechnics. It moved to the bar and placed one hoof upon the brass rail.

"The usual."

As Martin drew the beer, Tlingel looked about.

"The place has improved, a bit."

"Glad you think so. Would you care for some music?"

"Yes."

Martin fumbled at the back of the piano, locating the switch for the small, battery-operated computer which controlled the pumping mechanism and substituted its own memory for rolls. The keyboard immediately came to life.

"Very good," Tlingel stated. "Have you found your move?"

"I have."

"Then let us be about it."

He refilled the unicorn's mug and moved it to the table, along with his own.

"Pawn to king six," he said, executing it.

"What?"

"Just that."

"Give me a minute. I want to study this."

"Take your time."

"I'll take the pawn," Tlingel said, after a long pause and another mug.

"Then I'll take this knight."

Later, "Knight to K2," Tlingel said.

"Knight to B3."

An extremely long pause ensued before Tlingel moved the Knight to N3.

The hell with asking Grend, Martin suddenly decided. He'd been through this part any number of times already. He moved his Knight to N5.

"Change the tune on that thing!" Tlingel snapped.

Martin rose and obliged.

"I don't like that one either. Find a better one or shut it off!"

After three more tries, Martin shut it off.

"And get me another beer!"

He refilled their mugs.

"All right."

Tlingel moved the Bishop to K2.

Keeping the unicorn from castling had to be the most important thing at the moment. So Martin moved his Queen to R5. Tlingel made a tiny, strangling noise, and when Martin looked up smoke was curling from the unicorn's nostrils.

"More beer?"

"If you please."

As he returned with it, he saw Tlingel move the Bishop to capture the Knight. There seemed no choice for him at that moment, but he studied the position for a long while anyhow.

Finally, "Bishop takes bishop," he said.

"Of course."

"How's the warm glow?"

Tlingel chuckled.

"You'll see."

The wind rose again, began to howl. The building creaked.

"Okay," Tlingel finally said, and moved the Queen to Q2.

Martin stared. What was he doing? So far, it had gone all right, but— He listened again to the wind and thought of the risk he was taking.

"That's all, folks," he said, leaning back in his chair. "Continued next month."

Tlingel sighed.

"Don't run off. Fetch me another. Let me tell you of my wanderings in your world this past month."

"Looking for weak links?"

"You're lousy with them. How do you stand it?"

"They're harder to strengthen than you might think. Any advice?"

"Get the beer."

They talked until the sky paled in the east, and Martin found himself taking surreptitious notes. His admiration for the unicorn's analytical abilities increased as the evening advanced.

When they finally rose, Tlingel staggered.

"You all right?"

"Forgot to detox, that's all. Just a second. Then I'll be fading."

"Wait!"

"Whazzat?"

"I could use one, too."

"Oh. Grab hold, then."

Tlingel's head descended and Martin took the tip of the horn between his fingertips. Immediately, a delicious, warm sensation flowed through him. He closed his eyes to enjoy it. His head cleared. An ache which had been growing within his frontal sinus vanished. The tiredness went out of his muscles. He opened his eyes again.

"Thank—"

Tlingel had vanished. He held but a handful of air.

"—you."

"Rael here is my friend," Grend stated. "He's a griffin."

"I'd noticed."

Martin nodded at the beaked, golden-winged creature.

"Pleased to meet you, Rael."

"The same," cried the other in a high-pitched voice. "Have you got the beer?"

"Why—uh—yes."

"I've been telling him about beer," Grend explained, half-apologetically. "He can have some of mine. He won't kibitz or anything like that."

"Sure. All right. Any friend of yours . . ."

"The beer!" Rael cried. "Bars!"

"He's not real bright," Grend whispered. "But he's good company. I'd appreciate your humoring him."

Martin opened the first six-pack and passed the griffin and the sasquatch a beer apiece. Rael immediately punctured the can with his beak, chugged it, belched and held out his claw.

"Beer!" he shrieked. "More beer!"

Martin handed him another.

"Say, you're still into that first game, aren't you?" Grend observed, studying the board. "Now, *that* is an interesting position."

Grend drank and studied the board.

"Good thing it's not raining," Martin commented.

"Oh, it will. Just wait a while."

"More beer!" Rael screamed.

Martin passed him another without looking.

"I'll move my pawn to N6," Grend said.

"You're kidding."

"Nope. Then you'll take that pawn with your bishop's awn. Right?"

"Yes . . ."

Martin reached out and did it.

"Okay. Now I'll just swing this knight to Q5."

Martin took it with the Pawn.

Grend moved his Rook to K1.

"Check," he announced.

"Yes. That *is* the way to go," Martin observed.

Grend chuckled.

"I'm going to win this game another time," he said.

"I wouldn't put it past you."

"More beer?" Rael said softly.

"Sure."

As Martin poured him another, he noticed that the griffin was now leaning against the treetrunk.

After several minutes, Martin pushed his King to B1.

"Yeah, that's what I thought you'd do," Grend said. "You know something?"

"What?"

"You play a lot like a unicorn."

"Hm."

Grend moved his Rook to R3.

Later, as the rain descended gently about them and Grend beat him again, Martin realized that a prolonged period of silence had prevailed. He glanced over at the griffin. Rael had tucked his head beneath his left wing, balanced upon one leg, leaned heavily against the tree and gone to sleep.

"I told you he wouldn't be much trouble," Grend remarked.

Two games later, the beer was gone, the shadows were lengthening and Rael was stirring.

"See you next month?"

"Yeah."

"You bring my plaster of paris?"

"Yes, I did."

"Come on, then. I know a good place pretty far from here. We don't want people beating about *these* bushes. Let's go make you some money."

"To buy beer?" Rael said, looking out from under his wing.

"Next month," Grend said.

"You ride?"

"I don't think you could carry both of us," said Grend, "and I'm not sure I'd want to right now if you could."

"Bye-bye then," Rael shrieked, and he leaped into the air, crashing into branches and treetrunks, finally breaking through the overhead cover and vanishing.

"There goes a really decent guy," said Grend. "He sees everything and he never forgets. Knows how everything works—in the woods, in the air—even in the water. Generous, too, whenever he has anything."

"Hm," Martin observed.

"Let's make tracks," Grend said.

"Pawn to N6? Really?" Tlingel said. "All right. The bishop's pawn will just knock off the pawn."

Tlingel's eyes narrowed as Martin moved the Knight to Q5.

"At least this is an interesting game," the unicorn remarked. "Pawn takes knight."

Martin moved the Rook.

"Check."

"Yes, it is. This next one is going to be a three flagon move. Kindly bring me the first."

Martin thought back as he watched Tlingel drink and ponder. He almost felt guilty for hitting it with a powerhouse like the sasquatch behind its back. He was convinced now that the unicorn was going to lose. In every variation of this game that he'd played with Black against Grend, he'd been beaten. Tlingel was very good, but the sasquatch was a wizard with not much else to do but mental chess. It was unfair. But it was not a matter of personal honor, he kept telling himself. He was playing to protect his species against a supernatural force which might well be able to precipitate World War III by some arcane mind-manipulation or magically induced computer foulup. He didn't dare give the creature a break.

"Flagon number two, please."

He brought it another. He studied it as it studied the board. It was beautiful, he realized for the first time. It was the loveliest living thing he had ever seen. Now that the pressure was on the verge of evaporating and he could regard it without the overlay of fear which had always been there in the past, he could pause to admire it. If something *had* to succeed the human race, he could think of worse choices . . .

"Number three now."

"Coming up."

Tlingel drained it and moved the King to B1.

Martin leaned forward immediately and pushed the Rook to R3.

Tlingel looked up, stared at him.

"Not bad."

Martin wanted to squirm. He was struck by the nobility of the creature. He wanted so badly to play and beat the unicorn on his own, fairly. Not this way.

Tlingel looked back at the board, then almost carelessly moved the Knight to K4.

"Go ahead. Or will it take you another month?"

Martin growled softly, advanced the Rook and captured the Knight.

"Of course."

Tlingel captured the Rook with the Pawn. This was not the way that the last variation with Grend had run. Still . . .

He moved his Rook to KB3. As he did, the wind seemed to commence a peculiar shrieking, above, amid the ruined buildings.

"Check," he announced.

The hell with it! he decided. I'm good enough to manage my own endgame. Let's play this out.

He watched and waited and finally saw Tlingel move the King to N1.

He moved his Bishop to R6. Tlingel moved the Queen to K2. The shrieking came again, sounding nearer now. Martin took the Pawn with the Bishop.

The unicorn's head came up and it seemed to listen for a moment. Then Tlingel lowered it and captured the Bishop with the King.

Martin moved his Rook to KN3.

"Check."

Tlingel returned the King to B1.

Martin moved the Rook to KB3.

"Check."

Tlingel pushed the King to N2.

Martin moved the Rook back to KN3.

"Check."

Tlingel returned the King to B1, looked up and stared at him, showing teeth.

"Looks as if we've got a drawn game," the unicorn stated. "Care for another one?"

"Yes, but not for the fate of humanity."

"Forget it. I'd given up on that a long time ago. I decided that I wouldn't care to live here after all. I'm a little more discriminating than that."

"Except for this bar."

Tlingel turned away as another shriek sounded just beyond the door, followed by strange voices. "What is that?"

"I don't know," Martin answered, rising.

The doors opened and a golden griffin entered.

"Martin!" it cried. "Beer! Beer!"

"Uh—Tlingel, this is Rael, and, and—"

Three more griffins followed him in. Then came Grend, and three others of his own kind.

"—and that one's Grend," Martin said lamely. "I don't know the others."

They all halted when they beheld the unicorn.

"Tlingel," one of the sasquatches said. "I thought you were still in the morning land."

"I still am, in a way. Martin, how is it that you are acquainted with my former countrymen?"

"Well—uh—Grend here is my chess coach."

"Aha! I begin to understand."

"I am not sure that you really do. But let me get everyone a drink first."

Martin turned on the piano and set everyone up.

"How did you find this place?" he asked Grend as he was doing it. "And how did you get here?"

"Well . . ." Grend looked embarrassed. "Rael followed you back."

"Followed a jet?"

"Griffins are supernaturally fast."

"Oh."

"Anyway, he told his relatives and some of my folks about it. When we saw that the griffins were determined to visit you, we decided that we had better come along to keep them out of trouble. They brought us."

"I—see. Interesting . . ."

"No wonder you played like a unicorn, that one game with all the variations."

"Uh—yes."

Martin turned away, moved to the end of the bar.

"Welcome, all of you," he said. "I have a small announcement. Tlingel, awhile back you had a number of observations concerning possible ecological and urban disasters and lesser dangers. Also, some ideas as to possible safeguards against some of them."

"I recall," said the unicorn.

"I passed them along to a friend of mine in Washington who used to be a member of my old chess club. I told him that the work was not entirely my own."

"I should hope so."

"He has since suggested that I turn whatever group was involved into a think tank. He will then see about paying something for its efforts."

"I didn't come here to save the world," Tlingel said.

"No, but you've been very helpful. And Grend tells me that the griffins, even if their vocabulary is a bit limited, know almost all that there is to know about ecology."

"That is probably true."

"Since they have inherited a part of the Earth, it would be to their benefit as well to help preserve the place. Inasmuch as this many of us are already here, I can save myself some travel and suggest right now that we find a meeting place—say here, once a month—and that you let me have your unique viewpoints. You must know more about how species become extinct than anyone else in the business."

"Of course," said Grend, waving his mug, "but we really should ask the yeti, also. I'll do it, if you'd like. Is that stuff coming out of the big box music?"

"Yes."

"I like it. If we do this think tank thing, you'll make enough to keep this place going?"

"I'll buy the whole town."

Grend conversed in quick gutturals with the griffins, who shrieked back at him.

"You've got a think tank," he said, "and they want more beer."

Martin turned toward Tlingel.

"They were your observations. What do you think?"

"It may be amusing," said the unicorn, "to stop by occasionally." Then, "So much for saving the world. Did you say you wanted another game?"

"I've nothing to lose."

Grend took over the tending of the bar while Tlingel and Martin returned to the table.

He beat the unicorn in thirty-one moves and touched the extended horn.

The piano keys went up and down. Tiny sphinxes buzzed about the bar, drinking the spillage.

Basileus

Robert Silverberg

Robert Silverberg's dozens of science fiction and fantasy novels have addressed such themes as overpopulation, alien invasion, drug use, man's use of technology, and the perils of sorcery. His many worlds of wonder and the fantastic, alien races and societies that he has created in great detail, have brought him four Hugo awards and five Nebula trophies. His best-known books are those set on the world of Majipoor, an immense planet of great beauty and strangeness.

IN THE SHIMMERING LEMON-YELLOW OCTOBER LIGHT, CUNNINGHAM touches the keys of his terminal and summons angels. An instant to load the program, an instant to bring the file up, and there they are, ready to spout from the screen at his command: Apollyon, Anauel, Uriel, and all the rest. Uriel is the angel of thunder and terror; Apollyon is the Destroyer, the angel of the bottomless pit; Anauel is the angel of bankers and commission brokers. Cunningham is fascinated by the multifarious duties and tasks, both exalted and humble, that are assigned to the angels. "Every visible thing in the world is put under the charge of an angel," said St. Augustine in *The Eight Questions.*

Cunningham has 1,114 angels in his computer now. He adds a few more each night, though he knows that he has a long way to go before he has them all. In the fourteenth century the number of angels was reckoned by the Kabbalists, with some precision, at 301,655,722. Albertus Magnus had earlier calculated that each choir of angels held 6,666 legions, and each legion 6,666 angels; even without knowing the number of choirs, one can see that that produces rather a higher total. And in the Talmud, Rabbi Jochanan proposed that new angels are born "with every utterance that goes forth from the mouth of the Holy One, blessed be He."

If Rabbi Jochanan is correct, the number of angels is infinite. Cunningham's personal computer, though it has extraordinary add-on memory capacity and is capable, if he chooses, of tapping into the huge mainframe machines of the Defense Department, has no very practical way of handling an infinity. But he is doing his best. To have 1,114 angels on line already, after only eight months of part-time programming, is no small achievement.

One of his favorites of the moment is Harahel, the angel of archives, libraries, and rare cabinets. Cunningham has designated Harahel also the angel of computers: it seems appropriate. He invokes Harahel often, to discuss the evolving niceties of data processing with him. But he has many other favorites, and his tastes run somewhat to the sinister: Azrael, the angel of death, for example; and Arioch, the angel of vengeance; and Zebuleon, one of the nine angels who will govern at the end of the world. It is Cunningham's job, from eight to four every working day, to devise programs for the interception of incoming Soviet nuclear warheads, and that, perhaps, has inclined him toward the more apocalyptic members of the angelic host.

He invokes Harahel now. He has bad news for him. The invocation that he uses is a standard one that he found in Arthur Edward Waite's *The Lemegeton, or The Lesser Key of Solomon,* and he has dedicated one of his function keys to its text, so that a single keystroke suffices to load it. "I do invoke, conjure, and command thee, O thou Spirit N, to appear and to show thyself visibly unto me before this Circle in fair and comely shape," is the way it begins, and it proceeds to utilize various secret and potent names of God in the summoning of Spirit N—such names as Zabaoth and Elion and, of course, Adonai—and it concludes, "I do potently exorcise thee that thou appearest here to fulfill my will in all things which seem good unto me. Wherefore, come thou, visibly, peaceably, and affably, now, without delay to manifest that which I desire, speaking with a clear and perfect voice, intelligibly, and to mine understanding." All that takes but a microsecond, and another moment to read in the name of Harahel as Spirit N, and there the angel is one the screen.

"I am here at your summons," he announces expectantly.

Cunningham works with his angels from five to seven every evening. Then he has dinner. He lives alone, in a neat little flat a few blocks west of the Bayshore Freeway, and does not spend much of his time socializing. He thinks of himself as a pleasant man, a sociable man, and he may very well be right about that, but the pattern of his life has been a solitary one. He is thirty-seven years old, five feet eleven, with red hair, pale blue eyes, and a light dusting of freckles on his cheeks. He did his undergraduate work at Cal Tech, his postgraduate studies at Stanford, and for the last nine years he has been involved in ultrasensitive military-computer projects in northern California. He has never married. Sometimes he works with his angels again after dinner, from eight to ten, but hardly ever any later than that. At ten he goes to bed. He is a very methodical person.

He has given Harahel the physical form of his own first computer, a little Radio Shack TRS-80, with wings flanking the screen. He had thought originally to make the appearance of his angels more abstract—showing Harahel as a sheaf of kilobytes, for example— but like many of Cunningham's best and most austere ideas, it had turned out impractical in the execution, since abstract concepts did not translate well into graphics for him.

"I want to notify you," Cunningham says, "of a shift in jurisdiction." He speaks English with his angels. He has it on good, though apocryphal, authority that the primary language of the angels is Hebrew, but his computer's audio algorithms have no Hebrew capacity, nor does Cunningham. But they speak English readily enough with him: they have no choice. "From now on," Cunningham tells Harahel, "your domain is limited to hardware only."

Angry green lines rapidly cross and recross Harahel's screen, "By whose authority do you—"

"It isn't a question of authority," Cunningham replies smoothly. "It's a question of precision. I've just read Vretil into the data base, and I have to code his functions. He's the recording angel, after all. So, to some degree, then, he overlaps your territory."

"Ah," says Harahel, sounding melancholy. "I was hoping you wouldn't bother about him."

"How can I overlook such an important angel? 'Scribe of the knowledge of the Most High,' according to the Book of Enoch. 'Keeper of the heavenly books and records. Quicker in wisdom than the other archangels.'"

"If he's so quick," says Harahel sullenly, "give *him* the hardware. That's what governs the response time, you know."

"I understand. But he maintains the lists. That's data base."

"And where does the data base live? The hardware!"

"Listen, this isn't easy for me," Cunningham says. "But I have to be fair. I know you'll agree that some division of responsibilities is in order. And I'm giving him all data bases and related software. You keep the rest."

"Screens. Terminals. CPUs. Big deal."

"But without you, he's nothing, Harahel. Anyway, you've always been in charge of cabinets, haven't you?"

"And archives and libraries," the angel says. "Don't forget that."

"I'm not. But what's a library? Is it the books and shelves and stacks, or the words on the pages? We have to distinguish the container from the thing contained."

"A grammarian," Harahel sighs. "A hair splitter. A casuist."

"Look, Vretil wants the hardware, too. But he's willing to compromise. Are you?"

"You start to sound less and less like our programmer and more and more like the Almighty every day," says Harahel.

"Don't blaspheme," Cunningham tells him. "Please. Is it agreed? Hardware only?"

"You win," says the angel. "But you always do, naturally."

Naturally. Cunningham is the one with his hands on the keyboard, controlling things. The angels, though they are eloquent enough and have distinct and passionate personalities, are mere magnetic impulses deep within. In any contest with Cunningham they don't stand a chance. Cunningham, though he tries always to play the game by the rules, knows that, and so do they.

It makes him uncomfortable to think about it, but the role he plays is definitely godlike in all essential ways. He puts the angels into the computer; he gives them their tasks, their personalities, and their physical appearances; he summons them or leaves them uncalled, as he wishes.

A godlike role, yes. But Cunningham resists confronting that notion. He does not believe he is trying to be God; he does not even want to think about God. His family had been on comfortable terms with God—Uncle Tim was a priest, there was an archbishop somewhere back a few generations, his parents and sisters moved cozily within the divine presence as within a warm bath—but he himself, unable to quantify the Godhead, preferred to sidestep any thought of it. There were other, more immediate matters to engage his concern. His mother had wanted him to go into the priesthood, of all things, but Cunningham had averted that by demonstrating so visible and virtuosic a skill at mathematics that even she could see he was destined for science. Then she had prayed for a Nobel Prize in physics for him; but he had preferred computer technology. "Well," she said, "a Nobel in computers. I ask the Virgin daily."

"There's no Nobel in computers, Mom," he told her. But he suspects she still offers novenas for it.

The angel project had begun as a lark, but had escalated swiftly into an obsession. He was reading Gustav Davidson's old *Dictionary of Angels,* and when he came upon the description of the angel Adramelech, who had rebelled with Satan and had been cast from heaven, Cunningham thought it might be amusing to build a computer simulation and talk with him. Davidson said that Adramelech was sometimes shown as a winged and bearded lion, and sometimes as a mule with feathers, and sometimes as a peacock, and that one poet had described him as "the enemy of God, greater in malice, guile, ambition, and mischief than Satan, a fiend more curst, a deeper hypocrite." That was appealing. Well, why not build him? The graphics were easy—Cunningham chose the winged-lion form—but getting the personality constructed involved a month of intense labor and some consultations with the artificial-intelligence people over at Kestrel Institute. But finally Adramelech was on line, suave and diabolical, talking amiably of his days as an Assyrian god and his conversations with Beelzebub, who had named him Chancellor of the Order of the Fly (Grand Cross).

Next, Cunningham did Asmodeus, another fallen angel, said to be the inventor of dancing, gambling, music, drama, French fashions, and other frivolities. Cunningham made him look like a very dashing Beverly Hills Iranian, with a pair of tiny wings at his collar. It was Asmodeus who suggested that Cunningham continue the project, so he brought Gabriel and Raphael on line to provide some balance between good and evil, and then Forcas, the angel who renders people invisible, restores lost property, and teaches logic and rhetoric in Hell, and by that time Cunningham was hooked.

He surrounded himself with arcane lore: M. R. James's editions of the Apocrypha, Waite's *Book of Ceremonial Magic* and *Holy Kabbalah*, the *Mystical Theology and Celestial Hierarchies* of Dionysius the Areopagite, and dozens of related works that he called up from the Stanford data base in a kind of manic fervor. As he codified his systems, he became able to put in five, eight, a dozen angels a night; one June evening, staying up well past his usual time, he managed thirty-seven. As the population grew, it took on weight and substance, for one angel cross-filed another, and they behaved now as though they held long conversations with one another even when Cunningham was occupied elsewhere.

The question of actual *belief* in angels, like that of belief in God Himself, never arose in him. His project was purely a technical challenge, not a theological exploration. Once, at lunch, he told a co-worker what he was doing, and got a chilly blank stare. "Angels? *Angels?* Flying around with big flapping wings, passing miracles? You aren't seriously telling me that you believe in angels, are you, Dan?"

To which Cunningham replied, "You don't have to believe in angels to make use of them. I'm not always sure I believe in electrons and protons. I know I've never seen any. But I make use of them."

"And what use do you make of angels?"

But Cunningham had lost interest in the discussion.

He divides his evenings between calling up his angels for conversations and programming additional ones into his pantheon. That requires continuous intensive research, for the literature of angels is extraordinarily large, and he is thorough in everything he does. The research is time-consuming, for he wants his angels to meet every scholarly test of authenticity. He pores constantly over such works as Ginzberg's seven-volume *Legends of the Jews,* Clement of Alexandria's *Prophetic Eclogues,* Blavatsky's *The Secret Doctrine.*

It is the early part of the evening. He brings up Hagith, ruler of the planet Venus and commander of 4,000 legions of spirits, and asks him details of the transmutation of metals, which is Hagith's specialty. He summons Hadranel, who in Kabbalistic lore is a porter at the second gate of Heaven, and whose voice, when he proclaims the will of the Lord, penetrates through 200,000 universes; he questions the angel about his meeting with Moses, who uttered the Supreme Name at him and made him tremble. And then Cunningham sends for Israfel the four-winged, whose feet are under the seventh earth and whose head reaches to the pillars of the divine throne. It will be Israfel's task to blow the trumpet that announces the arrival of the Day of Judgment. Cunningham asks him to take a few trial riffs now—"just for practice," he says, but Israfel declines, saying he cannot touch his instrument until he receives the signal, and the command sequence for that, says the angel, is nowhere to be found in the software Cunningham has thus far constructed.

When he wearies of talking with the angels, Cunningham begins the evening's programming. By now the algorithms are second nature and he can enter angels into the computer in a matter of minutes, once he has done the research. This evening he inserts nine more. Then he opens a beer, sits back, and lets the day wind down to its close.

He thinks he understands why he has become so intensely involved with this enterprise. It is because he must contend each day in his daily work with matters of terrifying apocalyptic import: nothing less, indeed, than the impending destruction of the world. Cunningham works routinely with megadeath simulation. For six hours a day he sets up hypothetical situations in which Country A goes into alert mode, expecting an attack from Country B, which thereupon begins to suspect a preemptive strike and commences a defensive response, which leads Country A to escalate its own readiness, and so on until the bombs are in the air. He is aware, as are many thoughtful people both in Country A and Country B, that the possibility of computer-generated misinformation leading to a nuclear holocaust increases each year, as the time-window for correcting a malfunction diminishes. Cunningham also knows something that very few others do, or perhaps no one else at all: that it is now possible to send a signal to the giant computers—to Theirs or Ours, it makes no difference—that will be indistinguishable from the impulses that an actual flight of airborne warhead-bearing missiles would generate. If such a signal is permitted to enter the system, a minimum of eleven minutes, at the present time, will be needed to carry out fail-safe determination of its authenticity. That, at the present time, is too long to wait to decide whether the incoming missiles are real, a much swifter response is required.

Cunningham, when he designed his missile-simulating signal, thought at once of erasing his work. But he could not bring himself to do that: the program was too elegant, too perfect. On the other hand, he was afraid to tell anyone about it, for fear that it would be taken beyond his level of classification at once, and sealed away from him. He does not want that, for he dreams of finding an antidote for it, some sort of resonating inquiry mode that will distinguish all true alarms from false. When he has it, if he ever does, he will present both modes, in a single package, to Defense. Meanwhile, he bears the burden of suppressing a concept of overwhelming strategic importance. He had never done anything like that before. And he does not delude himself into thinking his mind is unique: if he could devise something like this, someone else probably could do it also, perhaps someone on the other side. True, it is a useless, suicidal program. But it would not be the first suicidal program to be devised in the interests of military security.

He knows he must take his simulator to his superiors before much more time goes by. And under the strain of that knowledge, he is beginning to show distinct signs of erosion. He mingles less and less with other people, he has unpleasant dreams and occasional periods of insomnia, he has lost his appetite and looks gaunt and haggard. The angel project is his only useful diversion, his chief distraction, his one avenue of escape.

For all his scrupulous scholarship, Cunningham has not hesitated to invent a few angels of his own. Uraniel is one of his: the angel of radioactive decay, with a face of whirling electron shells. And he has coined Dimitrion, too: the angel of Russian literature, whose wings are sleighs, and whose head is a snow-covered samovar. Cunningham feels no guilt over such whimsies. It is his computer, after all, and his program. And he knows he is not the first to concoct angels. Blake engendered platoons of them in his poems: Urizen and Orc and Enitharmon and more. Milton, he suspects, populated *Paradise Lost* with dozens of sprites of his own invention. Gurdjieff and Aleister

Crowley and even Pope Gregory the Great had their turns at ampli-
fying the angelic roster: why then not also Dan Cunningham of
Palo Alto, California? So from time to time he works one up on his
own. His most recent is the dread high lord Basileus, to whom
Cunningham has given the title of Emperor of the Angels. Basileus is
still incomplete: Cunningham has not arrived at his physical appearance, nor his specific functions, other than to make him the chief
administrator of the angelic horde. But there is something unsatisfac-
tory about imagining a new archangel, when Gabriel, Raphael, and
Michael already constitute the high command. Basileus needs more
work. Cunningham puts him aside, and begins to key in Duma, the
angel of silence and of the stillness of death, thousand-eyed, armed
with a fiery rod. His style in angels is getting darker and darker.

On a misty, rainy night in late October, a woman from San Francisco
whom he knows in a distant, occasional way, phones to invite him to
a party. Her name is Joanna; she is in her mid-thirties, a biologist
working for one of the little gene-splicing outfits in Berkeley;
Cunningham had had a brief and vague affair with her five or six
years back, when she was at Stanford, and since then they have kept
fitfully in touch, with long intervals elapsing between meetings. He
has not seen her or heard from her in over a year. "It's going to be
an interesting bunch," she tells him. "A futurologist from New York,
Thomson the sociobiology man, a couple of video poets, and someone from the chimpanzee-language outfit, and I forget the rest, but
they all sounded first rate."
    Cunningham hates parties. They bore and jangle him. No matter
how first rate the people are, he thinks, real interchange of ideas is
impossible in a large random group, and the best one can hope for
is some pleasant low-level chatter. He would rather be alone with his
angels than waste an evening that way.
    On the other hand, it has been so long since he has done anything
of a social nature that he has trouble remembering what the last
gathering was. As he had been telling himself all his life, he needs to
get out more often. He likes Joanna and it's about time they got
together, he thinks, and he fears that if he turns her down, she may
not call again for years. And the gentle patter of the rain, coming on
this mild evening after the long dry months of summer, has left him
feeling uncharacteristically relaxed, open, accessible.
    "All right," he says. "I'll be glad to go."
    The party is in San Mateo, on Saturday night. He takes down the
address. They arrange to meet there. Perhaps she'll come home
with him afterward, he thinks: San Mateo is only fifteen minutes

from his house, and she'll have a much longer drive back up to San Francisco. The thought surprises him. He had supposed he had lost all interest in her that way; he had supposed he had lost all interest in anyone that way, as a matter of fact.

Three days before the party, he decides to call Joanna and cancel. The idea of milling about in a roomful of strangers appalls him. He can't imagine, now, why he ever agreed to go. Better to stay home alone and pass a long rainy night designing angels and conversing with Uriel, Ithuriel, Raphael, Gabriel.

But as he goes toward the telephone, that renewed hunger for solitude vanishes as swiftly as it came. He *does* want to go to the party. He *does* want to see Joanna: very much, indeed. It startles him to realize that he positively yearns for some change in his rigid routine, some escape from his little apartment, its elaborate computer hookup, even its angels.

Cunningham imagines himself at the party, in some brightly lit room in a handsome redwood-and-glass house perched in the hills above San Mateo. He stands with his back to the vast-sparkling wraparound window, a drink in his hand and he is holding forth, dominating the conversation, sharing his rich stock of angel lore with a fascinated audience.

"Yes. Three hundred million of them," he is saying, "and each with his fixed-function. Angels don't have free will, you know. It's Church doctrine that they're created with it, but at the moment of their birth, they're given the choice of opting for God or against Him, and the choice is irrevocable. Once they've made it, they're unalterably fixed, for good or for evil. Oh, and angels are born circumcised, too. At least the Angels of Sanctification and the Angels of Glory are, and maybe the seventy Angels of the Presence."

"Does that mean that all angels are male?" asks a slender dark-haired woman.

"Strictly speaking, they're bodiless and therefore without sex," Cunningham tells her. "But in fact, the religions that believe in angels are mainly patriarchal ones, and when the angels are visualized, they tend to be portrayed as men. Although some of them, apparently, can change sex at will. Milton tells us that in *Paradise Lost:* 'Spirits when they please can either sex assume, or both; so soft and uncompounded is their essence pure.' And some angels seem to be envisioned as female in the first place. There's the Shekinah, for instance, 'the bride of God,' the manifestation of His glory indwelling in human beings. There's Sophia, the angel of wisdom. And Lilith, Adam's first wife, the demon of lust—"

"Are demons considered angels, then?" a tall professorial-looking man wants to know.

"Of course. They're the angels who opted away from God. But they're angels nevertheless, even if we mortals perceive their aspects as demonic or diabolical."

He goes on and on. They all listen as though he is God's own messenger. He speaks of the hierarchies of angels—the seraphim, cherubim, thrones, dominations, principalities, powers, virtues, archangels, and angels—and he tells them of the various lists of the seven great angels which differ so greatly once one gets beyond Michael, Gabriel, and Raphael, and he speaks of the 90,000 angels of destruction and the 300 angels of light; he conjures up the seven angels with seven trumpets from the Book of Revelation; he tells them which angels rule the seven days of the week and which the hours of the days and nights; he pours forth the wondrous angelic names, Zadkiel, Hashmal, Orphaniel, Jehudiel, Phaleg, Zagzagel. There is no end to it. He is in his glory. He is a fount of arcana. Then the manic mood passes. He is alone in his room; there is no eager audience. Once again he thinks he will skip the party. No. No. He will go. He wants to see Joanna.

He goes to his terminal and calls up two final angels before bedtime: Leviathan and Behemoth. Behemoth is the great hippopotamus-angel, the vast beast of darkness, the angel of chaos. Leviathan is his mate, the mighty she-whale, the splendid sea serpent. They dance for him on the screen. Behemoth's huge mouth yawns wide. Leviathan gapes even more awesomely. "We are getting hungry," they tell him. "When is feeding time?" In rabbinical lore, these two will swallow all the damned souls at the end of days. Cunningham tosses them some electronic sardines and sends them away. As he closes his eyes he invokes Poteh, the angel of oblivion, and falls into a black dreamless sleep.

At his desk the next morning, he is at work on a standard item, a glitch-clearing program for the third-quadrant surveillance satellites, when he finds himself unaccountably trembling. That has never happened to him before. His fingernails look almost white, his wrists are rigid, his hands are quivering. He feels chilled. It is as though he has not slept for days. In the washroom he clings to the sink and stares at his pallid, sweaty face. Someone comes up behind him and says, "You all right, Dan?"

"Yeah. Just a little attack of the damn queasies."

"All that wild living in the middle of the week wears a man down," the other says, and moves along. The social necessities have been observed: a question, a noncommittal answer, a quip, good-bye. He could have been having a stroke here and they would have played it the same way. Cunningham has no close friends at the office. He knows that they regard him as eccentric—eccentric in the wrong way, not lively and quirky but just a peculiar kind of hermit—and getting worse all the time. I could destroy the world, he thinks. I could go into the Big Room and type for fifteen seconds, and we'd be on all-out alert a minute later and the bombs would be coming down from orbit six minutes later. I could give that signal. I could really do it. I could do it right now.

Waves of nausea sweep him and he grips the edge of the sink until the last racking spasm is over. Then he cleans his face, and calmer now, returns to his desk to stare at the little green symbols on the screen.

That evening, still trying to find a function for Basileus, Cunningham discovers himself thinking of demons, and of one demon not in the classical demonology—Maxwell's Demon, the one that the physicist James Clerk Maxwell postulated to send fast-moving molecules in one direction and slow ones in another, thereby providing an ultra-efficient method for heating and refrigeration. Perhaps some sort of filtering role could be devised for Basileus. Last week a few of the loftier angels had been complaining about the proximity to them of certain fallen angels within the computer. "There's a smell of brimstone on this disk that I don't like," Gabriel had said. Cunningham wonders if he could make Basileus a kind of traffic manager within the program: let him sit in there and ship the celestial angels into one sector of a disk, the fallen ones to another.

The idea appeals to him for about thirty seconds. Then he sees how fundamentally trivial it is. He doesn't need an angel for a job like that; a little simple software could do it. Cunningham's corollary to Kant's categorical imperative: *Never use an angel as mere software.* He smiles, possibly for the first time all week. Why, he doesn't even need software. He can handle it himself, simply by assigning princes of Heaven to one file and demons to a different one. It hadn't seemed necessary to segregate his angels that way, or he would have done it from the start. But since now they were complaining—

He begins to flange up a sorting program to separate the files. It should have taken him a few minutes, but he finds himself working in a rambling, muddled way, doing an untypically sloppy job. With a quick swipe, he erases what he has done. Gabriel would have to put up with the reek of brimstone a little longer, he thinks.

There is a dull throbbing pain just behind his eyes. His throat is dry, his lips feel parched. Basileus would have to wait a little longer, too. Cunningham keys up another angel, allowing his fingers to choose for him, and finds himself looking at a blank faced angel with a gleaming metal skin. One of the early ones, Cunningham realizes. "I don't remember your name," he says. "Who are you?"

"I am Anaphaxeton."

"And your function?"

"When my name is pronounced aloud, I will cause the angels to summon the entire universe before the bar of justice on Judgment Day."

"Oh, Jesus," Cunningham says. "I don't want you tonight."

He sends Anaphaxeton away and finds himself with the dark angel Apollyon, fish scales, dragon wings, bear feet, breathing fire and smoke, holding the key to the Abyss. "No," Cunningham says, and brings up Michael, standing with drawn sword over Jerusalem, and sends him away only to find on the screen an angel with 70,000 feet and 4,000 wings, who is Azrael, the angel of death. "No," says Cunningham again. "Not you. Oh, Christ!" A vengeful army crowds his computer. On his screen there passes a flurrying regiment of wings and eyes and beaks. He shivers and shuts the system down for the night. Jesus, he thinks. Jesus, Jesus, Jesus. All night long, suns explode in his brain.

On Friday his supervisor, Ned Harris, saunters to his desk in an unusually folksy way and asks if he's going to be doing anything interesting this weekend. Cunningham shrugs. "A party Saturday night, that's about all. Why?"

"Thought you might be going off on a fishing trip, or something. Looks like the last nice weekend before the rainy season sets in, wouldn't you say?"

"I'm not a fisherman, Ned."

"Take some kind of trip. Drive down to Monterey, maybe. Or up into the wine country."

"What are you getting at?"

"You look like you could use a little change of pace," Harris says amiably. "A couple of days off. You've been crunching numbers so hard, they're starting to crunch you, is my guess."

"It's that obvious?"

Harris nods. "You're tired, Dan. It shows. We're a little like air traffic controllers around here, you know, working so hard we start to dream about blips on the screen. That's no good. Get the hell out of town, fellow. The Defense Department can operate without you for a while. Okay? Take Monday off. Tuesday, even. I can't afford to have a fine mind like yours going goofy from fatigue, Dan."

"All right, Ned. Sure. Thanks."

His hands are shaking again. His fingernails are colorless.

"And get a good early start on the weekend, too. No need for you to hang around here today until four."

"If that's okay—"

"Go on. Shoo!"

Cunningham closes down his desk and makes his way uncertainly out of the building. The security guards wave at him. Everyone seems to know he's being sent home early. Is this what it's like to crack up on the job? He wanders about the parking lot for a little while, not sure where he has left his car. At last he finds it, and drives home at thirty miles an hour, with horns honking at him all the way as he wanders up the freeway.

He settles wearily in front of his computer and brings the system on line, calling for Harahel. Surely the angel of computers will not plague him with such apocalyptic matters.

Harahel says, "Well, we've worked out your Basileus problem for you."

"You have?"

"Uriel had the basic idea, building on your Maxwell's Demon notion. Israfel and Azrael developed it some. What's needed is an angel embodying God's justice and God's mercy. A kind of evaluator, a filtering angel. He weighs deeds in the balance, and arrives at a verdict."

"What's new about that?" Cunningham asks. "Something like that's built into every mythology from Sumer and Egypt on. There's always a mechanism for evaluating the souls of the dead—this one goes to Paradise, this one goes to Hell—"

"Wait," Harahel says. "I wasn't finished. I'm not talking about the evaluation of individual souls."

"What then?"

"Worlds," the angel replies. "Basileus will be the judge of worlds. He holds an entire planet up to scrutiny and decides whether it's time to call for the last trump."

"Part of the machinery of Judgment, you mean?"

"Exactly. He's the one who presents the evidence to God and helps Him make his decision. And then he's the one who tells Israfel to blow the trumpet, and he's the one who calls out the name of Anaphaxeton to bring everyone before the bar. He's the prime apocalyptic angel, the destroyer of worlds. And we thought you might make him look like—"

"Ah," Cunningham says. "Not now. Let's talk about that some other time."

He shuts the system down, pours himself a drink, sits staring out the window at the big eucalyptus tree in the front yard. After a while it begins to rain. Not such a good weekend for a drive into the country after all, he thinks. He does not turn the computer on again that evening.

Despite everything, Cunningham goes to the party. Joanna is not there. She has phoned to cancel, late Saturday afternoon, pleading a bad cold. He detects no sound of a cold in her voice, but perhaps she is telling the truth. Or possibly she has found something better to do on Saturday night. But he is already geared for party going, and he is so tired, so eroded, that it is more effort to change his internal program than it is to follow through on the original schedule. So about eight that evening he drives up to San Mateo, through a light drizzle.

The party turns out not to be in the glamorous hills west of town, but in a small cramped condominium, close to the heart of the city, furnished with what looks like somebody's college-era chairs and couches and bookshelves. A cheap stereo is playing the pop music of a dozen years ago, and a sputtering screen provides a crude computer-generated light show. The host is some sort of marketing exec for a large video-games company in San Jose, and most of the guests look vaguely corporate, too. The futurologist from New York has sent his regrets; the famous sociobiologist has also failed to arrive; the video poets are two San Francisco gays who will talk only to each other, and stray not very far from the bar; the expert on teaching chimpanzees to speak is in the red-faced-and-sweaty-stage of being drunk, and is working hard at seducing a plump woman festooned with astrological jewelry. Cunningham, numb, drifts through the party as though he is made of ectoplasm. He speaks to no one; no one speaks to him. Some jugs of red wine are open on a table by the window, and he pours himself a glassful. There he stands, immobile, imprisoned by inertia. He imagines himself suddenly making a speech about angels, telling everyone how Ithuriel touched Satan with his spear in the Garden of Eden as the Fiend crouched next to Eve, and how the hierarch Ataphiel keeps Heaven aloft by balancing it on three fingers. But he says nothing. After a time he find himself approached by a lean, leathery-looking woman with glittering eyes, who says, "And what do you do?"

"I'm a programmer," Cunningham says. "Mainly I talk to angels. But I also do national security stuff."

"Angels?" she says, and laughs in a brittle, tinkling way. "You talk to angels? I've never heard anyone say that before." She pours herself a drink and moves quickly elsewhere.

"Angels?" says the astrological woman. "Did someone say angels?"

Cunningham smiles and shrugs and looks out the window. It is raining harder. I should go home, he thinks. There is absolutely no point in being here. He fills his glass again. The chimpanzee man is still working on the astrologer, but she seems to be trying to get free of him and come over to Cunningham. To discuss angels with him? She is heavy-breasted, a little walleyed, sloppy-looking. He does not want to discuss angels with her. He does not want to discuss angels with anyone. He holds his place at the window until it definitely does appear that the astrologer is heading his way; then he drifts toward the door. She says, "I heard you say you were interested in angels. Angels are a special field of mine, you know. I've studied with—"

"Angles," Cunningham says. "I play the angles. That's what I said. I'm a professional gambler."

"Wait," she says, but he moves past her and out into the night. It takes him a long while to find his key and get his car unlocked, and the rain soaks him to the skin, but that does not bother him. He is home a little before midnight.

He brings Raphael on line. The great archangel radiates a beautiful golden glow.

"You will be Basileus," Raphael tells him. "We've decided it by a vote, hierarchy by hierarchy. Everyone agrees."

"I can't be an angel. I'm human," Cunningham replies.

"There's ample precedent. Enoch was carried off to Heaven and became an angel. So was Elijah. St. John the Baptist was actually an angel. You will become Basileus. We've already done the program for you. It's on the disk: just call him up and you'll see. Your own face, looking out at you."

"No," Cunningham says.

"How can you refuse?"

"Are you really Raphael? You sound like someone from the other side. A tempter. Asmodeus. Astaroth. Belphegor."

"I am Raphael. And you are Basileus."

Cunningham considers it. He is so very tired that he can barely think.

An angel. Why not? A rainy Saturday night, a lousy party, a splitting headache: come home and find out you've been made an angel, and given a high place in the hierarchy. Why not? Why the hell not?

"All right," he says, "I'm Basileus."

He puts his hands on the keys and taps out a simple formulation that goes straight down the pipe into the Defense Department's big northern California system. With an alteration of two keystrokes, he sends the same message to the Soviets. Why not? Redundancy is the soul of security. The world now has about six minutes left. Cunningham has always been good with computers. He knows their secret language as few people before him have.

Then he brings Raphael on the screen again.

"You should see yourself as Basileus while there's still time," the archangel says.

"Yes. Of course. What's the access key?"

Raphael tells him. Cunningham begins to set it up.

Come now, Basileus! We are one!

Cunningham stares at the screen with growing wonder and delight, while the clock continues to tick.

The Jaguar Hunter

Lucius Shepard

Lucius Shepard has elevated the art of fantasy literature with his lyrical stories and novels. He has been awarded the John W. Campbell award, the Nebula, and the World Fantasy award for his fiction. His characters, whose adventures usually occur in Central America, the Caribbean, or Southeast Asia, inhabit a bleak world where nothing and no one can be trusted, and even simple things are not what they seem. Any growth or progress they make is almost accidental, and their relationship with the jungles they usually find themselves in is a powerful symbol of the confusion and turmoil in their lives.

IT WAS HIS WIFE'S DEBT TO ONOFRIO ESTEVES, THE APPLIANCE DEALER, that brought Esteban Caax to town for the first time in almost a year. By nature he was a man who enjoyed the sweetness of the countryside above all else; the placid measures of a farmer's day invigorated him, and he took great pleasure in nights spent joking and telling stories around a fire, or lying beside his wife, Incarnación. Puerto Morada, with its fruit company imperatives and sullen dogs and cantinas that blared American music, was a place he avoided like the plague: indeed, from his home atop the mountain whose slopes formed the northernmost enclosure of Bahia Onda, the rusted tin roofs ringing the bay resembled a dried crust of blood such as might appear upon the lips of a dying man.

On this particular morning, however, he had no choice but to visit the town. Incarnación had—without his knowledge—purchased a battery-operated television set on credit from Onofrio, and he was threatening to seize Esteban's three milk cows in lieu of the eight hundred lempiras that was owed; he refused to accept the return of the television, but had sent word that he was willing to discuss an alternate method of payment. Should Esteban lose the cows, his income would drop below a subsistence level, and he would be forced to take up his old occupation, an occupation far more onerous than farming.

As he walked down the mountain, past huts of thatch and

brushwood poles identical to his own, following a trail that wound through sunbrowned thickets lorded over by banana trees, he was not thinking of Onofrio but of Incarnación. It was in in her nature to be frivolous, and he had known this when he had married her; yet the television was emblematic of the differences that had developed between them since their children had reached maturity. She had begun to put on sophisticated airs, to laugh at Esteban's country ways, and she had become the doyenne of a group of older women, mostly widows, all of whom aspired to sophistication. Each night they would huddle around the television and strive to outdo one another in making sagacious comments about the American detective shows they watched; and each night Esteban would sit outside the hut and gloomily ponder the state of his marriage. He believed Incarnación's association with the widows was her manner of telling him that she looked forward to adopting the black skirt and shawl, that—having served his purpose as a father—he was now an impediment to her. Though she was only forty-one, younger by three years than Esteban, she was withdrawing from the life of the senses; they rarely made love anymore, and he was certain that this partially embodied her resentment of the fact that the years had been kind to him. He had the look of one of the Old Patuca—tall, with chiseled featurs and wide-set eyes; his coppery skin was relatively unlined and his hair jet black. Incarnación's hair was streaked with gray, and the clean beauty of her limbs had dissolved beneath layers of fat. He had not expected her to remain beautiful, and he had tried to assure her that he loved the woman she was and not merely the girl she had been. But that woman was dying, infected by the same disease that had infected Puerto Morada, and perhaps his love for her was dying, too.

The dusty street on which the appliance store was situated ran in back of the movie theater and the Hotel Circo Del Mar, and from the inland side of the street Esteban could see the bell towers of Santa Maria del Onda rising above the hotel roof like the horns of a great stone snail. As a young man, obeying his mother's wish that he become a priest, he had spent three years cloistered beneath those towers, preparing for the seminary under the tutelage of old Father Gonsalvo. It was the part of his life he most regretted, because the academic disciplines he had mastered seemed to have stranded him between the world of the Indian and that of contemporary society; in his heart he held to his father's teachings—the principles of magic, the history of the tribe, the lore of nature—and yet he could never escape the feeling that such wisdom was either superstitious or simply unimportant. The shadows of the towers lay upon his soul as surely as they did upon the cobbled square in front of the church, and the sight of them caused him to pick up his pace and lower his eyes.

Farther along the street was the Cantina Atomica, a gathering place for the well-to-do youth of the town, and across from it was the appliance store, a one-story building of yellow stucco with corrugated metal doors that were lowered at night. Its facade was decorated by a mural that supposedly represented the merchandise within: sparkling refrigerators and televisions and washing machines, all given the impression of enormity by the tiny men and women painted below them, their hands upflung in awe. The actual merchandise was much less imposing, consisting mainly of radios and used kitchen equipment. Few people in Puerto Morada could afford more, and those who could generally bought elsewhere. The majority of Onofrio's clientele were poor, hard-pressed to meet his schedule of payments, and to a large degree his wealth derived from selling repossessed appliances over and over.

Raimundo Esteves, a pale young man with puffy cheeks and heavily lidded eyes and a petulant mouth, was leaning against the counter when Esteban entered; Raimundo smirked and let out a piercing whistle, and a few seconds later his father emerged from the back room: a huge slug of a man, even paler than Raimundo. Filaments of gray hair were slicked down across his mottled scalp, and his belly stretched the front of a starched *guayabera*. He beamed and extended a hand.

"How good to see you," he said. "Raimundo! Bring us coffee and two chairs."

Much as he disliked Onofrio, Esteban was in no position to be uncivil: he accepted the handshake. Raimundo spilled coffee in the saucers and clattered the chairs and glowered, angry at being forced to serve an Indian.

"Why will you not let me return the television?" asked Esteban after taking a seat; and then, unable to bite back the words, he added, "Is it no longer your policy to swindle my people?"

Onofrio sighed, as if it were exhausting to explain things to a fool such as Esteban. "I do not swindle your people. I go beyond the letter of the contracts in allowing them to make returns rather than pursuing matters through the courts. In your case, however, I have devised a way whereby you can keep the television without any further payments and yet settle the account. Is this a swindle?"

It was pointless to argue with a man whose logic was as facile and self-serving as Onofrio's. "Tell me what you want," said Esteban.

Onofrio wetted his lips, which were the color of raw sausage. "I want you to kill the jaguar of Barrio Carolina."

"I no longer hunt," said Esteban.

"The Indian is afraid," said Raimundo, moving up behind Onofrio's shoulder. "I told you."

Onofrio waved him away and said to Esteban, "That is unreasonable. If I take the cows, you will once again be hunting jaguars. But if you do this, you will have to hunt only one jaguar."

"One that has killed eight huntrs." Esteban set down his coffee cup and stood. "It is no ordinary jaguar."

Raimundo laughed disparagingly, and Esteban skewered him with a stare.

"Ah!" said Onofrio, smiling a flatterer's smile. "But none of the eight used your method."

"Your pardon, *don* Onofrio," said Esteban with mock formality. "I have other business to attend."

"I will pay you five hundred lemiras in addition to erasing the debt," said Onofrio.

"Why?" asked Esteban. "Forgive me, but I cannot believe it is due to a concern for the public welfare."

Onofrio's fat throat pulsed, his face darkened.

"Never mind," said Esteban. "It is not enough."

"Very well. A thousand." Onofrio's casual manner could not conceal the anxiety in his voice.

Intrigued, curious to learn the extent of Onofrio's anxiety, Esteban plucked a figure from the air. "Ten thousand," he said. "And in advance."

"Ridiculous! I could hire ten hunters for this much! Twenty!"

Esteban shrugged. "But none with my method."

For a moment Onofrio sat with his hands enlaced, twisting them, as if struggling with some pious conception. "All right," he said, the words squeezed out of him. "Ten thousand!"

The reason for Onofrio's interest in Barrio Carolina suddenly dawned on Esteban, and he understood that the profits involved would make his fee seem pitifully small. But he was possessed by the thought of what ten thousand lempiras could mean: a herd of cows, a small truck to haul produce, or—and as he thought it, he realized this was the happiest possibility—the little stucco house in Barrio Clarin that Incarnación had set her heart on. Perhaps owning it would soften her toward him. He noticed Raimundo staring at him, his expression a knowing smirk; and even Onofrio, though still outraged by the fee, was beginning to show signs of satisfaction, adjusting the fit of his *guayabera,* slicking down his already-slicked-down hair. Esteban felt debased by their capacity to buy him, and to preserve a last shred of dignity, he turned and walked to the door.

"I will consider it," he tossed back over his shoulder. "And I will give you my answer in the morning."

"Murder Squad of New York," starring a bald American actor, was the featured attraction on Incarnación's television that night, and the widows sat cross-legged on the floor, filling the hut so completely that the charcoal stove and the sleeping hammock had been moved outside in order to provide good viewing angles for the latecomers. To Esteban, standing in the doorway, it seemed his home had been invaded by a covey of large black birds with cowled heads, who were receiving evil instruction from the core of a flickering gray jewel. Reluctantly, he pushed between them and made his way to the shelves mounted on the wall behind the set; he reached up to the top shelf and pulled down a long bundle wrapped in oil-stained newspapers. Out of the corner of his eye, he saw Incarnación watching him, her lips thinned, curved in a smile, and that cicatrix of a smile branded its mark on Esteban's heart. She knew what he was about, and she was delighted! Not in the least worried! Perhaps she had known of Onofrio's plan to kill the jaguar, perhaps she had schemed with Onofrio to entrap him. Infuriated, he barged through the widows, setting them to gabbling, and walked out into his banana grove and sat on a stone amidst it. The night was cloudy, and only a handful of stars showed between the tattered dark shapes of the leaves; the wind sent the leaves slithering together, and he heard one of his cows snorting and smelled the ripe odor of the corral. It was as if the solidity of his life had been reduced to this isolated perspective, and he bitterly felt the isolation. Though he would admit to fault in the marriage, he could think of nothing he had done that could have bred Incarnación's hateful smile.

After a while, he unwrapped the bundle of newspapers and drew out a thin-bladed machete of the sort used to chop banana stalks, but which he used to kill jaguars. Just holding it renewed his confidence and gave him a feeling of strength. It had been four years since he had hunted, yet he knew he had not lost the skill. Once he had been proclaimed the greatest hunter in the province of Neuva Esperanza, as had his father before him, and he had not retired from hunting because of age or infirmity, but because the jaguars were beautiful, and their beauty had begun to outweigh the reasons he had for killing them. He had no better reason to kill the jaguar of Barrio Carolina. It menaced no one other than those who hunted it, who sought to invade its territory, and its death would profit only a dishonorable man and a shrewish wife, and would spread the contamination of Puerto Morada. And besides, it was a black jaguar.

"Black jaguars," his father had told him, "are creatures of the moon. They have other forms and magical purposes with which we must not interfere. Never hunt them!"

His father had not said that the black jaguars lived on the moon, simply that they utilized its power; but as a child, Esteban had dreamed about a moon of ivory forests and silver meadows through which the jaguars lowed as swiftly as black water; and when he had told his father of the dreams, his father had said that such dreams were representations of a truth, and that sooner or later he would discover the truth underlying them. Esteban had never stopped believing in the dreams, not even in face of the rocky, airless place depicted by the science programs on Incarnación's television: that moon, its mystery explained, was merely a less enlightening kind of dream, a statement of fact that reduced reality to the knowable.

But as he thought this, Esteban suddenly realized that killing the jaguar might be the solution to his problems, that by going against his father's teaching, that by killing his dreams, his Indian conception of the world, he might be able to find accord with his wife's; he had been standing halfway between the two conceptions for too long, and it was time for him to choose. And there was no real choice. It was this world he inhabited, not that of the jaguars; if it took the death of a magical creature to permit him to embrace as joys the television and trips to the movies and a stucco house in Barrio Clarin, well, he had faith in this method. He swung the machete, slicing the dark air, and laughed. Incarnación's frivolousness, his skill at hunting, Onofrio's greed, the jaguar, the television . . . all these things were neatly woven together like the elements of a spell, one whose products would be a denial of magic and a furthering of the unmagical doctrines that had corrupted Puerto Morada. He laughed again, but a second later he chided himself: it was exactly this sort of thinking he was preparing to root out.

Esteban waked Incarnación early the next morning and forced her to accompany him to the appliance store. His machete swung by his side in a leather sheath, and he carried a burlap sack containing food and the herbs he would need for the hunt. Incarnación trotted along beside him, silent, her face hidden by a shawl. When they reached the store, Esteban had Onofrio stamp the bill PAID IN FULL, then he handed the bill and the money to Incarnación.

"If I kill the jaguar or if it kills me," he said harshly, "this will be yours. Should I fail to return within a week, you may assume that I will never return."

She retreated a step, her face registering alarm, as if she had seen him in new light and understood the consequences of her actions; but she made no move to stop him as he walked out the door.

Across the street, Raimundo Esteves was leaning against the wall of the Cantina Atomica, talking to two girls wearing jeans and frilly blouses; the girls were fluttering their hands and dancing to the music that issued from the cantina, and to Esteban they seemed more alien than the creature he was to hunt. Raimundo spotted him and whispered to the girls; they peeked over their shoulders and laughed. Already angry at Incarnación, Esteban was washed over by a cold fury. He crossed the street to them, rested his hand on the hilt of the machete, and stared at Raimundo; he had never before noticed how soft he was, how empty of presence. A crop of pimples straggled along his jaw, the flesh beneath his eyes was pocked by tiny indentations like those made by a silversmith's hammer, and, unequal to the stare, his eyes darted back and forth between the two girls.

Esteban's anger dissolved into revulsion. "I am Esteban Caax," he said. "I have built my own house, tilled my soil, and brought four children into the world. This day I am going to hunt the jaguar of Barrio Carolina in order to make you and your father even fatter than you are." He ran his gaze up and down Raimundo's body and, letting his voice fill with disgust, he asked, "Who are you?"

Raimundo's puffy face cinched in a knot of hatred, but he offered no response. The girls tittered and skipped through the door of the cantina; Esteban could hear them describing the incident, laughter, and he continued to stare at Raimundo. Several other girls poked their heads out the door, giggling and whispering. After a moment, Esteban spun on his heel and walked away. Behind him there was a chorus of unrestrained laughter, and a girl's voice called mockingly, "Raimundo! Who are you?" Other voices joined in, and it soon became a chant.

Barrio Carolina was not truly a barrio of Puerto Morada; it lay beyond Punta Manabique, the southernmost enclosure of the bay, and was fronted by a palm hammock and the loveliest stretch of beach in all the province, a curving slice of white sand giving way to jade-green shallows. Forty years before, it had been the headquarters of the fruit company's experimental farm, a project of such vast scope that a small town had been built on the site: rows of white frame houses with shingle roofs and screen porches, the kind you might see in a magazine illustration of rural America. The company had touted the project as being the keystone of the country's future, and had promised to develop high-yield crops that would banish starvation; but in 1947 a cholera epidemic had ravaged the coast and the town had been abandoned. By the time the cholera scare had died down, the company had become well-entrenched in national politics and no longer needed to maintain a benevolent image; the project had been dropped and the property abandoned until—in the same year that Esteban had retired from hunting—

developers had bought it, planning to build a major resort. It was then the jaguar had appeared. Though it had not killed any of the workmen, it had terrorized them to the point that they had refused to begin the job. Hunters had been sent, and these the jaguar *had* killed. The last party of hunters had been equipped with automatic rifles, all manner of technological aids; but the jaguar had picked them off one by one, and this project, too, had been abandoned. Rumor had it that the land had recently been resold (now Esteban knew to whom), and that the idea of a resort was once more under consideration.

The walk from Puerto Morada was hot and tiring, and upon arrival Esteban sat beneath a palm and ate a lunch of cold banana fritters. Combers as white as toothpaste broke on the shore, and there was no human litter, just dead fronds and driftwood and coconuts. All but four of the houses had been swallowed by the jungle, and only sections of those four remained visible, embedded like moldering gates in a blackish green wall of vegetation. Even under the bright sunlight, they were haunted-looking: their screens ripped, boards weathered gray, vines cascading over their facades. A mango tree had sprouted from one of the porches, and wild parrots were eating its fruit. He had not visited the barrio since childhood: the ruins had frightened him then, but now he found them appealing, testifying to the dominion of natural law. It distressed him that he would help transform it all into a place where the parrots would be chained to perches and the jaguars would be designs on tablecloths, a place of swimming pools and tourists sipping from coconut shells. Nonetheless, after he had finished lunch, he set out to explore the jungle and soon discovered a trail used by the jaguar: a narrow path that wound between the vine-matted shells of the houses for about a half mile and ended at the Rio Dulce. The river was a murkier green than the sea, curving away through the jungle walls; the jaguar's tracks were everywhere along the bank, especially thick upon a tussocky rise some five or six feet above the water. This baffled Esteban. The jaguar could not drink from the rise, and it certainly would not sleep there. He puzzled over it awhile, but eventually shrugged it off, returned to the beach, and, because he planned to keep watch that night, took a nap beneath the palms.

Some hours later, around midafternoon, he was started from his nap by a voice hailing him. A tall, slim, copper-skinned woman was walking toward him, wearing a dress of dark green—almost the exact color of the jungle walls—that exposed the swell of her breasts. As she drew near, he saw that though her features had a Patucan cast, they were of a lapidary fineness uncommon to the tribe; it was as if they had been refined into a lovely mask: cheeks planed into subtle hollows, lips sculpted full, stylized feathers of ebony inlaid for eyebrows, eyes of jet and white onyx, and all this given a human gloss. A sheen of sweat covered her breasts, and a single curl of black hair lay over her collarbone, so artful-seeming it appeared to have been placed there by design. She knelt beside him, gazing at him impassively, and Esteban was flustered by her heated air of sensuality. The sea breeze bore her scent to him, a sweet musk that reminded him of mangoes left ripening in the sun.

"My name is Esteban Caax," he said, painfully aware of his own sweaty odor.

"I have heard of you," she said. "The jaguar hunter. Have you come to kill the jaguar of the barrio?"

"Yes," he said, and felt shame at admitting it.

She picked up a handful of sand and watched it sift through her fingers.

"What is your name?" he asked.

"If we become friends, I will tell you my name," she said. "Why must you kill the jaguar?"

He told her about the television set, and then, to his surprise, he found himself describing his problems with Incarnación, explaining how he intended to adapt to her ways. These were not proper subjects to discuss with a stranger, yet he was lured to intimacy; he thought he sensed an affinity between them, and that prompted him to portray his marriage as more dismal than it was, for though he had never once been unfaithful to Incarnación, he would have welcomed the chance to do so now.

"This is a black jaguar," she said. "Surely you know they are not ordinary animals, that they have purposes with which we must not interfere?"

Esteban was startled to hear his father's words from her mouth, but he dismissed it as coincidence and replied, "Perhaps. But they are not mine."

"Truly, they are," she said. "You have simply chosen to ignore them." She scooped up another handful of sand. "How will you do it? You have no gun. Only a machete."

"I have this as well," he said, and from his sack he pulled out a small parcel of herbs and handed it to her.

She opened it and sniffed the contents. "Herbs? Ah! You plan to drug the jaguar."

"Not the jaguar. Myself." He took back the parcel. "The herbs slow the heart and give the body a semblance of death. They induce a trance, but one that can be thrown off at a moment's notice. After I chew them, I will lie down in a place that the jaguar must pass on its nightly hunt. It will think I am dead, but it will not feed unless it is sure that the spirit has left the flesh, and to determine this, it will sit on the body so it can feel the spirit rise up. As soon as it starts to settle, I will throw off the trance and stab it between the ribs. If my hand is steady, it will die instantly."

"And if your hand is unsteady?"

"I have killed nearly fifty jaguars," he said. "I no longer fear unsteadiness. The method comes down through my family from the Old Patuca, and it has never failed, to my knowledge."

"But a black jaguar . . ."

"Black or spotted, it makes no difference. Jaguars are creatures of instinct, and one is like another when it comes to feeding."

"Well," she said, "I cannot wish you luck, but neither do I wish you ill." She came to her feet, brushing the sand from her dress.

He wanted to ask her to stay, but pride prevented him, and she laughed as if she knew his mind.

"Perhaps we will talk again, Esteban," she said. "It would be a pity if we did not, for more lies between us than we have spoken of this day."

She walked swiftly down the beach, becoming a diminutive black figure that was rippled away by the heat haze.

That evening, needing a place from which to keep watch, Esteban pried open the screen door of one of the houses facing the beach and went onto the porth. Chameleons skittered into the corners, and an iguana slithered off a rusted lawn chair sheathed in spider-web and vanished through a gap in the floor. The interior of the house was dark and forbidding, except for the bathroom, the roof of which was missing, webbed over by vines that admitted a gray-green infusion of twilight. The cracked toilet was full of rainwater an dead insects. Uneasy, Esteban returned to the porch, cleaned the lawn chair, and sat.

Out on the horizon the sea and sky were blending in a haze of sil-ver and gray; the wind had died, and the palms were as still as sculp-ture; a string of pelicans flying low above the waves seemed to be spelling a sentence of cryptic black syllables. But the eerie beauty of the scene was lost on him. He could not stop thinking of the woman. The memory of her hips rolling beneath the fabric of her dress as she walked away was repeated over and over in his thoughts, and whenever he tried to turn his attention to the matter at hand, the memory became more compelling. He imagined her naked, the play of muscles rippling her haunches, and this so enflamed him that he started to pace, unmindful of the fact that the creaking boards were signaling his presence. He could not understand her effect upon him. Perhaps, he thought, it was her defense of the jaguar, her calling to mind of all he was putting behind him . . . and then a realization settled over him like an icy shroud.

It was commonly held among the Patuca that a man about to suffer a solitary and unexpected death would be visited by an envoy of death, who—standing in for family and friends—would prepare him to face the event; and Esteban was now very sure that the woman had been such an envoy, that her allure had been specifically designed to attract his soul to its imminent fate. He sat back down in the lawn chair, numb with the realization. Her knowledge of his father's words, the odd flavor of her conversation, her intimation that more lay between them: it all accorded perfectly with the traditional wisdom. The moon rose three-quarters full, silvering the sands of the barrio, and still he sat there, rooted to the spot by his fear of death.

He had been watching the jaguar for several seconds before he registered its presence. It seemed at first that a scrap of night sky had fallen onto the sand and was being blown by a fitful breeze; but soon he saw that it was the jaguar, that it was inching along as if stalking some prey. Then it leaped high into the air, twisting and turning, and began to race up and down the beach: a ribbon of black water flowing across the silver sands. He had never before seen a jaguar at play, and this alone was cause for wonder; but most of all, he wondered at the fact that here were his childhood dreams come to life. He might have been peering out onto a silvery meadow of the moon, spying on one of its magical creatures. His fear was eroded by the sight, and like a child he pressed his nose to the screen, trying not to blink, anxious that he might miss a single moment.

At length the jaguar left off its play and came prowling up the beach toward the jungle. By the set of its ears and the purposeful sway of its walk, Esteban recognized that it was hunting. It stopped beneath a palm about twenty feet from the house, lifted its head, and tested the air. Moonlight frayed down through the fronds, applying liquid gleams to its haunches; its eyes, glinting yellow-green, were like peepholes into a lurid dimension of fire. The jaguar's beauty was heart-stopping—the embodiment of a flawless principle—and Esteban, contrasting this beauty with the pallid ugliness of his employer, with the ugly principle that had led to his hiring, doubted that he could ever bring himself to kill it.

All the following day he debated the question. He had hoped the woman would return, because he had rejected the idea that she was death's envoy—that perception, he thought, must have been induced by the mysterious atmosphere of the barrio—and he felt that if she were to argue the jaguar's cause again, he would let

himself be persuaded. But she did not put in an appearance, and as
he sat upon the beach, watching the evening sun decline through
strata of dusky orange and lavender clouds, casting wild glitters over
the sea, he understood once more that he had no choice. Whether
or not the jaguar was beautiful, whether or not the woman had been
on a supernatural errand, he must treat these things as if they had
no substance. The point of the hunt had been to deny mysteries of
this sort, and he had lost sight of it under the influence of old
dreams.

He waited until moonrise to take the herbs, and then lay down
beneath the palm tree where the jaguar had paused the previous
night. Lizards whispered past in the grasses, sand fleas hopped onto
his face: he hardly felt them, sinking deeper into the languor of the
herbs. The fronds overhead showed an ashen green in the moonlight, lifting, rustling; and the stars between their feathered edges
flickered crazily as if the breeze were fanning their flames. He
became immersed in the landscape, savoring the smells of brine and
rotting foliage that were blowing across the beach, drifting with
them; but when he heard the pad of the jaguar's step, he came alert.
Through narrowed eyes he saw it sitting a dozen feet away, a bulky
shadow craning its neck toward him, investigating his scent. After a
moment it began to circle him, each circle a bit tighter than the
one before, and whenever it passed out of view, he had to repress a
trickle of fear. Then, as it passed close on the seaward side, he
caught a whiff of its odor.

A sweet, musky odor that reminded him of mangoes left ripening
in the sun.

Fear welled up in him, and he tried to banish it, to tell himself
that the odor could not possibly be what he thought. The jaguar
snarled, a razor stroke of sound that slit the peaceful mesh of wind
and surf, and realizing it had scented his fear, he sprang to his feet,
waving his machete. In a whirl of vision, he saw the jaguar leap
back, he shouted at it, waved the machete again, and sprinted for
the house where he had kept watch. He slipped through the door
and went staggering into the front room. There was a crash behind
him, and turning, he had a glimpse of a huge black shape struggling to extricate itself from a moonlit tangle of vines and ripped
screen. He darted into the bathroom, sat with his back against the
toilet bowl, and braced the door shut with his feet.

The sound of the jaguar's struggles subsided, and for a moment
he thought it had given up. Sweat left cold trails down his sides, his
heart pounded. He held his breath, listening, and it seemed the
whole world was holding its breath as well. The noises of wind and
surf and insects were a faint seething; moonlight shed a sickly white

radiance through the enlaced vines overhead, and a chameleon was frozen among peels of wallpaper beside the door. He let out a sigh and wiped the sweat from his eyes. He swallowed.

Then the top panel of the door exploded, shattered by a black paw. Splinters of rotten wood flew into his face, and he screamed. The sleek wedge of the jaguar's head thrust through the hole, roaring. A gateway of gleaming fangs guarding a plush red throat. Half-paralyzed, Esteban jabbed weakly with the machete. The jaguar withdrew, reached in with its paw, and clawed at his leg. More by accident than design, he managed to slice the jaguar, and the paw, too, was withdrawn. He heard it rumbling in the front room, and then, seconds later, a heavy thump against the wall behind him. The jaguar's head appeared above the edge of the wall; it was hanging by its forepaws, trying to gain a perch from which to leap down into the room. Esteban scrambled to his feet and slashed wildly, severing vines. The jaguar fell back, yowling. For a while it prowled along the wall, fuming to itself. Finally there was silence.

When sunlight began to filter through the vines, Esteban walked out of the house and headed down the beach to Puerto Morada. He went with his head lowered, desolate, thinking of the grim future that awaited him after he returned the money to Onofrio: a life of trying to please an increasingly shrewish Incarnación, of killing lesser jaguars for much less money. He was so mired in depression that he did not notice the woman until she called to him. She was leaning against a palm about thirty feet away, wearing a filmy white dress through which he could see the dark jut of her nipples. He drew his machete and backed off a pace.

"Why do you fear me, Esteban?" she called, walking toward him.

"You tricked me into revealing my method and tried to kill me," he said. "Is that not reason for fear?"

"I did not know you or your method in that form. I knew only that you were hunting me. But now the hunt has ended, and we can be as man and woman."

He kept his machete at point. "What are you?" he asked.

She smiled. "My name is Miranda. I am Patuca."

"Patucas do not have black fur and fangs."

"I am of the Old Patuca," she said. "We have this power."

"Keep away!" He lifted the machete as if to strike, and she stopped just beyond his reach.

"You can kill me if that is your wish, Esteban." She spread her arms, and her breasts thrust forward against the fabric of her dress. "You are stronger than I, now. But listen to me first."

He did not lower the machete, but his fear and anger were being overridden by a sweeter emotion.

"Long ago," she said, "there was a great healer who foresaw that one day the Patuca would lose their place in the world, and so, with the help of gods, he opened a door into another world where the tribe could flourish. But many of the tribe were afraid and would not follow him. Since then the door has been left open for those who would come after." She waved at the ruined houses. "Barrio Carolina is the site of the door, and the jaguar is its guardian. But soon the fevers of this world will sweep over the barrio, and the door will close forever. For though our hunt has ended, there is no end to hunters or to greed." She came a step nearer. "If you listen to the sounding of your heart, you will know this is the truth."

He half-believed her, yet he also believed her words masked a more poignant truth, one that fitted inside the other the way his machete fitted into its sheath.

"What is it?" she asked. "What troubles you?"

"I think you have come to prepare me for death," he said, "and that your door leads only to death."

"Then why do you not run from me?" She pointed toward Puerto Morada. "That is death, Esteban. The cries of the gulls are death, and when the hearts of lovers stop at the moment of greatest pleasure, that, too, is death. This world is no more than a thin covering of life drawn over a foundation of death, like a scum of algae upon rock. Perhaps you are right, perhaps my world lies beyond death. The two ideas are not opposed. But if I am death to you, Esteban, then it is death you love."

He turned his eyes to the sea, not wanting her to see his face. "I do not love you," he said.

"Love awaits us," she said. "And someday you will join me in my world."

He looked back to her, ready with a denial, but was shocked to silence. Her dress had fallen to the sand, and she was smiling. The litheness and purity of the jaguar were reflected in every line of her body; her secret hair was so absolute a black that it seemed an absence in her flesh. She moved close, pushing aside the machete. The tips of her breasts brushed against him, warm through the coarse cloth of his shirt; her hands cupped his face, and he was drowning in her heated scent, weakened by both fear and desire.

"We are of one soul, you and I," she said. "One blood and one truth. You cannot reject me."

Days passed, though Esteban was unclear as to how many. Night and day were unimportant incidences of his relationship with Miranda, serving only to color their lovemaking with a spectral or a sunny mood; and each time they made love, it was as if a thousand new colors were being added to his senses. He had never been so content. Sometimes, gazing at the haunted facades of the barrio, he believed that they might well conceal shadowy avenues leading to another world; however, whenever Miranda tried to convince him to leave with her, he refused: he could not overcome his fear and would never admit—even to himself—that he loved her. He attempted to fix his thoughts on Incarnación, hoping this would undermine his fixation with Miranda and free him to return to Puerto Morada; but he found that he could not picture his wife except as a black bird hunched before a flickering gray jewel. Miranda, however, seemed equally unreal at times. Once as they sat on the bank of the Rio Dulce, watching the reflection of the moon—almost full—floating upon the water, she pointed to it and said, "My world is that near, Esteban. That touchable. You may think the moon above is real and this is only a reflection, but the thing most real, that most illustrates the real, is the surface that permits the illusion of reflection. Passing through this surface is what you fear, and yet it is so insubstantial, you would scarcely notice the passage."

"You sound like the old priest who taught me philosophy," said Esteban. "His world—his heaven—was also philosophy. Is that what your world is? The idea of a place? Or are there birds and jungles and rivers?"

Her expression was in partial eclipse, half-moonlit, half-shadowed, and her voice revealed nothing of her mood. "No more than there are here," she said.

"What does that mean?" he said angrily. "Why will you not give me a clear answer?"

"If I were to describe my world, you would simply think me a clever liar." She rested her head on his shoulder. "Sooner or later you will understand. We did not find each other merely to have the pain of being parted."

In that moment her beauty—like her words—seemed a kind of evasion, obscuring a dark and frightening beauty beneath; and yet he knew that she was right, that no proof of hers could persuade him contrary to his fear.

One afternoon, an afternoon of such brightness that it was impossible to look at the sea without squinting, they swam out to a sandbar that showed as a thin curving island of white against the green water. Esteban floundered and splashed, but Miranda swam as if born to the element; she darted beneath him, tickling him, pulling at his feet, eeling away before he could catch her. They walked along the sand, turning over starfish with their toes, collecting whelks to boil for their dinner, and then Esteban spotted a dark stain hundreds of yards wide that was moving below the water beyond the bar: a great school of king mackerel.

"It is too bad we have no boat," he said. "Mackerel would taste better than whelks."

"We need no boat," she said. "I will show you an old way of catching fish."

She traced a complicated design in the sand, and when she had done, she led him into the shallows and had him stand facing her a few feet away.

"Look down at the water between us," she said. "Do not look up, and keep perfectly still until I tell you."

She began to sing with a faltering rhythm, a rhythm that put him in mind of the ragged breezes of the season. Most of the words were unfamiliar, but others he recognized as Patuca. After a minute he experienced a wave of dizziness, as if his legs had grown long and spindly, and he was now looking down from a great height, breathing rarefied air. Then a tiny dark stain materialized below the expanse of water between him and Miranda. He remembered his grandfather's stories of the Old Patuca, how—with the help of the gods—they had been able to shrink the world, to bring enemies close and cross vast distances in a matter of moments. But the gods were dead, their powers gone from the world. He wanted to glance back to shore and see if he and Miranda had become coppery giants taller than the palms.

"Now," she said, breaking off her song, "you must put your hand into the water on the seaward side of the school and gently wiggle your fingers. Very gently! Be sure not to disturb the surface."

But when Esteban made to do as he was told, he slipped and caused a splash. Miranda cried out. Looking up, he saw a wall of jade-green water bearing down on them, its face thickly studded with the fleeting dark shapes of the mackerel. Before he could move, the wave swept over the sandbar and carried him under, dragging him along the bottom and finally casting him onto shore. The beach was littered with flopping mackerel; Miranda lay in the shallows, laughing at him. Esteban laughed, too, but only to cover up his rekindled fear of this woman who drew upon the powers of dead gods. He had no wish to hear her explanation; he was certain she would tell him that the gods lived on in her world, and this would only confuse him further.

Later that day as Esteban was cleaning the fish, while Miranda was off picking bananas to cook with them—the sweet little ones that grew along the riverbank—a Land-Rover came jouncing up the beach from Puerto Morada, an orange fire of the setting sun dancing on its windshield. It pulled up beside him, and Onofrio climbed out the passenger side. A hectic flush dappled his cheeks, and he was dabbing his sweaty brow with a handkerchief. Raimundo climbed out the driver's side and leaned against the door, staring hatefully at Esteban.

"Nine days and not a word," said Onofrio gruffly. "We thought you were dead. How goes the hunt?"

Esteban set down the fish he had been scaling and stood. "I have failed," he said. "I will give you back the money."

Raimundo chuckled—a dull, cluttered sound—and Onofrio grunted with amusement. "Impossible," he said. "Incarnación has spent the money on a house in Barrio Clarin. You must kill the jaguar."

"I cannot," said Esteban. "I will repay you, somehow."

"The Indian has lost his nerve, Father." Raimundo spat in the sand. "Let my friends and I hunt the jaguar."

The idea of Raimundo and his loutish friends thrashing through the jungle was so ludicrous that Esteban could not restrain a laugh.

"Be careful, Indian!" Raimundo banged the flat of his hand on the roof of the car.

"It is you who should be careful," said Esteban. "Most likely the jaguar will be hunting you." Esteban picked up his machete. "And whoever hunts this jaguar will answer to me as well."

Raimundo reached for something in the driver's seat and walked around in front of the hood. In his hand was a silvered automatic. "I await your answer." he said.

"Put that away!" Onofrio's tone was that of a man addressing a child whose menace was inconsequential, but the intent surfacing in Raimundo's face was not childish. A tic marred the plump curve of his cheek, the ligature of his neck was cabled, and his lips were drawn back in a joyless grin. It was, thought Esteban—strangely fascinated by the transformation—like watching a demon dissolve its false shape: the true lean features melting up from the illusion of the soft.

"This son of a whore insulted me in front of Julia!" Raimundo's gun hand was shaking.

"Your personal differences can wait," said Onofrio. "This is a business matter." He held out his hand. "Give me the gun."

"If he is not going to kill the jaguar, what use is he?" said Raimundo.

"Perhaps we can convince him to change his mind." Onofrio beamed at Esteban. "What do you say? Shall I let my son collect his debt of honor, or will you fulfill our contract?"

"Father!" complained Raimundo; his eyes flicked sideways. "He . . ."

Esteban broke for the jungle. The gun roared, a white-hot claw swiped at his side, and he went flying. For an instant he did not know where he was; but then, one by one, his impressions began to sort themselves. He was lying on his injured side, and it was throbbing fiercely. Sand crusted his mouth and eyelids. He was curled up around his machete, which was still clutched in his hand. Voices above him, sand fleas hopping on his face. He resisted the urge to brush them off and lay without moving. The throb of his wound and his hatred had the same red force behind them.

". . . carry him to the river," Raimundo was saying, his voice atremble with excitement. "Everyone will think the jaguar killed him!"

"Fool!" said Onofrio. "He might have killed the jaguar, and you could have had a sweeter revenge. His wife . . . "

"This was sweet enough," said Raimundo.

A shadow fell over Esteban, and he held his breath. He needed no herbs to deceive this pale, flabby jaguar who was bending to him, turning him onto his back.

"Watch out!" cried Onofrio.

Esteban let himself be turned and lashed out with the machete. His contempt for Onofrio and Incarnación, as well as his hatred of Raimundo, was involved in the blow, and the blade lodged deep in Raimundo's side, grating on bone. Raimundo shrieked and would have fallen, but the blade helped to keep him upright; his hands fluttered around the machete as if he wanted to adjust it to a more comfortable position, and his eyes were wide with disbelief. A shudder vibrated the hilt of the machete—it seemed sensual, the spasm of a spent passion—and Raimundo sank to his knees. Blood spilled from his mouth, adding tragic lines to the corners of his lips. He pitched forward, not falling flat but remaining kneeling, his face pressed into the sand; the attitude of an Arab at prayer.

Esteban wrenched the machete free, fearful of an attack by Onofrio, but the appliance dealer was squirming into the Land-Rover. The engine caught, the wheels spun, and the car lurched off, turning through the edge of the surf and heading for Puerto Morada. An orange dazzle flared on the rear window, as if the spirit who had lured it to the barrio was now harrying it away.

Unsteadily, Esteban got to his feet. He peeled his shirt back from the bullet wound. There was a lot of blood, but it was only a crease. He avoided looking at Raimundo and walked down to the water and stood gazing out at the waves; his thoughts rolled in with them, less thoughts than tidal sweeps of emotion.

It was twilight by the time Miranda returned, her arms full of bananas and wild figs. She had not heard the shot. He told her what had happened as she dressed his wounds with a poultice of herbs and banana leaves. "It will mend," she said of the wound. "But this"—she gestured at Raimundo—"this will not. You must come with me, Esteban. The soldiers will kill you."

"No," he said. "They will come, but they are Patuca . . . except for the captain, who is a drunkard, a shell of a man. I doubt he will even be notified. They will listen to my story, and we will reach an accommodation. No matter what lies Onofrio tells, his word will not stand against theirs."

"And then?"

"I may have to go to jail for a while, or I may have to leave the province. But I will not be killed."

She sat for a minute without speaking, the whites of her eyes glowing in the half-light. Finally she stood and walked off along the beach.

"Where are you going?" he called.

She turned back. "You speak so casually of losing me . . ." she began.

"It is not casual!"

"No!" She laughed bitterly. "I suppose not. You are so afraid of life, you call it death and would prefer jail or exile to living it. That is hardly casual." She stared at him, her expression a cypher at that distance. "I will not lose you, Esteban," she said. She walked away again, and this time when he called she did not turn.

Twilight deepened to dusk, a slow fill of shadow graying the world into negative, and Esteban felt himself graying along with it, his thoughts reduced to echoing the dull wash of the receding tide. The dusk lingered, and he had the idea that night would never fall, that the act of violence had driven a nail through the substance of his irresolute life, pinned him forever to this ashen moment and deserted shore. As a child he had been terrified by the possibility of such magical isolations, but now the prospect seemed a consolation for Miranda's absence, a remembrance of her magic. Despite her parting words, he did not think she would be back—there had been sadness and finality in her voice—and this roused in him feelings of both relief and desolation feelings that set him to pacing up and down the tidal margin of the shore.

The full moon rose, the sands of the barrio burned silver, and shortly thereafter four soldiers came in a jeep from Puerto Morada. They were gnomish, copper-skinned men, and their uniforms were the dark blue of the night sky, bearing no device or decoration. Though they were not close friends, he knew them each by name. Sebastian, Amador, Carlito, and Ramón. In their headlights Raimuado's corpse—startlingly pale, the blood on his face dried into intricate whorls—looked like an exotic creature cast up by the sea, and their inspection of it smacked more of curiosity than of a search for evidence. Amador unearthed Raimundo's gun, sighted along it toward the jungle, and asked Ramón how much he thought it was worth.

"Perhaps Onofrio will give you a good price," said Ramón, and the others laughed.

They built a fire of driftwood and coconut shells, and sat around it while Esteban told his story; he did not mention either Miranda or her relation to the jaguar, because these men—estranged from the tribe by their government service—had grown conservative in their judgments, and he did not want them to consider him irrational. They listened without comment; the firelight burnished their skins to reddish gold and glinted on their rifle barrels.

"Onofrio will take his charge to the capital if we do nothing," said Amador after Esteban had finished.

"He may in any case," said Carlito. "And then it will go hard with Esteban."

"And," said Sebastian, "if an agent is sent to Puerto Morada and sees how things are with Captain Portales, they will surely replace him and it will go hard with us."

They stared into the flames, mulling over the problem, and Esteban chose the moment to ask Amador, who lived near him on the mountain, if he had seen Incarnación.

"She will be amazed to learn you are alive," said Amador. "I saw her yesterday in the dressmaker's shop. She was admiring the fit of a new black skirt in the mirror."

It was as if a black swath of Incarnación's skirt had folded around Esteban's thoughts. He lowered his head and carved lines in the sand with the point of his machete.

"I have it," said Ramón. "A boycott!"

The others expressed confusion.

"If we do not buy from Onofrio, who will?" said Ramón. "He will lose business. Threatened with this, he will not dare involve the government. He will allow Esteban to plead self-defense."

"But Raimundo was his only son," said Amador. "It may be that grief will count more than greed in this instance."

Again they fell silent. It mattered little to Esteban what was decided. He was coming to understand that without Miranda, his future held nothing but uninteresting choices; he turned his gaze to the sky and noticed that the stars and the fire were flickering with the same rhythm, and he imagined each of them ringed by a group of gnomish, copper-skinned men, debating the question of his fate.

"Aha!" said Carlito. "I know what to do. We will occupy Barrio

Carolina—the entire company—and *we* will kill the jaguar. Onofrio's greed cannot withstand this temptation."

"That you must not do," said Esteban.

"But why?" asked Amador. "We may not kill the jaguar, but with so many men we will certainly drive it away."

Before Esteban could answer, the jaguar roared. It was prowling down the beach toward the fire, like a black flame itself shifting over the glowing sand. Its ears were laid back, and silver drops of moonlight gleamed in its eyes. Amador grabbed his rifle, came to one knee, and fired: the bullet sprayed sand a dozen feet to the left of the jaguar.

"Wait!" cried Esteban, pushing him down.

But the rest had begun to fire, and the jaguar was hit. It leaped high as it had that first night while playing, but this time it landed in a heap, snarling, snapping at its shoulder; it regained its feet and limped toward the jungle, favoring its right foreleg. Excited by their success, the soldiers ran a few paces after it and stopped to fire again. Carlito dropped to one knee, taking careful aim.

"No!" shouted Esteban, and as he hurled his machete at Carlito, desperate to prevent further harm to Miranda, he recognized the trap that had been sprung and the consequences he would face.

The blade sliced across Carlito's thigh, knocking him onto his side. He screamed, and Amador, seeing what had happened, fired wildly at Esteban and called to the others. Esteban ran toward the jungle, making for the jaguar's path. A fusilade of shots rang out behind him, bullets whipped past his ears. Each time his feet slipped in the soft sand, the moonstruck facades of the barrio appeared to lurch sideways as if trying to block his way. And then, as he reached the verge of the jungle, he was hit.

The bullet seemed to throw him forward, to increase his speed, but somehow he managed to keep his feet. He careened along the path, arms waving, breath shrieking in his throat. Palmetto fronds swatted his face, vines tangled his legs. He felt no pain, only a peculiar numbness that pulsed low in his back; he pictured the wound opening and closing like the mouth of an anemone. The soldiers were shouting his name. They would follow, but cautiously, afraid of the jaguar, and he thought he might be able to cross the river before they could catch up. But when he came to the river, he found the jaguar waiting.

It was crouched on the tussocky rise, its neck craned over the water, and below, half a dozen feet from the bank, floated the reflection of the full moon, huge and silvery, an unblemished circle of light. Blood glistened scarlet on the jaguar's shoulder, like a fresh rose pinned in place, and this made it look even more an embodiment of principle: the shape a god might choose, that some universal constant might assume. It gazed calmly at Esteban, growled low in its throat, and dove into the river, cleaving and shattering the moon's reflection, vanishing beneath the surface. The ripples subsided, the image of the moon reformed. And there, silhouetted against it, Esteban saw the figure of a woman swimming, each stroke causing her to grow smaller and smaller until she seemed no more than a character incised upon a silver plate. It was not only Miranda he saw, but all mystery and beauty receding from him, and he realized how blind he had been not to perceive the truth sheathed inside the truth of death that had been sheathed inside her truth of another world. It was clear to him now. It sang to him from his wound, every syllable a heartbeat. It was written by the dying ripples, it swayed in the banana leaves, it sighed on the wind. It was everywhere, and he had always known it: If you deny mystery—even in the guise of death—then you deny life, and you will walk like a ghost through your days, never knowing the secrets of the extremes. The deep sorrows, the absolute joys.

He drew a breath of the rank jungle air, and with it drew a breath of a world no longer his, of the girl Incarnación, of friends and children and country nights . . . all his lost sweetness His chest tightened as with the onset of tears, but the sensation quickly abated, and he understood that the sweetness of the past had been subsumed by a scent of mangoes, that nine magical days—a magical number of days, the number it takes to sing the soul to rest—lay between him and tears. Freed of those associations, he felt as if he were undergoing a subtle refinement of form, a winnowing, and he remembered having felt much the same on the day when he had run out the door of Santa Maria del Onda, putting behind him its dark geometries and cobwebbed catechisms and generations of swallows that had never flown beyond the walls, casting off his acolyte's robe and racing across the square toward the mountain and Incarnación: it had been she who had lured him then, just as his mother had lured him to the church and as Miranda was luring him now, and he laughed at seeing how easily these three women had diverted the flow of his life, how like other men he was in this.

The strange bloom of painlessness in his back was sending out tendrils into his arms and legs, and the cries of the soldiers had grown louder. Miranda was a tiny speck shrinking against a silver immensity. For a moment he hesitated, experiencing a resurgence of fear; then Miranda's face materialized in his mind's eye, and all the emotion he had suppressed for nine days poured through him, washing away the fear. It was a silvery, flawless emotion, and he was giddy with it, light with it; it was like thunder and fire fused into one element and boiling up inside him, and he was overwhelmed by a need to express it, to mold it into a form that would reflect its power and purity. But he was no singer, no poet. There was but a single mode of expression open to him. Hoping he was not too late, that Miranda's door had not shut forever, Esteban dove into the river, cleaving the image of the full moon; and—his eyes still closed from the shock of the splash—with the last of his mortal strength, he swam hard down after her.

Buffalo Gals, Won't You Come Out Tonight

Ursula K. Le Guin

Ursula K. Le Guin is considered one of the most influential authors in the science fiction and fantasy field. Her Earthsea novels have been favorably compared to J.R.R. Tolkien's work for their intricate detailing of a fantasy world. Like Tolkien, Le Guin makes her worlds come alive though the brilliant use of language. Her work in the field has been critically acclaimed as well, garnering her four Nebula awards, five Hugo awards, three Jupiter awards, and the Gandalf award. She has taught writing courses all around the world, and currently lives in Portland, Oregon.

i

"YOU FELL OUT OF THE SKY," THE COYOTE SAID.

Still curled up tight, lying on her side, her back pressed against the overhanging rock, the child watched the coyote with one eye. Over the other eye she kept her hand cupped, its back on the dirt.

"There was a burned place in the sky, up there alongside the rim-rock, and then you fell out of it," the coyote repeated, patiently, as if the news was getting a bit stale. "Are you hurt?"

She was all right. She was in the plane with Mr. Michaels, and the motor was so loud she couldn't understand what he said even when he shouted, and the way the wind rocked the wings was making her feel sick, but it was all right. They were flying to Canyonville. In the plane.

She looked. The coyote was still sitting there. It yawned. It was a big one, in good condition, its coat silvery and thick. The dark tear-line from its long yellow eye was as clearly marked as a tabby cat's.

She sat up, slowly, still holding her right hand pressed to her right eye.

"Did you lose an eye?" the coyote asked, interested.

"I don't know," the child said. She caught her breath and shivered. "I'm cold."

"I'll help you look for it," the coyote said. "Come on! If you move around you won't have to shiver. The sun's up."

Cold lonely brightness lay across the falling land, a hundred miles of sagebrush. The coyote was trotting busily around, nosing under clumps of rabbit-brush and cheatgrass, pawing at a rock. "Aren't you going to look?" it said, suddenly sitting down on its haunches and abandoning the search. "I knew a trick once where I could throw my eyes way up into a tree and see everything from up there, and then whistle, and they'd come back into my head. But that goddam bluejay stole them, and when I whistled nothing came. I had to stick lumps of pine pitch into my head so I could see anything. You could try that. But you've got one eye that's OK, what do you need two for? Are you coming, or are you dying there?"

The child crouched, shivering.

"Well, come if you want to," said the coyote, yawned again, snapped at a flea, stood up, turned, and trotted away among the sparse clumps of rabbit-brush and sage, along the long slope that stretched on down and down into the plain streaked across by long shadows of sagebrush. The slender, grey-yellow animal was hard to keep in sight, vanishing as the child watched.

She struggled to her feet, and without a word, though she kept saying in her mind, "Wait, please wait," she hobbled after the coyote. She could not see it. She kept her hand pressed over the right eyesocket. Seeing with one eye there was no depth; it was like a huge, flat picture. The coyote suddenly sat in the middle of the picture, looking back at her, its mouth open, its eyes narrowed, grinning. Her legs began to steady and her head did not pound so hard, though the deep, black ache was always there. She had nearly caught up to the coyote when it trotted off again. This time she spoke. "Please wait!" she said.

"OK," said the coyote, but it trotted right on. She followed, walking downhill into the flat picture that at each step was deep.

Each step was different underfoot; each sage bush was different, and all the same. Following the coyote she came out from the shadow of the rimrock cliffs, and the sun at eyelevel dazzled her left eye. Its bright warmth soaked into her muscles and bones at once. The air, that all night had been so hard to breathe, came sweet and easy.

The sage bushes were pulling in their shadows and the sun was hot on the child's back when she followed the coyote along the rim of a gully. After a while the coyote slanted down the undercut slope and the child scrambled after, through scrub willows to the thin creek in its wide sandbed. Both drank.

The coyote crossed the creek, not with a careless charge and

splashing like a dog, but singlefoot and quiet like a cat; always it carried its tail low. The child hesitated, knowing that wet shoes make
blistered feet, and then waded across in as few steps as possible. Her
right arm ached with the effort of holding her hand up over her
eye. "I need a bandage," she said to the coyote. It cocked its head
and said nothing. It stretched out its forelegs and lay watching the
water, resting but alert. The child sat down nearby on the hot sand
and tried to move her right hand. It was glued to the skin around
her eye by dried blood. At the little tearing-away pain, she whimpered; though it was a small pain it frightened her. The coyote
came over close and poked its long snout into her face. Its strong,
sharp smell was in her nostrils. It began to lick the awful, aching
blindness, cleaning and cleaning with its curled, precise, strong, wet
tongue, until the child was able to cry a little with relief, being comforted. Her head was bent close to the grey-yellow ribs, and she saw
the hard nipples, the whitish belly-fur. She put her arm around the
she-coyote, stroking the harsh coat over back and ribs.

"OK," the coyote said, "let's go!" And set off without a backward
glance. The child scrambled to her feet and followed. "Where are
we going?" she said, and the coyote, trotting on down along the
creek, answered, "On down along the creek . . ."

There must have been a while she was asleep while she walked,
because she felt like she was waking up, but she was walking along,
only in a different place. She didn't know how she knew it was different. They were still following the creek, though the gully was flattened out to nothing much, and there was still sagebrush range as
far as the eye could see. The eye—the good one—felt rested. The
other one still ached, but not so sharply, and there was no use thinking about it. But where was the coyote?

She stopped. The pit of cold into which the plane had fallen
reopened and she fell. She stood falling, a thin whimper making
itself in her throat.

"Over here!"

The child turned. She saw a coyote gnawing at the half-dried-up
carcass of a crow, black feathers sticking to the black lips and narrow jaw.

She saw a tawny-skinned woman kneeling by a campfire, sprin-
kling something into a conical pot. She heard the water boiling in
the pot, though it was propped between rocks, off the fire. The
woman's hair was yellow and grey, bound back with a string. Her feet
were bare. The upturned soles looked as dark and hard as shoe
soles, but the arch of the foot was high, and the toes made two neat
curving rows. She wore bluejeans and an old white shirt. She

looked over at the girl. "Come on, eat crow!" she said. The child slowly came toward the woman and the fire, and squatted down. She had stopped falling and felt very light and empty; and her tongue was like a piece of wood stuck in her mouth.

Coyote was now blowing into the pot or basket or whatever it was. She reached into it with two fingers, and pulled her hand away shaking it and shouting, "Ow! Shit! Why don't I ever have any spoons?" She broke off a dead twig of sagebrush, dipped it into the pot, and licked it. "Oh, boy," she said. "Come on!"

The child moved a little closer, broke off a twig, dipped. Lumpy pinkish mush clung to the twig. She licked. The taste was rich and delicate.

"What is it?" she asked after a long time of dipping and licking.

"Food. Dried salmon mush," Coyote said. "It's cooling down." She stuck two fingers into the mush again, this time getting a good load, which she ate very neatly. The child, when she tried, got mush all over her chin. It was like chopsticks, it took practice. She practiced. They ate turn and turn until nothing was left in the pot but three rocks. The child did not ask why there were rocks in the mush-pot. They licked the rocks clean. Coyote licked out the inside of the pot-basket, rinsed it once in the creek, and put it onto her head. It fit nicely, making a conical hat. She pulled off her blue-jeans. "Piss on the fire!" she cried, and did so, standing straddling it. "Ah, steam between the legs!" she said. The child, embarrassed, thought she was supposed to do the same thing, but did not want to, and did not. Bareassed, Coyote danced around the dampened fire, kicking her long thin legs out and singing,

"*Buffalo gals, won't you come out tonight,*
Come out tonight, come out tonight,
Buffalo gals, won't you come out tonight,
And dance by the light of the moon?"

She pulled her jeans back on. The child was burying the remains of the fire in creek-sand, heaping it over, seriously, wanting to do right. Coyote watched her.

"Is that you?" she said. "A Buffalo Gal? What happened to the rest of you?"

"The rest of me?" The child looked at herself, alarmed.

"All your people."

"Oh. Well, Mom took Bobbie, he's my little brother, away with Uncle Norm. He isn't really my uncle, or anything. So Mr. Michaels was going there anyway so he was going to fly me over to my real father, in Canyonville. Linda, my stepmother, you know, she said it was OK for the summer anyhow if I was there, and then we could see. But the plane."

In the silence the girl's face became dark red, then greyish white. Coyote watched, fascinated. "Oh," the girl said, "Oh—Oh—Mr. Michaels—he must be—Did the—"

"Come on!" said Coyote, and set off walking.

The child cried, "I ought to go back—"

"What for?" said Coyote. She stopped to look round at the child, then went on faster. "Come on, Gal!" She said it as a name; maybe it was the child's name, Myra, as spoken by Coyote. The child, confused and despairing, protested again, but followed her. "Where are we going? Where *are* we?"

"This is my country," Coyote answered, with dignity, making a long, slow gesture all round the vast horizon. "I made it. Every goddam sage bush."

And they went on. Coyote's gait was easy, even a little shambling, but she covered the ground; the child struggled not to drop behind. Shadows were beginning to pull themselves out again from under the rocks and shrubs. Leaving the creek, they went up a long, low, uneven slope that ended away off against the sky in rimrock. Dark trees stood one here, another way over there; what people called a juniper forest, a desert forest, one with a lot more between the trees than trees. Each juniper they passed smelled sharply, catpee smell the kids at school called it, but the child liked it; it seemed to go into her mind and wake her up. She picked off a juniper berry and held it in her mouth, but after a while spat it out. The aching was coming back in huge black waves, and she kept stumbling. She found that she was sitting down on the ground. When she tried to get up her legs shook and would not go under her. She felt foolish and frightened, and began to cry.

"We're home!" Coyote called from way on up the hill.

The child looked with her one weeping eye, and saw sagebrush, juniper, cheatgrass, rimrock. She heard a coyote yip far off in the dry twilight.

She saw a little town up under the rimrock, board houses, shacks, all unpainted. She heard Coyote call again, "Come on, pup! Come on, Gal, we're home!" She could not get up, so she tried to go on all fours, the long way up the slope to the houses under the rimrock. Long before she got there, several people came to meet her. They were all children, she thought at first, and then began to understand that most of them were grown people, but all were very short; they were broad-bodied, fat, with fine, delicate hands and feet. Their eyes were bright. Some of the women helped her stand up and walk, coaxing her, "It isn't much farther, you're doing fine." In the late dusk lights shone yellow-bright through doorways and through unchinked cracks between boards. Woodsmoke hung sweet in the quiet air. The short people talked and laughed all the time, softly. "Where's she going to stay?"—"Put her in with Robin, they're all asleep already!"—"Oh, she can stay with us."

The child asked hoarsely. "Where's Coyote?"

"Out hunting," the short people said.

A deeper voice spoke: "Somebody new has come into town?"

"Yes, a new person," one of the short men answered.

Among these people the deep-voiced man bulked impressive; he was broad and tall, with powerful hands, a big head, a short neck. They made way for him respectfully. He moved very quietly, respectful of them also. His eyes when he stared down at the child were amazing. When he blinked, it was like the passing of a hand before a candle-flame.

"It's only an owlet," he said. "What have you let happen to your eye, new person?"

"I was—We were flying—"

"You're too young to fly," the big man said in his deep, soft voice. "Who brought you here?"

"Coyote."

And one of the short people confirmed: "She came here with Coyote, Young Owl."

"Then maybe she should stay in Coyote's house tonight," the big man said.

"It's all bones and lonely in there," said a short woman with fat cheeks and a striped shirt. "She can come with us."

That seemed to decide it. The fat-cheeked woman patted the child's arm and took her past several shacks and shanties to a low, windowless house. The doorway was so low even the child had to duck down to enter. There were a lot of people inside, some already there and some crowding in after the fat-cheeked woman. Several babies were fast asleep in cradle-boxes in corners. There was a good fire, and a good smell, like toasted sesame seeds. The child was given food, and ate a little, but her head swam and the blackness in her right eye kept coming across her left eye so she could not see at all for a while. Nobody asked her name or told her what to call them. She heard the children call the fat-cheeked woman Chipmunk. She got up courage finally to say, "Is there somewhere I can go to sleep, Mrs. Chipmunk?"

"Sure, come on," one of the daughters said, "in here," and took the child into a back room, not completely partitioned off from the crowded front room, but dark and uncrowded. Big shelves with mattresses and blankets lined the walls. "Crawl in!" said Chipmunk's daughter, patting the child's arm in the comforting way they had. The child climbed onto a shelf, under a blanket. She laid down her head. She thought, "I didn't brush my teeth."

ii

She woke; she slept again. In Chipmunk's sleeping room it was always stuffy, warm, and half-dark, day and night. People came in and slept and got up and left, night and day. She dozed and slept, got down to drink from the bucket and dipper in the front room, and went back to sleep and doze.

She was sitting up on the shelf, her feet dangling, not feeling bad any more, but dreamy, weak. She felt in her jeans pockets. In the left front one was a pocket comb and a bubblegum wrapper, in the right front, two dollar bills and a quarter and a dime.

Chipmunk and another woman, a very pretty dark-eyed plump one, came in. "So you woke up for your dance!" Chipmunk greeted her, laughing, and sat down by her with an arm around her.

"Jay's giving you a dance," the dark woman said. "He's going to make you all right. Let's get you all ready!"

There was a spring up under the rimrock, that flattened out into a pool with slimy, reedy shores. A flock of noisy children splashing in it ran off and left the child and the two women to bathe. The water was warm on the surface, cold down on the feet and legs. All naked, the two soft-voiced laughing women, their round bellies and breasts, broad hips and buttocks gleaming warm in the late afternoon light, sluiced the child down, washed and stroked her limbs and hands and hair, cleaned around the cheekbone and eyebrow of her right eye with infinite softness, admired her, sudsed her, rinsed her, splashed her out of the water, dried her off, dried each other off, got dressed, dressed her, braided her hair, braided each other's hair, tied feathers on the braid-ends, admired her and each other again, and brought her back down into the little straggling town and to a kind of playing field or dirt parking lot in among the houses. There were no streets, just paths and dirt, no lawns and gardens, just sagebrush and dirt. Quite a few people were gathering or wandering around the open place, looking dressed up, wearing colorful shirts, print dresses, strings of beads, earrings. "Hey there, Chipmunk, Whitefoot!" they greeted the women.

A man in new jeans, with a bright blue velveteen vest over a clean, faded blue workshirt, came forward to meet them, very handsome, tense, and important. "All right, Gal!" he said in a harsh, loud voice, which startled among all these soft-speaking people. "We're going to get that eye fixed right up tonight! You just sit down here and don't worry about a thing." He took her wrist, gently despite his bossy, brassy manner, and led her to a woven mat that lay on the dirt near the middle of the open place. There, feeling very foolish, she had to sit down, and was told to stay still. She soon got over feeling that everybody was looking at her, since nobody paid her more attention than a checking glance or, from Chipmunk or Whitefoot and their families, a reassuring wink. Every now and then Jay rushed over to her and said something like, "Going to be as good as new!" and went off again to organize people, waving his long blue arms and shouting.

Coming up the hill to the open place, a lean, loose, tawny figure—and the child started to jump up, remembered she was to sit still, and sat still, calling out softly, "Coyote! Coyote!"

Coyote came lounging by. She grinned. She stood looking down at the child. "Don't let that Bluejay fuck you up, Gal," she said, and lounged on.

The child's gaze followed her, yearning.

People were sitting down now over on one side of the open place, making an uneven half-circle that kept getting added to at the ends until there was nearly a circle of people sitting on the dirt around the child, ten or fifteen paces from her. All the people wore the kind of clothes the child was used to, jeans and jeans-jackets, shirts, vests, cotton dresses, but they were all barefoot, and she thought they were more beautiful than the people she knew, each in a different way, as if each one had invented beauty. Yet some of them were also very strange: thin black shining people with whispery voices, a long-legged woman with eyes like jewels. The big man called Young Owl was there, sleepy-looking and dignified, like Judge McCown who owned a sixty-thousand acre ranch; and beside him was a woman the child thought might be his sister, for like him she had a hook nose and big, strong hands; but she was lean and dark, and there was a crazy look in her fierce eyes. Yellow eyes, but round, not long and slanted like Coyote's. There was Coyote sitting yawning, scratching her armpit, bored. Now somebody was entering the circle: a man, wearing only a kind of kilt and a cloak painted or beaded with diamond shapes, dancing to the rhythm of the rattle he carried and shook with a buzzing fast beat. His limbs and body were thick yet supple, his movements smooth and pouring. The child kept her gaze on him as he danced past her, around her, past again. The rattle in his hand shook almost too fast to see, in the other hand was something thin and sharp. People were singing around the circle now, a few notes repeated in time to the rattle, soft and tuneless. It was exciting and boring, strange and familiar. The Rattler wove his dancing closer and closer to her, darting at her. The first time she flinched away, frightened by the lunging movement and by his flat, cold face with narrow eyes, but after that she sat still, knowing her part. The dancing went on, the singing went on, till they carried her past boredom into a floating that could go on forever.

Jay had come strutting into the circle, and was standing beside her. He couldn't sing, but he called out, "Hey! Hey! Hey! Hey!" in his big, harsh voice, and everybody answered from all round, and the echo came down from the rimrock on the second beat. Jay was holding up a stick with a ball on it in one hand, and something like a marble in the other. The stick was a pipe: he got smoke into his mouth from it and blew it in four directions and up and down and then over the marble, a puff each time. Then the rattle stopped suddenly, and everything was silent for several breaths. Jay squatted down and looked intently into the child's face, his head cocked to one side. He reached forward, muttering something in time to the rattle and the singing that had started up again louder than before; he touched the child's right eye in the black center of the pain. She flinched and endured. His touch was not gentle. She saw the marble, a dull yellow ball like beeswax, in his hand; then she shut her seeing eye and set her teeth.

"There!" Jay shouted. "Open up. Come on! Let's see!"

Her jaw clenched like a vise, she opened both eyes. The lid of the right one stuck and dragged with such a searing white pain that she nearly threw up as she sat there in the middle of everybody watching.

"Hey, can you see? How's it work? It looks great!" Jay was shaking her arm, railing at her. "How's it feel? Is it working?"

What she saw was confused, hazy, yellowish. She began to discover, as everybody came crowding around peering at her, smiling, stroking and patting her arms and shoulders, that if she shut the hurting eye and looked with the other, everything was clear and flat; if she used them both, things were blurry and yellowish, but deep.

There, right close, was Coyote's long nose and narrow eyes and grin. "What is it, Jay?" she was asking peering at the new eye. "One of mine you stole that time?"

"It's pine pitch," Jay shouted furiously. "You think I'd use some stupid secondhand coyote eye? I'm a doctor!"

"Ooooh, ooooh, a doctor," Coyote said. "Boy, that is one ugly eye. Why didn't you ask Rabbit for a rabbit-dropping? That eye looks like shit." She put her lean face yet closer, till the child thought she was going to kiss her; instead, the thin, firm tongue once more licked accurate across the pain, cooling, clearing. When the child opened both eyes again the world looked pretty good.

"It works fine," she said.

"Hey!" Jay yelled. "She says it works fine! It works fine, she says so! I told you! What'd I tell you?" He went off waving his arms and yelling. Coyote had disappeared. Everybody was wandering off.

The child stood up, stiff from long sitting. It was nearly dark; only the long west held a great depth of pale radiance. Eastward the plains ran down into night.

Lights were on in some of the shanties. Off at the edge of town somebody was playing a creaky fiddle, a lonesome chirping tune.

A person came beside her and spoke quietly: "Where will you stay?"

"I don't know," the child said. She was feeling extremely hungry. "Can I stay with Coyote?"

"She isn't home much," the soft-voiced woman said. "You were staying with Chipmunk, weren't you? Or there's Rabbit or Jackrabbit, they have families . . ."

"Do you have a family?" the girl asked, looking at the delicate, soft-eyed woman.

"Two fawns," the woman answered, smiling. "But I just came into town for the dance."

"I'd really like to stay with Coyote," the child said after a little pause, timid, but obstinate.

"OK, that's fine. Her house is over here." Doe walked along beside the child to a ramshackle cabin on the high edge of town. No light shone from inside. A lot of junk was scattered around the front. There was no step up to the half-open door. Over the door a battered pine board, nailed up crooked, said BIDE-A-WEE.

"Hey, Coyote? Visitors," Doe said. Nothing happened.

Doe pushed the door farther open and peered in. "She's out hunting, I guess. I better be getting back to the fawns. You going to be OK? Anybody else here will give you something to eat—you know . . . OK?"

"Yeah. I'm fine. Thank you," the child said.

She watched Doe walk away through the clear twilight, a severely elegant walk, small steps, like a woman in high heels, quick, precise, very light.

Inside Bide-A-Wee it was too dark to see anything and so cluttered that she fell over something at every step. She could not figure out where or how to light a fire. There was something that felt like a bed, but when she lay down on it, it felt more like a dirty-clothes pile, and smelt like one. Things bit her legs, arms, neck, and back. She was terribly hungry. By smell she found her way to what had to be a dead fish hanging from the ceiling in one corner. By feel she broke off a greasy flake and tasted it. It was smoked dried

salmon. She ate one succulent piece after another until she was satisfied, and licked her fingers clean. Near the open door starlight
shone on water in a pot of some kind; the child smelled it cautiously, tasted it cautiously, and drank just enough to quench her
thirst, for it tasted of mud and was warm and stale. Then she went
back to the bed of dirty clothes and fleas, and lay down. She could
have gone to Chipmunk's house, or other friendly households; she
thought of that as she lay forlorn in Coyote's dirty bed. But she did
not go. She slapped at fleas until she fell asleep.

Along in the deep night somebody said, "Move over, pup," and
was warm beside her.

Breakfast, eaten sitting in the sun in the doorway, was dried-salmon-
powder mush. Coyote hunted, mornings and evenings, but what
they ate was not fresh game but salmon, and dried stuff, and any
berries in season. The child did not ask about this. It made sense to
her. She was going to ask Coyote why she slept at night and waked
in the day like humans, instead of the other way round like coyotes,
but when she framed the question in her mind she saw at once that
night is when you sleep and day when you're awake; that made
sense too. But one question she did ask, one hot day when they
were lying around slapping fleas.

"I don't understand why you all look like people," she said.

"We are people."

"I mean, people like me, humans."

"Resemblance is in the eye," Coyote said. "How is that lousy eye,
by the way?"

"It's fine. But—like you wear clothes—and live in houses—with
fires and stuff—"

"That's what you think . . . If that loudmouth Jay hadn't horned
in, I could have done a really good job."

The child was quite used to Coyote's disinclination to stick to any
one subject, and to her boasting. Coyote was like a lot of kids she
knew, in some respects. Not in others.

"You mean what I'm seeing isn't true? Isn't real—like on TV, or
something?"

"No," Coyote said. "Hey, that's a tick on your collar." She reached
over, flicked the tick off, picked it up on one finger, bit it, and spat
out the bits.

"Yecch!" the child said. "So?"

"So, to me you're basically greyish yellow and run on four legs.
To that lot—" she waved disdainfully at the warren of little houses
next down the hill—"you hop around twitching your nose all the
time. To Hawk, you're an egg, or maybe getting pinfeathers. See? It

just depends on how you look at things. There are only two kinds of people."

"Humans and animals?"

"No. The kind of people who say, 'There are two kinds of people' and the kind of people who don't." Coyote cracked up, pounding her thigh and yelling with delight at her joke. The child didn't get it, and waited.

"OK," Coyote said. "There's the first people, and then the others. That's the two kinds."

"The first people are—?"

"Us, the animals . . . and things. All the old ones. You know. And you pups, kids, fledglings. All first people."

"And the—others?"

"Them," Coyote said. "You know. The others. The new people. The ones who came." Her fine, hard face had gone serious, rather formidable. She glanced directly, as she seldom did, at the child, a brief gold sharpness. "We were here," she said. "We were always here. We are always here. Where we are is here. But it's their country now. They're running it . . . Shit, even I did better!"

The child pondered and offered a word she had used to hear a good deal: "They're illegal immigrants."

"Illegal!" Coyote said, mocking, sneering. "Illegal is a sick bird. What the fuck's illegal mean? You want a code of justice from a coyote? Grow up, kid!"

"I don't want to."

"You don't want to grow up?"

"I'll be the other kind if I do."

"Yeah. So," Coyote said, and shrugged. "That's life." She got up and went around the house, and the child heard her pissing in the back yard.

A lot of things were hard to take about Coyote as a mother. When her boyfriends came to visit, the child learned to go stay with Chipmunk or the Rabbits for the night, because Coyote and her friend wouldn't even wait to get on the bed but would start doing that right on the floor or even out in the yard. A couple of times Coyote came back late from hunting with a friend, and the child had to lie up against the wall in the same bed and hear and feel them doing that right next to her. It was something like fighting and something like dancing, with a beat to it, and she didn't mind too much except that it made it hard to stay asleep.

Once she woke up and one of Coyote's friends was stroking her stomach in a creepy way. She didn't know what to do, but Coyote woke up and realized what he was doing, bit him hard, and kicked him out of bed. He spent the night on the floor, and apologized next morning—"Aw, hell, Ki, I forgot the kid was there, I thought it was you—"

Coyote, unappeased, yelled, "You think I don't got any standards? You think I'd let some coyote rape a kid in my bed?" She kicked him out of the house, and grumbled about him all day. But a while later he spent the night again, and he and Coyote did that three or four times.

Another thing that was embarrassing was the way Coyote peed anywhere, taking her pants down in public. But most people here didn't seem to care. The thing that worried the child most, maybe, was when Coyote did number two anywhere and then turned around and talked to it. That seemed so awful. As if Coyote was—the way she often seemed, but really wasn't—crazy.

The child gathered up all the old dry turds from around the house one day while Coyote was having a nap, and buried them in a sandy place near where she and Bobcat and some of the other people generally went and did and buried their number twos.

Coyote woke up, came lounging out of Bide-A-Wee, rubbing her hands through her thick, fair, greyish hair and yawning, looked all around once with those narrow eyes, and said, "Hey! Where are they?" Then she shouted, "Where are you? Where are you?"

And a faint, muffled chorus came from over in the sandy draw, "Mommy! Mommy! We're here!"

Coyote trotted over, squatted down, raked out every turd, and talked with them for a long time. When she came back she said nothing, but the child, redfaced and heart pounding, said, "I'm sorry I did that."

"It's just easier when they're all around close by," Coyote said, washing her hands (despite the filth of her house, she kept herself quite clean, in her own fashion).

"I kept stepping on them," the child said, trying to justify her deed.

"Poor little shits," said Coyote, practicing dance-steps.

"Coyote," the child said timidly. "Did you ever have any children? I mean real pups?"

"Did I? Did I have children? Litters! That one that tried feeling you up, you know? that was my son. Pick of the litter . . . Listen, Gal. Have daughters. When you have anything, have daughters. At least they clear out."

iii

The child thought of herself as Gal, but also sometimes as Myra. So far as she knew, she was the only person in town who had two names. She had to think about that, and about what Coyote had said about the two kinds of people; she had to think about where she belonged. Some persons in town made it clear that as far as they were concerned she didn't and never would belong there. Hawk's furious stare burned through her; the Skunk children made audible remarks about what she smelled like. And though Whitefoot and Chipmunk and their families were kind, it was the generosity of big families, where one more or less simply doesn't count. If one of them, or Cottontail, or Jackrabbit, had come upon her in the desert lying lost and half-blind, would they have stayed with her, like Coyote? That was Coyote's craziness, what they called her craziness. She wasn't afraid. She went between the two kinds of people, she crossed over. Buck and Doe and their beautiful children weren't really afraid, because they lived so constantly in danger. The Rattler wasn't afraid, because he was so dangerous. And yet maybe he was afraid of her, for he never spoke, and never came close to her. None of them treated her the way Coyote did. Even among the children, her only constant playmate was one younger than herself, a preposterous and fearless little boy called Horned Toad Child. They dug and built together, out among the sagebrush, and played at hunting and gathering and keeping house and holding dances, all the great games. A pale, squatty child with fringed eyebrows, he was a self-contained but loyal friend; and he knew a good deal for his age.

"There isn't anybody else like me here," she said, as they sat by the pool in the morning sunlight.

"There isn't anybody much like me anywhere," said Horned Toad Child.

"Well, you know what I mean."

"Yeah . . . There used to be people like you around, I guess."

"What were they called?"

"Oh—people. Like everybody . . ."

"But where do my people live? They have towns. I used to live in one. I don't know where they are, is all. I ought to find out. I don't know where my mother is now, but my daddy's in Canyonville. I was going there when."

"Ask Horse," said Horned Toad Child, sagaciously. He had moved away from the water, which he did not like and never drank, and was plaiting rushes.

"I don't know Horse."

"He hangs around the butte down there a lot of the time. He's waiting till his uncle gets old and he can kick him out and be the big honcho. The old man and the women don't want him around till then. Horses are weird. Anyway, he's the one to ask. He gets around a lot. And his people came here with the new people, that's what they say, anyhow."

Illegal immigrants, the girl thought. She took Horned Toad's advice, and one long day when Coyote was gone on one of her unannounced and unexplained trips, she took a pouchful of dried salmon and salmonberries and went off alone to the flat-topped butte miles away in the southwest.

There was a beautiful spring at the foot of the butte, and a trail to it with a lot of footprints on it. She waited there under willows by the clear pool, and after a while Horse came running, splendid, with copper-red skin and long, strong legs, deep chest, dark eyes, his black hair whipping his back as he ran. He stopped, not at all winded, and gave a snort as he looked at her. "Who are you?"

Nobody in town asked that—ever. She saw it was true: Horse had come here with her people, people who had to ask each other who they were.

"I live with Coyote," she said, cautiously.

"Oh, sure, I heard about you," Horse said. He knelt to drink from the pool, long deep drafts, his hands plunged in the cool water. When he had drunk he wiped his mouth, sat back on his heels, and announced, "I'm going to be King."

"King of the Horses?"

"Right! Pretty soon now. I could lick the old man already, but I can wait. Let him have his day," said Horse, vainglorious, magnanimous. The child gazed at him, in love already, forever.

"I can comb your hair, if you like," she said.

"Great!" said Horse, and sat still while she stood behind him, tugging her pocket comb through his coarse, black, shining, yard-long hair. It took a long time to get it smooth. She tied it in a massive ponytail with willowbark when she was done. Horse bent over the pool to admire himself. "That's great," he said. "That's really beautiful!"

"Do you ever go . . . where the other people are?" she asked in a low voice.

He did not reply for long enough that she thought he wasn't going to; then he said, "You mean the metal places, the glass places? The holes? I go around them. There are all the walls now. There didn't used to be so many. Grandmother said there didn't used to be any walls. Do you know Grandmother?" he asked naively, looking at her with his great dark eyes.

"Your grandmother?"

"Well, yes—Grandmother—You know. Who makes the web. Well, anyhow. I know there's some of my people, horses, there. I've seen them across the walls. They act really crazy. You know, we brought the new people here. They couldn't have got here without us, they only have two legs, and they have those metal shells. I can tell you that whole story. The King has to know the stories."

"I like stories a lot."

"It takes three nights to tell it. What do you want to know about them?"

"I was thinking that maybe I ought to go there. Where they are."

"It's dangerous. Really dangerous. You can't go through—they'd catch you."

"I'd just like to know the way."

"I know the way," Horse said, sounding for the first time entirely adult and reliable; she knew he did know the way. "It's a long run for a colt." He looked at her again. "I've got a cousin with different-color eyes," he said, looking from her right to her left eye. "One brown and one blue. But she's an Appaloosa."

"Bluejay made the yellow one," the child explained. "I lost my own one. In the . . . when . . . You don't think I could get to those places?"

"Why do you want to?"

"I sort of feel like I have to."

Horse nodded. He got up. She stood still.

"I could take you, I guess," he said.

"Would you? When?"

"Oh, now, I guess. Once I'm King I won't be able to leave, you know. Have to protect the women. And I sure wouldn't let my people get anywhere near those places!" A shudder ran right down his magnificent body, yet he said, with a toss of his head, "They couldn't catch me, of course, but the others can't run like I do . . ."

"How long would it take us?"

Horse thought a while. "Well, the nearest place like that is over by the red rocks. If we left now we'd be back here around tomorrow noon. It's just a little hole."

She did not know what he meant by "a hole," but did not ask.

"You want to go?" Horse said, flipping back his ponytail.

"OK," the girl said, feeling the ground go out from under her.

"Can you run?"

She shook her head. "I walked here, though."

Horse laughed, a large, cheerful laugh. "Come on," he said, and knelt and held his hands backturned like stirrups for her to mount to his shoulders. "What do they call you?" he teased, rising easily, setting right off at a jogtrot. "Gnat? Fly? Flea?"

"Tick, because I stick!" the child cried, gripping the willowbark tie of the black mane, laughing with delight at being suddenly eight feet tall and traveling across the desert without even trying, like the tumbleweed, as fast as the wind.

Moon, a night past full, rose to light the plains for them. Horse jogged easily on and on. Somewhere deep in the night they stopped at a Pygmy Owl camp, ate a little, and rested. Most of the owls were out hunting, but an old lady entertained them at her campfire, telling them tales about the ghost of a cricket, about the great invisible people, tales that the child heard interwoven with her own dreams as she dozed and half-woke and dozed again. Then Horse put her up on his shoulders and on they went at a tireless slow lope. Moon went down behind them, and before them the sky paled into rose and gold. The soft nightwind was gone; the air was sharp, cold, still. On it, in it, there was a faint, sour smell of burning. The child felt Horse's gait change, grow tighter, uneasy.

"Hey, Prince!"

A small, slightly scolding voice: the child knew it, and placed it as soon as she saw the person sitting by a juniper tree, neatly dressed, wearing an old black cap.

"Hey, Chickadee!" Horse said, coming round and stopping. The child had observed, back in Coyote's town, that everybody treated Chickadee with respect. She didn't see why. Chickadee seemed an ordinary person, busy and talkative like most of the small birds, nothing like so endearing as Quail or so impressive as Hawk or Great Owl.

"You're going on that way?" Chickadee asked Horse.

"The little one wants to see if her people are living there," Horse said, surprising the child. Was that what she wanted?

Chickadee looked disapproving, as she often did. She whistled a few notes thoughtfully, another of her habits, and then got up. "I'll come along."

"That's great," Horse said, thankfully.

"I'll scout." Chickadee said, and off she went, surprisingly fast, ahead of them, while Horse took up his steady long lope.

The sour smell was stronger in the air.

Chickadee halted, way ahead of them on a slight rise, and stood still. Horse dropped to a walk, and then stopped. "There," he said in a low voice.

The child stared. In the strange light and slight mist before sunrise she could not see clearly, and when she strained and peered she felt as if her left eye were not seeing at all. "What is it?" she whispered.

"One of the holes. Across the wall—see?"

It did seem there was a line, a straight, jerky line drawn across the sagebrush plain, and on the far side of it—nothing? Was it mist? Something moved there—"It's cattle!" she said. Horse stood silent, uneasy. Chickadee was coming back towards them.

"It's a ranch," the child said. "That's a fence. There's a lot of Herefords." The words tasted like iron, like salt in her mouth. The things she named wavered in her sight and faded, leaving nothing—a hole in the world, a burned place like a cigarette burn. "Go closer!" she urged Horse. "I want to see."

And as if he owed her obedience, he went forward, tense but unquestioning.

Chickadee came up to them. "Nobody around," she said in her small, dry voice, "but there's one of those fast turtle things coming."

Horse nodded, but kept going forward.

Gripping his broad shoulders, the child stared into the blank, and as if Chickadee's words had focused her eyes, she saw again: the scattered whitefaces, a few of them looking up with bluish, rolling eyes—the fences—over the rise a chimneyed house-roof and a high barn—and then in the distance something moving fast, too fast, burning across the ground straight at them at terrible speed. "Run!" she yelled to Horse, "run away! Run!" As if released from bonds he wheeled and ran, flat out, in great reaching strides, away from sunrise, the fiery burning chariot, the smell of acid, iron, death. And Chickadee flew before them like a cinder on the air of dawn.

iv

"Horse?" Coyote said. "That prick? Catfood!"

Coyote had been there when the child got home to Bide-A-Wee, but she clearly hadn't been worrying about where Gal was, and maybe hadn't even noticed she was gone She was in a vile mood, and took it all wrong when the child tried to tell her where she had been.

"If you're going to do damn fool things, next time do 'em with me, at least I'm an expert," she said, morose, and slouched out the door. The child saw her squatting down, poking an old, white turd with a stick trying to get it to answer some question she kept asking it. The turd lay obstinately silent. Later in the day the child saw two coyote men, a young one and a mangy-looking older one, loitering around near the spring, looking over at Bide-A-Wee. She decided it would be a good night to spend somewhere else.

The thought of the crowded rooms of Chipmunk's house was not attractive. It was going to be a warm night again tonight, and moonlit. Maybe she would sleep outside. If she could feel sure some people wouldn't come around, like the Rattler . . . She was standing indecisive halfway through town when a dry voice said, "Hey, Gal."

"Hey, Chickadee."

The trim, black-capped woman was standing on her doorstep

shaking out a rug. She kept her house neat, trim like herself. Having come back across the desert with her the child now knew, though she still could not have said, why Chickadee was a respected person.

"I thought maybe I'd sleep out tonight," the child said, tentative.

"Unhealthy," said Chickadee. "What are nests for?"

"Mom's kind of busy," the child said.

"Tsk!" went Chickadee, and snapped the rug with disapproving vigor. "What about your little friend? At least they're decent people."

"Horny-toad? His parents are so shy . . ."

"Well. Come in and have something to eat, anyhow," said Chickadee.

The child helped her cook dinner. She knew now why there were rocks in the mush-pot.

"Chickadee," she said, "I still don't understand, can I ask you? Mom said it depends who's seeing it, but still, I mean if I see you wearing clothes and everything like humans, then how come you cook this way, in baskets, you know, and there aren't any—any of the things like they have—there where we were with Horse this morning?"

"I don't know," Chickadee said. Her voice indoors was quite soft and pleasant. "I guess we do things the way they always were done. When your people and my people lived together, you know. And together with everything else here. The rocks, you know. The plants and everything." She looked at the basket of willowbark, fernroot and pitch, at the blackened rocks that were heating in the fire. "You see how it all goes together . . . ?

"But you have fire—That's different—"

"Ah!" said Chickadee, impatient, "you people! Do you think you invented the sun?"

She took up the wooden tongs, plopped the heated rocks into the water-filled basket with a terrific hiss and steam and loud bubblings. The child sprinkled in the pounded seeds, and stirred.

Chickadee brought out a basket of fine blackberries. They sat on the newly-shaken-out rug, and ate. The child's two-finger scoop technique with mush was now highly refined.

"Maybe I didn't cause the world," Chickadee said, "but I'm a better cook than Coyote."

The child nodded, stuffing.

"I don't know why I made Horse go there," she said, after she had stuffed. "I got just as scared as him when I saw it. But now I feel again like I have to go back there. But I want to stay here. With my, with Coyote. I don't understand."

"When we lived together it was all one place," Chickadee said in her slow, soft home-voice. "But now the others, the new people,

they live apart. And their places are so heavy. They weigh down on
our place, they press on it, draw it, suck it, eat it, eat holes in it,
crowd it out . . . Maybe after a while longer there'll only be one
place again, their place. And none of us here. I knew Bison, out
over the mountains. I knew Antelope right here. I knew Grizzly and
Greywolf, up west there. Gone. All gone. And the salmon you eat at
Coyote's house, those are the dream salmon, those are the true
food; but in the rivers, how many salmon now? The rivers that were
red with them in spring? Who dances, now, when the First Salmon
offers himself? Who dances by the river? Oh, you should ask Coyote
about all this. She knows more than I do! But she forgets . . . She's
hopeless, worse than Raven, she has to piss on every post, she's a
terrible housekeeper . . ." Chickadee's voice had sharpened. She
whistled a note or two, and said no more.

After a while the child asked very softly, "Who is Grandmother?"

"Grandmother," Chickadee said. She looked at the child, and ate
several blackberries thoughtfully. She stroked the rug they sat on.

"If I built the fire on the rug, it would burn a hole in it," she said.
"Right? So we build the fire on sand, on dirt . . . Things are woven
together. So we call the weaver the Grandmother." She whistled
four notes, looking up the smokehole. "After all," she added,
"maybe all this place, the other places too, maybe they're all only
one side of the weaving, I don't know. I can only look with one eye
at a time, how can I tell how deep it goes?"

Lying that night rolled up in a blanket in Chickadee's back yard, the
child heard the wind soughing and storming in the cottonwoods
down in the draw, and then slept deeply, weary from the long night
before. Just at sunrise she woke. The eastern mountains were a
cloudy dark red as if the level light shone through them as through a
hand held before the fire. In the tobacco patch—the only farming
anybody in this town did was to raise a little wild tobacco—Lizard
and Beetle were singing some kind of growing song or blessing song,
soft and desultory, huh-huh-huh-huh, huh-huh-huh-huh, and as she
lay warm-curled on the ground the song made her feel rooted in the
ground, cradled on it and in it, so where her fingers ended and the
dirt began she did not know, as if she were dead, but she was wholly
alive, she was the earth's life. She got up dancing, left the blanket
folded neatly on Chickadee's neat and already empty bed, and
danced up the hill to Bide-A-Wee. At the half-open door she sang,

"Danced with a gal with a hole in her stocking
And her knees kept a knocking and her toes
  kept a rocking,

Danced with a gal with a hole in her stocking,
Danced by the light of the moon!"

Coyote emerged, tousled and lurching, and eyed her narrowly. "Sheeeoot," she said. She sucked her teeth and then went to splash water all over her head from the gourd by the door. She shook her head and the water-drops flew. "Let's get out of here," she said. "I have had it. I don't know what got into me. If I'm pregnant again, at my age, oh, shit. Let's get out of town. I need a change of air."

In the foggy dark of the house, the child could see at least two coyote men sprawled snoring away on the bed and floor. Coyote walked over to the old white turd and kicked it. "Why didn't you stop me?" she shouted.

"I *told* you" the turd muttered sulkily.

"Dumb shit," Coyote said. "Come on, Gal. Let's go. Where to?" She didn't wait for an answer. "I know. Come on!"

And she set off through town at that lazy-looking rangy walk that was so hard to keep up with. But the child was full of pep, and came dancing, so that Coyote began dancing too, skipping and pirouetting and fooling around all the way down the long slope to the level plains. There she slanted their way off north-eastward. Horse Butte was at their backs, getting smaller in the distance.

Along near noon the child said, "I didn't bring anything to eat."

"Something will turn up," Coyote said, "sure to." And pretty soon she turned aside, going straight to a tiny grey shack hidden by a couple of half-dead junipers and a stand of rabbit-brush. The place smelled terrible. A sign on the door said: FOX. PRIVATE. NO TRESPASS-ING!—but Coyote pushed it open, and trotted right back out with half a small smoked salmon. "Nobody home but us chickens," she said, grinning sweetly.

"Isn't that stealing?" the child asked, worried.

"Yes," Coyote answered, trotting on.

They ate the fox-scented salmon by a dried-up creek, slept a while, and went on.

Before long the child smelled the sour burning smell, and stopped. It was as if a huge, heavy hand had begun pushing her chest, pushing her away, and yet at the same time as if she had stepped into a strong current that drew her forward, helpless.

"Hey, getting close!" Coyote said, and stopped to piss by a juniper stump.

"Close to what?"

"Their town. See?" She pointed to a pair of sage-spotted hills. Between them was an area of greyish blank.

"I don't want to go there."

"We won't go all the way in. No way! We'll just get a little closer and look. It's fun," Coyote said, putting her head on one side, coaxing. "They do all these weird things in the air."

The child hung back.

Coyote became business-like, responsible. "We're going to be very careful," she announced. "And look out for big dogs, OK? Little dogs I can handle. Make a good lunch. Big dogs, it goes the other way. Right? Let's go, then."

Seemingly as casual and lounging as ever, but with a tense alertness in the carriage of her head and the yellow glance of her eyes, Coyote led off again, not looking back; and the child followed.

All around them the pressures increased. It was if the air itself was pressing on them, as if time was going too fast, too hard, not flowing but pounding, pounding, pounding, faster and harder till it buzzed like Rattler's rattle. Hurry, you have to hurry! everything said, there isn't time! everything said. Things rushed past screaming and shuddering. Things turned, flashed, roared, stank, vanished. There was a boy—he came into focus all at once, but not on the ground: he was going along a couple of inches above the ground, moving very fast, bending his legs from side to side in a kind of frenzied swaying dance, and was gone. Twenty children sat in rows in the air all singing shrilly and then the walls closed over them. A basket no a pot no a can, a garbage can, full of salmon smelling wonderful no full of stinking deerhides and rotten cabbage stalks, keep out of it, Coyote! Where was she?

"Mom!" the child called. "Mother!"—standing a moment at the end of an ordinary small-town street near the gas station, and the next moment in a terror of blanknesses, invisible walls, terrible smells and pressures and the overwhelming rush of Time straight forward rolling her helpless as a twig in the race above a waterfall. She clung, held on trying not to fall—"Mother!"

Coyote was over by the big basket of salmon, approaching it, wary, but out in the open, in the full sunlight, in the full current. And a boy and a man borne by the same current were coming down the long, sage-spotted hill behind the gas station, each with a gun, red hats, hunters, it was killing season. "Hell, will you look at that damn coyote in broad daylight big as my wife's ass," the man said, and cocked aimed shot all as Myra screamed and ran against the enormous drowning torrent. Coyote fled past her yelling, "Get out of here!" She turned and was borne away.

Far out of sight of that place, in a little draw among low hills, they sat and breathed air in searing gasps until after a long time it came easy again.

"Mom, that was *stupid*," the child said furiously.

"Sure was," Coyote said. "But did you see all that food!"

"I'm not hungry," the child said sullenly. "Not till we get all the way away from here."

"But they're your folks," Coyote said. "All yours. Your kith and kin and cousins and kind. Bang! Pow! There's Coyote! Bang! There's my wife's ass! Pow! There's anything—BOOOOM! Blow it away, man! BOOOOOOM!"

"I want to go home," the child said.

"Not yet," said Coyote. "I got to take a shit." She did so, then turned to the fresh turd, leaning over it. "It says I have to stay," she reported, smiling.

"It didn't say anything! I was listening!"

"You know how to understand? You hear everything, Miss Big Ears? Hears all—Sees all with her crummy gummy eye—"

"You have pine-pitch eyes too! You told me so!"

"That's a story," Coyote snarled. "You don't even know a story when you hear one! Look, do what you like, it's a free country. I'm hanging around here tonight. I like the action." She sat down and began patting her hands on the dirt in a soft four-four rhythm and singing under her breath, one of the endless tuneless songs that kept time from running too fast, that wove the roots of trees and bushes and ferns and grass in the web that held the stream in the streambed and the rock in the rock's place and the earth together. And the child lay listening.

"I love you," she said.

Coyote went on singing.

Sun went down the last slope of the west and left a pale green clarity over the desert hills.

Coyote had stopped singing. She sniffed. "Hey," she said. "Dinner." She got up and moseyed along the little draw. "Yeah," she called back softly. "Come on!"

Stiffly, for the fear-crystals had not yet melted out of her joints, the child got up and went to Coyote. Off to one side along the hill was one of the lines, a fence. She didn't look at it. It was OK. They were outside it.

"Look at that!"

A smoked salmon, a whole chinook, lay on a little cedarbark mat. "An offering! Well, I'll be darned!" Coyote was so impressed she didn't even swear. "I haven't seen one of these for years! I thought they'd forgotten!"

"Offering to who?"

"Me! Who else? Boy, *look* at that!"

The child looked dubiously at the salmon.

"It smells funny."

"How funny?"

"Like burned."

"It's smoked, stupid! Come on."

"I'm not hungry."

"OK. It's not your salmon anyhow. It's mine. My offering, for me. Hey, you people! You people over there! Coyote thanks you! Keep it up like this and maybe I'll do some things for you too!"

"Don't, don't yell, Mom! They're not that far away—"

"They're all my people," said Coyote with a great gesture, and then sat down cross-legged, broke off a big piece of salmon, and ate.

Evening Star burned like a deep, bright pool of water in the clear sky. Down over the twin hills was a dim suffusion of light, like a fog. The child looked away from it, back at the star.

"Oh," Coyote said. "Oh, shit."

"What's wrong?"

"That wasn't so smart, eating that," Coyote said, and then held herself and began to shiver, to scream, to choke—her eyes rolled up, her long arms and legs flew out jerking and dancing, foam spurted out between her clenched teeth. Her body arched tremendously backwards, and the child, trying to hold her, was thrown violently off by the spasms of her limbs. The child scrambled back and held the body as it spasmed again, twitched, quivered, went still.

By moonrise Coyote was cold. Till then there had been so much warmth under the tawny coat that the child kept thinking maybe she was alive, maybe if she just kept holding her, keeping her warm, she would recover, she would be all right. She held her close, not looking at the black lips drawn back from the teeth, the white balls of the eyes. But when the cold came through the fur as the presence of death, the child let the slight, stiff corpse lie down on the dirt.

She went nearby and dug a hole in the stony sand of the draw, a shallow pit. Coyote's people did not bury their dead, she knew that. But her people did. She carried the small corpse to the pit, laid it down, and covered it with her blue and white bandanna. It was not large enough; the four stiff paws stuck out. The child heaped the body over with sand and rocks and a scurf of sagebrush and tumbleweed held down with more rocks. She also went to where the salmon had lain on the cedar mat, and finding the carcass of a lamb heaped dirt and rocks over the poisoned thing. Then she stood up and walked away without looking back.

At the top of the hill she stood and looked across the draw toward the misty glow of the lights of the town lying in the pass between the twin hills.

"I hope you all die in pain," she said aloud. She turned away and walked down into the desert.

V

It was Chickadee who met her, on the second evening, north of Horse Butte.

"I didn't cry," the child said.

"None of us do," said Chickadee. "Come with me this way now. Come into Grandmother's house."

It was underground, but very large, dark and large, and the Grandmother was there at the center, at her loom. She was making a rug or blanket of the hills and the black rain and the white rain, weaving in the lightning. As they spoke she wove.

"Hello, Chickadee. Hello, New Person."

"Grandmother," Chickadee greeted her.

The child said, "I'm not one of them."

Grandmother's eyes were small and dim. She smiled and wove. The shuttle thrummed through the warp.

"Old Person, then," said Grandmother. "You'd better go back there now, Granddaughter. That's where you live."

"I lived with Coyote. She's dead. They killed her."

"Oh, don't worry about Coyote!" Grandmother said, with a little huff of laughter. "She gets killed all the time."

The child stood still. She saw the endless weaving.

"Then I—Could I go back home—to her house?"

"I don't think it would work," Grandmother said. "Do you, Chickadee?"

Chickadee shook her head once, silent.

"It would be dark there now, and empty, and fleas . . . You got outside your people's time, into our place; but I think that Coyote was taking you back, see. Her way. If you go back now, you can still live with them. Isn't your father there?"

The child nodded.

"They've been looking for you."

"They have?"

"Oh, yes, ever since you fell out of the sky. The man was dead, but you weren't there—they kept looking."

"Serves him right. Serves them all right," the child said. She put her hands up over her face and began to cry terribly, without tears.

"Go on, little one, Granddaughter," Spider said. "Don't be afraid. You can live well there. I'll be there too, you know. In your dreams, in your ideas, in dark corners in the basement. Don't kill me, or I'll make it rain . . ."

"I'll come around," Chickadee said. "Make gardens for me."

The child held her breath and clenched her hands until her sobs stopped and let her speak.

"Will I ever see Coyote?"

"I don't know," the Grandmother replied.

The child accepted this. She said, after another silence, "Can I keep my eye?"

"Yes. You can keep your eye."

"Thank you, Grandmother," the child said. She turned away then and started up the night slope towards the next day. Ahead of her in the air of dawn for a long way a little bird flew, black-capped, light-winged.

Bears Discover Fire

Terry Bisson

Terry Bisson's work contains elements of both science fiction and fantasy, and he blends them together like no one else. His novels examine such diverse topics as what might have happened if the slaves had actually rebelled during the Civil War to a future America where the only way to get to Mars is to have a movie producer bankroll the expedition as a film. His work frequently satirizes contemporary lifestyles and social conventions, often reaching into the past for certain ideas or mores. His novels include Talking Man *and* Voyage to the Red Planet.

I WAS DRIVING WITH MY BROTHER, THE PREACHER, AND MY NEPHEW, THE preacher's son, on I-65 just north of Bowling Green when we got a flat. It was Sunday night and we had been to visit Mother at the Home. We were in my car. The flat caused what you might call knowing groans since, as the old-fashioned one in my family (so they tell me), I fix my own tires, and my brother is always telling me to get radials and quit buying old tires.

But if you know how to mount and fix tires yourself, you can pick them up for almost nothing.

Since it was a left rear tire, I pulled over left, onto the median grass. The way my Caddy stumbled to a stop, I figured the tire was ruined. "I guess there's no need asking if you have any of that *FlatFix* in the trunk," said Wallace.

"Here, son, hold the light," I said to Wallace Jr. He's old enough to want to help and not old enough (yet) to think he knows it all. If I'd married and had kids, he's the kind I'd have wanted.

An old Caddy has a big trunk that tends to fill up like a shed. Mine's a '56. Wallace was wearing his Sunday shirt, so he didn't offer to help while I pulled magazines, fishing tackle, a wooden tool box, some old clothes, a comealong wrapped in a grass sack, and a tobacco sprayer out of the way, looking for my jack. The spare looked a little soft.

The light went out. "Shake it, son," I said.

It went back on. The bumper jack was long gone, but I carry a little

¼ ton hydraulic. I finally found it under Mother's old *Southern Livings,* 1978–1986. I had been meaning to drop them at the dump. If Wallace hadn't been along, I'd have let Wallace Jr. position the jack under the axle, but I got on my knees and did it myself. There's nothing wrong with a boy learning to change a tire. Even if you're not going to fix and mount them, you're still going to have to change a few in this life. The light went off again before I had the wheel off the ground. I was surprised at how dark the night was already. It was late October and beginning to get cool. "Shake it again, son," I said.

It went back on but it was weak. Flickery.

"With radials you just don't *have* flats," Wallace explained in that voice he uses when he's talking to a number of people at once; in this case, Wallace Jr. and myself. "And even when you *do,* you just squirt them with this stuff called *FlatFix* and you just drive on. $3.95 the can."

"Uncle Bobby can fix a tire hisself," said Wallace Jr., out of loyalty I presume.

"*Him*self," I said from halfway under the car. If it was up to Wallace, the boy would talk like what Mother used to call "a helot from the gorges of the mountains." But drive on radials.

"Shake that light again," I said. It was about gone. I spun the lugs off into the hubcap and pulled the wheel. The tire had blown out along the sidewall. "Won't be fixing this one," I said. Not that I cared. I have a pile as tall as a man out by the barn.

The light went out again, then came back better than ever as I was fitting the spare over the lugs. "Much better," I said. There was a flood of dim orange flickery light. But when I turned to find the lug nuts, I was surprised to see that the flashlight the boy was holding was dead. The light was coming from two bears at the edge of the trees, holding torches. They were big, three-hundred pounders, standing about five feet tall. Wallace Jr. and his father had seen them and were standing perfectly still. It's best not to alarm bears.

I fished the lug nuts out of the hubcap and spun them on. I usually like to put a little oil on them, but this time I let it go. I reached under the car and let the jack down and pulled it out. I was relieved to see that the spare was high enough to drive on. I put the jack and the lug wrench and the flat into the trunk. Instead of replacing the hubcap, I put it in there, too. All this time, the bears never made a move. They just held the torches up, whether out of curiosity or helpfulness, there was no way of knowing. It looked like there may have been more bears behind them, in the trees.

Opening three doors at once, we got into the car and drove off. Wallace was the first to speak. "Looks like bears have discovered fire," he said.

———

When we first took Mother to the Home, almost four years (forty-seven months) ago, she told Wallace and me she was ready to die. "Don't worry about me, boys," she whispered, pulling us both down so the nurse wouldn't hear. "I've drove a million miles and I'm ready to pass over to the other shore. I won't have long to linger here." She drove a consolidated school bus for thirty-nine years. Later, after Wallace left, she told me about her dream. A bunch of doctors were sitting around in a circle discussing her case. One said, "We've done all we can for her, boys, let's let her go." They all turned their hands up and smiled. When she didn't die that fall, she seemed disappointed, though as spring came she forgot about it, as old people will.

In addition to taking Wallace and Wallace Jr. to see Mother on Sunday nights, I go myself on Tuesdays and Thursdays. I usually find her sitting in front of the TV, even though she doesn't watch it. The nurses keep it on all the time. They say the old folks like the flickering. It soothes them down.

"What's this I hear about bears discovering fire?" she said on Tuesday. "It's true," I told her as I combed her long white hair with the shell comb Wallace had brought her from Florida. Monday there had been a story in the Louisville *Courier-Journal,* and Tuesday one on NBC or CBS Nightly News. People were seeing bears all over the state, and in Virginia as well. They had quit hibernating, and were apparently planning to spend the winter in the medians of the interstates. There have always been bears in the mountains of Virginia, but not here in western Kentucky, not for almost a hundred years. The last one was killed when Mother was a girl. The theory in the *Courier-Journal* was that they were following I-65 down from the forests of Michigan and Canada, but one old man from Allen County (interviewed on nationwide TV) said that there had always been a few bears left back in the hills, and they had come out to join the others now that they had discovered fire.

"They don't hibernate any more," I said. "They make a fire and keep it going all winter."

"I declare," Mother said. "What'll they think of next!" The nurse came to take her tobacco away, which is the signal for bedtime.

Every October, Wallace Jr. stays with me while his parents go to camp. I realize how backward that sounds, but there it is. My brother is a minister (House of the Righteous Way, Reformed), but he makes two thirds of his living in real estate. He and Elizabeth go to a Christian Success Retreat in Florida, where people from all over the country practice selling things to one another. I know what it's like

not because they've ever bothered to tell me, but because I've seen
the Revolving Equity Success Plan ads late at night on TV.

The school bus let Wallace Jr. off at my house on Wednesday, the
day they left. The boy doesn't have to pack much of a bag when he
stays with me. He has his own room here. As the eldest of our family, I
hung on to the old home place near Smiths Grove. It's getting run
down, but Wallace Jr. and I don't mind. He has his own room in
Bowling Green, too, but since Wallace and Elizabeth move to a different house every three months (part of the Plan), he keeps his .22 and
his comics, the stuff that's important to a boy his age, in his room
here at the home place. It's the room his dad and I used to share.

Wallace Jr. is twelve. I found him sitting on the back porch that
overlooks the interstate when I got home for work. I sell crop insur-
ance.

After I changed clothes, I showed him how to break the bead on
a tire two ways, with a hammer and by backing a car over it. Like
making sorghum, fixing tires by hand is a dying art. The boy caught
on fast, though. "Tomorrow I'll show you how to mount your tire
with the hammer and a tire iron," I said.

"What I wish is I could see the bears," he said. He was looking
across the field to I-65, where the north-bound lanes cut off the corner of our field. From the house at night, sometimes the traffic
sounds like a waterfall.

"Can't see their fire in the daytime," I said. "But wait till tonight."
That night CBS or NBC (I forget which is which) did a special on
the bears, which were becoming a story of nationwide interest.
They were seen in Kentucky, West Virginia, Missouri, Illinois (southern), and, of course, Virginia. There have always been bears in
Virginia. Some characters there were even talking about hunting
them. A scientist said they were heading into the states where there
is some snow but not too much, and where there is enough timber
in the medians for firewood. He had gone in with a video camera,
but his shots were just blurry figures sitting around a fire. Another
scientist said the bears were attracted by the berries on a new bush
that grew only in the medians of the interstates. He claimed this
berry was the first new species in recent history, brought about by
the mixing of seeds along the highway. He ate one on TV, making a
face, and called it a "newberry." A climatic ecologist said that the
warm winters (there was no snow last winter in Nashville, and only
one flurry in Louisville) had changed the bears' hibernation cycle,
and now they were able to remember things from year to year.
"Bears may have discovered fire centuries ago," he said, "but forgot
it." Another theory was that they had discovered (or remembered)
fire when Yellowstone burned, several years ago.

The TV showed more guys talking about bears than it showed bears, and Wallace Jr. and I lost interest. After the supper dishes were done I took the boy out behind the house and down to our fence. Across the interstate and through the trees, we could see the light of the bears' fire. Wallace Jr. wanted to go back to the house and get his .22 and go shoot one, and I explained why that would be wrong. "Besides," I said, "a .22 wouldn't do much more to a bear than make it mad.

"Besides," I added, "it's illegal to hunt in the medians."

The only trick to mounting a tire by hand, once you have beaten or pried it onto the rim, is setting the bead. You do this by setting the tire upright, sitting on it, and bouncing it up and down between your legs while the air goes in. When the bead sets on the rim, it makes a satisfying "pop." On Thursday, I kept Wallace Jr. home from school and showed him how to do this until he got it right. Then we climbed our fence and crossed the field to get a look at the bears.

In northern Virginia, according to "Good Morning America," the bears were keeping their fires going all day long. Here in western Kentucky, though, it was still warm for late October and they only stayed around the fires at night. Where they went and what they did in the daytime, I don't know. Maybe they were watching from the newberry bushes as Wallace Jr. and I climbed the government fence and crossed the northbound lanes. I carried an axe and Wallace Jr. brought his .22, not because he wanted to kill a bear but because a boy likes to carry some kind of a gun. The median was all tangled with brush and vines under the maple, oaks, and sycamores. Even though we were only a hundred yards from the house, I had never been there, and neither had anyone else that I knew of. It was like a created country. We found a path in the center and followed it down across a slow, short stream that flowed out of one grate and into another. The tracks in the gray mud were the first bear signs we saw. There was a musty but not really unpleasant smell. In a clearing under a big hollow beech, where the fire had been, we found nothing but ashes. Logs were drawn up in a rough circle and the smell was stronger. I stirred the ashes and found enough coals left to start a new flame, so I banked them back the way they had been left.

I cut a little firewood and stacked it to one side, just to be neighborly.

Maybe the bears were watching us from the bushes even then. There's no way to know. I tasted one of the newberries and spit it out. It was so sweet it was sour, just the sort of thing you would imagine a bear would like.

———

That evening after supper, I asked Wallace Jr. if he might want to go with me to visit Mother. I wasn't surprised when he said "yes." Kids have more consideration than folks give them credit for. We found her sitting on the concrete front porch of the Home, watching the cars go by on I-65. The nurse said she had been agitated all day. I wasn't surprised by that, either. Every fall as the leaves change, she gets restless, maybe the word is hopeful, again. I brought her into the dayroom and combed her long, white hair. "Nothing but bears on TV anymore," the nurse complained, flipping the channels. Wallace Jr. picked up the remote after the nurse left, and we watched a CBS or NBC Special Report about some hunters in Virginia who had gotten their houses torched. The TV interviewed a hunter and his wife whose $117,500 Shenandoah Valley home had burned. She blamed the bears. He didn't blame the bears, but he was suing for compensation from the state since he had a valid hunting license. The state hunting commissioner came on and said that possession of a hunting license didn't prohibit (enjoin, I think, was the word he used) *the hunted* from striking back. I thought that was a pretty liberal view for a state commissioner. Of course, he had a vested interest in not paying off. I'm not a hunter myself.

"Don't bother coming on Sunday," Mother told Wallace Jr. with a wink. "I've drove a million miles and I've got one hand on the gate." I'm used to her saying stuff like that, especially in the fall, but I was afraid it would upset the boy. In fact, he looked worried after we left and I asked him what was wrong.

"How could she have drove a million miles?" he asked. She had told him 48 miles a day for 39 years, and he had worked it out on his calculator to be 336,960 miles.

"Have *driven*," I said. "And it's forty-eight in the morning and forty-eight in the afternoon. Plus there were the football trips. Plus, old folks exaggerate a little." Mother was the first woman school bus driver in the state. She did it every day and raised a family, too. Dad just farmed.

I usually get off the interstate at Smiths Grove, but that night I drove north all the way to Horse Cave and doubled back so Wallace Jr. and I could see the bears' fires. There were not as many as you would think from the TV—one every six or seven miles, hidden back in a clump of trees or under a rocky ledge. Probably they look for water as well as wood. Wallace Jr. wanted to stop, but it's against the law to stop on the interstate and I was afraid the state police would run us off.

There was a card from Wallace in the mailbox. He and Elizabeth were doing fine and having a wonderful time. Not a word about Wallace Jr., but he didn't seem to mind. Like most kids his age, he doesn't really enjoy going places with his parents.

On Saturday afternoon, the Home called my office (Burley Belt Drought & Hail) and left word that Mother was gone. I was on the road. I work Saturdays. It's the only day a lot of part-time farmers are home. My heart literally skipped a beat when I called in and got the message, but only a beat. I had long been prepared. "It's a blessing," I said when I got the nurse on the phone.

"You don't understand," the nurse said. "Not *passed* away, gone. *Ran* away, gone. Your mother has escaped." Mother had gone through the door at the end of the corridor when no one was looking, wedging the door with her comb and taking a bedspread which belonged to the Home. What about her tobacco? I asked. It was gone. That was a sure sign she was planning to stay away. I was in Franklin, and it took me less than an hour to get to the Home on I-65. The nurse told me that Mother had been acting more and more confused lately. Of course they are going to say that. We looked around the grounds, which is only an acre with no trees between the interstate and a soybean field. Then they had me leave a message at the Sheriff's office. I would have to keep paying for her care until she was officially listed as Missing, which would be Monday.

It was dark by the time I got back to the house, and Wallace Jr. was fixing supper. This just involves opening a few cans, already selected and grouped together with a rubber band. I told him his grandmother had gone, and he nodded, saying, "She told us she would be." I called Florida and left a message. There was nothing more to be done. I sat down and tried to watch TV, but there was nothing on. Then, I looked out the back door, and saw the firelight twinkling through the trees across the northbound lane of I-65, and realized I just might know where to find her.

It was definitely getting colder, so I got my jacket. I told the boy to wait by the phone in case the Sheriff called, but when I looked back, halfway across the field, there he was behind me. He didn't have a jacket. I let him catch up. He was carrying his .22, and I made him leave it leaning against our fence. It was harder climbing the government fence in the dark, at my age, than it had been in the daylight. I am sixty-one. The highway was busy with cars heading south and trucks heading north.

Crossing the shoulder, I got my pants cuffs wet on the long grass, already wet with dew. It is actually bluegrass.

The first few feet into the trees it was pitch black and the boy grabbed my hand. Then it got lighter. At first I thought it was the moon, but it was the high beams shining like moonlight into the tree-tops, allowing Wallace Jr. and me to pick our way through the brush. We soon found the path and its familiar bear smell.

I was wary of approaching the bears at night. If we stayed on the path we might run into one in the dark, but if we went through the bushes we might be seen as intruders. I wondered if maybe we shouldn't have brought the gun.

We stayed on the path. The light seemed to drip down from the canopy of the woods like rain. The going was easy, especially if we didn't try to look at the path but let our feet find their own way.

Then through the trees I saw their fire.

The fire was mostly of sycamore and breech branches, the kind of fire that puts out very little heat or light and lots of smoke. The bears hadn't learned the ins and outs of wood yet. They did okay at tending it, though. A large cinnamon brown northern-looking bear was poking the fire with a stick, adding a branch now and then from a pile at his side. The others sat around in a loose circle on the logs. Most were smaller black or honey bears; one was a mother with cubs. Some were eating berries from a hubcap. Not eating, but just watching the fire, my mother sat among them with the bedspread from the Home around her shoulders.

If the bears noticed us, they didn't let on. Mother patted a spot right next to her on the log and I sat down. A bear moved over to let Wallace Jr. sit on her other side.

The bear smell is rank but not unpleasant, once you get used to it. It's not like a barn smell, but wilder. I leaned over to whisper something to Mother and she shook her head. *It would be rude to whisper around these creatures that don't possess the power of speech,* she let me know without speaking. Wallace Jr. was silent, too. Mother shared the bedspread with us and we sat for what seemed hours, looking into the fire.

The big bear tended the fire, breaking up the dry branches by holding one end and stepping on them, like people do. He was good at keeping it going at the same level. Another bear poked the fire from time to time, but the others left it alone. It looked like only a few of the bears knew how to use fire, and were carrying the others along. But isn't that how it is with everything? Every once in a while, a smaller bear walked into the circle of firelight with an armload of wood and dropped it onto the pile. Median wood has a silvery cast, like driftwood.

Wallace Jr. isn't fidgety like a lot of kids. I found it pleasant to sit and stare into the fire. I took a little piece of Mother's *Red Man*, though I don't generally chew. It was no different from visiting her at the Home, only more interesting, because of the bears. There were about eight or ten of them. Inside the fire itself, things weren't so dull, either: little dramas were being played out as fiery chambers were created and then destroyed in a crashing of sparks. My imagination ran wild. I looked around the circle at the bears and wondered what *they* saw. Some had their eyes closed. Though they were gathered together, their spirits still seemed solitary, as if each bear was sitting alone in front of its own fire.

The hubcap came around and we all took some newberries. I don't know about Mother, but I just pretended to eat mine. Wallace Jr. made a face and spit his out. When he went to sleep, I wrapped the bedspread around all three of us. It was getting colder and we were not provided, like the bears, with fur. I was ready to go home, but not Mother. She pointed up toward the canopy of trees, where a light was spreading, and then pointed to herself. Did she think it was angels approaching from on high? It was only the high beams of some southbound truck, but she seemed mighty pleased. Holding her hand, I felt it grow colder and colder in mine.

Wallace Jr. woke me up by tapping on my knee. It was past dawn, and his grandmother had died sitting on the log between us. The fire was banked up and the bears were gone and someone was crashing straight through the woods, ignoring the path. It was Wallace. Two state troopers were right behind him. He was wearing a white shirt, and I realized it was Sunday morning. Underneath his sadness on learning of Mother's death, he looked peeved.

The troopers were sniffing the air and nodding. The bear smell was still strong. Wallace and I wrapped Mother in the bedspread and started with her body back out to the highway. The troopers stayed behind and scattered the bears' fire ashes and flung their firewood away into the bushes. It seemed a petty thing to do. They were like bears themselves, each one solitary in his own uniform.

There was Wallace's Olds 98 on the median, with its radial tires looking squashed on the grass. In front of it there was a police car with a trooper standing beside it, and behind it a funeral home hearse, also an Olds 98.

"First report we've had of them bothering old folks," the trooper said to Wallace. "That's not hardly what happened at all," I said, but nobody asked me to explain. They have their own procedures. Two men in suits got out of the hearse and opened the rear door. That to me was the point at which Mother departed this life. After we put her in, I put my arms around the boy. He was shivering even though it wasn't that cold. Sometimes death will do that, especially at dawn, with the police around and the grass wet, even when it comes as a friend.

We stood for a minute watching the cars pass. "It's a blessing," Wallace said. It's surprising how much traffic there is at 6:22 A.M.

That afternoon, I went back to the median and cut a little firewood to replace what the troopers had flung away. I could see the fire through the trees that night.

I went back two nights later, after the funeral. The fire was going and it was the same bunch of bears, as far as I could tell. I sat around with them a while but it seemed to make them nervous, so I went home. I had taken a handful of newberries from the hubcap, and on Sunday I went with the boy and arranged them on Mother's grave. I tried again, but it's no use, you can't eat them.

Unless you're a bear.

Tower of Babylon

Ted Chiang

This is the story with which Ted Chiang burst onto the science fiction scene in the early 1990s, his first published tale, which won the Nebula that year for best novella. His fiction has appeared in such magazines as Omni, Isaac Asimov's Science Fiction Magazine, *and the anthology* Full Spectrum.

WERE THE TOWER TO BE LAID DOWN ACROSS THE PLAIN OF SHINAR, IT would be two days' journey to walk from one end to the other. While the tower stands, it takes a month and a half to climb from its base to its summit, if a man walks unburdened. But few men climb the tower with empty hands; the pace of most men is much slowed by the cart of bricks that they pull behind them. Four months pass between the day a brick is loaded onto a cart and the day it is taken off to form a part of the tower.

Hillalum had spent all his life in Elam and knew Babylon only as a buyer of Elam's copper. The copper ingots were carried on boats that traveled down the Karun to the Lower Sea, headed for the Euphrates. Hillalum and the other miners traveled overland, along-side a merchant's caravan of loaded onagers. They walked along a dusty path leading down from the plateau, across the plains, to the green fields sectioned by canals and dikes.

None of them had seen the tower before. It became visible when they were still leagues away: a line as thin as a strand of flax, waver-ing in the shimmering air, rising up from the crust of mud that was Babylon itself. As they drew closer, the crust grew into the mighty city walls, but all they saw was the tower. When they did lower their gazes to the level of the river plain, they saw the marks the tower had made outside the city: The Euphrates itself now flowed at the bottom of a wide, sunken bed, dug to provide clay for bricks. To the south of the city could be seen rows upon rows of kilns, no longer burning.

As they approached the city gates, the tower appeared more mas-sive than anything Hillalum had ever imagined: a single column that must have been as large around as an entire temple, yet it rose so high that it shrank into invisibility.

All of them walked with their heads tilted back, squinting in the sun.

Hillalum's friend Nanni elbowed him, awestruck. "We're to climb that? To the top?"

"Going *up* to dig. It seems . . . unnatural."

The miners reached the central gate in the western wall, where another caravan was leaving. While they crowded forward into the narrow strip of shade provided by the wall, their foreman Beli shouted to the gatekeepers standing atop the gate towers. "We are the miners who were summoned from the land of Elam."

The gatekeepers were delighted. One called back, "You are the ones who are to dig through the vault of heaven?"

"We are."

The entire city was celebrating. The festival had begun eight days ago, when the last of the bricks were sent on their way, and would last two more. Every day and night, the city rejoiced, danced, feasted.

Along with the brickmakers were the cart pullers, men whose legs were roped with muscle from climbing the tower. Each morning a crew began its ascent; they climbed for four days, transferred their loads to the next crew of pullers, and returned to the city with empty carts on the fifth. A chain of such crews led all the way to the top of the tower, but only the bottommost celebrated with the city. For those who lived upon the tower, enough wine and meat had been sent up earlier to allow a feast to extend up the entire pillar.

In the evening, Hillalum and the other Elamite miners sat on clay stools before a long table laden with food, one table among many laid out in the city square. The miners spoke with the pullers, asking about the tower.

Nanni said, "Someone told me that the bricklayers who work at the top of the tower wail and tear their hair when a brick is dropped, because it will take four months to replace, but no one takes notice when a man falls to his death. Is that true?"

One of the more talkative pullers, Lugatum, shook his head. "Oh, no, that is only a story. There is a continuous caravan of bricks going up the tower; thousands of bricks reach the top each day. The loss of a single brick means nothing to the bricklayers." He leaned over to them. "However, there is something they value more than a man's life: a trowel."

"Why a trowel?"

"If a bricklayer drops his trowel, he can do no work until a new one is brought up. For months he cannot earn the food that he eats, so he must go into debt. The loss of a trowel is cause for much wailing. But if a man falls, and his trowel remains, men are secretly relieved. The next one to drop his trowel can pick up the extra one and continue working without incurring debt."

Hillalum was appalled, and for a frantic moment he tried to count how many picks the miners had brought. Then he realized. "That cannot be true. Why not have spare trowels brought up? Their weight would be nothing against all the bricks that go up there. And surely the loss of a man means a serious delay, unless they have an extra man at the top who is skilled at bricklaying. Without such a man, they must wait for another one to climb from the bottom."

All of the pullers roared with laughter. "We cannot fool this one," Lugatum said with much amusement. He turned to Hillalum. "So you'll begin your climb once the festival is over?"

Hillalum drank from a bowl of beer. "Yes. I've heard that we'll be joined by miners from a western land, but I haven't seen them. Do you know of them?"

"Yes, they come from a land called Egypt, but they do not mine ore as you do. They quarry stone."

"We dig stone in Elam, too," said Nanni, his mouth full of pork.

"Not as they do. They cut granite."

"Granite?" Limestone and alabaster were quarried in Elam, but not granite. "Are you certain?"

"Merchants who have traveled to Egypt say that they have ziggurats and temples, built with huge blocks of limestone and granite. And they carve giant statues from granite."

"But granite is so difficult to work."

Lugatum shrugged. "Not for them. The royal architects believe such stoneworkers may be useful when you reach the vault of heaven."

Hillalum nodded. That could be true. Who knew for certain what they would need? "Have you seen them?"

"No, they are not here yet, but they are expected in a few days' time. They may not arrive before the festival ends, though; then you Elamites will ascend alone."

"You will accompany us, won't you?"

"Yes, but only for the first four days. Then we must turn back, while you lucky ones go on."

"Why do you think us lucky?"

"I long to make the climb to the top. I once pulled with the higher crews, and reached a height of twelve days climb, but that is as high as I have ever gone. You will go far higher." Lugatum smiled ruefully. "I envy you, that you will touch the vault of heaven."

To touch the vault of heaven. To break it open with picks.

Hillalum felt uneasy at the idea. "There is no cause for envy—" he began.

"Right," said Nanni. "When we are finished, all men will touch the vault of heaven."

The next morning, Hillalum went to the tower. He stood in the giant courtyard surrounding it. There was a temple off to one side that would have been impressive if seen by itself, but it stood unnoticed beside the tower.

He could sense the utter solidity of it. According to all the tales, the tower was constructed to have a mighty strength that no ziggurat possessed; it was made of baked brick all the way through, when ordinary ziggurats were mere sun-dried mud brick, having baked brick only for the facing. The bricks were set in a bitumen mortar, which soaked into the fired clay, and hardened to form a bond as strong as the bricks themselves.

The tower's base resembled the first two platforms of an ordinary ziggurat. There stood a giant square platform some two hundred cubits on a side and forty cubits high, with a triple staircase against its south face. Stacked upon that first platform was another level, a smaller platform reached only by the central stair. It was atop the second platform that the tower itself began.

It was sixty cubits on a side and rose like a square pillar that bore the weight of heaven. Around it wound a gently inclined ramp, cut into the side, that banded the tower like the leather strip wrapped around the handle of a whip. No; upon looking again, Hillalum saw that there were two ramps, and they were intertwined. The outer edge of each ramp was studded with pillars, not thick but broad, to provide some shade behind them. In running his gaze up the tower, he saw alternating bands—ramp, brick, ramp, brick—until they could no longer be distinguished. And still the tower rose up and up, farther than the eye could see; Hillalum blinked, and squinted, and grew dizzy. He stumbled backward a couple steps and turned away with a shudder.

Hillalum thought of the story told to him in childhood, the tale following that of the Deluge. It told of how men had once again populated all the corners of the earth, inhabiting more lands than they ever had before. How men had sailed to the edges of the world and seen the ocean falling away into the mist to join the black waters of the Abyss far below. How men had thus realized the extent of the earth, and felt it to be small, and desired to see what lay beyond its borders, all the rest of Yahweh's creation. How they looked skyward and wondered about Yahweh's dwelling place, above the reservoirs that contained the waters of heaven. And how, many centuries ago, there began the construction of the tower, a pillar to heaven, a stair that men might ascend to see the works of Yahweh, and that Yahweh might descend to see the works of men.

It had always seemed inspiring to Hillalum, a tale of thousands of men toiling ceaselessly, but with joy, for they worked to know Yahweh better. He had been excited when the Babylonians came to Elam looking for miners. Yet now that he stood at the base of the tower, his senses rebelled, insisting that nothing should stand so high. He didn't feel as if he were on the earth when he looked up along the tower.

Should he climb such a thing?

On the morning of the climb, the second platform was covered edge to edge with stout two-wheeled carts arranged in rows.

Many were loaded with nothing but food of all sorts: sacks filled with barley, wheat, lentils, onions, dates, cucumbers, loaves of bread, dried fish. There were countless giant clay jars of water, date wine, beer, goat's milk, palm oil. Other carts were loaded with such goods as might be sold at a bazaar: bronze vessels, reed baskets, bolts of linen, wooden stools and tables. There was also a fattened ox and a goat that some priests were fitting with hoods so that they could not see to either side and would not be afraid on the climb. They would be sacrificed when they reached the top.

Then there were the carts loaded with the miners' picks and hammers, and the makings for a small forge. Their foreman had also ordered a number of carts be loaded with wood and sheaves of reeds.

Lugatum stood next to a cart, securing the ropes that held the wood. Hillalum walked up to him. "From where did this wood come? I saw no forests after we left Elam."

"There is a forest of trees to the north, which was planted when the tower was begun. The cut timber is floated down the Euphrates."

"You planted an entire *forest*?"

"When they began the tower, the architects knew that far more wood would be needed to fuel the kilns that could be found on the plain, so they had a forest planted. There are crews who provide water and plant one new tree for each that is cut."

Hillalum was astonished. "And that provides all the wood needed?"

"Most of it. Many other forests in the north have been cut as well, and their wood brought down the river." He inspected the wheels of the cart, uncorked a leather bottle he carried, and poured a little oil between the wheel and axle.

Nanni walked over to them, staring at the streets of Babylon laid out before them. "I've never before been this high, that I can look down upon a city."

"Now have I," said Hillalum, but Lugatum simply laughed. "Come along. All of the carts are ready."

Soon all the men were paired up and matched with a cart. The men stood between the carts' two pull rods, which had rope loops for pulling. The carts pulled by the miners were mixed in with those of the regular pullers, to ensure that they would keep the proper pace. Lugatum and another puller had the cart right behind that of Hillalum and Nanni.

"Remember," said Lugatum, "stay about ten cubits behind the cart in front of you. The man on the right does all the pulling when you turn corners, and you'll switch every hour."

Pullers were beginning to lead their carts up the ramp. Hillalum and Nanni bent down and slung the ropes of their cart over their opposite shoulders. They stood up together, raising the front end of the cart off the pavement.

"Now PULL," called Lugatum.

They leaned forward against the ropes, and the cart began rolling. Once it was moving, pulling seemed to be easy enough, and they wound their way around the platform. Then they reached the ramp, and they again had to lean deeply. "This is a light wagon?" muttered Hillalum.

The ramp was wide enough for a single man to walk beside a cart if he had to pass. The surface was paved with brick, with two grooves worn deep by centuries of wheels. Above their heads, the ceiling rose in a corbeled vault, with a wide, square bricks arranged in overlapping layers until they met in the middle. The pillars on the right were broad enough to make the ramp seem a bit like a tunnel. If one didn't look off to the side, there was little sense of being on a tower.

"Do you sing when you mine?" asked Lugatum.

"When the stone is soft."

"Sing one of your mining songs, then."

The call went down to the other miners, and before long the entire crew was singing.

As the shadows shortened, they ascended higher and higher. With only clear air surrounding them, and much shade from the sun, it was much cooler than in the narrow alleys of a city at ground level, where the heat at midday could kill lizards as they scurried across the street. Looking out to the side, the miners could see the dark Euphrates, and the green fields stretching out for leagues, crossed by canals that glinted in the sunlight. The city of Babylon was an intricate pattern of close-set streets and buildings, dazzling with gypsum whitewash; less and less of it was visible as it seemingly drew nearer the base of the tower.

Hillalum was again pulling on the right-hand rope, nearer the edge, when he heard some shouting from the upward ramp one level below. He thought of stopping and looking down the side, but he didn't wish to interrupt their pace, and he wouldn't be able to see the lower ramp clearly anyway. "What's happening down there?" he called to Lugatum behind him.

"One of your fellow miners fears the height. There is occasionally such a man among those who climb for the first time. Such a man embraces the floor and cannot ascend further. Few feel it so soon, though."

Hillalum understood. "We know of a similar fear, among those who would be miners. Some men cannot bear to enter the mines, for fear that they will be buried."

"Really?" called Lugatum. "I had not heard of that. How do you feel yourself about the height?"

"I feel nothing." But he glanced at Nanni, and they both knew the truth.

"You feel nervousness in your palms, don't you?" whispered Nanni.

Hillalum rubbed his hands on the coarse fibers of the rope and nodded.

"I felt it, too, earlier when I was closer to the edge."

"Perhaps we should go hooded, like the ox and the goat," muttered Hillalum jokingly.

"Do you think we, too, will fear the height, when we climb further?"

Hillalum considered. That one of their comrades should feel the fear so soon did not bode well. He shook it off; thousands climbed with no fear, and it would be foolish to let one miner's fear infect them all. "We are merely unaccustomed. We will have months to grow used to the height. By the time we reach the top of the tower, we will wish it were taller."

"No," said Nanni. "I don't think I'll wish to pull this any further."

They both laughed.

In the evening they ate a meal of barley and onions and lentils, and slept inside narrow corridors that penetrated into the body of the tower. When they woke the next morning, the miners were scarcely able to walk, so sore were their legs. The pullers laughed, and gave them salve to rub into their muscles, and redistributed the load on the carts to reduce the miners' burden.

By now, looking down the side turned Hillalum's knees to water. A wind blew steadily at this height, and he anticipated that it would grow stronger as they climbed. He wondered if anyone had ever been blown off the tower in a moment of carelessness. And the fall; a man would have time to say a prayer before he hit the ground. Hillalum shuddered at the thought.

Aside from the soreness in the miners' legs, the second day was similar to the first. They were able to see much farther now, and the breadth of land visible was stunning; the deserts beyond the fields were visible, and caravans appeared to be little more than lines of insects. No other miner feared the height so greatly that he couldn't continue, and their ascent proceeded all day without incident.

On the third day, the miners' legs had not improved, and Hillalum felt like a crippled old man. Only on the fourth day did their legs feel better, and they were pulling their original loads again. Their climb continued until the evening, when they met the second crew of pullers leading empty carts rapidly along the downward ramp. The upward and downward ramps wound around each other without touching, but they were joined by the corridors through the tower's body. When the crews had intertwined thoroughly on the two ramps, they crossed over to exchange carts.

The miners were introduced to the pullers of the second crew, and they all talked and ate together that night. The next morning the first crew readied the empty carts for their return to Babylon, and Lugatum bid farewell to Hillalum and Nanni.

"Take care of your cart. It has climbed the entire height of the tower, more times than any man."

"Do you envy the cart, too?" asked Nanni.

"No, because every time it reaches the top, it must come all the way back down. I could not bear to do that."

When the second crew stopped at the end of the day, the puller of the cart behind Hillalum and Nanni came over to them. His name was Kudda.

"You have never seen the sun set at this height. Come, look." The puller went to the edge and sat down, his legs hanging over the side. He saw that they hesitated. "Come. You can lie down and peer over the edge, if you like." Hillalum did not wish to seem like a fearful child, but he could not bring himself to sit at a cliff face that stretched for thousands of cubits below his feet. He lay down on his belly, with only his head at the edge. Nanni joined him.

"When the sun is about to set, look down the side of the tower." Hillalum glanced downward and then quickly looked to the horizon.

"What is different about the way the sun sets here?"

"Consider, when the sun sinks behind the peaks of the mountains to the west, it grows dark down on the plain of Shinar. Yet here, we are higher than the mountaintops, so we can still see the sun. The sun must descend further for us to see night."

Hillalum's jaw dropped as he understood. "The shadows of the mountains mark the beginning of night. Night falls on the earth before it does here."

Kudda nodded. "You can see night travel up the tower, from the ground up to the sky. It moves quickly, but you should be able to see it."

He watched the red globe of the sun for a minute and then looked down and pointed. "Now!"

Hillalum and Nanni looked down. At the base of the immense pillar, tiny Babylon was in shadow. Then the darkness climbed the tower, like a canopy unfurling upward. It moved slowly enough that Hillalum felt he could count the moments passing, but then it grew faster as it approached, until it raced past them faster than he could blink, and they were in twilight.

Hillalum rolled over and looked up, in time to see darkness rapidly ascend the rest of the tower. Gradually, the sky grew dimmer as the sun sank beneath the edge of the world, far away.

"Quite a sight, is it not?"

Hillalum said nothing. For the first time, he knew night for what it was: the shadow of the earth itself, cast against the sky.

After climbing for two more days, Hillalum had grown more accustomed to the height. Though they were the better part of a league straight up, he could bear to stand at the edge of the ramp and look down the tower. He held on to one of the pillars at the edge and cautiously leaned out to look upward. He noticed that the tower no longer looked like a smooth pillar.

He asked Kudda, "The tower seems to widen further up. How can that be?"

"Look more closely. There are wooden balconies reaching out from the sides. They are made of cypress, and suspended by ropes of flax."

Hillalum squinted. "Balconies? What are they for?"

"They have soil spread on them, so people may grow vegetables. At this height water is scarce, so onions are most commonly grown. Higher up, where there is more rain, you'll see beans."

Nanni asked, "How can there be rain above that does not just fall here?"

Kudda was surprised at him. "It dries in the air as it falls, of course."

"Oh, of course." Nanni shrugged.

By the end of the next day they reached the level of the balconies. They were flat platforms, dense with onions, supported by heavy ropes from the tower wall above, just below the next tier of balconies.

On each level the interior of the tower had several narrow rooms inside, in which the families of the pullers lived. Women could be seen sitting in the doorways sewing tunics, or out in the gardens digging up bulbs. Children chased each other up and down the ramps, weaving amidst the pullers' carts and running along the edge of the balconies without fear. The tower dwellers could easily pick out the miners, and they all smiled and waved.

When it came time for the evening meal, all the carts were set down and much food and other goods were taken off to be used by the people here. The pullers greeted their families and invited the miners to join them for the evening meal. Hillalum and Nanni ate with the family of Kudda, and they enjoyed a fine meal of dried fish, bread, date wine, and fruit.

Hillalum saw that this section of the tower formed a tiny kind of town, laid out in a line between two streets, the upward and downward ramps. There was a temple, in which the rituals for the festivals were performed; there were magistrates, who settled disputes; there were shops, which were stocked by the caravan. Of course, the town was inseparable from the caravan: Neither could exist without the other. And yet any caravan was essentially a journey, a thing that began at one place and ended at another. This town was never intended as a permanent place; it was merely part of a centuries-long journey.

After dinner, Hillalum asked Kudda and his family, "Have any of you ever visited Babylon?"

Kudda's wife, Alitum, answered. "No, why would we? It's a long climb, and we have all we need here."

"You have no desire to actually walk on the earth?"

Kudda shrugged. "We live on the road to heaven; all the work that we do is to extend it further. When we leave the tower, we will take the upward ramp, not the downward."

As the miners ascended, in the course of time there came the day when the tower appeared to be the same when one looked upward or downward from the ramp's edge. Below, the tower's shaft shrank to nothing long before it seemed to reach the plain below. Likewise the miners were still far from being able to see the top. All that was visible was a length of the tower. To look up or down was frightening, for the reassurance of continuity was not provided; they were no longer part of the ground. The tower might have been a thread suspended in the air, unattached to either Earth or heaven.

There were moments during this section of the climb when Hillalum despaired, feeling displaced and estranged from the world; it was as if the earth had rejected him for his faithlessness, while heaven disdained to accept him. He wished Yahweh would give a sign, to let men know that their venture was approved; otherwise how could they stay in a place that offered so little welcome to the spirit?

The tower dwellers at this altitude felt no unease with their station; they always greeted the miners warmly and wished them luck with their task at the vault. They lived inside the damp mists of clouds, they saw storms from below and from above, they harvested crops from the air, and they never feared that this was an improper place for men to be. There were no divine assurances to be had, but the people never knew a moment's doubt.

With the passage of the weeks, the sun and moon peaked lower and lower in their daily journeys. The moon flooded the south side of the tower with its silver radiance, glowing like the eye of Yahweh peering at them. Before long, they were at precisely the same level as the moon when it passed; they had reached the height of the first of the celestial bodies. They squinted at the moon's pitted face, marveled at its stately motion that scorned any support.

Then they approached the sun. It was the summer season, when the sun appears nearly overhead from Babylon, making it pass close by the tower at this height. No families lived in this section of the tower, nor were there any balconies, since the heat was enough to roast barley. The mortar between the tower's bricks was no longer bitumen, which would have softened and flowed, but clay, which had been virtually baked by the heat. As protection against the day temperatures, the pillars had been widened until they formed a nearly continuous wall, enclosing the ramp into a tunnel with only narrow slots admitting the whistling wind and blades of golden light.

The crews of pullers had been spaced very regularly up to this point, but here an adjustment was necessary. They started out earlier and earlier each morning, to gain more darkness for when they pulled. When they were at the level of the sun, they traveled entirely at night. During the day, they tried to sleep, naked and sweating in the hot breeze. The miners worried that if they did manage to sleep, they would be baked to death before they awoke. But the pullers had made the journey many times and never lost a man, and eventually they passed above the sun's level, where things were as they had been below.

Now the light of day shone *upward*, which seemed unnatural to the utmost. The balconies had planks removed from them so that the sunlight could shine through, with soil on the walkways that remained; the plants grew sideways and downward, bending down to catch the sun's rays.

Then they drew near the level of the stars, small fiery spheres spread on all sides. Hillalum had expected them to be spread more thickly, but even with the tiny stars invisible from the ground, they seemed to be thinly scattered. They were not all set at the same height but instead occupied the next few leagues above. It was difficult to tell how far they were, since there was no indication of their size, but occasionally one would make a close approach, evidencing its astonishing speed. Hillalum realized that all the objects in the sky hurtled by with similar speed, in order to travel the world from edge to edge in a day's time.

During the day, the sky was a much paler blue than it appeared from the earth, a sign they were nearing the vault. When studying the sky, Hillalum was startled to see that there were stars visible during the day. They couldn't be seen from the earth amidst the glare of the sun, but from this altitude they were quite distinct.

One day Nanni came to him hurriedly and said, "A star has hit the tower!"

"What!" Hillalum looked around panicked, feeling like he had been struck by a blow.

"No, not now. It was long ago, more than a century. One of the tower dwellers is telling the story; his grandfather was there."

They went inside the corridors and saw several miners seated around a wizened old man. "—lodged itself in the bricks about half a league above here. You can still see the scar it left; it's like a giant pockmark."

"What happened to the star?"

"It burned and sizzled, and was too bright to look upon. Men considered prying it out, so that it might resume its course, but it was too hot to approach closely, and they dared not quench it. After weeks it cooled into a knotted mass of black heaven metal, as large as a man could wrap his arms around."

"So large?" said Nanni, his voice full of awe. When stars fell to the earth of their own accord, small lumps of heaven metal were sometimes found, tougher than the finest bronze. The metal could not be melted for casting, so it was worked by hammering when heated red; amulets were made from it.

"Indeed, no one had ever heard of a mass of this size found on the earth. Can you imagine the tools that could be made from it!"

"You did not try to hammer it into tools, did you?" asked Hillalum, horrified.

"Oh, no. Men were frightened to touch it. Everyone descended from the tower, waiting for retribution from Yahweh for disturbing the workings of creation. They waited for months, but no sign came. Eventually they returned and pried out the star. It sits in a temple in the city below."

There was silence. Then one of the miners said, "I have never heard of this in the stories of the tower."

"It was a transgression, something not spoken of."

As they climbed higher up the tower, the sky grew lighter in color, until one morning Hillalum awoke and stood at the edge and yelled from shock: What had before seemed a pale sky now appeared to be a white ceiling stretched far above their heads. They were close enough now to perceive the vault of heaven, to see it as a solid carapace enclosing all the sky. All of the miners spoke in hushed tones, staring up like idiots, while the tower dwellers laughed at them.

As they continued to climb, they were startled at how *near* they actually were. The blankness of the vault's face had deceived them, making it undetectable until it appeared, abruptly, seemingly just above their heads. Now instead of climbing into the sky, they climbed up to a featureless plain that stretched endlessly in all directions.

All of Hillalum's senses were disoriented by the sight of it. Sometimes when he looked at the vault, he felt as if the world had flipped around somehow, and if he lost his footing he would fall upward to meet it. When the vault did appear to rest above his head, it had an oppressive *weight*. The vault was a stratum as heavy as all the world, yet utterly without support, and he feared what he never had in the mines: that the ceiling would collapse upon him.

Too, there were moments when it appeared as if the vault was a vertical cliff face of unimaginable height rising before him, and the dim earth behind him was another like it, and the tower was a cable stretched taut between the two. Or worst of all, for an instant it seemed that there was no up and no down, and his body did not know which way it was drawn. It was like fearing the height, but much worse. Often he would wake to find himself sweating and his fingers cramped, trying to clutch the brick floor.

Nanni and many of the other miners were bleary-eyed, too, though no one spoke of what disturbed their sleep. Their ascent grew slower, instead of faster as their foreman Beli had expected; the sight of the vault inspired unease rather than eagerness. The regular pullers became impatient with them. Hillalum wondered what sort of people were forged by living under such conditions; did they escape madness? Did they grow accustomed to this? Would the children born under a solid sky scream if they saw the ground beneath their feet?

Perhaps men were not meant to live in such a place. If their own natures restrained them from approaching heaven too closely, then men should remain on the earth.

When they reached the summit of the tower, the disorientation faded, or perhaps they had grown immune. Here, standing upon the square platform of the top, the miners gazed upon the most awesome scene ever glimpsed by men: Far below them lay a tapestry of soil and sea, veiled by mist, rolling out in all directions to the limit of the eye. Just above them hung the roof of the world itself, the absolute upper demarcation of the sky, guaranteeing their vantage point as the highest possible. Here was as much of creation as could be apprehended at once.

The priests led a prayer to Yahweh; they gave thanks that they were permitted to see so much and begged forgiveness for their desire to see more.

And at the top, the bricks were laid. One could catch the rich, raw smell of tar, rising out of the heated cauldrons in which the lumps of bitumen were melted. It was the most earthy odor the miners had smelled in four months, and their nostrils were desperate to catch a whiff before it was whipped away by the wind. Here at the summit, where the ooze that had once seeped from the earth's cracks now grew solid to hold bricks in place, the earth was growing a limb into the sky.

Here worked the bricklayers, the men smeared with bitumen who mixed the mortar and deftly set the heavy bricks with absolute precision. More than anyone else, these men could not permit themselves to experience dizziness when they saw the vault, for the tower could not vary a finger's width from the vertical. They were nearing the end of their task, finally, and after four months of climbing, the miners were ready to begin theirs.

The Egyptians arrived shortly afterward. They were dark of skin and slight of build and had sparsely bearded chins. They had pulled carts filled with dolerite hammers, and bronze tools, and wooden wedges. Their foreman was named Senmut, and he conferred with Beli, the Elamites' foreman, on how they would penetrate the vault. The Egyptians built a forge with what they had brought, as did the Elamites, for recasting the bronze tools that would be blunted during the mining.

The vault itself remained just above a man's outstretched fingertips; it felt smooth and cool when one leapt up to touch it. It seemed to be made of fine-grained white granite, unmarred and utterly featureless. And therein lay the problem. Long ago Yahweh had released the Deluge, unleashing waters from both below and above; the waters of the Abyss had burst forth from the springs of the earth, and the waters of heaven had poured through the sluice gates in the vault. Now men saw the vault closely, but there were no sluice gates discernible. They squinted at the surface in all directions, but no openings, no windows, no seams interrupted the granite plain.

It seemed that their tower met the vault at a point between any reservoirs, which was fortunate indeed. If a sluice gate had been visible, they would have had to risk breaking it open and emptying the reservoir. That would mean rain for Shinar, out of season and heavier than the winter rains; it would cause flooding along the Euphrates. The rain would most likely end when the reservoir was emptied, but there was always the possibility that Yahweh would punish them and continue the rain until the tower fell and Babylon was dissolved into mud.

Even though there were no visible gates, a risk still existed. Perhaps the gates had no seams perceptible to mortal eyes, and a reservoir lay directly above them. Or perhaps the reservoirs were huge, so that even if the nearest sluice gates were many leagues away, a reservoir still lay above them.

There was much debate over how best to proceed.

"Surely Yahweh will not wash away the tower," argued Qurdusa, one of the bricklayers. "If the tower were sacrilege, Yahweh would have destroyed it earlier. Yet in all the centuries we've been working, we have never seen the slightest sign of Yahweh's displeasure. Yahweh will drain any reservoir before we penetrate it."

"If Yahweh looked upon this venture with such favor, there would already be a stairway ready-made for us in the vault," countered Eluti, an Elamite. "Yahweh will neither help or hinder us; if we penetrate a reservoir, we will face the onrush of its waters."

Hillalum could not keep his doubts silent at such a time. "And if the waters are endless? Yahweh may not punish us, but Yahweh may allow us to bring our judgment upon ourselves."

"Elamite," said Qurdusa, "even as a newcomer to the tower, you should know better than that. We labor for our love of Yahweh, we have done so for all our lives, and so have our fathers for generations back. Men as righteous as we could not be judged harshly."

"It is true that we work with the purest of aims, but that doesn't mean we have worked wisely. Did men truly choose the correct path when they opted to live their lives away from the soil from which they were shaped? Never has Yahweh said that the choice was proper. Now we stand ready to break open heaven, even when we know that water lies above us. If we are misguided, how can we be sure Yahweh will protect us from our own errors?"

"Hillalum advises caution, and I agree," said Beli. "We must ensure that we do not bring a second Deluge upon the world, nor even dangerous rains upon Shinar. I have conferred with Senmut of the Egyptians, and he has shown me designs which they have employed to seal the tombs of their kings. I believe that their methods can provide us with safety when we begin digging."

The priests sacrificed the ox and the goat in a ceremony in which many sacred words were spoken and much incense was burned, and the miners began work.

Even before the miners reached the vault, it had been obvious that simple digging with hammers and picks would be impractical: Even if they were tunneling horizontally, they would make no more than two finger widths of progress a day through granite, and tunneling *upward* would be far, far slower. Instead, they employed fire setting.

With the wood they had brought, a bonfire was built below the chosen point of the vault and fed steadily for a day. Before the heat of the flames, the stone cracked and spalled. After letting the fire burn out, the miners splashed water onto the stone to further the cracking. They could then break the stone into large pieces, which fell heavily onto the tower. In this manner they could progress the better part of a cubit for each day the fire burned.

The tunnel did not rise straight up, but at the angle a staircase takes, so that they could build a ramp of steps up from the tower to meet it. The fire setting left the walls and floor smooth; the men built a frame of wooden steps underfoot so that they would not slide back down. They used a platform of baked bricks to support the bonfire at the tunnel's end.

After the tunnel rose ten cubits into the vault, they leveled it out and widened it to form a room. After the miners had removed all the stone that had been weakened by the fire, the Egyptians began work. They used no fire in their quarrying. With only their dolerite balls and hammers, they began to build a sliding door of granite. They first chipped away stone to cut an immense block of granite out of one wall. Hillalum and the other miners tried to help but found it difficult: One did not wear away the stone by grinding but instead pounded chips off, using hammer blows of one strength alone, and lighter or heavier ones would not do.

After some weeks, the block was ready. It stood taller than a man and was even wider than that. To free it from the floor, they cut slots around the base of the stone and pounded in dry wooden wedges.

Then they pounded thinner wedges into the first wedges to split them and poured water into the cracks so that the wood would swell. In a few hours, a crack traveled into the stone, and the block was freed.

At the rear of the room, on the right-hand side, the miners burned out a narrow upward-sloping corridor, and in the floor in front of the chamber entrance they dug a downward-sloping channel into the floor for a cubit. Thus there was a smooth continuous ramp that cut across the floor immediately in front of the entrance and ended just to its left.

On this ramp the Egyptians loaded the block of granite. They dragged and pushed it up into the side corridor, where it just barely fit, and propped it in place with a stack of flat mud bricks braced against the bottom of the left wall, like a pillar lying on the ramp.

With the sliding stone to hold back the waters, it was safe for the miners to continue tunneling. If they broke into a reservoir and the waters of heaven began pouring down into the tunnel, they would break the bricks one by one, and the stone would slide down until it rested in the recess in the floor, utterly blocking the doorway. If the waters flooded in with such force that they washed men out of the tunnels, the mud bricks would gradually dissolve, and again the stone would slide down. The waters would be retained, and the miners could then begin a new tunnel in another direction, to avoid the reservoir.

The miners again used fire setting to continue the tunnel, beginning at the far end of the room. To aid the circulation of air within the vault, oxhides were stretched on tall frames of wood and placed obliquely on either side of the tunnel entrance at the top of the tower. Thus the steady wind that blew underneath the vault of heaven was guided upward into the tunnel; it kept the fire blazing and cleared the air after the fire was extinguished, so that the miners could dig without breathing smoke.

The Egyptians did not stop working once the sliding stone was in place. While the miners swung their picks at the tunnel's end, the Egyptians labored at the task of cutting a stair into the solid stone, to replace the wooden steps. This they did with the wooden wedges, and the blocks they removed from the sloping floor left steps in their place.

Thus the miners worked, extending the tunnel on and on. The tunnel always ascended, though it reversed direction regularly like a thread in a giant stitch, so that its general path was straight up. They built other sliding-door rooms so that only the uppermost segment of the tunnel would be flooded if they penetrated a reservoir.

They cut channels in the vault's surface from which they hung walkways and platforms; starting from these platforms, well away from the tower, they dug side tunnels, which joined the main tunnel deep inside. The wind was guided through these to provide ventilation, clearing the smoke from deep inside the tunnel.

For years the labor continued. The pulling crews no longer hauled bricks but wood and water for the fire setting. People came to inhabit those tunnels just inside the vault's surface, and on hanging platforms they grew downward-bending vegetables. The miners lived there at the border of heaven; some married and raised children. Few ever set foot on the earth again.

With a wet cloth wrapped around his face, Hillalum climbed down from wooden steps onto stone, having just fed some more wood to the bonfire at the tunnel's end. The fire would continue for many hours, and he would wait in the lower tunnels, where the wind was not thick with smoke.

Then there was a distant sound of shattering, the sound of a mountain of stone being split through, and then a steadily growing roar. A torrent of water came rushing down the tunnel.

For a moment, Hillalum was frozen in horror. The water, shockingly cold, slammed into his legs, knocking him down. He rose to his feet, gasping for breath, leaning against the current, clutching at the steps.

They had hit a reservoir.

He had to descend below the highest sliding door, before it was closed. His legs wished to leap down the steps, but he knew he couldn't remain on his feet if he did, and being swept down by the raging current would likely batter him to death. Going as fast as he dared, he took the steps one by one.

He slipped several times, sliding down as many as a dozen steps each time; the stone steps scraped against his back, but he felt no pain. All the while he was certain the tunnel would collapse and crush him, or else the entire vault would split open, and the sky would gape beneath his feet, and he would fall down to Earth amidst the heavenly rain. Yahweh's punishment had come, a second Deluge.

How much further until he reached the sliding stone? The tunnel seemed to stretch on and on, and the waters were pouring down even faster now. He was virtually running down the steps.

Stumbling, he splashed into shallow water. He had run down past the end of the stairs and fallen into the room of the sliding stone, and there was water higher than his knees.

He stood up and saw Damqiya and Ahuni, two fellow miners, just noticing him. They stood in front of the stone, which already blocked the exit.

"No!" he cried.

"They closed it!" screamed Damqiya. "They did not wait!"

"Are there others coming?" shouted Ahuni, without hope. "We may be able to move the block."

"There are no others," answered Hillalum. "Can they push it from the other side?"

"They cannot hear us." Ahuni pounded the granite with a hammer, making not a sound against the din of the rushing water.

Hillalum looked around the tiny room, only now noticing that an Egyptian floated facedown in the water.

"He died falling down the stairs," yelled Damqiya.

"Is there nothing we can do?"

Ahuni looked upward. "Yahweh, spare us."

The three of them stood in the rising water, praying desperately, but Hillalum knew it was in vain: Yahweh had not asked men to build the tower or to pierce the vault; the decision belonged to men alone, and they would die in this endeavor just as they did in any of their earthbound tasks. Their righteousness could not save them from the consequences of their deeds.

The water reached their chests. "Let us ascend," shouted Hillalum.

They climbed the tunnel laboriously, against the onrush, as the water rose behind their heels. The few torches illuminating the tunnel had been extinguished, so they ascended in the dark, murmuring prayers that they couldn't hear. The wooden steps at the top of the tunnel had dislodged from their place and were jammed farther down in the tunnel. They climbed past them until they reached the smooth stone slope, and there they waited for the water to carry them higher.

They waited without words, their prayers exhausted. Hillalum imagined that he stood in the black gullet of Yahweh, as the Mighty One drank deep of the waters of heaven, ready to swallow the sinners.

The water rose and bore them up, until Hillalum could reach up with his hands and touch the ceiling. The giant fissure from which the waters gushed forth was right next to him. Only a tiny pocket of air remained. Hillalum shouted, "When this chamber is filled, we can swim heavenward."

He could not tell if they heard him. He gulped his last breath as the water reached the ceiling, and swam up into the fissure. He would die closer to heaven than any man ever had before.

The fissure extended for many cubits. As soon as Hillalum passed through, the stone stratum slipped from his fingers, and his flailing limbs touched nothing. For a moment he felt a current carrying him, but then he was no longer sure. With only blackness around him, he once again felt that horrible vertigo that he had experienced when first approaching the vault: He could not distinguish any directions, not even up or down. He pushed and kicked against the water but did not know if he moved.

Helpless, he was perhaps floating in still water, perhaps swept furiously by a current; all he felt was numbing cold. Never did he see any light. Was there no surface to this reservoir that he might rise to?

Then he was slammed into stone again. His hands felt a fissure in the surface. Was he back where he had begun? He was being forced into it, and he had no strength to resist. He was drawn into the tunnel and was rattled against its sides. It was incredibly deep, like the longest mine shaft: He felt as if his lungs would burst, but there was still no end to the passage. Finally his breath would not be held any longer, and it escaped from his lips. He was drowning, and the blackness around him entered his lungs.

But suddenly the walls opened out away from him. He was being carried along by a rushing stream of water; he felt air above the water! And then he felt no more.

Hillalum awoke with his face pressed against wet stone. He could see nothing, but he could feel water near his hands. He rolled over and groaned; his every limb ached, he was naked, and much of his skin was scraped raw or wrinkled from wetness, but he breathed air.

Time passed, and finally he could stand. Water flowed rapidly about his ankles. Stepping in one direction, the water deepened. In the other, there was dry stone—shale by the feel of it.

It was utterly dark, like a mine without torches. With torn fingertips he felt his way along the floor, until it rose up and became a wall. Slowly, like some blind creature, he crawled back and forth. He found the water's source, a large opening in the floor. He remembered! He had been spewed up from the reservoir through this hole. He continued crawling for what seemed to be hours; if he were in a cavern, it was immense. He found a place where the floor rose in a slope. Was there a passage leading upward? Perhaps it could still take him to heaven.

Hillalum crawled, having no idea of how much time passed, not caring that he would never be able to retrace his steps, for he could not return whence he had come. He followed upward tunnels when he found them, downward ones when he had to. Though earlier he had swallowed more water than he would have thought possible, he began to feel thirst, and hunger.

And eventually he saw light and raced to the outside.

The light made his eyes squeeze closed, and he fell to his knees, his fists clenched before his face. Was it the radiance of Yahweh? Could his eyes bear to see it? Minutes later he could open them, and he saw desert. He had emerged from a cave in the foothills of some mountains, and rocks and sand stretched to the horizon.

Was heaven just like the earth? Did Yahweh dwell in a place such as this? Or was this merely another realm within Yahweh's creation, another Earth above his own, while Yahweh dwelled still higher?

A sun lay near the mountaintops behind his back. Was it rising or falling? Were there days and nights here?

Hillalum squinted at the sandy landscape. A line moved along the horizon. Was it a caravan?

He ran to it, shouting with his parched throat until his need for breath stopped him. A figure at the end of the caravan saw him and brought the entire line to a stop.

The one who had seen him seemed to be man, not spirit, and was dressed like a desert crosser. He had a waterskin ready. Hillalum drank as best he could, panting for breath.

Finally he returned it to the man and gasped, "Where is this place?"

"Were you attacked by bandits? We are headed to Erech."

Hillalum stared. "You would deceive me!" he shouted. The man drew back and watched him as if he were mad from the sun. Hillalum saw another man in the caravan walking over to investigate. "Erech is in Shinar!"

"Yes, it is. Were you not traveling to Shinar?" The other man stood ready with his staff.

"I came from—I was in—" Hillalum stopped. "Do you know Babylon?"

"Oh, is that your destination? That is north of Erech. It is an easy journey between them."

"The tower—have you heard of it?"

"Certainly, the pillar to heaven. It is said men at the top are tunneling through the vault of heaven."

Hillalum fell to the sand.

"Are you unwell?" The two caravan drivers mumbled to each other and went off to confer with the others. Hillalum was not watching them.

He was in Shinar. He had returned to the earth. He had climbed above the reservoirs of heaven and arrived back at the earth. Had Yahweh brought him to this place to keep him from reaching further above? Yet Hillalum still hadn't seen any signs, any indication that Yahweh noticed him. He had not experienced any miracle that Yahweh had performed to place him here. As far as he could see, he had merely swum up from the vault and entered the cavern below.

Somehow the vault of heaven lay beneath the earth. It was as if they lay against each other, though they were separated by many leagues. How could that be? How could such distant places touch? Hillalum's head hurt trying to think about it.

And then it came to him: *a seal cylinder.* When rolled upon a tablet of soft clay, the carved cylinder left an imprint that formed a picture. Two figures might appear at opposite ends of the tablet, though they stood side by side on the surface of the cylinder. All the world was as such a cylinder. Men imagined heaven and Earth as being at the ends of a tablet, with sky and stars stretched between; yet the world was wrapped around in some fantastic way so that heaven and Earth touched.

It was clear now why Yahweh had not struck down the tower, had not punished men for wishing to reach beyond the bounds set for them—for the longest journey would merely return them to the place whence they'd come. Centuries of their labor would not reveal to them any more of creation than they already knew. Yet through their endeavor, men would glimpse the unimaginable artistry of Yahweh's work, in seeing how ingeniously the world had been constructed. By this construction, Yahweh's work was indicated, and Yahweh's work was concealed.

Thus would men know their place.

Hillalum rose to his feet, his legs unsteady from awe, and sought out the caravan drivers. He would go back to Babylon. Perhaps he would see Lugatum again. He would send word to those on the tower. He would tell them about the shape of the world.

Copyrights for
The Fantasy Hall of Fame: